Gavin sucked in light to start making his rowing apparatus.

Unthinking, he tried to draft blue. While brittle, blue's stiff, slick, smooth structure made it ideal for parts that didn't undergo sideways stresses. For a futile moment, Gavin tried to force it, again. He was a Prism made flesh; alone out of all the drafters, he could split light with himself. The blue was there—he knew it was there, and maybe knowing it was there, even though he couldn't see it, might be enough.

For Orholam's sake, if you could find your chamber pot in the middle of the night and, despite that you couldn't see it, the damned thing was still there, why couldn't this be the same?

Nothing. No rush of harmonious logic, no cool rationality, no stained blue skin, no drafting whatsoever. For the first time since he was a boy, he felt helpless. Like a natural man. Like a peasant.

Gavin screamed at his helplessness.

Praise for the novels of Brent Weeks:

"*The Blinding Knife* by Brent Weeks was even better than *The Black Prism* (and that's saying something)!"

—BN.com on *The Blinding Knife*

"[*The Blinding Knife*] places Brent Weeks on comfortable footing beside contemporaries like Brandon Sanderson and Joe Abercrombie, if not a step above...one of the best fantasy books of 2012."

—Aidan Moher on *The Blinding Knife*

"Weeks manages to ring new tunes on...old bells, letting a deep background slowly reveal its secrets and presenting his characters in a realistically flawed and human way."

—*Publishers Weekly* on *The Black Prism*

"...A solid, entertaining yarn."

—The Onion A.V. Club on *The Black Prism*

"All in all *The Black Prism is* an A++ from me while the series has the potential to become one for the ages. The main flaw of *The Black Prism* is that it ends—despite 600+ pages and a reasonable ending point, I still wanted another 600 at least!"

—Fantasy Book Critic on *The Black Prism*

"Weeks has written an epic fantasy unlike any of its contemporaries. It is a truly visionary and original work, and has set the bar high for others in its subgenre."

—graspingforthewind.com on *The Black Prism*

"Weeks creates a rich blend of politics, culture and character...then throws in magic-using assassins. Brent Weeks is so good it's starting to tick me off."

—Peter V. Brett, *New York Times* bestselling author of *The Desert Spear*

"What a terrific story! I was mesmerized from start to finish. Unforgettable characters, a plot that kept me guessing, nonstop action and the kind of in-depth storytelling that makes me admire a writer's work."   —Terry Brooks on *The Way of Shadows*

"Kylar is a wonderful character—sympathetic and despicable, cowardly and courageous, honorable and unscrupulous…a breathtaking debut!"   —Dave Duncan on *The Way of Shadows*

Books by Brent Weeks:

Perfect Shadow (e-only novella)

THE NIGHT ANGEL TRILOGY

The Way of Shadows
Shadow's Edge
Beyond the Shadows
Night Angel (omnibus)

THE LIGHTBRINGER SERIES

The Black Prism
The Blinding Knife

The
Blinding
Knife

Lightbringer: Book 2

BRENT WEEKS

orbit

www.orbitbooks.net

Copyright © 2012 by Brent Weeks
Map by Jeffrey L. Ward

Orbit
Hachette Book Group
237 Park Avenue, New York, NY 10017
www.HachetteBookGroup.com

Originally published in hardcover by Hachette Book Group.

First trade edition: August 2013

Orbit is an imprint of Hachette Book Group, Inc. The Orbit name and logo are trademarks of Little, Brown Book Group Limited.

The Hachette Speakers Bureau provides a wide range of authors for speaking events. To find out more, go to www.hachettespeakersbureau.com or call (866) 376-6591.

The publisher is not responsible for websites (or their content) that are not owned by the publisher.

Library of Congress Cataloging-in-Publication Data
Weeks, Brent.
    The blinding knife / Brent Weeks. — 1st ed.
        p. cm. — (Lightbringer series ; bk. 2)
    ISBN 978-0-316-07991-4
    1. Emperors—Fiction.   2. Brothers—Fiction.   3. Secrets—Fiction.
4. Magic—Fiction.   I. Title.
    PS3623.E4223B575 2012
    813'.6—dc23
                                                        2012009016

10 9 8 7 6 5 4 3 2 1

RRD-C

Printed in the United States of America

ISBN 978-0-316-06814-7 (pbk.)

For my wife, Kristi,

And for all the others who keep faith
when the time for giving up seems long past.

Contents

The Great Desert

Crater Lake

Kolfing

Tyrea

REKTON

The Badlands

Karsos Mountains

Umber River

Atan's Teeth

GARRISTON

Seers Island

The Everdark Gates

The Cerulean Sea

SMUSSATO

WIWURGH

PERICOL

Ilyta

White Mist Reef

The Deeps

S

CRAVOS

Abornea

ODESS

The Narrows

AZÛLAY

TABES

MELOS

Paria

Aslal

Ruthga

φ AGHBALU

The Verdant Plains

The Seven Satrapies

Hellmount

IDOSS

The Red Cliffs

The Cracked Lands

Atash

Ruic Head

◈ Ru

The Chromeria

Big Jasper

Little Jasper

Blood Forest

◈ Green Haven

THE FLOATING CITY

Rath ◈

The Great River

◈ VERIT

Chapter 1

Gavin Guile lay on his back on a narrow skimmer floating in the middle of the sea. It was a tiny craft with low sides. Lying on his back like this, he'd once almost believed he was one with the sea. Now the dome of the heavens above him was a lid, and he a crab in the cauldron, heat rising.

Two hours before noon, here on the southern rim of the Cerulean Sea, the waters should be a stunning deep blue-green. The sky above, cloudless, mist burned off, should be a peaceful, vibrant sapphire.

But he couldn't see it. Since he'd lost the Battle of Garriston four days ago, wherever there was blue, he saw gray. He couldn't even see that much unless he concentrated. Robbed of its blue, the sea looked like thin, gray-green broth.

His fleet was waiting. Hard to relax when thousands of people were waiting for you and only you, but he needed this measure of peace.

He looked to the heavens, arms spread, touching the waves with his fingertips.

Lucidonius, were you here? Were you even real? Did this happen to you, too?

Something hissed in the water, a sound like a boat cutting through the waves.

Gavin sat up on his skimmer. Then stood.

Fifty paces behind him, something disappeared under the waves, something big enough to cause its own swell. It could have been a whale.

Except whales usually surface to breathe. There was no spray hanging in the air, no whoosh of expelled breath. And from fifty paces, for

1

Gavin to have heard the hiss of a sea creature cutting through the water, it would have to be massive. His heart leapt to his throat.

He began sucking in light to draft his oar apparatus—and froze. Right beneath his tiny craft, something was moving through the water. It was like watching the landscape speed by when you're riding in a carriage, but Gavin wasn't moving. The rushing body was huge, many times the width of his craft, and it was undulating closer and closer to the surface, closer to his own little boat. A sea demon.

And it *glowed*. A peaceful, warm radiance like the sun itself on this cool morning.

Gavin had never heard of such a thing. Sea demons were monsters, the purest, craziest form of fury known to mankind. They burned red, boiled the seas, left fires floating in their wake. Not carnivores, so far as the old books guessed, but fiercely territorial—and any interloper that disrupted their seas was to be crushed. Interlopers like ships.

This light was different than that rage. A peaceful luminescence, the sea demon no vicious destroyer but a leviathan traversing the seas, leaving barely a ripple to note his passing. The colors shimmered through the waves, grew brighter as the undulation brought the body close.

Unthinking, Gavin knelt as the creature's back broke the surface of the water right underneath his boat. Before the boat slid away from the swell, he reached out and touched the sea demon's skin. He expected a creature that slid through the waves to be slimy, but the skin was surprisingly rough, muscular, warm.

For one precious moment, Gavin was not. There was no Gavin Guile, no Dazen Guile, no High Luxlord Prism, no scraping sniveling dignitaries devoid of dignity, no lies, no satraps to be bullied, no Spectrum councilors to manipulate, no lovers, no bastards, no power except the power before his eyes. He felt small, staring into incomprehensible vastness.

Cooled by the gentle morning breeze, warmed by the twin suns, one in the sky, one beneath the waves, Gavin was serene. It was the closest thing to a holy moment he had ever experienced.

And then he realized the sea demon was swimming toward his fleet.

Chapter 2

The green hell was calling him to madness. The dead man was back in the reflective wall, luminous, grinning at Dazen, features squeezed skeleton-thin by the curving walls of the spherical green cell.

The key was to *not* draft. After sixteen years of drafting only blue, of altering mind and damaging body with that loathsome cerulean serenity, now having escaped the blue cell, Dazen wanted nothing more than to gorge on some other color. It was like he'd eaten breakfast gruel morning, noon, and night for six thousand days, and now someone was offering him a rasher of bacon.

He hadn't even liked bacon, back when he'd been free. Now it sounded lovely. He wondered if that was the fever, turning his thoughts to sludge and emotion.

Funny how he thought that: 'Back when he'd been free.' Not 'Back when he'd been Prism.'

He wasn't sure if it was because he was still telling himself that he was the Prism whether he was in royal robes or rancid rags, or if it simply didn't matter anymore.

Dazen tried to look away, but everything was green. To have his eyes open was to be dipping his feet in green. No, he was up to his neck in water and trying to get dry. There was no hope of dryness. He had to know that and accept it. The only question wasn't if he was going to get his hair wet, it was if he was going to drown.

Green was all wildness, freedom. That logical part of Dazen that had basked in blue's orderliness knew that sucking up pure wildness while locked up in this luxin cage would lead to madness. Within days he'd claw out his own throat. Pure wildness, here, would be death. He would finally accomplish his brother's objective for him.

He needed to be patient. He needed to think, and thinking was hard right now. He examined his body slowly, carefully. His hands and knees were lacerated from his crawl through the hellstone tunnel. The bumps and bruises from his fall through the trapdoor and into this cell he could ignore. They were painful, but inconsequential. Most worrisome was the inflamed, infected slash across his chest. It nauseated him just looking at it, oozing pus and promises of death.

Worst was the fever, corrupting his very blood, making him stupid, irrational, sapping his will.

But Dazen had escaped the blue prison, and that prison had changed him. His brother had crafted these prisons quickly, and probably put most of his efforts into that first, blue one. Every prison had a flaw.

The blue prison had made him the perfect man to find it. Death or freedom.

In his reflective green wall, the dead man said, "You taking bets?"

Chapter 3

Gavin sucked in light to start making his rowing apparatus. Unthinking, he tried to draft blue. While brittle, blue's stiff, slick, smooth structure made it ideal for parts that didn't undergo sideways stresses. For a futile moment, Gavin tried to force it, again. He was a Prism made flesh; alone out of all drafters, he could split light within himself. The blue was there—he knew it was there, and maybe knowing it was there, even though he couldn't see, might be enough.

For Orholam's sake, if you could find your chamber pot in the middle of the night and, despite that you couldn't see it, the damned thing was still there, why couldn't this be the same?

Nothing. No rush of harmonious logic, no cool rationality, no stained blue skin, no drafting whatsoever. For the first time since he was a boy, he felt helpless. Like a natural man. Like a peasant.

Gavin screamed at his helplessness. It was too late for the oars anyway. That son of a bitch was swimming too fast.

He drafted the scoops and the reeds. Blue worked better to make the jets for a skimmer, but naturally flexible green could serve if he made it thick enough. The rough green luxin was heavier and created more drag against the water, so he was slower, but he didn't have the time or attention to make it from yellow. Precious seconds passed while he prepared his skimmer.

Then the scoops were in hand and he began throwing luxin down into the jets, blasting air and water out the back of his little craft and propelling himself forward. He leaned far forward, shoulders knotting with the effort; then, as he picked up speed, the effort eased. Soon his craft was hissing across the waves.

The fleet arose in the distance, the sails of the tallest ships first. But at Gavin's speed, it wasn't long before he could see all of them. There were hundreds of ships now: from sailing dinghies to galleasses to the square-rigged three-masted ship of the line with forty-eight guns that Gavin had taken from the Ruthgari governor to be his flagship. They'd left Garriston with over a hundred ships, but hundreds more that had gotten out earlier had joined them within days for protection from the pirates who lay thick in these waters. Last, he saw the great luxin barges, barely seaworthy. He himself had created those four great open boats to hold as many refugees as possible. If he hadn't, thousands of people would have died.

And now they would die regardless, if Gavin didn't turn the sea demon.

As he sped closer, he caught sight of the sea demon again, a hump cresting six feet out of the water. Its skin was still placidly luminous, and by some good fortune it wasn't actually cutting straight toward the fleet. Its path would take it perhaps a thousand paces in front of the lead ship.

Of course, the ships themselves were plowing slow furrows forward, closing that gap, but the sea demon was moving so quickly, Gavin dared to hope that it wouldn't matter. He had no idea how keen the sea demon's senses were, but if it kept going in the same direction, they might well make it.

Gavin couldn't take his hands away from the skimmer's jets without losing precious speed, and he didn't know how he would deliver a signal that said, "Don't Do Anything Stupid!" to the whole fleet at once even if he did. He followed directly behind the sea demon, closer now.

He'd been wrong; the sea demon was going to cut perhaps five hundred paces from the lead ship. A bad estimate, or was the creature turning toward the fleet?

Gavin could see lookouts in the crow's nests waving their hands violently to those on the decks below them. Doubtless shouting, though Gavin was too far away to hear them. He sped closer, saw men running on the decks.

The emergency was on the fleet far faster than any of them could

5

have expected. In the normal order of things, enemies might appear on the horizon and give chase. Storms could blow out of nowhere in half an hour—but this had happened in minutes, and some ships were only seeing the twin wonders now—a boat traveling faster across the waves than anyone had ever seen in their lives, and the huge dark shadow in front of it that could only be a sea demon.

Be smart, Orholam damn you all, be smart or be too terrified to do anything at all. Please!

Cannons took time to load and couldn't be left armed because the powder could go bad. Some idiot might shoot a musket at the passing form, but that should be too small a disturbance for the monster to notice.

The sea demon bulled through the waters four hundred paces in front of the fleet and kept going straight.

Gavin could hear the shouts from the ships now. The man in the crow's nest of Gavin's flagship was holding his hands to his head in disbelief, but no one did anything stupid.

Orholam, just one more minute. Just—

A signal mortar cracked the morning, and Gavin's hopes belly-flopped in the sea. He swore that all the shouting on every ship in the fleet stopped at once. And then began again a moment later, as the experienced sailors screamed in disbelief at the terrified idiot captain who'd probably just killed them all.

Gavin had eyes only for the sea demon. Its wake went straight, hissing bubbles and great undulations, another hundred paces. Another hundred. Maybe it hadn't heard.

Then his skimmer jetted right past the entire beast as the sea demon doubled back on itself faster than Gavin would have believed possible.

As it completed its turn, its tail broke the surface of the water. It moved too fast for Gavin to make out details. Only that it was burning red-hot, the color of iron angry from the forge, and when that span—surely thirty paces long—hit the water, the concussion made the signal mortar's report sound tinny and small.

Giant swells rolled out from the spot its tail had hit. From his dead stop, Gavin was barely able to turn his skimmer before the waves reached him. He dipped deep into the first wave and hurriedly threw green luxin forward, making the front of his craft wider and longer. He was shot upward by the next swell and flung into the air.

6   The skimmer's prow hit the next giant swell at too great of an angle

and went straight into it. Gavin was ripped off the skimmer and plunged into the waves.

The Cerulean Sea was a warm wet mouth. It took Gavin in whole, chomped his breath out of him, rolled him over with its tongue, disorienting him, made a play at swallowing him, and when he fought, finally let him go.

Gavin surfaced and quickly found the fleet. He didn't have time to draft an entire new skimmer, so he drafted smaller scoops around his arms, sucked in as much light as he could hold, threw his arms down to his sides, and pointed his head toward the sea demon. He threw luxin down and it threw him forward.

The pressure of the waves was incredible. It obliterated sight, blotted out sound, but Gavin didn't slow. With a body made so hard by years of working a skimmer that he could cross the sea in a day, and a will made implacable by years of being Prism and forcing the world to conform to his wishes, he *pushed.*

He felt himself slide into the sea demon's slipstream: the pressure suddenly eased and his speed doubled. Using his legs to aim, Gavin turned himself deeper into the water, then jetted toward the surface.

He shot into the air. Not a moment too soon.

He shouldn't have been able to see much of anything, gasping in air and light, water streaming off his entire body. But the tableau froze, and he saw *everything.* The sea demon's head was halfway out of the water, its cruciform mouth drawn shut so its knobby, spiky hammerhead could smash the flagship to kindling. Its body was at least twenty paces across, and only fifty paces now from the ship.

Men were standing on the port rail, matchlocks in hand. Black smoke billowed thick from a few. Others flared as the matches ignited powder in the pans in the instant before they fired. Commander Ironfist and Karris both stood, braced, fearless, glowing luxin forming missiles in their hands. In the gun decks, Gavin saw men tamping powder into the cannons for shots they would never get off in time.

The other ships in the fleet were crowding around like kids around a fistfight, men perched on gunwales, mouths agape, all too few even loading their muskets.

Dozens of men were turning from looking at the monster approaching to see what fresh horror this could be shooting into the air—and gaping, bewildered. A man in the crow's nest was pointing at him, shouting.

And Gavin hung in midair, disaster and mutilation only seconds away from his compatriots—and threw all he had at the sea demon.

A coruscating, twisting wall of multicolored light blew out of Gavin, streaking toward the creature.

Gavin didn't see what it did when it struck the sea demon, or even if he hit it at all.

There was an old Parian saying that Gavin had heard but never paid attention to: "When you hurl a mountain, the mountain hurls you back."

Time resumed, unpleasantly quickly. Gavin felt like he'd been walloped with a club bigger than his own body. He was launched backward, stars exploding in front of his eyes, clawing catlike, twisting, trying to turn—and splashing in the water with another jarring slap, twenty paces back.

Light is life. Years of war had taught Gavin never to leave yourself unarmed; vulnerability is a prelude to death. He found the surface and began drafting instantly. In the years he'd spent failing thousands of times while perfecting his skimmer, he'd also perfected methods of getting out of the water and creating a boat—not an easy task. Drafters were always terrified of falling in the water and not being able to get out again.

So within seconds Gavin was standing on the deck of a new skimmer, already drafting the scoops as he tried to assess what had happened.

The flagship was still floating, one railing knocked off, huge scrapes across the wood of the port side. So the sea demon must have turned, must have barely glanced off the boat. It had slapped its tail down again as it turned, though, because a few of the small sailing dinghies nearby had been swamped, and men were jumping into the water, other ships already heading toward them to pluck them from the sea's jaws.

And where the hell was the sea demon?

Men were screaming on the decks—not shouts of adulation, but alarm. They were pointing—

Oh *shit*.

Gavin began throwing luxin down the reeds as fast as possible. But the skimmer always started slow.

The giant steaming red-hot hammerhead surfaced not twenty paces away, coming fast. Gavin was accelerating and he caught the shockwave caused by such a massive, blunt shape pushing through the seas. The front of the head was a wall, a knobby, spiky wall.

But with the swell of the shockwave helping him, Gavin began to pull away.

And then the cruciform mouth opened, splitting that entire front hammerhead wide in four directions. As the sea demon began sucking water in rather than pushing it in front of it, the shockwave disappeared abruptly. And Gavin's skimmer lurched back into the mouth.

Fully into the mouth. The open mouth was easily two or three times as wide as Gavin was tall. Sea demons swallowed the seas entire. The body convulsed in rhythm, a circle that squeezed tighter and then opened wider, jetting water past gills and out the back almost the same way Gavin's skimmer did.

Gavin's arms were shaking, shoulders burning from the muscular effort of pushing his entire body, his entire boat across the seas. Harder. Dammit, harder!

The sea demon arched upward just as Gavin's skimmer shot out of its mouth. Its tetraform jaws snapped shut, and it launched itself into the air. He shut his eyes and screamed, pushing as hard as he could.

He shot a look over his shoulder and saw the impossible: the sea demon had breached. Completely. Its massive body crashed back down into the water like all seven towers of the Chromeria falling into the sea at once.

But Gavin was faster, up to full speed. Filling with the fierce freedom of flight and the luminous lightness of life, he laughed. Laughed.

The sea demon pursued him, furious, still burning red, moving even faster than before. But with the skimmer at full speed, Gavin was out of danger. He circled out to sea as the distant shapes of men cheered on the decks of every ship of the fleet, and the creature followed him.

Gavin led it for hours out to sea; then, circling wide in case it headed blindly in the last direction it had seen him go, he left it far behind.

As the sun set, exhausted and wrung out, he returned to his fleet. They'd lost two sailing dinghies, but not a single life. His people—for if they hadn't been his before, he owned them heart and soul now—greeted him like a god.

Gavin accepted their adulation with a wan smile, but the freedom had faded. He wished he, too, could rejoice. He wished he could get drunk and dance and bed the finest-looking girl he could find. He wished he could find Karris somewhere in the fleet and fight or fuck

9

or one and then the other. He wished he could tell the tale and hear it retold from a hundred lips and laugh at the death that had come so close to them all. Instead, as his people celebrated, he went belowdecks. Alone. Waved Corvan away. Shook his head at his wide-eyed son.

And finally, in his darkened cabin, alone, he wept. Not for what had been, but for what he knew he must become.

Chapter 4

Karris hadn't joined the revelers celebrating surviving their brush with the sea demon. She woke before dawn and made her ablutions, and brushed out her hair to give herself time to think. It didn't help.

The secret was rubbing Karris like a burr under the cinch strap. She bound hair black as her mood back in a ponytail as usual. She'd spent the last five days putting pieces together: Gavin "falling ill" after the last battle of the war against his brother Dazen; Gavin breaking their betrothal; Gavin being astonished at learning about his bastard son Kip; Gavin being *different*.

Then she'd wasted time wondering how she'd been so dense. She—and everyone else—had attributed the changes to the trauma of war, the trauma of killing his own brother. His prismatic eyes had been proof, *proof* that Gavin was Gavin. Gavin was brilliant and quite the liar, but he shouldn't have been able to fool her. She knew him too well. More to the point, she knew *Dazen* too well.

That was finished. She made her way to the forecastle as she had every morning and began stretching. She went crazy if she didn't do some calisthenics every day. Her superior, Commander Ironfist, had thoughtfully brought her two sets of blacks to wear, and both tunic and pants were cotton infused with luxin—snug in spots, flexible everywhere, made for movement foremost and secondly to show off the Blackguards' hardened physiques. But though grunting and sweating were part and parcel of her life, that didn't mean she wanted to share it with every cretin on deck.

"May I?" Ironfist asked, coming onto the deck. The commander of the Blackguard was a huge man. A good leader. Smart, tough, and intimidating as hell. When Karris nodded, he removed his headscarf and folded it neatly. It was a Parian religious custom, the men covering their heads in respect to Orholam. But there were exceptions, and like many Parians, Ironfist believed the injunction only applied once the sun had risen fully above the horizon.

Ironfist had once plaited his wiry black hair, but after the Battle of Garriston and the death of so many of his Blackguards, he'd shaved his head completely bald in mourning. Another Parian custom. The headscarf that had once covered his glory would now cover his grief.

Orholam. All the dead Blackguards, many of them killed at the same time by one exploding shell, a lucky shot that cared nothing for their elite skills in drafting and fighting. Her colleagues. Her friends. It was a yawning pit, devouring everything but her tears.

Coming to stand parallel to Karris, Ironfist brought his hands together, then separated them to a low-high guard. It was the beginning of the Marsh ka. A suitable beginning, when muscles weren't warm, and the ka didn't range far, so their moves could fit within the small confines of the forecastle. Sweep low, turn, back kick, roundhouse, land on the other foot, balance—not as easy a task as usual on the bobbing deck.

Ironfist led, and Karris was glad to let him do so. The sailors assigned to the third watch stole glances at them, but Karris and Ironfist weren't much visible in the predawn gray, and the gazes were unobtrusive. The motions were second nature. Karris focused on her body, the aches of sleeping on a wooden deck quickly worked out, the older aches more stubborn—the training injury that always made her hip ache, the stiffness in her left ankle from when she'd sprained it fighting a green wight with Gavin.

Not Gavin. Dazen. Orholam curse him.

Ironfist moved to Korick's ka, ramping up the intensity quickly, again, a good choice for this tight of a space. And soon Karris was focusing on getting just a little more length on her spinning roundhouse kick, getting full extension and height on the back kick. She wasn't nearly as tall as Ironfist, but he could flick his long limbs out into kicks and spear hands with unbelievable speed. She had to work hard to keep up with the pace he set.

The sun rose and they stopped only when it had almost cleared the horizon. Apparently Ironfist had wanted some hard work, too. As she breathed and gasped, leaning over with her hands propped on her thighs, he mopped his brow, made the sign of the seven to the new-risen sun, breathed a short prayer, and put his ghotra on his shaven head.

"You want something," he said.

He picked up another cloth and threw it to her. Of course he'd brought two. He was conscientious like that. It also told her that he'd not joined her morning calisthenics by accident. He'd come to talk.

Classic Ironfist. Comes to talk, and says five words in the course of an hour.

Still, he was right. So Karris said, "The Lord Prism is going to leave the fleet. He'll either try to do so without your knowledge or he'll at least try to get you to agree not to send any Blackguards with him. I want you to send me."

"He told you this?"

"He didn't have to tell me. He's a coward; he always runs away." Karris thought she'd worked out the rage in her calisthenics, but there it was, hot and crisp, ready to fling her skyward in an instant.

"Coward?" Ironfist leaned against the railing. He looked at it. "Hmm." Not a pace from where they stood, the railing was broken. Had been broken by a rampaging sea demon.

A rampaging sea demon that Gavin had faced down.

She grunted. "That last part wasn't supposed to come out."

Ironfist wasn't amused. "Come here. Eyes."

He took her face in his big hands and stared at her eyes in the rising sunlight, measuring, intense. He said, "Karris, you're the quickest drafter I have, but you're also the quickest *to* draft. Uncontrollable rage? Saying things aloud you didn't intend? Those are the hallmarks of a red or green who is *dying*. Half my Blackguard is dead, and if you keep on drafting like you have, you'll break the halo in—"

"Hope I'm not interrupting," a voice intruded. Gavin.

Ironfist was still holding Karris's face in both hands, staring into her eyes. Standing on the deck in the soft warm light of dawn, they both realized at the same time what it probably looked like.

Commander Ironfist dropped his hands, cleared his throat. Karris thought it was the first time she'd ever seen him embarrassed. "Lord Prism," Ironfist said. "Orholam's eye grace you."

"And a good morning to you, Commander. Karris. Commander,

I'd like to meet with you in an hour. Please summon Kip as well; I'll require him after our conversation. I believe he's on the first barge." Gavin's white tunic, accented with gold embroidery, was actually clean—on a ship, in the middle of fleeing from a battle, someone had laundered his clothes. He mattered that much to people. Things just magically worked out for Gavin without his even trying. It was infuriating. At least his face looked drawn. Gavin never slept well.

Ironfist looked like he wanted to say more, but he simply nodded and walked away.

Which left Karris alone with Gavin for the first time since she'd thrown a fit after learning he'd sired a bastard during their betrothal. She had jumped out of their boat then. It was the first time they'd even been face-to-face since she'd slapped his smiling face—in the middle of the Battle of Garriston, in full view of his entire army.

Maybe she *had* been drafting too much red and green. Anger and impulsivity shouldn't be a Blackguard's most prominent traits. Or a lady's. "Lord Prism," she said, determined to be civil.

He looked at her silently, that restless intelligence in his eyes weighing, always weighing. He looked at her almost mournfully, eyes touching her hair, her eyes, pausing at her lips, traveling quickly down her curves and back up to her eyes again, maybe flicking just for a moment to the sides of her eyes, where the wrinkles were starting.

He spoke softly: "Karris, you look better when you're a sweaty mess than most women look in their Sun Day best." Gavin was handsome, charming, and willful in all senses of the word, but something people often forgot was that he was smart, too.

He didn't want to talk. He was stalling. Getting her confused and defensive about something that had nothing to do with anything. Bastard! She was sweaty, sticky, stinky, how could he compliment her now?

How dare he be nice after she'd slapped him in the face?

How dare his stupid little gambit work despite that she knew what he was doing?

"Go to hell," she said, and walked away.

Nicely done, Karris. Professional, ladylike, civil. Bastard!

Chapter 5

How could a woman make you want to throw her ass into the sea and kiss her breathless at the same time? Karris walked away and Gavin couldn't help but admire her figure.

Damn woman.

He saw that some of the sailors on deck were appreciating her figure, too. He cleared his throat to get their attention and lifted an eyebrow at them; they quickly found work to do.

"Is this perfectly necessary, Lord Prism?" a voice asked, coming up behind Gavin. It was his new general, the man who'd worked with him sixteen years ago when he'd been Dazen's most effective general, Corvan Danavis. They'd had to do some clever work to make everyone believe Gavin's "enemy" would now take orders from him.

"By *this*, you mean this?" Gavin pointed at the rope ladder up to the crow's nest.

"Yes." General Danavis was the kind of man who prayed before a battle, just in case, and then went about his business as if he had absolutely no fear of death. Gavin didn't think he experienced fear in the way other men did—but he absolutely hated heights.

"Yes," Gavin said. He climbed up the rope ladder first. As he pulled himself into the observation box, he was struck once again by a thought he had regularly: his whole life was based on magic. He climbed this height fearlessly because he knew that if he fell, he could draft quickly enough to catch himself. Though he might appear fearless, he wasn't. There was simply hardly ever any danger for him—totally unlike most people. People would see him do incredible things, and think him incredible. And they would be totally misunderstanding.

The sudden stab of fear was so sharp that he thought for a moment someone actually had hit him in the gut. He took a deep breath.

Corvan came up, eyes locked on the crow's nest, hands in a death grip on each rung. Gavin hated to do this to his friend, but there were some conversations that one simply couldn't risk having overheard.

Gavin helped him into the box. He let the general catch his breath. At least the safety rails up here were nice and high and stout. Below, the sailors were going about their work. The morning wind was rising, and the first watch was out, checking lines and knots, the captain on the poop with a sextant, making sure of their position.

"I've lost blue," Gavin said. Get it out. Clean it up afterward.

He could tell from the expression on his face that Corvan Danavis had no idea what he was talking about. He stroked the red mustache he was growing back. He'd been known for dangling beads from that mustache, back during the Prisms' War. "Blue what?"

"I can't see blue anymore, Corvan. It's a sunny morning, I'm staring at the sky and the Cerulean Sea—and I can't see blue. I'm dying, and I need your help deciding what I should do."

Corvan was one of the smartest men Gavin knew, but he looked lost. "Lord Prism, such a thing isn't—wait, tell me one piece at a time. Did this happen during your fight with the sea demon?"

"No." Gavin looked over the waves. The rocking of the ship was soothing, perfectly complemented by the harmonious blues of sky and sea. He could remember the color so clearly he could swear he almost saw it. He was a superchromat, one who could differentiate colors much more finely than other men. He knew blue from its lightest to its darkest tones, from its violet hues to its greenest ones, blue of every saturation, blue of every mixture.

"After the battle," Gavin said. "When we sailed away with all the refugees. I woke the next day and I didn't even notice for a while. It's like looking at a friend's face and realizing you don't know her name, Corvan. Blue's there; it's close. It's like the color is on the tip of my eyes. If I don't concentrate, I don't even notice it, except that the world seems washed out, flat. But if I concentrate as hard as I can, I can see gray where the blue should be. Exactly the right tone and saturation and brightness, but...gray."

Corvan was silent for a long minute, red-haloed eyes squinting. "The timing isn't right," he said. "Prisms are supposed to last some multiple of seven years. You should have five years left."

"I don't think what's happening to me is normal. I was never ordained the Prism. Maybe this is what happens when a natural polychrome doesn't go through the Spectrum's ceremony."

"I don't know that that's quite—"

"Have you ever heard of any Prism going blind, Corvan? Ever?" The last Prism before Gavin—the real Gavin—had been Alexander Spreading Oak. He'd been a weak Prism, hid in his apartments mostly, had likely been a poppy addict. The matriarch Eirene Malargos had 15 been before him. She'd lasted fourteen years. Gavin had only the barest recollection of her from the Sun Day rituals when he was a young boy.

"Gavin, most Prisms don't last sixteen years. Maybe the Spectrum's ceremony would have made you die *earlier*. If you'd died after seven years or fourteen, you'd never have experienced this. We can't know."

That was one problem with being a fraud. You can't elicit information about something that's terribly secret that you should already know. The real Gavin had been initiated as Prism-elect when he was thirteen years old. He had sworn never to speak of it, not even to once-best-friend and brother Dazen.

It was one oath that, so far as Gavin could tell, each member of the Spectrum had honored. Because in the sixteen years he'd been impersonating his brother, no one had said a word about it. Unless, of course, they had made sidelong references to it—which he never picked up, and thus didn't respond to, and thus let them know that he valued the secrecy of the ceremony highly and they should, too.

In other words, he was caught in a trap of his own devising. Again.

"Corvan, I don't know what's happening. I may wake up tomorrow and not be able to draft green, and the next day and not be able to draft yellow. Or maybe I've just lost blue and that's all, but I have lost blue. Best-case scenario, if I manage to stay away from the Chromeria and am absent during every blue ritual, I've got one year left—until next Sun Day. There's no way I could maintain a fraud through the ceremonies, or skip them. If I can't draft blue by then, I'm dead."

Gavin could see Corvan realizing all the consequences. His friend expelled a breath. "Huh. Just when everything was going so well." He chuckled. "We've got fifty thousand refugees that no one is going to want; we're running low on food; the Color Prince has just had a major victory and will now doubtless gather thousands more heretics to his banners; and now we're losing our greatest asset."

"I'm not dead yet," Gavin said. He grinned.

Corvan grinned ruefully back, but he looked sick. "Don't worry, Lord Prism, I'm the last man who would count you out." Gavin knew it was true, too. Corvan had accepted disgrace and exile to make Dazen's defeat look credible. He'd spent the last sixteen years in a backwater village, poor, unknown, quietly keeping an eye on the real Gavin's bastard, Kip.

Another problem.

Corvan looked down, blanched at the height, and gripped the rail tightly again. "What are you going to do?"

"The more time I spend with drafters, the more likely it is that someone will notice something's wrong. And if I'm at the Chromeria too long, the White will ask me to balance. If blue goes under red, I might not even be able to tell, much less balance it out. They'll remove me."

"So…"

"So I'm going to go to Azûlay to see the Nuqaba," Gavin said.

"Well, that's one way of keeping Ironfist from accompanying you, but why do you want to see her?"

"Because in addition to their capital having the largest library in the world—where I can study without the entire Spectrum knowing what I've looked at within an hour—the Parians also keep oral histories, including many that are secret and some that are doubtless heretical."

"What are you looking for?"

"If I've lost control of blue, Corvan, that means blue is out of control."

Corvan looked momentarily confused, then aghast. "You can't be serious. I've never read a serious scholar who thought the *bane* were anything other than bogeymen the Chromeria invented to justify the actions of some of the early zealots and the luxors."

The bane. Corvan used the old Ptarsu term correctly. The word could be singular or plural. It had probably meant temple or holy place, but Lucidonius's Parians had believed they were abominations. They'd acquired the word itself as they'd acquired the world.

"And if they're wrong?"

Corvan was quiet for a long time. Then he said, "So you're going to show up on the Nuqaba's doorstep and say, 'As the head of your faith, please show me your heretical texts and tell me the stories which I of all people am most likely to find deserving of death,' and expect them to do it? I guess it qualifies as a plan. Not a good one, mind you."

"I *can* be awfully charming," Gavin said.

Corvan smiled, but turned away. "You know," he said, "what you did yesterday with the sea demon was…astounding. What you did in Garriston was astounding, and not just the building of Brightwater Wall. Gavin, these people will follow you to the ends of the earth. They will spread word of what you've done to anyone they meet. If it came down to a fight between you and the Spectrum…"

"The Spectrum already has more malleable candidates lined up to be the next Prism, Corvan. If I defy them now, I'll be in as bad of a spot as *Dazen* was seventeen years ago. I won't put the world through that again. The people can love me, but if all their leaders unite against me, I'll win nothing except for death for my friends and allies. I've done that once."

"So, what? You're just going to leave us? What are you going to do about Kip? He's a tough kid, but he's damaged and I think you're the only thing he's holding on to. If he finds out you're not who you say you are, he could shatter. There's no telling what he'd turn into. Don't do that to your soul, Gavin. Don't do that to the world. The last thing the Seven Satrapies need is another young polychrome Guile, mad with rage and grief. And what are *we* supposed to do? Where are we supposed to put all these people?"

"Corvan, Corvan, Corvan. I've got a plan." Sort of.

"Somehow, my friend, I was afraid of that." The crow's nest swayed hard as the ship caught a rogue wave, and Corvan looked down at the deck far below, swallowing. "I don't suppose it includes an easy way for me to get down?"

Chapter 6

Ironfist grimaced at the missive in his hand. Usually, that expression, from him, toward Gavin, would be a quick twitch, quickly smoothed away. This time, his face twisted as if he were eating steak smoked in poisonwood. "You're having me deliver *orders*. To the White," Ironfist said.

Gavin had summoned the big bodyguard to his stateroom after trying several rooms to see which suited his purposes best. "Regarding my son. Yes." As Prism, Gavin didn't have any authority over the White, but she had to be careful not to offend him. Both of them had to choose their battles with each other. He thought this was one she wouldn't choose.

"You want Kip made a Blackguard." Ironfist kept his voice flat. He was the Blackguard's commander. Technically, he alone was supposed to decide who was invited to try to join. "Lord Prism, I'm struggling to find where to start explaining how wrong and destructive that would be."

It was a sunny day out, but the gleaming dark woods of the stateroom soaked up light, made Gavin have to concentrate to see the commander's expressions. "I hope you know, Commander, that I have supreme respect for you."

Slight eyebrow twitch. Disbelief. It actually was true, but Gavin supposed he hadn't given Ironfist many reasons to believe that.

Gavin continued, "But we find ourselves in a situation that requires quick action. Refugees. Aggrieved satraps. A city lost. Rebellion. Ring a bell?"

Ironfist's face turned to stone.

Gavin needed to handle this better. Tell the man you respect him, and then treat him like he's an idiot? "Commander," he said, "how many Blackguards did you lose at Garriston?"

"Fifty-two dead. Twelve wounded. Fourteen so close to breaking the halo that they'll have to be replaced."

Gavin paused long enough to be respectful of the loss. He'd already known the number, of course. Knew the faces and the names of the dead. The Blackguard was the Prism's personal guard, and yet not under his control. He was treading on that line. "And pardon me for speaking so bluntly, but that number must be replenished."

"Three years at least, and the quality of the Blackguard as a whole won't recover for ten or more. I'll have to promote people who are inadequately trained. They'll not be able to train those beneath them as well. You understand what your actions have done to us? Killed a generation and retarded two. I'll leave the Blackguard a shadow of what it was when I got it." Ironfist kept his voice level, but the fury beneath it was unmistakable. Uncharacteristic for him.

Gavin said nothing, jaw clenched, eyes dead. This was the hell of leading: to see a man as an individual with hopes, families, loves, favorite foods, more alert in the morning or at night, fond of hot peppers and dancing girls and singing off key. Then the next hour to see him as a number and be willing to sacrifice him. Those thirty-eight dead men and fourteen women had saved tens of thousands of people, had almost saved the city. Gavin had put them in a place where he knew they might die, and they had. He'd do it again. He held Ironfist's gaze.

Ironfist looked away. "Lord Prism," he added. There was no remorse in his voice, but Gavin didn't require unquestioning obedience. Just obedience.

Gavin glanced up at the open space above the rafters between his stateroom and the next. "The Blackguard requires recruits. The autumn class probably hasn't even started yet, and Kip is ideal. You've seen him draft."

"It's too physically demanding. Twenty weeks of hellish training and fights every month that purge the deadwood. From forty-nine to the seven best. He'd never make it even if he hadn't burned his hand. If he slims down, maybe in a year or—"

"He'll make it," Gavin said. It wasn't an expression of confidence.

Silence as Ironfist grappled with the implication. Then disbelief. "You want me to induct him undeservedly?"

"Do I need to answer that?"

"You'll publicly make him a favorite? You'll destroy that boy."

"Everyone will think he's favored regardless." Gavin shrugged and made sure he was speaking forcefully. "He'll serve the purpose for which he was made, or he'll break in pursuit of it, just like the rest of us."

Commander Ironfist didn't reply. He was a man who understood the power of silence.

"Come with me, Commander." They walked together out to a balcony. The door between the rooms was thin, and there were open spaces beside the rafters, perhaps so the captain could yell orders to his secretaries who in normal times had their offices in the cuddy. The exchange hadn't gone exactly how he wanted, but it would serve. Kip should have overheard everything.

Now Gavin had some words for Ironfist, out of Kip's hearing. "Kip is my son, Commander. I acknowledged him as such when I could have instead let him die without anyone knowing better. I'm not going to destroy Kip. He's fat, and he's awkward, and he's a powerful polychrome. He's going to grow up fast when he gets to the Chromeria. He can become a laughingstock or he can become a great man. He's getting a late start. The satraps' sons and daughters will devour him. I want you to soak up every hour of his time, remake him physically, make him tough mentally, make him learn the measure of himself. When he's earned the respect of the Blackguards, when he doesn't care what the vipers think of him, I'll ask him to quit the Blackguard and jump in the vipers' den."

"You're grooming him to be the next Prism," Ironfist said.

"Why, Commander, Orholam alone chooses his Prisms," Gavin said.

It was a joke, but Ironfist didn't laugh. "Indeed, Lord Prism." Gavin kept forgetting that Ironfist was a religious man.

"I'm not going to go easy on him," Ironfist said. "If he's to join my Blackguard, he has to earn it."

"Sounds perfect," Gavin said.

"He's a *polychrome*." Polychromes were strongly discouraged from such dangerous service.

"He wouldn't be the first exception," Gavin said. He would be the first in a long, long time.

Unhappy silence. "And somehow *I* have to convince the White to allow this."

"I trust you." Gavin grinned.

Ironfist's glare could have soured honey. Gavin laughed, but he noted it again. Ironfist respected him, but Gavin's charm did nothing to this man.

"You're leaving us," Ironfist said slowly. "After you got half my people killed, you're planning to leave, and leave us behind, aren't you?"

Damn.

Ironfist took his silence for assent. "Know this, Prism: I won't allow it. I won't do anything at all for you if you don't let me do my job. If you make my work meaningless, why should I help yours? Is this what you call supreme respect?"

Ah. Note to self: charm is less effective on people who have good reason to kick your ass. Gavin raised his hands. "What do you want?"

"Not want. Demand. You take a Blackguard with you. My choice. I don't know what your mission is, but where one can go, two can. Note that I would much rather you travel with an entire squad, but I'm a reasonable man."

It actually *was* far more reasonable than Gavin would have expected. Maybe Ironfist wasn't as good at politics as Gavin had thought. Of course, he was probably too busy figuring out how to kill things efficiently to get as much practice in politics as Gavin got. Ironfist probably meant to come with Gavin himself—which would definitely not work, but after Ironfist thought about all the work he had to do rebuilding and training the Blackguard, he would realize that. Too late.

"Done," Gavin said quickly, before the man could reconsider.

"Then it's a deal," Ironfist said. He extended a hand, and Gavin took it. It was an old Parian way of sealing deals, not much used anymore. But Ironfist looked Gavin in the eye as he clasped his hand. "I've already had someone request the assignment," he said.

Impossible. I didn't even tell him I was leaving until—

"Karris," Ironfist said. And then he smiled, toothily.

Bastard.

Chapter 7

Kip sat in the secretaries' office, fiddling nervously with the bandage on his left hand as Ironfist and Gavin talked on the balcony off the ship's stern. He had been seated with his back to the wall between the office and the Prism's stateroom, but having overheard too much, he quietly moved to one of the secretaries' chairs, farther back from the wall, so it wouldn't look like he'd been eavesdropping.

A Blackguard. Him. It was like winning a contest he hadn't even known he was competing in. He hadn't really thought about his future yet; he figured the Chromeria would take the next few years of his life and he'd go from there. But the toughest people he knew in the world were Blackguards: Karris and Ironfist.

The stateroom door opened and Ironfist stepped out. He gave Kip a sharp look. A disapproving look. And all at once Kip realized he was being imposed on Ironfist—the man didn't want Kip the fatty debasing his Blackguards. His heart dropped so fast it left a smoking crater in the deck.

"The Prism will see you now," Ironfist said. And he left.

Kip stood on weak knees. He walked into the stateroom.

The Prism Gavin Guile, the man who'd made Brightwater Wall and faced a sea demon and sunk pirates and crushed armies and cowed satraps—his father—smiled at him. "Kip, how are you feeling? You did some pretty amazing things the other day. Come. I need to see your eyes."

Feeling suddenly awkward, Kip followed Gavin out onto the stern balcony. In the bright morning light, Gavin looked at Kip's irises.

"A definite green ring. Congratulations. No one will ever mistake you for a non-drafter again."

"That's...great."

Gavin smiled indulgently. "I know it's a lot to get used to, and I suppose someone's already told you this, but you used a lot of magic in the battle, Kip. A lot. Going green golem isn't something we teach anymore because a person can generally only do it two or three times in their life. It burns through your power—and your life—at an incredible rate. The power's intoxicating, but beware of it. You've seen some of the greatest drafters in the world work, and you can't assume that you can do everything they can do. But look at me, lecturing. Sorry."

"No, it's fine. It's..." It's the kind of thing a father does. Kip didn't say it out loud. He swallowed the sudden lump in his throat.

Gavin looked over the waves at his fleet following them. He was somber, pensive. Finally, he spoke. "Kip, I don't get to be fair to you. I can't spend the time with you that you deserve, that I owe you. I can't tell you all the secrets that I wish I could. I can't introduce you to your new life the way I wish. You've chosen to be known as my son, and I respect that. That's how you'll be known. As my son, I have work for you to do, and I need to tell you what that work is now, because I'm leaving today. I'll come to the Chromeria every once in a while, but not often. Not for the next year."

There were too many thoughts at once. Everything Kip knew had been turned on its head too many times. In the last few months he'd gone from being a child with a haze-addled single mother to losing his village, his mother, his life. He'd been flung into the Chromeria, and into the company of the best drafters and fighters in the world.

And on the very day his father had accepted him, recognized him as a son instead of a bastard, he'd found a note from his mother claiming Gavin Guile had raped her. She'd begged Kip to kill Gavin. She'd probably been high when she wrote it, of course. So it had been the last thing she'd written. It didn't magically make it different from all the other lies she'd told Kip over the years.

She said she loved me. Kip quickly rejected the thought and the well of emotions it tapped.

Some of it must have shown in his face, though, because Gavin said quietly, "Kip, you have every right to be angry, but I have something impossible to ask of you. I'm going to send you on to the Chromeria. I expect you to do well in all your classes, of course. But honestly, I don't care, so long as you learn as much and as quickly as you can. What I really want is..." He trailed off. "This has to be our secret, Kip. I'm putting my very life in your hands by even asking you this. And you may, of course, fail or choose not to do this, but—"

Kip swallowed. Why was his father dancing so carefully about asking him to join the Blackguard? "You're scaring me more by hedging than you would if you just told me," Kip said.

"First, you have to impress your grandfather without me there. He will summon you. He will not be pleasant. We'll count it a victory if you avoid wetting yourself." He grinned that Guile grin, then sobered. "Do your best. If you can impress him, you'll have done more than I ever could. But whatever you do, don't make an enemy of him."

"And that's going to be impossible?"

"No—well, maybe—but I was starting with the easy assignment. I want you to destroy Luxlord Klytos Blue."

Kip blinked. That wasn't "Join the Blackguard" either. "That thing about being more scared by your hedging than the assignment? I take it back."

"By destroy, I mean do whatever you have to do to make him resign his seat on the Spectrum. I need that seat, Kip."

"For what?"

"I can't tell you. What you should ask is, what do I mean when I say, 'Do whatever you have to'?"

"Right, then, *that*," Kip said. He was hoping this was all some kind of joke, but the feeling in his stomach told him that it wasn't.

"If you can't get Klytos to resign of his own will, or through blackmail, kill him."

A chill radiated from Kip's spine to his shoulders. He swallowed.

"Your choice. I'm trusting you with that. This is war, Kip. You saw what happens when the wrong man is in power. The governor of Garriston could have prepared his city. He knew what was coming. Preparing the city would have made him deeply unpopular and it would have cost him a fortune. So instead, he chose to let them all die. One man caused all that carnage, simply by his inaction. If we hadn't been there, it would have been much, much worse. This is like that. That's all I can tell you."

It was impossible, but Kip felt a calm. The impossibility didn't matter right now. He could grapple with that when his father was gone. "Does he deserve it?" he asked.

Gavin took a deep breath. "I want to say yes to make it easier on you, but 'deserving' is a slippery concept. Does a coward who deserts his comrades deserve to be shot? No, but it has to be done because the stakes are so high. Klytos Blue is a coward who believes lies. If a man believes lies and repeats them, is he a liar? Maybe not, but he has to be stopped. I don't believe Klytos is an evil man, Kip. I don't believe he deserves to die out of hand or I'd kill him myself. But the stakes are high, and they're rising. Do what you must. Get in the Blackguard first. I've secured a tryout for you. Get in, and the position will help you accomplish the rest."

Sure. Simple as that. Of course, for Gavin Guile, it probably *was* as simple as that. Things were so easy for a man of his powers, he probably thought they were easy for other people. "What are we trying to do?" Kip asked. "Ultimately, I mean."

"War is a spreading fire. And every old grudge is dry wood, begging for flame. When I fought my brother, men joined me who hated me, but they hated their neighbors more, and those neighbors then sided with him. We killed two hundred thousand people in less than four months, Kip. I had a chance to stop this new war at one city, a few thousand dead. I failed. There are satrapies that wouldn't mind seeing Atash burn, that wouldn't mind that fire spreading to Blood Forest, that don't want their sons to die defending Ruthgar, that don't want their daughters to have to be Freed after defending Paria, that don't want to raise their taxes for Ilytian heathens, that don't want to send their crops to those filthy Aborneans."

Kip understood. "Which leaves no one."

"We're trying to stop the war before it engulfs everyone."

"How do you stop a war?" Kip asked.

"You win. So you do your part, and I'll do mine."

"How long do I have?" Kip asked. A small part of him rebelled. It wasn't fair to ask a boy to do this. It wasn't what you'd ask of a son. But Kip was only a son by his father's grace. He was an unwanted bastard, and if Gavin held the boy he'd never known at arm's length, how could Kip blame him?

"Depends on how long the Color Prince licks his wounds in Garriston. It's probably too much to hope he'll stay the winter, so he'll most likely head west. I imagine Idoss will hold him off for a few months. Losing Idoss should be enough to move the Spectrum. If not...six months, Kip. Eight if we're lucky. If we don't save the city of Ru, he'll get their saltpeter caves and iron mines and we'll be plunged into a war worse than the False Prism's War, and unlikely to be as brief."

Kip was in so far over his head he couldn't even see the surface. "Why me?" he asked.

"Because audacity is a young man's sword. Daring is a gun. And, to be blunt, if you fail in non-spectacular fashion, you'll merely look like a petty child. That would damage your reputation but not mine. And it won't get either of us killed. You're a good weapon because to look at you, you look like a child, an affable boy who wouldn't hurt a fly."

Affable. Code for "fat and nice." Next I'll be "jolly." "I'm so unlikely that I'm perfect?" Kip said.

"Exactly."

"I thought that once, right before I ran away from Garriston." Kip had thought no one would think a child would come to spy on the Color Prince and rescue Liv. That had turned out well.

"But you're stronger now."

"That was two weeks ago!"

Gavin laughed.

"Doesn't that tell you something?" Kip insisted.

Gavin smiled. "It should tell you something, too."

"What?" Kip asked.

Gavin got serious. "That I believe in you."

Kip wasn't sure what to do with that, not when Gavin delivered it straight. He couldn't laugh it off, couldn't make a joke out of it. It was too obviously true, and it warmed him. Kip grimaced. "You're really good at this, aren't you?"

Gavin rubbed Kip's head. "Almost as good as I think I am." He grinned. "You know, Kip, when this is all over..." He let the words fall away, and his good humor went with them.

"It's never going to be over, is it?" Kip asked.

The Prism took a deep breath. "Not the way I'd like."

"Are we going to lose?" Kip asked.

Gavin was quiet for a while. He shrugged and smirked. "Odds are." He wrapped an arm around Kip's wide shoulders, squeezed, released him. "But odds are for defying."

Chapter 8

Karris had all the gear packed and ready. Gavin, she assumed, would draft another skimmer rather than take one of the ships. He always was an impatient man. She checked her gear again to calm her nerves. She hated thinking she'd forgotten something. Hated not knowing what to prepare for but trying to pack light.

Of course, Gavin would come out and say, "Let's go!" and try to leave immediately. As if, having invented a way to cross the entire Cerulean Sea in a day and save a month of sailing, he didn't have an extra hour or two for packing.

Why had she volunteered for this again?

Because you don't have anything better to do than saving the world and revealing the cancer at its heart.

There was that.

Gavin came onto the deck, and Karris was struck once again by how every eye turned to him. She supposed that most of the people on this ship were common folk, and they would have turned to see even Garriston's Governor Crassos, hated as he had been. And perhaps they would have stared as worshipfully at any Prism, but she doubted it. Gavin's title was special, but something in her believed that he would have attracted every eye on deck even if he'd been a cabin boy. Now that he'd saved all their lives again, she was surprised that they didn't spontaneously burst out into applause.

The sailors burst out into applause.

Son of a bitch.

Two Blackguards fell in beside him as he came out the door. Someone must have shouted the word that the Prism was making an appearance, because in moments, people were piling out onto the deck. The captain, a stalwart rotund Ruthgari, made no attempt to stop them or get his sailors back to work. They nearly trampled each other on their way out of the cabins below, and sailors, soldiers, traders, nobles, and refugee peasants alike came out to get a look at their Prism.

He'd been on board with them for the last week, and he'd been in Garriston with them before that. It wasn't like he'd changed. But somehow where he'd been an important man before, now he was

27

theirs. Their savior. Pitting himself against a sea demon and winning had made Gavin larger than life.

If Karris hadn't seen with her own eyes how close Gavin had come to getting eaten, she might have had the cynicism to think he had arranged the whole thing.

The people were packed on the deck—every ship had been filled to bursting in order to get the refugees out of Garriston before the Color Prince took over—and all of them were talking to each other, sharing inanities like, "Do you see him? Is he saying anything?"

Gavin made his way over to Karris, Blackguards in tow. They, like she, scanned the crowd for threats. Gavin said, "Milady, would you do me the honor of accompanying me on a small expedition?"

What do you do when someone asks you kindly to do what you've already wheedled and schemed for? "I would be…delighted," Karris said.

"Excellent." Gavin smiled without any hint of irony. He did have a nice smile. The worm.

He raised his hands. "My people!" he said. He had a commander's voice, an orator's voice with the trick of somehow speaking so loudly and clearly that everyone could understand him without his seeming to shout. "My people! I leave you today, but only for a time. I go to make a place for you. I go ahead of you. And now I ask you to be fearless and grow strong. There are days ahead that will test us all. There is work that only you can do, though I will help as I can. I'm leaving General Danavis in charge. He has my full trust. He will lead well."

The words walked a narrow line, and he surely knew it. What he was describing without precisely saying was that he was their *promachos*—the title a Prism could be given during war. But the *promachia* could only be instituted by the order of the entire Spectrum. Gavin had been promachos during the war with his brother, and had been relieved of the title in less than six months. To be a promachos was to be emperor in truth.

It was one of the very things the Blackguard had been created to protect against.

At the same time, what else was Gavin going to tell all these people? That he was leaving and they were going to have to fend for themselves? They had nothing. They'd left everything in Garriston.

He kept talking, and Karris kept scanning the crowd. Ironfist had taught them the telltales for spotting an assassin, of course. Someone who was sweating profusely, shifting awkwardly, anyone who was keeping their hands concealed in such a way that they might be hiding something. For Karris, it was more of a feeling. An assassin would feel out of place. Someone who wasn't listening, because they didn't care what was said. Someone who only cared about his own mission. Karris realized two things at the same time. First, that was exactly what she was doing. Second, there were at least fifty Blackguards on deck. Not to mention a couple of hundred fanatical common folk who would tear apart anyone who even dared *offend* their Prism. If there were a perfect moment to *not* attempt an assassination, this would be it.

Gavin drafted a set of steps from the deck down to the water and drafted a yellow-hulled scull onto the water, complete with rowing apparatus for two.

The Blackguards on duty were Ahhanen and Djur. Neither man looked pleased, but they saluted Karris, transferring protection to her. Life, light, purpose.

Gavin descended the steps and took his place. He didn't offer Karris a hand onto the scull, which she appreciated. Now, in this, they weren't some lord and a lady. She was *his* protector, thank you very much.

As she took her place on the oars, she said, "No blue this time, huh?" The last time they'd sculled together, she'd accused him of using blue luxin for the hull because blue was practically invisible against the waves and it had unnerved her.

He grunted.

She shouldn't have said it. He'd doubtless drafted the scull from yellow to be kind to her. She'd complained about what he'd done last time, so this time he was doing it differently. And she'd thrown it in his face. Nice, Karris.

They pushed off and sculled together in silence, heading west. When they were half a league out, Gavin signaled that they should stop.

"I showed them all the skimmer yesterday, but there was a lot going on," he said. A lot going on. She supposed that was one way to describe the panic fifty thousand helpless people felt when they realize they're under attack by a sea demon and then watching their Prism lure it away from them single-handedly, using magic the likes of which no one had ever seen. "I didn't want to give all the drafters a tutorial today in how to make one for themselves. Just because a secret's going to get out eventually doesn't mean you need to shout it 29 from the rooftops." He stopped, seeming to realize that she might not be the person to say that to.

"So where are we going?" Karris asked. She didn't want to talk about that now either.

"I told my people I'd go prepare a place for them."

"You tell people things all the time."

Gavin opened his mouth, hesitated. Licked his lips. Didn't say whatever he was going to say. "I deserved that. Point is, I've got fifty thousand refugees. If we put them in one of the little Tyrean coastal towns, they'll overwhelm the locals, and still be just a short march down the road for the Color Prince. They'll be defenseless, and they'll starve to death even if he doesn't come after them. Point is, mostly for unfair reasons, no one will want to help a bunch of Tyreans."

"So you've come up with an elaborate solution."

"Not elaborate. Elegant. Fine, I suppose you could call it elaborate, too." He began drafting the scoops and straws for the skimmer. "I'm going to put them on Seers Island."

He was officially mad. Karris said, "That entire island is ringed with reefs. No one can get ships in there."

"I can."

"And how do the Seers feel about this?" she demanded.

"Surprised, I'd guess. I haven't told them yet."

"Oh, wonderful."

"Who knows?" Gavin said. "They *are* Seers. Maybe they've foretold my coming." His grin withered in the heat of her disapproval. He handed over one of the reeds and they began skimming.

Last time they'd skimmed together, they had held hands, Karris squeezing out the rhythm so that they would be in time with each other. This time he didn't even extend his hand toward her. Good, it saved her the trouble of rejecting it.

Regardless, they found their rhythm and began cruising across the surface of the sea. Within half an hour, the mountains of Seers Island came into view. But they were farther away than they appeared, and it took hours before Gavin and Karris approached the island. Even then, Gavin didn't head straight in. He turned south of the island, keeping between it and Tyrea, whose Karsos Mountains were just visible, purple in the distance.

Finally, Gavin turned them north, toward a huge bay. It was a shallow crescent, big enough for Gavin's entire fleet to fit into, but too wide in Karris's half-educated opinion to offer protection from the winter storms that would rip between the island and the mainland in a few months.

There were no known settlements. This island was taboo, forbidden, holy. Lucidonius had given it to the Seers hundreds of years ago. And, of course, it was surrounded by reefs that would destroy any ship with a greater displacement than a canoe or a skimmer, and even those could only make it in at high tide.

As they came in closer, skimming a mere hand's breadth over the coral, Karris saw an enormous pier jutting from the undeveloped shore. A pier that gleamed like gold—a pier of solid yellow luxin. She was about to comment to Gavin about it—Had he created this? Was this where he'd been going in the last few days?—when she saw something else.

There were a couple of hundred armed men and women standing on the beach in an unruly mob.

"Gavin, those people look angry."

Amused, Gavin lifted his eyebrows momentarily. "Not as angry as they're going to be." And then, heedless, he beached the skimmer directly in front of the mob.

Chapter 9

"Commander, could I talk with you for a moment?" Kip asked.

After Gavin and Karris left, Commander Ironfist and the Blackguards had taken over the fastest galleass in the fleet and, taking Kip, had headed for the Chromeria.

Everyone had been busy all the time for the first few days, with the Blackguards following the sailors' lead and trying to learn their craft. Commander Ironfist didn't want his Guards to sit idle, and given the chance to master some new skill, they dove right in. The sailors grumbled at first, but were eventually won over by how quickly the Blackguards learned.

For those who weren't on duty, Ironfist supervised shifts of sparring 31 and calisthenics on the galleass's small castle. Kip was allowed to watch, but mostly he tried to keep out of the way. It had taken him days to figure out when the commander would have a few empty minutes for Kip to bother him.

The commander looked at Kip. Nodded. Walked back into the cabin the captain was sharing with him for his work.

Kip had mustered his courage, but now he found it leaking away as they came into the small room and sat at a little table. "Sir, I...During the battle at Garriston, I—Well, some of it doesn't seem real, like I'm remembering things that couldn't really have happened, do you know what I—But that's not what I..." Kip was being stupid, inarticulate. He flexed with his bandaged hand. It hurt. "I killed the king—satrap—whatever. When I did it, Master Danavis—I mean, General Danavis—shouted at me, saying I'd fouled everything. I didn't mean to disobey, it just didn't—I don't know, maybe I did mean to disobey." The words wouldn't come out right. He felt like he was veering all over the place. He'd killed people, and part of him had liked it. Like he was smashing in the faces of those who wouldn't take him seriously. Except that he had literally smashed faces in, and when he thought about it, he felt wretched. But that was too hard to say. "I still don't know what I messed up, and what it cost. Can you tell me?"

Commander Ironfist drew a deep breath. Seemed to reconsider. "Hand," he said.

Kip presented his right hand, not sure what the imposing commander wanted.

Commander Ironfist looked at him flatly.

"Oh!" Kip presented his left hand. The commander unwrapped the bandage. He said, "I was fourteen years old when I killed my first man. My mother was the *deya* of Aghbalu—a regional governor—and she was angling to depose Paria's satrapah and become satrapah herself, though I didn't know that then. I was walking past her chambers one day, and I heard her cry out. I had first drafted perhaps two weeks before. I went in, and I saw the assassin. Small man, features of the despised Gatu tribe, teeth stained from chewing *khat*, and poison on the wavy blade of his *kris*. I remember thinking that only if I drafted could I stop him in time. But the drafting didn't just happen as it had two weeks before. He stabbed my mother, and while I stood there, not believing what I'd seen, he jumped out the window he'd climbed in and tried to escape over the roofs. I chased him, and I beat him with my fists, and I threw him off the roof."

Kip swallowed. Ironfist had chased an assassin, unarmed, across rooftops, and killed a man armed with a poisoned blade—when he was *fourteen*?

Ironfist paused, examining Kip's burned hand. He gestured for the ointment the chirurgeons had given Kip and rubbed it on the raw skin. Kip hissed and clenched every muscle in his body to keep from crying out.

"You need to stretch your fingers," Ironfist said. "All day, every day. If you don't, your fingers will tighten up into claws in no time. The scars will freeze your palm and fingers, and you'll have to split your skin open just to move. Take a little pain now or a lot later."

This was a *little* pain?

Commander Ironfist went back to his story as he wrapped Kip's hand in fresh bandages. "The point isn't that I'm a hard man, Kip. The point is I made mistakes. My mother was trained in *dawat*, our tribe's martial art. Not highly proficient, but trained well for a civilian. If I hadn't come in the room and she hadn't been worried for me, she could have fended him off until her guards came. And once I chased him down, I shouldn't have killed him. We could have found out who sent him."

"But you were just a boy," Kip said. Having his hand wrapped back up and immobile was like crawling back into a warm bed on a cold morning.

"And so are you," Commander Ironfist said. Kip started to protest, but Commander Ironfist wasn't finished. "Even if you weren't, I've seen grown men and women make worse mistakes in battle. If we naturally made good decisions in battle, there'd be no need to train for it."

"Did I get people killed? I killed a king, and I still can't figure out if it was a good thing or not." The anguish leaked through and Kip's eyes welled up. He looked away and gritted his teeth, blinking. Stupid. Get control of yourself.

"I don't know," Commander Ironfist said. "But the Color Prince exposed King Garadul on purpose. He wanted him killed. Maybe he'd planned it well in advance. Certainly us capturing Garadul rather than killing him would have tripped him up. General Danavis is very, very good at what he does. He understood in a moment. Most people wouldn't have. Especially not fifteen-year-old boys who've never been in a battle before."

"But I ignored him. I wanted to kill the king so much I wouldn't listen to anyone. Anything." Kip had crushed the king's head. He could remember the feeling of the man's skull cracking, brains squishing, blood splurting.

"You were deep in the grip of your color, Kip. So you blundered. Maybe you precipitated a wider war. Maybe. Maybe the general was wrong. Maybe King Garadul would have been far worse than this prince. We don't know. Can't know. It happened. Do better next time. That's what I do."

That's why you train.

"Did you ever find out who sent him?" Kip asked.

"The assassin? My sister thought she did. Let's head to the galley. It's time for supper, though not as much as either of us would like."

"But did she get her vengeance on the killer?" Kip asked.

"You might say that."

"What'd she do to him?"

"She married him."

Chapter 10

~Gunner~

Tap. Superviolet and blue. As his thumb touched, it was like someone had blown out a candle. The world went dark. Eyes useless. But then, a moment later, there was sun, waves washing over him, blinking, bobbing. Seeing his perspective shift while he felt his body utterly motionless made him queasy.

Tap. Green solved that in a rush of embodiment, touch restored. He was swimming. A strong body, wiry, naked to the waist. The water is warm, strewn with flotsam.

Tap. Yellow. Hearing restored, the shouts of men calling to each other, others screaming in pain or terror. But yellow is more than that; it is the logic of man and place. But the yellow in this one isn't quite right. Disbelieving. The Prism came out of nowhere. Dodged all his cannon shots. Even when Gunner finally started shooting both at once. That little boat the Prism made moved at speeds he wouldn't have believed if he'd heard another telling the tale. Ceres is going to take this out on him. Damn Gavin Guile.

But this mind skips around. There's something—

Tap. Orange. The smell of the sea and smoke and discharged powder, and he can sense the other men floating in the water, and below them, around them— Oh, by the hells. Sharks. Lots of sharks.

His finger is already descending. *Tap. Red-and-sub-red-and-the-taste-of-blood-in-his-mouth-and-it's-too—*

The trick with sharks is the nose. Not so different from a man. You bloody a bully's nose, and he goes looking elsewhere right quick. Easy, right? Easy.

Gunner ain't no easy meat. The sea's my mirror. Fickle as me. Crazy as me. Deep currents, and monsters rise from her depths, too. What others call sea spray, I call her spitting in my face, friendly like. Unlike most of this lot, I can swim. I just don't like it. Ceres and me do our admiring best at a bit of a distance.

She must be ragging something fierce.

The shark she's sent after me is a tiger shark. Good hunters. Fast. Curious as a crotch-sniffing hound. Mad as a starving lotus eater. Usually twice as long as a man is tall. But the sea's shown me respect, as she ought. My shark's bigger. Three times as long as I am tall, looks like. Hard to tell through the water, of course. Don't want to exaggerate. Hate exaggerators. Fucking hate 'em.

I'm Gunner, and I give it straight.

The scraps and shrapnel lines and barrels of the shipwreck litter the sapphire waters everywhere, but that tiger's coming back. Depending how tenacious she is, it'll take me a few minutes to swim to an appropriately sized—

"Oy, Ceres!" I shout as a thought occurs to me. "I know why you're mad!" Not many people know it, but the Cerulean Sea is named for Ceres. Not for the color. Those tits and twits at the Chromeria think everything revolves around them and their colors.

The tiger shark is circling me, dorsal fin cutting beautiful arcs on the open water. I'm on the edge of the wreckage. I got out first, saw that the fires were headed for the powder magazine. But being on the edge means that shark don't have to go through the distraction of all the other meat to get to me.

"Ceres! Easy, Ceres. Come on now!"

I turn constantly, keeping my face to the beastie. Sharks are cowards—like to pull you down from behind. These big bastards float along with these tiny little moves, like soaring buzzards, making you think they're ponderous, but when they strike, their speed is pants-drenching. The wedge-shaped head circles a bit closer, veers. And...now!

Gunner is the master of timing. None finer. Got to be when the seas are bucking under your feet and the linstock is in hand, slow match smoking, breathing burning saltpeter and lye in your face like a lover's breath, and a corvette is pulling to broadside and if your chain shot doesn't take her mast this time, she's going to sink you and geld you and sell you as a galley slave after you've been made a bung boy for every man on deck with a grudge and a hunger.

I kick, stabbing one foot hardened to leather and bone by a life barefoot right at the tiger shark's nose. I see a flash of the milky membrane over its eyes as I'm thrown, almost lifted out of the water by the force of its strike.

The shark shivers, stunned. Sensitive nose, my father told me. Looks like he told me right.

Gunner ain't no easy meat.

"Ceres! You think I did this? I didn't! It was the Prism! Gavin Guile! That damn boy blew up the ship, not me. Go get *him*, you dumb broad!" Ceres hates it when you dirty her face with exploded ship, and I've done that more than a time or three.

The shark recovers, darts away. For one second, I think I'm safe, that Ceres is going to be reasonable. There's other meat out there. Then the shark turns, starts swimming back.

This is grudge. This is Ceres herself. And she's used to crushing those who defy her by sheer brute force.

"Ceres! Don't do this!"

I got a pistol still. Lost my musket when it blew up in my hands during the fight with the Prism and his Blackguards—which is infuriating, impossible, I've never double-charged a musket in my life. But that's something to worry about later. The pistol might even still work, despite my plunge into the water. I've been trying to make a pistol that's proof against Ceres's spit for years. Nothing's worked against a full plunge, though, and shooting into the water is a fool's game anyway. Ceres's sea skin shields her kin. So I pull my knife instead, its blade three hands long.

"Damn you, Ceres. I said I was sorry!" Sea demons are Ceres's sons. I killed one, years back. She hain't forgiven me yet. Won't, until I sacrifice something surreptitiously special.

The tiger shark comes straight at me. No subtlety, and I got her timing now.

She strikes, and my heels collide with her soft nose one more time. This time, I absorb some of the blow in my knees, still giving the beast a good shock, but not letting myself be thrown so far. I stab for the eye, miss, and bury the knife in its gills. Pull it out with a crimson gush following the blade like fire from a cannon's throat.

A mortal blow, but not a fast death. Damn. Meant it to be quick.

The wound stains the water in the high sun, and the tiger shark veers away. I swim like a furious goddess is on my heels. I get to the dinghy just as some younger tiger sharks arrive. They're shorter than Ceres's hellhound, their stripes more pronounced.

It's a miracle the dinghy survived—a miracle only slightly tainted by the fact that *there's no goddam oars*. I stand up, wide-legged, see that there are other men swimming for the dinghy. The first is a Parian with something shy of six teeth. His name is Conner, and for good reason.

That damned shovel head has got his grubby paws on two oars. He don't look pleased to see that I'm in the dinghy already.

"You look wet," I says. I got no oars, but I'm not swimming with sharks. And sharks don't eat oars.

"First mate," Conner says. "You're captain. And we need us a crew. Take it or leave it. The winds and waves aren't like to blow you to shore from here."

He's quick. Always hated that about Conner. Dangerous one, he is. Still, how good of a con man can he be? He let hisself get daubbed *Conner*.

"Hand me the oars then, First Mate, so I can help you up," I says.

"Go to hell."

"That was an order," Gunner says.

"Go to hell," Conner says, louder, heedless of the tigers.

I give in. I never give in.

Conner insists on holding the oars as I pull him in the dinghy—which 37 is good. It keeps his hands busy while I stick my knife through his back, pinning him to the gunwale.

Even as the men watching from the water curse, surprised at the sudden betrayal, I pry the oars from Conner's fingers. He's dead already, hands convulsed, locked tight. I have to use the butt of my pistol to smash his grip open and drop the oars into the dinghy.

I stand easily despite the dinghy bobbing like a cork in the waves. I hold my pistol, waving it carelessly as I address the swimming, desperate men who've just seen me murder Conner.

"I am Gunner!" I shout, more to Ceres than to the men in the water. "I have done what satraps and Prisms only dream. I am cannoneer of the legendary *Aved Barayah*! I am sea demon slayer! Shark killer! Pirate! Rogue! And now, I am captain. *Captain* Gunner is on the look for a crew," I say, finally turning to the men swimming, scared, surrounded by sharks. I rip my knife free of the gunwale and Conner's body drops into the hungry sea. "Must be willing to take orders!"

Chapter 11

"I hope you got your rest, little Guile," a short, thick Blackguard woman named Samite said. She was stationed with him near the back of their column of Blackguards. The galleass had just arrived at Big Jasper this morning, and the Blackguards were the first off. "It's going to be a long day for you."

Rest? Kip had been trying to figure out how to conceal his big secret, his inheritance, the last and only gift his mother had ever given him. He had a large, ornate jeweled white dagger that no one knew about, and he had a large, ornate polished dagger box. He could put the dagger in the dagger box, of course, but some paranoid corner of his brain was certain that the first thing a person would ask when they saw the box was if he would open it.

How could he say no?

So late into the night, he'd sat in his little bunk in the darkness, trying not to wake the Blackguards sleeping in the other bunks. He'd found twine and he tied the dagger to his back, a process that took a good ten minutes with his bandaged hand. Its point hung down to his butt, under his clothes, held in place by his belt.

It wasn't a great solution, but it was the best he could come up with. After his night, a long day was just what he needed now. Still, he mustered a rueful smile for Samite. She was nice, despite her crooked, oft-broken nose and prominently missing front tooth. She was short and solid as a seawall.

They were some of the last to join the column, and once formed up, the Blackguards set off at a slow jog.

Kip thought that he wouldn't be quite as awestruck the second time he saw the Chromeria. He was wrong. He was still awed even by Big Jasper Island, which was entirely covered by a city. The city was all multicolored domes on top of whitewashed square buildings. Every intersection was adorned with a tower at the top of which hung a mirror, polished and geared so that the mirror could direct sunlight or even moonlight into any part of the city. The Thousand Stars, they called them. The streets were laid out in straight lines with mathematical precision so as to cut off as few beams of light as possible.

Seeing him studying the structures, Samite said, "There is no darkness on Big Jasper, they like to say." She grinned her gap-toothed grin. "Not literally true, but more true here than anywhere else in the world."

Kip nodded, saving his air for the jogging. In simply looking over at her for an instant, he almost collided with a black-robed luxiat.

The streets were packed with thousands of people—not for market day or any particular holy day, Kip realized. This was normal for Big Jasper. And the people themselves came from every arc of the Seven Satrapies. Red-haired pale savages from deep within the Blood Forest to woolen-doublet-wearing midnight Ilytians, light-skinned Ruthgari in their wide straw hats to shield them from the sun, Abornean men and women virtually indistinguishable from each other in their layers of silks and earrings.

But regardless of their lineage, the people on the streets had one thing in common: their awe for the Blackguards with whom Kip was jogging. People got out of the way for them, and the Blackguards took it as their due.

At first, Kip tried not to look too conspicuously out of place among all the hard-muscled physiques around him, but soon he was just trying to keep up.

"Don't worry," Samite said. Infuriatingly, despite her own body being nearly as wide as it was tall, she wasn't even breathing hard. "If you can't keep up, we have orders to carry you."

Carry me? The mortification of the mental image was enough to keep Kip going. Plus, if they carried him, they'd discover the dagger.

Finally they crossed the Lily's Stem, the transparent blue-and-yellow-luxin-covered bridge between Little Jasper Island and Big Jasper Island.

Ironfist gave some sort of signal that Kip didn't see as the Blackguards came into the great yard between the six outer towers of the Chromeria, and the troop disappeared in half a dozen different directions. Kip leaned over with his hands on his knees, trying to catch his wind. He flinched, bit back a curse, and took his weight off his left hand.

"Concealed weapons are most useful if you can draw them on short notice," Samite said.

Kip stood up abruptly. Of course. Leaning forward had pressed the outline of the dagger against his clothes, and because of their work, of all people, Blackguards would be the best at noticing concealed weapons.

Excellent, Kip. Outstanding. You couldn't even hide the dagger for one hour.

Still, she said nothing further.

Kip looked after the departing Blackguards. Ironfist was gone, too. "Uh, what am I supposed to do?" he asked Samite.

"I'll take you to your new quarters, and then to your lectures."

Kip's stomach dropped. A class full of people who all knew each other and would stare at him when he came in. He'd be dropped into the middle of some subject he knew nothing about, and he'd look stupid. He swallowed.

I've seen a sea demon, faced color wights, been in battle, and killed...and I'm nervous about being the new boy. Kip grimaced, but it still didn't make him feel any better.

He followed Samite up into the central tower, up one of the counterweighted lifts. "You get the layout before?" she asked.

"The commander took me straight to the Threshing. Not really."

"We don't have time today, sadly. I like watching the fresh meat gawk." She grinned, but it was friendly. "In short, each tower houses its own color of drafters and most of the training facilities for them, though everyone shares some barracks, some offices, some store-rooms, some libraries. At the base of each tower there are more specialized functions: under the blue tower are the smelters and glass furnaces, under the green are gardens and menageries, under the red is the mirth hall and conservatories, under the yellow is the infirmary and discipline areas, under sub-red are the kitchens and the stockyards, under the Prism's Tower is the great hall. Got it?"

He hoped she was joking. He smiled uncertainly as they stepped out into an empty level, not far up. She walked him down the hall and opened an oak door to a barracks. "Find an empty bed," she said.

There was no one inside, empty pallets stretching from wall to wall. At the foot of each one was a chest for personal items.

"Please tell me there isn't some kind of pecking order for who gets what bed," Kip said.

"There isn't some kind of pecking order for who gets what bed," she said in a monotone.

"You're lying?" he asked.

"Correct."

"What's the worst bed in the room?"

"In the back. Farthest from the door."

Kip began walking to the last bed when he realized something. He stopped. "I don't really have any stuff." He only had a cloak, the ornate knife box, and the knife.

Samite cleared her throat.

"What?"

"You're not going to class armed."

Oh hell.

"We'll also be taking you to the tailors to get you Chromeria garb."

What was he supposed to do? Leave a priceless dagger in a barracks? Samite only knew that he had a knife. They'd just left a war zone, so that was no surprise. But if he showed it to her, she'd surely report it. He had to make it uninteresting even to her.

"I'm going to, um, have to take off my shirt to get my knife off. Can, uh, you turn your back?" Kip asked.

She turned her back, without even making any cracks or grinning.

Kip moved quickly to his pallet and stripped off his shirt and untied the dagger. He pulled the shirt back on and folded his cloak clumsily. He opened the chest. Inside was a thin, folded blanket. Kip set the cloak and the dagger box into his chest, and put the chest at the foot of the bed.   41

"Done yet?" Samite asked.

"Um, no! Just a minute."

Kip looked over the beds. There were maybe sixty pallets in the room. The unoccupied beds—those nearest Kip—were unmade and had the chest underneath them. The occupied beds were made and had the chest at the foot.

There were no hiding places, just as there was no privacy.

Kip tucked the dagger under the mattress. He made the bed quickly, trying to smooth out the wrinkles so the lump wasn't obvious. Then he started walking back toward Samite.

"So you know," Samite said, "best way to get something stolen is to hide it under your mattress. It's where the bullies and thieves always look first."

I'm *terrible* at this! I should have told my father about the dagger. Even if he took it away from me, that would have been better than having some sixteen-year-old butt fungus steal it. Damn it, mother, couldn't you have given me a locket?

Kip went back to his pallet, grabbed the dagger, and looked around. He walked down five rows to one of the unoccupied pallets, opened the chest under that bed, and tucked the knife under the blanket. Better than nothing. He slid the chest back under the bed, grimacing.

"Fantastic," he said. "What's next?"

Next was the tailors', where Kip had to strip down for the fitting. The tailors were women. One of them was attractive, and as she knelt in front of him standing in his underwear, he could see straight down her cleavage. He spent the next half hour staring at the ceiling and praying. And just when Kip was finally leaving, thanking Orholam that his body hadn't done anything to mortify him, the other woman cleared her throat and handed him an extra pair of clean underwear. "You *can* wash them once in a while," she said conspiratorially. "And your armpits, too."

He almost died.

They made him go sponge bathe—he angrily waved off the slave who tried to help him—and change into his new white tunic and new white pants, and new underwear, and a tower slave took his clothes to the barracks. Then they went and registered with some official who made Kip sign his name on a bunch of forms, and then Samite took him to the dining hall where he was allowed a very small and very fast lunch, and then she showed him where the toilets were on each level of the towers.

And then she took him to his first class. "I can come inside or I can wait outside. Your choice," she said.

"Outside. Please, outside." He was already embarrassed enough that he had a bodyguard. He looked into the lecture hall, trying to hide his nerves, while other students streamed past him. He was hungry. What wouldn't he give for a pie right now. He asked, "Anything I should, uh, know?"

"You're expected not to know anything."

Ah, then I might even exceed expectations.

Chapter 12

"Every time you draft, you're hastening your death," Magister Kadah said. She wasn't yet middle-aged, but she already seemed wizened, mousy, with hunched shoulders, hair that hadn't seen a brush or a pick in weeks, green spectacles on a gold chain around her neck, and a thin switch of green luxin in her hand. "Your death doesn't matter, but depriving your satrap of an expensive tool does. Your death doesn't matter, but depriving your community of what it needs to survive does. We who draft are slaves. Slaves to Orholam, to light, to the Prism, the satraps, and our cities."

Cheery sort. Kip tried to keep his expression neutral as he sat in on his first class at the Chromeria.

"Lies first, lessons later," a boy said behind Kip.

"What?" Kip asked. He looked over his shoulder. The boy was, oddly, wearing clear spectacles with thick black mahogany frames in front of thicker black brows. The lenses made one eye look bigger than the other. But more intriguing than his Ruthgari looks—curly light brown hair, small nose, tan skin, brown eyes—were the mechanical spectacles themselves. Two colored lenses, one yellow, one blue, rested on hinges, ready to be clicked down over the clear lenses at a moment's notice.

The boy grinned, seeing Kip's stare. "My own design," he said.

"It's genius. I've never—"

Something struck Kip's desk with a sound like a musket shot. Kip almost jumped out of his skin. He looked at the green luxin switch in the magister's hand. She'd slammed it across his desk, missing his fingertips by a thumb's width.

"*Master* Guile," she said.

She let the words sit in the air, announcing to anyone in the class who hadn't known who he was that he was indeed a Guile, and she knew it.

Next she proves she doesn't care.

"Do you think you're better than the rest of the class, Master Guile?"

The temptation was strong, but Kip had his orders. He was to do well in his classes. Getting kicked out of them would not help him achieve that. "No, Magister," he said. He thought he even made it sound sincere.

She wasn't an imposing figure, neither tall nor wide, but she loomed over Kip's seat. He leaned as far away as his seat allowed. "Do we understand each other, young man?" she asked.

It was an odd way to put it, since she hadn't made any explicit threat, but she didn't have to. "Yes, Magister," Kip said.

"Discipulae, I'm *sure* you've noticed your new classmate." The way she said it made it unclear whether or not she was referring to Kip being fat. There were a few nervous titters. "His name is Kit Guile and—"

"Kip," Kip interjected. "Not a woody tub for toys, a tubby wooden boy." He knew it was a mistake as soon as the words were halfway out of his mouth.

"Ah. Thank you. I'd forgotten that gutter Tyrean has its own definitions for words. Put out your hand, Kip."

He extended his hand, not quite guessing why he needed to do so until she cracked the green switch across his knuckles.

It yanked his breath away.

"Don't ever interrupt a magister, Kip. Even if you are a Guile."

He looked down at his knuckles, fully expecting them to be bloody. They weren't. She knew exactly how hard she could hit with that thing. At least she'd hit the knuckles of his right hand. His raw left hand would have been far worse.

Magister Kadah turned and walked back toward the front of the room, muttering, "Kip. Ridiculous name. But then what can one expect an illiterate slattern to name her bastard?"

It was a trap. Kip knew it was a trap. It yawned open right in front of his feet. She hates you and she has a plan, Kip. Just keep your mouth shut, Kip.

He raised his hand. It was the best compromise his brain could negotiate with his mouth.

She didn't call on him. He kept his left hand up. Wrapped in white bandages, it was impossible to miss. It might have looked like a flag of surrender, if it weren't so patently a rebellion.

"As you all should remember from yesterday's lecture, drafting is the process of turning light into a physical substance, luxin." She saw that Kip's hand was still up, and her mouth tightened momentarily, but she ignored him. "Each color of light can be transformed into a different color of luxin, each of which has its own smell, weight, solidity, strength."

Orholam's beard, this? They were this far back? What a waste of—

"Kip, are we wasting your time?" she asked sharply. "Are we boring you?"

Trap, Kip. Don't do it, Kip.

"No, my eyes glaze over like this all the time. Comes from having a mother who was always smoking haze."

Her eyebrows shot up.

"I have this condition," Kip said. Stop it, Kip. Stop. "See, I'm not just fat, I'm also slow—you know, mentally—so when I get fixated on one thing, I'm not able to go on to the next subject until all my questions are answered. Maybe I'm not advanced enough for this class. Maybe I should be moved elsewhere."

"I do see," she said. He knew she wasn't going to let him go to another class. He didn't even know if there was another class. "Well, Master Guile, this is a novice class, and we pride ourselves on not leaving behind even the slowest cattle in the herd, and obviously, you really want to say something, don't you?"

"Yes, Magister." He hated her. He barely knew her, and he wanted to beat her ugly face in.

She smiled. It was a deeply unpleasant smile. Small woman, so pleased to be the mistress of her domain, so proud to bully a class full of children. "Then I'll make you a deal, Kip: you say whatever you want, but if I find it impertinent, I'll smack your knuckles again. You see, class, this will be a nice object lesson. An analogue for drafting—there's always a price, and you have to decide if you are willing to pay it. So, Kip?"

"You called my mother illiterate, and that's about as true as me calling you a decent human being." Kip's heart was welling up, blocking his throat. "My mother sold her soul to haze. She lied and cheated and stole, I think she even whored herself a few times, but she wasn't illiterate. So if you're going to slander my mother to make me look pathetic, there's plenty of true things you can say. But that is not one of them." You *bitch*.

The class goggled at Kip. He didn't know if he'd just defanged a hundred rumors, or spawned them. Maybe both, but he'd kept a level tone, and he hadn't called his magister a liar or worse. It was sort of a victory. Sort of.

"Are you quite finished?" the magister asked.

And now the price of the victory. "Yes," Kip said.

He put his hand on the desk for her to smack—his left hand, wrapped in bandages.

Stupid, Kip. You're just daring her. Asking for it.

Crack! Kip jumped as the switch slammed into the table so hard it made the surface jump—just two thumbs away from his hand.

"Class, sometimes with drafting as with life, you don't have to pay the price for misbehaving," Magister Kadah said. "Especially if you're a Guile. Kip, I don't like your attitude," she said. "Go wait in the hall."

Kip stood and walked out into the hall, followed by twenty pairs of eyes. His fellow students were from all over the Seven Satrapies: dark-skinned Parians, the girls with hair free, the boys wearing ghotras; olive-skinned Atashians with sapphire-bright eyes; and lots of Ruthgari, small-nosed, thin-lipped, and lighter-skinned, one even a blonde. Kip was the only Tyrean, though he looked more mutt than anything: hair kinky like a Parian, but without the lean, fluid build; eyes blue like an Atashian, but skin darker than their olive complexions, nose not prominent. He even had a few freckles visible through his skin like he was part Blood Forester.

"They'll hate you for me," his father had told him. Then that lopsided, winsome Guile grin had struck. "But don't worry, eventually they'll hate you for you, too."

It was his first day, so Kip was guessing he was being hated for Gavin Guile this time.

Samite was gone when he got out into the hall. Kip supposed the Blackguards worked on shifts. She'd probably thought he could get through one lecture without getting in trouble.

Oops.

Go ahead, he thought as he sat on the floor in the Chromeria's hall, feel sorry for yourself. You've been acknowledged as a bastard of the most powerful man in the world. He saved your life many times, and he gave you the choice. You could have entered the Chromeria anonymously. You chose this.

Kip had thought he'd have at least one friend here, though. Liv had been here—until Garriston. She'd been nice to him, though she saw him as a little brother. But now she was gone, fighting for the Color Prince, choosing to believe comforting lies. Kip hated her for that, despised her for seeking the easy way out—but most of all he missed her.

He sat close to the door, trying to overhear Magister Kadah's lecture, trying to think about magic so he didn't think about anything else. The magister was saying something about the properties of green luxin? He thought about trying to draft some right here in the hall. It would be a bad idea, though. Green made you wild, made you disregard authority. Now would be a bad time for that. He smiled, though, thinking about it.

"Are you Kip?" a voice intruded, breaking Kip out of his fantasy. The speaker was a tiny, clean-shaven, very dark Parian man in a starched headscarf and a slave's robe of fine cotton.

"Uh, yes." Kip stood and the ball of dread that dropped into his stomach told him who'd sent the slave.

The man eyed him for long moments, clearly judging him, but not letting the verdict show in his face. Andross Guile's head slave and right hand was named Grinwoody, Gavin had told Kip. Grinwoody said, "Luxlord Guile requires your presence."

Luxlord Guile, as in Andross Guile, one of the richest men in the world, with estates throughout Ruthgar, Blood Forest, and Paria. On the ruling council known as the Spectrum, he was the Red. Father of two Prisms, Gavin and the rebel who'd almost destroyed the world, Dazen. Andross Guile was, Kip thought, the only man in the world Gavin Guile feared.

Grandfather.

And Kip was a bastard, a blot on the family honor. Felia Guile, Kip's grandmother and the only person who could massage Andross Guile's tyranny, was now dead.

But before Kip ran face first into that wall, he had another problem. He couldn't leave the hall without giving Magister Kadah fresh reasons to hate him, and he couldn't show Andross Guile disrespect by making him wait.

"Uh, will you tell my magister that I've been summoned?" Kip asked.

Grinwoody looked at him, expressionless.

Kip felt foolish. Like he couldn't take one step, poke his head in the door himself, and say, "I've been summoned." He opened his mouth to explain himself, remembered Gavin's orders: Remember who you are.

He was going to apologize, or say please, but he stopped himself.

After another moment of weighing Kip, Grinwoody acquiesced. He rapped on the door and stepped into the classroom. "Luxlord Guile requires Kip's presence."

He didn't give Magister Kadah a chance to respond, though Kip would have given his left eye to see the expression on her face. Grinwoody was a slave, but a slave authorized to do his duty by one of the most powerful men in the world. Nothing the magister said mattered. Grinwoody was a man who remembered who he was.

The real question was, who was Kip? Grinwoody had referred to him only by his first name. It hadn't been, 'Luxlord Guile requires his grandson.'

What had Gavin said? 'We'll count it a victory if you avoid wetting yourself'?

Kip cleared his throat. "Uh, you mind if we stop by the privies on the way?"

Chapter 13

Gavin smiled as he stepped off the skimmer onto Seers Island. Karris had her *ataghan* drawn, and was pointing her pistol at the nearest man.

The people stood in an unruly mob, but they were armed with

swords and muskets, makeshift spears. There were few commonalities between them: they had come from all seven satrapies, light-skinned and dark, dirty and clean, dressed in silk and wool. Several had an extra eye drawn on their forehead with coal. Though even among those, some had exquisitely drawn, others rough, lopsided.

What these men and women had in common was only this: each one had the religious devotion to cross reefs in a small outrigger canoe to get here, and every one of them was a drafter.

A woman stepped through the crowd. She was little, barely taller than Gavin's waist, arms and legs short, her trunk the size a woman of average height would have. She had a flaring eye tattooed exquisitely on her forehead.

"You will not draft here," she said.

"I'll decide that," Gavin said.

Instead of looking irritated, she smiled. "It is as foretold."

Seers. Excellent. "Someone foretold that I'd say that?" Gavin asked.

"No, that you'd be an asshole."

Gavin laughed. "I think I'm going to like this place."

"You'll come with us," she said.

"Sure," Gavin said.

"It wasn't a request."

"Yes it was," Gavin said. "When you don't have power to compel obedience, by definition you're making a request. What's your name?"

"Caelia. When I tire, you'll carry me," she said, unimpressed.

"Happy to."

The sound of a cocking hammer interrupted them. Karris pointed her pistol straight at Caelia's third-eye tattoo. There was a rattle as the other men pointed their muskets at Karris, cocked them.

"Try anything," Karris said, "and I'll hollow out your skull."

"The White Blackguard. We were told you'd be *forceful*."

Karris uncocked her pistol and tucked it away, sheathed her sword.

"I've changed my mind," Gavin said. "Who are you taking me to see, and how far away is she?" The "she" was a guess. He knew little about the Seers' religious belief, indeed, he thought there was no unified belief here, but when faced with biological facts, cultures had to make their own interpretations. Female drafters tended to draft more successfully because more of them could see colors more accurately, and they tended to live longer than male drafters. Those cultures that had decided this meant Orholam favored women didn't like it being assumed that they would be led by a man.

"The Third Eye resides at the base of Mount Inura."

Gavin pointed to the tallest mountain. It was green, not so tall that it had a tree line, but still quite a walk. "What is that, a five-hour walk from here?"

"Six."

"Don't suppose you have horses?" Gavin asked.

"We have some few horses, but one walks when one goes to see the Third Eye. It is a pilgrimage. It gives one time to reflect and prepare the soul for the meeting."

"Uh-huh. Well, when the Third Eye comes to see me, she can ride. I want her to be in the right frame of mind."

Caelia appeared to be chewing on the insides of her cheeks. "So it was foretold."

"She foretold I wouldn't come?" Gavin asked.

"No, still the asshole part." Her men chuckled.

"If it helps, I'm not being capricious. I've work to do. I'll be here, doing it."

Caelia looked around at the two hundred armed men who surrounded Gavin and Karris. "I could insist, you know. These men are not just armed, they are drafters, too."

"I'm the Prism," Gavin said, like she just wasn't getting it. "Do you think two hundred men can keep me from doing what I Will?"

Caelia hesitated. "I think you seek out conflict needlessly."

"Hear, hear," Karris said under her breath.

Sometimes Gavin thought the world was full of morons. Power could be a knife, but often it had to be a bludgeon. A man like Commander Ironfist could speak gently, because simply by standing he overawed other men with his physical presence. Gavin had to draw lines and enforce them, because he didn't trust others to do it for him. He had to do it because if others were allowed to start basing their decisions on the assumption that he was weak, it would take blunt force to get them to change their minds. Deterrence is cheaper than correction.

But what he'd said about Will wasn't thrown in heedlessly. Drafters always imposed their will on the world. The most powerful drafters always included more than their share of madmen, bastards, divas, and assholes. And because everything depended on them, they were tolerated. Gavin most of all.

But the more power you have, the harder it is to recognize what's beyond your power.

And there was a pleasure in seeing others do what you want. Gavin felt it now as Caelia gave orders, rounding up her men and leaving. He could tell himself that it was important to establish the power dynamic because of what he had to do, and to prepare the Seers for the bitter pill that they were going to have to swallow. That was true, but he had to watch himself, too.

Before they were even gone, Gavin headed back down the beach. He'd left the skimmer sealed.

"We have one week," he told Karris. "This bay is too wide, so we'll need to build seawalls off that point and from there to there. I'm going to have to clear out the reefs. I'm thinking of clearing them in a zigzag pattern so that if an invading navy comes here, they'll be destroyed, but we'll have marked the safe way so that the locals can direct traffic. Buoys that can be moved? I also haven't decided how wide the safe path should be. If it's too narrow, you keep supplies from getting into the city and it simply becomes too expensive for many people to live here, but too open and the reefs no longer serve as a deterrent. So your thoughts are more than welcome. Other than that, I'll need your help prioritizing what things I need to build to give my people a running start. Do we clear the jungle—and if so, how? Do we need to build a wall against the native animals, against the native people? Should we try to build any houses, or would that be too much work?"

Karris was just looking at him. "You know, every time I think I know you... You're really doing this, aren't you? You're founding a city. Not just a village. You're planning for it to be a major center."

"Not during my life." Gavin smiled.

"You know, if you keep changing everything you touch, nothing's going to be the same five years from now."

Five years. It was supposed to be the remainder of his term as Prism. But he was already dying, and pretty soon Karris would notice. "No," he said, "I hope it's not."

Five years, and five great purposes left. Except now he only had one year.

Chapter 14

The only thing this place needs to make it creepier is cobwebs blowing in the wind. Kip stared into the pitch black of Lord Andross Guile's room with something less than glee.

"You're letting in light," Grinwoody said. "Are you trying to kill my lord?"

"No, no, I'm—" I'm always apologizing. "I'm coming in." He stepped forward, through several layers of heavy tapestries that blocked light from the room.

The air inside the room was stale, still, hot. It reeked of old man. And it was impossibly dark. Kip began sweating instantly.

"Come here," a raspy voice said. It was low, gravelly, like Lord Guile hadn't spoken all day.

Kip moved forward with little steps, sure he'd trip and disgrace himself. It was like a dragon's den.

Something touched his face. He flinched. Not a cobweb, a feathery light touch. Kip stopped. He had somehow expected Andross Guile to be an invalid, seated in a wheeled chair perhaps, like a dark mirror of the White. But this man was standing.

The hand was firm, though with few calluses. It traced Kip's chubby face, felt the texture of his hair, the curve of his nose, pressed his lips, went against the grain of Kip's incipient beard. Kip winced, terribly aware of the pimples he had where his beard was coming in.

"So you're the bastard," Andross Guile said.

"Yes, my lord."

Out of nowhere, something nearly tore Kip's head off. He crashed into the wall so hard he would have broken something if it hadn't been covered in layers of tapestries, too. He fell to the carpeted floor, his cheek burning, ears ringing.

"That was for existing. Never shame this family again."

Kip stood unsteadily, too surprised to even be angry. He didn't know what he had been expecting, but a blow out of the darkness hadn't been it. "My apologies for being born, my lord."

"You have no idea."

There was silence. The darkness was oppressive. Whatever you do,

Gavin had said, don't make him an enemy. Could it get any hotter in here?

"Get out," Andross Guile said finally. "Get out now."

Kip left, having the distinct feeling that he'd failed.

Chapter 15

The Color Prince was rubbing his temples. Liv Danavis couldn't take her eyes off of him. No one could. The man was practically carved of pure luxin. Blue plates covered his forearms, made spiky gauntlets for his fists. Woven blue luxin made up much of his skin, with yellow flowing in rivers beneath the surface, constantly replenishing the rest. Flexible green luxin made up his joints. Only his face was human, and barely at that. His skin was knotted with burn scars, and his eyes—halos so broken as to be absent—were a swirl of every color, not just his irises, but the whites as well. Right now, those sclera swirled blue, then yellow as he sat on the great chair in the audience chamber of the Travertine Palace, deciding how to split up the city he'd just conquered—and found nearly empty.

"I want the twelve lords of the air to oversee redistribution of the city. Lord Shayam will preside. First, the plunder. Those who fled Garriston took almost nothing with them—it's all here. Some of it will travel with the army, but the rest shouldn't be left to rot. Sell what can be sold, and distribute the rest in the most equitable way possible among the remaining Garristonians. The twelve lords are to decide who among the new settlers will be given leases to which properties. The richer areas and homes will require a fee up front; the poorer will be allowed six months before they begin paying.

"Lady Selene," he said, turning to a blue/green bichrome who hadn't yet broken the halo. She was Tyrean, with wavy dark hair and a dusky complexion, striking but odd, eyes too far apart, small mouth. She curtsied. "You're in charge of all the greens until we leave the city. Six weeks. In that time, I expect you to dredge the key irrigation canals and repair the locks on the river. I want this city to flower next spring. The first rains of autumn may come any day. Consult with Lord Shayam. New plants will need to be brought in, perhaps soil as well. Do what you can with the labor provided in the time we have."

Lady Selene curtsied deeply and left immediately.

And on it went, all morning. Liv sat among five advisers to the Color Prince's left. Other than those advisers, no one else was allowed into the great hall. The prince wanted few people to see the entirety of his plans. Why Liv was one of the privileged few, she had no idea. She was the daughter of General Corvan Danavis, and the Color Prince had made no secret of the fact that he hoped he could recruit Gavin's old enemy to his side, but Liv thought it was more than that. She'd switched sides before the Battle of Garriston, even fighting for the army trying to reclaim the city—but she'd done it in return for the Color Prince saving her friends. She didn't deserve this kind of trust.

But she did find the whole thing fascinating. Often, the prince would call forth a courtier to give him more information on some point. He cared nothing for previous laws, and little for how things had been done traditionally, but he showed a keen interest in commerce and trade and taxation and agriculture: all the things needed to provide for his people and his army.

Summoning his military commanders, he elevated one of his most talented young commanders to general, and then tasked him with securing Tyrea's roads and rivers. He wanted trade to be able to flow unfettered up and down the whole of the Umber River, and bandits to be stamped out mercilessly.

In some ways, Liv knew, it was merely trading many bandits for one. The prince's men would doubtless collect taxes just as the bandits charged passage fees. But if they did it fairly, and didn't murder the farmers and traders for their goods, the country would still be better off, whatever you called it.

He set more greens and yellows to clear the river itself, under their own command. If the prince was a bad man, he was a bad man taking a long view, because even though Liv didn't understand everything that he was ordering, it was clear to her that he was sacrificing a huge number of his drafters and fighting men for the benefit of Tyrea. In the long run, her cynical superviolet nature told her, that would benefit him. An army on the march doesn't make its own food, and can't

54

always count on plunder to pay its men, so having a strong economic base would magnify his power later.

"Lord Arias," the Color Prince said, "I want you to select a hundred of your priests, young enough to be zealous, old enough to have absorbed the basics, and send them out to every satrapy to spread the good news of the coming freedom. Concentrate on the cities. Send natives where possible. Let them know what kind of opposition they'll face. Expect martyrs in Dazen's cause, and begin preparing another wave of zealots. I want regular reports, and send handlers with them. We'll contract the Order of the Broken Eye where persecution is too great, yes?"

Lord Arias bowed. He was Atashian, with his people's typical bright blue eyes, olive skin, and a plaited, beaded beard. "My prince, how would you like us to proceed on Big Jasper and in the Chromeria itself?"

"The Chromeria you leave alone. Others will handle that. Big Jasper should be handled with utmost care. I want our people there to be more eyes and ears than mouths, you understand? Your best people only on Big Jasper. I want them to grumble in the taverns and the markets, or join those who are already grumbling, barely whispering that our cause might have some merit. Identify those with grievances whom we might recruit, but take greatest care. They're not fools there. Expect the Chromeria to try to plant spies."

"Will you authorize the Order there?" Lord Arias asked.

"The Order's best people are already there or on their way there," the prince said. "But I expect you to use them like a needle, not a cudgel, understood? If our operations are exposed too early, the whole enterprise is doomed. The fate of the revolution lies in your hands."

Lord Arias stroked his beard, making the yellow beads click. "I believe I should base my own operations from Big Jasper, then."

"Agreed."

"And I'll need financing."

"Which, quite predictably, is where we run into problems. I can give you ten thousand danars. I know it's a fraction of what you'll need, but I have people who need to be fed. Be creative."

"Fifteen thousand?" Lord Arias countered. "Simply buying a house on Big Jasper..."

"Make do. I'll send more in three months if I can."

Most of the rest of the day was more mundane: orders for how the army was to camp and where, money requests for food and new clothing and new shoes and new horses and new oxen, and money owed to smiths and miners and foreign lords and bankers who wanted their loans repaid. Others came asking to be authorized to press the locals and the camp followers into service clearing roads, putting out fires, and rebuilding bridges.

Alone out of the advisers, Liv was never asked to consult on anything. The bursar was consulted most often. She wore gigantic corrective lenses and carried a small abacus that she was constantly worrying. Or at least Liv thought she was merely nervously fidgeting with the abacus. After a while, as the woman gave a report about a dozen different ways the prince could structure his debts so as to maximize his own take, Liv realized the little woman was doing figures ceaselessly.

Finally, the prince asked one of the advisers to tell him what other business was waiting, and deemed that it could all keep until tomorrow. He dismissed the rest of his advisers and beckoned Liv to join him.

Together they walked upstairs and out onto the great balcony from his room.

"So, Aliviana Danavis, what did you see today?"

"My lord?" She shrugged. "I saw that governing is a lot more complicated than I ever would have imagined."

"I did more for Garriston today—and more for Tyrea—than the Chromeria has done in sixteen years. Not that everyone will thank me for it. Forced labor to clean up the city won't be popular, but it's better than letting the goods rot or be taken away by looters and gangs."

"Yes, my lord."

He took out a thin *zigarro* of tobacco rolled inside a ratweed skin from a pocket in his cloak. He touched it to a finger full of sub-red to light it and inhaled deeply.

She looked at him curiously.

"My transition from flesh to luxin wasn't perfect," he said. "I've done better than anyone in centuries, but I still made mistakes. Painful mistakes. Of course, starting from a charred husk didn't make things any easier."

"What happened to you?" Liv asked.

"Some other time perhaps. I want you to think about the future, Aliviana. I want you to dream." He looked out over the bay. It was clotted with garbage, the docks littered. He sighed. "This is the city we've taken. The jewel of the desert that the Chromeria did its best to destroy."

"My father was trying to protect it," Liv said.

"Your father's a great man, and I have no doubt that's exactly what he thought he was doing. But your father believed the Chromeria's lies."

"I think he was blackmailed," Liv said, feeling hollow. The Prism she'd so admired had used *Liv* to blackmail her father into helping him. She didn't even know how, but it was the only thing she could imagine had brought her father to fight for his sworn enemy.

"I hope that's true."

"What?" Liv asked.

"Because if so, it isn't too late for him, and I'd love to have your father stand at our side. He's a dangerous man. A good man. Brilliant. We'll find out. But I'm afraid, Liv, that he's been listening to their lies for so long that his whole system of understanding has been corrupted. He might see a few weeds on the surface and reject those, but if the soil itself is fouled, how can he see the truth? This is why the young are our hope."

The sun was going down, and a fresh breeze had kicked up off the Cerulean Sea. The Color Prince took a deep drag on his zigarro and seemed to relish the redder light.

"Liv, I want you to think of a world without the Chromeria. A world where a woman can worship whichever god she sees fit. Where being a drafter isn't a death sentence with a ten-year wait. A world in which an accident of birth doesn't put fools on thrones, but where a man's abilities and drive are all that determines his success. No lords but those whose nature establishes them. No slaves—at all. Slavery is the curse of the Chromeria. In our new world, a woman won't be despised because she came from Tyrea—no, nor will it be a badge of honor. I'm not fighting to make Tyrea supreme. In our new world, it simply won't matter. Your hair, your eyes, whatever it is that sets you apart will merely make you interesting. We will be a light to the world. We will open the Everdark Gates that Lucidonius closed and cut passes through the Sharazan Mountains. We will welcome all.

"In every village and every town, magic will be taught, and we'll find that many, many more people have talents that can be used to better their lives and the lives of those around them. It won't be in the corrupt hands of governors and satraps. As we learn, I think we'll find that everyone, *everyone*, has been kissed by light. Someday everyone will draft. Think what geniuses of magic are out there even today—geniuses who could change the world! But right now, maybe they're Tyrean, and they can't afford to go to the Chromeria. They're Parian, and the deya doesn't like their family. They're Ilytian, and they're mired in superstition about magic being evil. Think of the fields that lie fallow. Think of children starving for the bread that they don't have because they don't have green drafters to fertilize the crops. The Chromeria has their blood on its hands—and none of them even realize it! It's a quiet death, a slow poison. The Chromeria has drained the life from the satrapies one drop of blood at a time. That's our fight, Aliviana. For a different future. And it won't be easy. Too many people gain too much from the current corruption for them to give it up easily. And they'll send the people to die for them. And it breaks my heart. They'll sacrifice the very people we want to set free. But we'll stop them. We'll make sure they can't do it again, that generations yet unborn receive a better world than the one we have."

She hesitated. "Everything you're saying sounds good, but the proof's in the eating, isn't it?" Liv said.

He smiled broadly. "Yes! This is what I want from you, Liv. Draft. Right now. Superviolet. And think. And tell me what you're thinking. You won't be punished. Regardless."

She did, soaking up that alien, invisible light and letting it course through her, feeling it peel her away from her emotions to a hyperrationality, an almost disembodied intelligence. "You're a practical man," she said, her voice flat. Intonation seemed an unnecessary frill when you were in the grip of superviolet. "Perhaps a romantic, too. An odd combination. But you've been accomplishing tasks all day, and I wonder if I'm not merely the last on the list. I can't tell if this is the prelude to a seduction or if you simply like the admiration of women." Part of her was appalled at what she'd said—the presumption! But instead of yielding to her blushes, she huddled deeper in the superviolet's dispassion.

Archly, the prince said, "Rare is the man who won't swoon over women swooning over him."

"So I'm trivially correct on the latter." He enjoyed her attention, her growing awe, but he had barely touched her, even when he had excuses to do so. He didn't lean toward her as they spoke. He was engaged intellectually but not bodily. "But this is no seduction."

He didn't look entirely pleased. "Alas, the fire that took so much else has denied me the simpler pleasures of the flesh. Not that I despise such. But no cavorting like a green for me." Between the immobilization caused by the burn scars on his face and the immobilization of the luxins he was weaving into his skin, it was difficult to read any but the most overt expressions on his face, but she reminded herself that this didn't mean he didn't *feel* readily or deeply. His eyes swirled freely with colors, but Liv thought they, too, were only good indicators of his emotions when he felt something strongly. It made him something of a cipher.

Superviolet loved ciphers. Cracking ciphers.

"Do you know who I was?" the Color Prince asked.

"No."

"And I'm not going to tell you. Do you know why?"

"Because you don't want me to know?" she hazarded.

"No. Because superviolets love digging up secrets. And if I don't set you to work digging up something that doesn't matter to me, you might be smart enough to dig up something I don't want known."

"Diabolical," she said appreciatively.

Luxin shot out of him, slamming into her chest. She staggered, lost her grip on superviolet, and found something tight around her neck.

Kicking, Liv realized she'd been lifted off her feet. No, not just off her feet. She was suspended, off the edge of the balcony, held by a fist of luxin around her entire head. She grabbed at the fist, trying to pull herself up, trying to breathe, trying to loosen its grip—panicking, not even realizing that loosening its grip was the last thing she ought to want. If she fell from this height, she'd die. Her head felt hot, all the veins bulging, her eyes feeling like they'd explode.

The Color Prince's eyes were stark red, glowing like coals. He blinked. Yellow flooded to the fore, and she felt herself swung back onto the balcony, released.

She fell, coughing.

"I...The Chromeria has demonized what we do," the prince rasped. "Literally. They have made us into actual devils, and I won't tolerate those who call good evil and evil good. I...reacted badly."

Liv was shaking, and embarrassed of it. She thought she was going to cry, and was furious with herself for it. She was a Danavis. She was brave and strong and she would not break down like a little girl. She was a woman, seventeen years old. Old enough to have children of her own. She would not break down.

She stood and curtsied, wobbling only a little. "My apologies, my lord. I didn't mean to offend."

He looked out over the bay, putting his hands on the rail. He'd lost his zigarro. He lit another. "You needn't be embarrassed of the trembling. It's the body's reaction. I've seen the most fearless veterans do the same. Your embarrassment of it makes it look like weakness. Ignore it. It passes."

Painting a placid expression on her face as if it were the stark lines of kohl, Liv drafted superviolet. It helped. She folded her arms, as if against the evening chill but really to bury their shaking. "So, my lord?"

He cocked his head. "So?"

"So you have a plan for me."

"Of course I do."

"And you're not going to tell me what it is."

"Such a smart girl. I'm going to assign you a tutor to answer almost every one of your questions."

"Except for that one?"

He grinned. "There will be other omissions as well."

"Who is this tutor?"

"You'll know when you see him. Now go. I have grimmer tasks to accomplish before the light dies."

Chapter 16

Ironfist was standing outside Andross Guile's chambers when Kip came out. As ever, he was huge and intimidating, but Kip was getting to know the commander of the Blackguard, and the look on Ironfist's face was more curious than anything else.

"I've seen satraps come out of that room looking worse," Ironfist said.

"Really?" Kip asked. He felt destroyed.

"No. I was trying to cheer you up." Ironfist started down the hall, and Kip fell in step beside him. "Kip, I'm inviting you to train for the Blackguard."

Oh, right. Because my father demanded it. Not on my own merits.

Kip thought he'd only thought those words, but by the time he said "merits," he realized he'd stepped in a big pile of his tongue once again.

Ironfist stopped cold. Turned to Kip, glowering, threatening. "You were eavesdropping?" Ironfist asked.

Kip swallowed. Nodded. I didn't mean to!

But this time the words didn't weasel their way past his lips. Excuses dried up in the blast furnace of Ironfist's disapproval.

"Then you know I have to induct you at the end. It's up to you how much of an embarrassment you want to make that for both of us."

It was like someone had put a great chain around Kip's chest, dropped him in the sea, and told him to swim home. Ironfist headed off once again, and didn't pause or slow as they left the Prism's Tower and crossed the great yard between the seven great towers of the Chromeria to a broad staircase that disappeared into the ground.

As they descended, Kip got a notion of just how massive the Chromeria was. It wasn't merely the huge towers, the spindles that connected them in midair, and the great yard covered with thousands of people going about all the business of the Seven Satrapies. All of it extended below the ground as well, into a huge chamber. The ceiling was fully twenty paces above the floor. Each of the seven towers had its roots down here, and yet more entrances. Buildings and storehouses, barracks, inns, and even a few homes crowded the chamber, reaching in many places from floor to ceiling. Some were constructed of stone, others of luxin. Vibrant colors rioted everywhere, and though the whole area was underground, it was neither dark nor musty. Crystals scintillated in every color like torches, taking sunlight from above and splashing it liberally through the chamber. Great fans set in the ceiling at either side sucked in and blew out air, sending a constant slight breeze over the whole area. There was a great hall in the center, and exercise yards off to one side.

"Beginning of each new class, there's a lottery. Some numbers are random, but legacies and those who finished just below the cut of the previous training class get to challenge in last. Big advantage. You fight for your spot, but you only have to fight three times. So if you choose spot ten, you might have to fight ten, eleven, and twelve. It's only a starting point, though; it's easy to move up in the coming weeks, and easier to move down. I can do this much for your father: you get to choose last. Don't choose too high or you'll pay for it in blood, but don't go too low. We cut the bottom seven each month."

Ironfist moved purposefully, unfazed by the subterranean splendor. Kip followed, tense. He was squeezing his burned hand. He consciously straightened it, grimaced against the pain. Soon he found himself standing with Ironfist in front of forty-nine young men and women. They were all dressed in loose tan shirts and pants. Everyone wore at least one armband with the color he drafted on his right or left arm. Though Kip knew that women outnumbered men in the Chromeria substantially, this class of potential Blackguards had only ten women.

Everyone was older than Kip, but still young. Kip would guess most were sixteen to eighteen years old. They each had a symbol affixed to their left breast in an old Parian script that Kip could mostly guess at. Numbers, he thought. It looked like they were lined up according to that number, seven lines of seven.

Among all the new things to look at, the thing that stuck out to Kip was the look in his new classmates' eyes. They barely even noticed him; they were too busy watching Ironfist like he was a god. The class's teacher hardly looked less impressed than the rest of them. He was a muscle-bound, short man, shaved bald and wearing a sleeveless black uniform that showed off massive biceps.

Ironfist gestured and the class melted, re-forming into a large circle in moments. It wasn't flawless, as a few jostled to move from one place to another, but it was pretty impressive for what Kip knew had to be a fairly new class.

"Kip." Ironfist gestured that Kip was to step into the circle.

Oh no.

Kip stepped in.

"This is Kip Guile. He's joining the class. As you know, that means one of you scrubs will be leaving. The Blackguard is elite. We've no room for deadwood. So, Kip, choose. Fights are five minutes or until one combatant cries mercy or is knocked out. As at all testings, inflicting permanent damage on your opponent will result in your expulsion from this class."

Kip knew he was going to lose. He barely understood the rules. The only fighting he'd done in his life had mostly been confined to flailing against Ramir, back in their village. And losing, always losing. His greatest skill was taking punishment.

"Do you have any questions, or are you ready to choose your place?" Ironfist asked.

"So if you lose, do you swap places with the person who beat you, or do you just move down one spot?"

"It's not an arithmetic problem, Kip."

But that was precisely what it was.

Ironfist grimaced. "You move down one," he said.

Kip put on a misty look and gazed into the distance. "I see pain in my future." He jauntily pointed his forefingers like pistols at the tall, slim young Parian who bore a number one on his chest. No one laughed. Maybe they'd laugh when Kip got his ass beat.

The young man stepped into the circle looking concerned—for Kip. "Match rules, Commander?" he asked.

"No spectacles," Ironfist said.

Kip and Number One handed over their spectacles. The young man was a green/blue bichrome.

Ironfist cleared his throat. "I mean that both ways, Cruxer."

Cruxer? His name was *Cruxer*?

"Of course, sir," Cruxer said. "Sir, his bandaged hand? Can I block it?"

"Don't target it. But if it gets hurt, it gets hurt."

The taller youth nodded quickly and moved opposite of Kip. Kip saw flashes of incredulity on the other students' faces as they looked at him. He supposed he didn't cut much of a figure. No one believed he could win. Hell, *he* didn't believe he could win. Lose with dignity, Kip. Lose in a way that will make them respect you for being plucky.

Plucky? I'm a *moron*.

Cruxer looked up and made the triangle: thumb to right eye, middle finger to left eye, forefinger to forehead. Then he touched the three to his mouth, heart, and hands. The three and the four, perfect seven. A religious young man. Hopefully he'd remember the virtue of mercy.

Cruxer turned and saluted Kip, fists touching over his heart and bowing slightly. Kip returned the salute.

"Begin," Ironfist said.

The tall youth moved—fast. He was on top of Kip before Kip could react. He shot into Kip and locked a leg behind Kip's, blocking Kip's punch and throwing his hips into Kip's. Kip went down hard, grabbing to try to pull Cruxer with him.

The slender boy let himself fall. His long limbs wrapped around

Kip. Kip threw an elbow, but Cruxer was so close, he barely got any force into it.

Then, somehow, the young man had control of Kip's arm and rolled him over. Cruxer's legs scissored around Kip's head. Tightened and—darkness.

Kip had no idea how long he was out. He blinked rapidly. Not long, he thought. Everyone was still standing around.

"That's one loss," Ironfist said. "You've got ten seconds until your next bout."

Kip struggled to his feet. A number of classmates were slapping Cruxer on the back, congratulating him on his effortless victory. Kip couldn't summon any ill feeling for the boy. He'd destroyed Kip without malice and without causing any unnecessary pain.

The second boy was stocky, blue-eyed like Kip, maybe only half Parian, because his skin wasn't much darker than Kip's. He bowed to Kip. Kip returned the bow, wondering what fresh pain was coming his way.

Kip and Number Two circled each other warily, but the boy kept looking up and away from Kip. At first, Kip didn't know why. Then he saw the boy's eyes. There were little wisps of blue appearing and disappearing in the whites of his eyes. Down, into his body. Gathering in his fists. If the boy hadn't been lighter-skinned, Kip wouldn't have been able to see it. It was one of the disadvantages the lighter-skinned had. It was why, nominally, the Blackguard were black.

But because they weren't wearing spectacles, the boy could only draft tiny sips of blue light at a time. He had to take his eyes off of Kip, look at one of the blue crystals overhead, take what he could, and look back to Kip. Without blue spectacles, it made for a slow process.

And Kip circling slowly was giving the boy all the time he needed.

"Ah hell," Kip said. He charged.

Kip threw a punch. It was blocked. The second punch hit the boy's shoulder—but Kip had thrown the punch with his left hand. He felt cuts rip open. It was like he'd dipped his palm in fire.

A fist caught him in the stomach, and another grazed his arm as he hunched forward. Kip staggered back, his motion taking most of the force out of a punch that caught his nose.

It still made his eyes water, though. He blinked and lurched, surprised the boy had let him go rather than press his advantage.

Then Kip realized the reason why the boy would do such a thing. A blue staff was forming in the boy's hands, slowly stretching out like molten glass.

Kip darted in and grabbed at the unfinished staff. He caught it, and as his fingertips sank into the crystallizing structure, he felt suddenly as connected to it as if he'd drafted it himself.

He could feel the other boy through the open luxin, his will, so focused a moment before, now scattered and confused by Kip's invasion. Kip tore the staff away from the boy and sealed it.

The blue luxin staff was bent from where the boys had grappled for it, but it was still as tall as either of them and as big around as Kip could comfortably hold in his hand. Ignoring the pain as he grabbed it with his bandaged left hand, Kip swung the bottom of the staff for the boy's knees.

It connected with a crack, and the still-stunned boy dropped. He hadn't even tried to move. Just stood there like a dumb ox. He crumpled, and Kip stepped over him, putting one end of the staff on the boy's throat.

"Match!" Ironfist called out.

Kip stepped away. Drafting blue made it much easier to obey orders than drafting green did.

The boy on the ground moaned, dazed, only slowly coming back to himself.

"Commander, sir," Cruxer asked, "what was that?"

Ironfist was scowling. "Something we don't teach until a year from now. Kip, who showed you that?"

Kip turned his hands up, helpless.

"Willjacking or will-breaking. Trainer Fisk?"

The muscle-bound teacher stepped forward. "Technically, it's called forced translucification. Luxin has no memory. There is no your luxin or my luxin. Once a drafter makes physical contact with open luxin of a color that she can draft, she can use it. What just happened here was two drafters fought will to will, and Kip broke Grazner's will."

The boy Kip had just defeated said, "But, but, I didn't know what he was doing!"

The trainer said, "He didn't know what he was doing either. Did you, Kip?"

"Uh, no, sir."

"You're just lucky you weren't left a blithering idiot, Graz," Trainer Fisk said.

A boy in the crowd whispered, "Blithering, no. Idiot? Weeelll..."

Several people snickered. A few had the decency to try to cover it with coughs.

"So Adrasteia, you want to challenge Kip?" Ironfist asked.

"Ah hells," the boy murmured. He was the one who'd made the crack about Grazner.

"Sir, I thought if I won I was done," Kip said.

"Whatever would make you believe such a thing? The winning is just the beginning."

Kip swallowed.

Adrasteia didn't look terribly pleased to be fighting Kip either. Alone of all the fighters, he wasn't wearing an armband showing what color he drafted.

He had straight, shoulder-length dark hair, bound back with a gold scarf. Skin just dark enough for the Blackguard, with Atashian features and striking blue eyes. Short and slender, but wearing a baggy shirt and baggy pants, he looked maybe thirteen years old. Odd haircut, but then Kip wasn't exactly a man of the world. Maybe long hair was in fashion now. Strange name, too, and rather full lips.

"Oh! You're a girl!" Kip said. It just slipped out.

The class hooted. Ironfist rubbed his forehead.

Not *trying* for an insult, but succeeding. Oops.

"No mercy, chubs," Adrasteia said. Now he could tell she was his age. Fifteen, maybe sixteen, petite, no curves. Fairly pretty, but no knockout.

He *hoped* she wasn't a knockout, anyway.

"Form up," Trainer Fisk said. "Same rules as before—and no will-jacking, but then, that shouldn't be a problem with you, Teia, should it?"

Adrasteia grimaced toward the trainer, face intense. She turned toward Kip, gave a very perfunctory bow.

Kip bowed back. "Sorry, I didn't—"

"Save it, Lard Guile," she said.

Several students laughed aloud.

"Oh, I get it, you're jealous 'cause I have bigger boobs than you," Kip said. He covered the stab of self-loathing with a condescending grin.

"I can see you naked," she said. "And I'm not jealous of *that*." She sniffed with distaste at his body.

Huh?

But Kip didn't have time to think about what she could possibly mean, because she attacked him.

He wasn't in a ready stance, and he wasn't ready, period. Especially not for her foot to go from the floor to the side of his head in the blink of an eye.

The flexibility! The grace!

The astonishing feeling of blood flying from his face!

Kip was looking at the world sideways. He was lying down, without having been aware of the whole *falling* part. As ever when hurt, he did a quick inventory: just how bad was it? Not that bad. He'd bit the hell out of his cheek and tongue, but he'd gone down mostly from the surprise.

Getting your head torn off by a little girl will do that to you.

She came into his view, still in a fighting stance, close to his head. Flat on his back, he asked, "That all you got?"

It enraged her, and she stepped toward him.

He rolled toward her, fast, hoping to catch her feet and trip her.

She jumped, trying to leap over him, but he slowed, grabbed one foot while she was in midair. He got lucky and snagged the inside foot.

Adrasteia clawed, catlike, twisting, but she couldn't recover. She landed flat on her hip and cried out.

Kip scrambled, trying to pin her—something, anything to use his weight to win somehow.

He was halfway on top of her when her small fist caught him straight in the throat. He coughed, collapsed.

In a moment, he was lying facedown and she was on top of him with her arm around his neck.

An adult was shouting, but Kip could only hear the roar of blood in his ears.

Then Adrasteia disappeared, feet kicking in midair as Ironfist lifted her bodily off him, literally hauling her off by her collar.

Ironfist dropped the furious girl in front of him. "I said, *Enough!*" he bellowed. Adrasteia was shocked to stillness. Then she wilted. Everyone in the class shrank back, wide-eyed and suddenly quiet.

"Kip!" Ironfist roared.

Kip swallowed a few times. "Yes, sir?" he asked, pulling himself to his feet for what felt like the hundredth time of the day.

"All the scrubs have a partner. You just found yours."

Chapter 17

At dinner, Kip took his food and sat at the end of a long table by himself. You can't get rejected if you don't try to fit in.

Adrasteia came over and sat across from him. "I'm supposed to spy on you," she said.

"Um, good sausage?" Kip said.

"It's not bad. You should see what the full Blackguards get."

"Good?" Kip asked.

"Fantastic," she said. She picked at her food. "I'm serious."

"You really love food, huh?" Kip asked.

"I meant about the spying, sheep-for-brains."

"I know." Sheep for brains? After the time he'd just spent with sailors and soldiers, it was insufferably cute to hear someone swear with euphemisms.

"Oh." She flushed. Looked down at her food.

"Why does anyone want to spy on me?" Kip asked.

"You're a Guile." She shrugged as if that explained everything. Kip supposed it did.

"Who are you spying for?" Kip asked.

"My sponsor, of course."

"Well, I sort of figured." Kip had had no idea. "But who's your sponsor?"

"That's kind of a personal question, isn't it?" she said.

"You're spying on me, but I don't get to ask slightly personal questions?" Kip asked, incredulous.

She laughed. "It's not really a personal question, Kip. I was just testing you."

Oh, and I failed.

"So does that mean you're going to tell me?" he asked, bullish.

"Tell you what?" Playing dumb.

"You are really impossible, aren't you?" Kip asked.

She grinned. "Lady Lucretia Verangheti of the Smussato Veranghetis is my sponsor."

"You're from Ilyta? You don't look Ilytian. Plus, I thought the Ilytians don't like drafting. Heretics and all."

Her eyebrows shot up. "You just say the first thing that pops into your head, don't you?"

"I'm getting better," Kip said. What had he done?

"*This* is the better?"

Maybe I'll just shut my fat face for the rest of my life. Kip slowly cut off another piece of sausage. His fingers were healing, so gripping wasn't very painful. Stretching, however, was murder. Of course, using his hands to fight with hadn't made anything better. "Tell you what," he said. "How about you tell me about *you*—and that way I can spend a few seconds not getting myself into trouble?"

"What's there to tell?" Adrasteia said. She hadn't eaten a bite of her dinner yet. "Father's a merchant sailor. Does the spice/silk circuit when he can. Gone more often than not. Mother's a brewer in Odess. She wanted me to take over the stills. Instead, here I am."

"Isn't Odess in Abornea?" Kip asked. His mother hadn't taught him much about geography, but he did know that Abornea and Ilyta were different satrapies.

"Head of the Narrows, one of the biggest cities in the world."

"So how come your sponsor is Ilytian?"

"Because she's the one who bought me last."

Bought? Kip tried not to let his surprise show.

She tapped the top of her ear. It was snipped vertically and cauterized. "You not see this?" she said.

"Oh!" he said. She was a slave—and he was stupid.

But she didn't mock him. She said, "They like to say that among the Chromeria's pupils, there is no slave and no free. They like to say all sorts of things, of course, but if you can make it into the Blackguard, it's actually true." She didn't say it bitterly, though. She shrugged. Who you were mattered here, and there was no getting around it.

"So that's why you're trying to get into the Blackguard?"

"You're joking, right?" she asked.

Kip's look must have been enough. She sighed.

"Do you know why almost everyone in our training group is older than you, Kip?"

"Do you see this blank look on my face? Assume it applies for everything," Kip said.

She grinned for a moment. "Getting a spot in the Blackguard is the most coveted appointment most of us can dream of. In our training group alone, there are four legacies: children of Blackguards. Cruxer, Rig, Aram, and Tana. I can guarantee you that all of them have been training in martial arts since they could walk. If you're a slave and you test in, you're freed—though you do have to swear your service to the Blackguard. If you're the owner of that slave, the Chromeria pays you a fortune for the transfer of your property. The Veranghetis have placed dozens of Blackguards over the years. It's one of their more lucrative businesses. I came in a little sideways. The family that owned me had a daughter who was my age. They wanted her to be able to defend herself. I was trained with her, so she'd have a sparring partner. When they realized I might be able to draft, they sold me to Lady Verangheti. She had me train for the last year, all day, every day, with a variety of top masters, so that I might make it in."

A whole life, spent as property, spent training for this? "So you're telling me I shouldn't feel bad for getting beat up by a girl."

"Watch it, chunky."

He grinned a moment late, not realizing right away that she was teasing.

Her face fell. "I'm sorry, that wasn't— I didn't realize you were sensit— I shouldn't have . . . I'm sorry."

There was a sticky silence.

"I heard you almost passed the Threshing," she said.

"Almost." Kip Almost. Another reminder of failure. But she'd clearly meant well. "Actually," he said, "I've got one special talent."

"What's that?"

Kip lowered his voice. "It's a secret. You can't tell anyone. Highly valuable."

"All right," she said, leaning close.

He looked left and right, as if nervous. "Plate cleaning," he whispered.

Pure puzzlement. He could see her thinking, Did I hear him right? He gestured to his empty plate.

She laughed. "That one is going right to my sponsor!"

She was cute. Damn she was cute. Her smile punched right through Kip's chest and stirred that same stupid, awful, ridiculous place that Liv had. Kip sighed. "I know you're just being nice to me because you've been ordered to, but I like you."

Something died in her eyes. She looked away. He saw a wave of suppressed emotion crest in her lips, which went through about four expressions in a second. She blinked rapidly. Stood up and left without a word.

So, Kip, sweetie, how was your first day?

I made my teacher hate me; I got slapped by an old man and beat up by a little girl; I told my class that you were a whore; I destroyed someone's dream of joining the Blackguard; and I made a nice girl cry. Other than that, great!

And my hand hurts. He pushed it against the tabletop, trying to straighten it like he was supposed to be doing all the time. It took his breath away. He stopped immediately. Breathed. Had to concentrate so tears didn't leak out.

Kip got up and walked out of the hall. His Blackguard followed him. The man was tall and skinny, his irises haloed in red behind square-lensed red spectacles, pistol tucked behind his back, ataghan on one hip, katar on the other. He wasn't one of the Blackguards who'd been to Tyrea.

It wasn't even dark when Kip got to the barracks. He didn't care. He crashed into his bed, not even pulling the blanket over himself. He was finished.

But the day wasn't finished with him.

Something jabbed him. "What are you doing in my bed?" a voice demanded.

Really?

Kip didn't even open his eyes. "I'm farting in it to warm it up for you."

"Get out." This time whoever it was punched Kip in the shoulder. It didn't hurt much. Kip was looking through slit eyes and saw the movement toward himself and had braced for it. "I want to sleep in this bed tonight."

"It's a bit small, but I guess we can cuddle," Kip said, sitting up.

The bully was big but doughy-looking. One of those boys who gets his height and weight early, and doesn't really notice when everyone else catches up with him.

"Out of my bed, fatty," the bully said.

Kip rubbed his eyes. The other boys in the barracks were watching, pretending to be readying their bunks, stripping off their tunics. "Problem with being a bully," Kip said. "You never know how tough the new boy is. Bet it scares you a little, doesn't it?"

"What? Get out, fatty!"

Kip stood up wearily. The bully had short-cropped brown hair, a heavy jaw, big nose, chubby, but a big frame. "You think I've never seen a bully before? That I've never been bullied? We both know how this goes: I'm going to draw a line—like, 'Don't hit me.' And then, because you're a bully, you're going to *have to* hit me. And then..."

Or I can sidestep all that nonsense.

Kip punched the bully in the nose as hard as he could—and actually connected. A most satisfying pop. The bully went down hard, stunned. Blood gave him the mustache and beard that age hadn't yet.

"What's your name?" Kip asked the boy at his feet.

"Erio," the boy said, plugging his nose, still stunned. He got up on all fours, or all threes actually, since one hand was occupied.

"Elio?"

Elio started to stand. "I am going to kill you, you little—" Fighting manners dictated that Kip let him stand before they fought.

Kip slugged the boy in the face, knocking him sprawling. He jumped on top of Elio, squashing the breath out of him and trapping his arm in a wristlock. He sat on the boy.

Abruptly, Kip was cold, in control.

Elio said, "I'm going to kick your ass, you little puke. I'm going to make you regret the day you were born." Apparently he'd recovered from his shock, then. "Let go of my arm!"

Elio jerked and jumped, trying to throw Kip off, but Kip merely ground forward until the boy cried out and stopped fighting. He knew wristlocks well, though it had always been from the other side. Back home, Ramir used to grind Kip's face in the ground, make him cry, furious, humiliated. Made him kiss the dirt and say nasty things for his amusement before he'd let him get up.

The bully didn't stop: "I'm going to kill you, you fat little bastard. You can't hold me forever, and once I get out, you're going to have to watch your back. I'll be there. I'll be waiting for you, and you won't get off with a sucker punch next time."

Kip realized suddenly that he was riding a tiger. There was no winning here. He was in a position of power, so he'd look the bad guy if he used it to his advantage. The normal course of things now was that he would give Elio an ultimatum, like Take it back! or something similarly stupid. Elio would refuse, and Kip would be stuck. If Kip let him get up, Elio would come back tomorrow—and he probably would beat the snot out of Kip. If Kip tortured Elio by grinding his arm, it wouldn't do permanent damage, but many of the boys wouldn't know that, and even if Elio submitted, Kip would look like a cruel bastard to everyone in the barracks. Or worse, someone would interfere before Elio submitted, and Kip would look cruel *and* weak.

Stalling, Kip said, "Elio, I might not look it, but I'm tougher than you, I'm meaner than you, I'm smarter than you, and I will always go further than you dare."

"Save it, shit-eater," Elio said, sensing weakness in Kip's hesitation. "Oww! Start begging now, you little bitch."

Kip was suddenly so tired of it all. What had Ironfist said: 'The winning is just the beginning'?

"Elio, I was going to give you one more chance to take it back. But you're not going to take anything back. You're too damn stupid, and I'm too tired to keep playing this game. But I want you to remember something after you go to the infirmary: this *is* me being merciful."

Still holding Elio's wrist in the wristlock, Kip brought his left forearm down sharply with his weight behind it.

Elio's arm broke with a crunch. Everyone gasped. A bit of bloody bone speared through the skin. Elio screamed. It was a high-pitched sound. Not what you would have guessed the boy would sound like at all.

Kip got off. As forty boys watched, wide-eyed, Elio crawled away, bleeding, weeping. He stood and lurched out of the barracks, cradling his broken arm. None of the boys helped him. No one in authority ever came.

As Elio careened out of the door, Kip saw that his Blackguard—the slim, tall young man—was standing in the dark corner, leaning against the wall. He'd watched everything, no doubt ready to move if Kip's life were in danger. Other than that, he wouldn't interfere. He just watched, eyes glittering, face blank.

With feigned nonchalance, Kip lay back down in his bed and pretended to go back to sleep instantly. Just leave me alone. He turned his back toward the boys who were whispering to each other, amazed, repeating the story that didn't need repeating. They'd all seen it.

73

Kip's sleep was a lie. Eventually the boys snuffed their candles. In the darkness, Kip relived the battle at Garriston.

The man he'd thrown into the campfire, skin tearing off his face like chicken sticking to a pan. The eyes of men, faces contorted with fury, trying to kill Kip, hefting weapons as Kip fell through the gap in the wall. Fell, fell. Feet kicking at him from a hundred sides.

The taste of gunpowder in the air.

The joy of sweeping a blade into a man, his flesh parting, the blade winning free of his flesh, liberating blood and soul.

Surrounded by soldiers, matchlocks coming up. Kip shooting their own musket balls in their faces.

An eyeball, blue as the sea, sitting on a paving stone, the head it had been blown out of nowhere to be found. Staring at Kip, staring. Accusing. Killer.

What have you done?

He remembered losing fights to Ramir, the village bully. They'd thought Ramir was going to be pressed into King Garadul's army. Kip had killed soldiers—boys—no older than Ramir at Garriston. Boys who'd probably been pressed into service. Innocents doing guilty work.

He'd thought he wanted to kill Ramir, sometimes, back when he was a boy. Back when he didn't know what it meant. Back when he didn't know how easy it was.

What kind of monster have I become?

Chapter 18

Gavin put the fist-sized charge into the tube and began spooling out a narrow finger of green luxin, pushing it under the waves. In the last two days, he'd gotten pretty good at this, but he still couldn't rely on the charges, which were made of intermixed layers of yellow and red luxin wrapped around a bubble of air. The trick was making that innermost layer improperly—in exactly the proper way. The luxin bubble decayed, exposing the unstable yellow luxin to air. That unstable luxin flashed into light, igniting the red luxin. The successive layers did the same and made an explosion big enough to clear the reefs. But handling explosives that you'd deliberately made unstable was tense work. And sometimes the charges blew as soon as they touched the reef; other times they didn't blow up for several minutes, or at all.

Karris was steadying the boat, sometimes poling, sometimes rowing.

This time, the explosion came before Gavin had pulled away the placement tube. The tube shot out of his hands, and the sea jumped beneath their boat. Gavin had been braced for the wave, but the tube shooting up into the air pulled him off balance. He stumbled backward. Ordinarily, falling in the water would have been fine, but at the moment it was full of razor-sharp chunks of coral boiling up to the surface from the explosion.

Karris snagged Gavin's belt as his foot plunged into the water. She heaved. He swung abruptly back toward the boat and swept her feet out from under her as he crashed onto the deck.

Gavin rolled hard to keep from capsizing their little craft, and ended up on top of Karris. He laughed. "Nice catch!"

The look in her eyes was so intense that he thought his heart was going to stop.

"Get. Off," she hissed. Her body was rigid. He must have misinterpreted that split-second look. For a sliver of an instant he could have sworn—

"Sorry," he said. He pushed himself up. "Good catch," he said again. Did she cling to him just for a moment there? Did her body rise with him, keeping the contact for just one moment more? He looked at her.

The sun was baking the bay and had been for the last two days. Gavin had stripped off his shirt to cool down immediately, and after modestly sweating through the first day, Karris had followed his lead on the second, wearing only her tight Blackguard's chemise. The sight of her on her back, lean stomach exposed, legs on either side of him, skin radiant from golden sun and sweat—his breath stopped, thoughts scattered. He tried not to—failed—looked at her breasts.

Briefly, but she noticed.

Gavin could hear his imprisoned brother's voice, sudden, sharp: 'So you'd take this, too, huh, brother? Make love with her, as if you were me? You want to hear her scream *my* name when she's in the throes of passion?'

75

If she were any other woman, he would force the moment to its crisis: he would kiss her right now and let her decide. She wanted to say no? Fine, to hell with her. He'd move on. Or, more likely, she'd say yes, and he'd bed her and leave her with a smile on her face—but leave her. At least he'd do something.

Karris was the only woman who paralyzed him.

He remembered lying beside her in her room in her father's house, so long ago. He remembered kissing that breast, caressing her body, talking as the dawn approached. They'd made love half a dozen times through the night, urgency and passion winning through the awkwardness of inexperience. He had to be gone before her maid came to wake her in the morning.

They'd both known their romance was doomed, even then, even as the children they'd been. "I'll come for you," Dazen had promised.

He'd come back as he'd sworn, and she'd been gone—taken away by her father, though he hadn't known it then; he'd thought she had betrayed him—and her brothers had ambushed him. And he'd started the fire that killed them all: brothers, servants, slaves, children, treasures, hope.

"I've done you many wrongs," Gavin said now. He stood. "And I regret every one of them. I'm sorry."

He extended a hand to Karris, to help her stand. He thought she was going to refuse for a moment, but then she took his hand, popped to her feet, and didn't release his hand. She stood close, but her proximity was a challenge. "Do you want to specify what you're asking my pardon for?"

At Garriston, she'd said, 'I know your big secret, you asshole.' And slapped him.

Which hadn't actually clarified that much. He'd kept a lot of secrets over the years, and whatever she thought she knew could be leagues away from the worst truth. His central secret had necessitated all sorts of other ones over the years.

And by secrets, I mean lies.

So how cold are you, Gavin? How committed to your goal? You've killed for it before. Can you do it again?

They were hundreds of leagues away from the nearest Chromeria spy. If Gavin told Karris the whole truth and she swore to expose him or ruin him, he could kill her.

Simple. Easy.

In a fair fight, she'd have a fair chance against him. Her Blackguard training had made her quite a weapon. But there was no fair fight against a Prism.

"I'm just sorry," Gavin said. He looked away.

She didn't let go of his hand. She clamped down on it until he met her fiery gaze. "It's not an apology if you won't take responsibility. If you can't even name what you're apologizing for, you've given me *nothing*. You will not buy absolution on the cheap, not after what you've done. Not from me."

Gavin tried to take his hand back. She refused to let go.

"Let go, or swim," Gavin said coldly.

She let go.

Damn woman. She made him so furious. More furious because she was right. Damn her!

But he couldn't kill her, and he knew it. He'd let the world burn down first.

She picked up the luxin tube he'd been using to place charges and handed it to him. "Five more charges should finish the channel," she said. "But we'll have to hurry to get it done before low tide. Then we can work on the seawall footings."

They worked until there was no longer enough light in the sky for Gavin to draft. Karris steadied the boat, and made the forms, and made sure that they were keeping within the lines they'd planned.

The seawall would actually be three seawalls, with two wide gaps: one for ships coming into the bay, and one for ships leaving. The channels through the coral that led to the openings zigzagged, the turns marked by buoys. If they came under threat of attack, the locals could remove the buoys. It was going to be rough work, Gavin thought. He'd learned some things from building Brightwater Wall, but there he'd also had thousands of workers and dozens of drafters to help him.

Lovely that I made such a defensible refuge for the Color Prince.

Well, second time's the charm. He would leave this for the people of Tyrea—now his people—and he would do a few other things to give them a head start on establishing a city. Then he would leave.

They had a small campfire, and Karris cooked some fish she'd snared while Gavin slept. She woke him and they ate together.

"Sorry," he said, "I should have helped with dinner."

She looked at him like he was being stupid. "You're making the Ninth Wonder of the World this week; I can make dinner."

"It's not really fair, is it?" Gavin said. "I couldn't do this without you, but it'll be the Thing Gavin Built, just like Brightwater Wall was."

She shook her head. "You're a mystery to me, Lord Prism."

He didn't remember falling asleep, but when he woke in the middle of the night, there was a blanket over him. He saw Karris in the low light of the fire, watching the darkness. He felt an immense gratitude toward her. She'd worked hard all day long, too, and now she was staying up all night.

Her back was to him and to the fire, maintaining her night vision, of course. Gavin and most sub-reds could control their eyes well enough to attain full night vision quickly, but Karris didn't like to lose even a few seconds of night vision.

Gavin sat up and was right on the edge of calling out to tell her he would take the next watch when he saw her shoulders shake.

Not a shiver. She was crying. Gavin hadn't seen Karris cry in years.

He knew she wouldn't be pleased to find out he'd noticed, but he stood and put his hands on her shoulders. She tensed.

"I'll take this watch," he said gently.

"Don't, Gavin," she said. Her voice was raw, right at the edge.

Don't *what*? Don't touch her? Don't say anything? Don't leave?

"Today was Tavos's birthday," she said, struggling to get the words out clearly. "I almost didn't even remember." Tavos, her brother. He'd died in the fire. He'd been a terrible person, violent, unstable, one of the boys whose jeering had made Dazen believe that if he didn't fight back that night, he would be killed. But Karris hadn't seen that, had maybe never seen that side of her brother. Even if she had, he'd still been her brother. "I just miss them all so much. Koios . . ." She sounded like she wanted to say more, but couldn't.

Koios had been her favorite brother. He was the only one Gavin regretted killing. The only halfway decent person among them.

And then she did weep. She turned to him, and he held her. He said nothing, still not certain he wasn't dreaming the whole thing, knowing only that if he said anything, he would say the wrong thing.

Bewildered as he might be, sometimes a man's highest calling is simply to stand, and hug.

Chapter 19

In his dream, Kip was a green wight, chasing down screaming children and murdering them with blade and fire. He woke alternately furious, weepy, and bloodthirsty, the rage from those phantasms sometimes still clinging to him.

When he got up to go urinate in the middle of the night, a Blackguard accompanied him. It was a man Kip had never met, and he said nothing. Merely walked with Kip, and held him back for a moment while he checked that there were no assassins in the toilet. Ridiculous.

It was a relief to get out of bed in the morning, though Kip didn't feel rested in the slightest. Several older, second-year students came and herded the new students toward the dining hall.

Kip was ravenous, but he got no more food than anyone else in the serving line. He reached the end of the line in dread. Tables were laid out in long rows, and students clumped together with friends.

Which I don't have.

In fact, Kip had quite the opposite. He caught sight of Elio, whose arm was wrapped in thick bandages and hung in a sling. The boy was talking with his friends when he saw Kip. He shut up instantly and blanched.

I should go over there. I should go and sit with them, disarm them with small talk, pretend nothing happened, but assert my right to sit with the toughest boys in the class.

But he didn't have it in him.

It was only then that he realized there was no Blackguard following him this morning. He looked around at the lines of students, tables, food, servants, and slaves. No Blackguards anywhere. For some reason, it took what little, tottering confidence he had and knocked it over with a breath. They'd seen what he'd done. They'd decided he wasn't worth protecting.

Then Kip saw some kids he recognized: the boy with the strange spectacles who'd sat behind him in class yesterday and some others from the Blackguard training class. They were the outcasts—Kip could tell immediately. They were the awkward, the intelligent, the ugly, with those Blackguard hopefuls who were destined to fail out early and were merely trying to get in from some vain hope of their own or their masters'. There was, of course, space at their table, and space around them, as if they were contagious. Kip went over.

"Can you read?" the boy asked as Kip came close. His flip-down spectacles currently had the blue lens down over one eye, and the yellow down over the other.

Kip hesitated. Did they not want him? "Um, yes?"

"You need to get to lecture if you can't. If you can, you need to check the work schedule. Hold on, you had that— Oh, never mind, of course you can read. You told Magister Kadah to go stuff herself."

"Really?" a homely girl asked.

Kip ignored her and tucked into his food.

"Why are you sitting with *us*?"

"You looked nicer than them," Kip said, gesturing with a toss of his head toward the tough boys. "You want me to leave?"

They all looked at each other. Shrugged. "No," the boy with spectacles said.

"So, what are your names?" Kip asked.

The bespectacled boy pointed to himself, "I'm Ben-hadad," then to the homely girl, "Tiziri," then to a gangly, gap-toothed boy, "that's Aras, and—"

They were interrupted by a girl's voice. "Hey, did you all hear about Elio getting his halos tapped by the new—" She cut off as she saw Kip.

"And...that would be Adrasteia. Classic, Teia."

"We've met," Kip said dryly.

Teia opened her mouth, then sat down silently, defeated.

"I didn't hear," Aras said. "What, new who? What happened?"

"*Aras*," Teia said through gritted teeth.

"What? Was there a fight?" Aras asked.

"I don't know if I'd call it a fight," Kip said.

"You? You were in a fight? With Elio?" Aras said.

"You broke his arm in three places!" Adrasteia—Teia?—said.

"I did?" Kip asked.

"Wait, you broke Elio's arm?" Ben-hadad asked. "I hate that kid."

"Is that how you hurt your hand?" Tiziri asked. She had a birthmark over the left half of her face. She wore her kinky hair flopped over that way to try to hide it, but it was a futile attempt.

Kip looked at his bandaged hand. He was supposed to get a fresh poultice smeared on it every day. He'd forgotten this morning. He didn't even know if he could find the infirmary from here. "No, uh, this. I kind of got thrown into a fire."

"Wait, wait, wait. You have to start from the beginning," Benhadad said. "Aras! Stop staring over there or they'll know we're talking about—"

Aras, Teia, Tiziri, and Kip all glanced over at Elio's table at the same time—and saw that Elio's friends were all staring at them. Caught.

Ben-hadad scrubbed his chin where his beard was just coming in. "Hopeless," he said. He flipped up both of the color lenses on the spectacles. He fixed his gaze on Kip, one eye looking slightly larger than the other. Kip had heard of the lenses that corrected bad vision before, but he'd never seen them. It was unnerving. "So," Ben-hadad said to Kip, "spill."

"About Elio? He came over and hit me a few times, and I punched him in the nose."

They waited.

Kip spooned in more gruel.

"Worst. Storyteller. Ever," Teia said.

"You punched him in the nose so hard his arm broke in three places?" Ben-hadad prompted.

"Look," Kip said, "it wasn't a big thing. I was really scared and I knew he was going to hit me, so I—you know? I hit him first. I kind of panicked."

"And broke his arm?" Teia asked.

Kip shrugged. "He said he was going to kill me."

Their looks were somewhere between dubious and totally impressed.

Kip decided to defuse it with humor. "I've only got one good hand. Now if he comes after me, we'll be even."

Not funny.

"Holy shit," Aras said. "I saw you at the tryouts, but I had no idea you were that good."

"You don't look like a badass," Ben-hadad said. "But I guess it proves you're a Guile."

"I heard after the fight was over, you broke his arm because he called you Lard Guile," Tiziri said. She hadn't been at Kip's tryouts, obviously.

Teia sank into her seat.

"It wasn't like that," Kip said. "Really. It was just really fast, and then it was over in like three seconds. I got lucky. Seriously. Ask Teia. She's tougher than I am. She kicked me in the face yesterday."

"What? What? What?" Ben-hadad said. "Teia?"

"Kip was assigned to be my partner," Teia said. She grimaced. Oh, thanks.

Ben-hadad asked her, "Partner? You tried out? I thought you weren't going to try out until next year." He looked momentarily hurt, but then covered it. "I would have come! Ha, scrub!"

Kip's lifted eyebrows asked the question for him.

Aras said, "Ben-hadad got here too late for the drafting lectures year last spring, but he did test into the spring class of the Blackguard." He turned to Teia. "But you said you thought the Blackguard was stupid. Standing in the path of swords to protect idiots is *for* idiots, you said."

"Aras, you're sitting next to Kip *Guile*," Tiziri said.

"I know. I heard the first time. What's the— Oh, oh! I'm sure Teia didn't mean your father's an idiot, Kip. She probably meant the White. I mean, I guess it's gotta be one or the other of them, huh? Maybe the Red? Oh, wait, that's your grandfather."

"*Aras!*" Teia said.

Ben-hadad said, "Teia, you said you didn't want to hurt people for a living." He seemed to take Teia's secrecy about trying out as a personal betrayal.

"I don't!" Teia said, defensive.

"Then, what? When I argue for you joining the Blackguard, what they do is garbage and idiocy, but Kip comes along and—"

"That has nothing to do with anything! Not all of us are bichromes, Ben. You might even be a poly. You can go wherever you want, do whatever you want. You're going to be powerful enough that no one will care who your parents are. I don't even have a real color."

"Your color is just as real as anyone's. People just don't recognize it yet, Teia, we've talked—"

Teia shot back, "If no one recognizes it, no one's going to recruit me for it either. Maybe in five years more people will think like you do, but for now I've got no other options. It's all I'm good for. Don't you understand? I tried to find another sponsor. I failed, and my mistress ordered me to try out for the Blackguard."

"I didn't know your mistress ordered it. I'm sorry," Ben-hadad said.

She'll make it in, Kip thought, but he said nothing. He was the one who'd unwittingly revealed the secret. He was just hoping that by being quiet he might avoid further wrath.

"And you, *partner*, thanks a lot," Teia said.

Chapter 20

Kip finished his breakfast, still feeling hungry. Teia got up and went over to the lists on the wall. She left her bowl and spoon and glass on the table, as it seemed that most everyone did.

Ben-hadad and Tiziri got up and left, too, heading in different directions. Only Kip and Aras were still sitting at the table. The gangly boy was a slow eater. The apple of his throat was distractingly large, making him look like a large, kind vulture.

"Are we supposed to do anything with our bowls?" Kip asked.

"Huh?" Aras had been looking over at some girls. Pretty, in the same plain uniforms as everyone else, but with jewelry at their wrists and throats. Rich girls. Out of reach, but not out of the reach of dreams, from Aras's distant look. "Bowls? What?"

"Are we supposed to put away our bowls?" Kip asked. Back home, no one would tolerate a fifteen-year-old shirking washing up.

"Slaves do it. You should go. First shift starts soon." Aras went back to staring at the girls.

Leaving the table felt like abandoning safety to go back and play in the fields of the wolves. But there was no putting it off. Kip stood and headed toward the wall of lists. He passed by some older discipulae just coming to eat. A boy and a girl walked by, their arms down at their sides, eyes intent with concentration, their food held on blue trays that they each were drafting. Each raised their hands slowly as they walked, trying to adjust the open luxin without spilling their food and drink. Then they sealed their trays, almost simultaneously.

"Oh no, oh no, oh no," the boy was repeating. He'd sealed the luxin badly, and even as he reached the table, his tray disintegrated, dropping his bowl and glass, both of which shattered.

"One for the girls!" his opponent said, setting down her perfect tray easily.

The boy swore under his breath as some other boys, clearly his friends, groaned. A magister piped up, "You're cleaning that yourself, Gerrad. No slaves."

Teia intercepted Kip before he got to the lists. "We've got mirror duty, blue tower."

"What?" Kip asked.

"You weren't here for bearings week when they show us how things work. You don't know anything," Teia said. "So I switched chores with someone. I'll be on your crew all week."

"Really?" Kip said. It was a ray of normal piercing his black clouds of utter cluelessness.

He was about to thank her when she said, "No. Don't."

"I was going to—"

"I'm not doing it for you. Partners often have to share each other's punishments. The punishments usually mean you miss class. So if you botch things, it hurts my chances to make it into the Blackguard."

Great, something else to feel guilty about.

Teia walked him to one of the lifts, where they joined about fifty other students waiting. Teia's hair wasn't tied back today and now Kip felt foolish for mistaking her for a boy in the first place. Moron.

He wondered what Liv was doing now. He wondered if she was even still alive. Stupid worry. She was probably murdering people by now. Kip had stood there, on the eve of the Battle of Garriston. He'd heard all of the Color Prince's lies and known them for what they were: smears and half-truths. High-minded talk used to cloak cowardice.

Magic was hard. It made you a master of the world for a decade or two, and then it mastered you. Drafters went crazy. When vastly powerful people go crazy, they endanger everyone. Killing them wasn't nice, but it was necessary.

The Color Prince said, "We won't murder our parents who have served for years!" He meant, "I don't want to die when it's my turn. I want all the privileges we're afforded because of our gifts, but I don't want to pay the price." Kip could see that, and Kip was a moron. Why hadn't Liv?

After a few minutes, Kip and Teia were able to get on the lift with

twenty other students.

"We're lucky," Teia said. "The mirrors are boring, but when you have to spend all morning on the counterweights and then you go to Blackguard tryouts and you can barely lift your arms? That's awful."

"Thanks, tell me about it," another student said. Kip thought he recognized the boy from the Blackguard class. His name was Ferkudi, maybe? "I've got the counterweights all week!"

"We'll trade you," Teia said.

"You will?!"

"No," Teia said. The students laughed.

The lift stopped about halfway up the tower, and almost all the students spilled out to cross the walkways. Kip and Teia went with them. The six outer towers of the Chromeria were connected to the central tower by a series of spindly walkways hanging high up in the air. Kip had crossed one of these bridges before. He *knew* that they were safe.

After all, the Chromeria wouldn't put drafters at risk, right?

Kip swallowed and followed. The blue tower was finished with blue luxin cut into facets so that the whole surface gleamed in the sun like a million sapphires. It would have been breathtaking, if Kip had any breath.

"Don't like heights, huh?" Teia asked after they got across.

"Not my favorite," Kip admitted.

"This might not be that much fun, then."

Kip forced a weak smile.

"You have a bad experience or something?" Teia asked. "With heights?"

"Fat assassin lady tried to throw me off the yellow tower," Kip said.

She looked at him, dubious. "Look, if you don't like heights, that's fine. You don't have to make fun. I was just making conversation."

Kip opened his mouth. No, he wasn't going to win this one.

Had they ever figured out who wanted him dead?

If so, no one had ever told him. Which reminded him of his Blackguard escort—there still wasn't one. It gave Kip the feeling—again—of being tangentially involved in Big Things. Someone tried to kill him; no one explained why. He got a Blackguard escort; the Blackguard escort got taken away, and no one figured to clue Kip in.

Go play in the corner and don't bother the adults, Kip.

Teia led half a dozen students to the blue tower's lift and they took that up to the top. There was a big, sturdy door and a nice hallway.

"Other half of the top floor is for satrapahs and nobles and religious festivals," Teia said. "On Sun Day, this whole floor rotates so that their half faces the sun, rather than ours."

Beyond the sturdy door was a room full of gears and pulleys and ropes and sand clocks and bells, with enormous windows. It was so bright that Kip was momentarily blinded. Teia handed him a pair of large round spectacles with darkened lenses. Once he put them on, he was able to see again.

Weary students who'd pulled the dawn shift got up from their chairs and handed off thick coats to the next shift. Some of them muttered instructions about the states of certain gears or ropes. A few traded jokes. Kip was lost.

Eventually, they got sorted. Kip and Teia took their coats and both took a chair. There were six stations, two students per station, two chairs, four sand clocks, four bells, one giant mirror per station that was bigger across than Kip was tall, and three smaller mirrors.

"The whole Chromeria rotates over the course of the day so that it's always facing the sun more or less directly," Teia said. "So mostly we only have to move the mirrors up and down as the sun rises. First rule, never touch the mirrors with your hands. If there's a problem, we summon the lens grinders. They're the best in the world, and they get furious if they find handprints on their mirrors."

But as impressive as the mirrors and pulleys were, they weren't what seized Kip's attention. There were half a dozen massive holes in the floor: one huge central hole, with six mirrors above it, and then numerous smaller ones.

"Lightwells," Teia said. "So that drafters in the tower below us will always have enough light available, no matter if they're on the dark side of the tower, or if it's early or late in the day. Take a peek over the side."

So every team used their big mirror to send light to another big mirror over the central hole, where other mirrors shot the light downward.

Kip poked his head over the side. The walls of the hole were perfectly sheer, covered in silver polished to a mirror sheen, and it plunged on forever. In the glare of the gathered sunlight, he couldn't even see the bottom.

As he was watching, about four floors down, a section of the wall opened and a mirror three feet across popped out into the light stream. Kip saw that farther down, other mirrors were similarly gathering light, offset from each other by careful degrees so that mirrors above wouldn't block light to the mirrors below.

Kip stepped back, swallowing. It was mind-blowing, genius—and there was no railing to keep the mirror-tenders from falling straight down.

A tiny bell rang, startling him. Teia turned over the sand timer connected to the bell and grabbed a rope over one of the smaller side mirrors. She pulled a ratcheting lever, which moved the mirror by some tiny degree.

The smaller mirrors fed light to smaller holes. "Special laboratories, or polychromes' or Colors' chambers," Teia answered Kip's unspoken question. "There's only so many private lightwells in each tower, so you have to be pretty important to get your own. But our work is pretty mindless. Once you get used to it, anyway. We don't calibrate anything. Mirror slaves do that, setting things every dawn, and then we just move the ropes so much every time a bell goes off. Teams of two so we stay awake, and in case we have to open the windows, and for the zenith switchover."

"Sure. Zenith switchover," Kip said, having no idea what she was talking about.

The work seemed complicated at first, but pretty soon Teia was letting Kip pull the levers and turn the sand timers.

"Anyone ever fall down the holes?" Kip asked.

"A boy fell down one of the smaller lightwells last year. It was four floors down to the Blue's mirror. Broke his back. Lived for six months. A few years ago, it's said some boys fought up here, and one pushed the other one into the great well. Died instantly. The killer swore it was on accident. They didn't believe him."

"What'd they do?" Kip asked.

"Orholam's Glare."

Kip's face apparently said it for him: I have no idea what you're talking about. Again.

"There's a pillar at the base of the bridge on Big Jasper. You know the Thousand Stars?"

The mirror towers all over the city. "Sure."

"Right, all those mirrors, plus all the mirrors on Chromeria towers, are all focused on that one point. They put the condemned at the focal point at noon. Drafter's got a choice then. You can cook to death like an ant under a glass, or you can draft. If you draft, it's like pushing too much water through a straw. You burst."

"That sounds...unspeakably awful," Kip said.

"It's not supposed to be fun. Come on, it's time for lecture. You think you can get through it today without causing an incident?"

Kip's brow wrinkled, not ready to let it go. "But I thought that they slaved the Thousand Stars onto the Prism every Sun Day."

"Yes?"

"Well, how does *he* not die?" Kip asked.

"He's the Prism. He can do anything."

Chapter 21

I can't do this.

Seven years, seven great purposes.

It was a fantasy, a fairy story, a fool's errand. What Gavin wanted was impossible.

He lay next to Karris, close enough to share body heat. He'd slept fitfully, as always, had nightmares, as always. Last night, no doubt because of his waking fears about losing blue, he'd dreamed of his brother escaping the blue hell. He shook it off, ignored the stabbing pain and tightness in his chest. Dawn was close. Karris would wake any minute, and she would move away. They would get up; they would work. Sooner or later, the people of this island would either come to stop him or to talk. If they came to kill him, they would come at night. With dawn coming, he thought it unlikely they would attack now. Gavin would live another day.

The first of his purposes was easy enough, though he'd persistently failed: tell the whole truth to Karris. When the city had fallen to the Color Prince, he'd almost abandoned the second: saving the people of Garriston who had suffered so much because of him. Now that salvation was within sight. Other purposes, he had achieved: learning to travel faster than any man alive; undermining certain Colors on the Spectrum, the ruling council of the Chromeria. Others were still in process. All except telling Karris the truth ultimately built toward one goal, one grand design that he barely even dared to think about, lest somehow thinking it would make it even more impossible than it already was. As if, in thinking it, he would spill the secret and it would escape beyond his grasp forever.

He owed his dead little brother Sevastian better. He owed his mother better. He owed Gavin better.

He wasn't sure, even as he thought it, if by "Gavin" he meant himself, or his brother.

Karris snuggled close to him, but the very movement seemed to raise her consciousness above the waterline, and she started. He breathed evenly, feigning sleep. She pulled back, scooted away gently so as not to wake him. She might hate him—deservedly so—but she was still kind. It was one of the things he loved about her.

He'd held her while she mourned her brother last night. Held her until she slept, and then got up and kept watch. He'd envied her tears even as it warmed him and made him ache for her. He'd envied her for clean grief for a dead brother rather than his horror and guilt over a living one. No wonder he'd dreamed about Dazen when it had been his turn to sleep. Regardless, last night changed nothing between them. He expected a brusque thank-you today, if anything. Then things would be back to normal.

Except normal couldn't hold. Karris wasn't stupid: pretty soon she'd notice that he couldn't draft blue. And her questions had already been unsettling.

The truth was, all his purposes were focused in one direction, except for the one about telling Karris the truth, which ran directly opposite. Karris was the greatest threat to his plans. And she was immune to flattery or pressure. She had nothing but her own sense of justice. If she thought ruining him was the right thing to do, she'd do it regardless of the cost.

The smart thing to do was to treat her like any other obstacle, and take her out.

It didn't mean killing her. He could take her to one of the outer islands, where even merchants came only once a year, and simply leave her there. Then whatever happened with him, she couldn't interfere. But stealing a year of the life of a woman who had, quite likely, only five years left to live was no small offense.

He sat up. This was going nowhere.

Karris was just coming back from making water in the woods.

"Any itch weed?" Gavin asked.

She blushed, remembering that misadventure. "I'm a touch more careful about that these days."

"Once bit twice shy, eh?" Gavin asked, standing and stretching. He had to go make water himself.

"In some things." She had an odd look in her eyes.

He stepped into the woods and started to urinate. It had been awkward, fifteen years ago, to have someone standing two paces away while he relieved himself. Having Blackguards protect him made him have to get over that fast. Especially when they traveled in wilderness, a Blackguard wasn't going to let him out of her sight.

"Gavin? Thank you," Karris said.

Gavin pissed. He knew better than to talk, better than to laugh in amusement at being right. He cleared his throat. "So, you figure this Third Eye is going to come today?" he asked.

"Safe bet," Karris said, voice suddenly tense. He heard her pistol cocking.

Chapter 22

"You may not know it now, but this class will be the most important topic some of you will ever study," Magister Hena said. She was both impossibly tall and impossibly skinny, with bad posture, bad teeth, and thick colorless corrective lenses that made her eyes look different sizes. "For most of you boys, it will be the only time you get to taste the greatness of making real structures with luxin, so it will behoove you to pay attention, so you know what the women for whom you work are doing. If you're good at it, you may be allowed to do the arithmetic, of course, so a large part of this class will have to do with the decidedly mundane task of teaching the abacus and the skills of drawing. Engineering is knowing. Building is an art. Everyone can do the former, the latter is reserved for the best women."

One of the boys, scowling, raised his hand. She called on him.

"Magister Hena, why can't we build?"

"Because only superchromats are allowed to build with luxin. You boys, your eyes are inferior. In some applications, you can cover your flawed drafting with enough will and by spraying enough luxin at the problem. But not in a structure people have to trust. Only women, and only superchromat women, are allowed to build. It's not worth death to risk trusting a man."

"But why, Magister Hena? *Why* can't we draft as well?" the boy asked. He sounded whiny. Even to Kip, who thought it was unfair, too.

"I don't care," Magister Hena said. "Ask a luxiat or one of your theology teachers. For today, I'll isolate the superchromats. Yes, I know you already tested this, but an engineer doesn't trust, an engineer tests. If it's not demonstrable, it's not real. On your slate before you, there are seven sticks of luxin. Only at one place on those sticks is the luxin drafted absolutely perfectly. Make a mark beneath that spot with your chalk. I'll come around and check your work, and the superchromats will move to the front of the room."

Kip looked at the sticks of luxin and picked up the chalk. He was damned if he did and damned if he didn't, he knew. He was a superchromat and a boy. A freak. Being in the *in* group wasn't going to help him at all, because none of the other boys would be in it with him. They'd hate him for being with the girls, and the girls wouldn't treat him like he belonged either. He'd be different, no matter what.

And because Magister Hena had seen the earlier test results, if Kip failed, she'd ask him if he'd failed on purpose. She didn't look like the type to think that "It's too embarrassing to be a superchromat boy" would be an acceptable answer.

Kip made his marks. It was easy. Around the room, boys and girls both were squinting, looking at the sticks from different angles, holding them up to the light. Kip suddenly felt sorry for the girls who didn't make it. It was one thing for boys to fail. No one expected them to pass. But *half* of girls passed. That was a big enough number that failing was embarrassing. To fail was to be like the boys. It was to be a second-class drafter. He could see them agonizing.

"It's not a test you can pass by trying harder," Magister Hena said. "You either see the differences or you don't. It's a failure, but it's not a personal one. There's nothing you can do to pass it. Either you were born blessed, or you weren't. Chalk down."

Either you were born blessed, or you weren't? Thanks. That makes it *so* much better.

Magister Hena walked around the room. She ticked through the students. "Up front, up front, stay here, stay here. Stay, stay, stay." She walked behind Kip's place, "Stay—er..."

She looked at his slate, then at the slates of his neighbors. Kip guessed that there were only so many tests, and she was seeing if he could have cheated off of a real superchromat to get the correct answers.

Apparently, she *hadn't* heard about him. Great.

"The boy next to you, take his test," Magister Hena ordered.

Kip grimaced to himself as the class looked at him. He picked up his chalk and quickly marked the spots on the boy's slate—of course, the boy's marks had been all wrong.

"Hmm, a superchromat *boy*. It's been years," Magister Hena said. "Very well. Up front."

She separated the rest of the class, and then went back up front herself to address those who had passed. "Very well. Girls...and boy... you've been moved up front because you're favored by Orholam. You can appreciate the beauties of Orholam's creation in ways the rest of this class and most of the world is blind to. However, that means more will be expected of you. That is why I've had you come to the front, not because I care what accident of birth gave you better eyes than the rest. You do have better eyes than the rest, so you have a responsibility to Orholam and *to me* to use those eyes well. Understood?"

"Yes, Magister," the girls said weakly.

She raised her eyebrows and peered at them over her goggly lenses. They repeated it, louder. Kip joined them, lest he be even more different.

"Good. Now, the abacus. Any of you here from Tyrea?"

"No? Oh, the boy, of course," she said as Kip raised his hand. She went on, "Tyrea was, despite all evidence to the contrary, once the seat of a great empire, long before Lucidonius came. Perhaps it was crumbling by the time he did come, or perhaps he hastened its demise. That is for another class. The Tyrean Empire gave us a few gifts and a few curses. The only one I care about for this class's purposes is the base twelve number system. Tyrea is the reason our day is broken into twelve-hour halves, and sixty-minute hours. Some of you Aborneans and Tyreans may have been taught to use the base twelve system in counting and in arithmetic. If so, this class will be much, much harder for you. That number system is unholy, and you will not use it hence-forth. Unholy? you ask. Yes, blasphemous. How can a number system be unholy? Well, how can a number system be based on twelves? What is our number system based on, anyone?"

"Ten," a girl in the front row said.

"Correct. Why does ten make sense?"

No one answered. "Fingers," Kip said, being a wiseass.

"You think you're joking, but even fools can be right."

Kip scowled.

"It's true. Fingers and toes. So if fingers and toes are the easiest way for primitives and morons to count"—she glanced at Kip—"especially before parchment or vellum or paper, how does a society count based on twelves?"

Kip scowled harder.

A girl at the back raised her hand. Magister Hena called on her. "The Tyrean gods had six fingers and toes."

"Exactly. That's why you'll hear stories of children who have six fingers and toes being venerated in certain superstitious corners of the world. You've heard of such things, right, boy?"

"It's *Kip*, and no, I've never heard of any such thing."

"Well, then perhaps your parents were particularly enlightened for Tyrea. Or ignorant even of the ignorance, I suppose."

Kip opened his mouth, then shut it. Don't, Kip. It doesn't matter. He suddenly felt hungry.

The next hour was spent learning how to use an abacus. The four beads on the bottom row were called the earthly beads, and the one bead on the top row was the heavenly bead. And first they simply counted, up and down, adding by ones, subtracting by ones. Then adding by twos and subtracting by twos, then fives.

Some of the students clearly were bored, having learned this long ago. Others, like Kip, struggled to keep up with even basic arithmetic. But the children who did the worst were the few who had learned to use the abacus on the base twelve system. They seemed frozen; everything they'd learned was wrong.

The next lecture was better. It was Properties of Luxin, taught by a ferret-faced Ilytian magister who leaned on his cane in between making points. Kip was surprised to find that half of the auditors were non-drafters. And the non-drafters were all smart and driven. These were the future architects and builders of the Seven Satrapies. Like the drafters, these boys and girls had their tuitions paid for by the satraps. Some were connected—second and third sons of nobles who had to be given some way to support themselves. But even they had passed competency tests in order to be accepted.

Kip could tell right away that these children wouldn't need any training on the abacus.

The tutorials were pretty basic today, though. Sheets of blue luxin one foot by one foot and one thumb thick were placed on supports, then weights added to the center until they shattered. The same was done with green, and superchromat-drafted yellow.

Magister Atagamo then had those students who were able to do so draft their own sheets of blue luxin. He tested each of those. They all failed at much lower weights—especially the boys'. "Later, I will have you memorize the theoretical weakest blue luxin that will still hold a solid so that you know the full range. For now, be aware that we are establishing maximum strengths. The luxins we have to work with are superchromat-drafted. Your own luxin will be weaker than this. Boys, yours will usually be substantially so."

Then Magister Atagamo's assistants put a cubit tub on a scale, showed how it measured one foot per side, zeroed the scale, and filled it with water. Kip noticed that all of the other students were writing everything down.

The weight of the water within that small tub was a seven, the basic unit of measuring weight. Of course, that was too big of a weight to be useful for a lot of things, so it was broken into sevs: one-seventh fractions of a seven. Kip weighed twenty-nine sevs, or four sevens and one sev, usually expressed as four sevens one.

But the magisters weren't finished. They poured out the water and had three superviolet drafters fill the tub with superviolet luxin. That was when Kip knew he was in real trouble—they were measuring everything! When they unsealed the superviolet and it dissolved into feather-fine, nearly invisible dust, they swept that out into a tiny cup and measured it. Everything that could be quantified was.

For a while, with the rest of the students, Kip simply wrote down the numbers without knowing why. Then they asked them to add the weights of all the colors together. The students who were already proficient with their abacuses did so quickly. Kip barely got through adding the first two before those students were finished.

Magister Atagamo said, "Now, subtract the weight of the cube of green luxin from that total, and add the weight of a small woman, let's say eleven sevs."

Four girls—non-drafters all—had the total practically as soon as the magister was finished talking. Kip was aghast.

"Excellent," the magister said. "Now, a practical example. You're a blue drafter, manning the counterweights for the lift in one of the towers. One of the counterweights breaks in half. It is made of iron, and weighs thirty sevs six. How much blue luxin will you have to draft to replace the counterweight? If your counterweight is more than three sevens heavier than the original when combined with the weight of the delegation, the pulley will break, killing everyone. When you have your answer, come show it to me. For the sake of our example, we'll pretend that the delegation is coming from your home satrapy, and if you don't have the lift ready by the time they arrive, you will shame them and lose your sponsorship. So you have thirty minutes to get your solution. If you get the answer quickly, you can leave, take the rest of the morning off. If you can't, there will be a mark against you for today. Go."

The other students set to work immediately, and Kip saw that the easy answer was impossible. He couldn't just add full-size blocks of blue luxin together, because that would make the counterweight too heavy. The arithmetic here was to find the exact fractional volume of blue luxin he would need to make a new counterweight.

The best girls and boys were already working their abacus beads back and forth. Kip wasn't good enough with the abacus. He'd never make it in time. He didn't know how to figure fractions. He could work the entire time and still not— Oh.

Got nothing to lose, do you, tubby?

Kip scribbled something on his paper, stood up, and walked to the magister's desk.

The magister looked at him tolerantly, like he was a student who hadn't understood the question and was about to ask for clarification. Kip held up the paper.

He'd drawn a quick sleeve of blue luxin to go around the original counterweight to hold the broken halves together.

"You're Guile's by-blow, aren't you?"

"Yes, Magister."

"I can tell. Those boys cheated magnificently, too."

Kip swallowed. The rest of the class stopped working on hearing "cheated." "You taught them, sir?"

Magister Atagamo's mouth twisted. He ignored the question. "You'll have to learn to use the abacus eventually, you know."

"Yes, sir."

The old man snorted. "Goodbye, little Guile."

"So I pass?"

"Highest marks of the day. And don't ever do it again."

Chapter 23

"Give us privacy," the White said.

Ironfist stood in the White's chambers, atop the Prism's Tower at the center of the Chromeria. The wheels of her chair were tall enough that she could push on them directly to move around her room, which she insisted on doing, despite the delicacy of her wrists.

"My blanket, please," she said.

He brought over her blanket—something she'd woven decades ago with her own hands. Like many who make their livelihood with their minds, she had an outsized pride in the few things her hands had crafted. It was perhaps the only thing for which Ironfist could consider her a silly old lady. He tucked the blanket around her legs and was surprised to feel how thin those limbs had become.

"You see?" she said. "You can tell, can't you, Commander?"

Silly old lady indeed. She'd set him up. Sharper than he was, still. It was a good reminder, both ways. Weak physically, but not mentally. Not in the least.

"Tell what, my lady?"

"Psh," she said. A little eye roll. "It is a hard place, for those who are not prepared." I'm dying, she was saying, prepare yourself so that when I do you won't fall prey to your enemies.

It was both terrifying to imagine a world without Orea Pullawr as the White, and warming to learn that she considered him a friend.

"Tell me again, Commander, about your coming to Garriston, and the preparations for battle there."

So he did, again. He tried to tell it differently, knowing that she was sifting his words, looking for something. He told her about the movement of troops, about how many men and drafters each side had, about the disposition of the Ruthgari garrison that had been there. She'd been interested in that, the first time. But now those were mere numbers to her. She already had memorized them, and analyzed what they meant about the Ruthgari commitment to Tyrea, and who had been bribed. Now she was looking for something else.

He spoke for two hours. He told her about General Danavis coming alone—unmustached—to the Travertine Palace, and how Ironfist had been expelled from the meeting. He spoke of Gavin moving the wagon that had blocked the gates, making the men help in doing what he could have done by himself, thereby somehow cementing them to his own cause.

She smiled at that, a small, knowing smile. Perhaps the smile of one leader approving of another's nice play.

He wasn't sure what she was looking for, though, and pretty certain that he wasn't supposed to know.

"You don't gamble, do you, Commander?" she asked.

"No, my lady." How did she know that? He supposed it wasn't the kind of thing that would be hard to find out, but that she had, that she cared about it, and that she recalled it was what made the White both alien and a little frightening.

"Always thought that was strange. You seem like the kind who would."

"I used to," Ironfist admitted. "I had a bad experience." He kept his face even. Equanimity was all a man could aspire to. Knowing what you had control over, and what you didn't. The Nuqaba had no place in his thoughts.

"My husband used to play Nine Kings. He maintained that he was a mediocre player, though he rarely walked away from a table with much less than he brought to it. He had a reputation as an amiable player who served fine liquor and excellent tobacco, though, so he played with all sorts of men from all over the Seven Satrapies. We were married three years—and I was only beginning to really fall in love with him—before he got me to come to one of his parties. It wasn't the night he would have chosen for me to see.

"A young lord came. Varigari family. From a line of fishermen before they were raised in the Blood Wars. He came in, new and cocksure, and over the course of the night he went through a small fortune. The lords my husband played with that night were wealthy, and decent men, not wolves. They could see what was happening. They told the young Varigari to quit. He refused. He won often enough that he kept hope, and I could see the resignation on their faces: he loses a small fortune, and perhaps it teaches him a lesson, so be it. Dawn came, and he had nothing, and there was this moment where he bet a small castle in order to stay in. I saw this look on his face. It's etched into my memory. Do you know what he was feeling?"

Ironfist could feel it right now, the memory was so hot and sharp. "Terror, but elation, too. There's something potent in knowing that you have pushed your life to one of its pivots. It is insanity."

"I glanced at my husband, unable to believe what I was seeing. Everyone else was looking at the young Varigari. My husband was looking at everyone else. And I realized a few things all at once." She coughed into her handkerchief, then glanced at it. "Keep worrying I'm going to cough blood one of these times. Not yet, thank Orholam."

She smiled to defuse his worries, and continued, "First, about the young man: the small fortune he'd lost was not a small fortune to him, and the small castle he'd bet was probably the last thing his family owned. To him this wasn't a lesson; this was *ruin*. Second, my husband was no mediocre player. He had the winning hand, and he had the wealth to risk playing it. He was an expert, but an expert who took pains to rarely win, because he'd found something that was more valuable to him than winning small fortunes and becoming known as a great player of Nine Kings. What he was really doing every time he played was taking the measure of those he played with. Finding not just their tells, but how they reacted to the whims of fate and fortune. Was this satrap greedy? Did this Color get so focused on one opponent that she ignored a true threat? Was this one smarter than anyone knew?"

Scary to think of the White paired up with a man as smart as she was.

She said no more.

"And?" Ironfist asked.

"And?" she asked.

"There was a lesson in there somewhere," Ironfist said.

"Was there?" she said, but her eyes danced. "I'm so old."

"I know you too well to think your mind is just wandering."

She smiled. "When the big bets are on the table, Commander, it's good to know which character in that little drama you are."

Problem with being surrounded by brilliant people: they expect your mind to be as nimble as theirs. Ironfist had no idea what she was talking about. He'd get there eventually, he always did, but he'd have to mull it over for a while. "If I may, my lady?"

"Please."

"Did Lord Rathcore ever play against Luxlord Andross Guile?"

She chuckled. "I guess it depends what you mean. Nine Kings? Never. He knew better. You don't play against those to whom you can only lose. I've seen Andross play. He uses his stacks of gold like a bludgeon. There is no gracefully losing a little bit of gold to Andross. It's win big or lose bigger against him. For my husband to play Andross was to lose a fortune or to lose the whole purpose of his games by exposing how skilled he was."

"And if I wasn't asking about Nine Kings?" Ironfist asked. He had been, but she obviously meant to tell him more.

She smiled, and he was glad that he served her. To be the commander of the Blackguard was to stand ready to give your life for those you protected, regardless of your feelings. But for this woman, even frail and with few days left, Ironfist would gladly trade his life. She said, "All I'll say is this: Andross Guile isn't the White, and it galls him deeply."

But the White was chosen by lot. Orholam himself moved his will through that.

But if Andross Guile had thought being the White was a victory within his grasp, maybe that was because it actually had been. Surely to corrupt the election of a White was the work of a heretic—worse, an atheist. Ironfist couldn't comprehend it.

The further implication—that Lord Rathcore had stymied Andross Guile by instead getting his wife Orea selected—was almost worse. If the White's election had been tainted by the machinations of men, was it thereby void? How could Orholam tolerate such a thing?

And yet the White was a holy woman, a good woman. Perhaps she hadn't been involved, or hadn't known, or hadn't figured it out until many years later. And then what would you do? Abdicate because there was some blight on your election that no one else had ever noticed and that even you hadn't known about? Perhaps that would bring greater disrepute on the Chromeria than simply to let it lie.

But it shook Ironfist's faith. What had Gavin said on the ship? Some jest about being chosen by Orholam—a jest that only made sense as a jest if you didn't believe Orholam really did choose.

Lord Rathcore had blocked Luxlord Guile from becoming the White, but couldn't block him from having his son made the Prism.

It almost took Ironfist's breath away to think of it in such nakedly political terms. He was no naïf. He served these people. He knew that even the greatest had their foibles. He knew they all had vast ambition. But surely, *surely* some few things must be held holy.

He remembered again holding his mother's bleeding body, screaming his prayers to Orholam, praying until he thought heart and soul would burst. Praying that Orholam would see him, just for one moment of his life. Hear him, just once. And his mother died.

"Who won? That night. What happened?" he asked.

She was quiet for a moment. "My husband let the young man win. No matter." The White waved a frail hand, as if to shoo the example away. "Commander," she said quietly, "I've upset you. I'm sorry. Let this be my absolution: as important as it is for you to know what character you are in this little drama, perhaps right now it is more important for you to know which character *I* am. I am the gambler, Commander, just waiting for Orholam's eye to rise over the horizon and reveal the truth. I am the gambler, and I've bet the family castle, and I'm waiting for the cards to turn."

"There's war coming, isn't there?" Ironfist asked.

She sighed. "Yes, blind though the Spectrum is to it. But I wasn't talking about the war."

He walked to the door, stopped. "What happened to that young man?"

"He gambled again later with someone else and lost everything, as gamblers do."

Chapter 24

"Skill, Will, Source, and Movement. These are the necessaries for the creation of luxin," Magister Kadah was saying. She had a gift. A great gift. She could make even magic seem boring.

Kip sat in the back of the lecture hall today, stomach growling, but absolutely determined not to open his big yapper. Adrasteia sat in the seat next to his, paying attention, and Ben-hadad was next to her, one yellow lens of his glasses continually swinging down in front of his eye, no matter how he tried to keep it up.

Together, they took up one of the little wooden tables. Sitting together, almost like friends.

It wasn't real, not yet. They didn't know Kip. They let him sit with them. It was different. But it was closer than Kip had felt to friendship in a long time.

He looked over at Teia. She saw him looking and glanced over at him, a question in her eyes.

And at exactly that moment, Magister Kadah looked up and caught them. Rotten luck. "Kip, do you have something to share with the class?" she asked.

Don't do it, Kip. No smart remarks.

Problem was, he had no idea what the magister had been talking about, and his mind had drifted. "I was thinking about the instability of imperfectly crafted luxin," Kip said. Magister Kadah had been talking about Skill, Kip thought, so it seemed like it might be close to a real question.

"Hmm," Magister Kadah said, as if disappointed she hadn't caught Kip napping. "Very well." She ran long fingers along the edge of her stick, flipped it over. On the back side, there was a color spectrum. She considered it for a moment, rejected it, walked over to the wall.

She opened a panel on the wall. It was dazzlingly bright. The light-well, Kip realized. There was a slide with a mirror mounted on it, and she pushed that into the light stream. A pure beam of white radiance shot across the room onto a bare white wall behind the students.

"This is light as it is. It is the keystone, the base on which all else is born. And this is how we imagine light is—" She held up a screen over the light stream. Brilliant colors were cast upon the wall, cerulean blue immediately next to jade green abutting on vibrant yellow next to an orange to make fruit jealous next to a clear red.

"These are the colors we draft—minus sub-red and superviolet, of course, which most of you can't see. We'll talk about them later. This is how the colors are in a rainbow, right, discipulae?"

There were some mutters. The colors were in the right order.

"Right, discipulae?" she repeated, irritated.

"Yes, Magister," most of the class answered.

"Morons," she said.

"*This* is light in our world—" She held a prism in front of the stream, and it sheared the light into the whole visible spectrum. Unlike the screen, which had the most vibrant colors immediately next to each other, the colors of the natural spectrum were broken into a continuum—but the continuum wasn't even. Some colors took up more space than others.

"In some ways, drafting is like anything else. If you sit in a poorly crafted chair, it breaks and you fall. It fails its purpose. Poorly crafted luxin is the same. On the color line, there are resonance points. Seven points, seven colors, seven satrapies. This is as Orholam has willed. At these resonance points"—she pointed to the places on the color line that corresponded to the bright colors she had put on the screen earlier—"at these places, luxin takes on a stable form. Becomes itself. Becomes useful." She pointed to places on the color line, in order. "Why, smarter auditors might ask, why those colors?" Magister Kadah smiled unpleasantly. She did that a lot.

Likes making people feel stupid, doesn't she?

Kip had noticed that the distances between the colors weren't even. Some colors were wide bands—blue stretched over a huge area, and red, too, but yellow and orange were tiny.

"Why does blue cover so much area? We might point to this"—she pointed deeper in blue—"in our humanness, and call it violet. Why can't we draft violet? Anyone?"

No one said anything. Not even Kip.

"It's simple, and it's a mystery. Because luxin doesn't resonate there. You can't make a stable luxin from violet. It doesn't work. Seven is the holy number. Seven points, seven colors, seven satrapies. Instead of demanding that the mystery surrender itself to the hammer blows of our intellects, we align ourselves with the mystery, and when we find perfect alignment with the piece of his creation that Orholam has given us, we draft perfectly. This is what we strive for. When you're not exactly in the center of his will, your blue will fall to dust, your red will fade, your yellow will shimmer away to nothingness. Those points, that perfection, that alignment with Orholam himself is what we seek, every time we draft. And when we do it perfectly, we become conduits of his will. This is what makes us better than the dullards out there, the munds, the norms, the non-drafters who only absorb light rather than reflect it. This is why bichromes—those who can draft two colors—are honored more highly than those who can draft only one. Bichromes are closer to Orholam, they partake of more of his holy creation. Each color has lessons to teach us, lessons about what it is to be human, and lessons on what it is to be like Orholam.

"And this, of course, is what makes the Prism so special. He is the only man on earth to commune perfectly with Orholam. He alone sees the world as it is. He alone is pure." She stared directly at Kip, walked toward him. "And this is why we oppose any who would taint the Holy Prism's light, or any who would dim his glory and bring shame upon him."

It took Kip's breath away. She hated him because she revered his father and Kip brought shame upon him?

The worst part of it was that it made sense. It wasn't fair. He hadn't chosen to be a bastard, but it did make sense.

"Remember, Kip," Magister Kadah said quietly, "you're not untouchable now."

What?

Ben-hadad raised his hand, rescuing Kip, and Magister Kadah called on him.

"Isn't that a bit dogmatic?" Ben-hadad asked. "With the whole color spectrum being so wonderfully *not* even, *not* regular, not arrayed right around the seven colors, doesn't that suggest that there's room for ever greater understanding? I mean, what about the other resonances?"

Other resonances?

"I already said we'll talk about sub-red and superviolet later." The brief, ugly look that passed across her face told him that she had hate enough in her for Ben-hadad as well. Here Kip had thought he was special.

"Your pardon, Magister, but I didn't mean those. I meant the secret colors," Ben-hadad said.

Teia buried her face in her hands.

"Friend of Kip's, are you?" Magister Kadah asked.

"What? No. I mean, not really." Ben-hadad scowled as if that came out harsher than he meant. "I mean, I barely met him."

"Uh-huh," Magister Kadah said. "This is one of the early lectures. It's to cover basic topics. Yes, there are other, weaker resonances. Some believe, as I do, that the use of those resonances are examples of man forcing nature to do things Orholam never intended. Some even call those who use the unnatural colors heretics."

Kip couldn't help but glance at Teia. She was pale, but her jaw was set.

Magister Kadah said, "The seven colors are in Orholam's will. The seven are strong. This we know. If you want to have fifth-year debates, you can wait until fifth year."

Chapter 25

Kip caught up to Teia on the way to Blackguard practice. "What was that all about?" he asked.

She didn't answer immediately. Didn't look at him.

They came to the lift and had to wait, and Kip thought she wasn't going to answer him, that he'd somehow been rude without knowing it. He would have started up a conversation about something else, but he couldn't think of anything to say.

"You know how you're a superchromat?" she said quietly.

"Freak," he said. Though other than making him different, as far as he knew, it was a pure advantage, with no drawbacks. "And how did you know?" She wasn't in his engineering class.

"Everyone knows everything about everyone here, Kip, especially about the new kids, especially when the new kid has a grandfather who's a Color . . . or a father who's the Prism."

Oh.

"Anyway," she said, setting her scarf on her head to pull back her hair, but still not making eye contact. "I'm a subchromat. Colorblind. It happens as rarely for girls as superchromacy does for boys, so I'm as much of a freak as you, but you're a freak in a good way."

"But, but, how's that work?"

"Reds and greens look the same to me. Sometimes, I try really hard and convince myself I can tell the difference. But I can't." She flushed, as if she hadn't meant to say so much. "Our lift." She gestured.

"But what's that got to do with the secret colors?"

"Nothing."

"And what are the secret colors?"

She stared hard at him. "Our lift, Kip."

"Do you draft one of the—"

"Kip!"

They got on the lift. An older student took care of counterweights. They didn't let first-year students operate the lift. Too many fatalities, they said.

Not reassuring.

"So, while we're trying to join the Blackguard, what is everyone else doing?" Kip asked.

"Work," Teia said. "And after we're done, there's *practicum* until dinner. Then another work period every other day of the week. On alternating days, they assign readings. Color theory, mechanics, drawing, religion, arithmetic, hagiographies, politics, lives of the satraps, that sort of thing. It's a lot of work to maintain the Chromeria, and they say it's good for us to know what all of that work is, so that when we take over one day, we know it all."

"What other kinds of work are there?"

"For dims? Mostly cleaning. Every floor, every window, every study mirror. If you're unlucky or being punished, you get latrines or stables or kitchens. If the older students are busy, we help in the jobs that take more skill or are more physically demanding: lifting the counterweights and the water, manning the great mirrors, carrying magisters' books back to the libraries. Later still, students who are rich or have good sponsorships are able to bring slaves to do their work for them. Or hire servants or poor students."

Like you, Kip realized. But not like me, not anymore. A Guile would definitely go into the rich category.

"You should have some sponsors coming around soon, Kip. Just make sure you don't sell out cheap. They'll act like they're your friend, but at the end of the day, they don't care about you. They're just scouts, and they get paid out of the difference between what the sponsor is willing to pay and what the drafter is willing to take."

They emerged from the Prism's Tower into the sunlight. Kip said, "But I'm not going to have to worry about a sponsor, am I? I mean, I thought my father was going to pay for everything."

She stopped dead. "What are you talking about?"

Kip raised an eyebrow, lifted his hands, befuddled. "I already told you I'm a Guile. I mean, a bastard, but my father has recognized me."

105

Her mouth dropped open. "You mean you don't know? I thought that's why you came and sat with the rejects today."

"What are you talking about?" Kip said. His throat felt suddenly tight.

"Andross Guile disavowed you. And he's the Red. His word is law. That's why you don't have a Blackguard escort anymore. That's why you have to work with the rest of us. That's why Magister Kadah treated you like she did. You're like everyone else now, Kip. Except with more talent. And a lot more enemies. You're not a Guile anymore."

Inexplicably, Kip laughed. It was the best news he'd heard in weeks.

Chapter 26

The Third Eye was, Gavin thought, quite beautiful for an otherworldly mystic. Her light brown hair hung in dreadlocks, pulled back on top with a spiky sandalwood crown, points lacquered with gold leaf. A very artistic sun, perhaps? Light brown to go with her hair; she had to have some Ruthgari blood in her for that. She wore a knee-length white dress, secured with golden ropes, wrapped around her body ingeniously in order to cross over the body's power centers in old pagan mysticism. Loose ends dangled from the last knot at her groin, the next crossed over her belly, the next crossed between her breasts, the ends looped over her shoulders. Gold makeup crossed her cheeks to her lips to suggest a knot there, and a few last streaks suggested a knot at her third eye in the middle of her forehead. She wore a bracelet on each hand connected to rings on each finger—sort of a fingerless glove—gold, suggesting knots there. Her sandals, covered now in sand as she walked the beach, would doubtless be the same.

Seven knots, or nine, depending on how you counted. It was a pagan paradox.

Heresy, maybe, but what it reminded Gavin of most at the moment was that he hadn't had sex for far too long. The knots might be religious symbolism, but the practical effect was that they pulled the dress tight around a fine-looking woman. He glanced at her breasts, briefly, then back to her face. Damn woman, not fighting fair.

He'd thought that she must have more gold paint on her forehead from how it glinted in the rising sun, but as she came to stand before him with her motley bodyguard of ten men, Gavin saw that the Third Eye had the most elaborate, remarkable tattoo he'd ever seen.

The third eye tattoo wasn't merely exquisitely drawn, it glowed. She'd infused yellow luxin into the tattoo: it caused the eye to emit golden light, making it even more reminiscent of Orholam's Eye, the sun.

Her own eyes declared her a yellow drafter, yellow near the halo, a pretty brown beyond it. She was in her late thirties, trim, but curvaceous. Gavin glanced at her breasts again. Dammit. He supposed after he finished the harbor here, it would be good to go by the Chromeria. He needed to go there anyway to make sure his orders were being followed and the satrapies were preparing for war, but spending some quality time in bed with his room slave Marissia would help him tolerate a few more weeks with Karris Blue Balls.

If the Third Eye weren't standing right there, Gavin would have drafted blue in order to give himself the cool rationality blue always brought.

Wait, no, I wouldn't have. I can't draft blue anymore.

Orholam's hairy ass. Gavin's throat tightened.

"Greetings," Gavin said. "Light be upon you."

The Third Eye was staring at him intently, and Gavin could swear that the tattoo was actually glowing brighter—not an impossible trick, but a good one regardless. "You're dying," she said, her voice mellifluous. "You're not supposed to be dying yet."

Chapter 27

The Blackguard training went about how Kip expected: a lot of running (not very fast), a lot of jumping (not very high), a lot of punching in time (not very timely), a lot of push-ups and sit-ups (not a lot). The vomiting, however, was a surprise. Not a pleasant one.

He stood, bent over, by one of the chalk lines, his whole body hot and cold and flushed. He felt like he was going to die.

"The good news is that this is as bad as it gets," a familiar voice said.

Kip could barely lift his eyes from Ironfist's shoes. He was purely focused on breathing. In, out.

"If you want it to stop, Kip, it can."

Kip spat, trying to clear the acrid sludge from his mouth. It didn't work. It seemed to cling to every crack and crevice. "What?"

"If you hate this. If you think it's pointless, you can quit. In fact, I've been asked to cut you."

"Cut me?" Kip's brain wasn't working very well.

"The Red is demanding that you be cut from the Blackguard. He cast aspersions on whether you would have been selected if you weren't... if the Prism hadn't requested it."

Which was, of course, true.

So Commander Ironfist was caught between what the Prism had asked him to do and what the Red was demanding now—but Andross Guile was here, and Gavin Guile wasn't.

"I guess my meeting with him went even worse than I thought, huh?" Kip said.

"You're a couple years before you can play those games with these people, Kip. Don't worry why they're doing what they're doing. It probably has nothing to do with you anyway. What you need to do is figure out *you*. Do you want to quit, or do you want to stay?"

Kip straightened up. Teia handed him a cup of water. She'd heard everything, but her eyes were a cipher. Kip's arm felt wobbly even as he lifted the water to his lips. He swished. Spat it aside.

He was the worst person in the class. Of forty-nine people, he did the fewest push-ups. He ran the slowest. He finished last. He couldn't do a single pull-up. If he stayed, he would probably vomit every day. Every week, he would get his ass kicked more times than he could count. Every month, he'd get beat up in the testing, probably many times.

It wasn't even a fair contest: his left hand was still injured, raw, tight, painful to fully open, agony to put pressure on.

His father had put him in this position, against the express wishes of Ironfist, expecting Kip not to be good enough to make the cut on his own. Expecting him to fail. And now his grandfather wanted to destroy him.

"Am I even going to be able to stay at the Chromeria?" Kip asked. "If I'm not a Guile, I don't have a sponsor, do I?"

A brief, satisfied smile flickered over Ironfist's face. "The funds had already been transferred to your account. Your tuition is fully paid. And believe me, once the money goes in, the abacus jockeys over there don't let it go out."

The funds had already been transferred. Past tense. So Kip's grandfather had tried to go after them, but had been foiled. And the quick smile meant Ironfist had done that—and was pleased to have stymied Andross Guile in this one small thing.

"But the situation is worse than that," Ironfist said. "From here on out, it's all you. You understand?"

Kip understood. Ironfist was being delicate because Teia was standing right there. He wouldn't help Kip. Couldn't stack the odds for him. If Kip got in to the Blackguard, he'd have to get in on his own. It was impossible.

And yet freeing. If Kip did this, he'd do it on his own. Not because of his father, but on his own merit.

So, it comes to this: an easy life as a student who doesn't even need a sponsor, or a terrifically hard life as the worst of the scrubs, and a slim chance to actually make it into the Blackguard on my own and be something.

"Fuck 'em," Kip said. "I'm staying."

"Good," Ironfist said. A fierce pleasure filled his eyes. He took a deep breath that expanded his giant chest and brought his massive shoulders proudly back. "Good. Now, five laps. Blackguards guard their tongues, too." Suddenly he was back in command, sharp and stern and all professionalism.

"F-five?"

The commander said, "Don't make me repeat myself. Adrasteia, you, too. Partner runs, you run."

Chapter 28

The next day, the girls in Blackguard scrubs class were split off from the boys and brought into another training area. As in many of the training areas, one wall was covered in weapons, but here the weapons were bows of various sorts, from short horse bows to the great yew longbows from Crater Lake, to the composite bows of Blood Forest that packed as much power as those yew bows into a much smaller frame. Crossbows of a dozen sorts completed the armory. There were numerous targets in the area where the girls were walking. Several female Blackguards were at the front, standing with arms folded, waiting for the girls to approach. As Adrasteia followed the other nine girls, she studied the women. Though their body types ranged from the squat thick Samite to the willowy Cordelia, they all had something that Adrasteia wanted badly: they were confident, at ease in their bodies, with the world and their place in it. Somehow, that made even the plain look luminous.

Not sure what else to do, the girls lined up before their teachers.

Petite, curvy Essel spoke. "There is a legend about warrior women of old on Seers Island. They were peerless archers, but—" She picked a bow off the wall, drew a practice arrow from a quiver over her shoulder, and aimed between Adrasteia and Mina.

At first all Adrasteia felt was alarm. The target wasn't very far away from her, and she had no idea what the Blackguards were trying to teach. It could well be How to Take an Arrow and Keep Fighting.

"Anyone see a problem?" Essel asked.

Aside from you pointing an arrow at me?

"Your breast's in the way," Mina said. Teia felt a surge of jealousy—first, that Mina wasn't fazed by having an arrow nearly pointed in her face, too, and had been able to answer, and second, that Mina had probably thought of it because she had breasts, too. Unlike Teia, whom Kip had thought was a boy.

But Essel had obviously been chosen to give this talk exactly for her large bosom. She grinned and took tension off the bowstring. "Ah, you've trained with the bow?" she asked Mina.

Mina nodded, suddenly shy. "Yes, my lady. It was, um, fine until one day when I was thirteen and I near tore my..." She trailed off, blushing. "My father hadn't thought to teach me to bind my chest. I think it made him feel more awkward than me."

"Well, those warrior women of legend were called the Amazoi. Literally, the Breastless, so perhaps you can think of their solution to the problem," Essel said.

Eyebrows shot up, though at least a couple of the girls seemed to already know the story.

"Of course, they only actually cut off their right breast—or their left if they were left-handed—and perhaps they didn't make the flat women join them. But the Breastless makes a better name than the Women Who Cut Off One Breast, Sometimes, If Their Breasts Were Big Enough to Interfere with Archery."

The girls giggled.

"The story isn't true, of course," Essel said. "It endures, probably, because men are fascinated with breasts, and men are fascinated with women who don't have to take their shit, and because women are fascinated with women who don't have to take men's shit. I personally can't imagine a woman dumb enough to cut off what she could bind with a strip of cloth."

Again, more grins.

"Regardless, the bow is the symbol of the women of the Blackguard. That much is known to all, but what follows is not to be shared with any man—even if you fail out, even after you retire. Men think the bow is our symbol because a bow is used to kill from distance, because women aren't as strong as men. Some say the bow is a coward's weapon. Some say as Orholam made women better at drafting, so men are better at fighting. They say that because men are more muscular, in this, women should defer."

Essel stopped, and Teia and all the others waited, expecting her to say something withering. Instead, Essel shook her head slowly. "They may be right. Generally. Thing is, I don't care. To be a Blackguard is to be the exception to the rules. Put me in a room with fifty men off the street, and I'm the best fighter there. Put me in a room with fifty soldiers from any army in the world, and I'm the best fighter there. But if Commander Ironfist fell in battle, big as he is, most of the men in the Blackguard would still be able to carry him off the field. Alone. I couldn't. Samite here, she could. I've seen her."

So what's the lesson? Teia wanted to ask. She could tell from the sidelong glances that the other girls were thinking the same thing.

"The bow is our symbol because the bow represents the sacrifices we have to make to be Blackguards—and the sacrifices we don't have to make. You could cut off your breast if you wanted to be an archer. Or you can bind it. Your choice. Both have their drawbacks. It's an annoyance that none but the fattest of men have to deal with. Fine. That's how things are. I see it. I accept it. I deal with it. I don't expect a man to consider the world as if he had breasts—though a good leader might. Mina, if your father could have seen past his own embarrassment, he would have been able to give you simple advice that would have spared you pain. He didn't. That's fine. We all have limitations, and we all see our own needs first.

"There are things about combat that are harder for women, and there are some few things that are easier. We'll talk about those, and we'll train you in what sacrifices you need to make and what you don't. These sacrifices are not the fault of men, they are the fault of the bow. What it is to be a Blackguard, what it is to be an elite warrior, what it is to be a powerful woman, is all the same: it is to stare unflinching at what is, and then move what *is* toward what you *will*."

Samite stepped forward. "Let's be blunt and practical. The Blackguard will make the minimum possible accommodation for any warrior. You have horrible cramps during your moon blood? You can switch guard shifts without asking your commander. Men are not allowed to do that. But you *will* make up the shifts you miss, and your sisters will expect you to be more willing to switch with them when their turn comes. In the barracks, women have a separate room—though the door between the rooms usually stays open. We have separate baths and toilets. But in the field, if your commander says battlefield rules, you bathe and change and piss where the men do, and anyone who gives you trouble gets punished severely. We're never allowed to have relations with other Blackguards, man or woman. You want to get married, one of you retires first. You're caught sleeping together, both of you are bounced out, ostracized, and fined equal to what replacing you costs the Blackguard. You are to think of the men as your brothers—your little brothers. You take care of them, they take care of you, but they don't get any say over your life. You spend your money and your time off how you want. You drink as much as you want. You bed who you want. Obviously, not all choices are equally wise, and sometimes the men get their roles as brothers confused and think they can tell you what to do in your off time. We will stand together with you and correct them. Mostly, they understand the rules and do their best.

"Out in the world, things can be different. Where village toughs or bullies might try to start a fight with a Blackguard man for status—because win or lose, a bully wins respect from his fellows simply for daring to fight a Blackguard—that won't happen to you. Even if a bully beats you, to his fellows, he's only beat a woman. And if he loses, he loses everything. You may, however, get groped or spit on or slighted. We'll talk about how you deal with that, and you'll find there are no fiercer defenders than your brothers.

"There are privileges for the sacrifices we make, sometimes privileges in their own right, and sometimes privileges that merely negate the privileges of others. Essel, you want to share about the governor's ball?"

Essel grinned at the memory. "We escorted the White to a ball at the Atashian embassy—so the grounds are technically Atashian soil. The ambassador thought that gave him rights. He liked me. In fact, I liked him. I was on break and he found me. He kissed me—which wasn't unpleasant, but it was unprofessional. I felt it would reflect badly on the Blackguard if we were found. So I told him so. He thought I was being coy. I told him I wasn't. But he got aggressive. He kissed me again. I told him I wouldn't warn him a third time. He put his hands on me in a way I found objectionable. So I broke his fingers. Most of them."

Teia didn't know what impressed her the most: that Essel could break the man's fingers so easily, that she would dare to do so, or that she was so nonchalant about it.

Continuing, Essel said, "When he recovered, he went to the White, furious. Demanded redress. He told some ridiculous story. The White didn't even ask for my side. She asked, 'Essel, did you act improperly?' I said no, and she told him that he was going to be lucky if she didn't decide to have him expelled from Big Jasper."

Samite said, "If anything, the Prism is even harsher with those who interfere with us. We occupy an odd position. In some ways, we're mere slaves who must be ready to die for those above us in an instant, deserving or not. In other ways, not even ambassadors, not even the Prism himself can interfere with us.

"Now," Samite continued, "after Essel has just spent time warning you about generalities and how they often don't apply, I'm going to use some. Because some generalities are true often enough that we have to worry about them. So here's one: men will physically fight for status. Women, generally, are more clever. The why of it doesn't matter: learned, innate, cultural, who cares? You see the chest-bumping, the name-calling, performing for their fellows, what they're really doing is getting the juices flowing. That interval isn't always long, but it's long enough for men to trigger the battle juice. That's the terror or excitation that leads people to fight or run. It can be useful in small doses or debilitating in large ones. Any of you have brothers, or boys you've fought with?"

Six of the ten raised their hands.

"Have you ever had a fight with them—verbal or physical—and then they leave and come back a little later, and they're completely done fighting and you're just fully getting into it? They look like they've been ambushed, because they've come completely off the mountain already, and you've just gotten to the top?"

"Think of it like lovemaking," Essel said. She *was* a bawdy one. "Breathe in a man's ear and tell him to take his trousers off, and he's ready to go before you draw your next breath. A woman's body takes longer."

Some of the girls giggled nervously.

"Men can switch on very, very fast. They also switch off from that battle readiness very, very fast. Sure, they'll be left trembling, sometimes puking from it, but it's on and then it's off. Women don't do that. We peak slower. Now, maybe there are exceptions, maybe. But as fighters, we tend to think that everyone reacts the way we do, because our own experience is all we have. In this case, it's not true for us. Men will be ready to fight, then finished, within heartbeats. This is good and bad.

"A man, deeply surprised, will have only his first instinctive response be as controlled and crisp as it is when he trains. Then that torrent of emotion is on him. We spend thousands of hours training that first instinctive response, and further, we train to control the torrent of emotion so that it raises us to a heightened level of awareness without making us stupid."

"So the positive, for us Archers: surprise me, and my first reaction will be the same as my male counterpart's. I can still, of course, get terrified, or locked into a loop of indecision. But if I'm not, my second, third, and tenth moves will also be controlled. My hands will not shake. I will be able to make precision movements that a man cannot.

But I won't have the heightened strength or sensations until perhaps a minute later—often too late.

"Where a man needs to train to control that rush, we need to train to make it closer. If we have to climb a mountain more slowly to get to the same height to get all the positives, we need to start climbing sooner. That is, when I go into a situation that I know may be hazardous, I need to prepare myself. I need to start climbing. The men may joke to break the tension. Let them. I don't join in. Maybe they think I'm humorless because I don't. Fine. That's a trade I'm willing to make."

Teia and the rest of the girls walked away from training that day somewhat dazed, definitely overwhelmed. What Teia realized was that the women were deeply appealing because they were honest and powerful. And those two things were wed inextricably together. They said, I am the best in the world at what I do, and I cannot do everything. Those two statements, held together, gave them the security to face any challenge. If her own strengths couldn't surmount an obstacle, her team's strengths could—and she was unembarrassed about asking for help where she needed it because she knew that what she brought to the team would be equally valuable in some other situation.

The Archers were uncompromising and unapologetic and yet in total balance. They respected each other and they respected themselves. Some of the Blackguards, Teia knew, had come from slave stock, others had come from noble blood. Some were blues, some were yellows or greens or reds. Some were bichromes, some were tall, some were skinny, some were as muscular as Commander Ironfist. They were different from each other—but the Blackguards looked at those differences and asked where they were useful, not who they made better than whom. Being a Blackguard was the central fact of their identity. All else came behind that.

For a girl who was a slave and a color-blind drafter of a useless color, that was like the impossible dream, dangled in front of her nose. She'd been ordered to join the Blackguard by her owner, she'd been trained for it for years at the direction of others and for the profit of others—but now she wanted it for herself, for her own reasons. And she wanted it with all her heart.

Chapter 29

Kip and Teia finished their laps—for Teia punching a boy who'd dismissed her as a 'little girl,' this time—and had no time to clean up before heading to practicum: drafting practice, Teia called it. She seemed to dread it. Kip was looking forward to it—even if he was a sweaty, stinky mess.

As usual, Teia led the way. It was on a different floor than their other class, sun side of the Prism's Tower. But when they got to the room, Kip saw that Grinwoody was waiting outside the door.

Oh no.

"Kip," the wizened slave said. "You're late. The Red will not be pleased."

And I care so much about his pleasure. "What does he want with me?" Kip asked.

"You've been summoned."

"What if I don't want to go?" Kip asked.

Grinwoody's eyebrows tented. "You wish me to communicate your refusal to the Red?" His belief that Kip was a buffoon was written all over his face. The man clearly didn't like him, and now that Kip had been disavowed, he felt no need to hide it.

It made Kip want to dig in his heels and tell the man to go to hell.

"Kip?" Teia said. She waited.

Kip looked over at her.

Teia said, "Don't be an idiot."

Kip frowned. "Let's go," he told Grinwoody.

He followed the man up to Andross Guile's room and found himself trying to hold on to his anger, but getting more and more nervous. Grinwoody opened the door and gestured to the heavy blackout curtains.

So help me, if that old bastard hits me today, I'm hitting him back.

Kip was pretty certain that he would do no such thing, but it made him feel better to think it. He stepped inside.

Cloying odors. Old man and incense. Dust and sour armpits. Oh, that last was *him*.

"You reek," a voice said in the darkness, thick with distaste.

"So do you," Kip shot back. Brain engaging two seconds late.

Silence. Then: "Sit."

"On the ground?" Kip asked.

"What are you, a monkey?"

"More monster than monkey. You and I are related, after all," Kip said.

Silence again. Longer this time. "I'd forgotten how reckless the young can be. But perhaps you're not rash, perhaps you're simply stupid. Sit. In the chair."

Kip groped around in the darkness until he found the chair. He sat.

"Grinwoody!" the old man barked.

The slave came in and hung something on a hook above Kip's head. He left wordlessly.

"Lantern," Andross Guile said.

Lantern? But it wasn't on. Was Kip supposed to light it? Wouldn't that defeat the whole point of sitting in a darkened room with blackout curtains over every window and door? Besides, Kip didn't have so much as a flint.

Was it a drafting test to see if Kip could—

Moron. It's a superviolet lantern.

Kip tightened his pupils, and the room jumped into alien, violet, superfine relief. It was a larger room than he'd thought. Portraits of the Guiles' ancestors hung on every wall. Viewed solely in superviolet light, the portraits were lifeless, monochrome. Kip could distinguish the ridges and bumps from the brushstrokes, but seeing the faces made thereby was more difficult. There was an enormous four-poster bed barely visible through the doors in a second chamber, and of course the heavy velvet curtains everywhere. Ivory and marble sculptures sat on the mantel, on the harpsichord. Kip couldn't pick a single style from all the art, but it all seemed very, very fine.

There were a number of chairs, divans, and tables. A clock with spinning gears and a swinging pendulum of the kind Kip had only heard of.

Last, Kip looked at the man in front of him, expecting some horror. Despite the darkness, Andross Guile wore enormous dark spectacles. He'd been a big man, before age robbed him. His shoulders were still broad, but skinny. His hair, flat, desaturated violet in the lantern light, must be silvery gray, almost white. It was sparse, disheveled—befitting a man who lived without mirrors. His skin, too, was washed out, loose. Naturally darker than Gavin's, but bleached by age. His nose straight, deep wrinkles. There was an old scar along his neck up onto his jawline.

He had been a handsome man. Clearly a Guile.

"You play Nine Kings?" Andross Guile asked.

"My mother never had that kind of money," Kip said. It was a card game. The cards themselves were often worth their weight in gold.

"But you know how to play."

"I've watched others."

"The deck lies before you," Andross Guile said. "Let it not be said I'm not fair: the first game will have no stakes."

"It will not be said," Kip said. He picked up his deck, and was hit with another reminder of how different of a world he'd stepped into. Depending on the seriousness of the players, there were many different variants of Nine Kings. There were more than seven hundred cards, from which each player constructed his own deck. In villages like Rekton, soldiers passing through might have a deck built by a small-town artist. The main requirement there was that the cards should have no markings on the back side by which players could cheat and draw the card of their choice. Nobles would play with cards made by artists and drafters together at one of the six branches of the Card Guild. Those cards were beautifully drawn and lacquered with blue luxin, guaranteeing every one was uniform.

These weren't those cards. Each card was electrum—a mixture of gold and silver. Parian cuneiform numbers denoted each strength and ability, and each was adorned with masterful art and signed. Some were inlaid with tiny jewels. All were sealed with perfect crystalline yellow luxin. Jeweled knucklebones and ivory counters and stained glass sand clocks completed the set.

Kip tried to ignore the treasure in his hands and awkwardly shuffled the cards.

"How'd you cripple yourself?" Andross Guile asked. He was expertly shuffling his own cards.

Kip was surprised the old man asked. "I got robbed. I fought, and someone pushed me into a fire. I caught myself with this." Kip held up his hand, then realized he was holding up his hand to a blind man. "Um, my hand. The wood was still hot."

" 'Still hot'?"

"Oh, I drafted the fire when I fought them."

Andross Guile *mm*ed that.

They played, and Kip lost spectacularly, barely even recalling the rules. He could hardly decipher the Parian numbers because he'd only just learned them from seeing the Blackguard scrubs stand in order. Andross, on the other hand, played blind. His cards had small bumps and ridges on the face that must have been code to tell him what the card was. It wasn't cheating, and it wasn't any advantage, but it told Kip that the makers of the cards were making them specifically with Andross Guile in mind.

No wonder Kip hadn't done any damage at all to Andross. The man was serious about his game.

The old man was expressionless, though. "Another. This time, there are stakes."

"What are they?" Kip asked.

"High," the old man said.

"I don't have any money," Kip said.

"I know what you have."

Kip thought instantly of the dagger. Chose to ignore it. Chose to answer as if it were obvious that he had nothing at all. "Then what are we playing for?"

"You'll find out when we finish. Play to win."

Kip took a deep breath and played better the second time, but still got massacred. When his last knucklebone turned over to zero, Andross Guile sat back and folded his hands over his little paunch.

"Today, you sat with a small group of young people who call themselves the Rejects. Among them was a girl named Tiziri. It was observed that you made no particular connection with her."

Kip remembered her. She was the homely girl at the table. Big smile, overweight, birthmark across her face. "What are you going to do?" Kip asked.

"Her parents sold six of their fifteen cattle to pay for her passage to the Chromeria. She's going home tomorrow. Because of you."

"What? Why? That doesn't make any sense. That's not fair!"

"You lost," Andross Guile said. "We'll play again. Next time the stakes will be higher."

Chapter 30

"And you," the Third Eye said, turning to Karris, "The Wife. You're not right either."

"Excuse me?" Karris said.

Gavin felt like he'd been kicked in the stomach, so it was nice to see Karris equally stunned.

But the Third Eye looked genuinely confused. "What are you here for, Prism?"

"I have fifty thousand refugees in need of a home. If I put them anywhere else, they'll either be held hostage to the politics of satrapies, or massacred outright by the Color Prince."

"You plan to put them here?"

"You're the Seer."

"You'll destroy the community we've built here," she said.

"You built a community to serve Orholam. Serve him by saving his people."

"You don't even know what you're destroying," she said.

"Nor is it in me to care overmuch. When the emperor sends a ship to Paria, he doesn't concern himself with the comfort of the rats in the hold. If you want to serve Orholam, start putting together food. 'Faith without deeds is dust,' is it not? Fifty thousand starving people are going to arrive in three days."

The men surrounding Gavin and Karris bristled. He shouldn't have said it, but the sun was up and he needed every minute of daylight to finish the harbor before the fleet arrived. They would most likely have run out of food today. If he didn't clear the coral and make a safe port, the ships would run aground, the men and women and children die.

"Are you a man or a god, Gavin Guile?" the Third Eye asked.

"I'm *busy*," Gavin said. "Join me or get out of the way, because I'm going to do what I will, and if you oppose me, I'll do what I must."

"I don't think I like you very much, Gavin Guile."

"In another time, I think you would. Now pardon me, but I've a harbor to build."

"Dinner," the Third Eye said. "After the sun has set, of course. Join me for dinner. You've given me much to think about, and I would like to return the favor. Unless dining with *a rat* is beneath you?" She lifted a challenging, cool eyebrow.

A very palpable hit. "I would be...delighted," Gavin said.

He walked down the beach, drawing in light. He stripped off his tunic. It wasn't so warm yet that it was necessary, but he wanted the Third Eye and her men to see the waves of color flooding through his skin as he walked away. Yellow first, making his body glow golden. He threw a spout of yellow up into the air, and had it formed into a skimmer by the time it hit the waves.

Karris stepped onto the skimmer with him. "Not sure why you always put yourself in a position where you have to turn your back on armed men," she said.

"All the world is armed," Gavin said. "I've got to have my back to half of it."

She grunted. "Which means I walk backwards a lot."

He looked over at her. She was smirking.

"You're not mad at me?" he said. He thought he could have handled things better.

"You're the Prism," she said, making a gesture as she said "the Prism," as if the words themselves sparkled. "How can I be mad at the Prism?"

He laughed. He spent his whole life with women, and he still didn't understand them. "No, really," he said.

She joined him on the oars. "I don't know what your ultimate objective is with Tyrea's refugees. I'm sure you have some endgame in mind. But I don't care. You really are doing this to save people who right now don't have anything to give you in return. People who are terribly inconvenient. People you *could* ignore. You're not ignoring them. That's—that's a good thing. I don't need to take that away from you."

So there's something in you that *wants* to take it away from me, though. "Thank you," Gavin said. He meant it, but his heart ached, too.

One year. Maybe it's a good thing I've only got one year left. I don't think I could take this for another five.

They worked, and gradually the pain faded. Gavin drafted the great posts that would support the seawalls. There was more blasting to clear the sea floor and dig deep enough to give the posts a solid foundation, but it was mostly brute drafting. Layers of yellow for strength and green for flexibility. He would have loved to use blue, but he thought this would work.

121

By night, they'd finished all the posts. Tomorrow, the seawalls. The next day finishing touches and double-checking that everything was working the way he'd intended. Then he could get the hell out of here.

They rowed to shore after sunset. Gavin was thinking that after today's labors, he should probably bathe before meeting for dinner with the Seer.

"Are you going to bed her?" Karris asked.

Gavin coughed. "What?"

"Is that a 'yes,' or a 'yes if the opportunity presents itself'?"

Gavin flushed, but had no words.

Karris turned away first, though. The muscles in her jaw jumped, relaxed. "I'm sorry, Lord Prism. Inappropriate question. I apologize."

Well, that takes that off the table.

I can't bed you, but I sure as hell better not bed anyone else, huh? Perfect.

The Third Eye greeted him at the beach, her walk an *aristeia* of corporeal grace, sensuous, sinuous, suggestive without seeming practiced. Standing, she was striking. In motion, she was a woman for whom the world reveled that Orholam had given bodies to his creation, that he had given light that man might see beauty. She was smiling, lips full and red and inviting, eyes bright and large. She was made up exquisitely and wearing a white gown so thin that he could see the dark circles of her nipples through it.

Just. Fucking. Perfect.

Chapter 31

Kip went back to the barracks dismayed. He didn't know what to do. If he told the Rejects that he was responsible for getting Tiziri sent home, they might turn on him, afraid that they would be next. And it was a rational fear, too.

What else could higher stakes next time mean? Kip had no money. All that could mean was that Andross would send home someone closer to Kip—or do something even worse.

The barracks was empty, though. Evidently the other students weren't back from practicum yet. Kip walked toward his own pallet at the back, double-checking that no one else was present. Four down from his own, he threw open the chest at the foot of one of the empty beds. He dug under the blankets.

He heaved a deep sigh. The dagger was still there.

Covering it back up, he closed the box carefully, making sure nothing looked different than it had before. Then he went to bed.

He slept, dreamlessly for once. He woke amid excitement the next morning. Students were chattering with each other, making no attempt to be quiet for those who were still in bed—though Kip realized as he sat up that he *was* the only one still in bed.

"What's going on?" he asked, voice scratchy from his long sleep.

"It's Sponsor Day," a boy said a few beds down. "No lectures or practicum today. We all meet with our sponsors."

Kip shuffled to the communal bathroom and washed, gargled with salt water, and ran a comb through his hair a few times until it had something approximating order.

He walked downstairs alone and went to the dining hall. It was still serving food—much finer food than normal, he noticed—but there were few students. Those who were present were sitting with adults. One or two of the adults might have been older siblings, or parents.

It felt like a fist in the middle of his chest. Kip stood with his tray, looking for a place. It didn't matter where he sat, he was going to be alone. Mother dead. Grandfather disavowed him. Father gone, as he'd been gone Kip's whole life.

He sat, alone. Ate, alone. He forced himself not to hurry, some part of him not quite enjoying the pain, but reveling in it nonetheless.

These are the hammerfalls that shape a man. And he accepted the blows. So be it.

He finished and went to the library. The librarian, a surprisingly attractive woman, perhaps a weak yellow from her eyes, said, "I'm afraid all our private meeting rooms have been taken by sponsors already, young man."

"I don't need a room. I need books. On strategies for Nine Kings."

"Ah." Her face lit up. "I think we can help you."

Rea Siluz was the fourth undersecretary. Usually worked the late shifts. Before Kip would be allowed to even view the books, he had to sign a contract swearing not to bring fire or to draft red luxin in the library. That done, she seated him at a desk on the shade side of the library, though of course there was plenty of artificial light from yellow lanterns throughout the space. Then she brought him half a dozen books.

"You play much?" Rea asked.

"Only twice. Lost both times, badly."

She laughed quietly. Her dark hair, tightly curled, was massed in a huge, careful halo around her head, setting off a narrow face, full lips. "Most people lose the first *twenty* times they play."

Ugh. "That's not an option for me," Kip said. "Where should I start?"

"Read these two first, and then study this one. This one has all the cards copied out, so you can refer to it when you don't understand. The sooner you memorize them, the better you'll be."

Oh, boy. Kip settled in.

He read for twelve hours. When he went to the toilet once, as he was coming back, he saw a man hovering over his table, writing down the titles of the books piled there. He saw Kip coming and disappeared. Kip thought briefly of chasing him, but realized that he didn't know what he would do if he caught the man.

Great, so they're spying on what I read. Kip didn't know who "they" were, but he figured it didn't matter too much.

When he got up to get a late dinner, he went to Rea's desk. "Can I come back after I eat?"

"You haven't eaten yet?" She looked tired from working two shifts.

"No, but I'm starving now."

"I'm sorry, then, but the library is closing in a few minutes."

Kip looked at the students, who seemed to be giving no indication of leaving anytime soon, and gestured helplessly.

"Those are third- and fourth-years, Kip. Higher years and Blackguard trainees get to study whenever and wherever they want. With so many other duties, some of them don't even get here until midnight. First-years aren't trusted that much. You can only be here when librarians are."

So Kip studied for a few more minutes. When he finally left to go to bed, he was stopped in the hall by Grinwoody. The man grinned wolfishly at him.

Kip hadn't learned enough. There was no way he could win.

124   Andross Guile's chambers were exactly like before, and when Kip

sat, there was a superviolet lantern and a deck of cards. Kip looked through his own cards. The twelve hours had done him no good at all.

"What are the stakes?" he asked.

"Higher, I told you." Andross Guile said nothing else. He played his first card, setting the scene.

Kip played. He played one of his good cards too early—which he only realized at the end of the game—and got slaughtered. He would have lost regardless, but it was the first time he caught a glimpse of something beyond his own helplessness.

"So what are you going to do to me this time?" he asked.

"Pathetic. Not a drop of Guile blood in you, whinger. You don't have to lose. You are losing because you choose to lose."

"Right, I'm choosing to lose. Because it's so fun."

"Sarcasm is the sanctum of the stupid. Stop it. The stakes this time were the privilege of eating tomorrow. Tomorrow, you fast. Maybe it will focus your mind. Now, another game."

"What are the stakes?" Kip asked, stubborn. It told him how little Andross Guile thought of him, though, that he thought not eating was a greater loss to Kip than a girl being sent home and losing everything she'd worked for.

"Higher." Andross Guile began to shuffle his cards.

"No," Kip said. "I don't trust you. I think you're making up stakes after the fact. I'm not playing until you tell the stakes."

A thin smile curved Andross Guile's lips. "Practicum," he said. "You lose this time, you lose your practicum."

"I lose that every time you make me come up here," Kip said.

"Permanently," Andross Guile said.

Losing the right to go to practicum meant losing the one place where Kip could learn to draft in any sort of organized way. "Can you even do that?"

"There is very little I cannot do."

If Kip couldn't learn to draft properly, he had no future. "That's not fair," he said. He knew he'd lose.

"I have very little interest in fair. Guiles are interested in victory, not sportsmanship."

"And if I refuse to play?"

"I'll have you expelled."

You asshole. "What do I win if I win?" Kip asked.

"I'll send that bully Elio home."

"I don't care to send him home."

"Maybe you should," Andross Guile said.

What was that? A warning?

"I hate you," Kip said.

"Breaks my heart," Andross Guile said. "Draw."

Kip drew. He recognized his opening hand as spectacular. He'd seen this hand in one of the books.

But three rounds in, he lost it. Got befuddled, didn't move before his timer ran out. He didn't know how to use even a great hand correctly. Andross Guile had obviously drawn a terrible hand—but he survived the damage Kip was able to do in the early rounds, and then demolished him.

Kip turned over his last counter as he lost, and said, "So what am I supposed to do while everyone else goes to practicum?"

"What do I care?" Andross Guile said. "Figure out other ways to be a failure and a disappointment. By the time my son gets back, he'll be ready to relinquish this." He gestured toward Kip, as if he were a cockroach to be swept away.

"You're old," Kip said. "How long before you die?"

The Red grinned a feral grin. "So, there's a little bastard in the little bastard. Good. Now get out."

Chapter 32

Adrasteia was a slave, not a victim. She had crossed the Lily's Stem, the bridge between the Chromeria and Big Jasper, before the sun had come up. Today was Sponsor Day. That meant no lectures, though the Blackguard would still practice. The Blackguard was too important to take days off. Every student was supposed to meet with her sponsor today, and slaves were no different from anyone else in this.

The difference was that Adrasteia's sponsor never met with her. Instead, she gave Teia secret little jobs to do on Sponsor Day. Lady Lucretia Verangheti was not an easy mistress.

The vendors in the market were setting up their tents and stalls, laying out carpets, prodding their burros to try to get loads of produce or fish into position. There was a constant stream of people, but with the dawn it would become a flood as house slaves and wives attended to the daily shopping to feed their households. Adrasteia slipped through the mass of people as if she had somewhere to be. She kicked loose one of the laces of her boots and stopped by a wall, knelt on one knee, and pulled her skirt up enough to tie the lace.

She pulled the package out from its space between two bricks, slipped it into her boot, and went on her way. She took a few twisting alleys to make sure she hadn't been followed—not that she'd ever been followed, but it was part of her orders—and finally found a place between two taller buildings. She pulled the package from her boot, then unrolled the letter.

Lady Verangheti rarely wrote words. She didn't want to leave her own handwriting to tie her to the crimes she made Adrasteia commit, and she didn't like trusting slaves or scribes with any more than she had to.

It didn't matter. Adrasteia knew what was expected.

There was an uncannily accurate drawing of a man—Lady Verangheti could have been quite an artist if she hadn't thought it beneath her. The next page of impossibly thin rice paper had a drawing of a snuff box, inlaid with a family crest: Herons Rising over a Crescent Moon.

From doing this before, Teia knew she was supposed to steal the snuff box, before tomorrow morning.

Adrasteia was a slave, not a fool: she knew that half the time, the victims were men or women working for Lucretia Verangheti. She'd been caught before, back home.

But she never knew which marks were real and which were decoys. It made sense, she supposed. Training worked best if failure was possible, but not catastrophic. If your trainee failed once and then was useless, you'd lose all the time you'd put into training her. If you weren't willing for your trainee to ever fail, then you wouldn't stretch her skills, you wouldn't teach her where the line was.

But Teia didn't know which was which. It didn't matter that much, honestly. She couldn't treat any of them like they were decoys. The difference being that if she were caught thieving from one of Lucretia's men, she'd be thrashed, and if she were caught stealing from anyone else, she'd be thrown out of the Blackguard and the Chromeria and put in jail.

And of course, her father was counting on her. Things went well for the father of a slave doing excellent work. The other half of the statement didn't even have to be breathed. A slave knew. Her father was a free man; she hadn't lied to Kip about that part. But that didn't mean that Lady Verangheti didn't have power over what happened to him and his debts.

So Teia studied the portrait, memorizing the man's features. Landed noble, most likely, from the clothes. Balding, short-cropped hair, wide nose, fat necklaces, wide cloak, sword belt, wide sleeves, leather gloves.

Dressed like that, Teia wouldn't be surprised if he traveled with a bodyguard. She glanced down the alley both ways. Saw no one. She folded up the rice paper. The corners had red and yellow luxin under a thin layer of wax. She rubbed them together, scraping away the wax, and the paper ignited and burned up in a flash. Teia blew away the dust and headed back toward the market.

Like every other intersection in the city, each entrance to the market was straddled by arches that supported one of the city's Thousand Stars. Though they were primarily intended to extend the power of drafters, in between the drafters' uses each district could employ the great elevated mirrors for whatever they chose.

This market had rented out its stars to whatever merchant paid the most. So some focused beams of sunlight on particular shops. Others had colored filters fixed over them and focused on luxin jugglers who wandered the market, doing tricks and promoting one shop or another. Adrasteia made her way to the base of one of the stars, unlocked the tiny door with a key, closed and locked the door behind her, and crawled up the painfully narrow shaft. She had an arrangement with the tower monkeys, the slaves who kept this arch. As long as she didn't get in their way or do any damage, they let her use one of the ventilation windows partway up as a lookout.

She opened her bag as she waited. Ordinarily, she hated her flat, lifeless hair, but this was why she kept it cut short. With a few clips, she was able to fasten a wig to her head with no problem: this time, long, wavy Atashian. Bound it with a red handkerchief. She fished about twenty bracelets out of the bag. Gaudy, flashy—anything to take attention off her face. She put rouge on her cheeks and lips, and

128

folded her other handkerchiefs. She tucked her shawl into the bag, loosened some ties on her dress, and pulled it down—when she left the arch, she would put on tall shoes that would disguise her height, and the hemline needed to hang low enough to disguise the shoes. She pulled on a bodice and cinched it loosely around her ribs and stuffed the folded handkerchiefs into the bodice to give the appearance that her breasts were larger than mosquito bites.

Almost everything she hated about her body made her good at this work, she knew. It was doubtless part of why she had been chosen. Not too short, not too tall, skinny—that was easier to disguise with clothes than fat was—facial features pleasant, but not so pretty as to stand out from a line of other girls. As much as Kip had peeved her for saying it aloud, she could—and had—even disguised herself as a boy.

When she was finished today, though, she thought she probably looked like a woman. Lower-class Atashian wife, mid-twenties, tallish, bad taste, one tooth blackened with a mixture of ash and tallow. Which tasted awful.

The disguise wasn't flawless, but Adrasteia wasn't trying for perfection. The best thing about this disguise was that if she were pursued, she could take it all off in a couple of seconds.

Finished changing, she waited. Finding one nobleman among the human stockyards of Big Jasper would have been impossible on her own, much less stealing a particular item within that same day. But Adrasteia wasn't required to find her target. He would come to her, and he would come marked.

She waited for an hour, dilating her eyes every minute. Her vision, as she'd told Kip, was alternately average, incredible, and terrible, with no logic behind which was which that she could divine. Superviolet didn't register at all, her perception of violet, purple, and blue was merely average, green possibly average, yellow average, and then red indistinguishable from green. But then, below the spectrum that was visible to mundanes and many drafters, her sight sharpened. She couldn't draft sub-red, but she could see it better than most sub-red drafters. Teia barely had to consciously dilate her eyes to see it; as long as she was relaxed it was as easy to her as going from focusing on something near to something far.

But when she did dilate her eyes, she saw something altogether different. Below sub-red, below sub-red as far as sub-red was below the visible spectrum, farther, was her color—if color it was. The books called it *paryl*. Paryl was pure and beautiful and mostly useless. It was so fine it couldn't hold anything. So fine the few books she'd ever found that tried to make some translation of paryl called it spidersilk.

Except, of course, spiders could hang from their webs. Teia knew better than to try that with her color.

She was starting to get nervous about the mirror slaves' shift changing. They didn't mind her being in their tower, but they couldn't get out while she was inside. And the moment when she left the tower in her disguise was the most vulnerable time of her day. She'd dilated her eyes all the way to paryl when something flickered at the corner of her vision.

A wisp of paryl smoke swirled and disappeared over the crowd, a hundred paces away.

No one noticed it, of course. No one *could* notice it. Teia hadn't even met anyone who could see paryl, much less draft it.

It had to be her target. That was how her targets came marked: wisps of paryl in their hair or on top of their hat, burning like flameless fires. It made a perfect beacon, invisible to anyone but Teia. But she'd never seen her counterpart; the man or woman who marked Teia's targets for her had always kept well out of sight.

Teia watched, looked everywhere. There! A beacon, passing below the foot of her tower. She couldn't quite get the angle to see her target, but this was going to be easier than usual.

She slid down the ladder with her bag slung over her back. At the bottom, she pulled out the tall shoes, put them on, put her bag over one shoulder, and made sure that the straps hadn't displaced her "breasts." She breathed deeply. Confident but not aggressive, Teia. No, not even confident. Just busy. Enough sway to make it look like I have hips, but not so much that I look like a prostitute. Checking her wig one last time, she exhaled, opened the door, stepped out, and closed it unhurriedly behind her.

The foot of the arch here was right next to the side of a building, so she was able to step into a narrow side street quickly. She scanned the crowd once she got away from the arch, and relaxed her eyes briefly. It was as important for her to look for people who had noticed her stepping out of the arch as it was for her to find her target.

She found the beacon in seconds. But it wasn't on her target. It was in a woman's hair, and it was knotted, tight. Not loose and fiery.

Teia knew it was a bad decision, but she followed the woman immediately.

If what Teia had seen was this woman being marked, the other paryl drafter might be here.

But rather than pure excitement, Teia felt that she'd stepped into something dangerous. Whoever had marked this woman didn't know that anyone else could see her. It was like stumbling across a secret message and opening it. Whoever had sent the message wouldn't be pleased to have their correspondence read—even if the words meant nothing to Teia.

There were powerful undercurrents in this city, and a slave could get sucked down into the weakest of them. It was a rare morning on Big Jasper that the Cerulean Sea didn't carry away at least one body.

Teia kept her eyes open, but didn't draft. Any drafting would alert the other paryl to her presence. The woman was perhaps fifty paces ahead of her, and not in any particular hurry, browsing the stalls, moving deeper into the market. Her very lack of haste made it almost impossible to find the other drafter. If she were heading somewhere, the number of possible followers would be limited to the people who were heading in the same direction and at roughly the same speed. With the woman browsing and impossible to lose because she had a beacon on her head, the woman's pursuer—her spy?—could focus on blending with the shifting crowd.

Trying not to be obvious, Teia circled to get a better look at the woman, who was now chatting with a textiles dealer, gesturing to a silk scarf checkered with bright greens and black. The woman was petite with a heart-shaped face, frizzy hair, well dressed in a pale blue dress, big earrings. Attractive, perhaps late thirties.

No hint why someone would be following her.

Nothing to do with me. I should get the hell out of here.

But Adrasteia couldn't help herself. Her mother had always said that she was the kind of girl who needed to burn her hand on the stove twice before she was convinced it was hot.

A vendor selling clay jars glazed with garish snarling animals approached Teia. "Ah, the lady has excellent taste," he said.

She smiled neutrally. "Just looking, thank you."

"Any particular uses you're looking—"

"I'll let you know," she said. She sort of surprised herself. She wouldn't be so rude in real life, but wearing a disguise was strangely freeing.

131

"Very well," the merchant said, giving her a false smile. He turned away and cursed her under his breath, none too quietly.

She had more important things to worry about, but it made her blush nonetheless. What an—

She almost missed it. A quick pulse emanating from near the fountain. She looked for the source, but couldn't narrow it down between three men standing there, all of them looking toward the pretty woman. Teia knew that pulse. She'd used it herself. It was, in fact, the only reason she had a chance at getting in the Blackguard. The special thing about paryl that no other color could do was that it went right through clothing. With paryl, you could see exactly where anything metal was on a person's body. If they wore mail concealed beneath a tunic, or had a concealed dagger strapped to their thigh, it wasn't concealed to Teia. That, and marking things with beacons no one else could see, seemed to be the only practical uses of the color that Teia had found. One book had discounted it from being a true color at all for that very reason, calling paryl "singularly ephemeral, and singularly useless."

It was easy to get tunnel vision when hunting, and Teia's fighting masters back in Odess had beaten her for it a number of times. So she tried to breathe deeply and be aware of her surroundings. That intense focus could give you away or cause you to make mistakes.

And just in time, too.

Glancing up and down the main street of the market, through the swirl of humanity—traders from every satrapy, slaves, luxiats, beggars, and nobles—Teia saw the last thing she wanted to see. Her own target—her target for Lucretia Verangheti—was walking straight toward her. Worse, the direction he was going would take him straight in front of the other paryl drafter. Her target had the familiar paryl beacon woven into his hair. If he walked down the street with that intact, the other paryl drafter couldn't miss him. And that might set *him* hunting *Teia*.

Teia was moving before she was sure what she was going to do. If she had one flaw, it wasn't passivity.

She shot out a pulse of superfine light herself, making it as brief as possible. A couple of the best things about paryl were that it could be drafted faster than any other color and it was everywhere, even on the cloudiest day, so there was rarely any problem finding a source. It was present weakly even at night, so long as you were outside. Her focused stream cut through her target's clothes, making them look like shadows shaking in the wind.

From long experience, Teia was able to pick out the fuzzy shapes of all the metal items he carried. Sword, knife, belt buckle, silver worked into belt, narrow chain links to secure his purse to his belt (paranoid about being robbed, then), coins within the purse, tips of the laces on his shirt, necklace, cloak chain and gold thread worked into the cloak's mantle, an earring, and—finally!—a snuff box in his cloak's chest pocket.

It was an easy spot to pickpocket from. She crossed the street. At the last moment, to make it convincing that her running into the target was accidental, she glanced back.

Mistake. She saw one of the men by the fountain—slight, plain, a fringe of red hair around a bald spot, tradesman's clothes—bring his hands together in front of him. A needle of paryl luxin leapt from his hands and stuck into the side of the neck of the woman he was watching, twenty paces away. It was an amazing shot through the press of massed bodies and passing carts. It hung in the air, anchored on one side to his hands and on the other to her neck. He was bent forward in concentration.

A passing pedestrian walked through the spidersilk thread and snapped it, but the man was unperturbed. He released the paryl and walked away without a second glance.

Teia caught a glimpse of the woman, frowning and rubbing her neck for a moment, then going back to looking at a melon in the cart before her.

Then someone collided with Teia. She would have gone sprawling, but a strong hand snatched her arm.

"Watch yourself there, sweetcheeks," her target said. He cupped her butt and gave it a squeeze as he helped her regain her balance.

"Oh—I—" Teia didn't have to feign her confusion. It took a little more effort to regain her balance with her tall shoes, and a little more effort than that to regain her mental balance.

"I'll be at the Red Six Inn later, if you're looking for some entertainment, gorgeous," the man said. His hand was still on her butt.

She swatted his hand away. "No, *thank you*, my lord. Excuse me."

He laughed and didn't try again. "Think about it," he said. "I'll show you a better night than your husband ever could."

She ducked her head shyly and walked away, feeling violated. She 133 swore she could still feel his hand on her. She wanted to punch him in his grinning face for groping her.

Instead, she contented herself with dropping the snuff box into her bag. He'd caught her off guard, but Teia had recovered quickly.

She turned as he walked on and, drafting, snatched the beacon off his head. If she was smart, she should get the hell out of here, but she couldn't help trying to peer deeper into the market to catch sight of the woman.

It wasn't hard to spot her. She still had her beacon glowing on her head, though it was already dissipating, and her skin was pale enough that it evinced the slight tea green tint of a longtime drafter. She crossed the main street of the market, carrying the melon. One of her arms fell and she dropped the melon. She smiled, as if surprised and confused, but only half of her face moved. She staggered and suddenly fell.

A couple of people grinned and chuckled. But the woman didn't get up. She started having a seizure. Apoplexy. A stroke.

The smiles disappeared, and people began running toward her.

"Someone, help! Chirurgeons!" a bystander shouted.

Dread shot through Teia. Orholam have mercy, what had she just seen?

Chapter 33

The great hall of the Chromeria was converted every week into a place of worship. Every student, drafter or not, was required to attend. Kip shuffled into his place in the pew between Ben-hadad and Teia. Ben-hadad was flicking down the colored lenses of his odd spectacles, staring from the white marble of the arches to the many-colored stained glass panels of the clerestory.

Kip was too absorbed in what was happening on the floor to even begin to parse the scenes depicted above them in the stained glass.

"So what do we do?" he asked.

"Mmm?" Ben-hadad asked.

"We listen," Teia said. Her tone was short, withdrawn, unusual for her. "It's the second week of the cycle, so I think the Blue himself will be speaking."

"Oh no," Ben-hadad said. "He's the worst. I heard from one of the glims that last year Gavin Guile preached on the Blue day and that he was amazing. But what's-his-name is awful."

"Klytos Blue," Kip said. He felt a weight of dread. His target. "He tries to be scholarly because he thinks that's how blues are supposed to be, but I've heard the real scholars mocking him."

Kip didn't care, though he hoped he could dislike the man he had sworn to destroy. It would be his first chance to see Klytos Blue in person. He found that his heart was pounding.

The great hall slowly filled, with a big rush of people coming in at the last minute before noon. Even as the people were still entering, a low choral chant rose from a pit hidden near the front. "What's that?" Kip whispered.

"The sub-reds' men's choir," Ben-hadad said, still staring up at the light pouring in through the clerestory.

"Shh," Teia said, intent on the music. Cranky.

"Why don't the blues do their own music?" Kip asked Ben-hadad.

"Don't know. It's just a special thing they do." Ben-hadad grinned suddenly and pulled his eyes down from the ceiling. "Sub-reds are always passionate, of course, but the men are almost always sterile. Both of which make them quite popular with the ladies."

"Musically talented doesn't hurt either," Teia said wistfully.

"What?" Kip asked Ben-hadad. "Why?"

Ben-hadad's eyebrows shot up.

"Why Kip, hasn't your father explained the Seventy Ways of a Man with a Maid to you?" Teia asked.

"That wasn't what I meant. I was—?" Oh, she knew that. She was grinning as he blushed.

Seventy?

She relented and, speaking low, said, "No one knows why they're sterile. It's just part of their burden and their sacrifice to Orholam."

"Shh!" a girl in the row in front of them said, turning around, irritated.

The choir began a new song, and this time many of the congregation joined in. Kip had no idea what they were saying. He could only guess that it was archaic Parian. It was beautiful, though, and he was glad that he didn't understand it. He could soak in pure music.

Two great skylights lit up suddenly with more than the noonday sun. Kip guessed that two of the great mirrors on top of the other towers had been turned toward the great hall, which of course had an entire tower above it, so it couldn't let in light from straight above. So the mirrors stood in to let Orholam's light shine upon his people.

There was more singing, and then a procession of blue-robed men and women, some swinging censers full of smoking incense. Kip watched as Klytos Blue, dressed in a blue silk robe with a high starched collar and wearing a strange blue hat, walked within several paces of him. The man looked uncomfortable, barely enduring this.

Kip didn't like him.

Orholam, *Seventy* Ways? Kip could only really imagine two.

Who could you ask about that sort of thing? They'd laugh at him like he was a bumpkin.

There was kneeling and prayers and readings and responses from five thousand throats. Kip moved his mouth and pretended to know what was going on. His mother had never had time for luxiats. She'd feared Orholam's judgment, mostly saying that if you kept your head down, you might escape the wrath you deserved.

Then Klytos Blue came to the lectern and began speaking so softly that even the people in the front row probably couldn't have heard a word. He was so awkwardly shy that Kip felt a stab of cruel compassion for the man. One of the luxiats approached him quietly and whispered to him.

Klytos raised his voice to a mumble: "...under cye of...this forty-ninth day..."

Kip saw the luxiat eyeing another luxiat, communicating with glances. The other luxiat got up and murmured to Klytos Blue, who spoke sharply back to the man, flushed, and then turned back to his papers.

"As I was saying," Klytos shrilled, finally speaking loudly enough that even those in the back could hear him. He sneered, "It is part of the Chromeria's work to bring the most recent work of scholars to blinkered corners of our world. Not long ago, it was considered heresy to speak of our world as if it were anything but a rolled-out parchment. People believed that the world had actual corners—luxiats most of all. Thanks to the blues and to the blue virtues, we now know this to be superstition and not in conflict with the scriptures which were speaking only metaphorically of the satrapies being the center.

The center of Orholam's will is a metaphorical statement, not a spatial one."

Kip had no idea what he was talking about, but a couple of the luxiats didn't look particularly pleased with this turn. Kip guessed that if Klytos lowered his voice another time, none of them was going to remind him to raise it again.

"In the last few years, there has been some exciting work done by your compeers in the Tower of Reason regarding the Great Schism and the events that flowed out of the Deimachia, the War of the Gods which most scholars now agree is better translated the War *on* the Gods. The 'dei' of course is the ablative, and in most of our translations, there's simply not enough contextual evidence to support overturning the generally accepted 'war of.' However, in Tristaem's *On the Fundaments of Reason*, he points out that with only a few changes in how we understand old Parian grammar, our entire hermeneutics is shifted. These shifts are under way now."

Kip's eyes began to glaze over. There were simply too many words he didn't understand. Even if he did think grammar was interesting, he couldn't have followed if he'd wanted to. He lost the stream and began looking around the room instead. One old luxiat in her rumpled black robe looked like she was chewing on a lemon. Several of the older students actually looked fascinated, and Kip despaired. Am I going to turn into that?

He'd thought that the Chromeria was a place of learning, yes, but a place of practical learning. He began studying the stained glass mosaics that lined the entire clerestory. There was Lucidonius himself, white-robed and soft-looking, surrounded by his Parian warriors, but his skin a couple of shades lighter than theirs. That was interesting. Kip had always heard he was a Parian outsider.

Oh, maybe he was an outsider even to the Parians.

Kip suddenly imagined furious arguments over exactly what color Lucidonius's skin color had been when the stained glass had gone in. He knew the Parians claimed him, especially over their rivals in riches and power, their neighbors the pale-skinned Ruthgari. The darker Lucidonius was, the more of a poke in the eye it would be to the Ruthgari.

And now, despite that the stained glass had gone in hundreds of years after Lucidonius died, people would look at the windows and assume that because they were old, they must be accurate.

137

Fascinating. Kip wished he knew.

Oh, hell. That's exactly what old windy up there is doing, isn't it? Turning the world on the parsing of a word, like Kip was imagining the world turned on a bit of pigment in a window.

The Blue had lowered his voice again, and Kip had to lean forward to hear him now. But he'd said a word that had caught Kip's attention: Lightbringer. "... which is why the Lightbringer is best understood as a metaphor for each one of us. Each of us is to bring light into the dark corners of the world. Not through missionary zeal. If the religions of those beyond the Everdark Gates are serving the barbarians out there well, who are we to change who they are? Are they not also the children of Orholam? We are to bring light into the dark corners of our own lives, by being kind and generous, by speaking well of others, by loving extravagantly. The Lightbringer is not coming. Hear O Children of Am, the Lightbringer is not one. We are Lightbringers all."

The luxiats' eyes all seemed ready to pop out of their heads as they ran screaming from the room to bathe themselves in milk.

Kip almost burst out laughing at the image.

Holy shit, Kip. Gotta get more sleep.

The High Luxiat took the dais. He didn't even look at Klytos Blue. "Choir," he said, "I wonder if you could close us with 'Father of Lights, Forgive Us.'" It wasn't, apparently, the song that had been planned.

Oh, nice.

But the men sang it, and they sang beautifully.

Everyone shuffled out after the song and Kip asked Ben-hadad, "So what was all that?"

"A lie from the pit of hell," Ben-hadad said. Two girls in the row in front of them turned and glanced at him, but he was heedless. "There have always been fights about the Lightbringer. Who he is, or will be, or if he already came. The Chromeria says he already came, that Lucidonius was the Lightbringer. His name means 'light giver,' after all."

"But you don't buy that?" Kip asked.

"I don't know all the arguments, but my parents don't believe it."

Kip looked at him. It was one of the dumber things he'd ever heard, and by the sudden glum look on Ben-hadad's face, he could tell the boy knew it, too.

138   "I don't want to live after history is settled," Ben-hadad said.

Which was also dumb: I don't like how the world is, so it isn't that way? At least this time Kip was able to keep himself from saying it.

"The Lightbringer is going to be a genius of magic," Teia suddenly said. She'd been unusually quiet until now. "A warrior who sweeps all before him. He will be great from his youth. He's going to do things no one ever thought was possible, and bring us back to the true path. Lucidonius wasn't even a good drafter. He figured out how to make colored lenses, but that hardly makes him a genius, does it? The Lightbringer will protect us. He will slay gods and kings."

I killed a king.

A chill washed down Kip's back.

"There are no kings anymore," an older boy said, butting in. "Lucidonius killed the last of them. And the last gods."

"Lucidonius's people did that," Ben-hadad said. "Not Lucidonius himself."

"It's the same thing," the boy said. "When you say, 'The Color Prince seized Garriston,' you don't mean he picked it up. You don't even mean that he took it by himself. You mean it was done at his will. It's—"

"Children!" a black-robed luxiat said, disgusted. Kip wondered how long the man had been listening. "Wielding half-remembered foolishness from your parents and superstitions from the benighted. Get to your lectures. I'll not have your blasphemies in this holy place. Now! Out!"

Chapter 34

"That dress doesn't do justice to your beauty," a young man said to Liv as she emerged from a warehouse some of the displaced women and their children had taken over in Garriston. "Nor do those quarters do justice to your gifts." He smiled the smile of a man who knows he's gorgeous. "I'm Zymun. I'm your tutor."

And he would have been gorgeous, had not his entire look been spoiled by the bandage over his nose, and two black eyes. Zymun looked maybe sixteen or seventeen, Liv's age, but maybe older, or maybe he simply carried himself like he was older. He had a mop of curly black hair, an aquiline nose made even bigger by the bandage over it, a wide mouth, and perfect bright white teeth. Atashian skin, heavy brows, light blue eyes with a ring of many colors beneath the halo. He wore a new white shirt—who had new shirts, just after a huge battle?—and over his sleeves, his forearms were covered with multi-colored vambraces with five thick bands of color against a white background. He wore a sparkling clean cloak that echoed the pattern, from a black fuzzy band for sub-red to red, orange, yellow, and green. A five-color polychrome. Five!

There were only perhaps twenty five-color polys in the Chromeria. Maybe a few more still in training. If this boy was cocky, it was for good reason.

Insufferable.

"You lose a fight?" Liv asked. How rude!

"Failed an assassination attempt, actually. Took a punch in the face. And got beaten for my failure when I got back. After swimming through shark-infested waters." He smiled.

"You're joking."

"Terrible sense of humor, if I were. It's not very funny, is it?"

"You're serious?"

"Second time's the charm, I guess. Come, we need to get you out of those rag—those clothes and into something more becoming."

He was her tutor, put over her by Lord Omnichrome himself, so Liv supposed that meant she had to obey him. She shrugged and followed him through the city. The warehouse wasn't far from the Travertine Palace, because it felt safer to be close to the soldiers. Being a woman alone during wartime meant never being off your guard.

But as Liv followed Zymun, she saw that his garb was better than armor. "Is everyone so afraid of drafters here?" she asked.

"Afraid? They respect us, which is only right, don't you think?"

"I suppose so."

"You suppose so? Ah. So this is why you needed a tutor."

Well *that* was patronizing, and Liv didn't appreciate it one bit.

"The Chromeria makes slaves, Liv. It depends on making those it trains being so indebted to them that you become at best an indentured servant—with the term of your indenture being the rest of your life. A slave, in other words. The Free reject that. We recognize instead the natural order as it is. Did you choose to be born a great beauty? Of course not. But you are. You can do with that what you will. Similarly, you were born a drafter. We can wish that all were born with our gifts, and the Color Prince is investigating how this might be done. But the fact remains, we are special. We have a gift that other men and women don't. We didn't do anything to earn that gift—we can't choose to be drafters. But we are. We don't ask those who have gifts to chain themselves, as we don't ask those who are skilled in running to get fat so they don't make us feel bad for being slow. We are what we are, as wild and free as nature made us. When you walk the streets as a drafter, men know that if they accost you, you can kill them. They can fear that or simply respect it like they'd respect a woman carrying a pistol. With the advantage, of course, being that a pistol only has one shot."

They passed workers clearing rubble-strewn streets and finally arrived at a little store undamaged in the fighting. An old woman greeted her. "So good to have business! Thank you, thank you, oh, and so beautiful you are! A marvel I'll make you. I have an order for three dresses, yes?" she asked Zymun.

"If that's what Lord Omnichrome ordered," Zymun said.

"Very well then, strip down," she told Liv.

Liv looked at her, then over at Zymun, who showed no inclination to leave. "Do you mind?" she asked him.

He looked her up and down, grinning mischievously. "Very much, but as you wish. Can't fault me for trying."

He stepped outside and left her in the capable hands of the seamstress. The woman took her measurements quickly, compared it to her height, had her turn around a few times, and then allowed her to dress. She made three quick sketches and showed them to Liv. "Everything is to be the finest possible for you, my lady. This first will be wool, but it's a goat's wool from the Abornean mountains. Warm, but so soft you won't believe it."

"That sounds…" Wonderful? Amazing? "…expensive." Liv hated herself for saying it, but she'd been poor for so long, she couldn't help it.

"Ha! That's not the start of it. I'm doing the trim of your silk dress with true murex purple. The finest silk, too, of course. Who's going to waste true purple to dye bad silk? Ten thousand murex shells harvested just for you."

Liv felt a little sick to her stomach. Silk? True purple? "I meant…
I'm really sorry. What I meant is, I don't have any money. Maybe
plain wool? Just one dress?" Truth was, she didn't even have the
money to pay for that, but her pride couldn't take admitting utter
poverty.

"Oh, you pretty little thing, you don't have to pay! The Lord
Omnichrome is taking care of everything. One warm dress, one for
everyday wear—that one will be upland Atashian cotton—and one
to dazzle. Looks like you could use some new shifts and undergarments, too?"

"Please! I don't generally… well, war, you know."

"Of course, of course. And we'll get you a clean dress to wear in the
meantime."

That offer turned into a clean dress and a hot bath, ostensibly
because the old woman didn't want her getting the dress dirty, but Liv
thought the seamstress was happy to have someone to spoil, someone
to talk to.

As she scrubbed herself with a sponge and let the hot water unknot
her muscles, Liv fought the rush of tears just below the surface. She
blew out a breath, feeling like she could cry and she would feel better
afterward, but she didn't want to look all splotchy and swollen. She
was sure the old woman wouldn't care—she had the air of someone
who'd understand—but Zymun would come back to pick her up later,
and he'd ask. And how can you explain *why* you were crying when
the answer would either take an hour or one word? Neither would
make him understand. She'd just look like a weak girl.

Liv blew out another breath.

"That's a lot of sighing," the old woman said. Liv hadn't noticed
her come in.

"Have you ever realized that everything you ever believed was
a lie?"

"Everything? The sky is green now?"

"I didn't mean—"

"Teasing, child." The old woman paused, then heaved a little sigh
of her own. "I believed my husband was faithful to me. When that
fell, it seemed like all the world did with it."

Liv hesitated.

"No, child. Don't tell me. I'm a stranger. Take my kindness, but
don't trust so much, so easily. You're a beautiful young woman in a

perilous place. Put on some armor. Just remember what's armor and what's you, so when it's time to take it off, you can."

The old woman walked out, and Liv knew that she'd done her a kindness greater than she could have by listening to her churning thoughts.

Liv had joined the enemy. She could excuse herself and say that she'd hoped her action might inspire the Color Prince to save Kip and Karris, and it had, but in truth she'd lost faith in everything the Chromeria had taught her. If the fruit is poison, why respect the tree?

But if the Chromeria itself was corrupt, how deep did that corruption go? If they'd taught one lie, how many others had they espoused? It made her feel sick to her stomach, like she was looking into the abyss. If the Chromeria was corrupt, and the Chromeria was supposed to be a central font of Orholam's will, what did that say about Orholam himself?

How could he let such corruption be? Either he didn't care, or he didn't have the power to do anything about it, or he didn't exist. Liv felt a chill despite the hot water. It was a thought that couldn't be called back.

But there was no answer. Doesn't care, can't fix, or doesn't exist. No matter what, things were not as Liv had believed. It was like having a nice warm cloak of comforting suppositions ripped off her shoulders.

So be it. This was what it was to be an adult, to be a strong woman. Her father had raised her to believe certain things, but her father wasn't omniscient. He could be wrong. And if he was, Liv wasn't going to be a moral coward. She would face the world as it was.

She'd once heard an old philosopher quoted in one of her classes: 'The truth is so dear to me that if Orholam stood on one side and truth on the other, I would turn my back on my creator himself.'

So be it. Fealty to One, that was the Danavis motto. Liv's fealty would be to the truth.

Simply considering that was scary, terrifying as she thought about the decisions she made all the time based on what was right—which was based on what was holy—which was based on what the Chromeria taught was holy—which was based on what the Chromeria believed about Orholam. Taking out that linchpin?

But at the same time, it was tremendously freeing. She would be strong. This was hard, but she would do it. She wouldn't shrink from hard truths or embrace comforting delusions. She would be a warrior for truth.

She finished bathing, the impulse to tears forgotten, steel in her spine. And then she ate what the old woman brought her, though it was only a thin broth dotted with a few potatoes.

"It isn't up to my normal standards, but well, war, you know," the old woman said, a twinkle in her eye.

Liv laughed.

"After I finish your dresses, I'll be able to serve you something much better, I promise."

When she was finished, Liv felt a thousand times better. She thanked the old woman and stepped outside.

Zymun was sitting on a crude bench, tossing little blue disks out of one hand into the air and shooting them with green from the other.

"You were waiting for me the whole time?" Liv asked.

He tossed a blue disk up and blasted it into oblivion, harder than necessary.

"Oh. I forgot about you," she said. Oops, that didn't come out quite like she meant it.

"You get away with that shit because you're beautiful?" Zymun asked. "If so, quit it."

"You keep saying that. I don't know if you're trying to make a backhanded compliment or a stupid forehanded insult." She wasn't beautiful. She knew that. On her best day, she could manage a bit of *cute*. Anyone who said different was trying to get something from her.

Zymun looked like he was going to tear into her, but then his mouth twitched. " 'Forehanded insult'?" he asked. "That your own invention?" But he grinned.

"I was hoping you wouldn't notice." She scowled, feeling stupid. "I thought you weren't a blue," she said quickly. He had five colors on his cloak and vambraces, but not blue and not superviolet.

"Not yet," he said. He drafted another blue disk. Liv could tell the color was off, and in barely more than a second it frayed apart and dissolved. "Hoping I grow into it. It's so close it's infuriating. Blue has so many uses. Plus, as nice as it already is to be a five, I can't help but dream of being a full-spectrum polychrome."

He was reaching to be a seven-color drafter with exactly the same kind of statements Liv had used a few months ago when she was longing to have her second color recognized. It was never enough, was it? There's always someone better than you.

Still, if seven colors might be within reach for Zymun, that meant the boy was on another plane altogether.

"Sorry about forgetting," Liv said, looking at her feet. "I didn't think I was important enough for you to wait around for me."

He smiled, and broken nose, black eyes, and all, he was terribly handsome. "Come on," he said. "I've got something to show you."

Chapter 35

It was strangely freeing to be so busy that he had no time for friends— or his lack thereof. Over the next weeks, Kip spent his mornings in class and working, spent hours more on the Blackguards' field, and then headed to the library. He got to know the staff, and they him. As often as not, a stack of books was waiting for him—the ones he requested every day, plus whatever ones Rea Siluz thought he might find helpful.

He would find an isolated desk, and not leave for eight or ten hours, depending on when the last librarian left. Every day he scowled at the older students, and stayed late with them a few times—until he was discovered and banned from the library for a week. Students also weren't allowed to reshelve their own books. Apparently so many had done so incorrectly for so long that it became a nightmare for the librarians. Now, after being read, books were to be deposited at one of the two desks for the purpose on each level of the library. Kip also quickly learned that despite taking up three full levels of the Prism's Tower, this library was only a small sliver of the total number of books the Chromeria owned. Many more were kept below ground. Dims were not allowed in the secondary libraries, period.

All of which combined to make Kip's other searches nearly impossible to even begin. He had sworn to avenge his mother—and crushing King Garadul's head somehow hadn't made that ache go away.

Then he'd sworn to find out if his mother was lying about Gavin Guile. He couldn't imagine the man had actually raped her, but liar and addict and horror though she was, she still deserved that of her son.

Of greater concern, though, was that he'd sworn to make Klytos Blue step down.

He really had to stop swearing.

The problem with both goals was that he barely knew where to start. He couldn't exactly ask, "Pardon, can you tell me where the damning evidence about the currently serving Colors and Prisms is kept?" And with his books being checked up on, any wider reading he did want to do had to be done carefully. Kip had found several books of genealogy to learn about Klytos Blue, and then waited until he saw one of the young women who assisted the libraries reshelving books and slid his books into her stacks.

At this rate, he'd never find anything. There was only one shortcut to get to the libraries that might have the information he needed: make it into the Blackguard.

So what had begun as something he attempted to please his father whose ultimate purpose he didn't understand now became the only possibility. Kip trained and studied and read books in the library and didn't sleep much, nightmares interrupting his rest every night, until he would crash and sleep for a day or two straight.

There was no punishment for missing class. The Chromeria let the sponsors handle that. It made Sponsor Day deeply unpleasant for those students who loafed. But Kip didn't have a sponsor. He went to class, though, even when he hated it. To miss would be to disappoint his father, to be a failure.

And then fight day came, the culmination of the month's training.

Though Kip was clearly the worst in class, by entering at number four he'd made it terribly unlikely that he could fail out this month. But the entire system was designed to force the cream of the class to rise. On testing day, each student was given a fight token. The testing started at the bottom, with the lowest-ranked students given a chance. Number forty-nine would go first. He could only challenge someone within three places, and if he won, he would be awarded that person's fight token, which he could immediately use again to keep climbing.

Before they started, a boy asked the trainer, "Trainer Fisk, sir?

Why do we have to fight with the spotlights instead of giving us spectacles?"

The trainer said, "You ask now? Why not ask when you started?"

"I, uh—everything was new," the boy said. Kip could tell the truth. The boy had been too intimidated to ask then.

"Anyone have a guess?" the trainer asked.

"Spectacles could break in training, and they're worth a fortune," Teia said.

"And the glass could blind us if it broke," someone else chimed in.

"True, but those aren't the most important reasons," Trainer Fisk said. "Let me tell a little story. Far as I know, it's true. Back in the days of Prism Karris Shadowblinder, just after Lucidonius himself had introduced colored lenses to the world, there was a young man who joined the Ilytian Heresy, though the same could have happened to anyone. Blue drafter named Gilliam. He had his blue lenses, and he never took them off. It was a time of wars to make ours look paltry, so none blamed him. The lenses were a symbol of power, and of status, of course. The technology to create colored lenses was known to only a few, so having the lenses showed that you were wealthy as well. He was in many battles over the years, mostly on the wrong side, but that's neither here nor there. A number of years later, he tried to assassinate Prism Shadowblinder. He cut through her guards handily, and then he faced the Prism herself. She berated him for using the spectacles her own husband had given him to fight *her*. She berated him for using them too much.

"But of course he thought she was stalling, and he tried to kill her again. She snatched the spectacles from his face. It was an overcast day; there was no blue for him to draft, and in moments he was hamstrung. She asked him then if he understood. He didn't. She picked up a simple iron spear and told him to stop her. Of course it was impossible. He looked everywhere for blue. There was none. And then, as she came closer, he felt the reds and greens and yellows sliding into his eyes. He was a full-spectrum polychrome, and he'd never known.

"But having never used the colors, he couldn't control them, couldn't bind them to his will in the time he had. And she slew him as he screamed. He who has ears, let him hear."

Kip looked around. Some of the scrubs were nodding, like this all made perfect sense. Others looked like he felt.

"He who looks through only one lens lives in darkness," Teia murmured. He could tell she hadn't just made that up. It had a weight of antiquity to it.

"Enough questions, we've got work here. Places!" Trainer Fisk said. And that was it. No explanation. Fantastic.

Forty-nine, a slight, awkward boy with crooked teeth, challenged forty-six as everyone expected he would. Forty-six was a beefy girl, nearly twice his size, but slow. If she lost, she would lose her fight token and her chance to challenge those above her, so it was do or die for both of them.

"What's your strategy?" Teia asked Kip.

Forty-nine and forty-six approached the great wheels, each spinning one. Depending on where the whizzing counters landed, they would have different rules for their fight. It was another aspect of the Blackguard ethos: you never knew under what circumstances you might have to fight, or with what weapons. You could get lucky or unlucky, and you had to deal with it.

The boy's roll landed at yellow and green. The girl's at staves.

"What do you mean?" Kip asked, entranced by what was happening in front of them.

Shutters were drawn and the battleground was bathed in yellow and green light. The boy and girl walked to Trainer Fisk, who stood by a small podium, and they both pushed their fingers onto two points of black rock and then were given staves. They saluted each other and began fighting. They were awkward, so bad that even Kip might have had a chance against them.

The girl attacked, her first shot rattling hard against the boy's block, and her very next swing going through and catching him on the side of the head. He fell heavily, not unconscious, but jellied.

The boy got up to his knees, then fell over again.

The girl was declared the winner, and forty-nine burst into tears. There was no way he could stay in the Blackguard. He was done.

"Don't feel sorry for him," Teia said. "Failing out may keep him from getting killed, either next month or down the line. The Blackguard can only be the best."

"Someone is going to go home today for me," Kip said.

She looked at him, quizzical. "So, you don't have a strategy?"

He stared back. She wasn't getting it. "Teia, I'm terrible. I'll fight the best I can, but I'll lose. It's that simple." He wasn't going to disappoint Gavin any more than necessary.

Forty-eight went next—and instead of challenging forty-five, instead he challenged the girl at forty-six.

"Why'd he—"

"She's already fought once, so she might be tired," Adrasteia said.

And so it was. Forty-eight and forty-six fought a purely mundane fight—the colors he'd spun were colors that neither of them could draft. Forty-six won, and challenged forty-three. She won again, and challenged forty, but lost.

As he watched and pieced together why people were sometimes choosing to fight three places up and sometimes only the person directly above, Kip asked Teia questions. Pretty quickly he figured out that there was as much strategy here as at Nine Kings.

Oh hell no.

People would sometimes not fight their friends, because they didn't want to make them lose places or challenge tokens. Other times people would fight those whom they thought were tired, or if there was a particular low-ranked fighter whom people thought was better than his spot, sometimes people would fight below him so that they could then leapfrog him.

In the bottom seven were people who'd already lost and were definitely going to fail out—those were assumed be less likely to fight hard, so others were more likely to challenge them.

With this setup, as Teia explained it to Kip, if someone was ranked lower than their ability deserved, they had a chance to climb all the way to the top, if they were that good. Practically, of course, it almost never happened. Fighting was exhausting, and having to fight again immediately if you won meant it was rare that anyone jumped up the rankings very far.

At the same time, it put tremendous pressure on those at the top not to lose even once. If they did, and the person they'd lost to also lost, they could lose numerous places by losing a single fight.

Whoever had designed the tests wanted to get Blackguards who performed well under tremendous pressure.

"By getting into the hierarchy higher than people think you deserve, Kip, you've pretty much guaranteed that you're going to get challenged a lot," Teia said.

Of course. If there was a safe fight in your block of three, you take that one. Kip would always be that safe fight.

"What do I care?" Kip asked. "It's just beatings."

"You know," Teia said, "I can't decide if you're brave or stupid."

Huh?

"If I fight you again, I'm going to win," she said.

"You never know," Kip said. "I might get lucky."

She left. He barely noticed; he was watching the fights. Because he didn't get any time in drafting practice, this was Kip's first glimpse of what he assumed was normal drafting.

But most of the Blackguard trainees were monochromes, and the odds of drawing their color on the wheel weren't good, so most of the fights were purely hand-to-hand or weapon-to-weapon. Or sometimes the wheel would give them their color, but weakly, so instead of trying to draft a color slowly, they'd go for a straight fight. Not many of the children were able to fight effectively while also slowly drawing in enough light to be able to use it after two or three minutes of fighting. Most of the fights didn't last that long.

The fighters got a lot better quickly, though.

The last fighters in danger began their fight. A muscular boy got unlucky and fought a blue-drafting girl in blue light. She used bars of blue luxin to choke him out before he could cross the distance to her.

When he got up, furious, instead of going toward her, he marched over to Kip and shook his finger in his face. "You! You're worse than me! *You* should be going home, you lardass. Not me."

"You're right," Kip said quietly.

"You're damn right I'm right! Why are you even here? Because your mother's some whore who spread her legs for Gavin Guile? You're a bastard. I'm the son of the dey of Aghbalu! This is bullshit!"

Kip knew what he should do. He should punch the boy. Destroy him somehow with a ferocity that let everyone know, once again, that Kip was not to be crossed. He'd already done it with the bully Elio. Apparently once wasn't enough. One story, people could disbelieve.

But Kip didn't want to be the boy who was the crazy, erratic bastard. The one whom people tiptoed around because he might hurt someone with little or no provocation. He looked inside himself for that fury he knew was there for the boy insulting his mother, but today it was just an ache. He had no violence in him now.

"Is this what I am to be?" Kip asked. Some part of him wanted to weep.

"What?" the boy snarled. "I wasn't done with you."

"You're nothing," Kip said sadly. "And I'm less. I'm the violent madman."

The other Blackguard trainees were gathered, of course, eager to see what would happen. The trainer, Kip thought, was notably slow to come break it up. Perhaps pecking orders were best established early in the Blackguard.

Kip stood up. He needed a spark of fury, but he had nothing. It was too hard to think of coldly sucker-punching another boy. Especially one who was rightly angry at him.

"Wait, wait, wait," Kip said. "What's your name?" I won't fail my father.

"Tizrik, and you'd better remember it, you—" The boy's eyes were suspicious.

"Tizrik Tamar, of Aghbalu? Tizrik!" Kip spread his arms out to hug the boy like he was long-lost family. "Tizrik! My uncle said—"

"No, it's not Tamar— I'm—"

Kip embraced the boy, who tried to push his hands away, irritated. But then Kip seized both of the boy's sleeves and yanked fiercely, throwing his forehead into the taller boy's face. With his own hands off to the sides, trying to stop Kip from hugging him, Tizrik didn't have a chance.

Face met forehead. Stuff crunched. Blood showered over Kip's head.

The boy collapsed, mostly onto Kip. Kip pushed him off. The boy fell to the ground, his nose streaming blood even as he lay whimpering. His nose was crooked, clearly broken, his lips mashed. He more mouthed out than spit out blood, and a tooth came with the torrent.

Kip felt like he was watching himself from afar as he stepped over the boy and put a foot on his neck, holding him prone.

Murmurs and gasps raced through the crowd. Trainer Fisk pushed through them. He looked at the bleeding young man, then at Kip. "Chirurgeons! You, too, Kip."

Kip was stunned that he didn't appear to be in trouble, and apparently the others were, too. "But . . . but I haven't fought yet today."

"You've fought enough," the trainer said, pulling Kip back away from Tizrik.

"He cheated!" Tizrik said, holding his nose.

Trainer Fisk said, "Blackguards don't cheat. Blackguards win."

Their questioning looks obviously irritated Trainer Fisk. "This is real life," the trainer said. "Our coin is violence. Sudden, sharp, 151 breathtaking, leaving no hope of revenge. That is what we do, when we must. Kip understands and some of the rest of you obviously don't. That's fine. We've got time to cut the rest of you deadwood out."

Teeth bared, Trainer Fisk stared around at the young people. No one dared meet his eyes, not even Kip, who for some reason felt embarrassed, though he couldn't have explained why.

"Next up!" Trainer Fisk shouted.

Kip was checked out by the chirurgeons, and as he'd known, nothing was wrong with him. But by being caught up with them, his space was passed. He lost two places as others above him lost challenges, but he realized that by not having to fight this week, his chances of staying in the Blackguard had pretty much been doubled. He had a chance.

But he was going to have to win *some* fights.

Chapter 36

Teia walked into the ring, praying. She was lean, with quick reflexes. Slippery. What she wasn't was strong, not compared to the boys in the Blackguard. Luckily, the training favored cutting and slashing weapons. The Blackguard didn't have any bias against crushing weapons— war hammers, bludgeons, maces—indeed, those were often the best against heavy armor. But those weapons weren't safe to train with.

They could blunt the edges of a mace, but if one of the monsters like Leo—with the shoulders of a draft horse and arms of banded iron—hit you with a mace, it wouldn't matter if you had pillows wrapped around it. Bones would break. So they didn't train with them.

She supposed that the muscular boys thought that wasn't fair. On the other hand, at least *their* colors might come up on the wheel.

And what would I do if my color did come up on the wheel? Stab it through someone's neck and kill them?

The thought turned her stomach, sent shivers of dread down the back of her neck. She saw the look on that woman's face again, dropping the melon, looking startled, not understanding that she was about to die horribly.

How had that happened?

Her opponent was Graystone Keftar. He was very dark-skinned, cute grin, green drafter. Nice boy. He'd flirted with her a few times. Already going bald, though. Tragic. He was short and athletic, a son of a rich family that had paid for him to be trained before he came to the Chromeria.

Graystone winked at her and spun his wheel. She grimaced and spun hers. Next time he flirted, she'd give him nothing. You only wink at someone you're about to fight if you don't take them seriously. What'd the boys think? That she was training to be cute?

The wheels came up green or red. From Graystone's self-satisfied expression, she knew it was green—dammit!—and rapiers.

She and Graystone took their weapons. He fumbled with his a bit, but she knew he was playing around. The Blackguards threw their trainees full into the water. If you didn't realize that these fights were all about watching everyone else and figuring out who was good at what, you were wasting your time. The monthly fights were as much about scouting threats as they were about maintaining your position. Graystone was a competent hand with the rapier. Not good. He was much more familiar with an ataghan or other, heavier blades, and treated the rapier like those all too often. But he knew his basic blocks and stances.

She could win—would win, definitely, if he hadn't spun green on the wheel.

They took their places in the circle, faced each other, saluted. He winked at her.

Seriously, if he winked at her one more time, she was going to punch him in the face.

She grinned at the thought.

He seemed to take that as encouragement.

The circle was flooded with green light as the overseers slapped the green filters over the crystals high above.

She launched a furious attack immediately. She drove him back, and back. He stepped out of the green spotlight, into the darkness. She pressed harder.

He was just recovering from his surprise when his back foot stepped past the edge of the circle. If he stayed out for five seconds, he lost.

Graystone looked down. Teia's next strike pushed his block wide—and the next slapped down hard on his hand.

153

His rapier clattered to the ground and the blunted point of Teia's rapier came to rest under his chin a moment later.

A win.

"Nice one," Graystone said.

"Shut up."

She stormed off. She could challenge one of the boys above her. But she was in the top seven already, and both of those boys were truly excellent. Realistically, at best she could hope to maybe finish number two unless she got spectacularly lucky against Cruxer, who was head and shoulders above everyone else in the class. More honestly, she was probably about tenth best in the class. If she was to make the top seven, she'd have to be a little lucky in what colors came up in the next three testings.

But the more she fought now, the more chances the others had to scout her abilities. She wanted to finish strong, not be strong *until* the finish.

So she didn't challenge anyone. It was perhaps a little dirty, but it was clever, too. They all had chances to scout each other during their training time, but they all tried to hold back their best, too. Until they were in.

Teia watched the last bouts, noting the artistry of the best fighters. Everyone was unlucky in the last six rounds—none spun his own color, so it was pure fighting technique.

They were about to be dismissed when Trainer Fisk told them that Commander Ironfist himself was going to address them.

Teia's heart beat faster just seeing the commander. It was said he hadn't lost a single bout in his own training. His little brother, entering with the Blackguard a few classes below him, had also gone undefeated. When the two finally fought in an exhibition, it was as if giants clashed. The training yards had been crammed with thousands. And though the fight was close, with every weapon Ironfist had won.

Then there were still legends of his exploits during the False Prism's War. And now stories were coming out about what he'd done at the Battle of Garriston. They were saying that he'd gone through King Garadul's entire army, infiltrated the wall behind him, taken out all the cannon crews—by himself!—and then turned the cannons back on the king's army, managing to shoot one of the great wagons loaded with black powder and killing scores if not hundreds. Then he'd escaped an entire furious army, but not alone. No, simple escape wasn't good enough for Ironfist. He'd done all of that to serve as his own distraction—and had then rescued Kip and Karris White Oak, running across the surface of the sea, where frenzied sharks were already feeding, only to return in time to foil an assassination attempt. If there was one man who encompassed all that every one of the gathered young people wanted to be, it was Ironfist.

"Well done," Ironfist said, addressing them. "Well fought, and just as important, well thought. I saw some real cleverness today, and some glimpses of real ability. But I've come today to lay a greater challenge before you than perhaps you can surmount. You're not going to like it. I don't like it, but circumstances demand it. We Blackguards judge circumstances with equanimity. We are unmoved. And we overcome."

Everyone was suddenly on the edge of their seat.

"As you may know by now, the Blackguards were involved in action at the fall of Garriston. They performed heroically, as expected. And our losses were grievous. Bullets don't bypass the brave. The Blackguard has always been an elite force, and our numbers have always been small. We can't sustain huge losses and still achieve our mission. Therefore, instead of your class only graduating the top seven into our ranks, we'll be taking the top fourteen."

The first feeling was one of relief. Fourteen spots! Teia could do that!

There were a few cheers—but they came from the students who thought they could make the top fourteen and knew they couldn't have made the top seven. The boys who had been certain they were going to make it didn't look as pleased.

Ironfist pursed his lips. "Yes," he said. "The Blackguards in previous classes are going to look down on you. I want you to take that on, as a class. I want you to make everyone in your top fourteen as good as the earlier classes' top seven. We have a mission. We need Blackguards to accomplish it. I will still expel anyone who can't handle the mission. I'm expanding Blackguards' remuneration immediately, too. You'll be elites, and you'll be paid as such. If you have friends who are excellent fighters or have the potential to be such, encourage them to join the next class. We'll be running four classes a year from here on, not two. If I'm right, the next few years may see all of us needing trustworthy comrades. Not all of us will make it."

Ironfist took off his ghotra. His head was shaved bald in mourning, and his face was mournful but stern. "Your predecessors have died defending the Seven Satrapies, defending the Prism, defending the

White. Many people will look at you and see children, but I'm asking you to make an adult decision. Are you ready to die, maybe alone, far from home, with no one even knowing what a hero you were? I can't even promise that your lives or your deaths will accomplish victory. All I can promise you is that as long as I draw breath, as long as I lead you, I won't let you be wasted. That's all you get. That, and the brothers and sisters you see around you. If you don't want that, good for you. Go lead a happier, safer life somewhere else. Don't show up tomorrow. Because tomorrow everything gets harder."

He tossed his ghotra on the ground and walked out.

The students watched him go.

A few clapped, but others looked toward Cruxer. He put out his hand, palm down: no, don't clap. And that—with a dozen students deferring to Cruxer, and Cruxer taking that deference and doing the right thing with it—was when Teia realized Cruxer would be the commander of the Blackguard someday.

"It's war," Cruxer said. "The Color Prince has invaded Atash. By now the city of Idoss has probably fallen. And his heresies are spreading. He says the oaths we swear to the Chromeria aren't binding. It's a lie from the pit of hell. Go talk to your sponsors and figure out where your loyalties lie. Don't come back until you know. If you're not back in a week, you're cut." He hesitated. "If that's acceptable, sir?"

Trainer Fisk had held his tongue the whole time, and now the students looked to him. He was, after all, in charge. He nodded.

Cruxer walked through the trainees with all eyes on him. He picked up Ironfist's ghotra reverently and folded it carefully, then walked away.

With silence heavy upon them, the rest of the trainees left, too.

Chapter 37

Gavin followed the Third Eye to a clearing not far into the jungle. There was a fire to fend off the coolness of the evening and cheery lanterns hung from the limbs of a jambu tree, the light showing its ripe, pink fruit. Rugs were spread on the ground. A bowl of wine and a larger bowl of figs and jambu and other fruits sat in the middle of the rug.

The Third Eye sat cross-legged on the rug, the movement exposing her legs to the knee. She gestured to the place opposite, and Gavin sat.

"So how did you come here to Seers Island?" Gavin asked. "How does one gain an eye?" He gave her a wry grin.

She ignored him, turning her face to the heavens, praying, blessing her meal. He tried not to stare at her breasts as she took a deep breath. He glanced over at Karris, who was standing guard in the jungle. She glanced at the Third Eye's breasts, then back to Gavin, nonplussed. You think that was on accident? she asked him with the barest twitch of one eyebrow.

Gavin closed his eyes so as to appear to be praying, too. Some people didn't like to think their Prism was irreligious.

Nice spot you've put me in here, Orholam.

He pretended to finish praying. When he opened his eyes, she was leaning forward—which did distracting things with her low neckline. She said, "I think you'll want to dismiss your...bodyguard? There are things I wish to speak with you about alone."

Gavin turned to Karris, who had of course heard everything the woman had said.

"I'm not leaving," Karris said, "unless those two women with muskets you have stationed in the forest withdraw and I search you for weapons."

The Third Eye looked off into the jungle. She stood, gracefully. Apparently light-blinded by the lanterns, she didn't look the right direction. "Clara, Cezilia, is that you? I told you my life is not in danger. My virtue, perhaps. Please withdraw now." She turned to Karris. "Be my guest," she said.

Briefly, and not roughly, Karris patted her down. She was a professional. Plus, in that dress, there weren't that many places the woman could be hiding a weapon.

Before Karris finished, the Third Eye leaned close and spoke to her, too low for Gavin to hear.

Karris blanched. Started, looked at the Third Eye, looked over at Gavin to see if he'd heard.

"You can't know that," she said. She was trying to speak low enough that Gavin didn't hear, but there was too much emotion for her to keep the reins tight. She shot a look over at Gavin as the Third Eye continued.

Then the Seer finished, and a long moment passed.

"I'll be nearby if you need me, Lord Prism," Karris said stiffly. Then she withdrew.

The Third Eye took her place across from Gavin once more. His eyes were tight, disturbed. Very few people had that kind of effect on Karris.

"Please," she said. "Drink. Eat. You're my guest."

He began, and she joined him, not saying a word. There was goat cheese with the fruit. A woman came with a loaf of flatbread and a bowl of beans and rice and wild pig in a spicy sauce. Following the Third Eye's lead, Gavin tore off chunks of bread and used it to scoop up the mixture. She said nothing, though she studied him intently. His attempts at starting conversation met silence. If he didn't know better, he would have assumed she was deaf.

"What are you doing?" he asked finally.

"I'm waiting," she said.

"Waiting?"

"It's coming, sometime tonight. I thought it would be by now, but clearly..."

"So you really do see the future," Gavin said.

"No," she said.

Gavin raised his hands. "And yet here you are, predicting the future." She raised a finger to object, but Gavin cut her off. "Even if not well."

She smiled. Gleaming white teeth, perfect smile. "Gifts can be curses, can't they, Lord Prism?"

"I suppo—"

"You're beautiful," she said, cutting him off. "Always did like a man with muscles, and the sight of yours has been filling my mind all day. Quite distracting."

"Um, thank you?"

"Are you a swimmer?" she asked, glancing at the breadth of his shoulders.

"Only when I make mistakes skimming. Which isn't often."

Her pupils flared. "I see. You know, that masterful, cocky thing you do makes me want to tie you to my bed and ravish you." Her eyes trailed over him and Gavin knew she was picturing it in her mind.

Gavin swallowed. There's no subtle way to adjust yourself when you're sitting cross-legged. He glanced guiltily over at Karris.

"Exactly," the Third Eye said. "You need her more than she needs you, Prism. She makes you human."

She tilted her head down and closed her eyes. The tattoo-and-luxin yellow eye on her forehead glowed, then she opened her eyes as it continued to pulse like a heartbeat. Then it faded.

"I see outside of time. And if that doesn't make sense to you, it doesn't to me either. Nor is it perfect, how I see. I'm not Orholam. I still have my own desires and prejudices that can color what I see or how I interpret what I see—how I put into words those visions that come before my eye. Tell me, Prism, do you think mercy is weakness?"

"No."

"Wrong question; your pardon. What I meant was, do you think justice is better, or mercy?"

"It depends."

"Who decides?" she asked.

"I do."

"Are pity and mercy the same?" she asked.

"No."

"What's the difference?"

"I don't believe in pity."

"Liar." She grinned.

"Excuse me?" Gavin said.

"There are two kinds of people who make excellent liars: monsters with no conscience, and those who become excellent liars from practice and necessity because they're deeply ashamed. I don't think you're a monster, Lord Prism. You've played beautifully. Your mask is compelling, gorgeous, alluring. It makes me want to get naked and subdue you with pleasure until you're too exhausted to maintain that façade and I can rip it off and show you what's underneath. Because I already know, and I judge that man beneath your mask much less harshly than you do."

Fortune-teller tripe. Albeit tripe with a fine sexual edge to it.

"Are you sure you're not trying to seduce me?" Gavin asked lightly.

"Ah, Prism, you always do like to cut corners, don't you? It's a strength, I suppose. Remember it. But then, you remember most everything, don't you?"

He was confused.

She smiled. "What I'm sure of is that bedding you would be a disaster for you and for Karris and for the Seven Satrapies. I'm also pretty sure it would be really, really good for me. Both in the moment and in the long run. Which is why I'm doing everything I can to be completely over the top and disgust you with my wanton ways. If I make you uninterested, then that disaster won't be an option anymore."

He laughed—and could tell she wasn't joking. She was acting as sex-starved as he felt, and something about her relentlessly frank style convinced him that she would be the best he'd ever had. He said, "The 'wanton ways' gambit is having an effect, but perhaps not the one you'd planned." Orholam's royal blue balls, Karris wasn't ten paces away. Gavin was going to die.

The Third Eye stared up at the sky and scowled. "I really thought it would start by now, hmm. What do you think is the worst decision you ever made in your life, Lord Prism?"

That was easy. Not killing his brother. "I had pity once."

"You're wrong. You didn't spare Gavin out of pity. And you wouldn't do any differently than you did if you could do it again."

She said it so matter-of-factly that he almost missed it. And then it yanked him up short, like a dog catching scent of a rabbit and charging heedless—right until he got to the end of his chain. She'd said sparing *Gavin*. She knew both that he wasn't that Gavin and that he had spared his brother. The air got dense, hard to breathe. Gavin's chest tightened.

"What, did you think I was a charlatan? Adjust to the new reality, Dazen, and move on to the real point."

There was no denial. No point. She hadn't ventured it as a guess, or a trap, and if he made her repeat it, Karris might hear. Gavin's heart was thundering. He swallowed, took some wine, swallowed again.

"My worst choice was not telling her." Gavin was in a fog, a fugue. He didn't want to say Karris's name. They were far enough away that their voices should be a murmur to her, but hearing one's own name tended to pique the ears.

"No, not that either. If you'd told her the truth when she was younger, she'd have exposed you. What you did wasn't kind, or perhaps fair, but it was wise, and I'd advise you not to apologize for what you did when the time comes. Karris is better at adjusting to hard realities than she is at forgiving. It's a character flaw."

It was true. Deeply true. Telling Karris, "I was doing my duty" would probably work better than, "I'm so sorry." She understood duty, cared about it. And yet something in Gavin bristled, wanted to defend Karris.

"So, what was it then?" Gavin asked.

"I don't know," she said. "I don't see everything. I just know what it wasn't. I know that you've been asking the wrong questions, so you've had no hope of getting the right answers. So my part is done, sadly with no cries of passion or clawing of your back. Aside from two things. First, your people may stay. They will, I'm fairly certain, destroy our way of life. But perhaps it will one day turn into something better. I have little hope of that, but I'm too close to see this clearly, and I know that pushing fifty thousand starving people into the sea is not what Orholam would ask of me, regardless of what they will do to us once they are no longer starving."

"And second?" Gavin asked. It was a huge victory. She was giving him everything he wanted, but you don't laud victories, you consolidate them and press forward.

"And second, you've lost control of blue, and your... *counterpart* has broken out of his blue prison. I'd advise you to do something about it, because without a Prism, strange things start happening. First, they're innocuous, weird little things. But they get worse." She seemed to retreat into herself.

Gavin felt naked. Not in a good way. The news about his brother— if it was true—was cataclysmic. Not just a terrible shock, and not just terrible news, but too coincidental. Gavin had woven alarums into the drafting, of course, but they were alarums to notify someone in his own room in the tower: Marissia when he was gone. There was no way he should have been aware, no matter how dimly or on how visceral a level, that Dazen had broken out.

He had sunk a huge amount of his will into that prison, in ways long forbidden, so maybe he'd felt that breaking of his will dimly over the leagues. But huge talent though he was, the Chromeria was halfway across the sea.

Perhaps his losing blue had weakened the prison or broken it. There need be no coincidence. The one could have caused the other—but he didn't know which way that causation flowed. Gavin felt like he was burrowing into the roots of a mountain, and the deeper he went, the faster he moved forward, the sooner the entire thing was going to come down on top of him.

But he didn't know any way out.

Orholam, his brother was out of the blue? Did Marissia even remember how to switch over the chutes? Maybe Dazen would starve to death. No...no, he'd shown her, years and years ago, how to do it, against just this eventuality. She had an excellent memory. She'd do it right.

Nonetheless, he had to get back. And going back meant heading right into the middle of everything that threatened him most.

"Aha!" The Third Eye sniffed. "Here it is."

Scrunching his forehead, Gavin glanced over at her. Noticed her nipples—dammit, got bigger things to worry about here, Gavin! She was leaning back, looking up again, this time not in prayer, though it again outlined her cold-stiffened nipples clearly against the fabric of her dress. He sniffed to see what she was talking about.

Smelled nothing. Sniffed again, and caught something very faint.

Something prickled on his skin, the lightest of touches. He looked over at the Third Eye.

She was grinning like a little girl. He didn't understand. Then something touched his arm. He brought it close, but it melted before he could get a look at it. Snow?

It was cool tonight, but it wasn't cold enough for snow. Not even close. He could smell it now—the familiar mineral, chalky odor. Blue luxin. More hit his upturned face, his arms. It was snowing.

"Blue delights in order," the Third Eye said. "I know you can't see it, but every flake is blue. Utterly beautiful, Lord Prism. I've never seen so stunning a harbinger of doom."

Gavin's heart dropped. Other than in the mountains of Paria and Tyrea, most of the Seven Satrapies went years without seeing snow. Gavin caught a flake on his sleeve, squinted at it. It looked like a snowflake. The blue luxin, free of his control, was running amok— but for blue, running amok meant randomly imposing order. Like organizing the crystals of a snowflake. It was a tenuous order; the unnatural snow was melting almost immediately.

"If it starts with this, what will it do next?" Gavin asked.

"Something worse," the Seer said. "And it's already doing it. We're simply so far away that this is all that's reaching us."

"The bane," Gavin whispered.

She nodded.

"Can you tell me where it is?"

"It's *moving*, and I see outside of time."

"So?"

"If something stays in one place, it doesn't matter *when* I see it. But if something moves, finding it inside a particular time is problematic."

"Which isn't the same as impossible," Gavin said, his heart leaping. If he could save himself the trip to Paria to see the Nuqaba, he could avoid all sorts of problems.

She scowled. "No, it's not."

Any time the Prism showed up in a major city, there were a thousand things that could only be done by him—not least endless rituals. The best he was ever able to get away with was doing one ritual for each color. And one of those would now expose him. He might be able to bluff his way past it, if he were there for only a week or two to find out what he needed, but the less he had to rely on his luck, the better. And if she could just tell him what he needed to know...

She looked over at him, and it obviously didn't take a Seer for her to know what he was going to ask her next. She sighed. "I don't see everything all the time all at once, Lord Prism. And I need light. I'll look for it for you tomorrow." She raised a finger. "I don't promise that I'll tell you all of what I see. I don't promise that knowing won't cost you something."

"Aha, so *now* comes the bargaining. You're going to save me at least two weeks and lots of awkward conversations with a powerful woman I once outmaneuvered. What's it going to cost me?" He was trying to set the floor low. The Third Eye would be saving him a whole lot more than that. And, being who she was, she could probably find that out, if she really cared to take the time to look. But as she'd said, she was human, and there was a lot of history and future for her to dig through.

But she shook her head. "I didn't mean that kind of cost. My help will be a gift. You don't need to earn it. But though truth is a gift, it's not always one people thank you for."

"Ah. That kind of cost," Gavin said, suddenly grim.

"Does the man who 'killed his brother' expect the truth to be easy?"

Killed my brother. If only. But of course, she knew that. She knew what it was costing him to maintain that deception and why he'd done it and what the truth would cost the world if it came out. She must also know the price of truth through her own gift in a thousand ways that Gavin would never know.

The Third Eye looked over at him, compassion in her eyes, and suddenly Gavin saw that she was a woman of tremendous depth. A leader in her own right. A woman who understood what Gavin was doing, why, and what he faced. He found her tremendously appealing. If his damn stubborn heart hadn't already been claimed, he could have fallen for her. She knew it, too. She hadn't been lying earlier: she really had been trying to make the attraction purely sexual—so that there wasn't the danger of something deeper.

As crystalline flurries spun around them, flecks of order spun in chaos, Gavin peered into the night as if he could unravel its mysteries. "So, you and me, disaster, huh?"

She smiled, full red lips, perfect teeth. Nodded, met his gaze. A remorseful twitch touched the corner of her mouth. "Utter." She gazed at him appreciatively, but as if saying farewell to the prospect of bedding him. "But I do have one prophecy for you already, Lord Prism, in the style you so love: Get there before noon. Three hours east, two and a half hours north."

Sounded simple enough. He did like that. And then he realized that she hadn't told him north and east from where. He said, "That's only going to be helpful in retrospect, isn't it?"

She grinned cryptically.

"You enjoy this, don't you?" he asked.

"Immensely."

"I haven't really had much use for prophecy," Gavin said.

"I know," she said. "It was one of the first things I saw about you. What happened?"

"Happened? I think I always thought it was—oh, no, there was something. When I was a boy and my brother stopped playing with me, I'd find these prophecies in old books, and I'd dream that I could decipher them. There was this one: how'd it go?"

He was asking himself, but the Third Eye said quietly,

> "Of red cunning, the youngest son,
> Will cleave father and father and father and son."

"How'd you...?" he asked.

"I see that line burning in bitter fire over your head, Lord Prism. What did you take it to mean?"

"The youngest son of red cunning—the youngest son of the red

Guile—the youngest son of the Guile who becomes the Red. So Andross Guile's youngest son. It was a prophecy about my little brother Sevastian."

"And then he died. Murdered."

"By a blue wight. He was everything that is good about my family with none of the bad. If he were alive, everything would be different."

He shook it off. "Your prophecies aren't like that. I mean, maddeningly vague. I mean, except for this last one." He grinned. "Why is that?"

She touched her third eye thoughtfully. "We're human, Gavin. My gift didn't come with a list of rules. I'm muddling through. I'm making it up as I go. But I feel the same temptations I'm sure all my predecessors have felt: to be important, to help those I love and harm those I hate, to be held as almost a god, to guide and be loved—or to say hell with it, I'm not responsible for this damned thing, and just spew everything I see. I hold my tongue when I'm not sure. I think others have spoken more, but more cryptically, hoping that they wouldn't be held responsible if things went wrong. And then, of course, there have been frauds: Seers who were not Seers at all."

"Can you tell me if that prophecy was a fraud?"

"I have no idea where to even start looking."

"You said you saw it in bitter fire over my head," Gavin said. "How about there?"

"I saw the words for a moment, yes. That doesn't mean they're true."

"You're honest to a fault, aren't you?" Gavin said.

"I hope not," she said. She smirked, a devious, playful twist on her full lips.

Gavin wanted to tear her clothes off.

He looked away and cleared his throat. "My lady, good night, and ahem, now that we've decided not to make a most delightful mistake together, I hope together we make our next meeting less...strained." He stood and brushed nonexistent crumbs off his lap pointedly. He grinned. But he wanted her agreement in this. He'd made mistakes that he knew were mistakes before.

She offered her hand and allowed him to help her stand. She stretched as if tired, but quite obviously to give him a chance to admire her while she looked away. He could tell what she was doing, and yet he admired her all the same. She gave a small, naughty smile. "You know," she said, "I'm actually really quite modest most of the time."

No, actually, I don't know that. He merely cocked a dubious eyebrow, quickly smoothed it away, and like a gentleman politely lying said, "Of course you are."

She laughed. "That you're impossible makes you somehow even more fun to play with," she said.

"When most people flirt with disaster, it's a figure of speech," Gavin said.

"Dangerous toys are the best toys. I pray you sleep well, Lord Prism."

Well, there was a prayer they both knew wasn't going to be answered.

Chapter 38

"The old gods weren't worshipped because the people of the Seven Satrapies were ignorant fools," Zymun told Liv. They were walking together to the outskirts of Garriston, heading through the Hag's Gate to the plain between the old wall and Brightwater Wall, where most of the drafters were camped. "The old gods were worshipped because they were real."

"Go on," Liv said, not doing a great job keeping her skepticism back.

A brief look of fury shot across Zymun's face, quickly smoothed away. He looked at her intensely. Who's the tutor here?

Liv blushed. Her instant reaction had been an artifact of her old beliefs. She'd always heard that the old gods were figments of the primitive imaginations of the peoples who lived around the Cerulean Sea before Lucidonius came. But if the Chromeria lied about other things, then that could be a lie as well. She cleared her throat. "I mean, go on."

"I think the peoples of the Seven Satrapies knew it, too. From nowhere, it seems, little statues of the gods have resurfaced. Hidden in attics, in cellars, in secret family shrines in the woods. Keep your eyes open as you walk the camp, you'll see little signs. Soon, there will be priesthoods reestablished, worship will become public. You look skeptical."

"I'm sorry, but, the old gods? Like Atirat and Anat and Dagnu?"
Again, a flash of irritation, and Liv felt stupid. But he spoke with kindness. "You know how you feel when you draft superviolet?"
"Of course. Alien, separated from emotion, and honestly a little proud of how clearly I see things."
"That isn't you," Zymun said.
"I'm not a terribly conceited person, I'll agree," Liv said. But you don't know me, so how would you know?
"I don't mean that isn't the 'real you.' I mean, that isn't you."
"Pardon?"
"Those aren't *your* feelings. Those aren't your perceptions. Indeed, those aren't your abilities. Ferrilux is invisible. He is behind many of man's greatest achievements, but he doesn't think much of most men. He is distant and disdainful, and he has chosen to share his powers with you."
The idea seemed repugnant to Liv. "There's an invisible man helping me draft? This is what the Color Prince believes? My drafting's mine."
Zymun's voice was cold, affect flat. "So you chose your colors? Superviolet, for an outsider, for the Tyrean girl who could never be part of the Chromeria, but who secretly despised the girls who would never let her join their petty circles. Yellow, for a clear thinker who couldn't decide whether or not to engage with all she saw around her. Hmm, sounds very, what's the word? Serendipitous."
"You're talking like a tenpenny soothsayer. If I'd been a sub-red, you'd say, oh, sub-red, for the girl so furious at being made an outsider. Or blue, oh, you envied the girls who did belong. Garbage." Liv folded her hands, took a breath, and squeezed her fingers against each other. "I mean...your pardon, my lord, but I'm not convinced. I know the Chromeria taught lies, but that doesn't mean I'm going to accept the first counterargument that comes along."
Zymun didn't seem to take it personally. "You're cute when you're mad. And when you do that with your arms, it shows off your bosom nicely."
Liv looked down and dropped her clenched hands like she'd been burned. "Excuse me?!" She stopped walking and he stopped, too, facing her. She almost slapped his silly face. "That is the most inappropriate thing anyone has ever said to me. And I expect your apology right this instant!"

"Inappropriate? Why? Who says? You're beautiful. I told you so. Who gets to decide that I can't tell you what I think? I'd tell you, but you're smart enough to already know. You've joined the Free, Aliviana. We decide for ourselves, and there's power in that. The Chromeria wants you to be modest. Why? If Orholam existed, why would he care how tight your dress is or who comes to your bed? Should have bigger problems to tackle, you'd think, wouldn't you?"

"Well..." But Liv didn't have anything to follow that monosyllable.

"The Chromeria teaches you to hate the very things about yourself that make you strong. You're beautiful. Use that. Use it however you wish. Don't you see? You *choose*. Now, you could choose to become a prostitute—no, don't take offense, dammit, it's a hypothetical! You could do very well, no doubt, and it wouldn't be wrong because Orholam says it's wrong: it's not wrong at all. It's just stupid. It's a poor use of all your gifts, and it limits your other choices, at least until the world changes. So it's a bad choice, but not a wrong one. That's how we draft, too. Some people break the halo before they're ready, choosing to share their body permanently before they can survive the union with their minds intact. They use their choice in a way that takes away their choice, like choosing suicide. It's a stupid action and it demeans them as moral agents. What we have here—the Free— what we offer, is a free-for-all. But it's not chaos. Free choices, freely made, but still with consequences. You choose to join the army, you have to obey orders until your time of service is ended. This is a harder world than what you left, Liv. Freedom is hard. If you don't want me to compliment you because someone told you that you shouldn't be proud of your beautiful curves, your full lips, your radiant skin, the graceful lines of your neck, your bright eyes, that's ridiculous. To hell with them. If you don't want to bed me because you don't like me, that's altogether different." He was terribly smart, wasn't he? And supremely willful. Powerful.

She pushed down a sudden surge of admiration, and a deep and silly pleasure at his outrageous flattery. She'd never been called beautiful at the Chromeria. Tyreans couldn't be beautiful, couldn't be fashionable, not after the False Prism's War. "You're used to getting your way, aren't you?" she asked.

"Hazard of being handsome and brilliant."

She sniffed. "So is getting punched in the nose."

He raised his hands and stepped back. "I didn't say I was brave, too." He offered her his arm, and she took it, not able to stop a grin from sneaking through her defenses. "Mm. Oh, just thought of something. Who was the Color Prince? Before he got burned?"

"Koios White Oak. Why?"

"Just curious." Karris's *brother*?

"No secret. What you were is less important to us than what you are, and what you will become. Now, you get to work on drafting. You have a lot to unlearn, and more to learn."

"I'm still not going to bed with you," she said.

"We'll work on that," he said with a wink and a big grin.

And with that, Liv's education began.

Chapter 39

When Kip shuffled out of the library at midnight, Ironfist was waiting for him at the lift. The huge commander said nothing, but gestured to him.

Kip was instantly alert. Hungry, but alert. He was surprised to see that Adrasteia was with the commander. They stepped into the lift together, and Commander Ironfist pushed a key into a lock, and took them to a lower level in the Chromeria than Kip had ever been to. He looked at Teia. She looked back, shrugged.

The commander poked his head into a dark hallway. He walked through the darkness. Kip opened his eyes wide, wider, to the sub-red spectrum. Ironfist radiated enough heat, his whole body gray, armpits and groin lighter, and his bare, uncovered head the brightest of all. He went down the hall.

"Kip," Teia said. Her voice was tight. He couldn't quite read her expression: sub-red light was inexact and Kip wasn't practiced with it, but he could tell she was nervous. Surely not scared of the dark. Not Teia.

But of course she was. Almost all drafters were afraid of the dark—even lots of sub-reds were. Light was Orholam's gift; darkness was akin to evil; blindness was powerlessness. Her hands were out, and Kip took one. He led her down the hall. Ironfist didn't slow.

Then Kip realized he was holding hands with Teia, and abruptly felt awkward. He sort of spasmed. She couldn't miss it.

"Uhm," he said. "Uh." He put her hand on his arm instead.

Oh, like a lord leading his lady to a dinner party. Much better. Moron!

Kip cleared his throat, but then thought that anything he said would be equally stupid. He scowled and shot a look at her.

She was smirking.

Though of course it was dark so she didn't know he could *see* her smirking, he still wanted to die.

She said, "I'm... I'm better now." Her tongue darted out to moisten her lips, an odd, hot point in the cool, dark hall. "I... have some trouble relaxing my eyes sometimes."

Oh, that was right. She could see sub-red. Her color was down farther on the spectrum that way. She would have gotten it on her own. She took her arm back, awkwardly.

Kip squared his shoulders, put his head down, and followed Ironfist down the halls. It was only a couple of turns before Ironfist took them into a room. He manipulated some mechanism Kip probably wouldn't have understood even if he'd been able to see it in visible light, and the ceiling began glowing, a warm radiant soft white.

It was a training room, but not like any Kip had ever seen.

Ironfist began rummaging in a corner while Kip and Teia looked around. There were beams for practicing balance, bars for doing pull-ups, punching dummies coated with luxin that would light up in various zones to train quickness, punching bags of sawdust and leather, wooden blocking trees, a pile of cushioned body armor for sparring, terry cloths, targets, and padded weapons of every sort.

"This is the Prism's training room. He allows us to share it," Ironfist said. He had long strips of cloth in each hand. "Give me your hands, Kip. Straight as you can, and firm."

Kip gave him his hands, and Ironfist began wrapping a strip of cloth around his wrist.

"It's time for you two to learn something," Ironfist said.

"What's that, sir?" Adrasteia asked.

"There are three scrubs I absolutely can't let fail."

"Who?" she asked.

"Kip, because his father asked me not to."

Teia looked over at him, obviously not happy with the injustice of that. Kip blushed, then scowled.

Ironfist continued: "Cruxer, because he's got the potential to be the best Blackguard in a generation."

"How would he fail out? He's the best of us by far," Teia said.

"Only through bad luck. But it could happen. Could, but I won't let it. And the third is you, Teia."

"Me?" she asked. She sounded genuinely shocked.

"Your color," Commander Ironfist said. "You can see through cloth, which means you can see concealed weapons. In a normal year, I could take you even if you had no legs. Your peers would be angry, but in the fullness of time they'd realize you're worth any five of them, even if you couldn't fight at all. I can't do that, not this year. If I pass you on and you're terrible, it'll be another blow to the Blackguards' confidence. It's important that we know we're elite. If I'm seen adding obvious mediocrities to our ranks, it hurts everyone. Thus, a bastard and an outer-spectrum girl have to look as good as everyone else. Teia, you've been hiding how good you are, but without drafting, you'll have to get lucky to make it at your current skill level, and Kip's a year behind the top students. So you both get extra practice, and less sleep."

He finished wrapping Kip's hands, scowling and being careful with the left, then helped Kip pull gloves on.

Under Ironfist's watchful eye, Kip started punching one of the sawdust bags. They'd trained punching forms in their lines during practice, but full contact was different.

"Not so hard, not yet," Ironfist said.

Kip got back to hitting the bag, quick but not hard. It hurt his left hand. But mostly keeping his left in a fist wasn't hard. It was straightening it that sent tears down his face. Ironfist set Teia to doing pushups, with claps in between. Teia was tiny, so she didn't have that much body to throw into the air, but even then she quickly tired. Ironfist had her continue doing it from her knees.

After they got going, Ironfist wrapped his own hands and stepped up to the bag next to Kip's and started working out himself.

Kip's hands hurt, but after ten minutes or so, they simply felt warm. He wondered if they were bleeding under the wrappings. Ironfist simply let him know that he could start hitting harder. He thought about Liv. He thought about his mother. He thought about the Prism.

And somehow, though his thoughts took him nowhere and he discovered nothing new, he felt better after beating the hell out of an inanimate object. But Ironfist kept going, and going. Kip followed. After an hour, Kip was the walking dead. Ironfist threw him a towel and said, "Kip, go to the lift. We'll be along in a minute."

Kip left. The temptation to eavesdrop was strong, but the idea of facing Ironfist's wrath was daunting. Plus, it just seemed disrespectful. He walked toward the lift, wiping sweat away with the towel.

He was hungry. It seemed like he was always hungry here. The glims, or second-year, and above students had lounges that were reputed to serve food for longer hours—or for the gleams and beams, the third- and fourth-year students, all day and night. But first-year students weren't allowed. You had to earn everything here, from library access to food.

Kip coughed, and in his sub-red vision the spray shot out in a cloud of little white and red dots.

He raised his hand, and he was in Garriston, covered in green luxin, the smell of gunpowder and blood and luxin and sweat and fear heavy in his nostrils. He held up his hand and shot out bullets at the soldiers massed around him. A man's cheek was blown off, head jerking around and then twisting back toward Kip, flinging teeth and blood droplets, the man staggering into him.

Kip put his hand on the man's forehead, as if blessing him. And shot a bullet into his brain, gore blasting back into his open palm.

He was pure will, and those who opposed him were nothing but chaff on a breeze blown about a titan's knees.

And then he was back, blinking, shivering.

It was like all this was so *thin*, so fragile. A lie. Kip was worrying about passing some test? About what fifteen-year-old children thought about him? Death was huge, towering, indomitable, victorious everywhere. One tiny lead ball away. A sliver of luxin, and all this was exposed as frippery and folly.

He barely had time to dab away the tears from his eyes—he wasn't crying, why were there tears?—before Ironfist and Teia came down the hall.

Ironfist glanced at Kip but said nothing. They got on the lift. Kip wanted to ask him something, but he couldn't even put it into words. How did Ironfist do it? How did he kill people, and come back, still himself? How did he straddle the worlds? Ironfist was a rock, unperturbed, solid, an island in a sea of madness.

Commander Ironfist ran his hand over his shaven, bare head. His voice came out low, gravelly. "While my mother bled out her life from that assassin's blade, I held her, Kip. I prayed. Prayed as I never had before, or since. Orholam didn't hear me. I believed I wasn't worthy of his gaze, that he sees only the good and great." His face twisted for a half second in some emotion, quickly suppressed. Grief? Desolation? But his voice was level. "Kip, the world doesn't explain itself. You go on."

"How?" Kip's voice sounded small and hollow in his own ears.

"You just do."

Kip looked at the commander. That was it? The answer was no answer? He felt his heart drop.

Teia looked from one to the other, mystified, but said nothing, asked nothing. Kip wished he could thank her for that.

The lift came to a stop at their floor.

Ironfist handed Teia the key. His voice was gruff, but not yet back to its old timbre. "Every night. I won't always be able to make it, but I'll be there as often as I can. Kip, I've heard you've been barred from practicum, and Teia, you need to work on your abilities, too, even though I can't help you much with your type of drafting. Tomorrow you both start practicing magic."

"Yes, sir."

Kip and Adrasteia went their separate ways, not sure what to say to each other. Kip washed up and went to bed. His body ached; his mind was numb, crying out for sleep, but every time he closed his eyes he saw blood, brains, the bullet blessing.

Dawn was a relief of the only kind he now knew: a move from one kind of fight to another. He got up to fill another day. If he was busy enough, he wouldn't have time to think.

Chapter 40

"She's a beautiful woman," Karris said.

Gavin said nothing. They were hiking back through the jungle to their own camp. This was the first thing Karris had said since exclaiming over the blue snow—which Gavin had claimed to know nothing about.

"She likes you," Karris said.

Gavin said nothing.

"You can spend the night with her, you know," Karris said.

Now she was starting to infuriate him.

"You've been edgy," Karris said. "Maybe it'll help calm you down if you go get it out of your system."

Gavin stopped. "You're saying this to me. Really. You?"

Karris gave a tiny shrug. "What I asked earlier . . . it wasn't fair. I've got no claim on you. You and I don't have anything that should keep you from . . . cavorting as you please. You're the Prism, there ought to be some benefits, right?"

"Please don't say stupid things to me, Karris." Cavorting?

"I was just—"

"I've made my decision." And it's you.

"And I'm telling you—"

"Shut *the fuck* up."

Usually, that would have made her explode. This time, she said nothing. They walked in silence. Made camp in silence. Slept in silence.

Somehow, he did sleep, but he dreamed of colored hells and his brothers. The dread inside him kept that sleep from leaving him rested. By the time Karris woke him for his watch, hours before dawn, the snow was gone. While Karris slept, Gavin sat up. For some reason, he was haunted by his dead little brother Sevastian. Little Sevastian, the good-hearted brother. The peacemaker between his constantly feuding older siblings.

Who would Sevastian have sided with in the Prisms' War?

In this insane world where Gavin was supposed to have some sort of holy link directly to a deity who didn't exist or didn't care, instead, he cared only about what his dead little brother would have thought of him. Who would you have been, Sevastian? Could I have killed Gavin and then handed over the reins to you and the world now know peace? What sort of world would this be, if that damned wight hadn't murdered you?

A blue wight, too. What did that mean? The very color Gavin had lost control of now was the color that had murdered Sevastian. It was the very color that Dazen had broken out of. Coincidence?

Yes, Gavin, that's what a coincidence *is*.

The sun rose, but there was only darkness in Gavin's heart.

Chapter 41

Dazen Guile stared at the dead man in the wall of the green prison. He and the dead man were picking scabs from their knees. They'd been in the green hell for days, a week? Surely not two weeks yet. They'd been quietly falling unconscious for unknown periods, quietly licking water off the wall, quietly starving. Maybe two weeks, from the scabs.

At some point before falling unconscious, he'd drafted tiny slivers of green. Whatever else it was, luxin was clean. Dazen had pushed luxin out—not out of his palms or under his fingernails, but out of his cuts. First he'd done the cuts on his hands and knees, then finally the inflamed, infected cut on his chest. The pain had been horrific. Yellow pus had preceded the luxin. When he woke, he'd licked the wall for moisture for an hour, then did it again, and passed out again. After a third time, only plasma and blood leaked from the wound.

Eventually, the fever had passed, leaving him passionless, empty, but finally aware again. Somewhat himself. A weaker self.

Like the blue prison, this green one was shaped like a squashed ball, a narrow chute above, a trickle of water down one wall, and a narrow drain below for the water and his waste.

His jailer—his brother—apparently hadn't yet figured out that Dazen had broken out of the blue prison. There must surely be some advantage to that fact, but Dazen couldn't figure out what it was. All he knew was that since he'd come to this prison, there had been no bread. He hated that thick, lumpy, coarse, dense bread—but now he would have begged, would have licked broken glass for it.

Perhaps his brother did know. Perhaps this was punishment.

Nonetheless, Gavin hadn't had the guts to starve him to death before, and he'd had sixteen years to do that, so Dazen didn't think Gavin would starve him now. At least not on purpose.

He felt weak, and that weakness was temptation. He hadn't drafted green since the fever passed, and green was strength, wildness.

Green had doubtless saved him, but it was death now. Because it was strength, and strength would be addictive here. Every time he drafted a tiny sip, he would want to draft more. And green was irrationality, wildness. Wildness in a cage meant insanity, suicide.

I'm close enough to that as is.

He started building the towers of suppositions again. That was the beauty of years spent drafting blue. It ordered your thoughts, smothered passion.

Blue still hated the illogic of how he thought of his brother as Gavin and himself as Dazen, but he'd held firm to that decision. Gavin was a loser. Gavin had lost the war, Gavin had let himself be imprisoned. Dazen had stolen Gavin's identity, so let him have it. "Gavin" was the dead man in the wall now, he the prisoner, he was Dazen now. He was a new man, and as Dazen, he would escape and he would win back all that should be his.

It was a touch of black madness, he knew. But perhaps a bit of madness is the only way to stay sane alone in a dungeon for sixteen years.

Recenter, Dazen. Dazed. Dozed. Dozen. Doozie. Double. Doubt. Certainty. T's. Bifurcations. Intersections. Directions. Direct. Deceased. Dead. Dozing. Dazed. Dazen.

He expelled a long, slow breath. Glared at the dead man, who glared back, defiant.

"I'd tell you to go to hell, but—" he told the dead man.

"I've heard that one before," the dead man replied. "Remember?"

Dazen grumbled into his beard. He held out his right hand. Either Gavin knows I'm in the next prison, or he doesn't.

No, back up.

Either Gavin had put into place a system that would tell him when I moved from one prison to another, or he hadn't.

If he'd gone to the trouble of making more than one prison, he'd have put a system into place to know when I went from one to the other.

Either his alarm worked, or it didn't work.

I'm betting it worked. Nothing Gavin has done has failed so far.

So if the alarm worked, it showed that I've come here.

If it showed I've come here, either Gavin hasn't seen the notice or he has.

But I've already established that he doesn't have the guts to starve me.

So maybe he hasn't seen that I'm here.

Which leaves another question: what does Gavin do when he travels? Either he never travels, or he's set up a system to get me fed when he does. There's no way he'd let himself be chained as much as I am, so he's set up a system.

Either he leaves someone else in charge of feeding me, or he has an automated system. Automated systems can easily break, and Gavin wouldn't want to kill me accidentally. But people can't be trusted. Tough choice.

Meh, Gavin believed in people. It was always one of his weaknesses. It was why Gavin had been able to foil his plan to escape with Karris.

That "Gavin" stuck in his blue brain irritated him. Made it hard to think about the time before the prison. Regardless, his brother's trust was why his brother's elopement with Karris had failed. Either the new Gavin had learned not to trust people from that failure or he hadn't. Hmm. Gavin had been successful in taking Gavin's place as Prism, which he couldn't possibly do on his own. So Gavin hadn't learned not to trust. So Gavin did trust *someone*.

So there *was* someone up there, who had either seen or not seen the warning that Dazen had moved from one prison to another. Either that someone was punctilious in fulfilling their duties or not. Gavin wouldn't have trusted someone who wasn't careful. So that someone was careful. Either that someone knew what the warning meant, and what he was supposed to do when he saw it, or he didn't.

Or...back up. Either that someone was a woman or a man. Not that it mattered, but somehow the thought of some woman running around panicking because there was a blinking green luxin light and she didn't know what to do about it pleased the prisoner immensely. He hoped she was a proud woman. How he missed humbling proud women.

Tangent, Dazen. And a tangent that stirred his lust. He couldn't afford lust, not here, not now. He had once loved to draft green while bedding a woman, loved the wildness, the intensity. But starvation and blue had blunted his carnal desires, and green was madness. And madness was death. So...

Gavin wouldn't have instructed for his brother to be starved to death, so eventually the woman up there would either do the right thing or the wrong. Or many wrong things in a row, looking for the right thing.

To do the right thing, she would have to either put bread in a different chute or manipulate the original chute so that it aimed toward Dazen's new cell. First, of course, she'd have to dye the bread green.

But would she know to dye it green?

She would only know to dye it green if Gavin had told her to do so. Maybe she was new. Maybe Gavin had kept her in the dark, not wanting to give away any details about the prison below, not wanting to stoke the woman's curiosity any more than necessary.

That was it. That was why it had been a week without food.

Gavin hadn't left her adequate instructions. She would know that there was food going down to someone. She would get desperate.

Either Gavin would come back before she did something wrong, or he wouldn't.

For the first time in perhaps years, a smile lit Dazen's features. All he had to do was wait. He would either wait until he died or he would wait until she made a mistake that led to his freedom.

Waiting was hell, but it was a hell he was comfortable in. He talked with the dead man to pass the hours. The dead man mocked him, and he mocked the dead man. It wasn't pleasant, but it was diverting. He could hardly wait until he broke out and left the dead man down here to die.

Days passed. Any of his suppositions could be wrong. Gavin might have trusted a woman to watch the prison who had reason to hate Dazen. She might be willfully murdering him, even though she knew exactly what to do. You never knew with women. Or there could be an alarm, but it had broken. How often would his brother check such things, anyway? Maybe after sixteen years he'd gotten careless. Maybe he inspected it every year, but the year had only recently expired, and he hadn't come yet. Despair set in. He had to try something.

Almost without willing it, he drafted green. It was warmth on a cold night. It was food to the starving. It was a shot of straight liquor that instead of warming his belly went from his eyes to every extremity, washing him clean of weakness and paralysis.

Not too much. Not too much! He cut off the flow before it overwhelmed. But already, looking at the walls made him terribly claustrophobic. His fingers twisted into claws and he found himself clawing at the green luxin wall.

Stop stop stop! He flung the excess luxin from his fingers. The strength, he knew, was only a veneer of strength. His body was horridly weak. He would pay for anything rash he did. And green was stupidly rash. He wanted to charge the far wall and break through it. If he gave in to that impulse, he'd knock himself unconscious, probably die.

What had he even drafted green for? He wasn't going to punch a hole in the green luxin wall with green luxin. His brother wasn't that stupid.

Orholam, his hunger! He shot a tendril of green luxin up the food chute, farther, farther. He pushed around a corner—this chute was shaped differently than the blue. Of course it was, it had to direct the bread, what, twenty, thirty paces farther away? He tried to hold his patience, but Orholam, there was food there. He needed it! There was freedom somewhere up there.

He pushed forward, slowly, but not nearly as slowly as the blue would counsel. He didn't feel the superviolet until it snapped.

Something swung sharply shut across the green arm he'd pushed so far, snapped it, snapped his will with it. He lost consciousness.

The next day—if day it was—he heard the grinding of gears in the chute. He sat up, expectant. Was it his brother, come to gloat, or food to save him?

His assumptions had been wrong. Either his brother did want to kill him, or the alarm had failed, or...he couldn't reconstruct the tower now. Not without fresh blue. He was stupid. He was an animal. He was wasted, thin. He was broken. If it wasn't bread, he was going to draft green. So it would be suicide. So what? What was so good about living, anyway?

Something rattled down the chute.

He waited, waited.

A loaf of bread shot out of the chute, and he caught it. He caught it and almost didn't believe. Though all the light in the cell was green, and blue lit only by green made for incredibly difficult drafting, in his hand was chromatic salvation. In a hell of green, the bread was blue. It was blue *enough*.

Chapter 42

Adrasteia had been summoned. Her mistress herself, Lucretia Verangheti, had ordered her to this dingy home on the far south side of Big Jasper, in the shadow of the walls. Not a pleasant neighborhood.

A pale, grumbling man opened the door and showed Adrasteia to a nook. He brought tea. Only one cup. Didn't put it in front of her. A woman Adrasteia didn't recognize came in ten minutes later. She was young and Ruthgari, with the vanishingly rare true blonde hair and blue eyes. It would have made her an exotic beauty if she didn't also have such a long, horsey face. She was dressed in a casual dress, well cut, and she wore only a few jewels. Her hair was long and gorgeous, but bound up in a practical bun right now. In all things, she looked like an extremely wealthy lady taking her ease in her own home. She sat. Sipped the tea.

"This isn't hot, Gaeros," she said.

The man apologized profusely and took it away. He returned almost immediately, put a hot cup in front of her. "We'll need privacy," the woman said.

"Yes, Mistress." He left and shut the door after himself.

"So," the woman said.

"So?" Teia asked.

"I'm your owner, my name is Lady Aglaia Crassos. You may call me Mistress."

"My owner is Lady Lucretia Verangheti."

"There is no Lady Verangheti. Or I am Lady Verangheti, depending on how you want to look at it. My family has enemies who would block us from placing slaves in certain households or positions—say, the Blackguard. The fiction of 'Lady Verangheti' helps me circumvent such pettiness."

"I'm sorry, Mistress, I don't mean to be rude, but out of loyalty to my mistress..." There had to be some way to say this. "Hrm..."

"You don't believe me," Lady Crassos said. She sounded amused, which Teia hoped was good. "It would be an interesting bluff, would it not? Of course, it would only work on slaves who never meet their mistress—meaning *my* slaves. Sad." She pulled out a single piece of vellum and handed it over. It was Teia's title; she recognized it instantly. Attached to it on a separate sheet was a writ of transfer, signed by Lucretia Verangheti and Aglaia Crassos. The handwriting was the same.

It took Teia a few moments to understand. If Aglaia wanted to keep her ownership of Teia secret, she couldn't own Teia's title under her real name or anyone who bothered to inquire could find out to whom Teia belonged. But she needed to have the writ of transfer already finished in case something came up that required her to prove ownership quickly—so she kept the writ and simply didn't file it at the Chromeria. Teia's throat tightened. Why would the woman reveal her ownership now?

"How good of a liar are you, girl?"

"I'm sorry?"

"Simple question. If you're willful, you will be beaten exquisitely."

Exquisitely? "I'm pretty good, when I try. Mistress."

Aglaia Crassos's face lit up. "Good. Good. Exactly what my sources have told me. Continue to answer honestly and your service for me need not be wholly unpleasant."

Fear stabbed through Teia. *Not wholly?*

Aglaia looked around, as if searching for something. She rang her little bell, and the serving man instantly came in. "My crop," she said.

Gaeros knuckled his forehead and disappeared. He was back in moments. He presented her with a riding crop, then turned his back.

She cracked the riding crop low against his back. He jerked, but said nothing.

Aglaia dismissed him with a wave. "My slaves must anticipate my needs. I believe in disciplining you personally when you don't. When a lady hands off discipline to someone else out of some misplaced sense of daintiness, she can't know if her discipline is being enforced with too much mercy or too much gusto. And slaves—like children or hounds—are best disciplined immediately. I will not always have an enforcer with me, but I carry my strong right arm wherever I go. So when we conclude our interview today, I will beat you. I think it's important for you to know how firm of a hand your mistress has. It will also let me know how easily you bruise, in case I have to beat you someday before you're to be seen in public."

Teia swallowed. The weight of dread made her knees quiver. "Yes, Mistress."

"Kip Guile is your partner in the Blackguard training."

"Yes, Mistress. Your pardon, but he was disowned weeks ago. He's no longer a Guile."

"I'm aware of this. But I have reason to believe that Kip may be welcomed back into his family when Gavin Guile returns."

Teia ducked her head, made her face show contrition. She was a slave, not a fool.

"Adrasteia, my brother was the governor of Garriston. He was

181

trying to save that worthless city when Gavin Guile shamed and murdered him and made him look like a traitor. And now my slave is partnered with his bastard. A bastard about whom he apparently cares. These are facts."

Teia scowled briefly, not sure what her mistress was implying. She didn't hold the expression. Some owners didn't like to see unpleasant expressions on their slaves. She also didn't smile with the vacuous impression that she was an idiot that so many other slaves had mastered. Aglaia had said she prized intelligence. It might even be true. Best to reinforce her mistress's feeling of superiority without overplaying it.

Aglaia rolled her eyes, like Teia was hopelessly stupid. "I want you to keep my ownership of you secret, understood? If it's found that I own you, because of the history between Gavin's family and mine, you'd likely be expelled from the Blackguard and made worthless to me. I'll sell you to a brothel at the silver mines in Laurion after I vent my frustrations on you. Understood?"

The silver mines were notorious, the first option for slaves who committed serious but not capital crimes, and the last resort for slave owners exasperated with slaves who rebelled or fled repeatedly. The mines were dangerous, the other slaves more so, and the brothels were worse. They were reserved for the use of the depraved gaolers and their favorite slaves: the best of the worst. Teia had a friend, Euterpe, whose owners had lost everything during a drought. Finding the local brothels already full with slaves and even free women who'd sold themselves into slavery so they could eat, Euterpe's owners had sworn to her that she would return after only three months. She'd been returned five months later, after her owners finally recovered. She never did. Never smiled. Flinched at the touch of any man, even her father, who'd gone mad and hanged himself.

Laurion was a curse among slaves. A byword. A threat whose mere existence was enough to keep most slaves in line.

Aglaia Crassos didn't mean it as a threat. Her eyes had as much pity as a rattlesnake's. "You think I wouldn't do that when you're worth a fortune if I let the Blackguard buy you?"

Teia licked her lips, but couldn't think of any response that mightn't plunge her further into hell.

"My brother's death means I'll inherit twice as much money now as I thought I would a few months ago. Vengeance is sweeter than gold.

Do you know the girls in Laurion service up to fifty men every day? Fifty! I didn't believe it myself, but I've known several people who've sworn it's true. They give the girls a measure of olive oil every day. Can you guess why?"

Teia blinked stupidly, ice in her guts.

"Because otherwise they get destroyed inside. Death by cock sounds so romantic, doesn't it? But I'm sure it's not. *Fifty* each day. And a pretty girl like you ... you might do even more. Not many pretty young girls there. Do you understand me?"

Teia's knees felt weak. She nodded. She had to get away.

"So now that we understand each other, tell me, have you seen anything worthwhile?"

Teia gave her report. Kip was fat, had few friends, spent most of his time in the library, apparently spending all his time reading about some game. He'd been summoned several times to speak with the Red, and had seemed distraught afterward. He thought the Red wanted to destroy him. The old man had taken away Kip's right to go to practicum in order to make Kip seem inept when Gavin got back. Teia had seen Kip draft green and blue. He didn't sleep well.

All that was fine. It was information Lady Crassos could learn through other avenues. But that wasn't good enough, and Teia knew it.

Feeling sick to her stomach, Teia also told her mistress that Commander Ironfist had told her that there were two trainees he couldn't let fail out of the Blackguard: Cruxer and Kip. She omitted herself.

That was obviously news to Aglaia. "That's good," she said. "That's very good. Is there ... anything else?"

"I train with Kip, after midnight, in a special room low in the Prism's Tower." Adrasteia shrugged. "The commander wants him to be good enough to make it into the Blackguard by himself."

Hold back what you can about Kip, too. Don't tell her about the dagger he has hidden. Keep what you can of your soul.

"Good enough," Aglaia said. "Anything else?"

Give *everything* else. A slave, not a hero. "I saw someone else using paryl when I was out on one of my special jobs."

Aglaia's eyebrows shot up, and she made Teia tell her everything about it.

"An assassination," she said. "Never liked her anyway, but that someone would ... hmm. I'll have to see if she died. Worrying, though, either way." She didn't explain who she was talking about. Teia knew better than to ask.

Aglaia seemed to push the thought out of her mind and turned back to the task at hand. She smiled, and it actually seemed genuine. "You've pleased me greatly, girl. I'll remember this. I know I'm a hard mistress, but if you perform well, you'll be rewarded well. Today, two rewards. First, I'll let you name one."

It could be a test, a trap. A slave knew there were certain rewards you didn't ask for. Asking too much made you seem lazy or ungrateful or greedy. But if your mistress were in a good mood, she might change your life on a whim—for the better. "Erase my father's debt," Teia said before she thought too much.

"How much does he owe?" Lady Crassos asked.

"Seven hundred danars." It was two years' wages for a laborer. Her father spent everything now simply paying the interest on it.

"Seven hundred danars? That *is* a substantial sum. How did your father run up such a massive sum? He a gambler?"

Teia ignored the patronizing tone. "He bought my sisters back." He'd been crushed when he came back from a trade journey to find that his wife had taken up with another man, had borrowed vast sums to fund a lavish lifestyle, and lost everything he'd worked for twenty years to accumulate, including their house, furniture, jewels, and brewery. His wife had finally sold their three daughters to pay her debts. And then only part of the debts. All while he'd been gone.

"He bought them back. But not you."

"I cost too much." It was Teia's fault. Her drafting had manifested after she'd been sold. If she hadn't drafted, everything would be different. Her mother had only been furious that she had sold Teia too cheaply.

After everything, Kallikrates hadn't even left his wife. Said she'd gone mad. Said it was his own fault that he'd married a woman who couldn't bear a trader's long absences.

"Do you know how much this bracelet cost me?" Aglaia asked. She held out a wrist, bangled with some ugly golden glittering thing.

"No, my lady." Guessing too high would be as bad as guessing too low.

"Guess." It was an order.

"Six, seven thousand danars?" Teia said. It couldn't be worth more than five thousand. Her father would have gotten it for four.

Aglaia's eyebrow rose for a moment. "Well done, little flower. I got it for five thousand six hundred, and I drove a hard bargain. I thought it would complement a necklace I have. It doesn't." Her expression made it clear that today was the last time she would ever wear it.

Teia said nothing. She knew better than to hope.

Aglaia said, "No, no, of course not. Seven hundred danars, for collecting snuff boxes and trinkets and a bit of information? That's far too rich. I will keep it in mind, though. Something else...?"

"Training in paryl," Teia said quickly. If she got in, the Blackguard would probably go to the expense of finding and hiring a private tutor for her. Otherwise, she'd have to wait until she was a gleam, or a third-year, when more specialized Chromeria training started. That was too long.

"Ah," Aglaia said. "That might well be more expensive in the long run than erasing your father's debts. But... it would make you more likely to get into the Blackguard, wouldn't it? An investment." She thought about it for a moment, while Teia's heart pounded. "Yes. Done." She smiled. "And an excellent request. Shows a good mind. For a slave. I want you to know, I'm quite pleased; if this weren't our first meeting, I'd skip the beating. But I can't have you thinking I'm soft. Strip down to your shift, girl. I like to keep one layer of cloth on so I don't leave marks, but there's no reason to give you more padding than necessary. Beatings can be so tiring in a stuffy little room."

Teia stripped, and Aglaia Crassos carefully beat her horrendously from her calves to her shoulders, and then, when Teia thought she was finished, she beat the front of her body from her collarbones to her shins.

Sometimes Teia fantasized about not weeping through a beating, of being as hard and implacable as Commander Ironfist or Watch Captain Karris White Oak, but she wept freely. Proud slaves were stupid slaves. And it hurt too much anyway. Though she claimed dispassion, once Aglaia Crassos got going, sweating as she beat the girl, her face lit up with glow that wasn't wholly perspiration. A small, fierce joy lit up her eyes when she snapped the crop across Teia's breasts one last time at the end.

Aglaia Crassos rang her little bell and Gaeros poked his head in the door immediately. Teia collapsed to the floor, every part of her aching. Gaeros carried in a platter with a goblet of chilled wine in it.

The foul hag took it and drank deeply. "Gaeros, help this one dress, 185 and"—she rubbed the beads of perspiration from her upper lip—"summon my room slave, the tall one, Incaros. I find I've worked up an appetite."

"He awaits you eagerly in the next room, Mistress."

"Ah, see! Anticipating my needs!" She turned and put the crop against Gaeros's groin. "If you were even a little bit handsome I might reward you for that." She slapped the crop against his crotch, as if it were playfully, but it connected hard.

A small grunt escaped as the man turned to the side and held himself still for a long moment. His eyes were watery when he opened them. But Aglaia had already forgotten about him. She turned to Teia and stood over her. Aglaia said gently, "You'll remember this, won't you, Teia?"

"Y-yes, Mistress."

"Gaeros, find out her favorite food and drink. We'll serve them to her next time. She's done well. Very well. Teia, I'll beat you again next time. Slaves are naturally slow to understand and need firm reinforcement of basic lessons. But after that, this won't have to happen again."

"Yes, Mistress."

"And you swear to serve me with your whole heart, don't you, girl?"

"Yes, Mistress," Teia said fervently. There was no trace of guile in her.

Was she a good liar? Aglaia had asked. Teia was a slave. Of course she was a good liar.

"Oh, I almost forgot. Your second reward." Aglaia Crassos rummaged through a little jewelry box. "You are to wear this at all times, understood?"

"Yes, Mistress." Teia had no idea what she was talking about.

Lady Crassos handed her a slender, pretty gold necklace with a little vial dangling from it. Seeing the puzzled look in Teia's eyes, Lady Crassos merely smiled broadly and left.

As Gaeros helped her dress, eliciting gasps and grunts and grinding teeth as cloth slid over inflamed skin, Teia heard the harpy noisily rutting next door, cries of passion not unlike pain. When Teia was all dressed and her tears dried, Gaeros gently took her tightly balled fist in his hand to take the necklace and put it on her.

With difficulty, Teia unclenched her fist and surrendered the vial. A vial of olive oil.

Chapter 43

Kip held a book open across one arm and rubbed his forehead, rubbed his eyes. He'd discovered a little trick to help his concentration. He was standing at the window, and now he closed the book, keeping a finger tucked in to hold his place. He looked left and right. No one was in sight. He turned the book over; its cover was bright blue, drafter's blue.

Blue sluiced through him, starting at his eyes, and cleared away every obstruction to logic: weariness, emotion, even pain from sitting scrunched. Kip breathed out and let the blue go. He grabbed another book, on the fauna of old Ruthgar when it was called Green Forest. It was actually a pretty interesting book, but he'd grabbed it for its cover as well: drafter's red. The primary colors—not in the sense artists used the term, but in the drafter's sense, the colors that were closest to their luxin counterparts—were endlessly popular. Kip looked at the cover and drafted a bit of red. It blew air on the dying sparks of his passion for learning about the cards. He set the book down. Grabbed orange. A thin tendril of that helped him be more aware of how objects related. He wasn't doing any of these colors perfectly, he knew. To be counted a drafter of a particular color, you had to be able to craft a stable block of its luxin. Kip couldn't do that. He could draft only green and blue. The sub-red had been a fluke, just that once. He'd taken the test. He was a bichrome.

But what he could do was pretty darn useful. He opened his book again and kept reading.

Over the last two weeks, he felt like he'd made a lot of progress learning Nine Kings. Now he had a good sense of the basic strategies—it was, after all, only a game. There were whole reams of information he could simply ignore as well—strategies when playing more than one opponent, game variants played using fewer cards or more, ways to wager money, drafts from common piles. All unnecessary for him.

Then, at some point, he had a realization that he'd learned basic strategy, but in studying accounts of great games, he still didn't understand *why* players wouldn't play their best cards immediately—and with a whoosh like drafting fire, the metagame opened up. Counters that he'd figured were unimportant, perhaps vestigial from the ancient versions of the game, suddenly came into play. Strategies to thin the opponent's deck. Theories as to how to balance play styles when addressing decks of certain colors. It became a game of mathematics, managing piles of numbers and playing odds. Playing against a certain deck in a certain situation, your opponent would have a one in twenty-seven chance of having the perfect card to stop you. If he played Counter-Sink now (and he was playing logically), you could infer that he didn't have it.

He walked up to the librarian with the huge black halo of hair, Rea Siluz, and handed her back the basic strategy book she'd told him to memorize. "Metagame," he said.

She grinned. She had beautiful, full lips. "That was quick."

"Quick? That took me weeks!"

"The next step shouldn't take you so long." She handed him a lambskin-bound book. "Hang in there with this one. It's a bit dry."

Kip took the book. She'd said the last one was *interesting*. If that had been interesting and this was dry...But he forgot his complaint as soon as he thumbed open the book. "What's this?" he asked.

The writing in the book was odd, blocky, legible, but unnaturally cramped. And unnaturally even. Every letter looked like every other letter, whether it was at the beginning of the word, the middle, or the end.

"It's an Ilytian book. Not more than five years old." She glowed, genuinely excited. "They've figured out how to copy books *with a machine*. Think of it! Apparently it's hideously difficult to make the first copy, but after that, they can make hundreds of copies. Hundreds! In a few days! The Ilytian scribes are up in arms, afraid their craft will go extinct, but the goldsmiths and clockmakers are flocking to it. They say even *tradesmen* own books in Ilyta now."

Strange. There was no personality to it. No human hand had inscribed these lines. It was lifeless, everything the same. No extra space after a difficult sentence to give a reader time to grapple with the implications. No space in the margins for notes or illuminations. No particular care taken on a memorable line or passage to highlight it for a tired reader. Only naked ink and the unfeeling stamp of some mechanical roller. Even the smell was different.

"I think I'm going to get bored even faster," Kip said. "It makes a book so...tedious."

"It's going to change the world."

Not to something better. "Can I ask something rude?" Kip asked.

"Generally when you preface a question that way, no, you shouldn't," Rea Siluz said.

Kip tried to figure out a more diplomatic way to ask if she was spying on him. He looked up, thinking. "Um, then... do lists of the books students are reading get passed on?"

"If librarians wish to keep their jobs, absolutely. Sometimes we neglect to write down all the titles, or miss things, however."

"Ah. Can you *miss* that I've moved on to this volume?"

"Want someone to underestimate your skills, huh?" she asked.

"I don't know if it's possible to underestimate my skill at this point," Kip said. "I'm hoping my skill takes a leap sometime soon and surprises everyone. Including myself."

"If you want to take a leap, you have to start playing."

Kip opened his hands, helpless.

"I'll teach you," she said. "At the end of my shift, I can stay late for an hour or two. I'll bring decks."

So now, a week later, he was waiting for Rea to come play against him as she had every day.

She came out and gestured Kip to follow her to one of the side rooms. "I've figured out your problem," she said.

"I'm not smart enough for this game?" Kip asked.

She laughed. She had a nice laugh, and Kip was nicely infatuated with her. Orholam, was he fickle or what? But the women here had been a handful of heavenly beads nicer to him than the girls back home. He wondered if things had been unfairly bad before because he'd had the baggage of his mother back home—or if they were unfairly good now because he had the father he had. He couldn't tell—and he never would. He was who he was, and nothing could change it, nothing could tell him how things would have been if his parents had been different, normal.

"I doubt it's that, Kip. Every card has a *story*."

"Oh no."

"Every card is based on a real person, or a real legend, anyway. But a number of the cards you've described to me are archaic, pulled from use years ago. They're sometimes known as the black cards, or the heresy cards. The odds of the entire game have shifted without those cards. Some cards can't be countered in ways they easily could have

189

when those cards were in play, and so forth. You can't tell anyone you've been playing with those cards, Kip. Playing with heresy is a good way to get a visit from the Office of Doctrine. But I'll tell you this: you won't win against someone playing with black cards. The basics are still the same, but all the deep strategy books in the last two hundred years have been written around the holes that yanking those cards has created."

"There're no books with those cards in them?"

She hesitated. "Not...here."

"Not here here, or not in the Chromeria?"

"The Chromeria prizes knowledge so highly that even horrid texts describing the rituals the Anatians used when they would pass infants through the flames haven't been destroyed. Indeed, when they've gotten so old that they need to be copied or disintegrate to dust, we still copy them. Albeit with rotating teams of twenty scribes. Each scribe copies a single word, and then moves on to the next book and the next, so that the knowledge may be preserved without contaminating anyone fully. Not everything that goes into the dark libraries is similarly evil—much is simply political, but only the most trusted people are allowed beyond the cages."

"Like who?" Kip asked.

"The Chief Librarian and her top assistants, of course. The Master of Scribes and his team. Some luxiats who've been given special dispensation by the White. Full drafters who have submitted applications for specific research are sometimes granted single books or are accompanied in there. Blackguards, and the Colors. And sometimes the Colors grant permission to certain drafters, but those have to be approved by the Chief Librarian, who answers to the White herself."

"Blackguards?"

"They're the most likely to have forbidden magic used against them as they protect the Prism or the White. And, unofficially, they're also the ones who need to know what longstanding feuds there are, so they can prepare defenses against the right people."

It was a light in darkness. A way Kip could kill about fifteen birds with one stone: he could learn the game, he could try to dig up dirt on Klytos Blue, and he could try to find out if his mother had simply been smoking too much haze or if there had been something to her accusations about Gavin. All it required was that he do what he'd already decided he had to do: get into the Blackguard. Easy. Ha.

"Blackguards being allowed in doesn't include scrubs, does it?"

She chuckled. "No. Nice try."

His immediate problem, though, was the games with his grandfather. And he knew, even though he'd been ignoring it because she was pretty and helpful, that he probably shouldn't share anything at all with Rea Siluz.

"So I've been wasting my time," Kip said.

"You can win, but you won't win consistently, even if you play well. The odds you'd judge from are the wrong odds." She shrugged.

"And I can't find the real odds by playing because no one plays with the heretical cards Andross Guile has in his decks, and I can't find out the real odds by studying because I'm not allowed into those libraries?"

"Pretty much." She looked like she wanted to say more, though.

"Or?" Kip prompted.

"There's someone who might help you, a woman named Borig."

"Borig?" It had to be the ugliest name for a woman Kip had ever heard.

"She's an artist. A little eccentric. Be respectful. The spies who check in on you are accustomed to you and me spending the next two hours playing in this room. If you leave by the back and take the stairs down a level, you can slip out without them seeing you. It's important, Kip, for her sake as well as yours, that you not be followed or overheard. The Office of Doctrine is more academic now than it once was, but with the recent troubles, there's been talk of appointing a few luxors. You don't want to run afoul of people who are afraid. Not now."

"Luxors?"

"Lights mandated to go into the darkness. Empowered to bring light by almost any means they deem necessary. There were…abuses. This White wouldn't stand for them to be appointed again, but Orea Pullawr is not a young woman, Kip."

It made Kip feel sick to his stomach. There were layers on layers of intrigue here, everywhere lurking under the surface. And any one of them could engulf him. "Where is she?" he asked.

Rea gave him directions, and he left immediately. Down the tower, across the bridge, into Big Jasper. He was walking through a narrow alley before he realized that sneaking away might be dangerous. Might be a setup. How stupid was he? Someone had tried to kill him once already. He didn't know Rea Siluz's loyalties, and she had both given him the problem (the existence of black cards) and the solution (visiting someone who might not exist, in a place far from safety).

He should go home right now. He should stop playing with Rea Siluz, and he should...What? Wait until he was a Blackguard? Ignore every summons from his grandfather? That wouldn't work. The old man wouldn't let Kip show him that kind of disrespect. Kip didn't know what Andross Guile would do, but it would be bad. Very, very bad.

If only Gavin would come back. Gavin could protect him. Even though Kip had heard people say that Gavin was afraid of Andross Guile—that everyone was afraid of Andross Guile—it felt like Gavin could arrive and solve all of his problems in an instant. Kip could go back to being a child again.

A child tasked with destroying the Blue.

Orholam have mercy. Kip couldn't count on anyone. He had to make the best of it. He had to go on.

It was late afternoon. The stars of this district had their light focused elsewhere. Here, the buildings were close, the shadows long. He looked over his shoulder.

Sure enough. A large, unkempt man was looming at the mouth of the alley. The man drew a knife from his belt. It was roughly the size of a sea demon.

Kip ran.

It was only twenty paces to the nearest lightwell. Kip skidded to a stop. He fumbled with his pocket, pulled out his spectacles as the big man charged after him. Put them on his face.

The big man pulled up short. Raised his hands. "Didn't see you there, drafter, sir. Was just running, uh, home. No offense."

Kip hadn't even started drafting. In truth, he probably wouldn't have had time to draft before the big man killed him.

But the man didn't know that. He backed away, as if from a wild animal, then ran.

Just a thug. Just a thief. Nothing personal. No conspiracy. No assassination attempt.

And Kip hadn't even thought of the fighting skills that Ironfist and Trainer Fisk had been beating into his skull. He looked down at his hands. His knuckles were chafed, fists bruised from constant use, and Kip had simply...forgotten it all. Hadn't even occurred to him that he could fight.

He tucked his spectacles back in a pocket, and saw that the door in front of him was labeled: *Janus Borig, Demiurgos.*

He knocked and swore he saw dark-clad figures up several stories on either side of the alley bob out of nowhere quickly and disappear. He felt the weight of hidden eyes.

Jumpy, Kip. Jumpy.

An old woman opened the door. She was almost bald, and she was smoking a long pipe. Long nose, few teeth, a scattering of liver spots amid faded freckles. Her dress was besmirched with paint. She would have looked like a vagabond, but she wore a thick gold necklace that must have weighed a sev. She was wrinkly and ugly as afterbirth, but plainly vigorous, and there was such warmth in her features, Kip found himself grinning almost immediately.

"So. You're the bastard," she said. "Rea told me you'd come. Come in."

Chapter 44

The first thing Kip noticed about Janus Borig's home was that it was home to the largest mess Kip had seen in his life. The mess had paws in every nook, had shed fur in every cranny. Piles of clothes like coughed-up hairballs hid the floor, and stacks of books stood like trees for the mess to mark its territory. The mess seemed to have little sense of human valuation, because old gnawed-on chicken bones shared floor space with strands of pearls and either jewels or colored glass close enough to jewels to fool Kip's eyes.

The second thing he noticed was the guns. Janus Borig liked guns. There was one attached to the door, swiveling toward the peephole, in case Janus decided to kill a visitor rather than welcome him. But others were scattered everywhere, as if the mess had gotten into them and tossed them about. Pistols, the latest flintlock muskets, matchlocks, blunderbusses—there were handy ways to kill people everywhere.

"Don't touch anything," Janus said.

Which was impossible, thanks.

"Half the things in here will kill you if you nudge them wrong."

Oh. Lovely.

She spun around and put something down on a shelf. It was a tiny pistol. She took a drag on her long pipe, contorted her lips into a quasi-smile, and blew smoke out of both sides of her mouth simultaneously. "Promise me something, bastard of the greatest Prism to ever live."

She turned over her pipe and tapped out the ashes into a small pile of the same. She picked up another pistol, cocked it, and then used the spur of the hammer to scrape out the remaining ashes from her pipe. With every scrape, the cocked—and for all Kip knew, loaded—pistol rotated from being pointed at Kip's forehead to being pointed at his groin.

To his left and right, there were piles; he couldn't move anywhere without touching something.

"Uh, yes?" Kip said.

"Promise me you won't kill me or report me to those who might."

"I promise," Kip said.

She sucked at her lips, making a squeaking sound, then spat. She put down the pistol and grabbed at a pile of tobacco, stuffed some in her pipe, eyeing Kip closely. He swore there was a pile of black powder right next to the pile of tobacco. She snatched a fuse cord from one of the matchlocks and stuck it onto the flame of a lantern, then used the fuse to light her pipe. "Swear it," she said from behind a curtain of smoke.

"I swear," Kip said.

"Again."

"I *swear.*"

"And thus are you bound. Come with me," she said.

Kip picked his way around piles that reached up to his knees. The woman wasn't right.

He followed her upstairs. It was, apparently, her workroom. The division between the rooms was stark. The mess didn't set one grubby paw beyond the stairs. There was no disorder here, none. Every surface was immaculate, all done in white marble with red veins. Jewelers' lenses and hammers and chisels hung beside tiny brushes, special lanterns, palettes, and little jars of paint. One desk was slate, with little bits of chalk and an assortment of abacuses, large and small. An easel sat opposite, with a blank canvas on it, a magnifying lens in front of it.

One wall was dedicated to finished cards. They were hung so densely that you couldn't touch the wall. And the wall was so big, so packed—from floor to ceiling—that if Kip hadn't spent the last weeks in the library, memorizing everything he could learn about these cards, he'd have no idea that every single one of them was worth a fortune. These were originals.

And there were too many of them. Kip sucked in a sudden breath.

"The Black Cards. The heresy decks," Janus said. She sat on a little stool in front of her easel. "You know of them."

"I've barely heard a whisper," Kip said. "I—not really."

"What colors have you drafted, Kip Guile?"

Kip felt a chill, displacement, sickness. "That's not my name," he said stiffly.

"There is no one else you can be, Kip. I've seen your eyes. You think you're smart, but the truth is—"

"Right, I know, everyone tells me—"

"—you're a lot smarter than you think you are."

Which left him dumbstruck. Ironically enough.

"You're a Guile to your bones, young man. Even if you're not a son, a bastard can go far in this world. The Guiles are cursed, don't you know? The family has few children, and has had few for generations. Intense lights all snuffed too soon. So goes the story, anyway. Now, what colors have you drafted?"

"Why do you want to know?"

"Because I'm starting your card."

She was speaking another language, or nonsense. Kip knuckled his forehead.

"I have a gift," Janus Borig said. "Curious, curious gift. Unusual. I have a host of gifts that are common enough, of course, though not common all together, and one gift as rare as a Prism's."

"I suppose you're going to tell me," Kip said. Someone is telling you something interesting, and you have to let your big yap interfere?

But she laughed. "Green, of course. But blue, too. What else? You're not merely a bichrome, I'm certain of that."

Want to play it like that?

"You can paint," Kip said. "Very skilled, and you're a jeweler, too. You can split a stone finely enough to fit it on your cards."

She chuckled. Smoked. "Here's the thing, this game is much easier for me. I only have nine colors left to guess from, and you may well be 195 able to draft more than one of those. You, on the other hand, have all the uncommon abilities in the world from which to guess."

Nine colors left? Eleven colors? What the hell was she talking about? "You're teasing me," Kip said.

"Maybe we'll know each other well enough someday that you'll be able to figure that out," she said. "Smoke?"

Huh? "Sub-red," Kip said, thinking she was guessing what he could draft.

She lowered her pipe. Oh, she'd been offering to share her pipe. But she said quickly, "You've drafted sub-red, or fire?"

"Same thing," Kip said.

"Answer the question."

"Fire."

"Do you know, a scheme can be useful without being true. You can see sub-red?"

"Yes," Kip said. Suddenly, he wasn't sure why he'd come. Curiosity? Maybe it hadn't been a good enough reason.

"Can you see superviolet?" she asked.

He nodded, grudgingly. He wasn't even sure why he was loath to give her more information.

"Do you want to be a Prism, Kip?"

It was like she had a trick of asking questions that he didn't want to ask himself. "Everyone probably thinks about that," Kip said.

"You don't know if you want it or not. Part of you does, but you don't think you could ever be the man your father is."

"That's crazy talk," Kip said. He swallowed.

"No, it's not. I know crazy talk. I know it well. I am a Maker. We are not mere artists; we are the caretakers of history. The cards are history. Each one tells a truth, a story. The Black Cards tell history that has been suppressed, because it threatens…" She looked up at the ceiling, thinking, looking for the right word. She gave up. "Well, it threatens. Take that as you will."

She smoked, thinking.

"What I'm about to tell you is heresy. Don't repeat it, if you value your life. Heresy, but true. Take these words, and bury them, treasure them. There are seven Great Gifts, Kip. Some are common. Others are given only to one person a generation, or one person a century. Light is truth, and all the gifts are connected to this foundation. To light, to truth, to reality. Being a drafter—one who works with light—is a great gift, but a relatively common one. Being a Prism is another. Being a Seer, who sees the essence of things, that is much rarer. My gift is rare as well: I am a Mirror. My gift is that I can't paint a lie. And my gift tells me that your father has two secrets. You, Kip, are not one of them."

Chapter 45

"So what's your real name?" Gavin asked the Third Eye, coming to stand beside her on the beach. She had kept her vigil on the southernmost point of Seers Island, and the descending sun bathed the woman in gold. "Or what was it, before? Who are your people?"

The Third Eye was dressed in a yellow cotton dress that made her look merely mortal, though she was still a striking, radiant figure. She hadn't sent for Gavin until late afternoon. Her associate, or servant, or friend, Caelia, told Gavin that seeing the future took time.

"Oh no you don't," the Third Eye said. "You're probably one of those men who accuses *women* of being capricious, too."

"Huh?"

"You ask me last night not to tempt you, to be more formal, and today the first thing you do is ask for greater familiarity. Uh-uh, Lord Prism. In your vanity you can take pleasure in breaking other hearts. Not mine."

Vanity? That was a little offensive, a little blunt, a little...accurate. He made to speak, then found he had nothing to say.

"I'm sorry," she said. "The aftermath of Seeing is...I forget myself. It's hard not to be honest. My apologies." She snapped open a hand-fan and fanned herself. "I'm afraid I've overheated, too. My skin doesn't well tolerate so much sun."

She did indeed look like she'd have a good burn.

"Seeing requires light, you said?" Gavin asked.

She nodded but didn't seem interested in explaining her gift any more than that.

"Did you find it?" Gavin asked finally.

"Many times, and down many paths. It's in the sea."

"Pardon?"

"The bane is floating, somewhere in the Cerulean Sea."

"That is..." Useless? Unhelpful? "...a large area," Gavin said. She'd said three hours east and two and a half hours north—which would be in the sea from here, but somehow he was sure this wouldn't be that easy.

"I'm aware of this. It is also fairly hard to find landmarks or time markers to tell you where to find it in the sea. It's moving through the water."

Gavin threw his hands up. "Where's it going? Where's it coming from?"

"I'm sorry," she said. "I think I can tell you it's heading toward center. A center? The center... I'm not sure." She looked apologetic.

"The center of the sea? Like White Mist Reef? Or the center like sinking?"

"Bane float, most of the times."

Times, plural. "That doesn't give me anything."

"It gives you enough." If the bane was floating toward White Mist Reef, then taking the calculations backward, it would be somewhere south of the Ilytian city of Smussato, perhaps floating in a line from the border between Paria and Tyrea. If he knew where it was going, and he could guess that it would go straight, and he knew where it was going to be at any one time, that should give him a line on which it must be.

"You mean I'm going to find it?" Sudden hope.

"Yes."

He couldn't believe it. There had to be a catch. This was going to take some figuring with a map and an abacus, but it seemed too easy. "How long is it going to take me?"

"If I tell you that, you'll stop looking until the day I said you were going to find it."

"No I wouldn't— Yes, yes, of course I would."

She sighed.

"Am I going to find it in time?" he asked.

"Even I don't know what you're asking by that."

"You can't do this to me," Gavin said.

"Please don't blame me for things I have nothing to do with."

Gavin licked his lips. She was right. Of course she was right: she could see everything. Unnerving still. "What *can* you tell me?" he asked.

"That you'll be here for a while, and that the Color Prince is looking for it, too, and that you better not let his plan come to fruition. It's growing, Lord Prism, and the more it grows, the more blues will be drawn to it. Blue wights most of all."

"Why, what happens? All I know is that the bane were tied in with the old gods' temples."

"You'll see. There's something else I should tell you."

"There's a thousand other things you should tell me!"

"If you take Karris when you go fight it, you're much more likely to succeed."

"I could have guessed that myself. She's a useful woman."

"And if she goes with you, she'll almost certainly die."

"Had to be a catch, didn't there?" Gavin said.

"I'm not trying to give you a catch; I'm trying to give you a chance."

He shrugged that off. " 'Almost certainly' as in ninety-nine times out of a hundred, or as in two times out of three?"

"When I see her go with you, I watch her die in dozens of different ways. It's not pleasant for me. Especially since I know that if she lives, we're probably going to be friends someday. Assuming you don't bed certain... you know what? I've already said too much."

"You called Karris The Wife," Gavin said. "But then you said it was wrong. What did you mean?"

"Knowing that if you know, it will change things... do you really want to know?"

Gavin scowled. "Well, yes."

"Tough. I'm not telling you."

"Some soothsayer you are," Gavin complained.

"I'm not a soothsayer. I'm a seer. I see; sometimes I say what I see. I'm not interested in soothing your feelings."

She meant it, too. Gavin could see the steel in her again. Doubtless it was the only way she could remain human and deal with her gift.

"Karris doesn't like to be left behind when I head into danger."

"You've brought me fifty thousand problems, Lord Prism. That, however, is not one of them."

A good shot, and completely fair. He took a breath to riposte, and then thought better of it. "My lady, your wit is as sharp as your beauty is radiant. Since the light has so clearly blessed you with its presence, the most I can do is bless you with my absence. Good day."

He bowed and left. He was only a few steps away when he thought he heard her murmur something. He shot a look over his shoulder, and swore he caught her staring at—

She pursed her lips, a quick look of consternation. "I can foresee the end of the world, but I can't tell when a man is going to catch me staring at his shapely ass."

Gavin could do nothing more than beat a dignified retreat, strangely aware of his ass with every step.

Chapter 46

The Color Prince had wanted to leave Garriston in six weeks. It had taken eight. Though Liv had spent half her waking hours with the Color Prince, she knew there were entire currents passing right beneath her eyes that she didn't even see. For a superviolet accustomed to seeing that which others didn't, it was discomfiting.

One day, a general was found hanged from the open portcullis of the Travertine Palace. Liv only found out after the fact that he had been one who'd advocated staying put, satisfied with regaining Tyrea and settling down in their new country.

The Color Prince had opened his court that day, saying, "While there is oppression anywhere, there is freedom nowhere."

Liv heard the statement repeated a dozen times that day, and the next day as they marched. He was too busy for her for weeks, spending all his time with his military commanders. Liv was on the outside, literally and figuratively. She rode close to the front, but not with the commanders or advisers. She wasn't certain of her place, and no one else was either.

The women and men who'd been with the prince since he'd left Kelfing didn't trust her. She was the enemy general's daughter. Again. How that infuriated her. In switching sides, her father had managed to make her be cast out from the opposite side than those who'd treated her like an outcast for her entire youth.

After two weeks on the road, one night the Color Prince summoned her to his tent, which was ostentatiously small and plain. A man of the people. Liv wondered how such transparent tricks worked. But work they did.

"So, Aliviana, have you learned your purpose yet?" he asked.

"You only have perhaps half a dozen superviolets in your whole army. I may be the best of them. I know that you're looking for more, and you're looking for a test that will help you identify superviolets. Your methods are crude compared to the Chromeria's. The general level of your drafters' abilities is poor, and you're hoping that the perspectives I bring might be valuable to you. That last is speculation, but well supported, I think. So I think you want me to train your superviolets."

Back in the Chromeria, the magisters had warned their disciples constantly not to rely too much on their luxin to shape their thoughts or their feelings. Here, it was encouraged, and Liv wasn't sure yet which approach was better. If you were burning away your life by drafting as the Chromeria taught, it made sense to train young drafters not to draft when they didn't have to. But it had never been clear to Liv that the prohibitions were solely utilitarian. They'd been moral warnings, as if luxin were wine and those who relied on it were morally weak.

If so, she was weak. But the superviolet gave her clarity, and distance from her feelings of inadequacy, of loneliness. She used it and then yellow to pull problems apart, examine them from new angles, and peer right through them, all the time.

He poured himself some brandy, held up a finger, watched it as it turned a dull hot red, and touched it to his zigarro. "That's all you have for me?"

"You were Koios White Oak," Liv said. Karris White Oak's supposedly dead brother.

"Past tense?" he said grimly into his brandy.

She had no answer.

"How'd you find out?" he asked.

"I asked," she admitted. Not exactly genius deduction.

"And what does this revelation tell you?" he asked.

"Not as much as I'd hoped."

He swallowed the rest of his brandy in a gulp. "Come with me." 201

They walked through the camp in the low light of the shrouded moon and a thousand campfires. As soon as he stepped out of the tent, two drafters and two soldiers clad in white fell in beside them.

"The Whiteguard?" Liv suggested. It smacked of desperation to be taken seriously, a mockery of the Prism.

"Are there no mirrors in nature?" he asked, seeming to read her thoughts. "There have been four attempts on my life. One by one of my former generals. Three by parties unknown. Light cannot be chained, but the Chromeria hopes it can be extinguished."

They passed the camp in its thousands. It was more organized than when it had marched on Garriston. Practice, Liv supposed. Few people even noticed their leader moving down the path, and those who did didn't seem to know how to salute him. Some bowed. Some prostrated themselves. Some gave a more military salute.

"The blues want me to standardize the response to me," the prince said around his zigarro. "But I only want to impose what order is needful. More order is needful while directing an army than I would like, but once we tear down what the Chromeria has built, the needs will change. All will be free in the light."

They stopped in front of a gallows on the western edge of the camp. Four men were hanged there. In the low light of torches, Liv couldn't see their faces, but she did see the unnaturally elongated necks. The prince held up a hand and a beam of yellow light shone on the dead men. There was dried blood down each man's chin. Their features were swollen. The birds had been feeding on them.

Liv didn't know much about how bodies rotted, but she knew enough to be able to tell that these men had been dead for more than a day. So they couldn't be criminals; the army had just arrived here.

"They're our zealots. Martyrs now. These were men I sent to spread the news to Atash, to prepare the way for us. They went unarmed. They were only to speak, to convince. Their tongues were torn out and they were tortured before they were hanged. The Atashians didn't even wait for them to cross the border. Invading our land to kill the unarmed? This is a declaration of war and commencement of hostilities. Atash has sown the wind. They will reap the whirlwind."

"You tell a lot of lies, don't you?" Liv asked. Then she swallowed. The superviolet made her understand structures, but not necessarily obey them.

The prince's guards stiffened. Liv saw glares of hatred from them.

But the prince looked over at her curiously. "I forget who you are," he said. Then his voice cooled. "But perhaps you do, too."

She swallowed again.

"I don't deny that I already intended to liberate Atash, but they have drawn first blood. Against innocents. And let me tell you this, Aliviana Danavis. It's time for you to step beyond the illusions of your childhood. A lie told in the service of truth is virtue. Do you know why Ilytian pirates have plagued the Cerulean Sea for centuries?"

"Because they have safe havens and the Ilytian coast is treacherous for those who don't know—"

"No. Because men are bad at judging their own long-term interests. Satraps hate the pirates. Traders hate the pirates. Families whose fathers are pressed into their service hate them. Parents whose sons are enslaved to pull an oar hate them. But though the pirates have been bruised a few times—and I'll be the first to acknowledge this is one good thing that the so-called Prism has done—they always come back. And why? Because satraps find it easier to pay them off than to crush them forever. There are currently four pirate lords in Ilyta, and each of them has signed contracts with the Abornean satrapah swearing not to attack ships flying the Abornean flag. Do you know what happens to the money that satrapah sends to those pirates?"

Liv grimaced. "It enriches the pirates."

"It finances more piracy, and the dreams of every pirate to become a pirate lord himself. Satraps have looked at the problem and despaired. From time to time, they'll go after one pirate lord who broke a treaty, and sometimes they're even successful in hanging a boatful of men. But it never sticks. No one is willing to put her money or men on the line to help others, so then when it's her ships getting stolen and scuttled, no one is willing to help her in return. Now, don't you think the Seven Satrapies would be better off if they worked together for once and simply took care of the problem? Not just better off now, but better off for a hundred years?"

"If you could really stop it. You really think you can accomplish what satraps and Prisms have failed to do?"

"Absolutely. It's purely a matter of will, and that I have in infinite supply."

His audacity was breathtaking.

"That's small, Liv," he said. "Slavery. Nature made not slaves, nor should man. You're Tyrean, and your land hasn't been tainted as much as others, but slavery's a curse. I'll end it. The Chromeria is the same. It comes and sweeps up the flower of a nation—its drafters—and takes them away. Indoctrinates them. Returns them only to those places it favors, and fools the young drafters into thinking they're doing it for their own good. Like slavery, a curse that corrupts those on both sides. Everyone has said these institutions are too big to change. I say they're too big not to change. I lie in pursuit of that. Say it will be easier than it will be. I admit it. I lie carefully, and only to motivate people toward their own good and the good of the Seven Satrapies."

Liv believed him, but the superviolet part of her compelled her: "Who decides which ends are worth lying for?"

He shook his head sadly. "You think I do this lightly? Look at what the Chromeria has wrought. Your father is a drafter. He's my enemy right now, but I can recognize him as a great man. A great soul. Would not almost anything be better than murdering him? Are your hands any cleaner because you ask someone else to do the murdering for you?"

She felt sick thinking about it. Her father was old for a drafter. He'd drafted little for most of her youth, but now, fighting, he would be drafting almost every day. He had a couple years at most. "Can't... maybe they can be convinced that the Freeing is unnecessary? That wights aren't evil? That—"

"Convinced? Liv. The Freeing isn't incidental to the Chromeria's order. It's the central pillar. Without the Freeing, there's no necessity for the Chromeria. If drafting isn't oh so very dangerous, you needn't send your daughter to a far country to learn it. Without that, there's no indoctrination, and no capture of the most valuable commodity in the whole world—drafters. Without control over and a monopoly on the drafters, the whole house comes down. That's why this." He pointed to the dead men.

A wind gusted and blew foul putrefaction into Liv's nose. She coughed and turned away.

"You might wonder why I haven't cut them down, given them a decent burial. I will. After all of our people march past this, and see what kind of animals we're fighting. Because I refuse to cover up the Chromeria's sins, and I refuse to take part in them." He stared at the bodies for another moment, sadness in his eyes, or at least Liv thought she read sadness there. He looked at her. "You have questions."

"Not about this. Not... now," Liv said, looking at the bodies, feigning hardness.

"I favor you because of your mind, Aliviana. You needn't restrict yourself to the lecture at hand."

She wondered at that. How much was true, how much was flattery? But it warmed her nonetheless. "The gods," she said, "are they real?"

A twist of a smile. "What does Zymun say?"

"He says they are."

"But?"

"But he's Zymun, and you're you."

The Color Prince laughed aloud. "Perfectly put. You ought to be an orange."

She thought he was teasing her for her ineloquence, but then realized he meant it. What she'd said was the safest thing she could have said: it could mean anything or nothing.

"Yes, they are real. Though I don't believe their exact nature is like either the Chromeria or the new priests think. I like you, Aliviana. You ask the right questions. You think big. But you don't think big for yourself. You're too modest. I need my drafters trained, of course. That is a purpose, and a worthy one—but it's not a great purpose."

"Does it have to do with Zymun?" she asked.

"Zymun? Oh, you fear that I'm trying to pair you off with him?"

"He's certainly doing his best, my lord."

"Yes, I'm not surprised. Zymun never underestimates himself. No, I put you with Zymun because you're of an age and I thought you'd appreciate that. And it keeps both of you busy. If you prefer another tutor...?"

"No, my lord. I've rather grown...used to him, I should say." So long as she didn't insult Zymun's own intelligence, which he couldn't bear, he was an unending fount of praise for her abilities, for how quickly she mastered abstruse concepts and remembered obscure history. He made her feel good about herself. Special. And his ceaseless attempts at seduction made her feel grown-up, womanly, desirable. "Only...he doesn't speak about his past much."

"The only important thing for you to know about Zymun's past is that he tried to assassinate the Prism," the Color Prince said.

"He really did? He said something, but I thought he was—"

"I gambled. Sent Zymun on a mission that had a low chance for success. He thinks he failed, which is good. It helps me keep him in line. Truth is, he only half failed. History may give him credit for midwifing..." His voice trailed off. He looked up at the sky.

"A new era?" Liv suggested. "Midwifing a new era?" She followed his gaze as the moon emerged, illuminating the nighttime clouds. They were spread across the sky in perfect lines, horizon to horizon, perfectly spaced, perfectly parallel. The vision—for such a thing couldn't be real, could it?—lasted for perhaps twenty seconds, then the clouds broke under the onslaught of the winds, smeared, scattered.

The Color Prince broke the silence. "New gods, Aliviana. New gods."

Chapter 47

"Secrets?" Kip asked. "What secrets?"

"I don't know. Yet," Janus Borig said. "That's why I brought you here today. I wanted to know if you were one of them." She sucked at her teeth. "You're not."

"So is that good news or bad news?" Kip asked.

"It is very, very bad news."

"I still don't understand," Kip said.

"Understatement."

"Huh?"

"Come here."

Kip came to her side. She showed him her sketches. The first was of a cloaked, hooded figure, lit from behind, long hair falling in front of his eyes in a dark curtain, eyes dimly gleaming from behind the mass, a beard with gleaming beads woven in, a dagger drawn. An assassin? Another showed a bald, ebony-skinned man, bleeding from a cut under one eye, wearing an eye patch, spinning short swords in both hands. Another showed—

"Wait, that's Commander Ironfist," Kip said.

"Ah, so it is. Thank you," she said. "What happened to his hair?"

"He's in mourning for his lost Blackguards."

"Ah yes, of course."

"Why are you asking me? Why does he only have one eye?"

"Does he not only have one now? Hmm. It's not always literal."

Her head tilted to the side. She scrawled an old Parian word on the paper below Ironfist.

"Guardian?" Kip asked.

"Sentry. Watchman. Guardian. Vigil Keeper. Strong Tower. Quiet."

"Quiet?" Kip asked. "How's that fit?"

"Not him. You. Be quiet."

"Oh, oh, sorry."

She drew a scrawl around his neck. A necklace. But her hand paused when it got to what was hanging from the chain. She sucked at her pipe, bringing the dormant coals back to life. Then she sighed. "Lost it."

"I'm still back at what you're doing with Commander Ironfist," Kip said. There was some corner of dread turning over in his soul. She turned her eyes on him, and his heart flipped over and convulsed, tried to crawl off the squeaky clean floor to the stairs, its palpitations making it hop like a deranged bunny, the worst escape attempt in history.

"Do you think being Prism is too small for you, boy?"

"You keep saying these things that make no sense to me," Kip said.

"Because I keep trying to draw you as the next Prism, and I can't. You won't be the Prism, Kip."

"I don't aspire to that," Kip said. A chill. Like being collared by history.

"Do you aspire to more?"

"There *is* no more, is there?" Kip asked. What could be bigger than being the Prism?

"Is there a name that the others call you?"

"You mean besides Kip? Sure: Fatty. Lard Guile. Bastard. Pokey."

"Something else. Maybe I've gone about this wrong. Maybe instead of trying to make your card, maybe I should try to decide which card is yours."

"Look, I just came here to learn how to play better. Can you help me or not?"

"What do you know about Zee Oakenshield?"

"Nothing," Kip said. He'd never even heard the name.

"Do you know anything about the cards?"

"I know all sorts of things about the cards. I've memorized seven hundred and thirty-six of them by name and ability. I've committed a dozen famous games to memory. I know twenty of the standard decks and why they work. Does that count for anything?"

"No."

"Oh hell." If Kip had honestly wasted all the time he'd spent studying, he was going to find the nearest tall building and throw himself off.

"I jest," she said. "It means you're ready to start."

"I feel a sudden, intense desire to throw a temper tantrum," Kip said.

She squinted at him. "The cards are true, young Guile. And that's why this game has been played by generations of fools and madmen and wise women and satraps. Take a moment and soak that up. The strengths and weaknesses on the cards are honest to the figures they depict. Not all-encompassing, of course—for a few numbers, a few lines, and a pretty picture can only tell so much—but not misleading. But that's only the beginning of the greater truth, the greater gift that is Mirroring." She walked over to the wall and grabbed a card. She sat on a stool and spun around twice like a little girl. "Come, look, and see. Taste of the light of Orholam."

Superstitious drivel, or magical invocation, or efficacious prayer? Kip had no idea. The old woman seemed half mad. Maybe every word she was telling him was a lie or a delusion.

The card was, Kip guessed, an original—a young woman, dressed in leathers, buttons of turquoise, pale skin, flaming red hair piled atop her head, caged between black ironwood thorns. Green stained the skin of her left arm, which was down at her side, leaves coiling about it. Her right hand was behind her back, as if she might be concealing a dagger. She stood straight-backed, and the smirk on her face was imperious, ready for anything.

"This is your great-great-great-great-grandmother, Zee Oakenshield. In most ways, she is the founder of your house, though the Guile name comes from elsewhere."

She was attractive, and there was nothing about her to remind Kip of himself—but that smirk was all Gavin Guile. It was like the artist had carried her expression over a century and dropped it on the man.

Instead of commenting on the startling similarity, and the obvious gift the artist must have had to have captured it so well, Kip said, "She doesn't even have a shield." Inane. Nicely done, Kip.

"She never carried a shield, oaken or otherwise. The name was for
something else. But I needn't tell you. You see the gems?"

Kip nodded. There were five tiny gems, framing the picture, one at each corner, one above her head. "Draft a bit, any color, and then touch all those gems at the same time." She pointed at a painting with broad bands of the drafting colors on one wall.

Kip stared at the blue. Blue was far less frightening than green. Within seconds, he felt the wash of cool rationality. Should he obey this woman? Well, if he didn't, he wouldn't learn anything. The only reason he'd come was to learn. Besides, what was she going to do with a card that she couldn't do to him with one of her many guns?

With the blue in his fingertips, he touched the gems.

Nothing happened.

Well, that was a little disappointing.

"Push harder," Janus Borig barked. "It needn't bleed, but it must be near enough to call to your blood. You've got soft hands. It shouldn't be hard."

Soft hands? Kip grimaced, but obeyed, tapping the blue jewel hard, his other fingers loosely over their corresponding jewels.

Zee blinks to clear her eyes, peering into the dawn. Filtering through the smoke of two burning cities on either side of the Great River, the rising light is red. It's disorienting, having his view cast this way and that, without his body moving, without any control.

There are enemy soldiers on both sides of the Great River. Kip can almost hear the whisper of thoughts attached to those men—who they are, what they do—but "enemy" is the only thing that drifts through to him.

She's on the high ground, and her siege-drafters are already at work, ropes and cranks at the ready, waiting for the dawn to get enough light to do the rest of their work.

Zee turns to a hulking brute of a man with one eye. He looks at her, a frightening visage, but deferring. An officer? A subordinate, certainly. He holds a great bow, an arrow the size of a ship's spar drawing back. Her mouth moves, but Kip hears nothing. He can only see.

The enemy is four hundred paces away, twenty paces downhill, downwind from Zee, to judge by the flapping of the standards. The Ruthgari army is jogging, keeping ranks. Some of Zee's horsemen—most still in their teens—are already charging. She sees officers waving at them angrily, calling them back perhaps?—and then, defeated, the officers follow them.

Her line is tearing, some of the clansmen on foot following after the horsemen, spoiling the shots for her archers.

Once the foot soldiers charge, the archers would have to leave off shooting. Instead of a dozen volleys of a thousand arrows each, it would be six.

She shouts something, looking toward the siege-drafters, who have already drafted the great green luxin crossbeam and are filling the barrels of flammable red luxin to hurl at the approaching army.

They—and a dozen other siege-drafting teams—may get off two rounds.

She jumps up on her horse, the sudden movement sickening Kip, shouting something to—Small Bear, that's his name!

Small Bear says nothing, adjusts his aim incrementally, and looses the huge arrow. A thousand archers follow his lead.

She grabs a torch and rides out in front of her men. Kip thinks she's shouting. Perhaps all the men are shouting. She throws the torch in a high arc, and her men surge forward.

Her thirty mighty men surround her in seconds.

Something is shifting, sinking deeper—

A flaming barrel of red luxin smashes into the front lines of the Ruthgari, bursting and cutting a vertical flaming slash, crushing men and setting them alight. I draft green off the grasses that will soon run red. To my left, Young Bull and Griv Gazzin are drafting blue and green respectively, swatting arrows and firebombs out of the air, keeping me safe.

I draft a lance of green luxin and kick my stallion's flanks.

"Enough."

The sound reverberates oddly.

I don't seem to notice. The taste of ashes heavy in the air is more noticeable by its sudden absence than it had been in its presence. When did she start tasting? Smelling? Then the smell of ash and sweat and horses—gone. The feel of the saddle between her knees, knuckles tight on the lance.

It goes dark.

Kip blinked, and found his hand held in the crone's. She'd pulled his fingers off the gems of the card one at a time.

Breathless, Kip looked into her eyes. He could feel the blue luxin leaving him, draining into nothingness, abandoning him, leaving him empty, lifeless.

"I'll be damned," she said. "You *heard* something there, at the end? Smelled? Tasted?"

"A, a little."

Her eyes lit. "They lied! Of course they lied. Of course. They're Guiles. But why would he send you here alone? He must have known you'd be discovered for what you are. We must know. Stare at the ceiling."

The ceiling, which Kip would have noticed earlier if it hadn't been for the profusion of original cards, was a full spectrum, enameled and shining. "Do you want me to do something? Draft or—"

She took his hand. "Keep looking up is all." She pressed his fingers onto a card, one at a time. She pushed his pinky down, hard. A whiff of tea leaves and tobacco washed over him. He was about to comment when he felt a bone-deep weariness settle over him. His body ached. Then, as if his ears had been unstopped, he could hear the creaking of wood and the whooshing of wind, the slap of waves.

He pondered the exact words. It was a cool evening, and the scent of gunpowder clung to the ship and the men. Somewhere on the ship, a woman was weeping, over the dead, no doubt. His room was dark, lit by only a single candle. Outside, silver streaks of moonlight cut the night like a sword. He rolled the quill between his fingers.

His naked hand lay across the parchment, holding it in place. No secretary for this. This was treason. There was a name the missive was addressed to, but the hand obscured it—it ended "-os," which meant it could be anyone Ruthgari, or one of thousands whose name was Ruthgari even if their blood no longer was.

Then Kip lost all awareness of himself.

"A more advantageous peace may be found on the opposite shore of war. Dagnu is—" I write, the scritching of my quill filling the little cabin until the last word, which is silent. Muted. Odd.

Then the cabin...dark. I feel—Kip feels—Kip felt dizzy. He was back, staring through his own eyes once more.

Janus Borig puffed on her pipe, looking angry. "At age fifteen? No."

"What the— What the hell just happened?" Kip demanded, yanking his hand back.

"You didn't tell me, or I could have made things easier for you."

"Tell you what? This is my fault somehow?" Kip was scared, angry. Was he crazy? What had she done to him?

"You're telling me you don't know? The cards make their connection through light, Kip. The more colors you can draft, the truer your experience."

"What happened to me?" Kip demanded.

"You saw more than you were supposed to. Let me leave it at that."

"Was it real?"

"That is a more difficult question than you know."

"Did she die?" Kip asked.

"Zee? Not in that battle, though she lost."

"She was fighting against..." Kip hadn't quite gotten it.

"Darien Guile. Fifteen years later she bought peace by having her daughter marry him. It was said that she wanted to marry him herself, but she was too old to bear children and she knew lasting peace could only be bought by binding the families together forever. There were rumors of an affair between Zee and Darien, but they weren't true. Darien Guile respected Zee enormously and might have preferred to marry her, but they both knew how much blood might be spilled over one man's broken oath and one woman's folly. A lesson your family had to learn the hard way some time later."

Kip didn't know what she was talking about, but he assumed from how she said it that the war Zee and Darien had been fighting must have been started by something personal. "Was he a good man?" Kip asked.

"Darien? He was a Guile."

"What was the second card?" Something about Dagnu. That was the old pagan god. Kip wondered how old that card had been.

"A mistake. I grabbed the closest real card, and I should have known better."

Which was no answer at all. "These cards all do that?" Kip asked, looking at the wall with awe and fear.

"Only the originals."

"Which ones are originals?" Kip asked.

"I'm not going to tell you. But I will tell you that many of the cards here are booby-trapped. If you try to take them off the wall, you'll have some very nasty surprises in store. If you get them off the wall and try to draft their truth, you most likely won't survive the hell they put your mind through."

"I thought you wanted to help me," Kip said.

"I do. I'm just letting you know that if you steal from me, you'll be left a gibbering idiot. Even the real cards, used correctly, have dangers. Not all truths are beautiful. These cards can make a man delusional. Make him lose himself. They can teach…hideous things to those who wed not wisdom to power." There was a bitterness in her tone, but before Kip could ask, she went on: "Regardless, a woman must needs protect herself. I don't care about your father, except to make his card. I don't care about you, except to make your card. This is what a Mirror does. It's who I am. It is my mission from Orholam himself, and I will do it well. If you help me do it, I will be happy to help you. You've let me know what you can draft. That helps enormously, so I'll give you this to start: if you play with the deck that Andross Guile gives you, you'll always lose."

Chapter 48

"Paryl is unique among the colors," Teia's tutor said. "And it is uniquely dangerous."

Teia scowled. She thought that despite being the weakest and the worst color, at least paryl wouldn't get you killed or drive you mad. Then she scowled again—because they were standing in one of the Blackguards' training halls. It was dinner time, and there weren't many scrubs in the hall. Mostly it was inductees from the classes ahead of Teia's, but Cruxer was nearby, kicking his shins methodically up against a post. He'd told Teia once that it lightly broke the bones in the shin, and that the body responded by building them up ever tougher. He'd showed her his lumpy shins. It was impressive—and kind of gross. She thought it was the greatest thing she'd ever seen. But right now, he'd slowed his training, obviously eavesdropping.

"What's dangerous about it?" Teia asked. Her private tutor, Marta Martaens, was more than fifty years old. Ancient for a drafter. Wavy dark hair gone platinum, olive skin, top front teeth missing.

"That you go blind or burn to death."

Teia took a sharp breath. Oh, is that all?

"To see paryl, you have to dilate your pupils much, much more than most people can. You can do this consciously, yes?" Magister Martaens sucked at her thin upper lip.

"Yes, Mistress."

"Do it. I need to see."

It took Teia a moment. It was hard to relax your eyes as far as paryl demanded when you were tense. But then it came.

"Good," Magister Martaens said. "Now, back to normal. I assume you've never seen your own eyes in a mirror when you've done that? No? Watch."

The woman stared at Teia, and her eyes dilated unnaturally wide, the iris a tiny band of brown around a huge pupil.

Teia made a moue of appreciation.

"That's to see sub-red," the old drafter said. Then her pupils flared again, stretching the sclera itself, her entire eye going an eerie black, pushing the white to nothingness.

Teia flinched and shrank back.

The woman's eyes went back to normal in a blink. "That's what your eyes look like when you're viewing paryl, Adrasteia. Our eyes themselves are different, the lenses far more malleable, blessed by Orholam to see differently. Can you see superviolet?"

"No. And I'm color-blind, red-green." Best to get it out right away.

"Unfortunate."

"Are you?"

"Color-blind? No, but it's more common among us. We can see a vast spectrum of light, far more than other drafters. But that doesn't necessarily overlap with what others see. My own mistress's master Shayam Rassad was completely blind in the visible spectrum, but navigated perfectly with sub-red and paryl. But, dangers. First, the physical: if you dilate your eyes so much in bright light too often, you will go blind. Slowly, usually, but you need to take extreme care with mag torches and bright sunlight. Now, enough talk. Let's see what you can do."

So they began practicing, Magister Martaens asking Teia what she could see, drafting substances of her own, picking out sources distant and near, asking Teia to draft it herself. The paryl as Magister Martaens explained it was more like a gel than anything, albeit a gel that was lighter than air. It made good markers because the gel floated and frayed apart, constantly emitting paryl light.

214   "So you made the markers for my mistress," Teia said. She was stu-

pid not to have realized it earlier. Of course the woman had! There weren't exactly hundreds of paryl drafters around.

The woman's face went very still.

"How many of us are there?" Teia asked.

"Only two right now," Magister Martaens said. She looked to either side as she spoke, glancing nervously over at Cruxer, who was still pretending to be working out, without moving her head. "You and me."

"But that can't be right," Teia said. "I saw a man craft solid paryl and—"

Marta Martaens hissed—actually hissed. Teia froze up.

Magister Martaens smoothed her features and calmly walked toward the exit, beckoning Teia to join her. When they were out into the huge, bright underground cavern beneath the Chromeria, she went around the corner of the building where they couldn't be seen. When Teia joined her, she saw the woman was livid.

"I don't know what you thought you saw," Magister Martaens said, "but you are never to speak of it again. Do you understand?"

"I—I'm sorry, but no," Teia said.

"You don't need to understand, you need to be silent. Especially about such things."

"No!" Teia said. "You're my tutor. Teach me. I need to know everything if I'm to get into the Blackguard. You can't hold back on me."

"I can and I will. You're my discipula; you will obey me."

"Then I'll take my questions to Commander Ironfist."

The woman went gray. "I want you to think very carefully about what you're considering, young lady."

"Going to someone I trust, someone in authority over me, with a simple question, that's what," Teia said, getting angry.

"Tell me what you think you saw. Quietly."

So Teia did.

Magister Martaens was shaking her head even before Teia was finished. "No. No. I've tried to make paryl solid a thousand times a thousand. It doesn't work that way."

"But what if it did?" Teia said.

"Yes, exactly," Marta Martaens said.

Teia lifted her palms, more mystified than angry now. Maybe drafting paryl really did make you crazy.

Magister Martaens looked around, again, though there was no one   215 to overhear them. "Think about what you're suggesting: a color that's invisible to nearly everyone, even every drafter—a color that could kill, without leaving a mark, without leaving any evidence, that looked like a natural death. Please use your *tiny brain* to think about how people would react to such magic."

Teia licked her lips. They would react exactly as she had, with terror.

"Anytime someone dies mysteriously, it becomes the fault of a paryl drafter. Anytime some obese noble keels over from a burst heart, people whisper that it's the work of his enemies—and every noble has enemies, and most of them are fat. Think first about what that does to nations, when *any* death could have been an assassination. Then think what that does to paryl drafters. When the Office of Doctrine sent out luxors to stamp out paryl drafters, they weren't authorized solely or even mainly because the Spectrum thought we were heretics."

The Office had sent luxors after paryl drafters? "So it does work. You're admitting it," Teia said, despite her tight throat.

"I'm admitting nothing. I've never seen solid paryl, and I can't make it. I don't believe it can be done. There were some of us, hundreds of years ago, who worked for the Order of the Broken Eye. Assassins. I think they probably killed with poisons, but by claiming that they could kill invisibly and without leaving any trace, they got many more contracts. But then, when people did die, it got out of control. That's why there aren't any paryl drafters anymore, you fool girl. Not because it doesn't work, but because everyone fears it might work better than it actually does. That's why we're still perilously close to being called heretics, why the libraries have been scrubbed of references to us, and why the present White has had to fight so hard to rein in the Office of Doctrine. She believes all light is Orholam's gift, but there are the superstitious people in every age. They call it darklight, *oralam*—hidden light. They say it is a gift from the lord of darkness. A darkness that can only be driven away with fire. Do you understand? A darkness that can only be driven away with fire."

"Burnings," Teia said quietly.

Magister Martaens seemed abruptly calm. "I met her once, you know. The White. She apologized. Said that drafters treat paryl drafters like the benighted treat all drafters. Said she was working to overcome it, but that it would be a labor of several generations. A good woman. Don't you dare overturn all her work with foolish rumors.

We may never have such a friend in the Chromeria again. This is bigger than you and me. This is for generations yet to come. Your mistress has already asked me all sorts of questions and I've had to lie a thousand ways to convince her you were delusional. When next you meet her, you tell her that just before you came to see her, you saw the paryl again. Describe it as a streak, but that there was no one there. That it originated from thin air. Be confused, and if she asks, tell her you haven't asked me about this yet, but you will. That you never said anything to me about the dead woman. I've told her that paryl drafters tend to see streaks at times, that it's a side effect of our drafting. You're to make her believe that what you saw was a coincidence. Because if you don't, our kind will be purged again."

"Yes, Magister."

"Then let's get to work. I want to see how far away you can place a beacon, and how tight a beam you can use to see through clothing," Magister Martaens said.

"Magister," Teia said, "how does it work? I mean, how does it supposedly work? I'll never speak of it again, I promise, but, please."

The older woman sucked on her thin lips. She looked around again. "In the stories, if she had the knowledge and tremendous will, a drafter could sharpen paryl not only to a solid, but into a needle so fine a person wouldn't feel it poke them. The drafter would then make a tiny stone inside their target's blood and release it. Supposedly, that eventually causes apoplexy—a stroke, the chirurgeons call it now. But there's no reason paryl should hurt anyone. I've cut myself and touched paryl to my blood; it isn't poisonous."

"But you're describing exactly what happened!" Teia said. At the woman's glower, she lowered her voice. "Sorry."

"And I'm telling you that you must have read the same story I did and forgotten it. Hallucinations are not uncommon among exhausted drafters. We who work with light sometimes have our eyes do strange things."

Teia couldn't believe the woman's willful blindness. She struggled to maintain a respectful tone. "Magister, does my mistress think it can be done? Does she believe you, or me? Does she want me to do *that* to someone?"

Magister Martaens looked like she'd swallowed vinegary wine. "I know two things about your mistress. She's more interested in who she can take to her bed than she is in dusty old tomes in forbidden libraries she'd have to pay a fortune to gain access to. Dangerous knowledge is often hidden under ponderous grammar and obscurantist vocabulary. She hasn't the patience to sift through mysteries. Everyone's heard silly stories about dark drafters and night weavers. No one knows anymore that those stories are about us. Which is why it behooves us not to remind them. Which is why I'd like you to wear darkened spectacles whenever you draft paryl publicly, or to always draft quickly so that no one sees your eyes."

"And the second thing?" Teia asked.

"There are those who can savor a silent victory. Your mistress is not one of them. She's not looking for quiet ways to kill the Guiles. But when she figures out whether helping the Prism's bastard or hurting him will hurt the Guiles more, you can expect to be used. No matter what it costs you, or her. She's insane with hatred. So don't get too close to that boy Kip. You'll probably have to betray him."

Chapter 49

Kip followed Grinwoody sullenly. Everything about the room was the same as always. Door, curtain, darkness. Andross Guile was already seated at the table.

As Grinwoody brought out the superviolet lantern, Kip took a seat across from the old man.

"Can I use your deck this time?" Kip asked.

"No," Andross Guile said. "You play the hand given you. You're a bastard. You get the bad deck."

"Oh, I'm a bastard now? So you don't doubt who my father is?" Kip swallowed. He shouldn't have said it.

But Andross Guile said nothing. He picked up his deck and began shuffling. "That my son sired you has never been in question, you fool. Even your voice sounds like his. The question was whether your mother was a concubine or simply a whore. If he's claimed she was a concubine merely to vex me, I shan't let it stand. I know for a fact there was no marriage, and I bet you know it, too."

"I didn't exist yet, so actually, no." Snotty. Dangerous, Kip.

"You still have that bandage on your hand?" Andross asked.

"Yes, my lord."

His eyebrows lifted above the dark glasses for a moment: Oh, it's "my lord" now?

Kip didn't know if he hated himself more for his earlier recklessness, or for his later deference to the old buzzard.

"Take off the bandage."

Untying the knot near his wrist took his fingers and his teeth, but soon Kip had unwrapped the linen. The burns were healing, but the skin was pink where it wasn't white with scars, and his fingers were bent permanently. He could tighten them into a fist, but it hurt to even try to straighten them. The chirurgeon and Ironfist both urged him to try, but it was agony.

"Put your hand out, bastard, I'm blind."

Kip put his hand on the table. The old man put his hand on top of Kip's. "Please," Kip said. "It's very painful."

Andross Guile hmmphed. He traced his bony, pale, long, loose-skinned fingers over Kip's hand, heedless of the oily unguent. It stung, but Kip held still.

"You'll lose the use of this hand quickly if you don't stretch your fingers," Andross said.

"Yes, my lord. I know."

Andross Guile turned Kip's hand over, palm down. "You know. So you've *chosen* to become a cripple? Why?"

Kip clenched his jaw. Swallowed. "Because it *hurts*."

"Because it hurts?" Andross mocked. "You're ashamed. I can hear it."

"Yes, my lord."

"You should be. Keep your hand on the table. Scream when it hurts too much."

What?

Andross pushed down on Kip's hand, flattening it slowly. Kip felt the new-formed skin at his joints tear open. A squeak escaped his lips, but he didn't scream.

I'm a big tub of lard, a shame, an embarrassment, but I am the fucking turtle-bear. You can go to hell, Andross Guile. You old, heartless, cruel—

The ligaments in Kip's hand were on fire, his whole palm was touching the tabletop, but his fingers were stubborn claws, arched up. 219

And then suddenly, the pressure stopped.

Tears were leaking down Kip's cheeks. He gasped and cradled his hand to his chest.

Andross Guile said, "That which you would have serve you, you must bend to your will. Even your own body. Perhaps especially your own body, fat one. Did the skin tear?"

It was a moment before Kip could trust his voice. "Yes, my lord."

"Smear the unguent back into the cuts. You don't want it getting infected."

With a trembling hand, Kip did.

"You know what I'm going to tell you next, right?" Andross Guile said.

"Keep doing it, all day, every day, so that it heals right," Kip said.

Then he felt another wave of shame. He did know what to do. He simply hadn't had the will to do it. Andross Guile didn't even have to say anything.

"You did well," the old man said instead.

"Huh?"

"You didn't scream. I expected you to. So this time, no stakes. A practice game. Next time is for your little friend, though, so I hope you're getting better."

With no further talking, Andross Guile dealt himself his cards. Six facedown, two up: a Stalker and a Green Warden.

That meant he was using his green and shadow deck. One of his best. Kip wrapped his bandages loosely around his hand and drew his own cards from the pure white deck Andross had given him to play. Kip had played with it twice before, and he was finally getting comfortable with its strategy. His up cards were the Eye of Heaven—a power enhancer—and the Dome of Aracles.

Kip cursed inwardly. No stakes? He'd just drawn this deck's best possible opening hand. His hand cards were good, too. He actually had a reasonable shot at winning. There were no choices for his first two rounds, and unless he drew something game-changing in the interim, all he had to do was survive until the sixth round, so Kip said, "When you say we play for my little friend, what do you mean?"

Andross played Cloak of Darkness, making Kip's gambit much less likely, and said, "That slave girl." He seemed to be at a loss to remember her name. Kip didn't supply it, for fear that he was being baited. Andross snapped his fingers.

"Adrasteia," Grinwoody said quietly from the darkness. Kip looked at him. The man was wearing odd, heavy spectacles Kip hadn't seen before.

"Adrasteia," Andross said as if he had remembered it, as if Grinwoody were an extension of himself. "I'll buy her, and if you win, I'll give her to you. You can take her as your room slave. I don't imagine your village gave a boy of your dubious charms many opportunities for the pleasures of the flesh, did it?"

Kip's stomach turned. "And if I lose?" he asked, hoping to steer far away from those topics.

"She'll be *my* slave. Worry about that as you will." His mouth twitched in a shadow of a smile.

Kip, I'm a slave, Teia had said. You don't even know what that means.

He did now. Kip was a fat bastard from the armpit of the Seven Satrapies, but he had choices. Teia didn't. Other people might look down on Kip, but they didn't even *see* Teia. Or when they did, it might not be in the way she'd want to be seen.

"What's your plan for me?" Kip asked.

Kip couldn't see the old man's eyes through his dark, dark spectacles, but Andross's head cocked to the side, brow twitched, surprised. "A question my own son would never have dared to ask. Are you bold or stupid, boy?"

"Both. And you're avoiding the question."

Andross Guile's lips pursed. He lifted two fingers, waved them forward.

A fist crashed across Kip's cheek. Grinwoody. May Orholam scratch out his eyes with sand.

Kip had fallen out of his chair and dropped his cards. He picked them up slowly, regaining his composure.

"It's amusing once in a while, Kip, but I don't tolerate much disrespect. Remember, or be reminded."

"So are you going to tell me or not?" Kip asked. He was treading the line, and he knew it, but Andross Guile let this one pass.

"It depends on how good of a Nine Kings player you are."

Kip was too smart for once to follow that up with, But what's the endgame, Rossie? Sure, the Guiles nearly rule the world, but Prisms don't last forever. Your family's almost gone. What do you *want*?

Maybe Andross Guile had been scheming so long that he didn't know how to not scheme. Maybe there was no winning, and he knew it, but losing was definitely possible, and his pride wouldn't allow him to lose. So he'd fight and fight and tear down a hundred other families and keep clawing until they finally nailed shut his crypt under the Chromeria.

"I don't have that much left that you can take away from me," Kip said. "So how many more times can we play?" After a while, with nothing to lose, I'll only be able to win.

But it was impossible to imagine Andross Guile putting him in a position where only good things could happen.

"Three more times," Andross said.

He had thought of it, the old shark.

Kip said nothing, and lo and behold, silence actually paid off. "Once we play for who owns Adrasteia. And then we play again, for your future."

"I don't think I like you very much," Kip said.

"That's a cryin' shame, because I mean for you to hate me as much as you hate your mother."

"Don't," Kip said, suddenly cold.

"Excuse me?" Andross Guile said.

"*Don't,*" Kip said.

Again, the head tilt, weighing Kip. "Your move," the old man said.

Kip made a mistake on the seventh round, not correctly calculating the cascading effect of the cards' abilities on each other, and watched Andross put together a brilliant series. Kip lost on the next turn.

With a sigh, Kip collected his cards. It was, as Andross Guile had said, a practice round, without even timers. But Kip could have won. With luck, he could win against Andross Guile. It was possible, even with Andross Guile's decks. Just unlikely. Kip flipped through the deck, seeing what cards would have come next, what might have happened if he hadn't botched it.

"How long do I have?" Kip asked.

"A drafter of your abilities? Maybe fifteen years," Andross Guile said. But he was grinning. He knew that wasn't what Kip meant.

So Kip didn't take the bait. For once.

"One week, then we play the first game. I'll arrange it with her present owner. And you can fantasize about what you'll do with her if you win. Of course, you have to win first." Andross Guile chuckled. "You think you'll free her, don't you? Truth is, you're not as altruistic as you think. No one who shares a drop of the Guile blood is. Blood is destiny, bastard. Don't forget it."

Kip heard the words, but suddenly they lost meaning, blew apart into irrelevance. The art on one of the white cards was different than he'd remembered. Or maybe because he'd been studying miniature portraits of all the cards, he simply hadn't noticed. Heaven's Finger. It was a dagger: white, veined with black, with seven colorless gems gleaming in the blade. It was the dagger Kip's mother had given him. He was stunned.

Hearing Grinwoody whispering something in Andross's ear, Kip looked up quickly.

"Hellfang," Andross Guile said. "You've seen it. Not the card. The real one."

It was a shot right in Kip's big soft stomach. He started. "I— No, what are you talking about?"

"Hellfang is its other name. Marrow Sucker. The Blinder's Knife. You've seen it. I'm right, aren't I?"

Kip said nothing, but he realized the last part wasn't to him. Grinwoody said, "He jumped when he saw the card, my lord. Definitely recognition." He made no effort to hide the smugness in his voice.

He'd been set up. Andross Guile had been playing him these games all this time simply to lure Kip into a false sense of security, complacency. Kip had played the White deck twice now, and the card had never come up. Andross Guile had been content to play him again and again so that Kip would be off guard when it did. All that time so that Kip would give an honest, startled reaction if he had seen the knife before. It had all been a trap.

"We'll talk more, when you're ready," Andross Guile said. "I know your mother stole it. I know she wanted to give it to Gavin, maybe in return for him making you legitimate. I want to know where it is and what my son knows about it. In return, I offer you the girl. Think about it. Not only will you get someone to warm your bed, which, face it, you have no hope of otherwise, but also a drafter's contract is worth a lot of money over the course of her life. Your tuition has been paid, but you have no other income. Maybe you can beg some scraps from Gavin, if he remembers you, if you want to be a beggar. Otherwise, tendering her services is the only way you'll be able to keep from having to find a sponsor yourself. All for a few bits of information that I'm going to find out regardless. If I learn it from somewhere else, you get nothing."

Kip was out of his depth. Playing his wits against Andross Guile was like playing Nine Kings with only two cards against an expert with a full deck. Kip's cards were Ignorance and Stupidity. Not winners.

"I'll see you in a week," Kip said. "Have Teia's papers ready. I intend to win."

Chapter 50

As soon as Kip got out of sight, he ran. He took the stairs down to his level and ran until he was within sight of his barracks.

There was a man standing outside the barracks. "Hello, sir," he said as Kip approached.

"Uh."

"I've been told to tell you that Lord Andross Guile wishes to reward you for your fine play. You've been given your own room. Your things have already been moved. Would you like to follow me?"

That old, decrepit, infuriating spider. He was magnificent. He'd just played a Scry and looked at Kip's hand. For one moment, Kip couldn't help but admire how well played it was. How better to go through all of Kip's possessions than by helping him move? And how could Kip object? He was getting a better room, for nothing.

So Kip did the smartest thing he'd done all day. He went upstairs—without making some excuse to first go into the barracks and check to see if the dagger was still in the chest five beds down. If they'd stolen it, it was already gone. If it was still there, he'd only be tipping them off. He'd come back later.

His new room wasn't large, but it did have a bed with new sheets and a warm blanket, a desk, a couple of chairs, and a small window to the outside. There was a lock on the door. The servant handed him a key. Nice touch.

The people most likely to steal from him doubtless already had
a copy.

"Thank you," Kip said. "Tell Luxlord Guile I was left speechless by his generosity. Tell him nice Scry."

"Nice...try, sir?"

"Nice Scry."

"Scry. Very well, sir."

The man waited near the door, and Kip realized he was supposed to give him a tip. "I'm terribly sorry," Kip said, "but I don't have any money."

The man glanced around the room, as if to say, Awfully nice room and situation you've got here for a pauper. As if to say, Liar.

Kip flushed. "Thank you, now goodbye." He nearly slammed the door on the man's face, suddenly angry, deeply embarrassed.

But as the door closed, he realized that Lord Guile had done this, too. He had plenty of slaves who could have brought Kip to his new room. Slaves weren't tipped, and the use of slaves so that your guests didn't have to worry about tipping was a courtesy often shown between the rich. Lord Guile was reminding Kip of his poverty, of his tenuous position. Rubbing his nose in it. Reminding him how badly Kip needed Teia.

Kip didn't know much about the economics of it, but he did know that some drafters never pledged themselves to any satrapy, instead being supported privately. Those lords or merchants then sometimes rented out the services of their drafters to whoever needed them— mercenaries. For those who couldn't afford the time and money it took to invest in developing a drafter, it was a bargain.

But...Teia's talent was worthless, wasn't it?

Or priceless, in the right quarters.

Gavin, Father, would you please come back? I'm afraid I'm going to do something awful here.

It was too late to go find Teia. She'd probably be done with her shift by now, but Kip couldn't stay here. He wasn't tired anyway. And he had four hours before his midnight training time with her and Ironfist.

He left the Prism's Tower and walked into Big Jasper. As he crossed through a market, he swore that for a few steps everyone's gait was synchronized, one, two, three steps all simultaneous—then it passed. He must have imagined it. A few people looked at each other, then went back to their business. In half an hour, he was back in front of Janus Borig's door. He knocked and waited patiently. He saw shadows shift on the rooftops nearby. Guards? The traps slid open, and he saw her peer out.

"Where can I get a deck of black cards?" Kip asked.

She laughed. "Back so soon. You see? I told you you're smarter than you thought. Come in. Come in."

Chapter 51

"You know I don't like to start fights," Karris said.

Gavin froze with a bit of rabbit stew on its way to his mouth. Clearly not an opening that boded well. He made a noncommittal noise. He and Karris were eating alone tonight in their little tent not far from the beach.

The weeks had passed in a blur of meaningful work and renewed friendship and fruitless searching and quietly growing dread. The Tyreans had landed in wonder and tears. The Third Eye's people had provided an enormous feast—and Gavin had put the Tyreans to work immediately. Within days, he had a plan and a routine. As much as possible, he handed over power to Corvan Danavis, supporting his decisions, deferring to him publicly, and bolstering the man until the Tyreans were almost as likely to turn to Corvan to settle disputes and give guidance when Gavin was there as when he was gone.

And Gavin was gone almost every day, scouring the seas for the blue bane with Karris. He'd sat with his abacus and his map, checked and double-checked his calculations and his assumptions—and then checked and double-checked the seas. The bane wasn't there. Wherever the two hours east and two and a half hours south started from, it wasn't from his beach on Seers Island. Nor, running it backward, was it simply two hours west and two and a half hours north of White Mist Reef, though that had taken him some time to figure out, too, because the reef wasn't simply one point on the map, it was an entire zone in the sea, five times larger than Seers Island. So did he measure that distance from the presumed center of the reef, or from some particular point therein, or from every possible point in a circle?

And it wasn't like his skimmer's speed was a simple constant either. Some days he was tired and he'd cover leagues less, though he thought he'd been traveling at the same rate.

"It's about Kip," Karris said.

That seemed safe enough. "Yes?" he ventured.

"What are you doing to that boy?"

"Pardon?" He hadn't even seen Kip in weeks.

"He's a boy, Gavin."

"I was under the impression he was a ptarmigan."

"Don't give me that," Karris said, flushing. She shifted on her stool and winced. Training with amateurs meant collecting bruises from where people weren't in control enough of their own bodies to pull blows short consistently.

"I have no idea what we're even talking about," Gavin said.

"You've given him some impossible task, haven't you?" Karris asked.

Gavin scowled. "How'd you know—"

"I know *you*!"

"You say that like it's a bad thing," Gavin said lightly, grinning, trying to defuse.

But Karris obviously wasn't in the mood to make peace. "He's a boy, not a weapon. You've loosed him like an arrow at some target. I don't know who. I don't even care. You're using him to advance some agenda."

Gavin absorbed that, pursed his lips, set his spoon down into his stew. "That's right. We all serve."

"It's not right. He's a good kid, and he deserves better. You've acknowledged him as your son—now be a father."

"What? What did you just say?" Gavin demanded.

"He's a *child*! You're treating him like he's another soldier. He needs your time, Gavin. He needs you to put him first."

"I don't put him first," Gavin said frankly.

"Exactly!"

"Exactly. And what *exactly* would you have me abandon so I can go have playtime with Junior? Clothing and housing fifty thousand refugees? Not important. Destroying a bane? Not important. Saving all seven satrapies? Not—"

"That's not what I meant and you know it! You've said Kip is your son. Are you going to treat him like he's your son or not?"

"Kip is not important!" Gavin shouted.

Karris sat back, defeated. "Then you are a smaller man than I thought you were."

"What would you have of me?" Gavin shouted.

"Decency," she said quietly.

He pounded the table with a fist so hard it bounced and spilled soup and wine everywhere. He roared, "Decency?! I do everything for others! *Everything!*"

"A lie," Karris said quietly. "But so very close to true. How is it that those closest to you get the worst of you, Gavin Guile?"

"Out! Get out!" he roared.

She got up and walked out. At the flap of the tent, she turned pitiless eyes on him and said, "You're a great man, but only when seen from afar." Then she was gone.

What the hell was that about?

He'd thought things were warming up with Karris as they worked together. They'd always worked well together, always enjoyed each other's company, even when they didn't speak. And now this. This *ambush*. Where had this come from?

Women. Gavin mouthed a few more curses. He could go after her. He should go after her.

And what? Tell her what? Tell her the whole truth?

The thought chilled his anger. He swore again and pulled out his charts. He had work to do, damn her.

He'd ended up abandoning his shortcut, which had probably put him two weeks behind what a methodical approach would have yielded, and narrowed the search through guesswork and good intelligence. He'd visited cities around the Cerulean Sea, asking if people had seen blue wights, and if so, what direction they were traveling. He'd even come across wights twice, one in a sailing dinghy, the other rowing a blue luxin dory of its own design. Both had been as unhelpful as possible, of course, trying to kill Gavin and Karris, but Gavin had found where each had come from, one from a little town outside Idoss in Atash and the other from Garriston. Taking the blues' penchant to move in efficient straight lines, he'd calculated where their paths should intersect—and found nothing there.

Clearly, one or both of them had either been a bad sailor or had been blown off course by the autumnal storms that were all too frequent now.

Blown off course by a storm from out of nowhere, pity the bastards. Ambushed. No wonder they say the sea is a woman.

Gavin had ended up dividing the Cerulean Sea into zones and grids, and he would skim as far as he could, checking every half hour on his sextant and compass that he was staying on line. Of course, at the speeds he was traveling, he could have gone off course for a half hour by a few degrees—easily done during the hard weather—then corrected himself, and the next day traversed that day's path perfectly and still have cut a wide enough berth that he would miss a small island.

The only other option was to stop every ten minutes and take the painstaking readings. He was adept in the tools' use, but stopping that often meant leagues and leagues that he didn't even get to. He also had to be aware that the bane was moving. If it moved too fast, it could go straight across his grid and he'd never be the wiser—even if all of his other calculations and guesses were accurate. It was infuriating.

Karris had suggested he build another condor and fly. It would have been a great suggestion, if he could still draft blue. It had taken him months to design the condor with the original materials, and it had still been a long way from perfect. Yellow luxin could be substituted for blue, but it was heavier, and infinitely more difficult to draft a stable version. He thought that within a couple of weeks he could figure out a design that would suffice. But made from solid yellow, it would be a permanent design. He couldn't make a new one every day, and he couldn't easily unravel it if he lost it to some enemy. So that meant finding a secure place to store it while he perfected it. And then, if something went wrong when he was in midair, he wouldn't be able to simply patch it quickly with blue. If something went wrong, he would crash, and all his work would be for naught. If he knew that he was going to be searching the sea for six months, it would be worth it. But he didn't know that.

Beyond infuriating.

And his Tyreans needed him. Their few drafters would burn themselves out helping with clearing forests and building shelters if Gavin didn't lend them aid. Corvan had convinced the Seers Islanders, who were almost all drafters, to help in exchange for future work, but there was still always more work to be done. Instead of trying to do it all himself, Gavin put his copious drafting abilities to work in a way that first amused himself, and then astounded everyone else: he built bricks.

Yellow luxin bricks. With what they'd learned building Brightwater Wall, his architects and laborers built forms for interlocking solid bricks. Gavin would walk around the forms every morning for an hour, filling them with yellow luxin, drafted perfectly, sealed perfectly, practically indestructible, and then he'd head out for the day. The laborers took the bricks and built everything out of them.

At first content to simply guard him on the island and while they traveled, Karris had eventually begun helping out on her own. She trained the best of the locals in fighting, sometimes organizing javelina hunts. Though javelinas and the rarer giant javelinas had long been native to Tyrea, there hadn't been any close to Garriston for decades, and facing the dangerous, unpredictable animals was the next best training to actual warfare.

Whenever Gavin and Karris returned to the island, he was always surprised. With plentiful free building supplies and fifty thousand willing workers and friendly locals and good governance, their little port went from a camp to a settlement in quick order. There were no walls, as per Corvan's agreement with the Third Eye, who thought that mutual vulnerability was a better guarantor of peace than mutual defensibility. But every other possible structure was springing up. Gavin felt proud to be part of building something for once.

He spent most evenings with Corvan, talking governance, mulling over problems, making plans, even playing a game or two of Nine Kings. It was good to talk, to jest, to drink too much wine every once in a while.

And he'd kept Karris at arm's length, desperate for her companionship, and desperately fearful of her. Treating those closest to him worst, indeed.

He set the charts down. He hadn't even been looking at them for the last few minutes.

This wasn't about Kip, he realized. At least not purely about Kip. For Karris, this was about the path not taken. Kip was of an age where he could have been their son, had Gavin not broken his and Karris's betrothal. Karris wasn't saying, How can you keep your distance from a bastard you unknowingly whelped on some peasant? She was saying, Is this the kind of father you would have been to our son?

Orholam have mercy. It was a punch in the stomach.

And she was right.

Kip was a good boy, but Gavin barely knew him. And he certainly didn't know what to do with him. He should have kept him here, should have trained him himself. It hadn't even really occurred to him. He'd seen Kip as baggage, a burden to be passed off to Commander Ironfist as quickly as possible.

Everyone had demands of the Prism, and that had been one too many. Kip was a good boy, but he wasn't Gavin's son. Gavin could tell the whole world that he was; he could take the disgrace of having fathered a bastard; he could even face his own father over it. But there was a difference between a grand gesture and daily decency.

Add Kip to the list of problems awaiting him when he got back to the Chromeria. Not waiting, festering—many of them problems that he desperately wanted to go tackle, but he felt trapped until he found the blue bane.

The next morning, Karris greeted him as if nothing had happened, and he let it lie, too. There was nothing he could do about Kip or anything else until he found the bane.

So he stopped whenever he saw ships out in the open sea, transformed the skimmer into a dory and rowed to them, asked his questions and deflected theirs, and kept searching. The problems elsewhere had to be growing. If he was gone too much longer, the Chromeria would declare him dead, despite the letters he sent with ship captains and the return letters from the Chromeria that he ignored. But he couldn't leave his search. He hated blues too much. This, too, was part of his five purposes—to destroy all wights. He owed Sevastian that. Nothing would keep him from it. Not even the Chromeria itself.

He took Karris with him almost every day, partly because she wouldn't let him leave her, and partly because he hoped she would feel the blue. The Third Eye had let slip that everyone in the proximity of a bane would be affected, but drafters most powerfully. Gavin's plan was to use Karris to find it, and then go back the next day without her to destroy it. She would be furious with him, of course, but he didn't care.

And the days passed, and passed, and passed. Two months passed. Three.

Chapter 52

"I can give them to you," Janus Borig said.

There had to be some catch, of course. No one was going to give Kip something he needed so desperately. The black cards had to be priceless.

"But it's going to cost me something," Kip said. She closed the door behind him, threw many latches and bolts home.

"No," she said. "Free gift. Which, come to think of it, is redundant, isn't it?"

"But..." he led.

She poked his chest with the stem of her long pipe. "But do you know what it's like to carry around an item of total wealth in your pocket? Walking down a back alley and knowing that you could buy every single house and shop on the block with what's in your pocket? It's terrifying. One of these cards is worth that, Kip. If I give you a deck, you'll be carrying more than you may make in your entire life. And the wealth isn't simply monetary. You'd be carrying history. History you could drop in a puddle and utterly ruin, or that could be quite literally stolen and gone forever. Do you have any idea how frightening that is?"

Kip was thinking of the dagger that might or might not still be in the chest in the barracks. He swallowed. "That's something that's been bothering me," he said. "Your home here. Don't get me wrong, it's nice and all, but...it's *here*. It's not where I'd expect to find fortunes." Which, he realized, might be the point.

"My husband and I built this house. Nigh unto fifty years ago now. I like it here." She shrugged. "I know it doesn't seem like a safe place to keep what I have here, but it's more secure than you know. I spend a fortune to make it secure. The Prism and the whole Spectrum couldn't come take something that I didn't want to give them." She grinned. "Now. Now. Now. Where were— Ah. The black cards. The question is, do you want the black cards because they're forbidden, or do you simply want to beat Andross Guile?"

Kip scowled. It felt like the wrong answer, but he said, "I just want to beat Andross Guile."

"In that case, you don't need a full deck of black cards." She groped on the counter for a jar with more tobacco while talking.

"I don't?"

"The cards weren't outlawed because they made good game cards, Kip. They were outlawed because they told stories that the Chromeria no longer wanted told. Just as when I release the new cards—the first new cards in many, many years—they will not be popular among those they depict."

"Can I use the new cards?" That would be one way to truly foil Andross Guile.

"No. Absolutely not. They're not finished, and when they are, my life will be in greater peril than usual. I'll accept that risk when the time comes, but not yet."

"Someone would kill you, over cards that are true, that *must* be true?"

"*Especially* over such things, Kip. If I could just make up whatever I wanted, then, well, who am I?" She tamped some tobacco into her pipe. It seemed awfully dark. "Some old woman. No one. Truth gives power. Light reveals—"

A sparkling, crackling whoosh of fire from the tip of her pipe interrupted her. It leapt up to the ceiling. She cried out a curse and dropped the pipe she'd loaded with black powder. She stamped on the scattered flames trying to set the garbage alight, but soon the gunpowder burned itself out.

"Dammit, second one this week."

Kip was round-eyed. "Are you—are you in danger?" he asked.

"Of course I am," she said. "But I'm very hard to find. And I'm very well protected."

"I found you no problem."

"That's because I meant you to find me, little Guile. Besides, haven't you seen my men?"

"Um..." Kip had thought he'd been watched.

"Black clothes, silver shield sigil? Hmm, say that six times fast. Well, good, then perhaps they're almost worth what I'm paying them." Janus grabbed another pipe off the wall and tamped it full of tobacco. "Now where were— Oh, never mind, come upstairs." Kip followed her as she kept speaking. "Here's the catch."

I knew it!

"I won't let you take a card until you've lived it."

"Lived it?"

"Lived the memory in the card. Like before. In case you lose it, I don't want those memories lost."

"How about, um, instead of taking your worth-a-fortune original cards, how about I take copies? You know, like people usually play with? Normal people, I mean."

Janus Borig scratched the side of her nose with her new pipe's stem. "That is . . . that is the most sensible idea I've heard in a long time. It would also allow me to put the blind man's marks on the cards, which would make Lord Guile far more likely to allow you to use them. Kip, you're brilliant."

Brilliant? She hadn't even thought of using cheap cards. Janus Borig was so smart, it was a miracle she could get dressed in the morning. Him thinking of the normal thing wasn't evidence of being smart; it was the opposite.

"Great," she said cheerily. "Well, let's make you a deck."

Chapter 53

Back into the same one. There was something important about this one. He had to find the right time. He had no idea what he was doing, but he had to learn. Tap, tap, tap, tap, tap.

~Gunner~

Captain Burshward is a bit crabbed this morning. That might have had something to do with us killing two of his men and presently attempting to make off with his fine galley, his excellent rowers, his rich cargo, and his miserable self.

"Captain Gunner is going to ask you one more time, Cap'n Burst Wart," I say. "I need that chain key." I scowl. "I suppose that wasn't a question, was it? But *that* was."

The captain and his brother and two officers are seated, hands tied behind their backs, on the gunwale. And on this galley, it is a gunwale. Their two cannons are propped up on it. It was only twenty years ago that all ships were thus, before some genius had the idea to make gunports. In a mere two decades, the idea spread all around the Cerulean Sea—but maybe not beyond it. Guns braced on the gunwale are less accurate left to right, and of course, they can't shoot low— ships have to stay far out, because if they get closer, they'd just be blowing away each other's rigging. When fighting oar-driven galleys, that isn't the best way to cripple a ship.

The captain looks furious, his brother gray despite his naturally ruddy complexion, the two sailors with them terrified.

They're Angari folk, from beyond the Everdark Gates. Big, burly men, wear their blond hair long and braided. Matrilineal. Sons a disappointment. Odd barbarian customs and strange cloying drink made with honey, but great sailors. Worthy of respect for being able to shoot through the Everdark Gates.

It is one thing that Captain Gunner hasn't done. Yet.

"Where is the chain key?" I ask, real nice like. A finger's breadth from his face.

The key is for the galley slaves' chains, belowdecks. Not to free them or some such silliness, but because the oars are locked in place. It isn't common, or I would have prepared for it.

'Course, it is just a chain. We can get through it. We have tools; we have powder. I can make a perfect charge in probably three minutes, and most likely not even set fire to the boat or kill anyone. But a key's faster.

And the majority of Burshward's men are coming back to the galley right now from shore leave in the city of Ru, their rowboat ambling over the waves, men hungover and sloppy. Not five hundred paces out. There isn't even a swivel gun on deck to take care of them. We've only found two muskets so far, old matchlocks that I don't want to trust my life to. If his men make it to the galley, they'll likely kill us all.

"Nice galley," I say. "Triple sweeps. Faster, but more likely to get the oars crossed, eh?"

"Tenth fastest in the blue god's fleet, which means it's the fastest fookin' galley in Ceres's piss puddle by a long tom's shot," he says. "Best oar boys in the world. Didn't foul the sweeps once, not even

235

coming through the Gates themselves." I've noticed his galley slaves aren't the usual skinny lot that stupider galley captains keep. You let your rowers waste away to nothing, and they get weak, and you get a slow boat. Burshward is smarter than that. His slaves are thick-muscled men, clean, no diseases, and big. Expensive to keep slaves in that good of shape, but worth it. Worth it double for a pirate, especially if they're well trained. I'm taking a richer prize than I'd realized. If I can get away with it.

"Chain key," I say. Real polite.

He says nothing. Brave man, balancing precariously on the gunwale. I can admire that.

"Rinky, sinky, dinky, or doe?" I ask.

"Rinky what?" Apparently he's not familiar with the game.

"Rinky 'tis."

I kick the first man in the chest. He flies overboard, lands with a yell and a splash. It isn't easy to swim with your hands tied behind your back, but it can be done, for a while.

But not by Rinky. He panics. Thrashes. Sinkies.

"Gimme a number, Captain."

"Wh-what?" A sudden look of fear.

"Ceres's tits, Gillan!" the brother says. "Pick a fookin' number!"

"Rinky, sinky, dinky, doe." I pull out my pistol and point at each man in turn as I singsong the words. "Once was a pirate by the name of Slow. Picked a sinner as a winner, and here's the way 'twould go—"

"Three!" the captain said.

"One . . ." I stick the barrel of my pistol against the captain's forehead. Cock it. Watch him shiver, go blank. Grit his teeth in defiance an instant later.

"Two . . ." I release the hammer and bring up my knife with the other hand, to the brother's throat. I draw the knife up to his chin through his thick braided blond beard. His eyes are squeezed tight shut.

"Three . . ." I pull the dagger back. "And this is the way it shall be."

"No no no!" the third man yells.

I poke him hard in the forehead with one bony finger instead of stabbing him. He tries to keep his balance, but I keep pushing. He tumbles off into the water.

236   "Cap'n, we ain't got much time," one of my men tells me.

I look at him. "This is me hurrying," I say. He swallows and shuts up.

"Gimme a number, Captain," I say. I aim the pistol at him first. Odd numbers will land at the captain, evens at his brother. Easy to figure, if you're figuring straight.

"That man had a family! He survived the—"

I start, "Rinky, sinky, dinky— Ah, fuck it." I shoot his brother in the knee.

A lead ball the size of your thumb hitting a kneecap and squishing will basically tear your leg off. I have to grab the brother to keep him from tumbling off the gunwale.

I say, "I'm tired of this game. Last chance, or I kill you both and fight. I like fighting. Tell me, and you live."

"In my cabin, above the doorframe," the captain says.

Worst hiding spot ever. If I had more men, I'd shoot one of them for missing it.

My first mate is already running for it.

He emerges a second later and heads belowdecks with a couple of others. They're following the plan. Should make a good crew. It'll take perhaps half a minute. We'll make it.

"You're going to kill us now, aren't you?" the captain says bitterly. His brother is barely conscious. I've heaved them both back onto the deck.

"Told you I wouldn't," I say. "And I'm the son of a whore and an apostate luxiat. My word is my bond." I grin crazily at him.

He goes white.

I tie a narrow rope tight around his brother's leg to stop the bleeding. "You want your brother to live a cripple, or die?" I ask.

He swallows. "Live."

I take the captain's sword—odd Angari thing, it's fat down at the point, sweeping broadly so there's no way you could put it in a scabbard. But I've used more awkward things to kill a man.

I slash the blade into the brother's leg, just above the knee and below the tied rope. I'm wiry, but I'm strong, and I know how to put a lot of speed into a blade. It lops the limb clean off.

Not *clean* clean. It still bleeds, of course. Tourniquet only does so much good.

The man screams and kicks. The captain looks like he's about to vomit. I toss the blade aside, check the progress of the rowboats. The men in those boats realize something is wrong; they heard my pistol shot, and now they're rowing with purpose. It'll be a near thing.

I roll One Leg over and pour black powder on his bleeding stump. He's whimpering, thrashing weakly. It takes three tries before I can get a spark to catch. Then it flares, filling the air with smoke and the smell of frying pork, cauterizing the stump. Odd how appetizing cooking man smells.

One Leg passes out. The captain is looking at me like he doesn't know what the hell I am.

"Lash 'em to barrels," I order those of my men who are just standing about. "Empty barrels, you morons!"

They do, just as fifty oars on each side rattle out. Triple sweeps. Puts more oars in the water, gives you more speed. I jump on the tiller—no wheel on this boat, sadly, just a straight tiller. Raiders can't be choosers, I guess.

Captain Burshward is staring at me still, shaking and shivering, but now with fury. "The old gods are being reborn," he says. "All of this is dying, pirate. The Everdark Gates will open, and we'll descend on you like the Raptors of Kazakdoon. We won't be exiled forever, thief. The White Mists will part for us. Our time is—"

I punch him across the face. Motion to my men.

"Mot is being reborn even now, pirate!" he shouts, bleeding. "Can't you feel it? We're here to announce his coming! Your days are over!"

Mot, the blue god. I've got my hands full with one blue goddess already.

My men throw the captain and his brother over the side. They land with a huge splash, and bob to the surface by the buoyancy of the barrels, but then roll underneath the water by them. Have to fight to breathe, as do we all, every day.

The Angari men in the rowboats are shouting now. The galley's oars dip and sweep, slow.

"That's your captain and his brother," I shout. "Save 'em or let 'em drown. It's all the same to me."

Giving the men in the rowboat the choice of rescuing their captain or coming after us divides their attention, gives us another few seconds. I see a couple of muskets come up. I duck.

The rattle of muskets. Ceres, I love the sound. A few men even blow chunks out of the wood. Excellent shots.

Wish I could have them on my crew.

The first rowboat has gone after the captain, the second is coming after us.

"Droose, tiller!" I order.

He takes it, and I leap up onto the gunwale and salute the men rowing after us.

"Good day, boys," I shout to the rowers. "You've just been bested by Captain Gunner. Ain't no shame in losing to the best. You'll tell your grandbabies about this day. And you'll live to do so! So turn back now. Because I'm Captain Gunner, slayer of sharks and sea demons, and I'll add you to the tally if you want."

I've made a makeshift grenado, but I'd rather not use it. The fuse is a rag with a bit of black powder rubbed into it. The grenado's a flagon full of black powder with a piece of wood shoved hard into the top. It'll just as likely blow up in my hand or not blow up at all. I need me a drafter. Magic makes me nervous as a virgin pillow girl, but sometimes even Gunner don't get what he wants. Sometimes you oil your bung, sometimes you oil your bunghole.

The men in the boat start cursing me. They've already fired their muskets, but a couple leave off rowing to charge their muskets. Good. Less men rowing means less speed.

I laugh at them, and another leaves off rowing. They're cursing at each other, screaming to row more, swearing they'll kill me.

The galley slaves sweep their big oars again, and again. It's enough. We pick up speed. I remove my hat with a flourish and bow, as the galley leaves its original owners behind.

A few seconds later, I hear a couple of gunshots. Love that musket music.

I've already turned to my men. "Take an inventory," I order. "Captain Gunner wants to take another ship within the week. I need to know if I'll have black powder for the job, or if I'll have to do it with my giant personality alone. And what the hell do these barbarians drink? Mead? Break out the mead. A measure for everyone, and two more tonight if you keep me chippy!"

Chapter 54

The thirty-five scrubs stood in neat lines, hands folded behind their backs, listening intently. Trainer Fisk usually handled their drills and conditioning, but today they were to be addressed again by Commander Ironfist. Two students had left after speaking with their sponsors about the impending war, but only two. Teia was proud of that; she was also keenly aware that being proud of ignoramuses who had no idea what they were getting into was probably silly.

Commander Ironfist walked to the front of the class, his head freshly shaven and oiled. His Blackguard garb, cotton fibers infused with luxin to make a stretchy second skin, showed the massive V of shoulders to waist, the gold piping down his sleeves emphasized arms as big around as some of his students' waists, the thick butt of a man who could run down a horse, and legs like towers of the Chromeria itself. He was astonishingly beautiful. The man's muscles had veins bigger than Teia's muscles. And all loose, easy, relaxed.

Teia knew that the relaxed, loose composure of a warrior meant speed. Trainer Fisk was shorter and thicker than Commander Ironfist, but literally muscle-bound. His heavy muscles actually slowed his motion—compared with Ironfist. Compared to Teia, of course, the trainer was fast as a loosed crossbow bolt.

"Your training is the best in the Seven Satrapies," Commander Ironfist began. No preliminaries, it wasn't his way. "Your training is necessary and good and effective. But your training—even here, even among the best—can hamstring you. When we practice punches, we pull them short, because if we don't, we'd lose you all to injuries. But when you pull punches ten thousand times, it's hard not to on the ten thousand and first punch: the punch that you throw at a real attacker.

"Our necessary safeguards can make you bad fighters. Blackguards can't be bad fighters. Your class will be called on to fight and perhaps to die, perhaps soon, and if you don't know how to kill your opponents first, a lot of you *will* die. Your class may have fourteen pass. May. Not will. So your class's training is going to be different. Accelerated. Harder. We will not allow you to be second-rate. There is no substitute for experience, so experience you will get. This experience will cost some of you injuries that will put you out of contention for those fourteen slots. We've never done this before because it's dangerous and it isn't fair. But we're out of time, so we're doing what we have to. For some of you, the tests will be easy. For some they will be boring. For others, they will be literal fights to the death. These experiences will not be safe, will not be controlled. They may be too hard. You may be crippled or die. If you can't accept this, you may leave. Now."

No one left.

"Failure on these tests will not automatically bar you from advancement. But it will matter. You fail, you drop three spots. Blackguards deal with what we get, not what we want. Here are the rules: You and your partner will be taken to a point in Big Jasper in one of the worst neighborhoods. You'll be given a handful of coins publicly, and then you must get those coins to the Great Fountain. You are forbidden to bring weapons or draft. To pass, you must bring back six of the eight danars you're given. However many you bring back, you and your partner get to keep. If you don't make it in three hours, we'll come looking for you. But don't expect any help. You're alone out there."

They drew straws for the order and an odd thing happened. The first team to draw drew number one, the second team number two, the third team number three. Trainer Fisk scowled and mixed the straws again. But the fourth drawers drew number four, the fifth number five. He mixed again, six, seven, eight, nine, ten. He frowned, but said nothing, and they dismissed it as a weird coincidence.

Adrasteia and Kip got a straw that put them in the last third. Not an auspicious beginning. Then they walked across town, led by Trainer Fisk and several of the older Blackguard trainees. Commander Ironfist didn't accompany them. He had duties elsewhere.

The first pair to go was the mountain Parian girl, Gracia. She was lean as a willow and taller than most of the boys. Her partner was another Parian, still tall and lean, but not so dark as Gracia, and a lot uglier, Goss. He was one of the best fighters, but he had a habit of *picking*—scabs, nose, earwax—and eating it. He was within a hair's breadth of earning the obvious nickname.

A sizable crowd had gathered to see what these Blackguards were doing in a bad neighborhood, and not all of the faces were friendly. Most were wary, but curious.

Trainer Fisk bade Gracia and Goss come forward, publicly handed them the eight danars, counting out the coins, then bound a red handkerchief around each one's forehead. "Bring these safely to the Great Fountain. No one in the Blackguard and no one in the Chromeria is going to help you. If you lose these coins, it's on your own head. You're not allowed to use weapons. You're not allowed to draft."

Murmurs went through the crowd watching them. It wasn't a fortune, but for an unskilled laborer it was as much as they could make in two weeks. And these children had it. And the watchers knew where the children were taking it, so they could guess what routes they'd take. And Trainer Fisk had just announced that the children wouldn't be protected from on high.

Gracia and Goss were smart, though. Smarter than Teia would have credited. They *ran*.

If they went by a direct route, they would travel faster than the news could. In fact, depending on how long Fisk made the teams wait in between attempts, the same strategy might work for the first few teams. Anyone hoping to ambush the Blackguards coming through would have to hear the news and then have to take the time to gather their gang to do so.

After five minutes, Trainer Fisk announced it all again, bound the red handkerchiefs around the brows of the second team, and handed them their money. They ran, too.

The crowd of the curious continued to grow, but Kip was watching the edges of the crowd to see who was leaving, and Teia followed his gaze. She saw several young men go different ways, each looking furtively back toward the circle, as if afraid that their payday would leave.

The scrubs were talking among themselves, trying to figure out strategies. If Teia was doing the arithmetic right, she and Kip had almost two hours before it would be their turn. When she thought about how many thugs could be gathered in that time, her mouth went dry. They would come for money like sharks came for blood.

She was still thinking about it when she noticed that Kip had walked away.

"Where are you going?" Teia asked.

"Where all of you should be going," Kip said.

"What?" she asked.

Every scrub's eyes were on Kip, and no few of the crowd's, now that he had been called out. "Scouting," Kip said.

The scrubs looked at Trainer Fisk. He shrugged. "No rules but the rules you were given," he said, bored.

Kip was brilliant. He'd seen it in a second: don't obey what the rules mean, obey what the rules say. *That* was the test as much as getting the coins through safely.

Within another ten seconds, all the scrubs scattered, except those who were up next. Ferkudi and Daelos went from looking excited to be going so early to looking stricken, keenly aware of their sudden relative ignorance.

Teia and Kip made a slow circuit of the nearby streets. They didn't speak.

After a while, they heard the sounds of a fight one block over. Teia ran toward the fight. Kip followed close after, though he was slower than she was.

"We don't even have the money yet, you morons!" a wide girl whose name Teia didn't know was shouting at some bloody-nosed tough on the ground in front of her. "Do you see the red kerchief?"

The girl's partner, Rud, a squat coastal Parian who wore the ghotra, didn't look angry or triumphant. He looked scared. He was bleeding from a deep gash in his shoulder.

"I should kill you!" the scrub girl shouted.

The tough scrambled back on all fours, then turned and ran.

Teia said, "We need to get you back to Trainer Fisk, Rud. Right away."

He nodded, and together the four of them walked briskly the four blocks back to the square. Rud leaned on his partner and then on Kip, too, as his blood loss made him nearly faint. Teia walked ahead of them, on the lookout for threats.

On catching sight of them, Trainer Fisk ran to meet them. The Blackguard scrubs were only steps behind him. They took Rud, made him lie down, and instantly began tending to the cut.

Teia heard someone say, "Bite down on this, Rud. This is going to hurt."

Then there was a quick flash of fire, and the stench of burned flesh and tea leaves and tobacco as they cauterized the cut with red luxin. Rud drummed his heels against the dirt and made a high-pitched whimper that trailed off quickly into deep, fast breaths.

One of the best boys in the class, Jun, came back into the square, pressing through the crowd. The next team was just about to leave, two skinny brothers who were in the bottom third of the scrubs.

Jun kept his voice down, but Teia heard him tell the brothers, "Don't take Low Street. There's a roadblock there. Twenty thugs, some of them armed. They already got Pip and Valor."

Oh, lovely, that was where Teia was hoping to go. Well, that left only—

"Corbine Street's blocked, too," Jun's partner Ular said.

Jun said, "The alleys through Weasel Rock looked clear, but they're so narrow, two men could hold them."

After making sure Rud was okay, and checking the wound, Trainer Fisk made his announcements again and handed the money to the Oros brothers.

"I've got a plan," Teia said.

"Huh?" Kip said. "What is it?"

She made a noncommittal noise. "You'll see."

"Teia? Teia, you're my partner. That means I'm *your* partner, too. You should tell me the plan."

She grinned. "And spoil it for you?"

He glowered. "Fine, then. You have any food while I wait? I'm hungry."

"No!"

"No, really, I am hungry. I wouldn't lie to you about that."

"Don't be thick," she said.

Kip held his hands up to himself as if measuring his thickness. He sighed. "Can't help myself."

She cracked a grin despite herself. "Give me your coins, when we start."

"So I can't buy a sweet roll?"

"No!"

"Yes, *sir*," he said, rolling his eyes.

"It's a good plan," she said, suddenly defensive, suddenly aware of who she was teasing. You're a slave, Teia.

"Mm."

"It'll work," Teia said. "Promise."

"Betcha anything it won't."

"What'll you give me if it does?" Teia challenged.

"A kiss," Kip said. Then his eyes got round. Like he couldn't believe what he'd just said.

Teia felt totally frozen. Was he making fun of her? Wait, a kiss if she was *right*?

Kip saw the look on her face. He said, "I...um..."

"Kip, Teia, you're up!" Trainer Fisk said. "Rud getting hurt put us behind schedule. Let's go."

Trainer Fisk ran through the announcement again, but Teia barely heard it. She handed her coins to Kip, not looking him in the eye. Trainer Fisk bound the red kerchiefs around their brows, and then Kip took off. Despite his bulk, Kip seemed to have no trouble keeping up with her as she snaked through the crowd. She went down one block and then turned into a cooper's shop, then through a smithy's yard connected to it, and then ducked into another shop.

Teia was already at the counter when Kip joined her. "At the Great Fountain within two hours?" she said.

"Our man's headed up that way in half an hour, so that's no problem," the grizzled old man behind the counter said.

Teia put the coins on the counter. "Delivery either to Kip here or Trainer Fisk, or Commander Ironfist?"

Kip tugged at Teia's sleeve. "What are you doing?"

"It was your idea that got me going. Now shut up."

She gave brief descriptions of Trainer Fisk and Commander Ironfist. Then she paid the courier fee—one danar—and asked, "Do you have a back door?"

The old man waved toward it.

"Thank you," Teia said. She took the red kerchief off, and motioned for Kip to do the same. It wasn't exactly a disguise, but with the Blackguard scrubs garb, she wasn't going to be able to get both of them into disguises. "Kip, take off your kerchief."

"Huh?"

"Off. Unless you want to get jumped."

Kip took off his kerchief, getting it.

"Hold on," Teia said.

"What?"

She licked her lips. "This was your idea, understand?"

"My...what? You know, I usually feel smarter than this."

"I want you to act like all this was your idea."

"Why?"

"Just do!"

He stood there, as mobile as a sack of paving stones, nonplussed.

She grimaced. "It's part of my strategy to make it into the Blackguard."

"Giving other people credit for what you do right? Ingenious."

"Look at me," she said. "I'm not tall, not muscular, not a bichrome. I'm fast, but I'm a girl and a subchromat. I want everyone to underestimate me, Kip. If they think I'm smart, they'll take me seriously. If they take me seriously, I won't make it in." She gripped the little vial on her necklace unconsciously. "Without my mind, I'm not good enough to make it in. Please."

He raised his hands. "I'll help you however I can. You're sure?"

"A thousand times yes."

He followed her lead. They walked to the Great Fountain via Corbine Street. They passed one group of young men who gave them hard stares, but by now the gangs had heard about the scrubs with money wearing the red kerchief, and because the scrubs' training clothes didn't have any pockets and Teia's and Kip's hands were open, it was clear that they didn't have anything.

The men, some of them bloodied from encounters with the other scrubs, let them through without saying a word.

When they got to the Great Fountain, though, only Commander Ironfist was there.

"You can show me your money," the commander said. He looked pointedly at their lack of red kerchiefs.

"Where are the others?" Kip asked instead. Teia watched him nervously. So rude!—and to Commander Ironfist!

The commander leveled his gaze on Kip and said nothing.

Kip looked away, glowered, but said nothing either.

Anything Teia said would just bring her between Rock and Hard Case, so she kept her peace. What did her father like to say? "She who gets in the middle of a pissing match will only get wet."

Then she realized Kip was doing it for *her*. He wasn't being obstinate, he was pretending to be obstinate to deflect any questions. He was alienating himself from Commander Ironfist—for Teia's sake. It almost made the brittle, fearful part of her soften. She knew how much Kip thought of the commander.

The Great Fountain capped the artesian well that provided much of Big Jasper's freshwater. Large underground pipes took water to four other public areas of the city and each of the embassies, and the Chromeria had its own well, but for the poorer residents, the Great Fountain was their sole source of water. Most made the trek at least once a day, if not multiple times.

The fountain itself was crowned by a glass statue of Karris Shadowblinder, the second Prism. She'd been Lucidonius's widow. Face upturned toward heaven, toward Orholam's eye, instead of standing, she was suspended by the twin jets of luxin pouring out of her hands toward the ground. Wearing only a shift, she had the lean body and the broad muscular shoulders of a fighter. Teia had always liked that about the statue. No soft lady of leisure, she. Like the drafters who would follow her, Karris the First's body had been shaped by the pure physical work of hurling luxin as much as she had shaped history by using it.

At all hours of the day, at least one of the Thousand Stars cast its light on the glass statue, illuminating it more brightly than the sun alone could. And several would illuminate it with the last and first rays of every day, making it a beacon in the darkness.

Around the merry splashing of the fountains' multiple jets, the seven-pointed star took water out to seven jets, allowing for lines to form easily and move efficiently.

At this time of day, there were only a few people in short lines, filling their buckets, setting them on yokes that they lay across their shoulders—or over their heads, in the case of the Atashians—and heading home. A number of shops lined the circle around the Great Fountain, and all of them were prosperous. No stalls were allowed here, nor beggars, which meant that both moved to clog the streets leading to the circle.

Teia sat on one of the benches at the fountain's edge. She wanted to touch the water, but she didn't. Jasperites were fiercely particular about their water. Some overzealous chirurgeon had given them notions that you would get sick if you so much as drank a cup of water from the same trough where you'd washed your hands. No arguing with people's superstitions, Teia supposed.

She hadn't been daydreaming for five minutes when she heard yelling. Triumphant vaunting. The rest of the scrubs. They were carrying Cruxer on their shoulders, almost the whole class—minus her and Kip.

The boys put Cruxer down in front of Commander Ironfist.

Cruxer beamed, but tried to put on a serious face.

Teia studied them. At least a dozen of them had obviously been in a fight. Clothes disheveled, a chipped tooth in a grinning mouth there, a bloody nose here, an eye swelling shut on one of the prettiest girls in the class, Lucia, a number of them favoring sore hands, bleeding knuckles.

Cruxer waved a hand forward. The class lined up before Commander

Ironfist, and now Trainer Fisk who rode in on a horse and dismounted to stand beside his superior. Each team came forward and presented Commander Ironfist with their coins.

It wasn't everyone. Eight teams had failed, and they glumly walked off to one side, empty-handed.

Teia searched the crowd and finally found Kip. He looked nervous. *Great.*

"Cruxer, report," Trainer Fisk said.

"Sir, after my partner Lucia and I brought our coins here, we went back and rallied the others. Together, we broke the gang's blockade and brought our coins through." He swallowed. "You did, um, say that the only rules were the rules you'd said."

"So you took what I'd designed to be an individual test and turned it into a corporate one," Commander Ironfist said flatly.

"It was too danger—"

"Yes or no."

"Yes, sir," Cruxer said. He swallowed again, but didn't look away.

Ironfist said, "Well done, Cruxer. This is exactly what I was hoping for."

A cheer broke out and Cruxer seemed to deflate with relief.

When the scrubs quieted again, Ironfist said, "You stood together and you accomplished a job you couldn't have otherwise. For the Blackguard, the job is all that matters. To the evernight with your pride. You accomplish your job in the most efficient way possible, and the safest way possible. We don't do this for valor or for glory, we do our job. Now, anyone else, or are we finished?"

The courier rode up then. She was a skinny Tyrean woman, wearing a sword and a brace of pistols. "Pardon me, my lords. Commander Ironfist?"

"I am he," the commander rumbled.

"This package is for you, from a Kip and Adrasteia." The courier handed over a bag and then left. The commander opened it, poured the coins out into his hand.

Murmurs. Not altogether appreciative.

"Kip," Commander Ironfist said. "I assume this was your idea?"

"Yes, sir," Kip said. Teia could practically hear Kip gulping from here. She said nothing, hoping the commander would ignore her. It simultaneously elated her that her gambit was working and broke her heart that Commander Ironfist assumed it had been Kip's idea.

248

"You took your coins to a courier, and then just walked through?"

"Yes, sir," Kip said.

Teia knew Ironfist's face would tell her nothing, so she looked at the faces of the other scrubs. Chagrin, consternation, irritation. *They* had needed to fight to get through. Or run like hell. Kip had cheated. *Kip* had cheated. They didn't even see her.

Of course, they had cheated, too, but their cheating had still involved fighting. *Their* cheating had been honorable. Surely Kip and Teia would be punished.

Commander Ironfist raised a hand, palm down. "Everything has a price. You lot chose to pay the price in flesh. Kip chose to pay in coin. Some of you got off without getting hurt, but some of you did. Our bodies are our coin. Our bodies, ultimately, are all that we Blackguards have. You chose to risk your bodies. Kip and Teia used their minds instead. If instead of coins, I'd given you the White to protect, which would have been better? Running a gauntlet and valiantly risking her death, or sneaking her through in some way no one expected? Kip, Teia, you did well. You each move up two places. Cruxer, Lucia, you each move up two places—of course, you're in the top spot, Cruxer, so you stay where you are. So we'll make it so that this week you can't be challenged out of first. Next week, you're back in the mix. Those of you who came back with no coins, you each move down two places. Tonight, we go out to a nice inn together—those of you who brought coins through can spend it all, but I expect you to also take care of those who don't get any coins. We're a unit. We're the best. We look after each other."

And so they did. They ate and drank—Commander Ironfist paying for their meals, the scrubs buying each other drinks until they all got tipsy and Trainer Fisk cut them off. They regaled each other with tales of their own heroics and reenacted epic fights, perhaps a little exaggerated. Eventually, both the commander and trainer excused themselves, no doubt to do more work.

At first there was some carping against Kip and Teia taking the easy way out, but when Cruxer came over and praised them as doing a smarter thing than even he had done, the complaining was ended, the rift was mended, and they became one class again, with Kip and maybe even Teia held in higher regard than before.

Teia barely spoke all night, but she soaked it up. It was light and life to her. She'd never felt part of something before, and she would pay anything to keep this. When she found herself stroking her necklace, she realized that for the first time, she was touching it with hope in her heart. Hope that she might actually throw the damned thing into the fire, and to hell with Aglaia Crassos.

Later, she was finally coaxed into drinking a single huge glass of ale. She felt like she was floating the rest of the night, drunk on companionship, drunk on belonging, maybe just drunk.

The scrubs walked home in a raucous pack, and no one even shushed them. But as they passed over the Lily's Stem, Kip and Teia walking at the back of the pack with Cruxer and his partner, Lucia, Teia remembered something.

"Hey, you know that Blackguards are forbidden to have relationships with each other, right?" Teia was talking to Kip, but Cruxer and Lucia shot startled, guilty looks at her.

Kip looked terrifically scandalized. "Um, yes? Sure. Of course."

"Then you should know that this isn't that," Teia said, still feeling warm inside. "This is just because of our ridiculous bet."

Kip shrank into himself. "Um, you really don't have—"

Teia put her hands on both sides of Kip's face and kissed him full on the lips. When she released him, he looked so poleaxed that she burst out laughing.

"Ooh, I want to make a ridiculous bet," Lucia said.

"No!" Kip said, jolted out of his stupor, hands rising defensively.

"Not with *you*, Kip!" Lucia said, laughing.

Kip put his hands over his face. "Let me die now, please."

Cruxer threw his arm around Kip's shoulders as the rest of the youths began to slow down and turn around to see what was so funny. "They do it to us all, Kip. They do it to us all."

Chapter 55

Gavin was out skimming at dawn again. Today he was alone. Karris had been training some of the Seers in self-defense yesterday, and a storm had kicked up in the evening, trapping her in their little town on top of the volcano's rim, Highland. Gavin yawned as the sun rose and took his eyes off the waves at just the wrong second. The skimmer turned a bit to the side and Gavin's hands came off the reeds.

The loss of speed made him pop up on the next swell. The skimmer landed sideways in a trough, and Gavin went flying. He hit the waves at breathtaking speed, skipped across the top of one, and then was crushed by another.

Gavin swam back to the skimmer, which was bobbing merrily in the waves without him, and, fully awake now, pulled himself up on the deck. What had he told the Third Eye? Something about not making mistakes often? He laughed quietly at himself. Then froze. She'd asked him if he was a swimmer; he'd said only when he made mistakes skimming; and she'd said, "I see."

Note to self: when a Seer says, "I see," pay attention.

He'd been heading west this morning, to start part of his grid from within sight of the Red Cliffs. He'd already been skimming for an hour.

The Third Eye had told Gavin, "Three hours east, two and a half hours north. Get there before noon." Five and a half hours from now put him an hour and a half *after* noon.

If she was talking about right now, there was no way he could get there before noon. So she must not have been talking about...

'You like to cut corners, don't you?' she'd said.

Clever witch. Playing with him.

He didn't need to go directly east and then directly south, he needed to go southeast... He did some figuring, his fingers flicking little imaginary beads. Taking the hypotenuse would take him... Four hours. Noon exactly.

Of course.

So he turned his little craft southeast and raced the sun.

Hours later, noon was nearly on him, and he thought he must have gone the wrong way or misunderstood the directions. It was a big sea, after all. But there was nothing for it but to keep going.

And then the sea changed, began to get calm. There was something odd about it. Gavin stopped the skimmer. He looked to either side. There was something like a shadow on the waves. It was as if a thin cloud were blocking the sun and he could see the edges of that shadow in the difference in color of the waves. But there were no clouds in the sky. This was some kind of slick, like oil calming the waters.

Gavin knelt on the edge of the skimmer and put his hand in the water and scooped up a handful. It was like thin slush, except it wasn't cold. Gavin looked at it closely. There were thousands, tens of thousands of tiny spars, like needles, like fragments of snowflakes, and they were all lined up the same way. He couldn't see blue, couldn't draft it. If he could, maybe there'd be no mystery here. He smelled the water: salt, and the faint ephemeral smell of resin, the chalky mineral scent of blue luxin.

The waves were awash in blue luxin, trying to form itself in crystals, somehow spontaneously coming together, rather than breaking apart and breaking down in the sunlight as it ought to.

As his hand cupping the water turned, he noticed that so, too, did the little spars, like a compass needle. One end pointed toward the outer edge of the slick. So the other way had to be pointing toward the center—where he needed to go.

He was as ready as he could be. He strengthened and narrowed the pipes that propelled the skimmer, thought again, and made them join to one pipe. He'd want a hand free. Then he skimmed toward the center.

The water thickened, though his scoop extended beneath the sludge and still propelled him at good speed. Then it thickened more until he could see that the scoop pipe was swirling the water like a spoon stirring soup.

Then the crystals of blue luxin began to clump together and form larger sheets. His passage made a sound like rumpling rice paper as he broke the luxin ice.

Ahead, he could see a blue island, floating where no blue island should be. It bobbed very slowly in the great, crusty water, cracking huge sheets of the luxin ice with every move. Some of it melted immediately in the sun, but other parts had become so infused with blue luxin that they held.

Then he saw something that made him stop drafting altogether and freeze. He was in shallows now, solid luxin ice floating maybe one pace beneath the waves. With that white background, he could see that there were bodies floating in the shallow waters. Dozens—no, *hundreds*—of bodies, bobbing at the surface, naked and encrusted with crystals.

Oh hell. Not bodies. Blue wights. Not dead, but absorbing the sun and the luxin. The water was so heavily infused with luxin it was helping them make the transition to blue wights.

"Get there before noon," the Third Eye had told him. Gavin suddenly had a sick intuition of what happened to the sleeping wights at noon.

He drafted an oar and maneuvered his way through the bobbing, unconscious wights until he reached the shore, his heart thundering in his chest. He threw his anchor ashore and jumped onto the ground. It was solid blue luxin.

It made an alien landscape. There were crystals as long as Gavin was tall. The action of the waves had shattered many of them, but the spars in general were pointed in the same direction—inland, always inland.

So Gavin began running. His goal was a huge spire at the center of the island, perhaps half a league distant. At first it was slow going, the ground simply so broken that he had to jump from gnarled crystal to odd glittering beam. Periodically, the ground would crack and a jet of blue crystals was shot into the air. Above, odd tornadoes circled, twisting top to bottom in mesmerizing mathematical motion. Twisted triangles like glass birds gyred on invisible zephyrs.

Crystal crunched beneath his feet like snow, but left glass behind, taking the heat and pressure of even his steps to make greater perfection.

As he moved inland, the order of blue began to assert itself more strongly.

He saw one spar, which was sticking at an angle to the ground, shiver. Then it slid even with the ground, seamless. The entire island here was flat, perfect. Ahead of him, he saw twelve shards of crystal, pillars arranged in a circle around the base of the great spire.

The twelve pillars were each three paces tall. As Gavin approached the nearest, he saw inside it the most perfectly formed blue wight that he'd ever encountered. It had fully sloughed off its human skin. In its place was a woven tapestry of gems, the weaves themselves altering for exactly how much motion the muscles beneath demanded of the skin at each point. It was terribly beautiful, like someone had painted a masterpiece with blood.

Gavin didn't hesitate. He ran toward the central spire. There were stairs up the outside of the thing in an odd square. No railing. Gavin ran up them, two at a time.

Ninety-seven steps to the top. The first thing Gavin noticed as he came around the corner was that he could see the White Mist from here. The mist, and the reef it hid, was legendary. Tales of its exact location varied, but all agreed it was somewhere in the middle of the Cerulean Sea. Maybe at its exact center, like a spider in the middle of its web.

What the hell was this floating island doing so close to White Mist Reef?

It could be a coincidence. Lots of those, recently.

Then his eyes fell on the pillar that shared the top of the spire with him. It was filled with bubbling water and churning gases—gray to Gavin's eyes, so he had to believe it was blue. There was something inside, but he couldn't see what it was. He leaned close. The sun, nearing its zenith, cut through the roiling gases. Gavin saw a curve at his eye level.

Oh no.

The sun reached the peak of the heavens and its pure light illumined the pillar fully. That curve at Gavin's eye level was a shoulder.

It was noon.

A tremor passed through the entire blue island. The ground cracked, shooting splinters of crystal into the air at high speed. Only the pillar itself didn't shake. In each of the twelve pillars surrounding him, Gavin saw movement. But he fixed his eyes on the one central pillar in front of him.

A huge figure was forming inside the pillar. Gavin was watching the birth of a god.

He drafted a yellow luxin sword, painfully slowly sealing it as the half-formed god's eyes flicked open, focused far away, then noticed Gavin all in a rush. Light swelled within the pillar, and finally the sword was sealed. Gavin rammed it through the pillar under the god's chin and out the back of its head.

Its eyes flared and exploded goo onto the glass.

Well, that was easy.

Gavin twisted the sword hard with both hands, feeling bones grind and yield. Then he drew the sword out. Goo slopped onto the ground at his feet. He pulled in intense sub-reds and red into his hand, set it afire, and punched his fist through the broken luxin. He found the creature's neck, grabbed it, and ripped the figure out of the pillar.

This was no wight. This was Mot himself. Human flesh becoming one with luxin, even the human skeleton distending, yielding to this new, larger shape. This giant was imperfect, not wholly formed. It had been coalescing, and Gavin had aborted it.

Gavin hacked off the god's head. He hacked off its skeletal arms, hacked off its legs—calves wholly formed, thighs still bony. He cut the spine—all in quick succession. There would be no resurrection. He picked up a gold necklace the creature had been wearing, adorned with a single black jewel, tucked it away, and sprayed the creature with pyrejelly, coating every limb. He set it aflame, stoking it with such deep sub-reds that it would be consumed utterly.

Mot melted, puddled, evaporated, burned completely away.

Only then did Gavin let his attention shift to what was happening on the island, *to* the island. Something was shrieking, distant, inhuman. The air was warmer. The triangle-birds were diving—no, falling, lifeless. The sun overhead had regained its normal hue. The tornadoes had turned to mist, and were everywhere blowing away.

Half of the twelve pillars had shattered. From one of them, a perfect blue wight was breaking free. The whole of the island seemed to be melting, and water was standing on the surface. The stench of released luxin was everywhere.

And in the distance, Gavin could see hundreds of blue wights standing from their pools, screaming.

Not least, he realized too late, the spire on which he stood was cracking.

Not good.

The spire split, and the chunk on which he stood sheared off to one side. It slid and then dropped fifteen feet, its jagged point stabbing into the island. For one second, Gavin thought he was just that lucky, and it was going to hold. Then the spire cracked again, and this time the fragment on which he stood leaned over crazily and threw him off.

Throwing jets of red luxin and fire downward worked only if you could find "downward." Gavin was tossed upside down, twisting, flipping. He barely found down and threw flames that direction before he splashed at high speed into the ground. High speed sideways, fortunately, and the luxin ground was evaporating, leaving water. Soft, glorious, nonlethal water. He plowed through the water for what seemed like forever.

When he came to a stop he found himself staring into the eyes of one of the perfect wights. Its head was cocked to one side. It was very much awake.

Blue wights are bad at acting before they understand a thing. Gavin had never shared that flaw. He came up out of the water and skewered the blue bastard. He splattered a ball of flame over its face, then decapitated the monster. He began running through the knee-deep water. He came out of the water and over a slight rise and found himself facing thirty howling blue wights. They raised their hands in unison, light flooding into their palms, projectiles forming in a fraction of second.

The whistling of dozens of flechettes passed over his head as he hit the ground. A moment later, he was up, sweeping his hand, bringing up a huge green shield in front of his body. He charged. The woody shield jumped and shivered in his hand as dozens of projectiles hit it and stuck.

Then some of the wights started shooting longer, larger projectiles at Gavin. Then all of them copied the first in a moment. Damn giists, always understood what other giists were thinking in an instant. Gavin took a second longer, his body understanding before his brain did.

The huge shield was getting heavier by the second, and the big projectiles put that much more mass on Gavin's arms.

Gavin's brain had almost figured it out before the shield dipped dangerously low. Too late. The bottom edge of the shield hit the ground at his feet and stopped abruptly, and he ran right over himself, flipping forward, exposed, dropping the shield. He splashed in ankle-deep water, caught his shoulder, and rolled.

He came up in fire. His arms swept left and right in great billows of flame. He dropped as the stronger of the blue wights still managed to get their blades through the wall of flame.

There was no way to keep this up forever, though. In about two seconds, they were all going to realize that he was lying down, and they'd aim their missiles at the source of the flame.

Then Gavin got incredibly, ridiculously, mercifully lucky. The ground dissolved fully beneath them, dumping them all into the ocean.

Gavin got one good breath in before he went under.

He never thought he'd thank a sea demon, but his little fight by his fleet had taught him how to make himself move through the water like a fish. Gavin put his hands down at his waist, opened his palms, and began shooting out disks of green, each shot propelling him through the water.

Steering around the mechanically swimming blue wights was simple, and in thirty seconds Gavin found his skimmer, still floating. He shot himself up out of the water, took a huge gasping breath, and then shielded himself. A few lonely missiles thunked into his shield, but in moments he was up manning the reeds, picking up speed. He could hear the wights' keening shrieks. Fury, from the depths of the supposedly purely rational blues. Fury that a *man* could best their blue perfection, fury that they could be wrong.

He circled the island as it broke up and sank, and divined from the wake even as it dissolved that the whole thing had been headed toward White Mist Reef, moving like a vast ship. Why?

But he didn't have time to think about that. Even now, some of the blue wights were trying to draft boats to escape. One would figure out how, then the others would copy it. Gavin couldn't let that happen.

Grimly, he drafted pontoons onto his skimmer and drafted yellow swords onto those, pointing downward into the water.

He skimmed in murderous circles at high speed, running over the swimming once-men, the sound of their glassine flesh being torn muted by the waters and his speed. Each death was announced by little more than a sound like a wagon wheel sliding off a particularly large cobblestone, sometimes accompanied by a rush of bubbles coming to the water's surface, always by a blossoming of blood.

The Prism was a peerless warrior, and slaughter, too, is the necessary work of war. He was a tireless worker, circling, circling, like a buzzard. He circled until there was no more shrieking, until there was no more hatred, until crimson blood no longer sluiced from the pure yellow decks of his skimmer, until the full harvest of death was brought to hell's gates.

Chapter 56

Aglaia Crassos found the visitor waiting in her parlor. He was fair, freckled, and bore a fringe of orangey-red hair combed over a knobby bald pate. He held a landed gentleman's petasos in his hand, and wore a fitted coat in the new Ruthgari fashion. He looked like a solicitor or a banker, but broad across the shoulders. But then, who knew about these monkeys from Blood Forest?

"Welcome to my home, Master Sharp," Aglaia said. "My man said you had some sort of proposal for me?"

"Indeed." He helped himself to a seat and crossed his legs. "I wouldn't usually do business with a total stranger, but your references were sterling."

"Mm. I went to a great deal of effort to *extract* those references." What an odd man. "Well then..." she said.

"Well then," he said. He stared at her with unsettling eyes. She hadn't noticed until now, but he had amber eyes. Not eyes dyed from a life as a drafter, simply the vanishingly rare true amber. "What is the worst deal you have ever accepted?" he asked. He was playing with a strand of pearls he wore under his shirt. Pearls, on a man? Was this a new fashion she hadn't seen, or a quirk?

"Pardon me?" she asked.

"Worst deal."

"How rude."

"You have something Lord Andross Guile demands," Master Sharp said.

"Pardon me?"

"The slave girl, Teia."

"Who? What? I have no such—"

"Did you think you could keep your ownership secret? My dear, you are so far out of your depth, the shore isn't in sight. You're going to sign over her title, and the more quickly you do it, the less bad it will be for you."

"You need to leave. Immediately," Aglaia said. She wanted to spit in this monkey's blithely smiling face. Andross Guile? She'd die first.

"The Red did tell me it might be like pulling teeth. How long should I give you to reconsider?"

Aglaia turned her back and strode toward the mantel where her slaves' bell sat. She wasn't even aware of Master Sharp moving, but suddenly he was holding her from behind, one arm around her ribs as if embracing her, but the hand a steel claw around her throat. His other hand stabbed behind her ear into a spot that eviscerated her with pain.

"I want you to know. I intend to enjoy this," he whispered in her ear. His breath was sweet, minty. "You have very. Nice. Teeth."

Then he released her. He was out the door before she even rang the

slaves' bell.

"Go after him," she told the muscular young slave, Incaros, her new favorite. "Take Big Ros and Aklos. Beat that son of a bitch. Badly. Break bones. Go. Now!"

She ordered her chamberlain to call up more guards and then went up to her chambers. She tried to comfort herself with the thought that even now Incaros, Ros, and Aklos were beating the hell out of that bastard, but he'd shaken her. She was trembling, and furious that she'd been so frightened. She closed her door and rubbed a kerchief across her brow.

A fist smashed into her forehead and her head slapped into the wooden door she'd just closed, stunning her. She fell, and hands guided her down. The man straddled her, and when she tried to scream, he stuffed something thick and sharp and metallic into her mouth. He strapped it onto her face quickly, expertly.

The gag held her tongue down and blocked air from her mouth, so she started screaming through her nose, and he simply pinched her nose, holding her down with one hand by her throat.

His amber eyes smiled.

She stopped screaming and he lifted her to her feet, mostly by her throat, and moved her to a chair.

How had he gotten here? Climbed up the outside of the house and broken in through a window as soon as she'd thrown him out? That fast? And no one had seen it?

Furious, she thrashed. He punched her so hard in the stomach that her breath whooshed out of her and she unwittingly bit down on the gag. It was like a horse's bit, but sharp, and it dug into her teeth and tongue cruelly. She had to keep her mouth open as widely as possible.

In moments, she was strapped to her own chair with broad leather straps.

Master Sharp stepped back, pushing his floppy fringe of red hair back over his head from where their wrestling had thrown it askew. His pearl necklace had come out of his shirt—and those weren't pearls.

"You can scream," he said quietly. "Anytime you want. But if you do, I'm going to punch you in the jaw. The gag you're wearing has tiny chisels above each tooth. If I've measured your jaw properly, it should break each tooth, top and bottom, neatly into four pieces. It's a bit of a rush job, so it may not be perfect. Sadly. And I'm afraid I won't be able to do the extractions myself, so you'll have that to look forward to with some other, less skilled hand on the pliers. But." He shrugged, 259 as if it couldn't be helped. He said, "Bottom line of the ledger. If you make my life difficult, I will break your teeth. In order. Molars first. I've never had anyone make it to the incisors." He breathed minty breath in her face. "But who knows? Maybe you'll be the first."

Chapter 57

Two days after their real-world testing, the scrubs had an elimination fight. Kip could only hope that some of the boys he would have to fight today might still have bruises enough to inhibit them from mopping the floor with his face.

But hope wasn't enough. He lost twice, quickly. He walked out onto the testing field again, flexing the fingers of his left hand lightly. It still hurt like small animals were gnawing at every joint and sprinkling salt on the flesh in between courses, but it hurt less than the beating that was to come. He stared at the youth across from him. Come on, turtle-bear, come on.

The wheels had come up Red, and Unarmed. Red was lucky, very lucky. Kip had just been practicing it last night with Teia. He could finally, finally make a stable red—though that was all he could do. He'd only figured out two ways to use the sticky stuff. One was flammable goo, and setting opponents on fire was decidedly frowned on. The downside was that the boy across from him, Ferkudi, was a blue/green bichrome, currently two places above Kip. There were about fifty people gathered around the circle, watching closely. Between injuries and nervous sponsors, there were now only twenty-eight scrubs left.

Ferkudi was short and thick through the chest, but strong as a bull, and deceptively quick. Kip had watched him fight, and the boy was better at grappling than almost anyone else. The fights that Ferkudi had lost, he'd lost because his reach was short. On a good day, and with the colors he had, he'd be in the top three or four fighters. It was just bad luck that he was fighting for position fifteen right now.

Kip shrugged his shoulders, rolled his head to stretch out his neck, and signaled that he was ready to fight.

The corner of Ferkudi's mouth twitched. He thought he was going to destroy Kip in a quick hand-to-hand fight.

No reason to let the other guy know what cards you're holding, is there? Thank you, Andross Guile.

Thank you, Andross Guile? Did someone slip haze into my breakfast?

The whistle blew and the circle was flooded with red light. Ferkudi came in straight.

Kip kept his hands up, between himself and Ferkudi so the boy wouldn't see Kip's eyes filling with red luxin. Then he threw his hand down and sprayed sticky red luxin at the boy's feet.

They stuck, and Ferkudi almost fell over. He rebalanced, brought his hands in, and Kip sprayed them with red luxin, too, gluing Ferkudi's hands to his chest. It worked just as Ironfist had taught him. Red was sticky, but it wasn't as strong as iron. Kip's will was. He threw all of his desire for the boy to be imprisoned into that drafting.

Ferkudi obviously hadn't been prepared for Kip to be drafting red, but Kip wasn't prepared for it either. The color breathed life onto the flames of his rage. He wasn't mad at Ferkudi, but red obliterated reason. He closed the distance and, before he even knew what he was doing, buried his fist in the astonished boy's face.

The late-night training sessions seemed to be doing something, because the punch went right where he wanted it to—he punched low, straight for Ferkudi's chin; and exactly as Commander Ironfist had said, the boy instinctively ducked his chin, and Kip's fist smashed his nose. With his feet stuck in red luxin, the boy toppled straight onto his back.

Kip sprayed red luxin around the fallen boy so he was stuck to the ground. He raised a foot to stomp on the boy's head—and barely stopped himself as the whistle shrilled.

Frightened at what he'd almost done, Kip flung away the red luxin. Orholam's beard, for a moment there, he wanted to kill the boy.

The red luxin disappeared, and Ferkudi sat up. "Oh," he said. "I think you broke my nose." He squeezed it gingerly, plugging its bleeding. "I 'idn't even owe you could draff red. Nice!" He grabbed the bridge of his nose, took a quick breath, and pulled it back into place. Groaning, he punched the ground twice. "Oww, oww." Blinking tears from his eyes, he extended his hands and some friends helped him up. "Nice one, Kip," he said.

Just like that? No anger?

"Uh...sorry," Kip said. "About your nose. The red sort of came over me."

"Ah, it's nuffin. 'Snot the first time."

"Nor probably the last, you big ugly mug," Cruxer said, coming up to join them. "Take a seat, Kip. I don't think you're going to have to fight again today."

"Really?" Kip asked. He was exhausted. The long workouts, the late nights, then not sleeping, then when he slept only having nightmares. He was hanging on by one frayed thread. He threw himself down into a camp chair.

Crack! The back legs of the chair snapped and Kip felt a stab of panic as he lost his balance and toppled flat on his back.

Fatty.

The scrubs laughed. Everyone laughed. Kip felt his face turning red as pyrejelly. Even Cruxer was laughing.

Kip jumped to his feet, but then couldn't move. Damn me. Just when I was making inroads. Just when I was starting to *belong* for once. Sick self-loathing shot through him, froze him. What could he do?

He hated them. He didn't want to be part of this anyway. They could all go to hell.

Cruxer raised his hands. "That clinches it! Kip, I already knew you needed a new name among us. Kip is no Blackguard name, and we've seen that *you* most certainly need one."

Was Cruxer making fun of him? What did he mean, "You need one"?

"I don't understand," Kip said quietly, wary of a trap.

Trainer Fisk was standing there, looking bemused. "I'm sure you're not the only one. How many of you lot grew up in Paria?" Less than half raised their hands. "Well then, story time. Not everyone's third-generation Blackguard, Cruxer."

"Yes, sir."

Trainer Fisk glowered at the ground, as if he didn't know exactly where to start. "When Lucidonius came, he was protected by thirty mighty men, some of whom he first had to defeat. Many of these men had been heroes and priests of the old gods and had names taken from those false gods, like El-Anat and Dagnar Zelan and Or-mar-zel-atir. They couldn't keep their old names, so they took new names. Though some of them went nameless until they felt they'd earned a new name in service of Orholam. El-Anat became Forushalzmarish for a time, but then as the light spread beyond Paria, more of them took names that the locals could pronounce—or fear. So Forushalzmarish changed his name again, and went by Shining Spear. Now, the Blackguard names don't mean quite what they used to now, because none of us is shedding a name associated with those old blasphemies. You can take a name, or not. If you're given a name, you can choose whether you want to use it all the time or just among the Blackguard. Names generally spread widest that are best earned, and best fit their wearer. It's up to you."

"But I'm not a Blackguard yet," Kip said. What if they gave him a name, and he didn't make it in?

"The tradition is that if the name is adopted, it's only used among your fellows until you become a full Blackguard." Trainer Fisk shrugged. "But then we get children whose parents give them Blackguard names before they even come to the Jaspers...like Cruxer here." He seemed amused. "So, Cruxer?"

"I say Kip is no Blackguard name, and I say he needs a good one." There were some murmurs of agreement. "But what name?" Cruxer asked. "It's got to fit, right?"

"Tiny!" someone shouted.

"Meh, too obvious," Cruxer said. "So what's he done? Arm-breaker, Will-breaker, Rule-breaker, Nose-breaker..." He paused for effect. "*Chair*-breaker." The scrubs roared.

With a flourish, he said, "Kip, we dub thee Breaker."

The scrubs cheered and laughed. It was the perfect Blackguard name: it could be used to laud or to lampoon. Kip rolled it over on his tongue. Breaker. Despite everything, despite how he could excuse how each of the incidents that led to him earning the name weren't really indicative of his character, just accidents, he liked it. It sounded *tough*.

A reluctant grin broke over his face like dawn over Atan's Teeth. "I'll take it," he said. "Among you, Breaker I am."

Chapter 58

"Breaker, huh?" Andross Guile said, sardonic. "I feel like I'm being visited by a high personage."

"And I feel like I'm visiting a bitter, hateful old man. Oh." Kip sat down in his chair opposite the old man.

Andross laughed. "So, *Breaker*, does your little friend Adrasteia know that we're playing for her future right now?"

"No."

"And which will you break, her heart or her maidenhead? Ha-ha! Mmm. You play like a failure, Kip. Do you know why you didn't tell her? Because you thought that if you lost, whatever happens to her could just be a tragedy that you could pretend you had nothing to do with. You didn't want her to hate you if you lost. Poor Kip. Poor orphan boy of a haze-addled mother."

"Shut up and play," Kip said.

"Kip the Lip. You never know when to stop, do you? Lean forward, lard boy."

He obeyed. The blind man groped, found his face, and slapped him heavily.

Kip accepted the blow. There was something purifying in pain. He was a madman. He spat bloody penance on Lord Guile's floor. Kip the Lip. Ramir had called him that, mocked him.

"Boy, your defiance is inspiring, but be aware that I set the rules, and I have no compunction about changing those when I please. You think you have nothing to lose? Fool. Don't vaunt until you've won, don't scream defiance until you've lost."

"Well then, I hope you'll accept my vaunting in about half an hour."

Andross said, "Let's get to it, then. Best two of three. Which deck would you like today? I'll be taking the red." He gestured. He had white and yellow decks set out for Kip.

"I'll pass," Kip said.

Thin eyebrows appeared briefly over the top of Andross Guile's huge dark spectacles. "Ah, your own deck? Show it to me."

"They've got the blind man's marks," Kip said. "Here." He handed over only one card.

Andross rubbed the corner where the marks were, as if looking for a reason to reject it, but it was perfect work. Janus Borig wouldn't do less.

Kip half expected the old man to tell him he couldn't use other cards. It was a rule that had never been addressed.

"If any of the cards don't have the marks, I'll reject the entire deck, and you lose, understood?" Andross said.

"Understood."

"Wondered how long it would be before you finally made your own deck," Andross said. "Slower than I thought you'd be."

"Mm-hmm," Kip said. The insult meant nothing, not in the same breath as the much larger victory of being allowed to use his own deck.

"Me first?" Hoping that the old man would contradict him and go first.

Indulgent smile. "Be my guest."

So Kip set the field of play to outside. Outside made it harder to control the light, which was usually a good call against red. So many of the sources of light indoors were torches or fires—light sources that gave yellow and red and sub-red easily—that it was harder for greens and blues to source their spells.

But Kip going first meant Andross got to draw an extra card.

They established the area quickly, the art on the cards giving them an imaginary space—outside the red walls of a castle. Grass, forest. Blue sky, of course. These were the sources. Either could draft from them, but Kip was on the forest side, so he could draft more quickly from it, powering his green drafting quicker, while the converse was true for Andross and the red walls.

Now that Kip knew the rules, Andross played a fast variant of the game. There were two tiny sand clocks, five seconds each. Absent the visual cues of seeing the grains drain through, the luxlord had a fantastically worked model that rang a bell each time a player ran out of time. If you didn't play during your five seconds, you lost your turn. As he liked to say, in real life, drafters fought each other simultaneously, each drafting as quickly as they could, deciding on the fly what to do, making mistakes.

Andross Guile's blindness was the one huge advantage Kip had. He could see his opponent's card as soon as it was turned over, where Andross had to reach across the table and feel for his. Kip put his new card in the same place every time so that the handicap was as little of one as possible, but it was still at least a second per turn extra that he had. And Andross had to remember everything on the play field.

In the normal variant, turns were taken in a leisurely fashion with no clocks, but Andross despised it, said it taught nothing. Life and death and drafting were *fast*, he said. The sands of our lives are always pouring out, always too fast.

"Ominous name," Andross said. The first few moves never took too much concentration.

"What's that?" Kip asked, trying to decide whether to spend his turn establishing more colors in the field or putting on his spectacles.

"Breaker."

Spectacles. He didn't want to be unarmed for any longer than absolutely necessary. "Ominous how?"

"You didn't put him up to it? Here I was giving you credit for doing that behind the scenes. Clever move, I thought."

Clever move? Apparently Kip's silence spoke for him.

"You'd have me believe you getting that name was a coincidence?"

"What're the two things that are coinciding?" Kip asked.

"Breaker's one of the epithets the prophecies apply to the Lightbringer."

"It was a joke. I broke a chair."

"Funny," Andross said, tone flat.

"And I broke a boy's nose. And a bit of drafting someone was doing."

The Lightbringer? Something in Kip's soul soared at the very thought. He was distracted by talking and almost missed his turn. He played quickly, putting Damien Savoss on the field and flipping Andross Guile's clock.

Oh hell. That was one of the forbidden cards. Kip had meant to hold on to those for another couple of turns.

Andross ran his fingers over the marks. Hesitated. Ran his fingers over the marks again. "This is Damien Savoss," he said. "This card is illegal." He was one to talk.

"Illegal to possess," Kip said quickly, "but the justiciars of the game never declared them illegal to play." He flipped his sand clock over.

"A fine distinction."

"A fine distinction? I only learned about the black cards because you play with them!"

"Some of the black cards were withdrawn, others were *outlawed*—"

The bell rang, signaling the end of Andross Guile's turn.

Kip played another card quickly, cementing the luxlord's missed turn.

Rage washed over Andross Guile's face. The loose flesh below his jawline quivered. But he said nothing. He played.

In five minutes, Kip won. The additional turn and the surprise of playing against cards he hadn't seen in more than a decade threw off Andross Guile's game. Still, it seemed like the man played defensively. Unusual.

"It was a good trick," Andross said afterward, while they shuffled their decks. "You shouldn't have wasted it on the girl. That's the kind of trick that only works once. You should have seen if you could beat me once, and then played that deck for the tiebreaker if you couldn't. Beyond that, you should have waited until your own future was in jeopardy, not spent it on a slave girl. Foolish."

Kip turned to Grinwoody. "Some water, please." He forgot again that you don't say please to a slave. He was always forgetting that.

But the water wasn't the point. Kip had figured out that the big spectacles Grinwoody wore somehow allowed him to see in the darkness. With them, Grinwoody was Andross's eyes. As soon as the old slave turned to grab the pitcher, Kip brought the other deck out of his pocket quietly, speaking to cover the noise of it. "There's a thousand things you could teach me, Luxlord Guile. You're brilliant and experienced. But right now you're my enemy, and you're trying to inflict horrors on someone who is dear to me. So I'll keep my own counsel, thanks."

Lord Guile's face cleared. "You are learning, aren't you? Ignorant, naïve, but not altogether as stupid as I thought. I know you may not believe this, Kip, but I actually like you. A little. How's your hand?"

It took Kip a moment to understand he didn't mean his cards, he actually meant his hand. "Better." His fingers still wouldn't straighten all the way, but his grip was strong, and he was working on them.

Andross Guile made some noncommittal noise and picked up the yellow deck that he'd set out for Kip earlier. He opened a box off to one side, grabbed out a few cards, took some out of the deck, and shuffled the new ones in. You were allowed to switch or modify your deck between rounds, to adapt to your opponent's strategies. "So have you thought about it? Most boys do, eventually."

"Thought about what?" Kip asked. The old man started speaking about whatever he was thinking of at times, not bothering to connect them for his listener.

"Whether you're the Lightbringer, of course." There was a savage, amused edge to Andross Guile's tone, like he was juggling fire and throwing it to Kip still burning.

"No," Kip said. Something in him seized up. "Let's play."

"He's supposed to be of mysterious birth, and yours is at least dubious—which could be close enough."

Kip flushed. "Your turn," he said.

"The old word that says he'll be a 'great' man from his youth could be a pun in the original Parian—another meaning of the word 'great' is 'rotund.' Which...*well.*"

Die, you old cancer. "Your turn," Kip said.

"But I am moving, don't you see?" Andross asked. "When the Lightbringer comes, he's going to upend everything. Anyone who has wealth, position, or power will fear him because he could take it all away. But everyone who doesn't have any of those will love him, hoping he'll give all that to them. So what part will you play, Kip? Garden."

Garden? Oh, he was declaring the setting.

Kip drew—and got lucky. A hand full of time control cards.

Using his first turns to gather the light he needed in various colors, he appeared to do nothing.

Andross played a Superchromat, a powerful card for a yellow deck, meaning his spells wouldn't fail, and then he drafted a yellow sword, which took two rounds, one to draft it and one to solidify it.

By the time Kip played Panic, the old man's lips were pursed. He wasn't aware of any green deck that used the strategy Kip was employing. Andross's five-second sand clocks were swapped out for four-second clocks.

And the pleasure of playing a Panic on the cold old man, who had probably never panicked in his entire life, was a joyous dagger-twist.

Andross attacked, and Kip didn't even try to stop it. It took off nearly half his life.

Kip played another Panic. Four-second sand clocks were replaced with three-second clocks.

It was, of course, a completely unfair strategy. It already took the blind man at least an additional second longer than a sighted man to tell what the card played was, and three seconds was no time to come up with any sort of good tactics.

He attacked again and took Kip within a hair's breadth of death. Then Kip followed up with a few weak attacks, barely staying alive. Between his own draw, reading his own card, and reading Kip's, Andross had no time at all.

Kip Disarmed him, playing his own cards as quickly as he could to deprive Andross of as much of his time as possible. Within five more turns, by a hundred weakling cuts, he'd killed the old man.

Andross's fist crashed onto the tabletop and he swept the sand clocks off the table, smashing several against the wall. He balled his hands and his fists shook.

"Give me your deck," he said, barely leashing his rage.

"It's on the table. In front of you," Kip said. His voice sounded thready and tight. Some dim part of him wondered why he was so terrified of an old, infirm man, but he was.

Andross went through the deck with surprising speed, given his blindness. "You switched decks," he said. "Grinwoody?"

"My lord, I didn't see him do it. It was my failure."

Andross screamed, voice raw, "I know it was your failure!" Kip was suddenly intensely aware that Andross Guile was the Red. He'd been using red luxin for twice as long as Kip had been alive. The darkness of the room was to keep Andross from becoming a color wight— and the man might be very, very close to the line. "Out, bastard! Out!"

Kip sat very still. Licked his lips.

"I said, *out!*" Andross roared.

Kip cowered. Very quietly and respectfully, he said, "I need Teia's writ, my lord. And my deck. Please."

Andross snarled and flung Kip's deck in his face. He whirled and stormed to his bedchamber. He paused at the open door, but didn't turn his back. "Grinwoody!" he barked.

"Yes, my lord," the slave said. After their years together, the little man was able to discern exactly what the Red wanted from the barest modulation of his voice.

The door slammed behind Andross, and Kip picked up his scattered cards. Grinwoody brought forth a sheaf of papers and Andross Guile's seal.

"Mother's name?" Grinwoody asked, voice low.

"Katalina."

"Full name."

"Katalina Delauria." Grinwoody nodded, as if he knew it all along and was merely receiving confirmation. Kip was dimly aware that even in this loss, Andross Guile was getting some information out of him. Kip had no idea what the information was good for, but he knew the spider was spinning silken snares with every breath.

Grinwoody filled out the forms, affixed the seal, and handed them to Kip. There was a brown stain on the papers. Blood? "Turn these in to the head scribe in the Prism's Tower. And congratulations, you're now the owner of a young slave girl. Enjoy."

Chapter 59

~Shimmercloak~

Tap, tap, tap, tap . . .
    Out of time. Out of place.
    Dissolving.

As his fingers touched each point, he felt as if a scroll unfurled. Not simply the senses: the five central colors offering sight, touch, hearing, smell, and taste, but more. Superviolet and blue came together through his thumb at the bottom left of the card: cities and superstructures, their outlines burning in tight, logical lines, then rising up out of the page, lines of reason, of thought, of history, causality lifting up—and still deeper he plunged.

Green through his forefinger at the top left of the card. Embodiment: the health, the shape of the body that he now knew he would inhabit, but also the bodies around him, the physical presences, the lives—the sick, the weak, the vivacious. Even the flashes of the fishes in the bay, the background light of the life in the waves, and the cool peace emanating from the grasses and the trees of this island. His body in this card was strong, a man in his prime, some aches, though. Perhaps a warrior of some sort? An old back injury, never quite healed. An ankle that he'd rolled a dozen times, always weak. And then, deeper, he felt the strength of his muscles, the grace of a fighter who'd grown up in a dance troupe, felt the dammed-up libido of a man traveling with a woman he desires.

The next finger to touch was his ring finger. Top right corner. Orange. Where green was life, the orange was the connections between the living. Those glowing blue lines of causality, of logic, now came alive. Those lines, without this, were meaningless. Some of those blue structures were the lies he'd told, the foundations he'd placed for falsehoods, false trails, deceptions that made sense to his inquisitors. And now, quite suddenly, the young man had a taste of how dangerous this man was. There was something *stunted* about him. He'd had a relationship with Niah, that was the woman, he now knew. His partner, a woman he can't help but eye: admiring, desiring, and hating. He'd coaxed her to bed, once, early on.

She'd said afterward that if he ever touched her again, she'd kill him. Said he'd been too rough—or something.

She just didn't like to admit how she liked it. Weak in that. Shy. She could fight, though. She'd asked their superiors to be reassigned after their one tryst, but she hadn't told them why. Too embarrassed, too weak. They'd refused.

He hadn't touched her since, though. She was good with a dagger, good with a gun, good with a grudge. Still, he couldn't help but fantasize about tying her up again. Normally, after he'd had a woman once, he lost interest. Not Niah. Maybe this is love, then.

Oh, Orholam help him. The young man was losing himself into the card, already, and he hadn't even touched all the—

His little finger, bottom right, sub-red and red at almost the exact same time his middle finger touched the top middle, the yellow.

Whatever disinterested study of the mechanics of the cards and how they connected a drafter to his subject was obliterated in the rush of Vox's crippled passions and Vox's single-mindedness. And Vox's shimmercloak.

I throw my bag over my shoulder and follow Niah down the pier. I hate the rotten seaweed stench of the sea, always have. But it's good to get off the corvette. Hate ships. If I'd stayed much longer, I would've opened that gangrenous captain from groin to gills. The thought puts a smile on my face, as do Niah's swaying hips in front of me. Niah's ass could make luxiats curse and eunuchs pop wood. Made up for her face, I suppose.

Niah shifts her own pack on her back and adjusts her belt. She extends a single finger down as she does so. A little token of her appreciation for my appreciation.

I laugh. Niah loves to flirt.

We don't even clear the taxmen's station out of the docks before Niah coughs. It's the signal that she'd been passed her orders. Our superiors always have the orders passed to her. Think she's better than me, for some reason. It keeps me attached to her, though. Keeps me from hurting her, they think. Like I'd hurt her.

She walks on ahead of me. Doesn't tell me the message, doesn't show it to me. It's in code anyway, a code they haven't taught me, and that Niah refuses to teach me. Smart woman, sometimes.

I look up at the Chromeria. It fills me with rage and loathing. They kicked me out in my first year, thirteen years old, and over what? A cat.

Who likes cats? Cats aren't even capable of loving you back. Why had they decided that damned beast was worth more than me? I was a budding green drafter. They couldn't have known then how special I would be, but who would throw any drafter away over a cat?

Still, that cat taught me something. Taught me to be careful. Invaluable in my occupation. It's why I'm still alive, twenty years later. My first three partners hadn't been as careful as I am. I barely recovered Gebalyn's cloak last time, and wasn't able to pull it out of the fire before it lost six precious thumb-widths off the hem. That cloak would always have to go to someone as short as Niah now. It was already hard enough to find lightsplitters—now my matron would have to find a *short* splitter.

Not my problem.

All I hope is that this job hurts the Chromeria. Atirat is far more accepting of my little quirks than Orholam and his Chromeria would ever be. The green goddess doesn't chain those who love her. Atirat saved me from a life of self-loathing. She gives me freedom, acceptance. These cattle, these chattel, would never know that.

The taxmen don't stop me, don't search my bag. Though they have the right to do so, the volume of people who come through is simply too high to effectively stop all of them. They do spot checks instead, pulling people out of the lines and searching for ratweed, for jewels, for saffron, for any items that are small enough and precious enough that individuals could smuggle an untaxed fortune's worth in their pockets.

Maybe I don't look the type, though in my experience smugglers do look as bedraggled as I must. My beard needs a fresh oiling at the least. If I can find an Atashian barber, I'll get the whole beard redone—unbraided, beads removed, combed out, face massage, dyed to cover the patchy gray, then rebraided and tied, with gold beads perhaps instead of the blue glass I have now, maybe some gold wire woven in. Gold wire, that's how I'll reward myself for this job, whatever it is.

I catch up with Niah an hour later, after both of us have taken rooms in an inn, separately. There are good operational reasons for doing so, but Niah didn't mention those when I suggested we save money by sharing a room; she simply said that she'd kill me if I ever came into her room.

Sometimes I think she doesn't like me much. Good partner, though. Capable, won't get me killed. In the end, that's what I care about, although I miss that look on her face when I started asphyxiating her after I tied her up. She panicked, but I knew she'd thank me as soon as she hit the peak. I couldn't wait to see her terror turn to delirious pleasure.

But she was frigid. Man can't help that.

I fall in beside her as she buys fruit at the market a block away from the inn. "Nice melons," I say.

She pretends I haven't said anything. "I translated the code. You're not going to believe it."

I'm much taller than she is, and I stand close, looking down the front of her blouse. "Mm, suspense."

"You know, Vox, there's a brothel across the street. You need to go take care of something before we can talk?" Spunky. Like that about her.

I glance back up to her eyes. "You don't want me to look, don't show 'em off. I'm free to look; you're free to cover up. What's the job?"

She looks around, making sure no one is close enough to listen in. She lowers her voice. "They want us to kill the Witch of the Winds. They want us to kill Janus Borig herself."

My eyes go dark even as I feel dread shoot down into my stomach. Sound ceases. I'm losing feeling, losing my train of thought. I'm being shot up and out and back.

I hover, suspended between my own body and the body of a fat young man. Ugh, *fat*, after the glorious utility of my warrior-assassin's frame, after the grace earned by ten thousand hours of training. I'm sitting in the—

What the hell?

What was—

He was back.

Chapter 60

"You won me? You won me in a *card game?*" Teia asked.

"Yes?" Kip said.

It was after their midnight workout and drafting practice. Teia had apparently noticed that Kip was acting strange and had cornered him. Now they were sitting in his new room. He was still hot from their exercise, wearing a towel around his shoulders, having a hard time making eye contact. He wasn't even sure why he felt ashamed.

"What did you bet against me? I mean, what stakes did you put up?" Teia asked. "You don't own anything. I mean, no offense. I don't either, but..."

"It wasn't really a bet like that. The Red was—I don't know— seeing how much strain he could put on me, I guess. It was you against...a secret that he thinks I have."

"I...see." Teia's nose wrinkled for a second. She saw that he wasn't going to trust her. "I'm sorry, I'm not at my best when I'm tired," she said. "They gave you my papers?"

Kip waved toward his desk where the stamped paper sat. "I already registered it with the head scribe. He said they have to query the Abornean satrap's embassy to make sure there's no liens on you, but with it countersigned by Andross Guile, he was sure there would be nothing wrong. He already entered it in the Chromeria's books."

Teia was still blinking like a child who's fallen and can't decide whether she's hurt or not. Is the right response tears, or just getting back up and walking away? "You *won* me?" she asked again. "What...what are you going to do with me?"

Her eyes flicked to his bed, back to his eyes, then down.

274

"No!" Kip said. "Like you said, that's forbidden for Blackguards. I..."

"For full Blackguards, not for scrubs," she said quietly. "Not until you take the vows."

No woman would ever take Kip to her bed willingly. Not for himself. He'd have to get a room slave to do it, or a prostitute. He was fat, a bastard, stupid, ugly, awkward, Tyrean, mixed-breed. He didn't know how to talk to girls like other boys did. This was his only chance. Teia wasn't exactly volunteering, but she didn't seem disgusted by him either. Andross Guile was right.

He could always free her later. Or if they both became Blackguards, they would take the vows, and it would end there.

Kip would get something for himself for once. He'd earned it. All those hours studying, memorizing decks and strategies when he could have been studying drafting instead. He'd known that he shouldn't use the black deck trick saving Teia. He should have held on to that to save himself. He was risking his own future for her. She owed him. Without Kip, she'd belong to Andross Guile. He'd saved her from that spider. What was so wrong with wanting a little gratitude in return?

Gratitude, huh? Is *that* what you've been fantasizing about, Kip?

Teia set her bag down. Her voice was distant, empty. "Do you want me to wash up first? Or I could bring up hot water and we could wash together. Or... I'm sorry, Kip. I mean, my lord. I've never done this before. I don't—I didn't expect my mistress to sell me. She seemed very set—I—I'm talking too much, aren't I?"

And he had fantasized about Teia. And felt awful afterward.

Kip scrubbed his towel over his face. She was a slave. He hadn't enslaved her; it was just how things were. All this wasn't his idea, and he had to pay penalties for how things were, too. He hadn't chosen to be a bastard, but he had to live with that, didn't he? He took his lumps, it was only fair that he get some of the rewards. He deserved this. Besides, just because it was a duty didn't mean it had to be unpleasant. Kip would be good to her. He would care about her. He would be better to her than any slave girl could hope a man would be.

Teia swallowed. "I'm a virgin, but the room slaves talked about their work—a lot." She blushed. "I think I know what to do." She swallowed again.

And really, what could she hope for that was better if he freed her? Did peasants have things so much better than slaves?

Temptation is a slow and subtle serpent.

I am the turtle-bear. I'm fat and ungainly and ridiculous, but at least I can be honest with myself. I want to take her because I'm terrified I'll never get the chance to bed anyone ever again. And I'll be nice to her because I don't want to feel guilty afterward. It's all lies.

Of course I want to sleep with you, Master. Of course you were good to me. Of course it's better than a girl could have ever asked for. Of course you are kind and generous and wonderful.

If you're not free to say no, your yes is meaningless.

"Have I displeased you?" Teia asked.

She wouldn't be so attuned to my every mood and whim if I weren't her master, would she?

She swallowed. "We don't need to wash up first. I didn't mean anything by it. I'm sorry. I'm all thumbs at this. I should shut up and—" She crossed her arms and grabbed the hem of her shirt.

Kip grabbed her arm before she could strip, stopping her. He ignored the bewildered look on her face, went to his desk, and grabbed the papers. He handed them to her, avoided her eyes.

"You're free. I won't be able to get it registered until the first transfer clears the embassy—I tried, but as far as I'm concerned, you don't belong to me." That sounded bad, for some reason. Kip rubbed his face with the towel. "No one had slaves where I grew up, so I don't know how people usually do this, but...I don't want to know how it works. The idea of compelling you to...to do the things that awful old man suggested...I hate myself enough already."

"You haven't been sleeping, have you?" Teia asked.

"What's that got to do with anything?"

"So you haven't."

Kip looked away. "I have...bad dreams." Bad dreams. That was putting it mildly. "Whether I sleep or not, I'm more tired in the morning."

"Go to bed, Kip. We'll talk about this in the morning."

"I'm serious, Teia."

"Me, too. To bed," she said firmly.

"I thought I was the master around here," Kip said. He regretted saying it immediately, but she laughed and swatted his butt. She'd laughed a little too hard, though, obviously at least as relieved as he was.

He went to bed and, miracle of miracles, slept.

In the morning, Kip felt ridiculously well. For ten seconds. He caught himself humming.

Then he thought about the dagger.

He sponged himself clean, put on fresh clothes, and then poked his head out of his door quickly. No spies, at least none that he noticed. He used the stairs to go down to his old barracks level. He still didn't have a plan, but he knew he couldn't leave a priceless relic in some random chest forever. He slipped into the barracks and walked quickly down the rows.

The bed under which he'd hidden the dagger had been claimed. The chest was moved to the foot of the bed, like all the other occupied beds. Kip's throat clamped shut.

He threw the chest open. A change of clothes, an extra blanket, a few coins. No dagger. Oh hell. Oh hell no. Dear Orholam no.

"What are you doing in my stuff?" a voice said from the latrine doorway. It was a new boy, someone Kip had never seen before. Pimply, scrawny, birthmark on his neck.

"I had some things in this chest," Kip said. "Where are they? What have you done with them?"

"What are you talking about? There was just the standard blanket when I got the chest. Are you stealing from me?"

"Oh shut up," Kip said.

"You're Breaker, aren't you?" the boy asked.

Great. Kip didn't say anything. He left.

He went downstairs and got in a student line. He was here during lectures, so the line was empty. The secretary obviously knew Kip was skipping lectures, too. He took his time coming over.

Kip bit his tongue.

"Are you lost, young man?" the secretary asked him. The man was holding a steaming cup of kopi.

"No, but something of mine is. Do you have an area where you keep lost items?"

"Indeed," the man said. "What have you lost?"

Kip swallowed.

"Please don't tell me you've lost a number of coins, but you can't remember exactly how many." The man smiled humorlessly and sipped at his kopi.

"No. Um." Kip lowered his voice. "A knife in a sheath, about this long, white ray skin on the um, grip, some um, glass embedded in the blade?"

"You boys and your games."

"I'm serious."

The man took another sip of his kopi, rolled his eyes, and went to a box behind his desk. He began rummaging through old cloaks and trousers. "Slaves clean the rooms, you know. Shifty lot. No morals. Thieves half the time. You really shouldn't leave anything out that—" He stopped speaking.

Kip heard the unmistakable sound of a blade sliding out of its sheath. His heart leapt.

The man came back to the counter and laid the blade on the counter. It was the real thing. His eyes were wide.

Kip swept it off the counter. "It might, uh, be wiser for you to not tell anyone about this," he said. "Um, I didn't mean that to sound like a threat. I meant it's kind of incredibly important, so if anyone else comes looking for it, maybe you haven't ever seen it and don't know what they're talking about? And if you ever find out which slave brought it here, tell them thanks. I probably owe them my life or something."

The man sipped his kopi nonchalantly. There were beads of sweat on his forehead, though.

I don't have anywhere to conceal a big knife.

As if it weren't terribly conspicuous, Kip took the knife and stuck it up his sleeve, the hilt concealed as much as possible in his hand. He swallowed and tightened his belt with one hand.

Girding up my loins, I guess.

Loins. Kip didn't like the word.

The secretary cleared his throat. "Is there anything else I can help you with?" he asked.

Oh, Kip was stalling.

"No. Thanks again." Then he was off.

He didn't know where to go. He didn't have any safe place to put something worth a fortune, but he found himself walking toward Janus Borig's house. She had things that were worth a fortune, hidden in plain sight. Maybe she could give him some advice.

When he got to the entry hall, he realized that everyone coming inside was soaking wet. He thought about going back up to his room and getting a cloak, but his room could well have a spy on it, and he already was doing a bad job of protecting the dagger. Getting lucky once was great, but expecting it to happen again was too much.

He'd just have to get wet. Orholam knew he had enough insulation to keep warm. He braced himself against the downpour and started jogging.

When he reached Janus Borig's house, sopping wet and freezing cold, he found the door bashed in, torn off its hinges, the iron twisted and ripped. He smelled something in the air. Blood. Blood and smoke.

Chapter 61

Kip could feel fear trying to paralyze him, but fear was slow. Fear could only perch on his shoulders and spread its black wings over his face if he gave it a place to roost. It flew around his head, stabbing its bloody beak for his eyes, but Kip was faster. He burst inside.

He ran into something as he stepped through the torn door. Something yielding and invisible. Not something. Someone.

Kip's weight did something useful for once, and he fell forward, staggering into Janus Borig's house and knocking over the invisible figure. He saw the flash of a trouser leg through an open cloak, as the man tumbled over a shattered bookshelf.

There was a small explosion of cards. The man must have had his hands full of them, and as he hit the ground, they went everywhere.

Then, in a rustle of cloth, he *disappeared*.

Kip jumped to his feet, slipped on the trash on the floor, and saw dead bodies. Armed men, perhaps half a dozen, all uniformed in black with a silver shield embroidered on their chests. Janus Borig's guards. All the dead were her guards. They hadn't killed anyone in return.

The sound of steel being drawn cut through the muted hiss of the rain and wind outside.

Kip widened his eyes to the sub-red spectrum—and the invisible man snapped into focus. Cloaked but still radiating more heat than his surroundings. He was walking straight toward Kip, not bothering to lower his own center of gravity. Kip must look like easy meat.

Looking around frantically like he had no idea what was going on, Kip waited until the cloaked man stepped closer. Apparently the cloak only concealed what was beneath it, so the man had only a short sword, and he couldn't lift it until the last second or it would be revealed, hanging in midair. So the man walked forward, sword point down. When the man was within two paces, Kip screamed. He leapt toward the man and to the side, left arm sweeping in a block that batted the man's sword arm even as it came up, and his right hand burying his own dagger in the man's chest.

Sub-red was bad for making out detail, or Kip was just clumsy, because his feet landed on books and apple cores and flew out from under him. He lost his dagger.

He popped back up to his feet, the battle rush making him shake. The invisible man was now very much visible, flopped on his back, arms wide, unmoving, Kip's dagger staked straight through his chest.

Kip looked around frantically. Janus had had a thousand muskets in here. Why couldn't he find any of them now? Nothing seemed to be on fire now, though the smell of smoke was heavy in the air. He also smelled the resinous, fresh cedar smell of green luxin. They'd smothered fires with luxin. Fires. Janus Borig had said she'd booby-trapped the cards upstairs. Maybe she'd laid traps down here, too.

"Vox?!" a woman's voice shouted from upstairs. "What was that?"

Snatching up his dagger from the dead man, Kip charged up the steps, as stealthy as a rhinoceros falling onto a crate of porcelain. The woman was standing at the wall of cards, pulling them down, sticking them into a wooden case with dividers, but she was already looking alarmed when Kip came into her view. She dropped the case onto a table and pulled her cloak around herself.

Without noticing, Kip had let his eyes go back to normal vision, and he saw the briefest glimpse of the upper room. Janus Borig lay in a bloody heap by her desk, dead. One smooth section of the wall had been broken open, revealing a hiding place that must have held cards or other treasures, and half the wall was bare.

The shimmer came toward him, and he relaxed his eyes. The invisible woman became a warm glow, coming fast toward him, raising her short sword at the last second. These assassins must be used to easy kills, because when Kip dodged, she was so surprised she didn't even try to adjust. He spun as he jumped past her and lashed out.

His dagger brushed something and then pulled through. Kip thought—hoped—that it was the side of her neck. He crouched low, out in the middle of the room.

"You're a sub-red," she said. "Always hated sub-reds." She shimmered back into visibility. She was a petite woman, blonde hair and pale skin, blue eyes made mostly green by drafting. Eyes narrow, face like a ferret. Her hair was pulled back into two braids. One of them had been cut halfway through by Kip's dagger. She drew a pistol.

Kip snatched up Janus's little chair and threw it at the assassin. She jumped aside, but had already pulled her trigger. The gun roared, its sound amplified in the small room. A series of loud whines, one on top of the other, rang out as the lead ball ricocheted off the walls.

The woman cursed and grabbed her leg, either hit by the bullet or faking it. Kip had no idea how badly it had wounded her. She threw the pistol at him, missed, and then attacked him with the short sword.

Her blade wasn't a fencing weapon by any means. Short and broad, it was meant for stabbing the unsuspecting, and making sure that single stab was lethal. Kip's blade was almost the same length, but narrower, sharper, and held by a much worse fighter and a much bigger target.

But the woman was hurt. Kip got into a knife fighting stance, trying to remember everything his trainers had ever said. The assassin might be feigning that her injury was worse than it was to lure Kip into doing something stupid.

Patience. If she was hurt, she'd do something reckless to try to end the fight quickly.

"People will be here any second," Kip said. "You might as well—"

She lunged at him and he batted her short sword aside and punched her in the face with his ruined left hand. At least it made a good fist— and good contact. She staggered back, wobbling a bit on her injured left leg.

If he'd followed hard after that strike, he could have ended the fight there, but he was tentative, worried she was tricking him.

She recovered, nose streaming blood, weaving. Maybe exaggerating the weaving a little.

"Every guard captain in five blocks has been bribed," she said. "And you hear that?"

Kip wasn't sure what she was talking about. Oh, the thunder.

"That means no one who's heard the shots will think anything of it. You're going to die here, fire boy."

"Why'd you do it?" Kip asked. Stalling. He could see a bloodstain spreading on her dark trousers. The ricochet *had* hit her.

There is no cheating in war; there are only survivors and victims. Trainer Fisk had pounded those lessons into his class. Blackguards weren't taught to duel; they were taught to kill.

Kip was no knife fighter, but he was stronger than this woman, especially as the blood loss weakened her. Their slow circling had brought him back within reach of the stool.

"Orders," she said. "And who the hell are you, so I can report who we killed?"

"Kip Guile," he said.

"Guile?"

Kip hurled his knife at the woman. It was never a good idea to throw your knife, unless you know how to throw knives. Kip didn't. But she wasn't expecting it—and it hit her, right in her chest. Hilt first.

But she jumped back, cursing, and Kip grabbed the stool, swinging it with both hands in a great arc.

The assassin tried to move back farther, but she was right against the wall, there was nowhere to go. Kip connected solidly, all of his strength in the blow. She tried to block it, but he crushed through her defense, breaking one leg of the stool, leaving it an awkward weapon.

But he didn't repeat his earlier mistake; this time he followed up his attack. The room was brighter than it had been earlier, and he could see that the assassin's arm was obviously broken, but she still somehow held on to her knife. She was reaching over to grab it with her left hand when Kip crashed into her, smashing her against the wall with his lowered shoulder.

He heard the whoosh of her breath being crushed out of her, and then they were both scrambling for her dagger.

"Niah!" A voice cried out from the stairs. "Get down!"

Kip turned to see the other assassin—the one he swore he'd killed—standing there, pistol leveled. The assassin, Niah, tried to wriggle away from Kip and dive to the floor, but he held her, absorbed by the tiny orange dot hovering above the man's pistol—a burning slow match. It slapped down into the pan.

Kip spun with Niah, face-to-face, abandoning all thought of the dagger between them.

A boom, and she snapped her head forward into his face. Her headbutt caught him in the nose and lip. His eyes instantly flooded with tears.

"Niah!"

Kip stumbled backward, tripped, fell on his ass. The assassin Niah dropped like a pile of meat, the back of her skull exploded. What Kip had thought was a headbutt was her brained skull snapping forward into him from absorbing a bullet.

He smacked his head on the wall as he fell, not so hard that it dazed him, but it still hurt.

I'm a moron. He reached into a pocket and snatched out his green spectacles.

The other assassin, Vox, was staring in horror at the shattered head of his partner, whom he'd just killed. But Kip's movement made him spring into action, leaping forward and kicking Kip in the head.

Kip's shoulder took most of the blow, and he rolled with the kick, putting as much distance between himself and Vox as he could. He saw the assassin snatching up Niah's short sword. Kip staggered to his feet, unarmed, trapped in a corner of the room, just as Vox settled into a fighting stance. From the stance alone, Kip could tell he was a warrior.

Kip's spectacles were bent but still in his hand. No time. He'd get them on his face about the time the sword ended his life.

Both he and the assassin lunged at the same time: Vox lunging for Kip, Kip lunging for the cards on the wall. Kip raked his hand down the wall, tearing off four, five, six cards.

A gush of flames shot straight out of the wall. If Kip had been standing in front of the cards, he would have been consumed. Instead, the flames made a wall between him and the assassin, who skidded to a stop. Kip pulled on his spectacles, bending them roughly into place and sucking in green. Vox saw what he was doing, and as the curtain of flame dwindled to nothing, they both threw up an open hand to fling luxin at each other.

The assassin was faster. His hand snapped out—and nothing happened. His palm was empty of color. He had one second to look down at his own hand, surprised. Then Kip's green missile speared through his stomach.

The man fell to the floor and wailed. "Atirat! Atirat, come back. What have you done to me?!" he shouted at Kip. He wasn't looking at his stomach. He wasn't looking at his death wound. He was looking at his *hands*.

Kip coughed. The wall holding the remainder of the cards had caught fire. Some of the cards sparked and spat, like tree sap in the blaze. Others sat placid in the flames. The fire was spreading, fast.

A breathy, labored voice said, "Kip."

It came from the corner. Janus Borig. She was alive.

"Get the knife, you fool," she said.

"What?" Kip asked, like a simpleton. Oh, his knife. The one he'd thrown away during the fight. *That* knife.

Kip had to step over Niah's body, her exploded head still leaking blood in an expanding circle. He looked away quickly so he didn't vomit.

The other assassin was babbling something about being unclean, unworthy, ruined. He was weeping, gasping, but he didn't seem like he had the strength to make any trouble. Kip found the dagger and stood up into the smoke just as he heard a scream.

He flinched, ducked low, and was in time to see Vox—who had taken off his cloak and his shirt for some reason—slash open the side of his own neck. Blood fountained out, and the assassin stared at Kip, his brown eyes full of hatred, for a single moment, then he slumped over, unconscious.

What the hell?

Kip ran back to Janus. "Cloaks, Kip."

"We can get you a cloak once we get out of here," Kip said.

"Stupid, wonderful boy. *Their* cloaks." Her voice was weak.

Kip obeyed. His brain didn't seem to be working correctly, so he was glad to have the direction—even if the direction didn't make sense in a house that was rapidly filling with smoke. The man had thrown his cloak off, so that was easy to grab, but the woman's cloak was still around her body. Kip looked away as he rolled her off it, but still it stuck, and he saw that the cloak was bound to a choker collar of gold around the woman's throat.

Focusing just on his fingers so he didn't get overwhelmed by the gore and lose control, he unclasped the choker and finally pulled the cloak away.

He took a deep breath in the less smoky air down by the ground, and moved over to Janus Borig. He lifted her in his arms. Then he saw the cards again, and it hit him.

The precious cards lining the walls were aflame, each a little torch as the luxins within them flared.

"Don't worry about them. Go," Janus said.

"But they're everything! They're worth a—"

"Go, Kip." Her voice was weak.

Kip stumbled down the steps, with the old woman in his arms, his head coming dangerously close to the open flames, the heat a wall.

The flames were crawling down the side of the stairs, and Kip saw garbage smoldering as they reached the ground level. Orholam have mercy, this room wasn't only full of garbage. It was full of *black powder*.

Kip pushed toward the door, having to step deliberately to get around the trash, his arms full of old lady, cloaks, and one big-ass knife.

"One moment," Janus said in Kip's ear right before he carried her out the door. Her voice was a whisper. "Turn a..." He turned her and she reached out toward her tobacco box.

"Are you kidding me?" Kip asked. "You want a smoke? Now?"

She rooted around in the box for one moment more, and from beneath the tobacco she pulled out a small lacquered olivewood and ivory box, only large enough to hold a single deck of cards.

"Ha! They didn't get 'em." She gave a wan smile. "What are you waiting for? This place is on fire."

Kip carried her out into the night. It was storming, hard, lightning flashing, thunder shaking the buildings, rain smothering the streets. No one had noticed that the small building was on fire yet. Kip carried Janus down the street and had barely turned into an alley when he heard an explosion from her house. Then another, much bigger. He stumbled, fell, barely able to cushion the woman's fall.

He propped her up in the wet, dirty alley, abruptly exhausted.

"I don't suppose you grabbed my brushes," she asked, eyebrows lifting. The rain had washed the blood from her face, but she was looking unhealthily pale, somehow luminous. "Because..." She smiled, her eyes unnaturally bright. "I know who the Lightbringer is now."

And then she died.

Chapter 62

The Color Prince's army had fought through the pass into Atash with few casualties. Liv hadn't seen any of the fighting, and all the evidence of it was gone by the time she'd gone through.

After they made it through the pass, everyone had assumed they'd head straight for Idoss, the largest city in southern Atash. Instead, while smaller parties of foragers fanned out through the Atashian countryside to feed the army, the prince had taken the bulk of the army south, deeper into the mountains. He cut across the river and the main road, and then marched upstream, instead of downstream to Idoss.

Eventually, they came to the great silver mines at Laurion. Liv had never seen anything like it. The hills for at least a league in every direction were studded with holes. Three hundred and fifty mines, the prince said, worked by thirty thousand slaves. The mines were owned by the Atashian government, but nobles throughout the Seven Satrapies leased them and paid rents and a share of their profits to the state. Liv had heard of slaves being sent to the mines, but she'd never had any real concept of what it meant, other than that it was something bad that owners could threaten rebellious or lazy slaves with. Some Atashian students had mentioned their families renting out their slaves for the months after harvest to rich slaveholders who would transport them to the mines, work them, and send them back before planting. Apparently, a lot didn't come back, and most families would only rent out their slaves that way if they desperately needed the money.

Around the hills beyond the mines was a ring of wooden towers. The area inside was too vast to enclose with a fence, but the land had been cleared of timber. Any escaping slave would have to cross a great deal of open ground. Each wooden tower had a small complement of guards, horses, and several slave-hunting mastiffs.

A small town called Thorikos sat below the mines on the river. Here, the ore was loaded onto barges, food was brought in from the surrounding countryside, trade was conducted between slaveholders, medical treatment and tools were sold, and disputes were adjudicated. Thorikos was mostly empty, though. Everyone who could flee had. Left behind were only an old assemblyman and those citizens too old or ill to make the trip. Liv wondered at the cowardice of their families. Who would leave his mother to an advancing army? War brings out the worst in many, and the best in few.

There was no battle. When the overlords of the mine saw the forces arrayed against them, they knew it would be suicide. The soldiers stationed at Laurion were guards who kept the slaves in and captured those who escaped, not disciplined fighting men. They had only half a dozen drafters, none of them women skilled in battle. All those had been withdrawn to Idoss.

The assemblyman met the Color Prince outside of town. He looked quite frightened by the sight of the prince. Liv had forgotten how overwhelming he was at first. But the old man surrendered gracefully and begged for mercy.

The Color Prince granted it. He swore no one would be killed or accosted, that nothing would be stolen except food and tools.

And he was true to his word, though it caused grumbling. It would have been harder, Liv realized, if the army had experienced any privation. Since their food stores were still well stocked and no one had yet died in claiming plunder, it was far easier to ask the army to go without.

The prince took great care in how he seized the mines themselves. He sent soldiers to circle through the hills to capture each wooden watchtower to keep the slaves from escaping in the chaos. If he really did mean to free the slaves as he'd claimed, he meant to do it at his own pace, in his own way.

And so it was. Koios White Oak loved a spectacle. As the evening sun set the sky alight with fire, he spoke to the thirty thousand gathered slaves. All would be released immediately as soon as they listened to his few, poor words. He would clothe and feed them all tonight. They were free to go wherever they pleased so long as they didn't steal from his people or join the Chromeria against them. Or, he said, they could march with him, and take equal shares of the plunder with the rest of his soldiers, and exact vengeance, and perhaps make enough to start a life, to earn a plot of land if they wished to farm or a grant of money if they wished to live in the cities. They had ten days to decide, but they had to decide before he assaulted Idoss. If they chose to march with the army, they would be choosing to live by the army's rules. But it was their own choice, freely given, and they would from this day never be slaves again.

With his own hands, he struck the chains off an old slave's hands.

It was a huge gamble, and the next day it looked like it was one that had failed spectacularly. The slaves sent to the silver mines weren't the best and most temperate men. They were the captured pirates, the violent, the disobedient, the lazy, the rebellious. They were the kind of men who hated having rules at all, and only perhaps a tenth showed up for the drills the next morning. The army spent that day training, and only began its march at noon the next day.

By the third day, Liv realized what the prince had been betting on. The freed men, though now clothed and unbound, had no food. The Color Prince's foragers had denuded the land of crops and livestock. No one would beat the freed men, but no one would feed them either. Of course, most of them were very familiar with privation; starving the slaves was seen as the best way to cure lustfulness and laziness. They could deal with the pain of an empty belly. For a while.

There was no traffic on the roads except other slaves, so there was no one to rob even if they wanted to. One small band had attacked the camp, making off with food, but not horses. They'd been hunted down, tied up, sprayed with red luxin, and set afire alive. As three days turned to four, large groups began traveling parallel to the slow-moving army.

On the fifth day, at dinner, thousands came into camp. They were given crusts, nothing more. Free men work for their meat, they were told. The next morning, thousands more were at the drills.

By the tenth day, twenty-two thousand men had been added to the army.

Of course, adding such huge numbers of untrained, undisciplined men to an already undertrained and undisciplined army caused huge problems. Liv would listen to the advisers bickering late into the night about it, even raising their voices to the prince. Should the slaves be put into their own units, or incorporated into existing ones? (The latter.) What was to be done about slaves who accosted women or men in the camp? (Immolation.) The slaves were all men, and only the camp overseers and their favorites—who'd all fled—had been allowed to visit the prostitutes in Thorikos. Could anything be done for them?

The prince had addressed that by bringing together representatives of the slaves, his generals, and the prostitutes—who hadn't been organized in any sort of a guild, but did so rapidly when they were told that they could thus make a fortune. Liv's ears burned as she listened, but the prince never asked her to leave. He got the Mother of the Companions, as the prostitutes wished to be called, to tell him how many clients their women could serve in a day. He had two-thirds that many chits made up, made of bronze, each stamped with a lewd act. Then he made up a much smaller number of silver chits that could be used for the best Companions—he left it up to the Mother to decide how she wished to choose those women. He distributed a third of the chits to the generals, a third to the head of the foragers, and a third to his bursar.

Chits were to be given to men who gave extraordinary service—either bringing in many more crops or volunteering for particularly hazardous assignments for the generals. At least half of the chits had to be distributed to slaves, and if there was any corruption in hoarding chits or dispensing them only to favorites, the corrupt man or woman would be drawn, hanged, and immolated. Then, every day, the Companions would turn in the chits for reimbursement. The last third could be purchased by anyone in the army for set prices, helping offset the subsidy for the others.

The prince said, "For the next two weeks, I want you to do your best to find ways to give out as many of these as possible, and not to the same men over and over. Give everyone a chance to earn one. After that, we'll scale back. We don't want riots or rapists this week, but we don't want financial ruin next week either."

The next day, it seemed the camp shrank by a third as the newly freed men went out on volunteer missions in every direction.

As they approached Idoss, the towns got bigger and the loot got better. None resisted until they were almost on the outskirts of Idoss itself. This city, Ergion, had a stone wall, archers, a few drafters. Liv couldn't figure what the people of the city were thinking—Idoss, which might be defended, was only a day's trip away for a family, two days for an army. An easy trip, when fleeing for your life. But somehow the city elders had convinced themselves they could scatter a slave army like chaff.

The headsman spat from the ramparts and instructed his archers to fire on the Color Prince when he came forward to parley. The Color Prince's drafters deflected the arrows easily.

With drafters providing cover from the archers, their sappers—former miners, half of them—placed gunpowder charges under the wall within an hour. They blew open a hole and had the city in flames in another.

This time, the Color Prince gave orders for no quarter to be given. This would be an example, he said. He only wanted five hundred women and children left alive.

The army went mad, and Liv stayed in the camp. Even dressed as a rich drafter and well-known as she was, it wasn't safe in Ergion for a woman alone. She didn't want to see what the freed men were doing to their former masters anyway.

That night, a hugely muscled man whose status as a former slave   289 could only be noted by his sheared ear was allowed into the prince's tent. He bowed and presented a sack. The city headsman's head was inside.

The Color Prince gave him a handful of silver chits, looked him in the eye, and nodded. As the brute left, leaving the disfigured head oozing blood on the prince's carpet, Koios White Oak simply said, "Amazing what a man will risk for a few minutes with the mouth of a talented woman."

Chapter 63

~Samila Sayeh~

Tap, superviolet and blue. Tap, green. Tap, orange. Tap, yellow. Tap, red and sub-red.

I've been having these waking dreams. Before the Guiles' War had come to Ru, my favorite little cousin Meena was given an Ilytian dragon. Everywhere she'd gone, the toy had bobbed along in the air above her, tied to her wrist with a string, never deflating in the two months she had it. Meena had skipped everywhere, singing. Seven years old, and already she'd been training for two years. Her voice had a purity that transfixed soldiers and courtiers alike, but as often as not she'd make up her own nonsense songs, skipping through town.

Meena is dead. She would have been twenty-three years old now. She wanted to go to the Chromeria with me. I told her no. Of course, her mother never would have let her go even if I'd asked. Most likely, I hadn't tried. Meena died in General Gad Delmarta's purge, her body tossed down the steps of the Great Pyramid along with those of the rest of our family. Fifty-seven dead at the pyramid alone. Many more within the city, though those deaths were more pedestrian, somehow mattered less—at least to my people.

I wonder if Meena would have become a drafter, a warrior like me. I had no interest in fighting until that butcher killed all my people. I became quite a warrior, though. But evidently not enough of one.

And now my time is done.

With the precision only the best blues can manage, I study the red tent that is my cell.

The battle for Garriston was to have been my last fight. Usef and I had been overwhelmed by the wights and separated from the other veteran drafters who'd volunteered to fight to the death instead of joining the Freeing.

Usef and I had fought on opposite sides of the Prisms' War, the False Prism's War, the War of Guiles. One of my best friends from the Chromeria killed Usef's first wife. And Usef had killed her in turn. Usef and I had ample reason to hate each other. Instead, we'd fallen in love. Two broken warriors tired of war.

We'd chosen to make our last stand together. All the veteran drafters had been broken into pairs, each armed with a pistol and a dagger. All of us were close to breaking the halo, so whoever broke first would have their partner put them out of their madness. And if she was left alive alone, each was responsible for ending her own life.

I wondered if Usef could kill me, when it came to it. Usef was a blue, but he was also a red. It was how he'd gotten his nickname, the Purple Bear. He hated that name with a passion, thought it made him sound ridiculous. But as I pointed out, it was really the only nickname possible. Usef was six and a half feet tall, barrel-chested, burly, and hairy, with a full, wild beard and long, wild dark hair and heavy brows. He was a bear, and a red and blue disjunctive bichrome. His growling in response to people calling him the Purple Bear had only made the name stick.

Usef's chest exploded when a shell hit the building behind them. Impossibly, he'd stood, looking for me, relieved to find me, relieved that I wasn't injured. His mouth moved. And then he'd died.

I'd picked up my musket, and his, but instead of turning it on myself, I attacked the bastards. Found the cannon team. Massacred them. And there I broke my halo.

At first I thought I'd been hit with musket fire. I lost consciousness, and fully believed I was dying. I was content with that.

I love you, my Purple Bear.

I woke in a blacked-out wagon, sick as a dim.

Eventually, perhaps weeks later, the wagon had been commandeered for other uses and set off from Garriston. I recovered, and now find myself daily in this tent. I pick up snatches of conversation from the soldiers and peasants who pass too close, but all I can construct is speculative. Obviously, we're marching at the direction of this Color Prince and covering a good distance daily, despite what seems a vast caravan.

From the excitement on certain days, and the smell of smoke that isn't woodsmoke, I know we must have cut far enough south that they avoided the Karsos Mountains, and that we have invaded Atash.

Every day, I'm chained and blindfolded carefully before we move, but otherwise I haven't been accosted. An odd mercy. I'm on the wrong side of forty years old now, but as a warrior, I long ago prepared myself for outrages, should I be captured. Weak men like to humble women, especially great women who make them feel as inferior. I do that constantly.

So what's the game?

I'm a formidable blue warrior, perhaps even a legend. And I've broken the halo.

And there it is. This Color Prince, whoever he is, wants me to join him. He thinks that the longer he lets me sit in my blueness, the more likely I am to go mad and join him.

It's been a long time since I've been underestimated. I don't like it any more now than I did as a young woman.

My tent isn't large; I can't stand up straight without brushing my head on the fabric. My hands are manacled in front of me, and the manacles attach to the iron collar around my neck. My legs are hobbled with chains around my ankles, held apart by an iron pole.

All in all, it gives me reasonable freedom of movement, but little possibility of attacking anyone. Truth is, I'm no Blackguard: I wouldn't know how to attack someone with my hands even were I free. Well, I know a few punches, but that's a far different thing than being dangerous. Truth is, without drafting, I'm simply another helpless woman.

But I'm not ready to give up drafting yet.

They haven't taken my ring—which absolutely must mean that the Color Prince intends to recruit me. They'd taken a long, hard look at the ruby on my finger, another at the broken, pure blue halo in my eyes, and let me keep it.

It takes me two days to form my plan. The tent is red, so the light that comes through it keeps me from panicking like darkness would, but it's worthless to me for drafting. However, the tent is also made of cloth. Standing on tiptoe, I can pull a bit of the tent that is usually covered by the frame underneath it and gnaw on it. It takes me two days to chew a hole big enough to let in a tiny spotlight of clear, white light—but still small enough to be hidden to the eyes of those who fold up the tent every morning.

The next day, I nearly panick when I find that the hole isn't there. But there is no punishment, no mention of it. There must be more than one blue drafter imprisoned as I am; our tents had merely been switched during the march.

I begin again. This time, I'm luckier: I keep my own tent. On the twelfth day, the army takes one of its daylong breaks, camping in one spot for some kind of festival I can dimly overhear. No matter: I'm ready, and the tent has been aligned north-south, the most advantageous way with where I'd chewed the hole. I can peek out.

Above the tents is a large white canopy. I'd thought it had merely been clouds overhead, diffusing the blueness. Clouds that might burn off under Orholam's gaze and give me the blessed blue of pure sky. It is white canvas instead, allowing in light, but blocking my color. If I had spectacles, it wouldn't matter. I don't. I'm no Prism; white is as useless to me as no light at all. So this Color Prince isn't stupid. He must know the tents are vulnerable. I hate him and admire him for it at the same time. But it doesn't dissuade me.

Silently blessing Usef for giving me the ring, I brace myself and begin slamming the "ruby" against my manacle. After a dozen attempts, I hit it right, and the top half of the jewel shears off, breaking the glue that held it in place. I spend the next twenty minutes searching my tent for the fragment that split off.

After I find it, I put it in my mouth, moistening the glue. The red half of the ring is useless to me, but if I'm interrupted I'll need to put it back onto my ring as quickly as possible.

The bottom half of the ring is sapphire blue. It's tiny, but if it were larger, it wouldn't have escaped my gaolers' notice. I pull the fabric of the tent to the left of the frame, slowly, carefully. Two hours before noon, the sun is high enough that pure light pours through it in a tiny speck, a spotlight, a pinprick of power. The fact that my hands are chained to my neck becomes another blessing, a gift from the distant Orholam. It allows me to rest my hands and yet keep them in place.

I bathe my ring in that tiny spotlight, and it sends me thready blue power.

It takes hours, hours of barely blinking, of shifting minutely every minute as Orholam's Eye climbs to the peak of the heavens and then begins its slow descent.

With evening coming, and the certain arrival of the steward who checks on me, I bring the red glass chip to the front of my mouth and slowly reaffix it to the ring. Then I carefully move the blue luxin around beneath my skin, packing it so that it will inhabit my skin only under my clothing. I haven't soaked up much, despite the hours, but if my steward sees it, all my efforts will have been in vain. So I move the luxin into my back and butt and thighs. They have respected my privacy so far, and if they do so for one more night...

The steward comes. He sniffs once or twice, but seems to think he is allergic to something in "this damned country." He leaves me the daily ration. Then comes and takes the plate away when I'm finished.

He will come again at curfew. It gives me two hours. Two hours is plenty of time to die.

With trembling hands, I draft a tiny, sharp knife of blue luxin. More like a nail, really. It isn't as dramatic as slashing my wrists, but cut wrists can be bound, my life saved. A nail driven through my own heart? That is irrevocable, and reasonably quick. Even if my flesh betrays me and I cry out, there will be no saving me.

I should have died in Garriston. I should have died with Usef. I hadn't told Usef that Gavin is really Dazen. I hadn't trusted how he'd respond. I regret that now. He should have known for whom he died.

But no. He died for me. He didn't care about this war. He didn't care about Orholam. He cared about doing what is right, gods or no gods, Chromeria or no. And he cared about me. I should have told him. I should have trusted him. It was a betrayal.

I'm sorry, Usef. I'll come see you and apologize in person. In person? In spirit?

Usef didn't believe in any of that. I hope the afterlife has been a pleasant surprise for my big bear.

I hold the point of the nail over my chest. Gavin Guile—well, Dazen Guile—gave a special dispensation to suicide for those who broke the halo, but it has been drummed into me for all my life that self-murder is as much murder as any other, and it is hard to disregard the thought. No, this isn't murder. I am a casualty of war.

"Lord of Light, if this be sin, forgive me. If this be sacrilege, forgive your errant daughter." Taking a deep breath, I brace myself.

But still I don't press the nail home.

I am a wight. I know it. I felt the halo break. I am doomed. I will go mad. I might already be mad.

But I don't feel mad. I feel remarkably like…myself.

Maybe that is the sign that I am mad—that I can't see my own madness. But that doesn't make sense. Anyone in the world might be mad if thinking you aren't mad is a valid criterion.

Maybe blue is seducing me. Yes. Maybe it is.

But if so, it is a logician's seduction, not a lothario's. If the blue is some separate spirit, whispering sweet sins in my ears, I ought to be hearing them. Instead, I simply have the vague reservation that what I've been taught doesn't align correctly with what I'm experiencing.

I consider a thought that I had found disgusting in the past: remaking myself with blue luxin.

Still sounds disgusting.

How about something more borderline, like making permanent blue caps for my eyes, to function as blue lenses?

That sounds difficult. If you cut off the eyes from air, they don't do well, that has been proven, but if you leave air holes—

I'm getting caught up in the problems. Just like I always have. So… not changed. Not changed at all.

Maybe it is the drafting that changes you. Maybe once you start drafting blue after breaking the halo, it runs away with you. But I drafted blue just now. Small amounts, sure. But I don't feel like I'm stark raving anything.

I *can* kill myself. I see that now. The path is open, and I can take it when it's time.

But to suicide for no purpose? That makes no sense. How would that honor Orholam, who gave light and life?

If I wait, I might get a chance to kill the Color Prince himself. I might be able to repay this man fully for murdering Usef. Yes, that. *That* is reasonable.

The hard knot in my chest finally relaxes. I dissolve the nail and draft a very small straw that I poke through the hole in the tent. If the tent smells like blue luxin, they'll search me, and they'll find the hole and the ring. I have to cover up even the faint smell of chalky luxin. I draw the blue dust into my mouth and puff it out into the night air. Then I swallow the gritty bits that remain, swishing the watered wine they gave me around my mouth so none remain stuck in my teeth.

295

I will live. I will fight another day. And I will unravel the mysteries of the halo. I lie down, at peace, and sleep.

As his fingers slowly came off the five points, he realized she didn't weep for Usef. Hadn't wept for him since he died. It never occurred to her.

Chapter 64

Kip was soaked to the skin. The cold was an invading army, crossing every border of his skin, laying waste. Maybe it had invaded his brain first, making him sluggish, stupid. His fists were the only points of warmth on his whole body, those fired by pain. He'd ripped open the scars on his left hand. Didn't remember how.

He felt something wash down onto his cheek from the rain, brushed it away. Looked at it in his hand. What the—

A chill deeper than the cold rain rushing down his spine. Orholam have mercy. It was a piece of Niah's brain, washed clean by the rain, gray and blue. It had been stuck to his face since her head had been blown apart. Kip convulsed, flung it away.

He had to get out of here. First, he wrapped the cloaks around his body. Without whatever magic had animated them before, they now seemed like very pale, worn cloaks. Nothing special. The gold chokers dangled quite naturally inside the cloak, as if they were often hidden from sight that way. Kip pulled the hood up. The woman's cloak was too small to fit him comfortably, but he made it work. They were very thin, almost silky, and not fully waterproof, but they were better than nothing. Kip didn't even open the box of cards—not in this rain.

Last, he picked up the knife. He hadn't put it in its sheath, just blandly, blindly carried both when he'd picked up Janus Borig and all the other stuff he'd pulled out of the burning house like a looter. But there was something off. He swore the sheath was too short for the blade. No, it couldn't be.

He sheathed the blade, and as he pushed it home, lightning flashed, illuminating the entire alley, blinding him momentarily. Blinking, he stared at the sheathed blade. The sheath fit perfectly. Still, he swore it looked longer and wider than it had been before.

"Fire! Fire!"

Someone went running past Kip's alley, and suddenly he was starkly aware that he was standing over the body of an old woman who'd been stabbed to death—with a knife in his hand, in an area that was going to be swarming with people soon.

And so it was. Kip took off, and saw dozens, hundreds of people come out into the streets. "Lightning strike! Fire!" people shouted, pounding on the doors of their neighbors.

In a city, fire was everyone's problem, even in a storm. The storm was a blessing, of course, the rains helping the crowds extinguish the fires, but everyone turned out to battle the blaze lest it spread.

Kip got out of the neighborhood, made his way back toward the great bridge, the Lily's Stem, but didn't cross. He'd gone to seek Janus Borig to ask her where to hide a great treasure: now he had four treasures.

What the hell was he doing with four treasures?

The more relevant question was what the hell was he *going to do* with four treasures?

He stood for a minute in the rain, probably wealthy beyond the dreams of satrapahs and queens, and he couldn't afford a dry place to lay his head.

Ironfist. If Kip could get to him.

He walked across the bridge, tucking the dagger in his belt and covering it up, but making sure he could reach it quickly if he needed to.

There was no one outside except a pair of guards standing in their sentry boxes to avoid the rain, and they didn't look interested, though Kip's imagination made him paranoid. He made it to the lift without incident.

Kip had been a child for too long. He'd come to the Chromeria, and as soon as Andross Guile had found out about him, an assassin had tried to throw him off the tower. By playing the black cards, Kip must have revealed that Janus Borig had helped him defeat Andross Guile in a game. And she'd been murdered almost immediately.

With the amount of time that Kip had spent with the old man, it was tempting to humanize him, to believe that Andross might feel something for Kip. It wasn't true. There were monsters in the world, and Andross Guile was one of them.

Kip got off the elevator a few levels short of the top of the Prism's Tower. The Blackguards made their barracks here.

The first man he saw was a skinny Ilytian with a burn scar across one cheek, sitting on his bed, reading. A few other men were dicing a ways back in a common area, others were sharing rumors about assassinations in Abornea from comfortable chairs. "This area is for Blackguards only, boy," the man said.

"I need to see Ironfist," Kip said. "I'm Kip, Gavin's bastard. It's an emergency. I may be in danger. And it's secret."

Blackguards didn't get to be Blackguards by being indecisive. The man stood. "No one will harm you here. I'll take you to the commander's quarters. He's out on rounds right now—he always works longer than any of us—but he's usually back by an hour after midnight."

An hour after midnight? Of course. Kip hadn't realized that his own midnight training sessions with Ironfist were actually part of the man's normal workday—he worked from dawn until an hour after midnight. Every day.

The Blackguard walked Kip past the others, who looked askance but didn't object, and took Kip to a small room. He opened the door, which wasn't locked.

"No one except the commander will get in while any of us live." He hesitated, then said, "Do please note that if you steal anything from this room, the consequences will be dire."

"Yes, yes, thank you. Of course," Kip said.

He felt a huge wave of relief, quickly replaced by exhaustion and then discomfort as he looked around Ironfist's room.

For some reason, it felt oddly intimate to be here. Kip had never really imagined the huge Blackguard commander as a person who *had* a room. Ridiculous thought, of course. Where'd you figure he sleeps, Kip?

The room fit the man: tidy, not large despite his exalted position, finely carved lean black oak chairs with no cushions, the narrow bed covered with a green-and-black-checkered blanket, a rack of many fine weapons on one wall and one gorgeous painting opposite the bed. It was of a young woman, hair knotted and piled atop her head, dark eyes glimmering with orange halos, beautiful, chin lifted, hint of a playful twist to her lips. Kip didn't know anything about painting, but it was clear even to his untrained eye that this was exquisite.

A knock on the door interrupted his reverie. He opened it. The solemn Blackguard handed him a towel. "He lets guests sit in that chair," the man said, pointing. "You can pull it by the fire. Is it the kind of emergency where we need to send runners for him, or can you wait?"

"Wait. Waiting is fine," Kip said. "Thank you."

The door closed with a click, and Kip's heart went out of him. He wanted to be a Blackguard so much he thought he'd die if he didn't make it. Quiet and calm in the face of an emergency, decisive in the face of uncertainty, dangerous, masterful, confident.

He toweled off as well as he could, then stretched the two cloaks out to dry and sat in the chair by the fire.

Standing there in the warmth of the fire, Kip was struck by a thought. He drafted sub-red directly from the fire and pulled it through his skin. He was warm instantly. He could, in fact, dry his clothes—though not too quickly or he'd burn himself. Hell, if he weren't such a moron, he could have gone back into the building when it was on fire. He could have drafted the heat away from himself—and then what? Recovered a few treasures and still been inside the building when it exploded? Maybe he could have drafted shields around the kegs of black powder. If he'd been thinking.

He hadn't even thought to draft himself an umbrella on his way back to the Chromeria to stay dry. It simply hadn't occurred to him. He just wasn't mentally fast enough for this. A failure, stupid, his mother would say.

But then, he'd been *not* a drafter for his whole life, and only a drafter for a couple months. Nothing was instinctive yet. He pushed the thought, the worries, his mother's lies, away.

The card box smelled of cherry cavendish, tobacco like fruit leather. Janus Borig had hidden her most valuable cards in her tobacco. And it had worked. Funny old coot.

Kip had liked her.

His quick grin faded. Orholam. She was *dead*. Murdered.

By Andross Guile. A soul-deep loathing settled in him. He stood. Go right to the gut, Kip. See if the man only has the balls to hire murderers. Kip put the card box on the table. Don't stop moving, Kip. Weakness and fear beckoned. He tossed his knife on the bed. It was safer here than anywhere.

He went out the door. "I'll be back in ten minutes," he told the skinny Ilytian standing guard by his door. He wanted to tell the man to guard that room with his life, but anything Kip said like that would sound melodramatic, hysterical. Besides, who was going to break into the commander of the Blackguard's room?

Kip hadn't seen or heard any signal, but before he got to the lift, Samite fell in place beside him. She was still buckling her ataghan belt.

"You're not trying to stop me?" Kip asked as they got on the lift.

"Not a Blackguard's place to stop her charges from making mistakes." Though her tone was light, Samite didn't grin.

Kip set his jaw, hunkered into himself. He thought about Janus Borig. I am not going to be afraid. She deserves better. When they arrived, he knocked firmly on Andross Guile's door. The door opened after a few moments, and Grinwoody appeared. With the open door, Kip heard harp music float out.

"I need to speak with him," Kip said.

"The High Luxlord is occupied."

"Now, Grinwoody."

The Ilytian's unpleasant expression turned angry at Kip using his real name.

"Now, Wormwood!" Kip said.

Grinwoody turned his back and closed the door. Kip stuck his foot in the crack. The man looked at him, furious.

"Try to throw me out, you simpering worm," Kip said. "Try."

Grinwoody looked from Kip to Samite. "The young master will keep the drapes closed," he said. Then he disappeared into the darkness of the spider's hole.

"You see superviolet?" Kip asked Samite.

"No." Her tone carried a slight accusation: If you'd needed someone who could see superviolet, you could have said so, knucklehead.

"My fault. Wait out here. If they kill me, you'll know who did it." Drafting his own superviolet torch, Kip went inside, not waiting for permission.

He almost collided with Andross Guile.

"You are not to come here without permission!" Andross shouted. He swung a slap at Kip. Kip dodged.

"You fucking murderer!" Kip shouted back in his face.

The harpist, a young woman sitting in the chair Kip usually occupied, stopped playing, looking terrified in the darkness.

"What?" Andross demanded.

"You killed Janus Borig, you fucking coward!"

There was a swift motion behind Kip. He hadn't even noticed Grinwoody slipping around him, and in an instant both of Kip's arms were knocked down, twisted, and put in elbow locks. Kip lost the superviolet and was plunged into blindness. He was driven to his knees.

"Janus Borig? How do you know her?" Andross demanded.

"You killed her! I just came from her house!" Kip was suddenly jagged, powerless, a furious child. Damn me, a furious child.

"Why would I kill Janus Borig?" Andross Guile asked.

"She gave me the black cards I used to beat you!"

"You think I'd kill a demiurge over a card game? Where was she? She was here? On the Jaspers?"

"Don't lie to me! You knew she was here. You've had me followed everywhere I go."

"I have? And every bad thing that happens in the world is my doing? What a simple world you live in," Andross Guile said. "She was killed? You're certain of this."

Kip realized suddenly that he was on the verge of making a tremendous mistake. Anything he said could give Andross Guile information he hadn't had before. Even coming here did that. "Why should I believe you didn't kill her?" he said.

"Because she did me two great favors a long time ago," Andross said. "We were friends, for a time. She had a history of that, you know. Befriending people, using them for her art, and then disappearing. She was doubtless using you, too."

No, she hadn't been doing that. Not to Kip. Lies. "What favors?"

"She was making new Nine Kings cards. Did she not— No, of course she wouldn't have told a child. She made my card first."

"So?"

"You've never seen the true cards, have you? The cards let a drafter live the memories of those they depict—but only up to the moment when the cards were drawn. Janus Borig enshrined me as important enough to deserve a card, and did it without threatening me. At best, an enemy could learn my thoughts and plans as of what, twenty-eight years ago? I am the only important person alive to whom those new cards are not a threat."

Which meant he would want Janus Borig to finish as many of her other cards as possible. Of course he would do anything to get his hands on the final product, but he wouldn't kill her before she finished.

"And the second favor she did you?" Kip asked. He was deflating, though, defeated already.

"You tell me what happened, and I'll tell you."

Kip slumped, and Grinwoody released him. "I went to her home tonight—"

"Where?"

"On Big Jasper."

"Where?"

Kip told him. "When I got there, the house was on fire. The whole neighborhood was trying to put it out before it spread. They thought it was a lightning strike, but they found her a couple streets over, with no cloak, and stab wounds all over her. I could barely even recognize her." If Kip had gotten there late, even if Janus Borig had taken something out of the house, there was no way to tell who might have found her first, who might have stolen what she had.

"Did you see anyone suspicious?" Andross asked.

"You know what?" Kip said. "Forget it. I'm not trading with you. You're better at this game. I don't need to play."

Kip drafted a superviolet torch and saw that Samite was standing behind Grinwoody, the point of a knife a finger's breadth from the back of his neck. In the utter darkness. She was that good.

"She gave me my card, Kip," Andross Guile said. "So I could see exactly what was in it. She could make copies, of course, but they're always weaker. She feared me. I know that. But I had no reason to hurt her."

And Andross Guile never did anything without a reason.

Chapter 65

~Skirting the Issue~

Tap. Superviolet-blue. Tap. Green. Tap. Yellow. Tap. Red, sub-red.

The young Blackguard steps back from the precipice. The smell of burning homes, burning livestock, and burning human flesh wafts up from the valley floor.

"I can make the jump, Commander," he says. Skinny, long-legged, hair perpetually askew, Finer is the young man I hope will succeed me as commander one day. If this kind of mission doesn't kill him. The boy says, "It'll take us twenty minutes if we go down the trail."

Normally so decisive, I hesitate.

"It's not incarnitive, sir."

"It's real damn close."

"Yes, sir."

What Finer has discovered is that if he stabs points of green luxin from the braces into his knees, it allows him to keep the luxin open, fluid. This itself is no great discovery, of course. As long as luxin is touching blood, it can be held open. But external, attached luxin with direct control? That's perilously close to what wights do.

With the seals held directly at his knees, Finer can run with the braces on and have them not encumber his motion, but when he falls, he can close the weave. The stiff springiness of the green luxin will keep him from destroying his knees. It also seems that with the luxin inserted at his knees it reacts faster, instinctively opening or closing for what the body knows it needs.

This is exactly what leads otherwise good men and women to become wights: the realization that luxin is better than flesh. At certain things. But the more you experiment with it, the greater a hold it gets on you. There's always a good reason to use more.

And yet.

Orholam hates war, and yet he allows war in certain exigencies. So.

"Do it," I breathe.

Finer pulls up the leg of his trousers and begins drafting green. He drafts braces of green luxin around his knees, stabs the points in, drafts a thick sheen around his thighs. Then more.

Orholam's balls, he's coating his entire body. Going green golem.

"Son," I say, "you let it go once you get down."

Finer turns to me and grins a wild grin. "Yes..." he struggles, "...sir." He grins again, gives a jaunty salute, and leaps off the precipice.

The glorious sonuvabitch. He does a *somersault* on the way down.

Chapter 66

Back safely in Ironfist's room, Kip studied the card box. It hadn't been moved, of course. And Ironfist still wasn't back. The box, the only thing that was left of Janus Borig's life's work, was made of olivewood and lacquered ivory inlaid with electrum. Kip rubbed his hands on his shirt to get as much of the oils off them as possible, then cracked open the box.

The cards slid into his hand. Originals. He could see the tiny brushstrokes on them; the paint had a thickness to it, rising from the surface of the cards where details had been meticulously applied. But they weren't just originals. The names on the cards were names—both people and game mechanic cards—that Kip knew had never been in the game before: Talon Gim, Deedee Falling Leaf, Izem Red, Orea Pullawr, The Prisoner, New Green Wight, Polychrome Wight, Orlov Kunar, Jing, Black Powder Charge, Luxin Grenadoes, Sea Demon Slayer, Flintlock, Shimmercloak, Heresy, Three-Eyed Ben, Usem the Wild, Ganesh the Bear—Kip stopped.

Shimmercloak? Orholam's balls. The painting depicted a sneering man with heavy brows: it was Vox. His gray cloak was visible at the neck where the chains bit into his throat, and then his body disappeared below that. The text read, "If Lightsplitter, grants invisibility except against sub-red and superviolet."

If Lightsplitter?

Kip stared at the two cloaks drying by the fire. The cards were real. They were of real things, and they told the truth. They were new cards—and they were of people who had been alive recently. Kip knew some of those names had been drafters whom he'd seen at Garriston.

And if the cards were of those who had recently been alive, it was possible that there were cards of those who were still alive.

Kip began flipping through the cards faster, not trying to grab all the details, not trying to savor the art—he was hunting.

The Fixer. The Shadow. Tala. Flamehands. Aheyyad Brightwater. Samila Sayeh. Halo Breaker. The Fallen Prophet. The Black Seer. Mirrorman. Mirror Armor. The Technologist. The Novist. The Color Prince.

This wasn't a deck. There weren't multiple copies of the cards, such as one would use when playing so as to maximize your chances of that card coming up. This was an entire new set. Kip was looking for his father's card. Where was it? What would it tell him?

Zymun the Dancer. Kors Angier. Enervate. Incarnidine. Black Luxin. Hellstone Dagger. Multicolored Spectacles. The Angari Serpent. Andross the Red.

Kip felt ice in his veins. It was a young Andross Guile, handsome, strong, a warrior, a white dagger in his hand, tattered cloak billowing around him, three young boys behind him, one to his right, the other to his left, one barely visible in the distance.

Orholam, he looks like a hero.

Putting the card aside, Kip kept going. The Color Prince's Rifle. Rifle? Kip didn't even know what the word meant. Not that that was terribly uncommon. Incarnidine? If he had time, he could probably figure some of them out from the pictures, but time felt compressed. Like someone was going to come along any moment and take the cards from him, and they'd be lost forever.

Skimmer. Condor. Incendiary Musket. Gan Guvair. Helane Troas. Viv Grayskin. Yras the Caster. Iron Elm. Pleiad Poros. The Butcher of Aghbalu. Flashbomb.

Again Kip stopped, went back. The Butcher of Aghbalu. The man was splattered with gore, a fiery scimitar in one hand, stylized blue fire around the other, no armor, just a torn, bloodied tunic, revealing massive ebony arms and shoulders. The bodies of the dead lay all around him, in a palace. The man was young, wearing no ghotra, his kinky hair worn in a braided style Kip had never seen before, but it was undeniably Commander Ironfist. Kip had thought Janus Borig was working on his card, a one-eyed man—and it hadn't looked like this, but this *was* Commander Ironfist. Younger, but definitely him. Kip's heart seized.

The *Butcher*?

Kip looked at the weapons rack on the wall. The scimitar from the card was there, at the top. Spine blackened, blade shining. Garnets and scrimshaw, turquoise and abalone.

Part of him wanted to draft and jump into that memory instantly, but he didn't. He needed to go through all the cards before someone interrupted him. Surely someone was looking for him, surely he couldn't be allowed to know everything; it was somehow too easy.

He tucked that card away with the others he wanted to examine later and shuffled through the rest quickly. The Butcher of Ru was the next card, the art paired with Ironfist's card. Kip's stomach turned. He knew about General Gad Delmarta's massacre. On that card, the grinning man on the front was swinging a man's head by its braided Atashian beard in one hand, and a woman's head by her long black hair in the other. Kip thought about what would happen to his mind if he jumped into that card. If he became General Delmarta, what would he see? What if getting into that mind wasn't terribly difficult?

This was living history. He could learn things from these cards that no one else knew, that no one else had any way of knowing. And even if Kip wasn't a real polychrome and couldn't draft his extra colors consistently, he could *see* them, which meant he could know the whole story of every one of them—as only a few other people in the world possibly could. Whoever controlled these cards would control the truth. This wasn't just a treasure with a titanic monetary value, it was insight; it was a stripping bare of lies.

Anyone in power would want it for what it could tell them about their enemies. Anyone with a secret would want to destroy it lest their enemies find it.

Anyone with a secret. Like being the Butcher of Aghbalu?

A black cloud demon of smoky despair ripped Kip's mouth open and crawled into his throat. Commander Ironfist had been the one man Kip thought he could trust. And now Kip was in his room, with treasures, vulnerable.

"It's not me," a deep voice said behind Kip.

Kip jumped, so startled he flung priceless cards both left and right.

"My apologies," Ironfist said. "Thought you might have fallen asleep waiting for me. Didn't want to wake you." He knelt to help Kip pick up the scattered cards.

He scowled at the very first one he picked up. Looked over at Kip. "These are...real?"

"Yes, sir." Kip finally got up and started helping the commander gather up the cards.

They stood, and Commander Ironfist handed Kip a stack of the cards. He kept one in his hand. "I've never seen originals before. Does it work? Like they say?"

"Yes, sir. If you draft while you touch it, you experience what they did. The more colors you can draft, the more you see."

Ironfist looked at the card in his hand. "This card. This is my brother, you know him?"

Kip nodded. Tremblefist.

"When my mother was assassinated—it's complicated. She'd been keeping me away from the Chromeria, and with her death the reasons for keeping me away died, too. Our father was gone, and we had a *dey* to rule. Both my brother and I were gifted, my sister was too young, so one of us had to stay home to rule. My brother was younger, but I was more gifted, and we had good advisers who would actually do most of the ruling for him. We thought that if I could become a full drafter, in the future I would have more pull with the Chromeria. After I came home, my brother would then take his turn at the Chromeria. So my brother stayed home. To stabilize his rule, we decided he should marry. The Tiru had the best claim, and we should have appeased them. Our advisers told us as much. But we were young men, and though the Tiru's candidate was not ugly, she was not a beauty to make the heart race either. We were young fools, and I cared what my brother thought. We chose the Tlaglanu princess Tazerwalt because she was prettier than any of the other candidates by far. Her tribe was hated, and though she fell madly in love with Hanishu— pardon, that was my brother's name, before—even though she loved him and respected him, she was haughty before everyone else. Despised them. It made them hate her more, and made them hate him, too. The competing Tiru had crippled her father during a raid when he was still young, and she was no peacemaker. She took every opportunity to snub and shame them."

He sighed, but continued, "I had just finished my training when the False Prism's War began. There was no question that we would support Gavin. Dazen made some abortive overtures to Paria, but we were too deeply indebted to Andross Guile and his father Draccos Guile to take those overtures seriously. You wouldn't know it from Gavin's coloring, but no small amount of Parian blood flows in the Guile veins. Anyway, we sent our entire army, and still Andross demanded more. Most of the palace guards went. They ended up barely making it in time, but that's another story.

"Seeing this weakness, the Tiru tribesmen came from the mountains and infiltrated the capital city of our dey, Aghbalu, as civilians, and then one day when my brother went out hunting with fifty of the few remaining soldiers with him, the Tiru attacked.

"Hanishu and his fifty were alerted by some refugees, and they came back to the city as fast as they could. The Tiru had already set up camp in the palace, feasting around the still-unburied bodies of those they'd massacred. My brother and his soldiers arrived in the middle of the night. The Tiru were scattered, sleeping, or drunk, and my brother fell on them like a lion. He was eighteen years old, and he already had two daughters and a son. He found his wife's and children's bodies. The Tiru had done . . . unspeakable things to them. My brother went mad. A warrior in his prime and a wild drafter.

"The Tiru panicked, attacked each other, and my brother slaughtered all those he found. They said that he fought like a god, like Anat had possessed him. He killed through the dawn. The people of Aghbalu rallied around him then, and they rounded up the Tiru tribesmen, the old men and the young, the traders and camp followers and the wives and the shepherds . . . and . . ." He swallowed. "And Hanishu slaughtered them all. Personally. The Tiru numbered two thousand families, and the Tiru are no more." He handed Kip the card. "Beware of what memories you choose to watch, Kip. You may carry what you find forever."

Kip knew he should keep his mouth shut, but he couldn't help it. "What if the truth in that card is different than what you were told?"

The big commander turned mournful eyes on Kip. "I don't think it would matter. I lost most of the people I cared about, and I lost my brother. Hanishu is no more. He was broken by what he did. Still a peerless warrior, but he doesn't trust himself anymore. He can't lead. He's not even a watch captain. Can't bear the weight of responsibility. Every time I go back into a fight with him, I lose him for weeks afterward." He ran a hand over his shaven, bare head. "I'm afraid I've eaten too much truth recently. So this is what you came to speak to me about?"

"Will you swear not to tell anyone else?" Kip asked.

"You can't ask me that, Kip. I need to do what I think is right."

"I'm asking," Kip said. "If you won't promise, I can't tell you everything."

Commander Ironfist heaved a deep breath. "You're as bad as any Guile, you know that?"

"Yes, sir. Sorry, sir."

Commander Ironfist stared at the floor for a while. "I don't know why you drag us in your wake. Even a child of the Guiles is pulling me along like a leaf in a gale." He shook his head, and there was bitterness in his sad eyes. "Very well, you have my word."

"Janus Borig made the cards. I was down at her house—"

"Janus Borig? She's a myth, Kip. The old Witch of Wind Palace?"

"I don't know what you're talking about," Kip said. "She's just an old lady with a little shop."

"A shop?"

"On Big Jasper." Kip looked at him, confused.

"You found a True Mirror, hiding in plain sight. You've been in this city two months? How'd you find her?"

"The librarian told me—"

"Which librarian?"

"Rea. Rea Siluz."

"Hmm. I'll check into that. But never mind that for now. Tell me."

"I went to Janus Borig's house tonight. She was murdered. By a man and a woman wearing those cloaks. Shimmercloaks. Made them mostly invisible, except in the sub-red and superviolet."

For a moment, Ironfist's face twisted like Kip was a little boy telling the most outlandish lies. Then he looked at the cloaks.

"Show me one of those cards."

"Which one do you—"

"Doesn't matter."

Kip pulled out a card at random and Ironfist drafted a sliver of blue and touched the card for an instant, then snatched back his finger.

"Another," he said.

Kip extended one, fanning out the cards, but Ironfist chose another. He drafted, touched it, and pulled his finger back as if burned.

"My apologies, I had to know for myself. They're real. They're all real. Tell me everything, Kip."

So Kip did. It was like an enormous burden being lifted from his shoulders. Abruptly, he felt like he was a child again—except it felt good. There were things in the world too big for him to deal with by himself, and trusting Ironfist felt really good. "So what's it all mean?" he asked.

"I thought war was coming, but I was wrong," Commander Ironfist said. "War is already here. And you're in tremendous danger, and so am I."

It seemed like as much of a global summary statement as Kip had ever heard, and he felt totally inappropriate when he said, "Oh, um. There's one more thing."

"Found some other artifact of world-altering power to go with two shimmercloaks and an entire set of original, new Nine Kings cards?" Commander Ironfist asked archly.

Kip's mouth worked.

"It was a joke, Kip."

Kip pulled out the dagger slowly and laid it across his palms. It was longer. He was sure of it now. The white seemed whiter, the black whorls seemed blacker. There was also another difference: of the seven diamonds embedded in the blade, one burned bright blue as it had since Kip had recovered it from Zymun, but now a second was lit from within, too. It was a dull green.

Swallowing, Kip looked up at Commander Ironfist.

Chapter 67

Dazen Guile was trembling, shivering. His eyes were dry, scratchy from not blinking enough.

He was in a race against his own mortality and a timer with some uncertain amount of sand in it. He'd recovered from his fever, but was still deathly weakened from it. His body, struggling to heal itself from the fever and from the dozens of cuts he'd sustained in crawling through the hellstone tunnel, was desperate and weak. Gavin's fool lackey kept dropping the blue bread down the tube. The more of it Dazen didn't eat, the better his source of blue and the faster he could draft. But the more he starved himself, the weaker he became.

And the bread only lasted so long. Once a week—assuming, always assuming that Gavin had arranged for him to be fed once per day, rather than some odd fraction thereof—once a week, the cell was flooded with water.

At first, so many years ago, Dazen had thought this was a mercy.

The water was soapy, warm. He could regain a modicum of cleanliness once a week. If he tried, he could comb the tangles out of his hair and beard. And then he'd tried saving his bread once—and saw the water bleached it, or stained it a dull gray. A blue-gray, it had been in the blue cell, of course, reflecting the blue light of the walls.

It had been a mercy. It had been Gavin's way of keeping his brother from getting some disease that fed on the muck and filth his own body produced. It had also been Gavin's way of making sure that whatever Dazen might have hidden away in a week, from his own body's effluents or from his food, would be washed away, leached of power.

Dazen had needed to swim before he'd broken out of the blue cell, holding the oily cloth he'd woven from his own hair out of the water several times when the torrent had come, and now, in this cell, the bleaching water threatened again. He was too weak to do more than float and save perhaps one blue loaf, so every week he would starve himself for the first couple of days and start drafting again, and his drafting would speed up as the week progressed. Then he would devour all the stale bread his belly could hold before the flood came to wash all away again.

My will is indomitable. Unshakable. Titanic. I cannot be opposed. I cannot be stopped. I will win. There is only winning. And I will crush my brother. This is the fire, this is the fuel, this is the hope that sustains my broken body.

Blue was harder than green. Blue was all Dazen needed to break out of this level of hell.

In another hour, Dazen's right arm was full. He scooted over to his seat against one wall. He nestled his back firmly against the green luxin and braced himself. For weeks now—months?—he had been shooting out blue projectiles at the highest speed his body could handle, and bracing himself against the wall kept him from being flung about and destroyed.

The green luxin wall opposite him was pitted and chipped to a depth of a hand. It had infuriated him at first. His brother had made the blue chamber thinner, and the blue drafter in Dazen had expected every chamber to have exactly the same dimensions. But his brother knew that green was weaker than blue, so of course he'd made the green walls thicker. It was logical. The blue in him had calmed.

He picked his targets with arithmetic precision to exploit the structural properties of green luxin. He didn't know, of course, if he'd picked the correct wall. The ball shape of his chamber prohibited that. If his brother had irrationally made one wall thicker than the others, Dazen might simply get unlucky and pick the thickest wall.

That infuriated him. The uncertainty of it. The imprecision. It was wrong. He'd wasted at least a day in a weak stupor trying to figure out if there was some way to tell which wall was the right one. Hours wasted in calculation when action was required.

It was a warning sign of how deep the blue had sunk into him.

But he'd overcome that, as he'd overcome every struggle. As he would overcome even his brother.

He breathed deeply, ten breaths, gathering his will. Every projectile he fired hurt him, crushed his weakened body against the wall. But Dazen couldn't yield, couldn't shoot weakly. Shooting weakly meant that he'd wasted the days it took to draft the blue he needed. The wall could give anytime. It could give to this very shot.

Or, of course, it could take another twenty, and at any time, Gavin could come back and—

No! Don't think it. Do this. Pain is nothing. Pain is an obstacle on the road to freedom. I cannot be stopped. I will not be stopped. I will have my vengeance and my freedom, and those who have done this will tremble.

He took the tenth breath, braced his right arm with his left, and gathered his power. Old scars ripped open on his palm as the blue luxin tore through his skin.

Dazen screamed rage and despair and hatred and pure, glorious will. A missile burst from him with incredible power.

During the False Prism's War, he'd been hit in the chest with a war hammer once. It had cracked his shield and a rib. With his weakened body, this was worse. He passed out.

But when he opened his eyes, he saw his victory. The green luxin was broken. A few fibrous tendrils held on, but it was broken. He could see darkness beyond. His prison was broken.

With a calm willpower that would have stunned a younger version of himself, he drank some water, ate a little of the bread. Not so much that his long-empty stomach would revolt.

Then, only then, did he draft a tiny thread of green. It was light, it was life, it was power and connectedness and well-being and strength.

Only then did he allow himself a moment of triumph. He had done it. He had done it. He really was unstoppable. He was a god.

He stood, grinning, legs trembling, but strong enough to allow him to stand, and tottered over to the hole. He tore away the green luxin with his bare hands, opened the hole enough to peer through. To crawl through, once he gained a little more strength.

Poking his head through the hole, he drafted some green imperfectly into his hand, bathing the darkness in weak green light. The green egg in which he'd been imprisoned was, it appeared, contained within a greater chamber, only a little larger than the egg itself. It wouldn't have mattered which wall Dazen broke through. All of them were equal.

For one stupid moment, he was furious at the time he'd wasted, wondering which side to attack. But then that passed. That day of vacillation was gone, it couldn't be called back, and it was illogical to fret over it, to waste more of the present on the past. He pushed it away, and his smile came back.

To one side of the chamber, he saw a tunnel, floor glittering with sharp shards of hellstone.

Dazen laughed, low, quiet. It was a laugh at finally, finally being underestimated.

No, brother, that won't work. Not this time.

Chapter 68

"Corvan, am I a good man?" Gavin asked.

"You're a great man, my friend."

"Not the same, are they?" Gavin asked. There had been blood in his dreams, blood staining the water from the blue he couldn't see to the red he most certainly could. Red on gray. In his incipient blindness, he'd traded blue beauty for blood, all unwillingly.

313

Corvan said, "When you move the world, some will be crushed. How could it be else? When you sank the pirates at Tranquil Point, the slaves chained to the oars died first. What else were you to do? Leave the pirates to capture and make slaves of thousands more? But that's not what I meant, my lord. You are a *great* man."

Gavin chewed on that, put it in the hold of his memory. "And you, Corvan? What kind of man are you?"

"I am simply competent. A red by training but not by nature. Not a leader except when leadership is lacking. But you know these things better than anyone." A quizzical, amused expression.

Not a leader except when leadership is lacking? It was true: Corvan had proven himself to be perfectly content to take orders—even orders he didn't understand—from those who had won his trust. Then, without changing his nature, he'd assumed command of entire armies. He knew what needed to be done, and did it, somehow without it changing his appraisal of himself. He probably really had been content as a small-town dyer.

Gavin wondered how Corvan did it. He himself had never been content in any place but the first. Even under those wilier than he, like his father, or those wiser than he, like the White, he'd chafed. Burned.

It was, no doubt, a flaw in his character.

"I'm making you a satrap," Gavin said. And let be crushed by that whoever may be.

Corvan coughed up tea. Most satisfying.

"Are you insane?" Corvan asked. "My lord."

"It's pretty much what you already are, and I am still the Prism. It is my prerogative. They'll try to stop me, but so long as you don't massacre the Seers, no one of the other satraps or members of the Spectrum are losing anything. I will propose that you get to name a Color on the Spectrum, but allow myself to lose on that point so they have some victory for their egos. Your new satrapy will be a second-rate satrapy for a few generations. Those will be political battles those who follow us will have to fight. Survival first."

"But why?" Corvan asked. "What do you get?"

"We've already discussed this. Food. Seeds. We already know things are going to be tight, but the island is big enough to keep us from starvation until spring. But if we don't get seeds for next year—"

314   "That's not what I meant."

"I give our people a sense of purpose, and I give them another reason to obey you, to make a new life here and stay, even once things start to go well enough that they could leave."

Corvan set his teacup down. "Your pardon, Gavin, but you forget how well I know you. There's more to it than that."

Gavin smirked. "I need you to believe in me, Corvan. When the time comes. There are crises coming, and I will need to move quickly. I need to know you have my back, instantly."

Corvan's back stiffened, brow darkened. Gavin hadn't seen the man angry in many years. "My lord, some men believe in Orholam, some believe in gold, but I believe in you, and to this I will hold. Fealty to One, as you should know."

"You think it unworthy of me to question you?" Gavin asked.

Corvan's lips were tight, eyes lidded.

"It is," Gavin said. "You've more than proved yourself. But your faith will be tested."

"And will come through the fire purer than before, doubtless."

"Thank you, Corvan. Your pardon. *Satrap* Danavis."

"My lord," Corvan said quietly. "Thank you for what you did. With the blue bane. I know...I know it must have been awful, but thank you for doing it."

Gavin stood, said nothing. Popped his neck right and left. He'd summoned the people to the great square. There were plans to build a stadium, but they hadn't progressed far on it yet. Regardless, he was going to have to give a talk. Bolster support for Corvan.

"Lord Prism," Corvan said quietly. "I don't know if I can be a satrap. Not even of a second-rate satrapy." It was a mercy, switching the subject, saying his piece about Gavin's slaughter and then letting it go.

"Nonsense. It's just like being a general, except that if you're any good at it, you'll rarely have to watch your people die."

The general snorted. It would be harder than that, in the environment he was leading his people into, and they both knew it. Then Gavin's friend squinted. "My lord," Corvan said. "The rebels have my daughter. You making me a satrap will make Liv a thousand times more valuable to them."

Corvan always was quick.

Gavin stood, and looked to the people crowding the stadium, gathering to listen to him, hoping he'd speak, but willing to just get a   315 glimpse of him. He said, "You know what you *can't* do with a satrap's daughter when you're looking for support among neutral parties?"

For once, Corvan didn't have a ready answer.

"Kill her," Gavin said. "I hold you in my eyes, Corvan. I won't forget."

The man's face contorted for an instant with sudden grief, sudden hope, and his shoulders heaved. He looked away from Gavin, trying to control himself. Then he dropped to his knees, and farther, lying prostrate at Gavin's feet. More than respect and thankfulness, it was veneration. Worship.

"You would do this, for me?" Corvan said.

"I do it for many reasons, my friend. There is no unadulterated altruism."

"But altruism abides. I know you, lord."

"Please stand, my friend, it grows awkward." And indeed, around the square, and from the wood-hewn balconies of golden buildings all around, men and women, and even children who couldn't have known to what they paid obeisance, were dropping to their knees, to their faces where there was room.

It touched Gavin's heart. They'd lost everything because he'd failed. Not one had eaten his fill for the last months, because they didn't know how long their food would last. Everyone had worked from dawn to dusk and beyond, every day. They lived in great longhouses, not homes, stuffed with strangers. They had no wealth, little hope, and lots of pain, and yet what little they had, they offered him freely.

"My people!" Gavin shouted, pitching his voice to his orator's tone, his general's tone. "Downtrodden, destitute, devastated but not dismayed. My people, dearest to my heart…" And so he spoke. He bade them rise, and they rose. He could bid them into the teeth of hell, and they would descend, singing praises all the way. He was good at this. Not born to it, but he'd stolen this crown and worked it so long in his hands that now it fit him.

He addressed their fears, and fired their desires, and acknowledged their sorrows and their sacrifices, and braced them for coming hardship and made them feel noble about it all.

By what right do I bend men to my will? Or is there no right, only ability? Are these women here mere slaves on my pirate ship? Are these children mere victims in the path of my plague?

But on he spoke, urging peace and honest dealing with the people of Seers Island, laying foundations, frankly assessing the difficulties coming their way, and throwing the full weight of his support behind Corvan.

He swore he would be with them when he could, and that when he left he would go to better protect them, and that he would always come back. He would work beside them, and prevent the suffering that he could, and mourn the dead beside them when death couldn't be avoided.

Gavin saw that there were at least two scribes copying his every word in shorthand. He was surprised that there were scribes here among the poor, but he shouldn't have been. Corvan would have, of course, scoured the refugees for scribes so they could distribute copies of his decrees to those camped far out in the woods and send messages to the Seers.

It made him temper what he would say. He hoped it would take months, but eventually, his father would end up with a copy of every word. Still, the good it would do in spreading support through the refugees was worth the damage it would do him later.

Not even you will be able to stop this, father.

And last, bracing them that the Spectrum and the other satrapies would look down on them—as if they should care about such things when their bellies were gnawing on their navels—he built up the audience and himself as their champion, and announced the new satrapy.

The people roared in approval.

I really am very, very good at this.

They looked radiant. Perhaps he was a gifted orator; he was a gifted drafter for sure, the best for many years, perhaps. Their respect, their admiration, these were his due, but he didn't deserve their love. He wondered that he was the only one who knew it.

Half an hour later, he and Karris skimmed away with little more than they'd brought with them three months ago. He didn't explain himself. She'd seen the blood on him when he got back last night. She'd seen the look on his face. She didn't berate him for leaving without her. She knew him. And without asking whether they were leaving, she'd said her goodbyes. She knew.

The crowds gathered once more as they walked to the beach, and they roared as he waved to them. Men and women wept for him. It was an insanity of kindness that Gavin couldn't understand, but he treasured it nonetheless. And then they left.

As Seers Island slowly disappeared into the distance behind them, Gavin examined it over his shoulder, discomfited. He and Karris talked little that day, each introspective, and camped on a beach near Ruic Head in Atash.

The next day, as Gavin switched the skimmer for the manual labor of the scull to close the final leagues to Little Jasper, he spied the towers, rising majestic against the noon sun. Against the stark colors of the other towers, the blue sat mute, gray. Its sister tower and neighbor, the green tower, was adorned with illusions beneath the luxin to make it look like a towering tree—this year they honored Atash by depicting the extinct atasifusta. But the color wasn't right. Before the war, Gavin had seen the last grove of atasifusta.

There were storm clouds gathering over the Chromeria, and at first Gavin thought perhaps it was simply a trick of the light, but as they got closer, he became certain that wasn't it.

Why would they make such a mistake? Surely some Atashian who remembered the trees would complain. The leaves of the giants were vibrant, radiant, a perfect complement to the green tower, not this sickly, gray-green mishmash.

Oh hells. Gavin drafted the green he needed for the scull's flexibility. He could still do it, but it was like he was building the whole damn Brightwater Wall all over again, just to give a few corners of his boat some flexibility.

In that moment, he knew: after all he'd just done to save the world from a blue calamity, now he was losing green.

Chapter 69

Commander Ironfist breathed. "Kip, do you have any idea..."

"No! I don't."

Commander Ironfist was already looking at the blade intently. "Strange. Why are two of the jewels colored and the others clear?"

"I was sort of hoping you'd tell me. Sir."

"Kip, I don't know that much about this blade except that it's important, that the Spectrum itself used to keep it, and that it was lost during the war. I don't know what it does besides look pretty, but people have killed for this knife. Literally. More than once. These materials—white metal, and black..." He reached a finger to touch them, but then stopped.

"Luxin?" Kip asked. "White and black luxin?"

Ironfist looked troubled. "I'd always thought black luxin was simply obsidian. Hellstone. This..."

Kip hadn't noticed, maybe hadn't really looked since he'd first examined the blade in the dim light of the barge, but the black metal threaded down the middle of the white blade looked different than he remembered. It looked like it shimmered dully, a tiny thready pulse.

Other discipulae had asked about white luxin and black luxin in Kip's classes. The response had been tart—you're not ready for those talks. All Kip knew was that no one had ever seen either, so he'd concentrated on more direct worries—like trying not to get his ass kicked and figuring out how to use a stupid abacus and memorizing seven hundred and thirty-six idiot cards that didn't even include all the forbidden cards that were, apparently, all the most interesting ones. Kip reached out.

"Don't touch the blade!" Ironfist said. "They call it the Marrow Sucker—and I don't want to find out why the hard way." Then his visage darkened. "This looks familiar. Where have I seen this?"

"Zymun, sir. This is the knife he tried to kill the Lord Prism with."

"The assassin boy? From the barge?"

Kip nodded.

"How do you know his name?"

"He tried to kill me back in Rekton."

"And how—never mind. You need to hide this, Kip. From everyone."

"I think it's too late for that," Kip said. "Andross Guile thinks I have it. Or at least he thinks I know where it is. I'm afraid what he'll do for it."

"As well you should be." Commander Ironfist went over to a closet and started rummaging through a box. He came back with something with numerous leather straps. He threaded them through the dagger's sheath. "Strap this on your calf, under your trousers. Now, Kip."

Commander Ironfist went to the door, then pointed Kip to stand out of the line of sight. Kip did, and Ironfist cracked the door.

"Jade, I'm occupied. Don't let in any messengers. Especially that damned snake."

"With pleasure, sir," a woman's voice answered.

"Snake?" Kip asked, trouser leg up, not quite having figured out the straps yet.

"Andross Guile's slave, Grinwoody. He was barely even a drafter, but Andross pulled strings and got him in to Blackguard testing, as a parting reward for good service, we supposed. He made it all the way through the training, made friends, learned secrets both personal and corporate, and on oath day decided to sign with Lord Guile instead. Who used those secrets. Twenty years ago, and still we remember. It's not terribly uncommon that someone leaves right before they sign, but it wastes a huge amount of our time and effort. We go to all the work of training someone, and they leave us high and dry."

"Grinwoody?" Kip asked. He couldn't get over it. "That old stump was almost a Blackguard?"

"He'd be dead by now if he had been a Blackguard, of course. The constant drafting. So maybe he's the smart one."

"Doesn't make it any less a betrayal," Kip said.

After Kip pulled down his trouser leg to conceal the sheath now strapped to the outside of his calf, he extended a hand toward the commander for the knife. Ironfist looked at him, eyes hard. "Kip, thank you. Thank you for trusting me. And now, don't ever do that again."

"Sir?"

"Kip I know you're lonely, and I know you want to trust someone. I understand. But you're not in that place anymore. You don't know what kind of pressure Andross Guile can bring to bear against me. You haven't known me for three months, and you've just handed four great treasures into my hands. I could take them from you now and have you thrown out. I could buy myself a satrap's seat with what you've got. You think I'm immune? You think I'm too good a man to do that?"

"Yes, sir," Kip said.

"But you don't *know.*"

"A man's got to act without knowing everything, or he'll never do anything."

Commander Ironfist's lip twitched. "So you're a man now?"

"I've taken lives, and I've taken my own life in my hands and trusted a friend with it. Yes, sir, I'd say that makes me a man."

"Neither makes you a man. The first makes you a killer. The second makes you a fool. Either may get you killed."

"But not today?" Kip asked. For all his bravado, he couldn't help but swallow, looking at the bare knife in Ironfist's hand.

"Not today," Commander Ironfist averred. He offered the blade to Kip.

Kip took it with a weak smile and sheathed it, then bloused his trouser leg over it.

"Now, let's talk about the other things that can get you killed here," the commander said. He picked up one of the cloaks. "One, shimmercloaks. Fantastic." Commander Ironfist sighed, as if he'd blown through his entire allowance of incredulity in one orgy of wild spending. "In legend, there are twelve shimmercloaks. Supposedly, they always worked in pairs. Assassins."

"Like the Order of the Broken Eye?" Kip asked.

"They were the pride of that supposed order."

"Were? Supposed? You hold the fabric of legends in your hand. Literally."

"So it seems."

Kip showed Commander Ironfist the Shimmercloak card. "This man was one of them. His name was Vox, and his partner a woman named Niah."

"And how did you kill two professional assassins, Kip?"

"He killed her. On accident. And I got lucky. They didn't expect me to see them, and I did. They kept their weapons down until the last second so they wouldn't displace their cloaks and then—"

"Rhetorical question, Kip."

"Oh."

Commander Ironfist sat on the edge of his bed. "Just when a man makes a decision that everything he's believed his whole life is a lie, something comes along tempting him to believe again. Vanity. Quicksand."

"Sir?"

Commander Ironfist rubbed his stubble-fuzzy scalp. "The pagans believed in separate gods, as you know. Either real, living entities that required their sacrifices and could be wooed by human gifts or, as other pagans believed, simply as facets of humanity itself—as greed is part of each of us, or ambition, or passion—they believed the gods should be acknowledged only for how they revealed truths about our own souls. But talking about pagans as if they were one camp is an oversimplification. Even if you talked about the worshippers of Atirat—as apparently Vox was—you'd be speaking too broadly. They all agreed on the existence of multiple gods, but the agreement didn't extend much beyond that.

"They were men like us: some were good, some evil, some believed nonsense. There were religious proscriptions that made no sense—like a deep suspicion that the use of spectacles was sinful, unnatural. But then some sects were happy to sacrifice their firstborn to bribe the gods to give them a fruitful harvest. Some venerated their color wights. Others drove them out. Others stoned them. The successful wights—for they claimed that such existed—would reign as demigods."

"I don't understand how this connects," Kip said.

"Just because a man bases his entire life on nonsense doesn't mean everything he believes is wrong."

Kip raised his eyebrows. So... "The suspense is torture, sir."

"Some pagans believed light splitting was a separate gift. Our teaching has been that light splitting is the sole gift of the Prism. It's not holy writ, but it has been the teaching for hundreds of years." Commander Ironfist waved the Shimmercloak card. "This is one card. It says, 'If Lightsplitter...' Which means light splitting is possible. Even if people denied what happened to you, these cards are true. They can't be denied. This one card wouldn't destroy the faith, but it would make every luxiat who's ever spoken about light splitting look like a fool. It will be like when Pevarc proved once and for all that the world is round two hundred years ago. A few scholars had been whispering the same things for five hundred years before him, but no one thanked him for making fools of the luxiats. The navigational corrections that his better calculations allowed all came about years after he was lynched."

"Lynched?" Kip asked, eyebrows climbing.

"For something else altogether—he proposed that light was an absence of darkness, rather than the inverse." Seeing the befuddled look on Kip's face, he said, "Don't worry about that. Point is, light splitting is real. Some of us had always suspected as much, which is why the Blackguard has always recruited drafters like Adrasteia. Not just because she can see concealed weapons, but because she could see an assassin who is invisible."

"But how does it work?" Kip asked. "I didn't think such things were possible."

"You're a dim, Kip. You don't have the background to understand—"

"And if I did, I'd only know wrong things. So you don't have to unteach me all the things I think I know."

A dip of the head and a momentary grin conceded the point. Iron-fist took a breath. "Light is power. The power always goes somewhere. Sunlight hits a cherrywood floor. We know that the sunlight is full-spectrum, from sub-red through superviolet, but the floor reflects only reddish brown. Where does the rest of the light go? It's absorbed. And years later, compare that wood floor with a section of the same floor that was covered with a rug, or a shadow. The sun-exposed part is bleached. The light very slowly changed the nature of the wood itself—broke it down. Just like light darkens a man's skin or lightens a woman's hair. Just like a color does to a drafter's body. Prisms don't break the halo despite drafting vast amounts of light because they're able to release *all* the light that hits them. The rest of us are less efficient, more susceptible to the damage. The point is that the light hitting a surface can't be changed unless you can put a lens over the sun. The energy is constant. It must be dealt with.

"If it works the way I've heard guessed at, a lightsplitter acts like a wedge in the stream of light, lengthening the long spectra and shortening the shorter, so that all the visible light hitting her is released above and below the visible spectrum. If she does it perfectly, she'll glow bright as a torch in the superviolet and the sub-red. I've heard tales of lightsplitters burning up if there's too much light to handle, say on a bright day—because they're turning so much visible light into heat, they can burn out. These cloaks make what they do easier. Like lenses make it easier for a drafter to draft her color."

Kip had seen so many wonders in the past months, he had no trouble believing it. "So you're telling me there may be hordes of invisible people walking among us?"

"Not hordes. Splitting light well enough to be invisible is probably close to impossible. And there are only—if the legends are right, which is a *big* if—twelve of these cloaks, created for the original Order of the Broken Eye, if not before. Some have surely been lost or destroyed, and we now have two of them. So at most there are five more teams of assassins out there. Maybe only two or three. Maybe none."

"At least we have these cloaks now."

"Which is better than our enemies having them, but they're probably useless to us. Having denied their existence, I don't think the Chromeria has any method of testing drafters to find lightsplitters. Even if someone knew of such a thing, could they be convinced to share it when the very idea verges on heresy? The Atashian luxors suppressed something uncomfortably similar a hundred ten, maybe a hundred twenty years ago now."

"And that's one card," Kip said.

"And you have a deck full. Breaker indeed." Commander Ironfist started laughing quietly.

"What's so funny?" Kip asked.

"I was just thinking that with how important these cards are and who can view them most clearly, you've probably just condemned a few of my least favorite people to spending the rest of their natural lives in a library somewhere, touching cards and taking notes."

"You realize," Kip said grumpily, "that that may well be *my* future you're laughing about?"

"Doubtful," a voice said behind Kip. "I imagine that you'll be killed within the next year or live forever."

Kip turned around, and there, in front of the most silent door in history stood Gavin Guile, his Gavin Guile smirk on his lips.

"But I wouldn't bet against the boy who convinced Janus Borig to give him her life's work."

Kip couldn't speak. Gavin's presence filled the room.

"How is the old goat?" Gavin asked.

"Dead," Kip said, his voice flat and lifeless. He hadn't realized how much he'd cared for the woman until now.

A respectful pause. "I should have gathered as much from the cloaks. No evidence who sent them, I suppose?"

Kip had nothing to say. Obviously, *his* first instinct had been wrong.

"Don't look at me, Lord Prism," Commander Ironfist said. "I wasn't there. I didn't kill them. Kip did."

Gavin shot a look at Kip. "*You* killed them? That's a story I'll want to hear. But later. Well done, son."

Son. Son! With one word, Gavin was overturning months of Lord Andross Guile's torment. Kip wanted to fall all to pieces. He wanted to shove all the cards and the knife into his father's hands and blubber.

Gavin raised a finger. "First things first. Commander, your Blackguards sent Grinwoody packing. I intercepted him. He was on his way back to my father. He seemed to think that when he returns, you'll be deprived of your position."

"I think that faithless worm is being optimistic," Ironfist said.

"I sent Karris to stall him, but if there's anything you need to do, I suggest you do it now. I'll intervene for you so far as I can, but you're not under my purview. You're certain he's wrong, and you've done nothing, and you're sure Carver Black will save you?"

Commander Ironfist's face clouded. "I suppose there are a couple things that could...cause problems."

"What?" Kip asked. "What have you done?"

"It's not what I've done," Ironfist said. "I've been looking into some old m— Lord Prism, Breaker, excuse me. I have urgent matters to attend to."

He stepped out the door, then turned. "Breaker," he said. "You can trust Cruxer. And...just so you know, you'd have made an excellent Blackguard."

He was leaving. Kip had the sudden fear that he'd never see the big man again.

Kip ran over and hugged him.

Ironfist grunted, surprised. Then he hugged Kip in return. After a moment, he pushed Kip back.

Gavin had an odd look in his eye at seeing Kip embrace the commander. A distance between them. But in a blink, it was gone. He tossed the man a coin purse. "Commander, just in case. And honestly, I don't know for certain that they're coming after you."

"I do," Ironfist said. "Orholam give you light, Lord Prism. Be well, Breaker." Then he was gone.

Chapter 70

Idoss was a city of ancient ziggurats. Some luxiats said they were man's attempt to scale to the heavens. They called them blasphemy. But those luxiats' attempts to have the ziggurats torn down had never been successful. There were thirteen of the great terraced pyramids in the city arrayed geometrically, six and six around one. The central one was easily taller than the Prism's Tower that Liv had thought was the tallest structure in the world.

Having surrendered to Dazen's general Gad Delmarta rather than fight during the Prisms' War, Idoss had escaped the torch and the sword and the flux. Most of the men pressed into service in Dazen's army—at least those who survived the Battle of Sundered Rock—had made their way home within a couple months and the city had recovered more quickly from the war than any other city on the southern rim of the sea.

The city's *corregidor* was the Atashian satrap's son, Kata Ham-haldita. The term was Tyrean, one of the few remnants left of the time when Tyrea had included what was now eastern Atash. When the corregidor came out to parley, the Color Prince had the central avenue up which the young man traveled lined with all the color wights in the army, and instructed them to all be outside and in full view, but to ignore the corregidor and go about their chores so that he might believe there were far more of them in the army than there were.

It doubtless made for a terrifying walk, and the boy arrived rattled. And boy he was, for though he nominally ruled one of the richest cities in the Seven Satrapies, he was only twenty years old, and clearly young for his age.

Liv met Corregidor Ham-haldita and his two bodyguards outside the Color Prince's tent. Her presence seemed to brace the young man. He smiled at her as if he was used to wooing women with that smile alone. He was a pretty boy, though skinny and narrow-shouldered. Liv preferred a man who looked like a man; she gave a pleasantly neutral nod. In truth, her heart was pounding—not from the boy, but with being trusted to be here. She'd worn the nicest of her dresses, and she could tell that the young man appreciated it.

"Corregidor, we're delighted that you've come to join us. The prince is resting within. Will you join us?" she asked.

He looked at his bodyguards, but Liv stepped inside the tent, not waiting for a response. After a short hesitation, the corregidor and his men followed her.

The tent was dark, darker than usual, darker than necessary. There was one chair inside, a throne, and nothing else, not even rugs. In the chair, slouching, sat the Color Prince. He didn't move when Liv came in. Then, when Corregidor Ham-haldita came in, the Color Prince lifted his head, and his eyes began to glow dull red, the color of new-forged iron. He stood, and the layers of luxin scraping across each other gave a sound like steel rasping over steel.

A shimmer of pale yellow light passed down his form, illuminating every crack and joint and seam, he flexed as if shaking himself from sleep, and every blue plate of armor on his body glowed, dimmed, then every red seam, then every green joint, all the way up to the barely visible pale violet that pulsed around his head in a crown.

The slack-jawed expression on the corregidor's face almost made Liv laugh aloud, but she tucked her chin and bit her tongue. His men were right on the verge of pulling their weapons, but they looked terrified, too.

"Corregidor," the prince said. "Welcome. Walk with me?"

The corregidor had to clear his throat before he could speak. "Of course."

Liv joined the leaders and their guards, walking as she'd been instructed on the corregidor's right while the prince walked on his left. Trapped between hope and fear, the prince had said.

Hope of what? Liv hadn't quite dared to ask.

She didn't think she was pretty enough to catch a future satrap's eye, though if the Color Prince was successful, this boy would never be a satrap. But *he* didn't know that yet. What then? A mistress? A night's entertainment? Liv was abruptly aware again that she was a woman alone. If the Color Prince wanted her to accept one of the whores' chits from Corregidor Ham-haldita, there was no way she could refuse. Not exactly the great purpose that the prince kept alluding to, but she wasn't the person who got to choose, was she?

A quiet fury rolled through her.

When they strode into the full sunlight, the corregidor missed a step again. Seeing the Color Prince's luxin form fully lit with natural light was at least as impressive as seeing him glow in a darkened tent. Again, not a mistake.

The Color Prince led the way through the camp, as if walking aimlessly, though Liv was sure he wasn't. He didn't leave much to chance.

"You've come with something to say," the Color Prince said. "A deal, perhaps."

"The city mothers have asked that I tell you we wish only peace, but if we must fight, you will pay dearly to take this city, and perhaps not before our reinforcements arrive."

"Which I'm sure you expect any day."

"Yes, we do." The boy colored, as if fearing he was being made fun of. "And we can hold you until they arrive and smash you against our walls."

They passed by Zymun, who was training with the other drafters. He stood shirtless, lashing an old tree with great whips of fire, awing his fellows. He stopped when they walked by, bowing respectfully to the Color Prince, his eyes full of jealousy at the sight of the other young man. Zymun's wounds had faded, and if his shirtless body didn't fill Liv with the speechless desire that Gavin Guile's once had, he was still quite handsome. Powerful, intelligent, charismatic—and always, always interested in her. Always flattering. Always flirting.

She'd flirted with boys at the Chromeria, of course—mostly before that disastrous Luxlords' Ball. But those had mostly been the flirtations of impossibility: playing at being adults. Playing at being outrageous. Zymun's flirtation was the flirtation of possibility. She had only to say the word, just once, one night when he came by her tent and asked politely if he could come in. That she *could* say yes, that none would stop her, that none would even question her was more of an erotic charge than that she could say yes to Zymun in particular, dashing as he was.

Her students would envy her the assignation, of course, for she had students now. Not discipulae, not among the Free.

"So Delara Orange has been successful in persuading the rest of the Spectrum to go to war? Or am I to be on watch for the elite Ruic troops?"

"Both," the boy said. Even Liv could tell he was lying.

"You are a young man," the prince said. "And I think you're a hair's breadth from being stripped of your position by those frightened old harridans."

They walked through a narrow alley between two tents, stepping over the guy wires. As they emerged, the corregidor's guards found themselves looking into the barrels of twenty loaded muskets and at half a dozen drafters with arms loaded with luxin.

"Disarm them, and keep them thirty paces away, but don't harm them," the Color Prince said. "Unless they do something stupid, in which case, shoot for the groin."

With the men thus detained, the Color Prince kept walking, as if nothing had happened. "Both of those men report to the mothers, and I think we can agree we don't need their interference, can't we, Corregidor?"

"How do you know that? Or are you just guessing?" the corregidor asked, trying to keep his voice level.

"Can't we?"

The corregidor choked down his fear. "Very well. I'm—I'm sure we can settle this together."

"Mmm. I believe in choices, Kata. We are free men, making free choices, and bearing the consequences. So here are yours: First, you can surrender. I will give you less than generous terms. You will free your slaves, the city will pay a million danars, and you will give us twenty thousand ephahs of barley, sixty wagons laden with fruit, ten thousand barrels of wine, and twenty thousand barrels of olives. You will give us five thousand swords or spears and a thousand working muskets, with five hundred barrels of gunpowder and a hundred barrels of shot or eight hundred bars of lead. You will send with us fifty smiths and fifty wheelwrights and half a dozen chemists, and you will pay them double wages while they're gone. You will empty your city of brothels—the prostitutes can make their own choice on if they travel with us, but you will not allow any of them within your city for one year so as to encourage them to choose wisely. You will send all of your drafters to speak with me. Same with the slaves. They will be allowed to choose whether to join us or to go elsewhere, but they won't be allowed to return to your city until the war is completed, on pain of death. You will arrange a parade through the city, welcoming us with trumpets and hailing us for giving you freedom. And before we come into the city, you will send all your luxiats out to this camp."

The details were washing over the young man, and he grabbed on to the last like a raft in a maelstrom. "What is to happen to them?"

"We'll kill them all," the Color Prince said bluntly. Then he continued as if the man hadn't interrupted. "Then, in every church, you will allow to be established new forms of worship: one for each of the old gods. You will not be required to maintain or attend services at any of these, however, and our new priests will abide by your laws so long as you don't interfere with their worship.

"In return, you and the city's mothers will be allowed to retain your lives, your estates, and your positions, unless you betray me. The city will be unmolested; the countryside will go unplundered; no men or women will be pressed into service. I expect you to communicate this offer to the city's mothers. I've put it in writing already.

"All of it is true, except one part. I don't trust the city mothers. I know what kind of women they are. I have reports on all of them. They aren't young, and smart, and flexible like you are. When I leave this city, you will rule alone. I am not a hard master with my friends. I hope you can be such."

The corregidor was pale. "And if we refuse?"

They had arrived at the place where Liv now realized the Color Prince had been heading all along. He gestured to a large group of wretched people behind them, guarded by soldiers. It was the five hundred women and children captured from the small town of Ergion. "These unfortunates were taken from the last city that opposed us. They will be herded in front of our army for the first attack. When your ballistae and cannons and catapults start, you will massacre them—or do you think perhaps the city mothers will instruct you not to fire? And there will be attacks within your city. You know I have people inside. You don't know how many. I know about your secret exits along the river and below the Great Abbey."

The corregidor's eyes widened for a fraction of a second. Either surprise that the prince knew about this or surprise that there was another exit he hadn't known about.

"You remember the stories about the massacres at Ru, which led to Idoss surrendering during the last war? I will simply do the same, in reverse. Idoss will be a beacon to the world, and you get to choose which kind—a beacon of my munificence, showing how kind I can be to those I conquer, or a beacon of my malfeasance, showing how ferocious I am with those who oppose me. The children in your city will be killed—too many mouths to feed, too likely to get sick or bear grudges when they're grown. The women will be killed or put to service if they're pretty or useful enough. The only men and women who will survive unmolested will be your slaves. And they will be free to keep any of their masters' goods they wish. My people in the city are already letting them know this now. How much do you trust your slaves, Corregidor Kata? If by some chance you do hold out for a week, two weeks, a month, do you think the slaves might join us? Or have you treated them so well that their loyalty is unshakable?

"You, I will do my best to capture alive. I will send your genitals to your father. I will cut off your arms and legs and dress you in purple and put a crown on your head. I may blind you. I haven't decided yet what makes a better example. Tongue, no tongue? It will probably depend on your attitude. Regardless, I'll take my time. You will live a long time, and in great pain, I promise you."

The corregidor looked positively sick. "You're insane," he said. "You talk one second like you're some luxiat and you have all these principles, and the next you're talking about murdering a hundred thousand people."

The same thought had struck Liv before, but now she had another one. There were only a few people in the entire world who were absolutely overawing in their abilities—and she'd met the best of them: Gavin Guile and now Koios White Oak. Those two, and perhaps a few others like the White were far above Liv. But no one else was. She could have done better here than this boy was doing—and he was two or three years her elder and had all the benefits of being raised as a satrap's son. The reason the Color Prince was treating her as a capable adult wasn't because he was flattering her—though he was, and they both knew it—it was because she deserved to be treated as such. It wasn't that she was so incredibly gifted; it was that the people she had always assumed were incredibly gifted were in fact no more gifted than she was. She was their peer. And she was young yet. In time, she would be superior to most. Why hadn't the Chromeria ever treated her this way?

Why hadn't her own father?

The Color Prince said, "We all make choices, and then we bear the consequences for those. Unfortunately, right now, you get to make the choices for those people and for me. They're *your* victims, not mine. When I'm in charge, they'll be free to choose for themselves. There's no way to overturn the Chromeria without people like you forcing massacres. If there were, I'd take it in a heartbeat. This is the only way I can bring the change needed, so this is how I will do it."

"You'll do it because you can," the corregidor sneered over his fear.

"Because I can. Because I will it."

"So might makes right?"

The Color Prince was steel. Unamused, unapologetic, unyielding. "Might doesn't make right. Might makes reality." He stared at the corregidor for long enough to drop the weight of certainty on the boy, then turned and looked at the women and children. His gaze was sad but resolute. He would march these people to their deaths to shield his own people's lives, and he would blame the corregidor for it.

If it was a bluff, it was as brassy a bluff as Liv had ever seen. But she didn't think it was a bluff. Neither, she could tell, did the corregidor. His face slowly worked through horror, revulsion, astonishment, and finally resignation. He wasn't facing a man, he was facing a force of nature. There was no reasoning with a cyclone, no pleading with a hurricano. You batten down the hatches and ride it out, praying you survive.

"We don't have close to a million danars," the corregidor said, and Liv knew he had surrendered.

"Not in your treasury, you don't. You'll let every rich and noble family in the city know that if they don't pay their share, they'll be first to die. Substitutions can be made on the food. I'm not unreasonable. You may not have that much barley. You can make it up in other grains. And the fruit will be difficult if you don't hurry. We won't take spoiled produce. One noble family will be killed for each wagon you're short."

The corregidor blanched. "I'll have to take this to the city mothers, of course. It'll probably take two days."

"In one day, our catapults will be constructed. We'll start hurling one woman of Ergion over your walls every quarter hour. We won't stop until the luxiats arrive. I know your guns will be able to reach our catapults, so please know that the women and children of Ergion will be camped around the catapults as well. Your gunners are half-trained at best. There's no way they'll be able to hit our catapults on the first shot—or even the tenth."

The corregidor swallowed. "I understand."

"My people will post lists of the women's names in the order they will be flung, so that people inside Idoss can know when to listen for their friends' deaths—or perhaps their enemies', I suppose. We're starting with known acquaintances of the city mothers. My engineers tell me that the forces generated in the catapult's sling will have an even chance of killing a woman before she's even released. I've told them to work on it. I want you to hear their screams as they fly."

Kata Ham-haldita cursed quietly and left. He glanced at Liv, glanced away, ashamed.

"So that's it?" Liv asked once he was gone. She wouldn't have dared ask, before. She would have been too awed, too frightened. But now she wasn't going to waste the opportunity to learn from the best.

The prince was still looking at the women and the children. The children were playing together, shrieking and squabbling, unaware of their probable impending deaths. "Most likely," the Color Prince said. "It all depends on how smart young Kata is. One of the city mothers is a shrewd old harpy named Neta Delucia. The guards were her men. If Kata isn't careful, he has just signed his own death warrant by meeting with me privately. She'll know immediately that I offered to buy him off. And I put Mother Delucia's enemies at the top of the list of women to be killed. With her friends right behind them. The mother and the corregidor will fight. If Mother Delucia wins, we'll fling half a dozen women into town, and suddenly Idoss will see reason. If Kata wins, it may take more or less time, depending on how decisively he moves."

"And either way, you win?" Liv asked.

"We choose freely, Aliviana. That doesn't mean we can't set up the choices so that both benefit us." He smiled, and that smile reminded Liv of Gavin Guile's crazy reckless indomitable smile, but without the warmth.

"That's not really freedom then, is it? Not for them," Liv said.

"Are you ready for another truth, then, Aliviana? You learn so fast. Very well. Freedom isn't the highest good. Power is. For without power, your freedom can be taken." He smiled again. It was a hard smile, but this was a hard world.

Chapter 71

Ironfist was on his way to the White's quarters on top of the tower when he saw Blackguards standing outside the Prism's apartments. Since he'd just left Gavin, they could only be hers.

The commander knocked on the door.

"Come in," the White said.

The White was in her wheeled chair. Before her, Gavin Guile's room slave Marissia was on her knees, laying her head in the White's lap. Tears streaked the room slave's face, and the White was soothing her.

"Gavin Guile's back. He's one floor down," Ironfist said. The sometimes fractious relationship between the White and the Prism didn't need the additional strain of Gavin finding the White in his room. Gavin liked his private space.

Marissia hopped to her feet, dabbing her eyes with a handkerchief. "Oh! I cry once a year and he invariably— Mother, thank you. I will do as you've said."

"Orholam bless you, child. We'll leave now so we don't make your life any more complicated than necessary," Orea Pullawr said. "Commander?"

He wheeled her out into the hallway. It was much faster for him to do so, but it was also evidence of her growing frailty. Not two months ago, she would have angrily refused to let anyone push her around like she was an invalid.

Nor did she take over when they went down the hall. She seemed tired.

One Blackguard preceded them, and the other took their backs. Even here, they guarded.

"One thing I never considered about getting old," the White said, as Ironfist rolled her in front of her desk and then released her, to sit opposite her. "It makes spying so much harder."

"I thought that you had people for such things," Ironfist said.

"You can never leave such things entirely in other hands. It puts you at the mercy of your own spymaster. Or spymistress, as the case may be."

Spymistress? What? Did she mean—"Marissia?" Ironfist asked, incredulous. "She's your—"

The White said nothing for a long moment, and Ironfist's mind whirled at the implications. Marissia did have unfettered access to this floor at all times, but she could also move freely among the other slaves in the tower. Her position as a slave to the most important man in the world made her exist in a social gray zone: if needed, she could mix socially with the lowest scullery boy, or she could chide the richest merchant on Big Jasper. A smart woman would exploit the advantages of such a situation, and Ironfist knew that Marissia was definitely a smart woman.

"No, she's not," the White said finally. "But just now, you were thinking as I must think all the time. As Gavin must think."

"That's harder than juggling the odds of a rival pulling a good card," Ironfist said.

"One gets better with practice. But I prattle." She tented her hands in her lap, sat quietly. She glanced at his bare head, then back to his eyes. Waited.

Ironfist rubbed his bare head, the stubbly hairs growing in like stubborn weeds of faith he could cut but not uproot. If he couldn't trust the White, who could he? Even if she was faithless. Of course, he was faithless now, too. Did that make him less trustworthy?

He laughed quietly to himself. Truth was, he didn't know.

"I may be on the verge of losing my position. What was your big gamble?"

"Cards on the table, huh?" the White said.

"I at least appear to have very little to lose."

"Those who fold have no right to see the cards of those who stay in the game," the White said.

"Metaphors break down."

The White was quiet for a long moment, staring into the depths of him. He was impassive under her gaze. "You've stopped wearing your ghotra. It's hard to fail to notice such a thing. How should I react to that, Commander? Personally, or politically?"

"What do you mean?" he asked.

"Politically, you may have just made it impossible for me to save you. You've gone apostate. Most people don't wear the evidence of their faith on their heads—or take it off when they have doubts. You do. If the Black lists your apostasy as a reason to remove you from office, you'll admit it's true. So, politically, you've put the knife to your own throat."

335

He hadn't even thought of that. His religion—or lack thereof—wasn't some public show. How could not the outer man reflect the inner?

"Of course, you could defang that by simply putting your damn hat back on. Explain to anyone who asks that you removed it in mourning for your lost, which is true. Partly. But you won't do that."

"To be a man is to bring together that which you should be and that which you are. Deception is darkness."

"And did not Orholam himself set the world to spinning, so that there may be both times of light and times of darkness? The greater light and its nightly mirror do not shine on all the world constantly."

"That's generally understood to allow for moral exceptions to the rule in the case of war," Ironfist said, a little stiffly.

"Do you think we have not been at war these sixteen years?" the White said quietly.

"Does being the White mean getting to define war as anything you want it to be?"

"You met Corvan Danavis, did you not?" she asked. "Oh yes, of course you did, at Garriston. He used to say, 'Not all sharks and sea demons swim Ceres' seas.'"

"We're awash in metaphors, Mistress. I'm a simple man."

"Simplicity has its own power, Harrdun. As well you know. Yes, then. Yes, being White means I decide what is war. And when to threaten it." She smiled thinly.

Ironfist waited.

"As you know, I select the commander of the Blackguard, and the Black has the power to remove you. It's meant to balance our power. Really, it's meant to diminish mine. But what perhaps you don't appreciate is that after you are removed, I could simply appoint you again."

"And he would remove me again."

"Precipitating a crisis. But if you stayed, retained your quarters, continued giving orders, assigning shifts, how many of your Blackguards would abide by your choice and mine, over Carver Black's?"

What she was proposing could precipitate civil war. Ironfist raised his hands. "Hold. Wait, wait, wait. I'm not worth the kind of carnage you're inviting here."

"No, you're not."

She wasn't making sense. Was she finally going senile? No, the intensity in her desaturated blue, gray, and green eyes showed that nothing had shaken her deep intelligence.

"So what is it? I'm another front in your war?" Ironfist asked.

"Precisely. Carver Black doesn't hate you. In fact, he likes you. Andross Guile has something over him. I haven't ever been able to find out what it is, but we can put the problem back in his court: ask him if he wants to destroy the Blackguard, now, over his dirty laundry."

"So you're hoping Carver Black blinks."

"That's right," the White said.

"Well, at least you realize that Andross Guile won't."

"Never."

"I don't want this on my head. I love my people. I don't want to gamble with their lives. That's a game for worse men."

"Or women," she said lightly. Meaning herself?

"Or women." He refused to be taken in by her self-deprecation. Her charm. She was smarter than he was, fine. He didn't have to play this game. "I am the best of the Blackguard for my position, but every man and woman is loyal to our task. Losing me is a serious loss, but not one from which the Blackguard cannot recover." He stood. He was finished with this. He wouldn't miss all of it.

"You assume your successor would be chosen from the Blackguard's ranks."

He blinked. "I suppose you can choose anyone you want. You aren't going to choose someone bad for the job simply to spite me. You can threaten it now, but I know you too well. Once I'm gone, there'll be no reason for you to hurt yourself."

"Stop playing against *me*, you simpleton! Understand how Andross Guile works. After stripping you of your position, and disgracing you, he will use your disgrace to besmirch my judgment. He will already have the four votes he needs to pass an injunction circumscribing my authority by this little bit: he will then, through Carver, appoint your successor."

"Surely—"

"It doesn't stop there. Your successor, perhaps young Lord Jevaros—perfect because he's a loyal idiot—will report his concerns about my deteriorating mental condition. Incidents will be arranged to make me look senile. My duties will be further circumscribed, and I will be strongly encouraged to withdraw until Sun Day."

She was making guesses, of course, but they all made sense to Ironfist. "But...what does he want? Lord Guile, I mean? Why go to so much trouble? What's his goal?"

"If I had to guess, I'd say he simply wants control. I know this man. If he could, he would dissolve the Chromeria, dissolve the satrapies, renounce the Prism, and become emperor of the known world. I think he would hold that position for one day. One. Then he would feel either the triumph of obliterating all before him or the emptiness of holding power for no reason other than his own lust—and he would kill himself. Because there is no reason *why* he wants to rule. He simply believes he should. It irks him that his lessers should rule where he believes he ought."

"You make it sound so simple, and empty."

"Evil is simple and empty. Evil has no mysterious depths. We stare into a dark hole and fill it with our fears, but it is only a hole."

"Do you believe in Orholam, or was that a necessary lie, too?"

"I have big questions for him; he hasn't deigned to answer them."

He'd believed something similar, as a young man. He thought Orholam heard the prayers of the great and the holy. He'd prayed with blood on his hands, so he hadn't been heard. Excuses. He'd been making excuses for Orholam for more than twenty years. Because the alternative was too terrible. But here it was. He would believe lies no more.

"But I do believe," the White said. "I believe profoundly, my friend." She held him with her gaze, and he was reminded that this was a woman of will. Will great enough to become the White, and great enough to not use her magic for years and years.

"Would you lie to me?" he asked.

"Absolutely. But not about this."

"You would turn me into a liar."

"You would not be the first good man I've seen live a lie."

"Riddles."

"Perhaps."

"You mean Gavin, presiding over all the rituals. He's an atheist, isn't he?" When he said "atheist," it was a slur. He realized he said it as a slur out of force of habit. He'd always thought it the worst thing a man could be. And now he was one himself.

"I prefer to think that he's struggling through a lack of faith," she said carefully.

He sneered. He'd come up here to tell her about the cards and the knife, but now—all this was double-talk. If he didn't deserve the full truth from her, then she didn't deserve it of him.

There was a knock on the door. "Mistress," one of the Blackguards, a stocky woman named Samite said, "now that the Prism has returned, the Spectrum is proceeding with that emergency meeting. We need to head down in ten minutes."

The White nodded to her, dismissing her. She looked burdened, bitter, for one second. "Your people are kind to me, Commander. Telling me about 'that emergency meeting' in case I'd forgotten that we have to decide whether we go to war today. But such kindness is dangerous when my body is betraying me and the Red is already trying to paint me as lost in my dotage."

"I'll speak with her."

"Delicately, if you will. I know she means well." She turned back to Ironfist. "I've already told the Black that he can't remove you. The Red hates you for reasons I don't know and that you won't tell me, but he can't have you while I breathe." She waved her hand, and that was that. Ironfist was saved. "Now. My bet. I can't tell you what it was, but I can tell you who it was on. I bet everything on Gavin. I bet the world on him, and I may not live long enough to find out who wins."

Ironfist exhaled. *Since when did I become a keeper of secrets and teller of half-truths?*

He fished in his pocket. He pulled out a white rock, the size of his hand. He tossed it on the White's desk as if it were trash.

Her eyes went wide. "Commander, is that...?" She reached for it. "White luxin," she whispered.

"Gavin drafted it at the Battle of Garriston. He doesn't know he did it."

She picked up the white luxin with trembling hands, and for the first time that Ironfist had ever seen, she quietly wept.

Lots of crying women today.

Chapter 72

"Aliviana, come, I have something for you," the Color Prince said. He turned to the engineer in charge of the trebuchet. "Ten chits if you make it into the city on the first shot. But you owe me five if she doesn't scream."

The engineer bowed low, almost prostrating himself. The people still didn't know how much deference to pay to the Color Prince.

The entire camp had turned out for this. Noon was coming, and everyone knew that noon was the deadline. The guns on the city's walls were trained on them, but they hadn't fired during the entire setup of the trebuchet, three hundred paces from the city's walls. Some of the prince's followers stayed farther away, fearing that the guns would open up and try to destroy the trebuchet first, despite the women and children of Ergion held hostage around its base. More, however, crowded close, wanting to see the spectacle for themselves, heedless of the danger.

Liv had joined them because the prince had asked her to. "I will not shield you from the realities of war, Aliviana. This is our path, and you must know it. I trust you with hard truths." She caught his implication: Unlike her father. Unlike the Chromeria.

She would be worthy of that trust. So she watched, from close up. The crowds didn't jostle her. Her violet and yellow drafter's dress guaranteed that. Drafters were treated as lords and ladies. They had power, and power was a virtue.

"You said you had something for me, my prince?" Liv said.

"A letter came for you," he said. "And before you ask, of course I read it."

He gestured, and a steward brought a letter. Liv knew the handwriting. She felt tingles up her arms, up her neck. It was from her father.

The Color Prince said, "It's time for you to decide who you are and who you will be, Aliviana Danavis."

The engineers began cranking the great counterweight up into the air, sticking long staves into a wooden gear, ratcheting it down. The counterweight rose, slowly racing the sun, which was approaching its own zenith.

Liv opened the cracked seal: "My Dearest Aliviana, Light of my Eyes." A rush of tears came to her eyes, just at seeing her father's hand. When Kip had told her Corvan had died in Rekton, Liv's world had ended. She blew out a slow breath, blinked.

The crowd was jubilant and nervous by turns. The cannons could open up at any moment, spraying death everywhere, or the gates might open in surrender, or in attack, or nothing at all might happen. Men laughed too loudly. Some placed wagers. Liv could hear the women who were in line to be thrown over the walls crying quietly. Quietly only because they were trying not to upset the children, who still had no idea what was happening.

She kept reading: "Daughter, please come home. I know you think I've forsaken my oaths. I have not. I can tell you no more in a letter that may be intercepted, but I will tell you when you come." What he said was true, but it was infuriating, too. She'd been with him. She'd asked him—and he wouldn't tell her what he was doing. And now he would?

Now that she wasn't under his control.

Wood groaning, ropes straining, the trebuchet's enormous counterweight made it to its height before the sun. The engineers didn't leave off their work, though, rushing around checking how their machine was bearing up under the pressure, preparing the basket for the woman, warning the crowds before and behind the trebuchet to move back.

Eventually, the chief engineer came to the Color Prince. "We're ready, sir, should we load the cargo?"

Cargo. Oddly impersonal verbiage, wasn't it? The prince nodded.

An older woman was led forward. There were tears on her cheeks, but she wasn't crying now. Her clothes had been rich, Liv could tell, and she had the pale skin of a woman who'd never worked outdoors in her life. Wavy, silvered hair, brown eyes. Out of all the people staring at her, she saw Liv, and met her gaze.

"It's a bluff, isn't it?" the old woman asked. "Or am I fooling myself?"

Liv looked away. Trust me, her father had said. Was that just another way of saying, *submit*?

The woman let herself be folded into the net, meek, powerless. "Keep your head resting on the ropes," the chief engineer said. "Relax."

Relax, we're trying to win our chits, lady.

"Ready," the chief engineer said quietly to the Color Prince. 341

The prince beckoned Liv forward. His eyes were swirling red, and then blue, and then red. "Tell me, Liv. Should I wait until noon, or show them what it means to cross me?"

It was less than a minute until noon. Liv saw at once that part of him wanted to punish the city for standing against him, wanted to make them pay, was afraid that they would surrender too soon. Liv hadn't finished her letter. She hesitated, somehow thinking it was important. "You might stiffen their resolve if they think you haven't been fair. You've set up a deadline and a consequence, let it be their fault if this woman dies." For some reason, she had to finish the letter before that woman died.

The Color Prince relaxed. "Yes, yes of course. It would be wrong to blink first." Then orange flooded his eyes, and suddenly he seemed to be enjoying the tension he'd created.

She'd been right, she realized. He had asked her opinion because her opinion was valuable. She—*she*—was smart enough, strong enough to be trusted. She was no child.

She read: "Livi, I don't know what lies they've told you, but you've joined monsters. If you stay with them, you'll become monstrous yourself. Our home is gone, but come home, Livi. No matter what's happened. No matter what you've done. I love you. Papa."

Come home, and admit you were wrong. I'll enfold you in all the old rules you understand. I'll embrace you into childhood again. And it will be warm and safe.

"It is monstrous, isn't it?" the Color Prince said quietly to Liv. He didn't turn from looking at the gate.

"I suppose it—"

"Monstrous how they keep a place like Laurion, and call *us* the beasts, because we're willing to punish one slave owner, this woman. How many slaves do you suppose she kept? How many did she beat, or send to the mines, or the brothels? Or allow her husband to dishonor? Monstrous, how they turn our very hearts against our own interests. They've trapped us in this, Aliviana. They made this system. They made it so that we can't change it from within. They made it so we must kill to break it. If we be monsters, we're monsters made in their image."

Every eye was turned to the city's great gates. The top of the city's walls was crowded with spectators as well.

342 "Regardless of whether they fight or surrender, Aliviana, fewer will

die here than died in one year in Laurion. And we ended Laurion forever. Sacrifices, Liv. Sacrifices must be made."

Though she knew better, Liv hoped that the gates would open at the last second, that a fluttering flag would appear. It didn't.

"Noon," an engineer intoned.

"Proceed," the Color Prince said loudly.

The old woman screamed, "No, please! I haven't done any—"

The release pin was pulled. The great counterweight came barreling down, swinging beneath the great groaning struts, and the longer arm whipped forward, the ropes pulling the basket skyward at incredible speed. The sound of the ropes whipping the air layered below the woman's shriek.

She flew through the three hundred paces between the trebuchet and the wall so fast it was hard to follow, but Liv could see the woman clearly flail for one moment before crashing headfirst into the wall, halfway up.

Gasps rose from the entire crowd simultaneously, and then cheers and laughing and cheerful insults for the engineers. To Liv, it was all distant and horrifying. There was a splotch on the great tan walls, like a giant had swatted a mosquito on its arm.

Liv drafted superviolet and felt the paradoxical relief of not feeling. There was logic here, logic to this horror. If they attacked the city, how many men and women would die in the first charge alone? Better for one woman to die noisily and horribly—but quickly for all that and without much bodily pain—than for thousands to die in taking the city. And tens of thousands to die when they took the city itself. Once the Idossians had spilled the blood of thousands of the Free Men, there would be nothing the Color Prince could do to keep those men from exacting a terrible vengeance. This wouldn't be like retaking Garriston, which had been the army's own city, a place they wanted to preserve as much as possible so they could live in it themselves. This would be annihilation.

Though slaves no more, the slaves of Laurion weren't blank slates, weren't merely innocent farm boys who'd been made slaves and now might revert to a peaceful life. Many had been brutes before being forced into the brutish life of a mine slave. Outlaws, pirates, rapists, rebels, and those who'd fomented revolt among slaves went to Laurion. What proportion those men made up of the total, Liv had no idea, but even in her drafter's robes there were times walking the camp late at night she felt nervous. Those men, cut loose in a city that had killed their friends?

This was better, for everyone except a few unfortunate women. Sacrifices. The city must be taken, and this was the best way to do it. It was better that a few should die than many, wasn't it? Averting those greater horrors demanded this of them. Given war, this was the most moral way to wage it, horrible though it still was.

With no return fire from the city walls, the atmosphere quickly relaxed. Men began taking bets, serving food, spreading blankets on the grass, making a picnic of the day.

The Color Prince turned to Liv. She was struck again by his visage, but now her shock lasted only half a second. He did look a monster at first glance. And yet he'd been nothing but honest with her, even when the truths were hard. Especially when they were hard. He'd seen her for what she was, for who she was. And though she was a young Tyrean girl, he'd treated her as she deserved. He said, "I'll give you a horse, two sticks of tin danars, and letters of passage."

"That's not—" Liv started.

"I'm not finished. If you go, you never come back. You'll be my enemy and I'll never trust you. And if you don't go now, you never go. You choose, one way or the other, today. I've been patient with you, but I need to know if I can count on you. So this is it. Look at us at our worst, and decide. You have until the city falls. Then march in with us, or go your own way."

The second woman screamed the whole time they brought her forward, shrieking loudly enough that Liv had no doubt she could be heard on the walls. The Color Prince told the men not to silence her. When she tangled her limbs into the ropes of the basket, the engineers were stumped for a moment. With the incredible forces applied, the woman would still fly out of the basket, but she could seriously hamper the distance and trajectory, making them fail again.

They solved the problem by pulling her out of the basket and crushing her hands with a rock. Then they broke her elbows for good measure. She shrieked and shrieked, and Liv found herself wishing the woman would shut her mouth and just die.

But the Color Prince waited until the fifteen minutes had passed. On the grain, he said, "Proceed."

The straining whomp of the counterweight falling and whooshing and the long arm flinging the basket forward drowned the woman's screams. Maybe it knocked the wind out of her, because for a moment she was silent. Then, airborne, they heard her scream again.

To be fair, this woman had much longer to scream. The engineers had shifted the release peg, and the woman flew high, high into the air, hundreds of paces deep into the city.

The crowd cheered, although some seemed a little disappointed not to get to see the woman die in such a spectacular fashion as the first one had.

The Color Prince seemed to have had enough. He retired to his tent, handing over control to one of his favorite blues, a powerful young man named Ramia Corfu. Liv was transfixed, the letter in her hand. There was nothing more. Reading it again changed nothing. There were no hidden messages.

Two hours and seven deaths later, the gates opened, and four hundred and fifty black-robed luxiats were marched out, under guard. The Color Prince's men met the guards in the very shadow of the walls. The prince's military adviser had suggested that the besieged might dress up armed men in luxiats' robes and then attempt an assassination when they got close to the Color Prince.

Instead, the hundreds of luxiats docilely accepted the change of guard, accepted being checked for weapons, and marched willingly to the Color Prince.

Odd, Liv thought. Suicidal. Using their freedom to lose their freedom. Surrendering power. Insane. She looked at the letter again.

When they were finally brought forward, the Color Prince met them himself. He was mounted on his spectacular white stallion Morning Star.

"Why Neta Delucia, I had no idea you'd taken the black robe," the Color Prince said, addressing a woman in the front row. "Your devotion, though deluded, is...refreshing."

Neta Delucia was the city mother who the prince had said would head the opposition. So apparently the young corregidor had been successful after all.

Neta spat toward the Color Prince. "You *bought* him. That little coward. That little traitor. I knew you would."

"I knew you were the only one who had a chance to stop him," Koios said. "So how he'd win, your bad luck?"

"He struck half an hour before my men were to arrive to take him to prison."

"I could use a smart woman willing to do what needs to be done," the prince said.

Neta looked like she couldn't believe she was being given a second chance. After a moment, she fell to her knees, heedless of all the condemned men watching. "My lord, I would be happy to— I would be delighted and honored to serve."

"Who's the traitor now?" the Color Prince asked. He turned his back on her.

"But my lord! You said you needed me!" she shrilled.

"Enough," the prince said.

"My lord! My lord! Please! Please!"

"Silence her," the prince said.

A soldier stepped forward and slashed a dagger across her neck. Blood sprayed out of her throat and she crumpled. She lay on the ground, gasping out her last breaths.

Liv felt a wave of nausea, and quickly drafted superviolet to gain control of herself.

"I didn't mean *kill* her!" the prince said. "I—it doesn't matter. She didn't deserve to be with these servants of Orholam anyway." He raised his voice. "Luxiats, I detest everything you love, and I hate what you've done to the Seven Satrapies. But I admire your courage. Your deaths will spare thousands on both sides. For this one act, I admire you. Die well."

The Color Prince turned to the soldiers guarding them. "Bind them, hand and foot. All of them." Some few wept, but none fought, none screamed. Then, as hundreds of soldiers descended with ropes and bound the unresisting luxiats, he turned to his own gathered people.

"My brothers and sisters, today is the first day of a new order!" Cheers interrupted him, and he had to wait while they quieted. "Today, we take our first steps out of darkness." More cheers. If anything, to Liv Koios looked irritated that he wasn't able to finish. She gathered that he hadn't spoken to huge groups very often, especially not huge and enthusiastic groups flushed with victory and bloodshed. "We have been kept chained by the Chromeria and by her luxiats. Are we going to stand for it any longer?"

"No!" a few men cried.

"Are we going to let the Chromeria tell us what to do?"

"No!" the crowd joined in, now catching on. It was like the old call and response, but this time against the luxiats, rather than with them.

"Are we going to go quietly into the darkness?"

"No!" This time, everyone joined, even those far enough back that they couldn't possibly have heard the prince's question.

This is the mob, Liv thought. This is the beast. But beasts can be harnessed.

"Our future lies before us. Our victories lie before us. They lie there!" He pointed to the city, where the gates were opening even now.

Nice timing, Liv thought. But then, maybe he'd been stalling until he saw the gates about to open. Well done, regardless. Well played.

A huge cheer, but the Color Prince wasn't done. "Between us and our future stand the luxiats." He pointed to them. "Are we going to let them stop us?"

"No!"

"Then I say we march. I say we march right over those who would stop us."

"Yes!"

"If sacrifices must be made, let them be their sacrifices!"

"Yes!"

"Are you with me?"

"Yes!"

He glanced at Liv and said quietly, "Are you with me?"

She swallowed. Looked at the letter one last time. Dropped it in the mud. "Let's go."

And, so help them Orholam, that's what they did. The soldiers laid the bound luxiats across the road, and the whole army marched over them. The army kept in lockstep, marching heedless, as if they were simply traversing difficult terrain, ignoring the living beneath their boots.

After the army passed, the Color Prince's white-robed drafters followed. Their long white robes and dresses trailed into blood and took on a scarlet edge.

Then all the rest of the people came. Some tried to step around the groaning, screaming men and women. Others deliberately stomped groins and fingers, carried rocks to crush heads. Soon, it didn't matter. The bodies turned to jelly, the road bloody mud as gore was churned with the uncaring soil. Liv heard later that through good luck or bad, some of the luxiats had survived until the heavy-laden wagons' iron-rimmed wheels passed over them at the tail end of the army.

The army entered the city, victorious, cheering, drunk on their own omnipotence. And soon they were marching on, but now they had names, names they'd won in blood and battle. Names for their implacability. Some called them blasphemers, and so they were. Some called them luxiat-hunters, and so they became. Some called them Red Robes, and saw the blood as a sign of their viciousness. They accepted them all, and marched. And among them, every drafter cherished the blood on the hem of her robe, and after washing, they would dip their hems in cow's blood to renew the stain. It gave a stench to them, especially when they passed en masse. But they called it the smell of freedom, the sacrifice of others. Some quietly called them animals. They called themselves invincible. They called themselves the Blood Robes.

Liv's status meant she stayed in one of the Idossian nobles' own apartments that night. She got drunk, and when Zymun came knocking on her door once again after midnight, this time she didn't turn him away.

Chapter 73

"You're going to take them from me, aren't you?" Kip asked. The words came out all raw and jagged. Harder and harsher than he intended.

"What?" Gavin asked. He scowled.

It was as if while Ironfist had been here, Kip was able to be the Kip who was training for the Blackguard, the Kip who had some tenuous friendships and was starting to be good at some things. And now, with Ironfist hinting that Gavin was going to yank him out of the Blackguard, everything else came flooding back. Not just nearly getting killed tonight and having Janus Borig die in his arms, but his mother dying in his arms, bitter and accusatory. "I knew it. I knew if I didn't look at them right away, someone would steal them. I just didn't think it would be you."

Kip knew he wasn't mad about the cards—he was mad at being helpless. Before Gavin Guile had come along, sweeping everything up in his wake, Kip had had his own shitty life in his own shitty town with his shitty, shitty friends. Ever since Gavin Guile had come into his life, he felt like he'd been plunged underwater. And now his last breath had escaped and he was panicking, flailing, punching whoever happened to be nearest.

"What are you doing?" Gavin asked.

"What do you mean?"

"Why are you acting like this? You were sane just two seconds ago!"

"You left me!" Kip said. The sense of abandonment made his throat feel tight. It was hard to swallow. He hadn't even known that was in there, but now he felt horribly exposed, weak, ashamed. It was the prospect of Commander Ironfist leaving forever—just like everyone left him.

"I—what?!"

"You left me here," Kip said. He was already recoiling from his own stupidity. Gavin had just come back, and Kip was taking this out on him? What had Kip just been saying to Ironfist? That he was an adult? "I'm sorry," Kip said. "I've failed. I haven't accomplished anything you asked of me." He couldn't look at Gavin. "You said I had six months, and the only way I could think of accomplishing anything was to get into the forbidden parts of the libraries, and the only way to that was as a Blackguard. And I haven't gotten there yet. I don't think I'm good enough. And I failed with your father, too. He hates me."

Gavin cursed under his breath. "I wish my mother was here," he said suddenly. "I'd ask her...Kip, there's probably nothing you could have done to please my father. Nothing. And that other thing...We got unlucky and the Color Prince moved faster than I thought he would. I still might be able to get around that obstacle we talked about anyway."

"So everything I've been doing is extraneous?"

"Kip, in a very short time you've become one of the most important arrows in my quiver. But you're not the only one. Orholam help me if you were."

It was a slap to his whiny, fifteen-year-old face. And a well-deserved one.

Gavin cursed again. "I didn't mean it like that. I meant I can't do what I have to do with one weapon, no matter how sharp. Kip, you deserve more of my time, but right now I have about three emergencies to deal with, and my enemies are probably moving fast. Can you wait?"

Emergencies. Important stuff, like saving the world, preventing wars—or maybe winning them—fates of hundreds of thousands in the balance. And Kip wanted him to what? Sit around and talk? Wrestle? Play a card game?

I'm needy. Weak. A distraction from the important things. People could die because of my pathetic whining. Orholam, Kip, be a man.

Kip swallowed and straightened his back. "Yes, sir. I'm fine."

Gavin hesitated. "If it...if it makes any difference, I, I should have taken you with me. I should have taught you personally. I didn't—I didn't think of it. I'm not used to thinking of anyone but myself. And...I'm sorry."

Kip didn't know what to say.

"How many colors can you draft now?" Gavin asked.

"Sir?" The question seemed out of nowhere.

"Colors?" Gavin insisted.

"Um, four, five? Your father made me wager my right to the practicum, so I haven't been able to work on it as much as I'd like."

Gavin frowned. "Tell me what you can do."

"Only blue and green are stable. Red's inconsistent. Yellow's all over the place, and I haven't drafted sub-red again since Garriston."

"You know they say the Lightbringer will be a genius of magic."

"I'm...I'm not that, sir." He'd said "will." That meant his father believed that Lucidonius hadn't been the Lightbringer, that the Lightbringer hadn't come yet.

"No, you're not, Kip. Not because you're not a genius. You may be. Not because you're not tremendously talented, smart, and gifted, and mentally nimble. You are. You're not the Lightbringer because there is no Lightbringer. It's a myth that's destroyed a thousand boys, and led a hundred thousand men to cynicism and disillusionment. It's a lie. A lie more tempting the more powerful you are. Like all lies, it destroys those who long entertain it. And that's why I lied to you."

"Huh?"

"You're a polychrome. If you're angry at me because your test didn't show that, I deserve your anger. You're both privileged and despised for your birth, for one parent or the other, depending on who's hating you at the moment. You've got a right to have a chip on your shoulder, but I didn't want you to become a monster. So I didn't want you to know how powerful you were going to be. That's why I falsified your test."

"Wh-what?" Kip had been denying all the evidence of his expanding colors because of that damned test. He'd been wasting his time practicing the bouncy balls of doom while he could have been working on other colors?

"I don't apologize for it, Kip. I wanted you to grow up a little. I wanted you to get the measure of yourself before we added the burdens of vast talent onto your new burdens of being the son of the Prism, having everyone you ever knew murdered, and moving to a new home and jumping into social circles you probably never imagined."

"So why do you get to decide? Because you're the Prism?"

"Because I'm your father. I had to grow up too fast, and I didn't do it at all well. You know what it is to start a war when you're seventeen?"

"I thought you were eighteen."

"Young, regardless," Gavin said, but a quick expression leapt across his face, a tightening in his eyes, passing so fast Kip couldn't read it. "Long time ago, but I remember wanting to be an adult so bad it stuck on my tongue. I wanted people to take me seriously, to care what I thought. To listen to what I said without that amused, tolerant look on their face—'Here goes the young lord again.' I've been there, Kip, and people died because I didn't handle it well. Orholam send that the price you have to pay is never so high, but I didn't want to force you into a position where any mistake you made could get you or others killed."

Kip glowered. "Well, when you say it like that it all makes sense and stuff."

Gavin took his cloak off. "Come. Fold those up tight," he said, pointing to the shimmercloaks. "We'll talk about them later."

Father and son folded up the cloaks carefully and bundled them inside Gavin's cloak. Gavin folded it over his arm nonchalantly. He grabbed the deck box in his hand, concealed again by the cloaks.

"You know," Kip said, "Janus Borig said I wasn't going to be the next Prism. Not that I really wanted to. I mean, I want you to be the Prism forever. But..."

"But if you're not going to be the Prism, and there's no such thing as the Lightbringer, then that means you're going to be nothing?" Gavin asked.

"Yes, sir," Kip said, averting his eyes. "Sounds... awful, huh?"

"Yes," Gavin said. "Let's go."

Kip was a muddle. No Lightbringer? But Janus Borig had said she knew who the Lightbringer was—when she was looking at me. Afterward, when he finally thought about it, Kip had dared to hope that meant...

Exactly what his father had thought Kip would hope it meant. She could have meant, I know who the Lightbringer is... the Lightbringer is no one. Or, the Lightbringer is Lucidonius. Or she could have just been wrong. Right?

She'd *said* that her paintings had to be true, but Kip didn't know that to be true. Even if her paintings had to be true, that didn't mean her words did. She could easily have been lying, or just wrong. Even if she was right, and Gavin was wrong, she hadn't painted the Lightbringer. Maybe she wouldn't have been able to. Or maybe it would have been too obscure to tell anything. Even then, she'd said that sometimes her paintings weren't literal.

Kip followed Gavin out of the Blackguard barracks. A man and a woman Blackguard fell in behind them, natural and unobtrusive. Kip wondered how they did that. Long practice, he supposed. Just like everything in the Blackguards' lives.

Maybe that was why being a Blackguard appealed so much to him. Everything they got was earned. Not like Kip's life. They didn't care whose son he was, they cared if he could do the work.

Gavin set the weights in the lift—Kip had never really noticed it before, but though the Blackguards guarded Gavin's life, they weren't servants. Kip wondered if that was because Gavin had established that he wanted to do things for himself, or if the Blackguards simply refused to do more than protect him. They headed up, surprising Kip, who thought Gavin would make him go back to his own room.

They were deposited on the top floor. Gavin's and the White's floor.

"So your grandfather gave you trouble?" Gavin asked.

"Sir," Kip said. "Your father...um, he's denied me, sir. You know, denied that I'm your son." Kip swallowed. Of course he knows what it means, moron. "That's what I meant when I said I failed."

"Really?" Gavin said. "This is going to be fun, isn't it?" There was no mirth in his tone. He turned to one of the Blackguards, a lanky Ilytian with a crooked smile. "Lytos, this is my son, Kip. Kip is my son."

"Yes, sir," the man said. He had a strangely high voice. "I understand." Oh, a eunuch. Kip had heard that some Ilytians believed eunuchs were better drafters than boys. His teachers had ridiculed the idea, though: cutting a man's balls off doesn't change his eyes, she'd said. Cutting off one end of a man doesn't change the other. On the other hand, it did obviously change a man's voice, so maybe the idea wasn't that ludicrous. Or maybe it kept a man's voice from changing, which obviously wasn't the same thing. Unless there was something about puberty that also changed a man's eyes—maybe imperceptibly, but enough to skew men's color vision and make their magic fail more often than women's.

Again, the problem was that you couldn't tell what exact tones another person perceived, so everyone made the best guess they could. And apparently some people were confident enough in their guesses to cut off a child's testicles.

Kip was living in a mad world, among people who were happy to do worse than he could dream. He shivered.

Gavin looked at him, and understood. He touched Kip's shoulder briefly.

Lytos peeled off as they walked through the security checkpoint and spoke to the officer in charge. Not five seconds later, Lytos was walking quickly to catch up with Gavin and Kip. Another Blackguard—Kip's Blackguard, he supposed—was with him. Samite. Kip was glad to see her again. He hadn't seen her much since the day he'd first arrived. He grinned at her. She simply raised an eyebrow.

They walked to Gavin's room, went inside. Gavin beckoned Kip to follow him. Like a particularly squat shadow, Samite followed Kip in and took her place behind the door. She was Kip's bodyguard now, and that meant guarding him even in Gavin's room. Even from Gavin, if it came to that?

A mad world.

The big, open room was spotlessly clean and as beautiful as the last time Kip had been here. But now he knew a lot more about drafting than the first time he'd been here. Knowing more, he was more impressed. There were hellstone panels in the walls that you could hit with superviolet luxin to control the windows and the artificial lights above. There was sub-red luxin woven through the floors and the ceiling to keep the room warm, counteracting the chill that invaded through the dozens of floor-to-ceiling windows.

But before Kip could marvel at the workmanship and luxury even of the windows themselves, he saw Marissia, Gavin's room slave. She must have had warning that Gavin was coming, because she was wearing finer clothing than Kip had ever seen her in before. He supposed that the gray color technically was in obedience to the sumptuary laws, and her hair was carefully kept free of her ears to show where they had been snipped vertically and cauterized in the Ruthgari style, but she looked astoundingly good. But the fitted cut and her lean curves hit Kip more like the background roar of ocean waves crashing to shore. He was arrested by the look on her face. She took a steadying breath, desperate for approval, eager for favor, eyes only for Gavin.

Kip had seen dozens, hundreds of people look at his father with adoration in their gazes. He'd seen people look at him with veneration in their gazes. This was love.

As fast as if he were trying to follow a cannonball in flight, Kip looked over to Gavin's face.

The Prism was obviously pleased. He smiled widely, and Kip saw his father's eyes sweep over Marissia's body appreciatively.

Ew. That's my father. Looking at a woman like—

Kip didn't want to think about it. He looked away.

"Marissia," Gavin said.

Marissia hurried over and knelt at Gavin's feet. She kissed his hand. "My lord."

Kip couldn't help but look back at them.

"You've been crying," Gavin said.

"Yes, my lord. I have much to tell you." She glanced over at Kip. Ah, in private.

Gavin handed Kip the cloaks and the card box. He walked to a
closet, rummaged for something.

Kip cleared his throat awkwardly and walked over to one side of the room where there was a table and chairs. Marissia had already risen by the time Kip sat, and was speaking quickly to Gavin, with her hand to the side of her mouth, in case Kip was a lip-reader, he guessed.

These people know what they're doing, and they're playing for keeps. Kip felt the familiar sinking feeling. He was so far out of his depth all he could do was flail.

"No!" she said, her voice rising just enough for Kip to hear it. "No alarms. I'm certain—" She lowered her voice again.

Gavin asked several quick, sharp questions, heard the low answers, then nodded a few times. There was a knock on the door. Gavin appeared to curse. "Yes?" he said.

The door cracked open. Kip couldn't see who it was, and Gavin made a very subtle gesture to him to stay where he was. Always keeping secrets, his father. Not letting anyone know anything that might endanger them all. Samite, blocked from sight as she was by the open door, remained silent, unseen.

"Gavin," an older woman's voice said. "I was hoping you might accompany me downstairs. It is *your* business that will be before the Spectrum, after all, but I'd enjoy a word first."

The White. Gavin was talking to *the White.* Kip swallowed again.

"Of course," Gavin said.

He turned around and addressed Marissia, but Kip could tell that he was really talking to him. "I'll be back in an hour. Stay out of trouble."

Marissia curtsied deeply. She knew when to play along. Gavin nonchalantly tossed something onto his bed, flicked his eyes to Kip to let him know it was for him, and then left.

After the door closed, Marissia turned to Kip. "It appears you're to stay here, young master. Do you have any needs?"

"Perhaps a bite to—"

"Excellent. Then if you'll excuse me, I have urgent errands for the Prism. Please do stay out of his things. He's not very understanding about those who violate this, the only sanctuary he knows."

"I under—"

But she was already gone, the door snapping smartly shut behind her.

"—stand," Kip said. He glanced, chagrined, at Samite beside the door. Her lips were pursed, trying to keep from grinning, no doubt, but otherwise her face was expressionless.

He sat down at the table. Stay out of trouble, huh? He looked over at the bed and then at the deck box, and, for one proud moment, thought of not opening it.

Hell with that.

The cards practically leapt into his hands.

The door opened, and Kip slammed the cards back into their box and hid it under the cloaks.

Oh, it was just Teia.

"Hey, Master," she said, eyes twinkling. "The Prism's slave told me you might still be here. We're supposed to go to practice."

"We need to talk about that master thing," Kip said.

"No, we need to talk about our strategies for the Blackguard testing. After practice."

"We don't need to talk about strategies yet, do we?" Kip asked.

"*We* don't."

"They sent you in here to distract me," Kip said, understanding.

"Commander said you'd just been through something traumatic. Your partner's supposed to look out for you. Now come on."

It was almost like having a real friend. But of course Teia had to look out for Kip. She was his slave. Kip gave a wan smile. "Almost a real friend" wasn't half bad, considering.

He picked up the card box again as he stood. Samite cleared her throat.

Kip looked at her. She returned his look blandly. He put the box down, feeling like a chastened child. He gestured toward the bed: Can I get that at least, Mom?

Be my guest, her expression said, tolerantly amused.

Kip picked up a little stick of ivory from the bed. He had no idea what it was.

"Oh, that's a testing stick," Teia said, coming over to stand beside him. "From the Threshing. It shows what colors you'll likely be able to draft. Why'd he give you a testing..."

The stick lay across Kip's open palm. It had all seven colors.

Chapter 74

Gavin greeted the White with a smile as their Blackguards fell into place behind them. Elessia, a petite woman, light-skinned for the Blackguard, was pushing the White's wheeled chair. This was a change. The White was weakening, then.

For some reason, though he had feared her for nearly two decades, the thought brought him nothing but dread. She was dying, and so was Gavin. And if she continued drafting so much, so, too, was Karris. Maybe this generation's time had passed.

Meanwhile, the heretics under the Color Prince grew strong. Kip wouldn't be ready in time. Not with Gavin dying at this rate. He'd lost two colors in what, four months?

"So you faked Kip's test so your enemies wouldn't know he was a full-spectrum polychrome?" the White said.

Yes, let's do jump right in. Anything to not give her a commitment to balance while she watched. "Pretty much, though someone sent an assassin after him immediately, so it obviously didn't work."

"It appears someone is trying to start up the Order again. There have been a few unexplained murders in the time you've been gone. But we can talk about that later."

They entered the lift together. Gavin took his time setting the weights. First, he wanted to get the weight exactly right so the stop wouldn't be jarring for the old woman. Second, he wanted her to hear what he had to say.

"If you told me your plans beforehand every once in a while, I could help you, you know, Gavin."

But that would require me to trust you.

"But that would require you to trust me," she said.

Scary. Too much time with the old goat. He wondered if he was becoming more like her, or she him. Now *there* was a scary thought.

"What's the endgame, Gavin?"

Endgame? He thought of his seven purposes. Seven purposes in seven years. He was two years in now. And he didn't have five years left anymore. He'd learned to travel faster than anyone ever had. Hell, he'd learned to fly. He'd failed at freeing Garriston—though if he followed Corvan's argument, he'd actually succeeded by saving the people. He still hadn't told Karris the truth, but he'd do that once he left here. And the other four? Well, he'd be working toward all of them in this meeting. And he certainly couldn't tell her about any of—

"So there is an endgame," she said. She lifted her eyebrows, coolly amused.

Shit. He'd forgotten who he was talking to here. Forgotten to guard his every expression. Forgotten to lie first and think later. Protect. Guard. Hide. The fugitive's motto. Honesty is death. Loneliness is weakness.

"War," Gavin said darkly. "The end is always war."

"I don't even know that they'll declare war, but if you think they're going to declare you promachos again, you're insane," she said as he applied the brake. He stopped them perfectly even with the level so that her wheeled chair could exit smoothly.

He strode ahead, not waiting for her.

"They're too afraid of you, Gavin."

Too afraid? They're not afraid enough.

Gavin stepped into the meeting room and took a seat on the far side. The table around which they met was a circle, but Gavin wanted to be able to see who came in the door. A few of the Colors were already seated. Sadah Superviolet, representing Paria, sat next to Klytos Blue. Sadah was from minor nobility in a clan that wielded little clout in Paria. Mountain Parian. She'd attained far more in her life than anyone would have expected through cold intelligence and fierce ambition. Indeterminate age, limbs lean, hands as gnarled as a yucca palm branches, skin as psoriatic as a yucca palm's trunk. She wore her kinky hair gathered in small knots and wore a tight-fitting cap of woven gold that sat tight against her scalp, with little gaps for each knot of hair. An odd style that, so far as Gavin knew, had originated with the woman herself. Like the superviolet she was, Sadah brought a dispassionate perspective to all her votes, and was often the swing voter because she was immune to any pressure but that of logic. Hated lies.

Klytos Blue was Ruthgari through and through, but represented Ilyta. He was a coward. Intelligent, but lacking substance, no gravitas. He did what Andross told him on most matters. Gavin sat next to Klytos, greeting him as if he didn't despise him. He was happy to sit next to the man—not for his company, but because it's hardest to surreptitiously study the expressions on the faces of those who sit right next to you. Klytos didn't matter; Gavin didn't have to be able to study his face.

Jia Tolver, the Yellow, nodded to Gavin, smiled. At the center of the color spectrum, yellows could be truly fearsome: great souls who brought under their power the appeals of emotion and reason in perfect balance. Jia was no great soul, though she liked to think she was. In truth, she really just ended up being perfectly susceptible to appeals of reason and emotion both. She was Gavin's, almost always. She'd been infatuated with him for years. His smile was enough to get her vote, though it had been a delicate act to keep her from trying to get into his bed. She tried her wiles on him every so often, and he deflected her propositions rather than rejected them. Vain creature. Good enough looking, but too much makeup, though she had cut back on the perfume after Andross made numerous explicit references to rooms smelling like cheap whores whenever she entered. She was proud of her unibrow, kept it perfectly coifed.

As he sat, Gavin smiled at the hairy caterpillar perched on her brow. Jia beamed.

The others came in together, chatting. They were friendly, but tense. Delara Orange, the red/orange bichrome whose bosom was so large it ought to have had its own vote, looked drawn, grim, older than Gavin had ever seen her. She represented Atash: her country had been invaded by the Color Prince, and doubtless she would advocate war. Doubtless, she had been advocating war since she'd first heard of the invasion.

The Sub-red was Arys of the Greenveils. She was perhaps eight months pregnant now, serially pregnant always. In her, the passions of sub-red were wedded to a cultural imperative for drafters to breed so as to replace the dead for the once-interminable wars between Blood Forest and Ruthgar. She was, Gavin thought, perhaps thirty-five, and she had twelve children. Not a one, if rumor was correct, by the same father. She had a curtain of straight red-red hair, freckles, and blue eyes sparkling with the crystalline detritus that marked a longtime sub-red. She had perhaps two years left. Her thirteen—or by then probably fourteen—children would grow up honored in Blood Forest. They would also grow up without a mother.

"Where's Lunna Green?" Gavin asked Klytos.

Klytos blanched. "I'm so sorry, Lord Prism..."

Lunna, despite being Ruthgari, was Gavin's. He'd carefully built up enough credits with her that if he called them all in, she would do almost anything for him.

"What?" Gavin asked. Oh no.

"She had a stroke. She died."

"She wasn't even forty-five," Gavin said.

"I'm so sorry, Lord Prism. She was right at the verge of breaking the halo for some time, and..." Klytos lowered his voice. "There were rumors she wasn't going to take the Freeing. You understand?"

That she was trying to become a green wight, and she'd failed. No, she wouldn't. Would she?

But that was the thing about facing death and insanity, wasn't it? You never knew what a person would do. Gavin had seen all sorts over the years.

This was a disaster. A declaration of war required a simple majority. Eight votes were possible—one for each Color, and one for the Prism. In case of ties, the White got a vote. Gavin's count had included Delara Orange, who was Atashian and would definitely vote for war, and Arys Greenveil, whose Blood Forest was directly on the warpath and who wasn't averse to war regardless. His own vote, with Lunna's, would bring it to four. That would kick it up to the White, who he thought would vote for it. She wasn't a fool.

But without Lunna, Gavin would have to sway Jia Tolver or Sadah Superviolet. Jia voted with him often, but the Aborneans had no stake in a war, and wouldn't mind seeing Atash burn for a while as they pretended that their reluctance to help put out the flames was born of pure, high-minded pacifism. Sadah Superviolet was even harder to judge. Paria was also far away from the fighting, and wouldn't want to send its young men or its wealth—but Sadah would do what was right. He hoped.

Gavin would have to move fast if he was going to have a chance.

Perhaps the new Green would be amenable. If she or he wasn't, Gavin could structure the vote. His father would have already sent in his vote on war as a no, but if Gavin was tricky and quick, he could make there be votes on issues that the Red hadn't sent his vote down for. By not calling a straight up-or-down vote on declaring war, Gavin might be able to outmaneuver the old spider. Difficult, but possible. He would turn the old man's proud disregard for the Spectrum on its head.

For all the satisfaction you get out of despising us, father, there are costs.

Lunna Green, though? She wouldn't have gone wight, would she? But if she hadn't...Dear Orholam, the murder of a Color? Surely the Order wasn't that good.

This wasn't the right way to do this. He knew that. He wasn't prepared for this meeting. Not that it was his fault—they'd called for an emergency session weeks ago, to be held as soon as he got back. So he couldn't wait, couldn't put it off. The longer he spent with these people, the more opportunities they had to notice that something was wrong with him. His eyes had still looked prismatic when he'd only lost blue—he'd asked Corvan. But then, his eyes' natural color was blue. Now that he'd lost green, wouldn't his eyes start changing color? This was all madness and stumbling in the dark.

There was conversation from the hall and, wearing a luxurious green silk cloak, in came none other than Tisis Malargos, the astoundingly beautiful young green who'd sabotaged Kip's test. The woman who hated Gavin, because her family had reason to hate the real Gavin. The woman whose father had been murdered on Felia Guile's orders, because he could have exposed that Gavin wasn't really Gavin.

She laughed at something her interlocutor said outside, then shot a look at the Prism. Hazel eyes, heart-shaped face, pale skin, the preciously rare blonde hair, generous curves. An exotic beauty who hated him for nothing he had actually done. Perfect. Very, very young to be on the Spectrum, though. How had that—

And then her interlocutor stepped into view, wearing large blacked-out spectacles under a crimson hood, and robes the color of blood.

"Father," Gavin said, his heart icing over. "What a surprise."

Chapter 75

Trainer Fisk was running the scrubs through takedown drills when Karris White Oak came in. Teia immediately took notice. For one thing, she wasn't very good at the throws they were practicing—it was one area where her lack of body weight made things much more difficult for her. She could still throw a boy who weighed twice as much as she did, but she had to get the leverage perfect. Getting things perfect seemed beyond her right now.

Second, Karris was her hero. Everyone respected Karris. She was known to be one of the best fighters in the entire Blackguard. Fast and tough, mentally and physically and magically. Smart, confident, and beautiful on top of it all. She was everything Teia hoped to be, even if some of those last things were out of reach.

Third, learning that Kip was a full-spectrum polychrome had kind of frightened her. And it had scared Kip, too. Attending Blackguard training? That was normal. She could handle that.

"Watch Captain White Oak, it's an honor to have you come," Trainer Fisk said.

"I wish I could visit more often. I hear this is a very talented class." She had? They were? Everyone perked up at that, even Kip.

"I wonder," Trainer Fisk said. "Would you be willing to show us a quick takedown? Some of the girls have been very quietly grumbling that these drills are too hard because they don't have the body weight."

"Really?" Karris said. "*Very* quietly, I might imagine. Or at least I hope." She arched an eyebrow at one of the girls, who withered. "I'd be happy to. Who's the best fighter in the class?"

"Cruxer," someone said. The rest of them mumbled agreement.

"Cruxer, defend yourself," Karris said.

She walked toward him and he got in a ready stance, one foot forward, hands lightly balled and held up. She snapped an attack, a knifehand, right at his eyes. His hands shot up to block, palms out.

Then his hands and hers entwined, and Cruxer dropped to his knees as fast as he could, yelping. He had barely touched them to the dirt before she was moving in, sweeping him off his knees to the ground, rolled over, facedown, one of his hands still clasped in hers, her knee on his neck.

Unhurriedly, she drew a pistol from her belt and put it to the back of his head.

It was over that fast. Against *Cruxer*. Teia looked over at Kip. He had the same wide-eyed look she did.

Then Karris tucked her pistol away and got up. The class started breathing again. Karris made it seem so effortless. She hadn't even gotten dirt on her knees.

"It's one of those tricks that works well against those who've never seen it," Karris said. "It's instinctive. You go for the eyes, and your target will open his hands to fend off the strike. A quick fingerlock, and you can drop him. From there, you've got all the leverage you need. Less weight and less strength just means you need to be smarter."

"Nicely done, Watch Captain. I haven't seen that one in years. I'm afraid it would have worked even on me," Trainer Fisk said.

"Mm, maybe," Karris said. She smiled. "Although I'm not too eager to reenact our last fight."

He shrugged. "Extenuating circumstances," he said. "You were tired. Not many people trade five fight tokens."

"Can I take one of your students for the afternoon?" Karris asked. "I've got some private training to brush up on."

"But of course."

Karris looked around the room. Then, finally, she pointed at Teia. "You, you'll do."

For some reason, Teia was sure that she hadn't been picked randomly. But that night, Karris just trained. She said nothing except to give instructions about how to hold the kick bags or which exercises she wanted Teia to do with her.

"Excuse me, Watch Captain," Teia said finally. "But why are you training with me? I can't hold a candle to a lot of the fighters you work with every day."

Karris said, "Sometimes it's good to fight people who don't know what they're doing. It reminds you how most of your opponents in real life flail. It's less predictable."

Oh. Well then.

Neither of them said anything else.

Chapter 76

Gavin had almost forgotten the visceral effect his father had on people. Andross Guile had sequestered himself by degrees starting almost a decade ago. Most men would be diminished by their absence.

Andross had grown in people's minds, in their dread. He'd become the bloated spider at the center of the web. And now, returning, weak, near blind, somehow he was still a titan. He was old. Drafters never got old. Becoming old meant you'd done the impossible. The casual destructions of age—the sagging translucent skin, the liver spots, the frailty—these had become badges of honor, proof of godlike will, self-discipline, power.

With the assistance of his lapdog slave Grinwoody, Andross Guile sat. He ignored the greetings of the other Colors and lifted his chin as if staring in the direction of the White, who alone seemed unmoved.

Well, if Andross Guile's presence swayed everyone else in the room against Gavin's proposal, at least it swayed the White toward it. But though her instinct would be to oppose anything Andross wanted, she wouldn't let that override her concern for what was right, what was best for the Seven Satrapies and the Chromeria. Even she couldn't be counted on.

Trying not to let how utterly furious he was show on his face, Gavin looked at his father. The bastard sat there, basking in his own excellence. The rules didn't apply to Andross Guile. He was above them. The world bent to his will. Ridiculous.

Gavin chuckled.

"Is something funny, Lord Prism?" Tisis Malargos asked.

"Just had a small personal revelation." He smiled indulgently, and didn't tell her more, just to infuriate her. You're playing with the big guns now, Tisis, are you sure you're ready?

"And that is?" she asked, insincerity oozing down her chin.

"Why you don't like me. Which isn't the reason you shouldn't like me."

"Perhaps we should get started," the White said quickly. Ever the peacekeeper, if not always a peacemaker. "Andross, it is so good to see you. It's been too long. Would you like to lead the invocation?"

"No," the old man said. He didn't elaborate, excuse, or apologize.

The White tented her fingers. Waited a long moment.

Klytos Blue couldn't handle the tension. "I—I would be happy to—"

"Are you feeling unwell, Andross? Too feeble for a prayer?" the White asked.

Gavin saw where that was going. Implied weakness, implied unfitness to remain on the Spectrum. It was unusually blunt for the White, who preferred a gentler hand. But she also didn't suffer rudeness.

Andross cocked his head, as if admitting a point scored by his opponent. "Of course not," he rasped. "My voice is no longer a thing of beauty. The ravages of many years in Orholam's service. I thought perhaps the mellifluous tones of Tisis Green's voice might be more uplifting for us all."

"Orholam judges the hearts of men, not their voices," the White said. "He hears any prayer lifted to him in humility."

So my father might as well save his breath.

Gavin let his bemusement show on his face. His father, his eyes shuttered even beneath his blacked-out spectacles, was literally playing blind. Taking on the whole Spectrum, without being able to see anyone's facial expressions? Balls.

Perhaps it was handicap enough to help Gavin.

But his father's words actually cast doubt into Gavin's mind. Why would Andross point to the new Green? Of course she was young and beautiful, and she did have a pretty voice, all things that Andross did appreciate, Gavin knew. But by singling her out, Andross suggested that Tisis was his.

Gavin had assumed she was. But why would Andross need to point it out to everyone, unless perhaps she wasn't? Or wasn't fully.

The tightness around Tisis's eyes, above her phony smile, told Gavin his father was pushing it. Greens hated to be bound, hated to be controlled. Careful, father. I might just pull that jewel away from you. Despite everything.

Relaxing his eyes into sub-red, Gavin looked at each member of the Spectrum in turn, doing his best to be subtle about it. In sub-red, the nuances of a person's facial expressions couldn't be seen: that spectrum of light was too fuzzy for fine details. What he could see was the temperature of each person's skin. It varied from woman to woman, of course, depending on their natural temperature and how close their blood vessels were to the surface of the skin, but if you could establish and remember a baseline for each person—and Gavin had very carefully done that over the years for everyone here except Tisis—you could tell when someone was feeling unusual stress. As their heart pounded faster, even if they were able to control more overt signs like swallowing, fidgeting, or clenching their jaws, they would glow hotter in sub-red.

Of course, a person could be nervous for dozens of reasons, and their temperature could be affected by any number of factors from drinking a glass of wine to wearing heavy clothes, but every once in a while it would give him a clue that nothing else would. With this group, he needed every advantage.

Andross Guile prayed. "Father of Lights, we humbly beseech you attend our supplication." Andross despised prayer, Gavin knew. He could do what he had to do, of course. He knew all the rituals backward and forward, and in front of the common folk was capable of all apparent sincerity. Here, among those he could almost consider peers, he had more trouble hiding his contempt. To him, the entire religion was a con, but a con on which all their power rested. Thus the faux-archaisms, delivered deadpan enough that one couldn't quite be sure if he was devout and old, or mocking them all: "Prostrate before you, we fall, O Lord. May our pretensions wither in the heat of your glory, may our presumptions fade in the light of your truth. May you bestow upon us clarity in counsel, obscurity in obfuscation, ocular acuity in action. Thus, in our wretchedness do we implore. May our young defer to old and our old defer to the grave. May our labors flower in your sight, with peace and truth and long-suffering."

Crotchety old bastard.

"Thus be it," Andross ended.

They all made the sign of the four and three. "So may it be," each murmured.

The White looked furious. But the sledge of her gaze had no effect on a blind man.

"Gavin," she said, "your meeting." *You want to sow the wind?* she was asking Andross.

His father's hatred of the White and his contempt had pushed her too far. Presiding was a huge advantage, enough of one to give Gavin a fighting chance. He took a deep breath. "Clearly some things have changed in the time I was gone." He stared at Tisis Green. "For all of us."

"I was rightly appointed to this body—" Tisis said, bristling.

"Tisis!" the White said. "Gavin is presiding. All Colors will be recognized in due course and heard fully, but we are a collegial body, and interruptions shall not be tolerated."

"As you are no doubt aware," Gavin said, as if the interruption and counterinterruption hadn't happened, "when last I met with you— that is, those who were present at that time, and those who were not have doubtless read the minutes of that meeting pursuant to diligent fulfillment of their duties—" That is, if you don't know what I'm talking about, you're lazy and bad at your job, Tisis. Gavin had no doubt that his father had memorized the minutes from the last meeting. He'd gotten his memory from the old man, after all. He continued: "When last I met with you, I warned you that King Garadul had rebelled, and would doubtless seize Garriston. I urged us to prevent war, though in a way that proved too painful for this council to countenance. This august body rejected my proposal, and war did indeed follow."

Klytos raised a forefinger, asking for recognition to speak. Gavin extended his hands out and downward, as if smoothing away the problem. "I don't come to refight old debates. I understand that there were excellent reasons to be skeptical of what King Garadul intended and what he would be able to do. I have no intention of dwelling on the past." Except to remind you all that I was right. "Merely summarizing for those who might not have noticed the nuances of the minutes." He looked at Tisis, as though this last comment were directed at her, and indeed, she flushed.

In truth, his summary was for everyone else, framing the old conversation for his own purposes. He who controls the past, and all that. Gavin could do all this with his brain handing over control of the ship to the first mate. He was thinking furiously. Orholam, Lunna. After all the work I did cultivating her.

Andross Guile moistened his lips. If anything, he looked perversely proud of his son.

Which didn't mean he wouldn't yank the rug out from under Gavin as soon as the opportunity presented itself.

For a moment, Gavin wondered. What if Lunna Green had been murdered, but not by the Order? What if his father had done it?

No, that wasn't Andross Guile's way. He would bribe a Color, or blackmail her, but not murder. On the other hand, it would be vintage Andross Guile to have a plan to replace each and every one of them, in case they did break the halo or resign. Andross would be ready. That didn't mean he would get an ideal candidate in place each time, only that he could steer the nomination. Perhaps that was why Tisis wasn't fully his.

If Andross really was willing to murder a Color, he would have made sure that he murdered one whose replacement was fully his. Right? Otherwise, why risk murder?

Gavin was taking too long. Take the facts as they are, and work with them. Move forward. Figuring out the past can wait. What advantages did having Tisis on the council give him?

The Spectrum expected Gavin to head straight for the discussion of a declaration of war. Then they thought he'd ask to be made promachos again. So Gavin said, "In truth, I don't think the first thing we should discuss today is the war raging in Tyrea and eastern Atash."

Klytos raised his finger again. Gavin motioned for him to speak.

"We've not established that the *troubles* in Tyrea and eastern Atash are war, Lord Prism," Klytos said.

He was about to go on, but Gavin knuckled his forehead and said, as if mystified by Klytos's stupidity, "Precisely. Which is why I said we wouldn't be talking about it first. We are a deliberative council; such matters should be discussed, but not necessarily first. Like I *just* said."

Delara's orange/red-haloed eyes narrowed. She wanted to talk about war, too, immediately. She clearly hoped Gavin would be the last vote she needed. She never had been very good at the arithmetic of these situations.

"The satrapy of Tyrea was a place of dishonor and war," Gavin said. "Since Satrap Ruy Gonzalo sided with my brother Dazen, his satrapy was doomed. It waged war, and destruction was visited by its sons on others, and by others' sons on it. After the war, Tyrea was stripped of her representation on this council and looted—" Seeing Delara's raised finger, Gavin amended, "—forced to pay reparations that left her destitute. For many good reasons and a few ill, Tyrea became a husk. Satrap Garadul doomed that husk. He made war on Garriston and the Seven Satrapies and this council thereby, and declared himself king. I fought him in Garriston, and I lost. Of course, the good news is that the so-called king was also killed in the last battle.

"There are many things we need to do today and I apologize for the many hours we're going to spend here—I've arranged for refreshments to be brought up in two hours—but the first item is very simple." Every one of them hated these meetings, and every one of them except Blue and Superviolet hated the formal order to them that made even the simplest resolution take half an hour. By raising the specter of being stuck in the meeting all day, Gavin hoped to make them a little careless. It would especially needle a green. He also did have a history when the White let him preside of tackling whatever business was before them in a logical manner—first agreeing on what everyone could agree on, and then moving forward as efficiently as possible while letting everyone have their say.

"There are people in Tyrea who have now been deprived of their leader—people who didn't care if he called himself satrap or king. They followed Rask's father and most of them liked the old man. In the course of a life that is rarely touched by politics, most common folk will simply go along with whoever is giving the orders. They had no reason to think Rask Garadul was illegitimate, and no reason to think his successor is, especially if we who divine Orholam's will say nothing against the new king—as this Color Prince will no doubt declare himself. So, before we get to the meat of today's proposals, I suggest we draft a simple resolution, condemning King Rask Garadul for waging war on the Seven Satrapies." Gavin opened the floor for comments and debate, as if he wanted to get this out of the way.

He stared at Tisis. Beautiful girl.

"It would certainly strike a blow against the legitimacy of this Color Prince," Delara said. The woman had drafted enough red in her life that her rage was overpowering. Anything that hurt the Color Prince was something she would vote for.

"And the man we're condemning is dead," Sadah said. "So we wouldn't be further alienating a man with whom we might need to make peace in the near future. If we're able to settle things down in eastern Atash with this man, it would put us in a better negotiating position. We would visibly have to move farther to meet him in the middle, making the halfway point effectively closer to our side of things." Ah, Sadah, seeing political problems as if they were points to be plotted on a graph. Orholam love her, the fool.

"No, no, no," Klytos Blue said. "I see what you're doing here, Lord Prism."

Gavin lifted an eyebrow, like, What is this moron doing? "Yes, I'm trying to weaken a rebellion before it sweeps up half the lands in the Seven Satrapies," he said.

"Which is a noble goal that I share," Klytos said. He glanced over at Andross, but without eyes, Andross couldn't give him subtle cues of whether Klytos was on the tack Andross wanted him to take. "But even if the man called himself a king, I think that gives him too much prestige."

"It is what he called himself," Jia Tolver said impatiently.

"We needn't give him that moral high ground; he was rebel, nothing more," Klytos said. In sub-red, he was clearly warmer than before. But Klytos always got nervous when he spoke, even in front of a group this small.

"What would you prefer, then?" Gavin said. "Illegitimate king, so-called king? Illegitimate satrap?"

"Clearly," Sadah Superviolet said, scratching at one psoriatic arm, "declaring oneself to be a rebel would vacate one's legitimacy, thus 'illegitimate satrap' would be an accurate descriptor." She clearly intended this as an olive branch to Klytos Blue.

Gavin turned his hands palm up toward Klytos, as if surrendering the issue to him. "Very well, we can back up further. Would you like to dictate the document, Klytos?" Gavin asked.

Klytos hated public speaking. As the Blue, he felt that he should get all the technicalities exactly right on the first try—and he never did. "No, please, go ahead," he said, as if he were being polite.

Gavin turned to the chief scribe in the room. "By order of the Color Spectrum, with the full imprimatur of the Prism, blessed by Orholam's radiance, etcetera."

The woman scribbled in a few lines, skipping space to fill in the official lines.

"I must confess," Gavin said to the Spectrum as she scribbled, "I'm disappointed something so simple wasn't done during my absence. Surely such a condemnation would seem pro forma—never mind. Please interject if you have any suggestions."

There was still some niggling done over the word "war." Gavin and Delara championed it, but eventually it was stricken in favor of a condemnation of "visiting violence upon the innocent peoples of the Seven Satrapies" and the illegitimate Satrap Garadul condemned, though the word "traitor" was also stricken. Gavin grimaced briefly, as if this were a setback, but not a huge one. It was a brief document, and he took care not to feign too much boredom.

The "war" bit was the canard. Let them think that he was angling subtly toward declaring war later in the meeting. But don't overplay your hand.

As soon as the scribe finished, Gavin signed the document and sent it around the table for signatures.

"Now," Gavin said, not waiting for the signatures, not giving them any weight. "The urgent matter. The reason we've come here today: refugees, and war. The fact of the matter is, I do have some personal investment in this issue. I'll put that on the table. I failed to stop Garadul, and Garriston was lost because of that. I went to fight—perhaps rashly—without the full weight of the Spectrum behind me, and I lost. In losing, I lost face, and some of the people for whom I was fighting lost faith in the Chromeria. Obviously, the former isn't a problem for this body, but the latter is. I feel a responsibility for the people who have fled. I would like to see this council make some efforts to provide for them. So, again, easy issues first: I'd like to draft another resolution that our satrapies send food, clothing, and supplies to those who've been displaced."

He recognized Delara. "And arms!" she said. "Those refugees will join the fight—at least some of them will—against the Color Prince."

"I agree with you," Gavin said. "But I would suggest we put the more contentious issues into a separate resolution, so that we can do the sane and humane thing in providing for those who've been attacked by the late Rask Garadul as soon as possible. Will the Spectrum agree to address these issues separately?"

"Let's agree to what's immediately obvious to all of us," Arys Subred said. "These refugees are doubtless starving. We can agree that we must send them help. Later we can argue about exactly how much of a share of that burden each of us should send." Ah, the brass tacks. Arys was ruthlessly practical, even in her charity. Gavin liked that about her.

They agreed by acclaim to consider the issues separately. The first resolution had made it halfway around the room. Gavin had passed it to Klytos, who'd signed it. The White had passed it on. Because she only voted in the case of ties, she never signed any resolution until at least a majority had. Delara signed it and passed it on to Sadah Superviolet. She paused, and Gavin couldn't tell if it was because she was thinking about the second resolution, or if she had some sudden qualm about the first.

Sadah Superviolet stared at Gavin. She didn't say anything, but she handed on the resolution without signing it. Arys did, Delara did, and she slid it to Tisis. Tisis gave one more glance to Andross, got nothing, and signed it.

And Gavin had his supermajority. Oh, Tisis. Lunna Green was almost a friend. I never could have done this to her. Do you know what you can do to an enemy but not to a friend? Stab her in the back.

Carver Black slid the paper over in front of Andross. Carver had a voice on the Spectrum, but no vote. Andross whispered to Grinwoody, who responded. Andross asked him another question in a whisper.

Gavin narrowed his eyes to sub-red. And instantly, he saw his father getting hotter, though the man's expression didn't alter in any other perceptible way.

Andross started laughing suddenly, and signed his name. Given his blindness, his signature was only in approximately the right place.

The discussion stopped instantly. It was rare to hear Andross Guile laugh.

Andross turned to Tisis. "Do you know what you've done, girl?"

"What?" she asked, suddenly worried.

Gavin leaned over and quickly took the parchment from in front of his father and cocked an eyebrow at Sadah. "Will you make it unanimous?" Gavin asked.

"Of course," she said. It was a moot point now. She signed it, handed it to the White, who sighed, and signed.

"What?" Tisis asked, more insistent.

"Why don't you explain, son?" Andross Guile suggested.

The head scribe brought the resolution to Gavin, who brought his stick of official sealing wax up to his finger, drafted sub-red directly to it, and pressed his seal on the document, making it official. "Of course, father," Gavin said. He handed the document to the head scribe, who handed it off to a secretary who would enter it in the annals and publish it.

When the door closed behind the man, Gavin said, "The fact is, we *are* at war. None of us wants this. I don't want it. You don't want to admit it because you're afraid I'll press you to declare me promachos again. I understand that fear. Surrendering power is terrifying, though Orholam knows I've not given you any reason to distrust me.

Tyrea is gone. I suppose that's just as well. We can fight about what to do next. We can fight about how we fight. But while we bicker, the people who fled Garriston have lost everything. I'm sure you know by now that they've found refuge upon Seers Island, and I will report on that fully later today, but winter is upon us. There's no time for them to plant a harvest. If we don't provide for them, they'll die. We brought this on them, and even if you reject that, they are still the subjects of the Seven Satrapies. It is our duty."

"The point being..." Andross growled.

"The point, dear father, dear friends, is that I won't stand for these people to suffer any more than absolutely necessary to make their new lives. In the resolution we just signed unanimously, this council has declared Satrap Garadul's satrapy illegitimate. Rask Garadul was installed legitimately, was corresponded with as a legitimate satrap for a time. If he became illegitimate, but not through his personal treason, it is because his satrapy itself is illegitimate. Which is a simple acknowledgment of truth. Tyrea has not been a real satrapy in sixteen years. It had caretakers in its former capital, and its seat on this council was seized by another satrapy. So this is as it should be. However, a satrapy can only be dissolved by a supermajority vote of this council. We have so voted."

"That's a lot of interpretation you're layering onto a simple document," the White said. She didn't, Gavin thought, necessarily disagree with him, but she didn't like at all how he'd done it.

"Yes. But it is the Prism's prerogative to define satrapies, and I have already done so. I settled the refugees of Garriston onto Seers Island— a place where they will not be flooding *your* cities with their destitute tens of thousands, for which I hope all your satraps thank you endlessly. And me. And I declared Seers Island a new satrapy. The new satrap, I'm afraid to say, could only be Corvan Danavis."

They knew he hated Corvan. They knew he'd fought against him, and had lost friends in those fights. That Corvan might be the new satrap was at least one thing that undercut Gavin's personal power— so they thought.

"By endorsing that we are indeed still seven satrapies, you've endorsed my new creation."

"This is an outrage," Carver Black said.

"I think we can all agree that what you've just tried to do is, is, is unacceptable," Klytos Blue said.

"Surely he doesn't have the power to establish new satrapies on his own," Tisis said. "High Lady Pullawr?"

The White shrugged. "Look at any history, it will tell you the Prism established the Seven Satrapies. Of course, things have changed greatly since those times, but it clearly *was* in the Prism's purview, of old."

"And has never been removed from the Prism's purview, as you put it, High Lady," Gavin said. Of course it hadn't. There wasn't anywhere else to put another satrapy, and no one would ever agree to splitting their own.

"Let's just vote to undo this," Tisis said.

Several other Colors voiced their approval.

"I agree," Gavin said, "but pardon me, I'm still presiding here today, and we'll still follow the proper procedure. You wish to dissolve Seers Island as a satrapy?"

"Yes!" Tisis said.

"Then you'll need a supermajority to pass your resolution. As we've just said, dissolving a satrapy requires a supermajority."

"Fine." He could see others looking around the table, sliding the beads. Would anyone hold out on this?

They brought the resolution. Several of the Colors looked at Gavin like he was insane. Why would he pull such a thing, and then allow it to be rescinded immediately?

The White knew. He could see it in the tightness of her face. And Andross knew. He was rubbing the bridge of his nose, where his heavy dark spectacles had worn lines into his skin.

Tisis, furious, dictated the resolution. Gavin made no objection. When the head scribe brought it to him for his inspection, he nodded and handed the document to Tisis first.

"And on whose behalf are you signing, Tisis?" Gavin asked.

"My own," she said, as if it were a trap.

"Our service on the Spectrum is never on our own behalf, child," the White said. She sounded tired.

Tisis sneered. Unwise. She was mad at Gavin, not the White, and it never paid to sneer at the White. "So be it. I sign on behalf of..." All the blood drained out of her face. Her voice dropped to a whisper. She was Ruthgari and her seat was used for Ruthgar's benefit, but it was a seat held in protectorship. "I sign for Tyrea," she whispered.

"There is no satrapy of Tyrea," Gavin said. "Your position no longer exists. As this meeting is a closed meeting of the Spectrum, you're excused."

Dead silence fell on the room.

"You can't do this," Tisis said.

"Not alone. We did it together. You helped."

Gavin's Blackguards were at his side, somehow sensitive to the imminent threats.

Tisis looked around the table in disbelief.

"Don't worry, you'll be right back," Klytos said. "We'll have the vote immediately. It'll be five minutes."

Tisis sneered. "You idiot, you think he took it this far without a plan?" She stood sharply and strode out of the room, slamming the door shut behind her.

"As the satrap of Seers Island hasn't yet appointed his Color, the Prism holds his vote in trust," Gavin said. "And believe me, he wouldn't want me to use his vote to disband his satrapy."

Two votes then for him. He gave them a second to finish the arithmetic. Tisis was gone. They needed a supermajority of five, so Gavin only needed four to stop them. No tie was possible, so the White couldn't vote. The Black could never vote. They knew Delara would vote with him because she needed his help on the war. Jia Tolver always voted with him. Four.

And that was if *all* the others broke Andross Guile's way.

"Is there anyone who wishes to call the vote?" Gavin asked. Daring them. Supremely self-confident.

"I do," Klytos said immediately, finding his courage somewhere.

"Is there a second?"

"*Raka*," Andross Guile said to Klytos. It was a heavy insult. "You want to put a loss in the records and establish precedent?"

Klytos paled, then stared around the room, looking for allies. Even those who might have voted with him turned away.

"I—I—wish—"

Rather than let him withdraw the motion, Gavin said quickly, "The motion fails for lack of a second."

"I move we adjourn," Arys said. "I've a babe to nurse, and I think all of us have messengers to send."

Gavin had expected as much. "One moment. I want to say one

thing," he said as the Colors were scooting their seats back, getting ready to leave. "You did this. It didn't have to be this way. If you'd listened to me, Tyrea would still exist, and the Color Prince wouldn't be rampaging across Atash. If you'd sent a bare thousand soldiers or a hundred drafters, we could have defeated King Garadul. But you, you sent a delegation to *study* the problem."

"Peace should be maintained at almost any cost," Klytos interrupted. "As the blessed Adraea Coran—"

"War is a horror, yes. I know. *I* know. And pacifism, which you claim to value so highly? Pacifism is a virtue indistinguishable from cowardice." He sneered. "This war could have been ended before it began in half a dozen ways. If you'd taken your boot off the throat of Tyrea one second before it got strong enough to throw you off, this wouldn't have happened. I tell you this, if you won't do what's right, *I will*. Things are going to change around here."

Andross Guile yawned.

"Starting with this," Gavin snapped. "Father, you've treated Kip like a bastard. He's not. His mother was a free woman that I elevated to a ladyship during the war. As promachos, that was my right. We married in secret because I was young and I was afraid of what you would say. But we did marry. That's why I've never married since. She's dead now, but she deserves this of me: Kip is my son, not a bastard, a full son. That you've cast aspersions on this, that you've doubted my own word is, I'm afraid, further evidence of your advancing senility. You'll join the Freeing this year, *my son*. If you don't feel you can hold out for another eight months I will be at your disposal for a more private ceremony sooner."

No one moved. No one even breathed. A small, detached part of Gavin marveled. He could dissolve an entire satrapy and unseat one of the Colors, and they were perturbed—but see him cross his father and they were flabbergasted.

"Senility?" Barely more than a whisper. Dangerously amused.

And now we find out how far gone to red he is.

But Andross Guile was as cold as an old red could be. He saw the trap. If he screamed, if he lost his temper, he'd be making Gavin's case.

"If that is what my Lord Prism believes, I shall of course go to the Freeing at the time you appoint. As must surely we all. I only wonder what I have done to offend you? Why do you lash out at me, my son?"

A nice seed to plant, father. Well played. *Yes, the Prism can send me to my grave. He can send any of us to our graves. Think about that.* Turn it so that *I* look unreasonable instead.

"No," Gavin said. "No. You endangered my son. On purpose. No more lies. Grinwoody, take him out."

"Son," Andross Guile said, and now his voice was tight. "You will show me the proper reverence."

"Ignoring you when you act the fool and removing you from the public eye when you disgrace yourself *is* the proper reverence. Grinwoody!"

Andross Guile's fingers trembled. His jowls quivered. But he controlled himself. After a long moment, he turned and left, led by Grinwoody.

No one said anything. No one met Gavin's eyes.

"It would behoove us," Gavin said, "to begin considering who may be the next Red. I will be amenable to suggestions." *I know I've pushed things; I know that I've frightened you, and to make up for it, I'll let one of you have what you want. I'll let one of you place your woman or man on the Red seat, and not try to place my own. Tit for tat.*

You want to plant seeds, father? Let's do.

"Now, before we adjourn this meeting," Gavin said, "unless there are any other motions?"

No one said anything.

"Delara?" Gavin prompted.

Her eyes widened as she caught his implication. "I move we declare war," she said.

"Seconded," Arys said.

"Seers Island votes for war," Gavin said. "The Prism votes for war."

"Atash votes for war," Delara Orange said.

"Blood Forest votes for war," Arys Sub-red said.

"But the Red is—" Klytos Blue said.

"You wish to leave the room during a vote to fetch him?" Gavin said. "If you go, your vote won't be recorded."

"You can't!" Klytos said.

Gavin spoke instantly, but slowly, enunciating each word, seizing control of even the speed of the conversation. "Those are very dangerous words to say to me."

Pregnant silence. Cowards sometimes find their spines at inconvenient moments. But then Klytos withered.

"Your vote and his are entered as no votes," Gavin said. Truth was, he couldn't let this vote be challenged after the fact. That would tangle things up for weeks more.

"Abornea votes no, with great personal regret," Jia Tolver said. Gavin expected as much. She was doubtless under strict orders.

Gavin needed either Sadah Superviolet or the White. He was certain the White would vote with him.

Apparently Sadah thought the same. She was looking at the White. "Paria votes for war," Sadah said. And that was the win.

Klytos blinked. "High Lord Prism, Ruthgar wishes to stand in unity with her neighbors. Ruthgar votes yes."

"Of course," Gavin said. He sent the declaration around the room, and everyone signed it. They allowed Andross an abstention, and the White signed it.

The room slowly emptied. No one said a word.

Oddly enough, Jia Tolver stayed behind. Gavin would have expected the White. Jia's single dark eyebrow was wrinkled. When the last person other than Gavin's Blackguards had left the room, she leaned over. "My Lord Prism, so you know, if they'd called the vote on your own personal satrapy, I would've voted against you. They'd have had their supermajority. Your arrogance always treads the line. Today, you overstepped. You won. You won everything. But don't count on me as a safe vote ever again."

She left. Gavin scrubbed his hands through his hair. He needed a drink. He looked at his Blackguards. They looked impassive. He wondered how they did that. They were the crazy ones around here.

He stood and went to the door. They said nothing, but one of the Blackguards preceded him, not a precaution they always took.

The White was waiting for him in the hall.

He didn't stop, and she motioned to her Blackguard to wheel her along at the same speed Gavin was walking.

"What have you done, Gavin?"

Gavin got onto the lift. "I'm going down," he said, turning to face her, trying to forestall her from joining him.

"That's what I'm afraid of," she said. She held him by the force of her personality, let her question hang in the air, demanding an answer.

"I lied and cheated and manipulated, and I won. And I did it all for good reasons. For once."

"*All* good reasons?" she asked.

He said nothing. Threw the brake open and dropped from sight.

Chapter 77

"I've got something to say. It's not going to be easy," Samite said.

Karris had barely finished washing up and getting dressed when Samite came into the Archers' side of the barracks. Samite was one of Karris's best friends in the Blackguard: squat, tough, smart, and unfailingly awkward when she tried to be tender. Karris paused, comb in hand. "What's going on?"

Samite sat heavily on the edge of Karris's bed. "K, you know how the lords and ladies of the great houses are always trying to get to us Blackguards and make us spies or deserters?"

"I— What does that have to do with anything?"

"One of them got to me. Years ago."

"What?! Sami, stop! What are you doing?"

"What I should have done a long time ago." Samite's face was grim but stubborn. She sat with her elbows on her thighs, hands clasped across each other.

"Who?" Karris barely breathed the word.

"Lady Felia Guile."

"Lady Guile subverted you?" Karris asked. She'd liked Lady Guile, a lot. Had thought for years that the woman would be her mother-in-law, and the closest thing to a mother Karris would ever know. "How'd she— No, never mind. I don't need to know. Sami, she's gone. You don't need to do this."

"It was nothing untoward. Two of my brothers were captured by Ilytian pirates and made galley slaves. My family didn't even know where to start looking, much less how they'd afford a ransom. I went to her. She had people track them down, and ransomed them herself. She brought them here so I could see they were well. She nursed them

379

back to full health, and paid for their passage home. I could never have paid her back; I mean, I used my big Blackguard payout to buy my family a store and a farm. I offered, and she refused. She knew it would ruin my family. She said nothing about it for months, and when she asked me for information later, there was no way I could refuse her."

A velvet leash, held only by Samite's sense of honor, of debt. Yes, that was Lady Guile's style. She'd been a gentle Orange, but an Orange nonetheless.

Samite continued, her voice a dull monotone, as if marching to her own death. "She said she was merely trying to protect her son, and I believed her. He's the Prism, so I figured we were sharing the same goal. It wasn't really a betrayal, right? I knew better in my heart, which is why I'm telling you now. But I can't bear to tell Commander Ironfist. I can't bear to see the disappointment in his eyes. Regardless, the last duty she entrusted to me was this: she said that after she died, I was to give you this note."

Samite handed Karris a small note on Lady Guile's stationery.

"I don't blame her, you know," Samite said. "She might have destroyed me, but it wasn't about me. It wasn't even about protecting her family. She did what she did for the Seven Satrapies. Sometimes, sacrifices must be made, and it's usually us small folk who pay, and we don't always get to know why. When I was young, I hated that, but I've made my peace. It's the way of the world." She cleared her throat again and stood. "I'll, uh, I'll wait for you outside."

"Dammit, Sami, why couldn't you have just left the note on my bed?"

"The secrets were eating me up inside. I can't live like that, Karris. Not anymore."

Karris rubbed her temples, trying to collect herself as Samite left. The Blackguard couldn't afford to lose a woman as levelheaded as Samite, not even normally, and definitely not now, not after they'd lost so many at Garriston. She opened the letter.

In Lady Guile's beautifully practiced hand, it read, "Dazen loves you, Karris. He's always loved you. If you've confronted him with the truth already, please take the time to ask him what really happened at your family's estate. I know you don't want to hear this, but a comforting lie has been poisoning your whole life, and that lie is this: that your brothers were innocent in the tragedy that destroyed your family. They weren't."

Karris felt like she'd been punched in the stomach. She was breathing fast and shallow, holding on to read it all. Lady Guile was not only admitting that Gavin wasn't Gavin, she was going from that point to tell Karris things Karris didn't know. And maybe didn't want to know.

"Your maid Galaea betrayed your elopement to your brothers. They laid a trap at the estate, and tricked Dazen into coming inside. They had chained all the doors shut and only had red light sources, knowing him not to be a red drafter. He alone got out, Karris. And perhaps he set the fires, but he didn't chain the doors. I don't wish to speak ill of the dead, Karris, but the blood spilled that night isn't on my Dazen's head.

"Of course, there was no easy way to let you know what really happened. I had several people over the years try to introduce the topic to you obliquely. You rebuffed any discussion. Please pardon my clumsy attempts to make peace.

"My dear child, Dazen thought you'd fallen in love with Gavin and that was why you'd become betrothed to him. He thought you could never forgive him for what you thought he'd done. After Sundered Rock, I urged him to marry you quickly before Andross could interfere. He refused, Karris. He said he could kill his own brother, and he could lie to all the world, but the one thing he would never do was take a woman to bed who loved his brother. He couldn't lie to you. Silly fool, he broke his betrothal to you because he loved you."

Karris wanted to be sick. She couldn't stop reading.

"And he loves you still, Karris. Believe me, I eventually gave up hope and urged him to marry other women, but he could never get you out of his heart. Please forgive him, child, and please forgive me, too. By putting these truths in writing, I've delivered our family into your hands. You can destroy Dazen if you so desire, and this will be proof. I would trust no one else with such power over my son, but I see no other way. I wish only that I'd had the opportunity to say this all to you myself, and that I had done better at making peace between you, that I might see my grandchildren before I died. May Orholam's light shine on you, Karris. Sincerely, Felia Guile."

Karris felt numb. She read the letter again, and wondered at herself. How had she believed such preposterous lies in the first place? On the night they were to elope, Dazen had sneaked around her family's estate and chained every door shut and then set the place afire? Or he'd arrived with a dozen men to do the same task—men who had never been found or mentioned again, after Gavin got the armies marching after his brother?

No, this made much more sense. Why else had her father insisted on getting Karris out of the city that very night? Because he knew about the trap his sons had planned, perhaps that he had helped them plan.

And then when it went bad, her father had gladly covered up his sons' murderous guilt in the deaths of everyone at the estate, and had done so with Andross Guile's complicity, because it rallied the other noble families around Andross's favored son Gavin. It *had* been a conspiracy, just not the one Karris had always thought.

The drums of war had started pounding, and Karris, young and weak, had simply believed that her elders must know things she didn't. Things that made the war inevitable, that made Dazen's guilt indisputable.

Since then, Karris had always struggled to bring together the two Gavins she'd known: the one who'd been betrothed to her but then used her cruelly and cast her off like she was garbage, and the later one who broke their betrothal and her heart but then treated her kindly. The inexplicability was what had twisted her into knots: if she'd known Gavin was a cruel cad, she could have written off her infatuation as the stupidity of a young girl deluded by a man's good looks and charm and power. It was the parts of his character that seemed totally contradictory that kept her in limbo.

And now, instead of the hard revelations prompting gales of tears at years lost and lies believed, Karris felt relieved. At peace.

She took each page of the letter and held it over a candle. Each burned in a flash.

Karris grinned at that. Fire paper. Lady Guile might have trusted her, but that didn't mean she wanted the letter to be hard to destroy.

Dazen loved her. Dazen had always loved her. And he was holding terrible secrets. Alone. His respect for her, his love for her, had made him keep her nearby. It had made a thousand hard tasks harder for him. If he'd wanted, he could have had her cast out of the Blackguard easily. He could have had her imprisoned. He had never taken the easy way out, not where she was concerned.

She stood, feeling lighter than she had in sixteen years, and walked to the door. Samite was standing there, waiting for her. She had her hands behind her back, as if hiding something.

Samite said, "Lady Guile said that after you read that note, you'd have need of some serious firepower, one way or the other." She brought her hands out from behind her back. In one hand was a large old pistol. In the other was a painfully beautiful lace chemise and a matching corset with short stays that would cost a Blackguard a year's wages. "So which is it going to be?"

Karris stared openmouthed. Lady Guile! Scandalous! And Sami was holding that up in the middle of the barracks, for Orholam's sake! "Who's on Prism duty tonight?"

"Think it's some of the new boys."

"Perfect," Karris said. She grinned.

"Karris, what are you…" Samite said.

"Are you just going to stand there, or are you going to help me with my hair?"

Chapter 78

Marissia's brief, whispered report had been terrifying. The old familiar panic tightened Gavin's chest. First had been news from all over the satrapies: twelve sea demons, swimming together in three precise ranks of four, circling all of Abornea five times before disappearing. A sheet of ice covering all of Crater Lake by Kelfing, though it was too warm. Herds of wild goats a thousand strong, standing all in precise rows. Poets struck dumb. Musicians writing a hundred pages of notation in a day, forgetting to eat or drink or sleep until they fell unconscious. Galley slaves rowing until they died, afraid of falling out of tempo. Captains plotting out constellations instead of piloting, running onto rocks. Mothers engaged in menial tasks abandoning their mewling infants until the tasks were complete.

There was a certain irony to order going out of control, but it wasn't one the dead would appreciate. And that wasn't the worst.

The alarm on the blue hadn't gone off. She hadn't known that Dazen had broken out. When was the last time Gavin had checked that mechanism? A year? A year and a half?

In the third year of Dazen's imprisonment, hoping it would alleviate his terrible nightmares, Gavin had built in fail-safes. He thought. If Dazen broke into any prison, that very action was supposed to activate a glowing warning at the top of the chute: the alarm.

Either Marissia had been turned—no, the shock on her face had been real—or Gavin's mechanism had failed.

If the chutes hadn't switched over, Dazen would have starved to death by now. Gavin had made it so that if Dazen tried to throw luxin up the chute, it would switch it over as well—but if one mechanism had failed, others might have, too. Dammit. He hadn't made them to last forever. Luxin decayed, even in darkness, and he'd crafted almost every part of the prisons from luxin.

If he's dead, I'd have felt it, wouldn't I? I knew something was wrong when Sevastian died. Surely...

The lift shuddered to a stop, just a couple floors down. Not many people had the keys to stop the Prism's lift.

It was Grinwoody, giving his thin, unpleasant smirk, happy to interrupt. He extended a hand silently. Gavin took the note from the slave. He already knew what it was going to say.

"Son, come to my chambers. This is not a request."

Pretty much as he guessed.

First, it was Kip and Samite in his room, keeping him from checking the chute's alarm immediately. Then it was the "emergency meeting." Now this.

But there was nothing for it. If Dazen had escaped, he was long gone by now. If he'd been starved, he was dead by now. Orholam have mercy, this put the wights' talk about Dazen Guile coming to save them in a different light, didn't it?

They knew. They'd been working to free him all along.

Peace, Gavin. Patience. If it's done, it's done. If not, don't tip off the most cunning man in the world by acting strangely. He went with Grinwoody. There was nothing to be gained by putting it off. He wouldn't be any more ready to face off with the tyrant later, and time wasn't going to make Andross Guile's anger cool. Indeed, getting to him now, when he was still fresh in his fury and hadn't had time to plan his vengeance, might be best.

Gavin made his way into the dark room. The air was oppressive, hot. He hated it in here. Even illuminated with his superviolet lantern, there was a darkness here that clung to the bones and weakened the will.

"Gavin," Andross Guile said. His voice was level, gravelly.

"Father." He mustered what respect he could.

"You stabbed me in the back in there." Andross Guile's face was covered, of course, but his tone was almost bemused. He relished this, Gavin realized. There was nothing left to the old man now except proving his mastery, and there was no game that could compare to Gavin challenging him.

Andross was also certain that he would win, which frightened Gavin.

"I did what you taught me, father."

"Stuck up for some wandering wretches from Tyrea?"

"Won. I won."

That earned some silence.

"So you get your own satrap. By itself, worthless. This new Tyrea may not even survive. So you get a vote on the Spectrum you can count on for a couple years. No subtlety, though. If you want to own Colors, there are better ways. Why did you defy me?"

"Funny," Gavin said. "That was exactly my question for you. Why oppose me, father? What do you care if we fight or not? It's not like anyone's going to ask you to take the field. What do you care even if I become promachos again? What could be better for our family?"

"You forget who asks the questions here," Andross snapped.

Gavin sat in one of the old armchairs. Once regal, it was now shabby. "So you've been playing Nine Kings with Kip? How good is he?" It was a petty defiance, asking more questions by misdirection when his father had laid down the law. But he thought Andross would find it irresistible. The man had nothing but his games now.

Andross smiled, a rictus bent upward. "After the war, you lost your focus, Gavin. You could have been as good as me. Now you're running out of time, and you'll never be my equal. I'm sorry I misjudged you."

Misjudged me? There's an understatement. You saggy-drawered monster. Mother took one look at me after Sundered Rock and knew me. You've talked to me a thousand times since, and still don't know me. You *never* knew me, you blind old fool. "You don't know what it does to me to consider that I might not be like you," Gavin said, tone flat.

"It's time for you to marry," Andross said.

Gavin had thought the old man might have forgotten. He himself nearly had. It was a shot in the gut.

"I'll only marry one woman," Gavin said.

"I'm only asking you to marry one. You've got five years. If you can give me four sons, perhaps one of them will have a spine on which I'll have a chance at rebuilding this family."

"I have a son," Gavin said. Kip, who was actually his brother's son. What a horrible mess.

"A bastard." Andross waved a hand. "He will be pushed aside in due time. Until your true heirs reach majority, Kip will serve in other ways. To serve as a focus for other families' assassination attempts and so forth. But Kip will never carry this family's name forward."

Gavin tented his fingers, sneering, but of course Andross couldn't see it. "What's your master plan, then?"

Andross Guile's lips thinned. He sat across from Gavin. "I was going to give you your choice of a wife. There were three strong contenders from families wealthy enough or connected in useful ways, and the girls young enough to give you children quickly. Young enough to be…malleable. Solicitous."

"You mean you could control them after I die."

"Of course. You bed a strong-willed woman and she might steal your future and disappear." Andross gave a malicious grin.

Gavin froze. From the tone and the smile, the sentence was meant to be a knife under his armor—under *Gavin's* armor—and he had no idea what his father was talking about.

Say the wrong thing, and he'll know.

So he said nothing, as if stricken. Which he was, if for the wrong reasons.

The knife. It had something to do with the knife.

"Are you curious who they were?" Andross asked.

"Please," Gavin said lightly. He swallowed.

"Your little temptress Ana Jorvis, Naftalie Delara, and Eva Golden Briar. I was even going to add Liv Danavis, if you'd managed to save Garriston with her father's help. Of course, now you've bound the Danavis clan to us forever in another way so it's a moot point. Regardless," Andross Guile said, "now you've destroyed that choice for yourself. I'll give you this, son, you present me with interesting challenges."

Grinwoody brought them tea. Gavin picked up his cup. "Father, speaking of moot, *all* of this is moot. I'm not going to marry—"

"Tisis Malargos."

The teacup hovered in front of Gavin's mouth. "Pardon?"

"She's nineteen. Not so young she'll get pregnant if you sneeze at her, but young enough to bear quickly. Pretty, too, or so Grinwoody says. Her older sister Eirene took over the family's financial affairs after Dervani didn't come back from the war. Brilliant merchant, Eirene. She's built the family into a financial juggernaut, and the dowry she's promised for Tisis, whilst enormous, pales in comparison to the wealth Tisis will inherit when Eirene dies."

"What? Why would Tisis inherit from her sister?"

"Eirene's a tribadist. And not fond enough of children to get on her back for any man. Smart enough, though, to carry on flirtations with many men in order to secure better business deals for herself, and, she thinks, to keep us in line if her sister does marry you. In this, she's partly correct: there will be no divorce or flagrant affairs while you are married to Tisis, Gavin."

"What?!" Gavin still hadn't processed the first part. His father wanted him to marry Tisis? She was the woman who'd sabotaged Kip's testing. She was the woman Gavin had just thrown out of the Spectrum.

Orholam have mercy. Gavin's mother had confessed to ordering Dervani murdered—because he knew Dazen's secret. And now his father wanted him to marry a woman whose father Felia Guile had murdered.

"You see the beauty of it? Eirene holds her inheritance against us, and we hold Kip against her. If she leaves our family to inherit everything, we disown Kip. It's not the only card we have to play, but it is always a good idea to make your opponent pay you to sacrifice a card you didn't want to play anyway."

In purely tactical terms, Gavin saw the appeal—not to his family, but to himself. Tisis was a beautiful woman, who might still be turned into a friend rather than the enemy he'd thought he'd just made. And by doing this, he'd keep his father from destroying Kip. At least he would buy Kip time. Gavin's own time was drawing to a close, and there would be no one to protect Kip when he was gone—and if Gavin died before Andross did, Kip would need that protection. But—

"Father, why don't you turn your mind to helping me for once? The only woman I'll consent to marry is Karris White Oak."

Andross Guile snorted. "And she brings what to this family? A few barren estates? Her family alliances allowed to wither while she plays Blackguard? Don't be ridiculous."

Gavin took a sip of his tea. When his nerves steadied, very calmly, very quietly, he said, "It's her or it's no one."

"You were always my favorite son, Gavin. Thought I saw myself in you. Thought I saw *will* in you. Perhaps I shouldn't complain too bitterly that you turn it against me now, though you have good reasons not to. You remember what we did to make you Prism. You owe everything you are to me, son. So now either you do exactly what I tell you or the cost will be more swift and grievous than you can imagine."

Gavin got up without saying a word.

"Son, let me hear you say it. Say you'll obey me in this."

Gavin walked to the door, parted the dark curtains, and stepped through, out of the cloying darkness.

"Gavin!" his father shouted. He sounded old. He sounded weak. "Gavin!"

Chapter 79

"Good evening," Gavin greeted the Blackguards at the door to his rooms. He didn't recognize either man. They were young, maybe eighteen. They looked like children—and when eighteen-year-old men look like children to you, it's a sure sign that you're getting old.

What did you do when you were eighteen, Gavin?

Too much. But that was a distraction. Here were two Blackguards he didn't know, despite knowing all the Blackguards. Two Blackguards, alone with him. This was how assassination attempts began. He'd been warned.

The men saluted him. "Lord Prism."

"What're your names?" Gavin asked.

"Gill and Gavin Greyling, sir," the elder said.

Brothers, of course. He should have picked it up. "*Gavin?*" he asked the younger.

The boy beamed. "Yes, sir, named after—"

"After our mother saw that he was a bit ill-favored, my lord," Gill said dryly.

"Hey!" Gavin Greyling said.

Gavin laughed. Of the two, Gavin was definitely the more handsome.

The younger Greyling looked relieved that the Prism had laughed. "I'm sorry my brother is horrifying, my lord. It is a real honor to serve you. A lifelong dream, my lord."

"An honor to have you in my service, Gavin, and even you, Gill. You two just raised?" A Blackguard, named after him. Good Orholam. He *was* getting old. And going blind to prove it. His chest tightened. He hadn't had the heart to go straight down to the back entrance to the tunnels after meeting with his father. He'd told himself that this would allow him to check the alarm first from his room. That it would give him warning if he'd been betrayed.

Really, he just didn't have the strength to go down there right now and face his brother—alive or dead.

"Yes, my lord," Gill said.

"Doesn't the commander usually have a veteran accompany the newly raised?" Gavin asked.

Gill flinched. "Yes, sir. With the personnel we lost at Garriston, it's been hard to cover all the shifts."

Gavin looked at each man in turn, widened his eyes momentarily to see how hot each looked. Both were pretty warm, nervous. Of course, with no baseline, and it being the first time they'd talked to him, that told him little.

Besides, now that he thought about it, he thought he did remember seeing these boys train. Gill was quite a hand with stabbing spears, if Gavin remembered correctly. And what kind of assassin would risk antagonizing the target by teasing him? Perhaps a very subtle one, but not likely one who was eighteen years old.

He bade them good night and stepped into his rooms. "Marissia?" he called. It was late, she might have gone to her bed in the little side room—more a closet, really. But she didn't answer. Which she wouldn't, if she'd betrayed him.

Behind him, Gavin Greyling was closing the doors. "Um, she left about half an hour ago, sir." She often worked late into the night when he returned from trips, giving him the most up-to-date reports the next morning and arranging the most pressing business on his schedule. And if she was loyal, she'd been doing everything she could to investigate her "failure." Yes, that was Marissia. That was the heart of the woman, dutifully looking to correct any error, even when it meant she'd forget that when he came home, he wanted her *here*. She didn't have betrayal in her.

"Ah." Shit.

"Is there anything we can do, my lord?" Gavin Greyling asked.

Gavin leveled a bemused gaze on the boy and said, "I have been traveling for the past four months with a woman I find incredibly seductive but whom I can never have. So no, I'm afraid that the duty I have for my room slave to perform is not one I would ask of you."

Gill started laughing. It took his brother longer.

"Are you talking about Watch Commander Ka— Ow!" he said as Gill slammed the butt of his spear onto his foot.

Gavin Greyling looked at his brother, peeved, and then blanched. "Oh. Oh. Um. I'm sorry, sir. Would you like one of us to go summon her? Her the room slave, I mean, my lord. Not her the watch commander... Although I suppose... Ahem."

Even though they were offering, Gavin knew he wasn't supposed to treat the Blackguard as his fetch-and-carry boys. It would, quite possibly, get these young men into trouble for having volunteered it. No, he'd spent the time talking with them to gain some rapport and to make sure they weren't assassins. He wasn't going to throw away that rapport just for his complaining loins.

But it was close. He shook his head.

The doors closed behind him and he shuffled toward the painting. He was exhausted, and there was a ball of despair swelling in his stomach. He looked at the painting closely, examined the hidden hinge, saw no sign of tampering. The frame of the painting needed a new coat of paint, though. The oils on his fingers had worn one edge smooth. He would have to disguise that. He pulled the frame open.

The panel under which sat the liquid yellow luxin was undisturbed, inert until the alarm injected air into it to make it glow faintly. The alarm hadn't gone off.

He drafted superviolet and reached deeper, pushed the superviolet into the hellstone panel, felt the brush of the filaments he'd left there, so thin they'd tear at the slightest touch—so thin they'd tell him if anyone had tampered with this. He felt the mechanism. It was undisturbed.

For one wild moment, he thought that it was all a mistake. Dazen was still in the blue prison! Nothing had gone wrong! He'd merely panicked because he'd lost blue. Because he'd had a bad dream about Dazen escaping—which he'd been fearing for sixteen years, so that was no wonder, in the aftermath of losing blue.

Except that the Third Eye had said his brother had broken out of blue, too.

But fortune-tellers are often wrong, right?

Not her.

Gavin drafted deeper down to the chute. It had moved over. It had moved to green.

So Dazen *had* broken out of blue, but he was still stuck in green. The blue alarm had failed, but eventually Dazen had gotten food. He'd been getting blue bread in the green prison, but he hadn't broken out. Either the green had made him too wild to think clearly enough or the blue bread when illuminated by green light had been too spectrally close to give him usable luxin. He was in green and he was alive.

Dazen could never be counted out, but it wasn't a catastrophe. Not yet.

The enormous weight didn't quite lift from Gavin's shoulders, but it shifted to a more comfortable position. This one emergency, at least, could wait until the morning. He wasn't ready to face Dazen, not after this day. He'd rest, and gather his wits, and then face his brother. Tomorrow.

He walked to his desk, took the folded shimmercloaks and the deck box, and tucked them in a closet. More problems for tomorrow. There were always more problems for tomorrow. He went to his bed, stripping off his clothes. He threw them willy-nilly, suddenly peeved. Where was Marissia, anyway? What does one have a room slave for, if not for some damned companionship once in a while?

Schedules could wait. He wanted her here. He cursed, feeling peevish and petty.

Truth was, he was angry at Karris for being so damned intractable. And he missed Marissia, and not only for her admirable bed skills. He didn't want to sleep alone tonight. He wanted to hold her body, to feel the soft comfort of her curves. To wake and embrace her and then sleep again. He wanted to take her in the bath in the morning, and then have her comb his hair, anoint him with oils, dress him, and send him off to conquer the world again with a clear head.

Instead, she was off doing whatever it was she did when she wasn't serving him.

That was ungracious, unfair. Most of the time that Marissia spent away from this room was to serve him. He crawled under the covers and thought dark thoughts for a few more seconds, then surrendered to sleep.

In the middle of the night, Gavin must have gotten hot and thrown the covers off, because he felt cold. Foggy-headed, he reached a hand to pull the blankets back on him, but then he felt the sweep of long hair over his thigh, and then a kiss. She took his hands and tucked them firmly at his sides, telling him not to interfere.

Oh, Marissia, if a man could fall in love with a slave...

Marissia pleasured him like she did everything: efficiently and well. She'd done this before when he'd come back from trips and she'd been out when he got back, or even just when she'd sensed that he was hungry for the pleasures of the flesh. She would wake him rapidly and pleasantly, and then ride him to a quick climax. It was like providing a meal on the march: she satisfied his hunger as quickly as possible, and interfered as little as possible with the business at hand. In this case, his sleep. Funny woman, but Gavin wouldn't trade her for the world.

Having roused him with admirable dispatch, Marissia crawled up Gavin's body. He reached for her breasts, but she grabbed his hands and pushed them above his head. Marissia's breasts got so tender some months that she didn't like Gavin to even touch them. She'd allow it if he insisted, of course—she served for his pleasure—but Gavin didn't want to insist tonight. Not when she was being so solicitous.

She quietly moaned as she lowered herself onto him a little at a time, and the pleasure of it almost blotted out all thought for Gavin, but he opened his eyes. Marissia rarely moaned. The room was dark. Gavin could of course change that, but pleasure blotted out will. It had been so long.

When she settled fully on him, though, even without hands, without sight, he knew this wasn't Marissia. As he came out of his stupor, it became more and more obvious. He knew Marissia's body, how she moved, the smell of her arousal and the smell of her perfume, and this was not—

That perfume. As his succubus began to rock her hips rhythmically, Gavin was entranced by the competing soporifics of pleasure and memory.

Karris almost never wore perfume. Only one day a year, and then only when she couldn't get out of it. She only wore perfume to the Luxlords' Ball. This perfume.

Orholam have mercy. That was how she'd gotten into his room. The Blackguards knew they weren't supposed to allow anyone in, but they wouldn't stop Karris. Especially not after Gavin had told them that...Ooh.

The very thought that it was Karris brought Gavin fully awake, inflamed him. His succubus was a little awkward, like she didn't really know what she was doing. Karris had only had two lovers that he'd heard about, and neither of them for long. She hadn't had all that much practice. Still, in most things she was more coordinated than this.

Gavin brought his hands to the softness of her hips to help guide her. Karris! After sixteen—

Soft? Karris's hips? A woman could be incredibly fit and still carry a little softness on her hips, of course, but...

She was moaning louder now, and her vocalizations almost covered the sound of voices outside Gavin's door. He stopped guiding her, but she only ground against him harder.

The door opened and a woman bearing a lantern walked in.

"Watch Captain," one of the Greylings protested, "I really think you—"

The light from the lantern showed Karris standing at the foot of Gavin's bed. The same light threw his succubus into shadow. Nor did the woman atop Gavin stop, grinding lascivious hips against him for several long, deliberate seconds after she must have become aware there were others in the room.

Karris flung the lever that opened the brightwater panels on the walls, flooding the room with light.

For one second, Gavin saw nothing as the light blinded him. Then, as his eyes adjusted, the young woman atop him was illuminated fully: Ana Jorvis, the student from the superviolets' class. Ana, the little temptress who'd tried to sneak into his bed before.

"You mind?" Ana demanded, looking over her shoulder. She was unashamed of her nudity before both Karris and the young Blackguards. Unabashed at being interrupted in coitus. Even proud. Defiant. Haughty.

But Gavin had no thought for her. He was staring at Karris, who looked suddenly dead. Her hair hung around her shoulders, not just loose, but carefully combed and curled. The rouge on her cheeks was the only thing that livened her pallid pallor. Her lips, too, were rouged. Karris never wore makeup. She was wearing a fine cloak that he'd never seen before, and where it was open as her hand held the lantern, Gavin saw lace.

A lace chemise. Karris. Midnight. His bed chamber. She had been planning—

"I said, do you mind? My lord and I are occupied," Ana said. She took one of Gavin's hands from where it sat limp on her hip and pressed it to her full breast. The breast she hadn't let him touch earlier—lest he realize who she was.

Karris bolted.

Gavin flung Ana off with a curse and ran after Karris, going right past the aghast Greyling brothers. "Karris!"

He heard the sound of glass shattering just as he got into the hall and saw that Karris had dropped her lantern in her haste. Its reservoir smashed and oil coated the hallway. Gavin stopped.

The still-burning wick tilted slowly, slowly, and before Gavin could draft, the hallway was alight. He smothered the flaring fire in seconds with great sheets of yellow. When he finally ran through, Karris had already gone down the lift. He hung out over the lift shaft, ignoring the Blackguards guarding it.

She'd stopped one level down, the Blackguard barracks.

"My lord!" the Blackguard Samite shouted.

"Don't even try to stop—" Gavin snarled.

She held her hands up. Peace. She tossed him her cloak to cover himself. "Good luck, sir."

Gavin tied the cloak around his waist and jumped into the lift shaft. He dropped down one level. He swung out of the shaft and stormed toward the women's side of the Blackguard barracks. The door was closed.

"Karris!" he shouted.

But as he approached, a dozen Blackguards, most of them only half dressed, formed ranks seamlessly in front of the door. They made a wall in front of him.

"That's far enough, my lord," Tremblefist said, gently. He was one of the half-dressed ones, and even though he wasn't quite as big as Ironfist, he was still bigger than Gavin. Enormous pectorals, shoulders broad enough to close the Everdark Gates.

"Out of my way!" Gavin shouted.

They said nothing, merely held ranks.

"Damn you all, you can't stop me!"

"Yes we can," Tremblefist said. "Now please, sir, leave. Leave before you shame your faithful servants any more than you already have. We've new men in our company. They can't understand."

Gavin screamed in frustration and stormed out.

The ride up one floor wasn't enough to cool his rage. His young Blackguards watched him closely, aghast, but said nothing as he strode past them and back into his room.

Ana should have been on her knees, weeping and begging for forgiveness. Instead, she stood in artfully meretricious pose that Gavin recognized from a famous sculpture, the Maiden's Gift. She'd even put on a fine silk shift identical to the statue's: back turned, hair spilling over her shoulder, curves in an S, the side of one breast visible. It was so obviously staged that Gavin would have laughed if he weren't so furious. Instead, it stoked the fires hotter.

"My lord," she said. "Shall we continue? I've so many pleasures yet to share with you."

Gavin's self-restraint had one last gasp. He closed his eyes, ground his teeth. Finally said, "Do you have any idea...I only—I thought you were her!"

"What?! Her? She's all muscly and gross. Karris is old enough to be my mother. I mean, if you want a sparring partner, I'm sure she's wonderful, but a lover? Bedding her would be like fucking dust. That old bitch—"

A sound like an uncaged tiger tore its way out of Gavin's throat. He hit the lever that dropped all the windows in his room open and was on top of Ana in an instant.

The night was moonlit, clouds being chased by buffeting winds.

"My lord, what are you doing?!" one of the Blackguards yelled, but Gavin didn't even hear him. He grabbed a handful of the girl's hair, walking her backward out into the cold night. "That *bitch*," he screamed above the howling wind, "is the woman I love!" With an inhuman roar, he flung Ana from him. Flung her so hard that she hit the railing of the balcony and flipped right over it.

And fell.

She didn't scream. She barely yelped, and Gavin barely heard it over the sound of wind.

Gavin's heart stopped, and the wind stopped, but he didn't hear her land. Maybe something had broken her fall? Maybe someone had saved her?

A fool's hope, and Gavin knew it.

Rushing to the edge of his balcony, he looked over.

Orholam have mercy. Hundreds of feet below, Ana had landed headfirst. Her body had crumpled all the wrong ways. From here she looked like a grape popped between your fingers: all the skin gathered and juices everywhere.

"My lord..."

Gavin turned and saw his two young Blackguards. The looks on their faces told him that Ana wasn't the only person who'd just fallen from heaven. He covered his face with his hands. He stepped back inside, and one of them, wide-eyed, closed the windows. Gavin sat on his bed, conscious for the first time of his near nakedness.

"Go tell who you have to tell," Gavin said. "I'll be here."

Of course, he lied.

Chapter 80

When the pounding started on the door of the women's side of the barracks, Karris thought it had to be Gavin come back again, but the voice was Watch Captain Blademan's. "Hey! Why's this door locked?! I said all hands on, dammit! I don't care if you're naked or on the shitter, I mean now!"

Karris threw the door open, instantly alert, tears forgotten. "What is it?" she asked.

Watch Captain Blademan looked at her, the cloak not covering her chemise, not covering her makeup, her perfume, her coiffed hair, her eyes puffy from crying. He hesitated only a moment, working through his surprise, then decided that whatever *this* was, it could wait. "All hands on, Karris. You're needed upstairs immediately. Some girl just took a dive off the Prism's balcony. She's dead. We think he threw her."

Gavin stared at the moon, drafting its feeble light slowly. His plan was simple—to draft a rope and dangle it out the window, making them think he'd escaped.

But he couldn't draft green or blue now. A rope was impossible. He leaned on the doorframe, swallowed with difficulty. He'd never had to think this way before. The simplest answer had always been the best. With every color in his palette, he'd simply had to figure out the best materials for the job. Now... now he was like some normal drafter, trying to solve a problem with a limited set of tools. It was a totally different way of thinking. He hated it.

As he turned the problem over, he grabbed fresh clothes from his closet and got dressed. He could, he supposed, draft a yellow chain, but that would beg them to ask why he would choose to draft only yellow, which was much more difficult and time-consuming. Questions like that could be more deadly than killing a powerful nobleman's daughter.

He pushed that out of his mind. No time.

Just an open window, then.

Then Gavin saw the shimmercloaks in his closet. He threw on the larger cloak. He knew the choker had to be important, so he put it on, drew it snug. He hated having things around his neck, and there were cold metal ridges along the inside that dug into his skin unpleasantly. He stepped in front of a mirror. He was still very much visible. He drew the cloak closed. Still visible. He closed his eyes and imagined being invisible, willed it, desired it, lusted after it, believed it. Cracked an eye. Still there.

A soft knock sounded on the door. Gavin drafted instinctively to defend himself.

Daggers stabbed into his neck from either side. What felt like a sheet of flame shot up and down his body: cheeks hot, scalp aflame, chest burning, arms burning, legs burning. Then the heat passed, leaving tingling, and the tingling turned to sensitivity, like a tooth shy of a cold drink.

He looked into the mirror—and saw through himself. His face was visible, and a V of his neck where the cloak wasn't fully closed. The collar had injected two needles into his neck. Gavin pulled the cloak fully closed, and found there were tiny hooks hidden in the fabric to keep the hood closed even over his face. Only his eyes remained. The rest of him was translucent—not perfectly transparent, but like looking through a dirty window. In low light, it would be more than acceptable. If he stayed still against a wall, it would be perfect. But moving fast in good light, he'd be easy to spot.

Louder knocking. "Sir, please let us in!"

Gavin ducked his head, to see if he could hide his eyes under the flap of the hood and thus be functionally invisible. When he did that, he saw nothing at all. Blackness so deep it struck a visceral fear into him.

So if he fell under piercing scrutiny, he'd have to make himself blind in order to be fully invisible. Lovely. Terrifying.

The window was already open. Gavin stood against a wall next to the door.

"Lord Prism," Commander Ironfist shouted, "we've come to take you to the Spectrum. Please open the door, my lord."

Thanks for the warning, old friend.

The Blackguards opened the door moments later. They had keys, of course. Ironfist led six men in. "Check the balcony," Ironfist said.

Gavin snuck through the open door right behind them. The wind gusting through the open window and the hall made the cloak flutter around his leg. But no one saw anything. He made it into the hall.

From there, instead of heading for the lift, he walked the other way and went to the stairs leading out to the roof. He cracked the door open, dealt with another quick gust of wind, and slipped out quickly. It was still hours before dawn. Gavin sat on a bench out of sight of the door. He had to see how bad things were before he did anything. But sitting, thinking, that was dangerous.

Orholam have mercy, he'd murdered that stupid girl. He rubbed his face. He wished he felt worse, but it wasn't his first murder. He'd been murdering people every year in that damned barbaric ritual—hearing their sins and stabbing them in the heart. What was one more soul on his tally?

If he looked harder at that girl, doubtless he'd find out some pathetic tale. Like Ana's family was on the brink of financial ruin, and she hoped that by seducing him they would be saved. Or that his father had blackmailed her into going to Gavin's bed so he could then blackmail Gavin. Andross had said that Ana was in the list of contenders for a marriage, hadn't he? Or... it didn't matter. What she'd done, why. How she'd gotten past his guards. It might have been a conspiracy; more likely, it was simply miscommunication and inexperience.

But Gavin didn't usually lose control of himself like that. He was steady, logical. For Orholam's sake, Gavin was the whole man. Was. Had been.

No longer.

He'd lost blue. That wasn't merely a magical fact, maybe it was a personal fact as well. He'd lost the cold, hard, passionless practicality of blue. There had been no reason to kill the girl, nothing but passion and hatred had impelled him to do such a thing. Passion and hatred unbridled by reason.

The loss of his powers wasn't only the loss of power; Gavin was becoming less. Less in control, less intelligent, less of a man.

He'd thrown a girl off his balcony. What kind of a man did that? He hadn't meant to—but that didn't matter. He'd done it. And maybe he *had* meant to do it.

And he'd lost Karris. She'd come to his room, at midnight, dressed to make love. His heart was in his throat. Orholam have mercy. He didn't know what she'd been doing, why she'd come now when they'd had every opportunity for months. But she'd come. Everything would be perfect if he'd done *anything* differently—had he not charmed his guards and told them he wanted companionship; had he awakened earlier; had he stopped an unknown woman before she mounted him, perhaps?

I saw what I wanted to see, just like I always do. And my self-delusion cost me the real thing.

He wondered how long it would be before he lost yellow. How long before he lost the rest. It was another eight months until the Freeing. When he'd found out he'd lost blue, he'd thought he could make it that long. That wasn't going to happen, he knew that now.

He thought of his goals.

Lucidonius, were things so bleak for you when the Ur trapped you in Hass Valley? Did you doubt yourself then? Or were you as willful as the tales tell? Were you just a man? You changed the world, but is this what you wanted to change it to?

Gavin had murdered his own mother, and she'd thanked him for it. What kind of broken world was this? She'd thanked him for it!

He remembered that artist, that damned genius addict artist, what was his name? Aheyyad Brightwater. He'd given the boy a name, and murdered him. Giving scraps with one hand, and taking away everything with the other. And Aheyyad had thanked him. Gavin had failed Garriston, lost them their city, their possessions, the lives of many they'd cared about—and they worshipped him as a god. They loved him.

How was he the only man who saw what he was?

There were no answers to be found in the waning stars. Like there were no gods, no Orholam, no light in the witching hour.

He could survive this, couldn't he? Maybe if Ana Jorvis had been a slave. She wasn't. Her father owned more than half of the barges that plied the Great River, and her mother was Arys of the Greenveils's sister. Arys, the Sub-red. A former ally, passionate, and not averse to war. Arys had loved Ana. Arys would make destroying the man who'd murdered her niece her life's work. With her passion and the recklessness that only having a couple of years of life left engendered? Hell, even Gavin losing her votes on the Spectrum meant...

Nothing was possible. It was all over.

The sun finally gripped the horizon with bloodied fingernails and pulled itself up. Gavin walked over to the great crystal mounted on its swivel and as the sunlight finally descended on him like Orholam's heavy hand, he pulled off his shimmercloak and dropped it at his feet, then pulled off the dust cover and put his hands onto the great cold rock.

He extended himself, feeling, sensing the light. He couldn't see the blue, but he could feel it. It wasn't precisely out of balance—blue was about equal with red right now—but it was out of control. It felt uneven, a checkerboard of total chaos and excruciating control. He could feel a knot, though, tiny, far out into the Cerulean Sea, maybe not even in physical form yet, knitting itself back together, floating like one of the fabled glaciers from the great seas beyond the Everdark Gates. Gavin had destroyed the bane, but it would never be finished. In six months, there would be another. He could destroy bane after bane, but they would slowly heal, build themselves anew—until a real Prism tamed them again.

Then he felt the green. There was no order there, no clear checkerboard. Green was running rampant, but only in random streaks. The Verdant Plains were blooming now, in autumn, because a huge streak of verdure covered them. Then, gaps. Huge blooms of algae in the sea, empty spaces, and then another knot, just forming to the southwest. Where was that?

Orholam. Just outside Ru. Right in the path of the Color Prince's advancing army.

Both...knots—whatever they were—were very slowly growing.

Putting his will into the great crystal, Gavin tried to balance, tried to impose the happy harmony on the entire world, as he had done so many times before.

This was what he was made for. This was what he had done, over and over, not even needing the crystal. This was his genius, his purpose, his aristeia!

Nothing. Vacuum. Emptiness. Lack. He was merely a man, merely a man pushing on a rock as if he thought he could squeeze liquid dreams out of it by wishing. A fool.

It was over. He was finished. A Prism who couldn't balance was nothing, and without a Prism who could balance, the world was doomed. The problems would only get worse. Things would go back to the way they had been before Lucidonius: gods being born, drafters flocking to the god of their color, trying to become gods themselves, and every god at war with every other, the world itself torn by massive storms that lasted decades, the sea choked and dead, monstrous beasts roaming the plains, glaciers spilling through the mountains to abut directly on deserts. Starvation, privation, and constant war over scarce resources that might disappear completely in the very next year. Nations broken down to tribes and clans. Cities burned. Libraries burned. Civilization ended.

If only half of what they said the world was like without Prisms was true, it would be a cataclysm to dwarf all others. Gavin sat and wrapped himself in the warmth of the cloak, drifting in and out of consciousness.

And slowly it came to him. In this insane world where nothing was as it was supposed to be, Gavin Guile wasn't the only Prism. The tightness in his chest told him what he had to do.

Even my selfishness must have an end.

Gavin stood, turned his back on the light, and went to see his brother.

Chapter 81

Dazen knew time was against him. Surely Gavin must have some way of knowing when he broke through his prisons.

Gavin. Dazen? Even I'm confused.

Dazen, though younger, had always been the smarter brother. *Well, I'm Dazen now. And I'll outsmart you this time.*

Dazen considered the easy way first. He could lay a plank of sealed green luxin on top of the hellstone in the hallway. So long as the luxin was sealed, the hellstone wouldn't leach it, at least not quickly. If done in many layers and many trips, he should be able to take green all the way to the next prison. If the next hallway was as long as the first, given how weak Dazen was now, it would probably be two or three days' work.

Did he have two or three days? He'd taken months to get this far, what was a couple more days?

He didn't know. Maybe it would be all the difference in the world. Maybe Gavin had met some grisly end out there, and it made no difference at all.

Did Gavin think that his prisoner would be so inflamed by green that he would just charge down the hallway, like a mad dog seeking freedom?

No, that wasn't how Gavin worked. He would know that Dazen, having been tricked into losing his luxin when he moved between the blue prison and the green one, would be extra cautious here. Surely the first thing Gavin would have thought of was the first thing Dazen was thinking of now.

And having thought of it, Gavin would have a plan. Gavin would have some kind of trap waiting. Once Dazen moved down that hallway, something would happen that would rob him of the green luxin.

So Dazen sat, thinking. The trigger on the trap—for surely, surely, there must be a trap—might be at any point in that hellstone tunnel. Until Dazen had a plan, he'd be a fool to go into the tunnel looking for it.

And he'd be a fool to sit too long waiting and planning. Gavin could be back at any moment. Coming to visit, coming to gloat. How Dazen wanted to smash that monster's grinning face in!

He sat and ate, casting his mind about, searching, searching.

Knowing it was second best, he got up after a while and stood at the mouth of that tunnel to hell, the tunnel to the yellow prison. Very carefully and very slowly, he drafted and sealed a long thin stick out of green luxin. He probed the mouth of the tunnel, looking for tripwires concealed in the darkness.

No, this was hopeless. If he was paranoid, he'd never get out of here. He had to act boldly, had to take his own fate in his hands and smash through Gavin's plans, destroy them. He couldn't let himself be trapped here. He had to go, now! He had to—

Slow down, Dazen. That's the green talking. You're weak, the luxin has more power over you when you're exhausted and sick.

Dazen released the green, emptied himself of it completely.

Without it, he felt wrung out, unbearably tired. No, the weakness was too great. If he didn't take the green again, he'd sleep, and sleeping, he'd give Gavin time to come back—

But if he took the green, he'd do something stupid, just as Gavin expected. He'd fall right into the next trap, and that might leave him in a worse place than ever before. A yellow prison could well be unbreakable. He'd been lucky in the green. Gavin had made a mistake, letting him get blue bread. Dazen couldn't count on that twice. He needed to make that one mistake count.

He imagined Gavin coming back down here, grinning that lopsided grin at him, taunting—

403

Wait. Gavin came down here. When Gavin came down here, he had to traverse this geometrical space.

Even without luxin, Dazen felt a burst of energy, life. Gavin came down here. That meant he had tunnels. He came close enough that he could talk to Dazen. That meant those tunnels were very, very close.

If Dazen could find one of those tunnels, he wouldn't simply get past the yellow prison, he'd break out of *all* of the prisons. He didn't have to break out of each in turn, he could simply *leave*.

Salvation was that close. His heart leapt. His heart burned within him. It was as if his fever was still burning him.

No, this was real joy. It had been so long since he'd felt it, he almost didn't recognize the giddy, skittish thing. He laughed aloud. Then he started moving around the chamber surrounding the great green egg that had been his prison, knocking on the walls.

Tap, tap, tap. Tap, tap, tap. Tap, tap, tonk.

Tonk, tonk, tonk. The hollow sound was like a choir singing the Sun Day salutations.

Just to be sure, just to be careful, Dazen checked the rest of the chamber. Nothing. This one section, almost four paces long, was the thinnest. He looked for hidden hinges, but he couldn't find any. Not that he expected them. After the prison was finished, Gavin doubtless would have fully sealed the tunnel. No reason to leave a weakness where Dazen might find it.

Going back to the green cell was like going back to scoop up his own vomit and eat it. But back he went. Shivering with revulsion, he clambered through the hole he'd made and grabbed the husk of his blue bread.

He'd left all of the crust, broken open now to give him the maximum surface from which to draft.

He climbed back out of the green cell, but stood in its light. It took him another quarter of an hour to draft enough blue. It was a relief, though, when it came. The clarity of blue was a boon. He'd lived with blue for sixteen years, and he needed it. With the blue slowly filling him, he became aware once again of how fragile his health was. It had only been months since his fever had passed. The nasty cut across his chest had mostly healed in a nasty scar. His body had won the fight against the infection, but that didn't mean he was up to full strength.

He didn't know how long he had. He needed to blast the wall open, draft green for the necessary strength, and go as fast and far as he could. Once he found a safe place, he could worry about healing. It was a gamble, and his blue self hated gambles, but this was a gamble he had to play or die.

He thought of going back to the stone wall to knock again, to double-check, but he didn't need to. He'd drafted blue for so long that he could practically see lines overlaying his vision that denoted the exact outline of the hollow space. He could envision the probable thickness of the stone. It was granite, and from some class he'd taken as a boy and had thought long lost, he remembered how granite broke.

That was blue for you, dredging up details from your own mind that you couldn't believe you remembered. Granite broke in predictable wedges, Xs at sixty degrees and one hundred twenty degrees. Of course, the blue couldn't tell him at what angle those wedges lay to him. So he braced himself and grasped his right wrist in his left hand. He gathered his will. The first missile would need to be about the size of his thumb or the granite might not crack and show him the appropriate angles.

He took a deep breath and gave the short, sharp cry. It tightened stomach, chest, and diaphragm, gave tension and a stable firing platform, and a small animal boost to the will. Mechanics meets the beast.

The blue bullet burst from him and smashed into the wall, in and through with a small explosion of granite dust and granite shrapnel.

No alarm sounded. At least none that he could hear. Dazen strode to the wall. It was too dark to see the hole well, but he traced his fingers around it, felt the fractures. Aha, tilted about twelve degrees.

His blue-enhanced mind laid the lines out easily, compensated for the angles, picked out lines along which it would fracture, and exactly where he would have to shoot the next missiles to make the hole big enough to climb through.

Taking his place back far enough that he wouldn't get hit with the shrapnel but would still easily hit his targets, Dazen braced himself, one foot back, turned, both hands up. Each hand would shoot two missiles simultaneously: there and...there.

He shouted, and the missiles blasted out from him, hitting the wall in a blue explosion as parts of the luxin were torn back into light. Dust filled the tunnel, and Dazen choked on it, feeling suddenly empty. He staggered over to the green cell and drew in liquid life.

Looking at the hunks of blue bread at his feet, he had the passing thought that he should draft in blue as well, at least some, some thread—he ate the bread. There'd be plenty more blue where he was going. He needed the strength.

A tiny part of him protested, but it was little, and weak.

He pushed through the dark hole into the dark tunnel. He drafted imperfect green into his hand. Green made lousy torches, and even in the state he was in, he knew not to use all of his luxin up just to make it slightly brighter.

The tunnel—Gavin's tunnel—was simple, rough-hewn. It was a workspace, barely wide enough for a man. Not really wide enough for a man with a torch, if he didn't want to risk burning the hell out of himself. Of course.

Gavin would have used a luxin torch. Bastard.

Dazen hesitated once inside the tunnel. One way might gently slope up, and the other seemed to gently slope down, but he couldn't be certain. His instinct was to choose the upward direction, but when he thought about it rationally, there was no guarantee that simply because this one tiny section of tunnel had a slope that the slope continued all the way to the surface. Really, he had no idea which way was out. If he went the wrong way, of course, he could simply turn around, but he'd be wasting time. Time that might be valuable. And he'd certainly be wasting energy, and even with the green alive inside him, he knew his bucket had holes in the bottom of it. He was emaciated, unhealthy underneath the veneer of wild energy green lent him. So he forced himself to hold still, wait.

The blue saved him. He wasn't drafting it, but it had changed him in all those years. He stayed still and held his meager green light. The granite dust, still settling from the explosion and still settling from his own passage into the tunnel, now resumed its natural patterns.

There was a slight breeze between the two newly connected passages, too slight for Dazen to feel on his skin, but enough to see the dust slide into the tunnel and...up. If the wind was blowing that way, that was the way that was open. That was his way out.

Dazen went up. Up was good. Up was out.

A sudden sob racked his frame. Up was out. Dear gods. Up was out.

Chapter 82

"Here's what I'm curious about," Teia said as they sat down in Kip's room. She was tired and her hair was askew from training with Karris White Oak. "I think Aram is the second best fighter in the scrubs."

"He's the tall kid, muscular?" Kip asked.

"And fast. And a yellow/green bichrome. He's gotten some unlucky matchups, but I'm wondering if he's playing sand spider."

"Sand spider?" Kip asked. She'd said it like it was a saying he should know.

"Hiding in his hole so he can jump out at exactly the right time. He is a yellow. Maybe he thinks that he's another Ayrad."

"When you use one reference I don't know to explain another I don't know..." Kip said.

"Ayrad was a Blackguard seventy, eighty years ago now. He entered at the bottom of his class, at forty-nine, and each month at testing, he barely made it into the next month. Forty-nine, to thirty-five, to twenty-eight, to fourteen. And then on the last week, he beat *everyone*. Turned out he'd taken a vow or something."

"So on the last week, he fought, what? Fourteen to eleven, eleven to eight, eight to five, five to two, and two to one? Orholam's balls, that's a lot of fights. I can't imagine facing the best guy in the class after having already fought four times." It was one of the controls that the tests had built in. Someone could technically fight from the last place to the first, but because they had to fight again immediately until they stopped winning fight tokens, the exhaustion piled on—and with each new fight, the challenger would be facing someone who was fresh.

"Kip, Ayrad didn't skip fighters. He beat all of them. From fourteen, he challenged thirteen, from thirteen, twelve."

"You're kidding."

"That's the story." Teia shrugged. "Karris did almost what you said, until she faced Fisk. She finished third, after four fights. And Fisk barely got her, they say."

With all his study of magic and history and the cards, Kip almost despaired as he saw that there was another gigantic area of lore that he hadn't even touched: the histories of the great Blackguards.

Teia picked up Kip's slate and began writing on it.

"So how did Lucretia Verangheti take it when she lost you?" Kip asked. "I never even heard how the Red got her to give up your title."

"I don't know," Teia said. "I haven't seen her since then. Don't want to." She shrugged, then pointed to the slate quickly. "This is what I think the true ranking of the Blackguard scrubs should be. What do you think?"

There was something about how she'd glossed over her slavery that caught Kip's attention, but then he got caught up in looking at the slate. Teia had Cruxer at first, Aram at second (second?), herself at twelfth, and Kip at...eighteenth. He raised an eyebrow at her.

"Um, sorry," she said. "Maybe you could do better than that."

"You're apologizing for the wrong thing," Kip said. "I don't belong at eighteenth, do I?" He'd put himself around twentieth.

Teia cleared her throat. "You're a polychrome, Kip. It makes a big difference. Huge, if you use it right."

Kip scowled. A polychrome. They'd guessed that for a while. A full-spectrum polychrome? That was different. Totally different. And yet, with missing the practicum every day, he didn't have nearly the skills he should have. In truth, as Teia had told him, if he really was a full-spectrum polychrome, all sorts of things would be different. They wouldn't let him be a Blackguard unless Gavin intervened—he was too valuable. And they would want him to marry, young. It still wasn't understood what made drafters, but enough people believed that drafters had children who could draft that the pressure for drafters to have children was intense. And more intense for the more gifted. Unless you got as powerful as Gavin Guile, and you could do whatever you wanted and everyone else could go to hell.

But he didn't want to think about all that right now. He went back to looking at the rankings. "How'd you even arrive at this?"

"Paying attention? Watching? First you have to take into account that everyone wants to finish as high as possible, but at least in the top fourteen. People also have friends that they don't want to knock out of the top fourteen, so lots of times people won't challenge three up from themselves if that's where their friend is. Because win or lose, either they or their friend will lose their challenge token. That's less important in the top ten where people will know they're safe, but people heading for getting kicked out aren't going to want to ruin their friends' chances." She started drawing lines. "Person at the bottom goes first, so they might challenge the weakest person in the three above them. So let's say Idus at twenty challenges Asmun at eighteen because even though he is allowed to challenge Ziri at seventeen, he thinks he can beat Asmun and not Ziri. If he wins, he moves up and then takes on Winsen, hoping to get lucky. So now the new person at twenty is more likely to challenge Asmun who is now at nineteen, even though that's only one place up."

"Why?" Kip asked. The numbers were spinning in his head.

"Because Asmun's already lost. He's got no challenge token, so he knows he can't make it in this season at all. He won't fight as hard because there's nothing at stake. See, you have to reshuffle the order every time someone wins, and keep track of who has and who doesn't have their challenge token. That way you can skip the more difficult fights. But of course, we have to keep in mind that some people will feign weaknesses until the last week so they have an advantage."

"Like you." That was why Teia had wanted Kip to take credit for the courier idea.

"Yes, like me."

"Oh hell no," Kip said. Talk about vast areas of lore he knew nothing about. "No, no, no, this is hopeless. I can't figure this all out!" He stood up. "No, I'm tired. Forget this—"

"Kip, if you don't figure this out, you're not going to make it into the Blackguard. You're not a good enough fighter, so you need to be smarter than people who are better fighters than you. *That* is what people admired about Ayrad."

"The man who defeated all the other fighters in the Blackguard wasn't admired because he was a good fighter? I find that hard to believe."

"Kip, he was able to figure out exactly how to finish last every month and still make it in. That means he was figuring exactly who would challenge whom and who would win those fights—every month. If he figured wrong once, he would have failed out early."

"So he's admired for losing intelligently? That's mad."

"He's admired for knowing his friends and knowing his enemies and outwitting them all."

"So what happened to him?" Kip asked.

"He became commander of the Blackguard and saved the lives of four different Prisms over the course of his career—and then someone poisoned him."

"So he wasn't perfect," Kip said grumpily.

"He was perfect for twenty-four years. That's a lot longer than most of us can even dream."

"Sorry," Kip said. He could tell that somehow the dead commander meant a lot to Teia.

"Don't pout. We've got work to do."

"Hold on, before we do all that, I want you to take your papers. You keep on avoiding this. Look, all you have to do is sign them and we can take them to be registered tomorrow."

"Kip, don't be an idiot."

Kip was so tired he wanted to cry. He lifted his hands helplessly. "What happens after you free me, Kip?"

"Uh, you're free?"

"And poor."

"Didn't we already talk about this?" Kip asked.

"What happens when a slave gets into the Blackguard, Kip?"

"They're freed, sort of."

"They're purchased, for a fortune. And as soon as a scrub passes the test, their contract goes into escrow until final vows. If you free me now, you get nothing."

"I don't want to own you, Teia. It doesn't feel right. Do you even want to be in the Blackguard?"

"Of course I do!"

"I don't even know if I should believe you. You can't tell me that you don't, can you?"

"What? I'm a slave, not a liar, Kip."

He scowled. "It's more complicated than that, and we both know it."

She looked at him like he was crazy for a long moment, then the façade crumbled. One second she was all breezy confidence and happiness, and the next she looked terribly vulnerable and frightened. "Kip... I've been thinking about this a lot. Ever since you said you'd free me. You know that the first thing I felt was angry—at you? Because as soon as you won me, I stopped getting my lessons in how to draft paryl. I'll get them again, but I'll have to wait years. Nothing in my life changed except that, and I was *mad* at you. Stupid, huh? Kip, part of me tells me to take those papers and run to the registrar. To take my freedom while it's sitting there in front of me. It tells me slave owners are notoriously fickle. Sorry."

"No offense taken," Kip mumbled.

"My family's in debt, Kip. My mother did some bad things, and my father lost everything, including me and my sisters. He was a trader like I said, but his creditors won't let him go on another voyage because they're afraid he'll flee, so he's stuck working as a day laborer. With what he's earning now, there's no way he can pay off what he owes. He can't afford to buy inventory to trade at home. If I take those papers now, I'm condemning him to poverty, and my sisters to early marriages to the first poor men my father can convince to take them."

"What happened?" Kip asked.

"Please don't ask me that."

But I already did ask— Oh, because she's my slave, if I insist, she'll have to answer. Kip said, "Forget it then. Sorry. You have a plan?"

"Hold on to my title for a few more weeks. Then when I go through final vows, you give me a fifth of what the Blackguard pays for me. That way, we both get something—and you'll need the money as badly as I do. I want to be a Blackguard anyway, Kip. There is nothing in life I want more. This way, the Chromeria pays us for it."

"That's...sort of...brilliant," Kip said.

"And what's the downside?" she asked.

I don't get to find out if you like me for me or if you like me because you need the money—until after final vows. But that was purely selfish, wasn't it? He wanted her to pay for him to feel good about himself.

"See?" she said. "But...I want you to swear something to me, Kip."

"Anything."

"Swear that you won't sell me back to...that you won't sell me. To anyone. I'll serve you in our off hours, I don't care. I've been a slave for years, I can do it for a few more weeks, just promise that."

"I swear to Orholam," Kip said, "on one condition."

She looked dubiously at him.

"That you take half of what we get for your contract."

"Kip, you're a terrible negotiator." She grinned, and Kip was struck again by how different she was from Liv. Liv had lived in bitterness over her station, which had been unjust, but it hadn't been as bad as being a slave. Maybe it was that Liv had seen how close a gloriously easy life had been, so she felt the sting of its loss. Or maybe Teia was simply naturally more positive, but if he had to go through bad and unfair stuff, he hoped that in the future he could be more like Teia and less like Liv. The thought somehow loosened something inside of Kip and he found himself both less angry with Liv and less interested in her. "I accept," Teia said. "Now, quit grinning...to work!"

Chapter 83

Dazen passed the first unlit torch in the tunnel without touching it. A torch could be a trap. He pressed on through the tight confines of the tunnel, breathing deeply to try to keep himself calm. The tunnel wasn't that tight, and the blackness wasn't the dark. He could go through worse. He would go through worse, gladly, to get out of here.

No going back. Never.

Perhaps a hundred paces later, he came to another torch, and he paused. The light of his green luxin ball was feeble, and it was consuming his only luxin. He didn't know how long it was going to have to last him. Hopefully only minutes, but just in case...

He studied the torch like it was a serpent. The tunnel was too tight to comfortably carry a normal torch with the attendant open flames and dripping pitch. To carry a normal torch without burning yourself down here, you'd have to hold it directly in front of you. In his usual profligately drafting way, his brother had made lux torches, made of a mundane shaft of wood. The ends had panels of imperfectly drafted yellow, covered completely by a thin layer of luxin or glass or even waxed leather. Sealed against the air, the yellow luxin lay dormant. When you wanted light, you simply peeled back the sealant and had a perfect, single-spectrum yellow light source. Depending on how much air was allowed through and how well the yellow had been drafted, the lux torch could last from an hour to four hours. Hideously expensive to buy and horribly difficult to craft; his brother had liked to draft them to show off his superchromacy.

This one was his brother's work, no doubt. Of course, his brother must have done most if not all of the work on this prison himself. The lux torch was set in a simple iron bracket. Dazen squinted at the little piece of iron as if it held the mysteries of the universe. But it was just iron. The fit didn't look particularly tight. It didn't look like there was any way it could be some kind of a switch so that when he lifted the torch it would pop up and trigger a trap.

But it felt wrong.

Dazen cursed. And then he cursed some more. He liked hearing the sound of his words echo down the tunnel, disappear into the distance, rather than simply bounce back at him from a few feet away.

"A little dumb to be hollering when you're trying to escape, don't you think?" a voice said.

Dazen felt a shock run down his spine. For one long instant he thought it was all over. Then he recognized the voice.

"Dead man," he said.

"But not as dead as you'll be soon, I think," the dead man said.

"I thought you were back in your wall, where I left you. I don't need you out here."

The dead man chuckled from the darkness. "Thought you could lose me so easily? You're an amusing little man, Gavin Guile."

"No, *you're* Gavin. You're the dead man. I'm done with that. I'm done with losing. Now go away, I'm burning light here."

"Bet the torch is trapped."

Dazen snarled. "I know the torch is trapped!"

But he didn't know the torch was trapped. That was fear, paranoia. But he couldn't shake it. Cursing quietly, over and over and over, he studied the torch. He couldn't touch it.

"Forget it," the dead man said. "You've probably got fifteen minutes left with the green. You might make it, if you don't sit around and talk to yourself." He laughed again, mocking.

Dazen stumbled down the hall. He was in bad shape. If he didn't get sleep and real food soon...

No, worry about that later.

The tunnel curved slowly, and Dazen thought he was spiraling slowly upward. It felt like it was taking forever. It felt unbearable, but it couldn't go on for too long, could it? How deep would Gavin have dug?

"Deeper than you can dig out, of course," the dead man said. "He was always that little bit smarter than you."

"Shut up!" Dazen's leg folded and he fell. He caught himself, but it almost cost him his concentration. He almost lost the green ball.

"You remember how you were father's favorite? I wonder if Gavin's his favorite now. You were always afraid father would realize how much smarter Gavin was than you, weren't you?"

"Shut up," Dazen said weakly. Orholam, he'd almost lost his only light. He couldn't imagine being trapped in utter darkness with only the voices in his head.

"Why don't you go back to that lux torch," the dead man said from the darkness. "Your green might last that long. Of course, that lux torch might be dead. Been there a long time. They don't last forever. Not even your brother's."

The darkness was getting stronger, closing in around the little wan circle of green light. Green was supposed to make him feel wild, and strong. But even wild animals can have their hearts burst. And the feeling of strength isn't the same thing as strength.

Dazen hobbled on, because there was nothing else to do. His body was betraying him. Black spots swam before his eyes. He stumbled again, and this time he fell, barely cradling his dwindling green globe to his chest. He stood, shakily, and even the dead man was silent.

Then, salvation.

He saw another lux torch. He moved toward it slowly, carefully.

"It's trapped, you know that, right?" the dead man said. "I bet the last one wasn't trapped. He probably is so much smarter than you that he knew you'd go past that one, and then get desperate. He's got you figured pretty—"

"Shut up! Shut up. Shut up!"

The green ball was smaller than Dazen's fist now. He had five minutes left, maybe.

Still, he didn't rush. He examined closely the iron bracket this torch sat in.

"It won't be a simple lever trap. Come now, Dazen would be more elegant than that, don't you think? Dazen—"

"I'm Dazen now!" Dazen hissed. But he didn't even turn. He was right, it couldn't be a simple lever trap. The bracket was solid. He stepped back and extended one finger and pressed on the bracket, ready to jump backward if anything happened.

Nothing.

He squinted his eyes, trying to see into the superviolet, but he couldn't tell if he was failing or there was simply no superviolet luxin to see.

He poked the torch. It shifted in the bracket and he jumped back. His leg betrayed him again and he tumbled to the floor, barely able to break his fall by pushing himself against the wall.

But other than a complete loss of his dignity, nothing happened.

"Loss of your dignity?" The dead man chortled. "You're bloody, and dirty, and naked, you smell like shit, and you talk to yourself. What dignity do you have to lose?"

"I want you to know," Dazen said, "when I get out of here, you're gone. I don't need you anymore."

" 'Need' is such an interesting word, isn't it?"

"Go to the evernight." Dazen stood wearily. "Let's see what you've got, brother," he said. He grabbed the lux torch.

And. Nothing. Happened.

He expelled a breath. He hadn't realized he'd been holding it. Orholam damn you, Gavin, I really thought you were that diabolically clever.

Dazen pulled back the little clay tab over one square face of the lux torch and a slow glow began emanating as the air got in through its many tiny holes. The torch was still half full of yellow luxin. With the quality of Gavin's drafting, that would be plenty.

Hope broke over Dazen's heart like the sun breaking over the hills as that pure yellow light blossomed. He jostled the lux torch and the light bloomed full. He peeled off another clay face and basked in the glow. There was no trap.

He was really going to make it. He'd dug a fathom below that bastard's petard.

Drafting from luxin was horridly inefficient. The light being cast was cast because the luxin had been drafted incorrectly, so the only correct yellows you got were those shed through spectral scattering, and even then, your own abilities and efficiency as a drafter dictated what was possible. But Dazen wasn't trying to draft something useful; he merely wanted to taste yellow.

It leaked into him in a slow swirl, and after sixteen years of its absence, it was glorious. He felt sharper, clearer, able to go on, carefully.

The bare fact that Gavin hadn't booby-trapped this lux torch didn't mean that there weren't traps in the tunnel. Even if he'd never guessed that his brother would get out this way, he might have worried that someone would find it from the other end. Yes, he'd have to be careful.

Thank you, yellow.

Invigorated, Dazen walked on.

Not three minutes more, and he saw the rays of the lux torch illuminate the mouth of a chamber. He slowed.

"This will be where he gets you," the dead man said.

"Shut up," he hissed.

He examined everything minutely. The walls of his tunnel before it emerged into the chamber; the floor; the ceiling—anything he could see, in every spectrum. His heart pounded, but there was nothing, no hidden tripwires, no hinges, no inexplicable holes in the wall that would shoot out some kind of gory death. He edged forward slowly. He could take his time. The torch would last.

Of course, his brother could be coming at any moment.

The chamber was perhaps ten paces wide in either direction. There was a small table, small chair, small cot. No food, though. This must have been a room where Gavin rested while he constructed the prison.

Dazen watched where he put every step.

"I'm telling you, this is where he gets you," the dead man said. "Go ahead, go lie down in that cot. Want to bet you never wake up?"

Dazen didn't touch the cot. He wasn't going to sleep anyway, not with the lux torch slowly burning out. He'd discarded the clay caps, hadn't even thought about keeping them, dammit. Stupid mistake. Not that he had pockets or free hands to carry them in. Still.

Something glimmered on the far wall, directly over the tunnel mouth.

"Oh, by all means, go look at the shiny. Right. That couldn't *possibly* be a trap," the dead man said.

"Why don't you stay here, and I'll go on without you?" Dazen said. "Then we'll both be happy."

"By all means, I'm not the one talking to myself. You can leave me behind whenever you're good and ready."

"Go to hell," Dazen said. "It's over by the tunnel. I have to go that way regardless."

Still, he went carefully. It was easy to get fixated, get tunnel vision.

"Ha! Punning!" the dead man said.

What? Oh. "Bugger off."

Dazen blinked, rubbed his eyes, studied the floor, tested every step. He couldn't go at this pace for long or he'd never get out. But it was worth it here. No matter that the dead man was mocking him, he *did* have a point.

Whatever the shiny was, it was etched into the rock. Perhaps a natural vein of some ore? Gold? Dazen knew nothing about mining, but he was deep under the earth somewhere. The distribution looked random at first, but as he got closer—

"Trap. I'm telling you. Trap," the dead man said.

"I'm not touching it, you asshole. Stop distracting me." Trap it might be, but Dazen wasn't going to put his head right underneath that thing to step into the tunnel beyond it if it was going to snap down without a moment's notice.

Keeping his distance, he stood up on tiptoe and held the lux torch high. Whatever it was, it sat deep in grooves, and only fell full under the torch's light when he lifted it. He heard a little hiss and he froze.

This was the trap. He needed to do something immediately, but he didn't know what.

In an instant, the luxin—for it was luxin—in the grooves ignited and glowed a dull, infernal red. Dazen remembered the formulation. Gavin's work, a blend of yellow and red so unstable that even being hit with light would cause it to combust. He felt a stab of fury—and then the whole design bloomed with light, ignited by the light of his lux torch.

It was a single, roughly shaped word, two paces across, drawn with a jaunty, cocky hand. It unfurled in yellow-red fire: *Almost.*

Dazen's feet became unstuck and he leapt backward and ran for the tunnel behind him.

The light of his lux torch, which had been directed solely forward as he'd entered the chamber, now cut into deep grooves in the wall back behind him that he hadn't even seen. These flashed to fire, the fires cut ropes, and the floor dropped out from under him.

He tumbled head over heels into the darkness down a tube, then abruptly dropped straight onto a flat surface. He impaled himself on several tiny spikes, not longer than his first knuckle. It took his breath—and his luxin. Hellstone!

Then that floor swung open and he tumbled down farther, farther. He smashed into a door that swung open and then shut behind him.

Dizzy, back and arms bleeding from tiny stab wounds and disoriented, Dazen nonetheless immediately knew where he was by the light that stabbed through his eyelids, mocking him.

He rolled over, opened his eyes. The room was shaped like a squashed ball, one hole above for food and water, one hole below for his waste. And in the round, curving wall of his new yellow cell sat the dead man.

In a mad falsetto, he said, "Told you so."

Chapter 84

The shimmercloak made it easy for Gavin to get back to his room. Indeed, he passed only a single Blackguard who glanced toward the door to the roof when a bit of wind gusted in, but Gavin closed it quickly behind him.

The young woman looked up the stairs but dismissed it. Gavin made it past her, and when she finally decided to go check, he used the opportunity to slip into his room.

Clearly, they'd searched the room for him, but it had been a cursory search. What had he been thinking, inviting a search of his room? They could have found the door in his closet.

Not that it mattered now. Gavin went to the picture of the blue colossus and pulled it open. He almost laughed. The alarm panel was glowing yellow.

His brother had broken out of green, *last night*. Insanely, Gavin felt proud of him. He was a fighter. Maybe enough of one.

Well, at least the second alarm worked. Gavin swung the painting shut and went to his closet and began moving his clothes.

"My lord, may I help?"

Gavin wheeled around to find Marissia. She was kneeling beside the bed, head down. Apparently waiting for him, paying some sort of penance by making her vigil here. Her face was drawn, haggard.

He felt a rush of warmth for the woman. She'd been more than his room slave. She'd served with her whole heart, and in difficult circumstances.

"Marissia, there's a letter in my desk drawer. I'm sure you've seen it. Please get it for me."

She got it for him while he continued piling his clothes out of the way in the closet. She brought it back, wooden. It was her letter of manumission. Instead of having the standard thing written up and then signing it, Gavin had written it all in his own hand. He'd heard tales of room slaves being accused of forging their own manumission papers and kept in slavery because of it. Marissia was beautiful and valuable for a dozen reasons. Gavin wasn't going to let them have her.

He looked it over, though he had the contents memorized. It was not only manumission, but also a grant of ten thousand danars. A fortune, enough to start a business and marry, or just to live off for the rest of her life. He signed it. Then he grabbed another scrap of paper and wrote down a series of letters and numbers. "My father might seize this money through some pretext or another. They know I care about you, so they'll suspect that I'd leave you something. This code will open another account to you. Speak to the Ilytian banker Prestor Onesto at Varig and Green."

"My lord, why are you speaking this way?" She sounded on the verge of tears.

"Please give five thousand of what's in that account to Karris and five thousand to Kip. The rest is for you." He handed the writ to her. "Memorize that sequence and then burn that; Onesto will release the money to anyone who has that number."

"Lord Prism..." She held the papers limply. She looked bereaved.

"I've freed you. You're supposed to be happy." Gavin looked away. Of course it stroked his ego that his slave didn't seem delighted to be free, but perhaps that was simply because she knew to cover her delight for his sake. In case it was a lie, he didn't want to see through it, so he looked away.

"This is my fault, isn't it, my lord?" she said. "I did something wrong, didn't I? I missed the alarm somehow."

He put his hands on her shoulders. "It's not your fault. My alarm failed. It was my work. Everything had to go right, for too long. Something happened. But it wasn't you."

"I should have been here for you. That Ana girl...I should never have left. I'm so sorry, my lord." She was right; if Marissia had been in his bed where Gavin wanted her, things would have been very different. But he was the master of his own fate. No one had forced him to throw that girl out onto his balcony.

What had he been thinking, anyway? Just that he wanted her out of his room? Just that he wanted to frighten her? Or had his rage been murderous all along?

Maybe intent didn't matter. She was dead. It was all finished.

"It's not your fault, Marissia. It's mine. You have been a good servant, a good companion, a good friend. I want you to go now so you don't get sucked down by the wreckage."

Her eyebrows tented in dismay. "My lord, you are a good man. Please don't—"

He snorted. "A good man would have freed you long ago. I was afraid of how you'd use your freedom, so I withheld it from you. I've a small and mean spirit. The master who fears the choices his people will make enough to take those choices away isn't worth serving. You've served me well, despite my shortcomings. Thank you, Marissia. Please take these two cloaks down to my secret room. Then go. I may not come back up alone. I may not come back up at all, but someone else will. You oughtn't be here when he does."

She turned her hands up, helpless for once. "My lord," she said plaintively.

He opened the closet and drafted the board for his feet—out of yellow luxin now, since he couldn't do blue.

"Tell Kip I'm sorry. Tell Karris . . . No, I suppose you can't. Fare thee well, Marissia." He stepped into the closet and closed the door.

He could hear her weeping as soon as the door closed, though she was trying to hold it back.

Gavin slid open the floor, found the rope, and fitted the board onto it. In moments, he was whizzing downward into the darkness.

When he got to the bottom of the shaft, he groped around until he found the lux torches, then pulled one off the wall. He hadn't been able to use them before because he hadn't wanted to cast yellow light into any of his brother's cells. Now that Dazen was in the yellow cell, it didn't matter anymore.

He found the controls and pulled the levers to bring the yellow cell up. It would take about five minutes for the cell to lift and rotate into position. He'd built it that way so that his brother would always think that the place where the window sat was a weakness in the design, when in fact he'd hardened that spot above all others.

The wait gave him time to think about the spasm of creative genius he'd had in constructing this prison. He'd built the first, blue cell in a month, and then spent the better part of a year constructing all the other cells. He wondered how much different the world would be if he'd simply killed his brother and turned his attention immediately to fighting the Spectrum and changing the injustices he saw them committing everywhere. A waste, all for one man.

Never had the guts to let him go. Never had the guts to murder him in cold blood.

Slowly, slowly, the orb came into view, and then slowly settled. There was a slide to pull back to reveal the window, but Gavin found himself looking blankly at that slide, afraid to pull it open.

Ridiculous. He was here to die. He was here to let his brother out. This should be easy. It was all finished. His heart hammered protests in his chest, and he thought it was going to seize up. His throat constricted. He was sweating.

He pulled back the slide.

A man charged from the other side and swung a club straight at his face.

Gavin threw himself backward. His brother's lux torch hit the yellow luxin window and shattered in a flash of released yellow brightwater. But the prisoner wasn't finished. He didn't laugh with cool resolve at scaring Gavin. Instead, he attacked with the fury of a rabid wolf, beating the lux torch against the window with great blows until the wood shaft splintered in his hands, broke.

"You motherfucker!" the prisoner shouted. "I am going to kill you and everyone you ever loved. I'm going to rip your fucking head off and sodomize you with it."

Gavin stood, brushed himself off, and put his own lux torch into a bracket.

"You hear me, *Gavin?*" the prisoner shouted. "You think you're so clever. Good! You know what? You are clever. You always wanted me to say you're the smarter brother. You know what? You are. You know what else you are? You're the weaker brother. You ever wonder why I'm father's favorite? Look at this. This prison. Ingenious. And *pathetic.* I thought you made this prison to prove you were smarter than me, brother. I know better now. You made it because you can't kill me. Because you're afraid.

"That's why father loves me. Oh, I'm a disappointment, too. He wishes his son were both smart and ruthless, fearless, but he had to choose one, and he chose me. And he chose right, you spineless, scrofulous sack of shit. Because I can hold a grudge. I can nurse it, feed it, grow it. And I will. You're going to sit out there, worrying. Just like when you were a kid, huh? You still get the bad dreams, don't you? You still wake up crying, don't you? You still piss yourself, *Gavin?* Now you've got a reason to. I'm coming!" The prisoner was so close, his spit flecked the window.

"You could kill me," he said, "but you won't. I bet you think about it every single morning when you send me my bread. I could poison this, you think. I could just not feed him, you think. But you can't. You don't have it in you. You know, Gavin, you're right. You don't.

But I do. If our positions had been reversed, I'd have killed you as you lay unconscious at Sundered Rock. I would have cut off your head and filled your mouth with your own feces and put you on a pike. Because that's how you win, Gavin. That's how you show you can't be crossed. Peace through terror, Gavin. That probably doesn't even make any sense to you, does it? No, you were always like mother, all sweet manipulations and bullshit. She—"

"Mother's dead," Gavin said. He didn't want Dazen to slur her in his moment of anger.

"Fuck her," Dazen said. "As good a liar as she was, she never even bothered to pretend she didn't love you more."

What?

"You killed her?" Dazen asked, seeing a chink in Gavin's armor in the shock on his face. "You shrive her first? What'd she tell you? Do you think she was honest with you, even then? Or was she angling you to do what she wanted, even then? She might be dead, but I bet she's not gone, is she? Little spider bitch."

"That's your mother you're talking about, you sick bastard," Gavin said.

"So what're you going to do, little brother? Make me stop? You'll do nothing, like always. You're going to wait for me, and have your nightmares. I got out of the other prisons, and I'll get out of this one. You know, I was worried at first, when I fell into the green. I thought that blue was the only one, and green—that was cruel, brother, brilliant. I thought then that there must be seven prisons, one for every color. But there aren't, are there?"

Gavin said nothing.

"You couldn't make a cell of superviolet. There's no way you can make one of sub-red. I don't think you could make one out of orange or red either. I think this is the last cell. I think I'm a hair's breadth from ending everything you've ever built."

"You might be surprised," Gavin said quietly.

"You're a failure, little brother. An embarrassment. An empty shell."

Gavin stood looking at his brother in the pitiless yellow light.

"Karris never told you about our night together, did she?" the prisoner said.

"You've regaled me with your sexual prowess before. I'm not interested," Gavin said. The prisoner wasn't in his right mind. He'd just fallen into the yellow prison in the last twelve hours, doubtless thinking that this time he was really going to escape. The disappointment, the heartbreak would be enough to make anyone lash out. But Gavin didn't want to hear it.

"So she didn't." Dazen laughed, an edgy, grating laugh unlike any Gavin had ever heard from him. "I used to be kind of ashamed of it, really. But I'm past that now. She wasn't quite so eager as I might have made out before. We were at dinner, my men and her and her father, and I was telling these outrageous jokes, and even her father laughed along, and I had this moment, Gavin, when I realized just how different I am. How I can do whatever I want. I put my big cock in the world, and the world shuts up and takes it. I talked about fucking Karris all night long and making sure she was up to my standards and that coward laughed along. Can you believe it? And Karris, little coward Karris, she just got drunk.

"Sad to say, it was nothing special. She didn't give me much of a ride after I got mounted. You ever try to finish while the woman's bawling? And I know it wasn't because I took her maidenhead. You took care of that, didn't you?"

"You sick piece of—"

"I didn't think I was going to be able to finish. I was drunk and she wasn't doing much for me, with all her tears. But then she said your name, and I knew I had to. To show *you* that you couldn't take what was mine. And do you know what's mine? Anything I want. Anyone. She kept crying afterward so I kicked her out. I was kind of embarrassed, to tell you the truth." He shrugged. "I got over it." He leered at Gavin, saw how aghast he was. "She never mentioned it, huh?"

Gavin couldn't speak.

"You never married her, did you?"

Gavin felt gutted. He'd told his brother a hundred lies about his happy little life and his happy little wife. "No."

The prisoner's face contorted. His eyes darted to the side, then back to his gaoler. "Sixteen years of lies, crumbling, huh? You're probably better off without her anyway. You think while she was making the rounds of the Guiles she slept with father, too?"

Begging his brother to stop or commanding him to stop talking about Karris would be equally ineffectual. "I thought... I always thought you were the good brother," Gavin said.

"Good brother?" the prisoner barked. "Like we're the good twin and the bad twin? We're not twins, Gavin, and neither one of us is good."

"Have you always been like this, or have you gone mad down here?" Gavin asked.

"You made me, little brother, just like I made you." Dazen tossed the shattered pieces of the lux torch away. "Now why don't we end this farce? Open the door. Release me." He spread his hands wide and leaned against the window, intent on Gavin.

Gavin could see blood trickling down his brother's chest from a thickly scarred wound, torn open in his fall. He could see another trickle of fresh blood from the little spikes of hellstone he had rigged to take away all of Dazen's luxin when he fell into yellow.

Dazen was thin, ragged, unhealthy. He was furious, as he had every right to be. Doubtless he was lying about Karris to hurt Gavin. Or exaggerating at the least. But though Karris had never meant anything to him, their mother should have.

I was mother's favorite? Of course I was. Maybe first she'd lavished more attention on me because she saw how much father's abandonment hurt me, how much I needed a parent. But we were kindred souls. She'd probably felt guilty that she loved me more. She'd certainly felt relieved when she learned Gavin was actually Dazen. He'd seen that in her face, sixteen years ago, and tried to deny it since.

I'm like the dog with a bone who crossed a low bridge in the fable. I see another dog passing beneath me carrying a bone, and I snap to take his bone—and drop my own into the water, into my reflection.

He looked at the prisoner, who was glancing at one wall of his cell repeatedly, as if in conversation. It might well have been Gavin's fault that his brother was mad. After all, he was the one who'd kept the man caged, alone, for sixteen years. But it wasn't the kind of transgression he could fix.

Gavin leaned against his own side of the window, hands pressing the immaculate, unbreakable yellow luxin opposite his big brother's hands. "I'm sorry, brother. I'm sorry if I drove you mad, and I'm sorry if you were always like this and I never knew it. But I don't think I can let you out. Not like you are. My world is falling apart. I won't lie to you about that. I murdered a girl. I'm losing my colors. I've lost the woman I love. I...I'm losing everything. But I haven't lost my mind, and in that, I'm up on you."

He felt a sudden wave of peace roll through him like a tsunami, obliterating everything in its path, burying his objections, smashing his protests. His brother deserved to be here. Maybe they didn't get to simply switch places—maybe Gavin didn't get to be the good brother in his own mind now that he'd determined that the prisoner was the bad brother. But his brother was *a* bad brother. A bad man. A danger. If the seed of megalomania had already been sprouting when he was nineteen years old, what would boundless power have done to him if Gavin had let him walk free all those years ago?

Maybe he'd even done the right thing, not just the least bad thing. Maybe locking his brother up had been just.

Maybe not. It didn't matter. He took a deep breath.

"You started the war on purpose to rally allies around you, didn't you? You wiped out that village where I'd been hiding and then men flocked to me. Just to oppose you. You could have gotten me to surrender. I would have. And after that first clash where my men won, you killed our messenger. Why'd you do that? All you had to do was grant clemency to my men, and you could have had me. Was that father's idea, or yours?"

Dazen shot a quick sneer over at the wall. "Look, brother, as nice as this little scam that Lucidonius pulled together is, it doesn't work for some kinds of threats. Take Ilyta. Which satrapies are going to vote to go to war to bring Ilyta back into the fold? None. But a promachos could do it. The Aborneans have been cheating their tributes for decades. The Parians barely pay attention to the Chromeria. The Ruthgari openly manipulate and dominate with their wealth and their lies. The Tyreans—well, I suppose I'm not in much of a place to say what's happened to Tyrea since the war changed everything. Am I right?"

"Yes," Gavin said. His stomach was churning. His joints felt weak.

"You think the Everdark Gates are going to stay closed forever?"

"Ah, the amorphous threat from beyond the Everdark Gates," Gavin said. "You're a student of history, at least. Wasn't it Prism Sayid Talim who nearly got himself named promachos to face the 'armada' that waited beyond the gates? That was forty-seven years ago. Long time for an armada to wait around."

"You look around, Gavin, and you tell me if what we have is working."

Gavin couldn't even get the Spectrum to declare war even after Tyrea had been lost and Atash invaded. How was that possible? His brother was right. Their system was broken, and it would take a man of will to make something new.

"War is the only way to be named promachos," Dazen said. "You need a great crisis. *You* were our perfect opportunity. We could look reluctant going after you. You were my brother. You were Andross Guile's son. No one would think it was a ploy. But you kept trying to end our war before it could really begin."

Gavin felt sick. "And General Delmarta. Was he your man all along?" It had been the general's slaughter of the Atashian royal family that not only mobilized the satrapies against Gavin but also got rid of one of the families that had opposed Andross Guile.

"It was fifty-seven people. You killed more than that in the skirmish at Tanner Creek."

"It's different when it's in cold blood."

"Is it?" the prisoner asked. "Do they end up less dead?" He blinked, looked over at the wall, as if someone was speaking to him.

Gavin didn't answer.

"You tell me, brother," the prisoner said. "Honest question, because I have no way of knowing the answer: how much trouble have you had from Atash since our war?"

It was a body blow. Before the war, the Atashian royals—last remnant of the orders that had existed before Lucidonius—had caused problems and small wars constantly. If the royal family had still been around with their money and influence, their safe havens and their smuggling ships, the Red Cliff Uprising would have been horrendous. As it was, the uprising had failed almost as soon as it began. The slaughter had *worked*.

"Let me out, brother," Dazen said. "You're finished, and you know it. Forgive me for what I said before. Threats and vileness. I didn't mean it. I just fell into this cell hours ago. I'd thought I was out, and you beat me again. You've got an excellent mind, little brother. But your time is done. I can see it in your eyes, and not just in the colors that you've lost. You have the smarts, but I have the will, and now the world needs will. There is a threat out there, and it is growing, and only I can save the Seven Satrapies."

"You were always willing to do what needed to be done," Gavin said. "That was the difference between us, wasn't it?" His breath escaped in a long sigh. "It's all coming apart. There's no way I can save it. Gavin," he said, and it was a relief to call his older brother by his real name. "Gavin, I want assurances. Swear to me, swear before Orholam that you won't take any vengeance on Karris. I don't know how she'll react, and I know you may have to exile her, but swear to me you'll see she's provided for. And Kip. Same terms."

Gavin—the real Gavin—squinted, as if considering the terms and the implications they would have on his reign, moving seamlessly from the mad prisoner to the earnest emperor. "In the sight of Orholam, I so swear."

Gavin the false reached his hand up to the node on the yellow window.

"Wait," the prisoner said. "Before you let me out. We've unfinished business, brother. What do I do with you?" He glanced quickly over at the wall again, a quick crinkle of irritation, instantly smoothed away.

Gavin hesitated. His brother really was magnificent. "I figured you'd kill me. While I'm alive, I'm a threat, aren't I?"

"You've only got a year or so left. Killing you isn't necessary. Father owns a little island off Melos that would be perfect for an exile. Used to keep a mistress there."

"That is . . . quite kind," Gavin said. "I, I've missed you, big brother." He raised his hand to the node and dissolved the window between them. Then he drew the dagger-pistols from his belt and pulled both triggers. The roar filled the little space as the lead balls blasted through the prisoner's body. One punched a perfect hole in his sternum. The other smashed through his teeth and blew out the back of his head. The prisoner's body dropped. Didn't even twitch. The acrid, comforting aroma of gunpowder followed.

Both pistols had fired. Ilytian handiwork. Gavin could admire that. The Ilytians made fine pistols.

He looked over at the wall, where the prisoner had been glancing repeatedly, but he saw nothing but the reflection of a dead man.

Chapter 85

Waiting was part of life for a Blackguard. It was service as much as throwing yourself in front of a musket or magic. But like most of the Blackguards, Karris hated waiting. She'd come upstairs and heard nothing, then had been instructed to wait for the White, who'd been gone for hours.

Another Blackguard eventually came and told the White's room guard that there had been an emergency session of the Spectrum called.

Now, after dawn, the White was finally being wheeled down the long hallway from the lift to her own room. Karris's impatience was quickly replaced by concern for the old woman. She shouldn't be made to stay up all night. The strain of it was evident on her face.

The White smiled at Karris as she was wheeled into her own room, but it was a perfunctory smile. The White had more Blackguards today than usual—two of the new inductees, and Jin Holvar, a woman who'd entered the same year Karris had, though she was a few years younger than Karris.

Karris and Jin helped the White relieve herself, having to support almost all of her weight. Karris had to help her clean herself.

"My apologies, child. The body fails," the White murmured, embarrassed.

The two young Blackguards, Gill and Gavin Greyling, studiously avoided looking back. The time would come when the young men would have to help with this. There simply weren't enough Archers in the Blackguard to have two women on every shift. But right now, they were no doubt simply having to adjust to the very fact that the White needed to relieve herself at all. Karris remembered being young and in awe.

Felt like a long time ago, now.

"You can go," Karris told the young men. "I'll meet you back in the barracks to talk. Jin and I will—"

"No, I want them to stay," the White said wearily. "Jin, you can go."

Jin left and Karris helped the White into her bedclothes. Karris helped the White totter toward bed, and then helped her sit up. It was, technically, not the Blackguard's duty, but the White's room slave was old and frail herself. The White didn't want to buy another slave when she said she had so little time left anyway, and didn't want to get rid of the one she had—little though the old woman did for her now.

The White sighed deeply. "Now," she said. "Work."

"You look exhausted, Mistress," Karris said. "And I need to interview these men. They were on duty, earlier—"

"I know where they were. Why do you think I took them with me?" the White asked.

Karris furrowed her brow.

"The Spectrum," the White said, "has declared war. Tonight we voted on the composition of forces."

"Pardon me?" Karris said.

"Blood Forest and Ruthgar had already mobilized their armies, and they're almost here. They've known this was coming as soon as Atash was invaded. But no one else will be able to get their armies into the fray before Ru's fate is decided, I'm afraid. Andross Guile will be in charge of directing the Chromeria's contribution and managing the Blood Forest and Ruthgari generals."

"So there's to be no promachos?" Karris asked. "And how is Lord Guile going to—"

"It is as it is," the White said. "It was cleverly done when Gavin couldn't be reached, so he and his new satrapy had no vote. The proposals were managed with Andross's typical skill. He knows his parliamentary maneuvering. It was war on his terms or let Ru fall. He wanted to be named promachos, and we had to call it a victory to stop him from that. I suspect he didn't expect to get it, but there you have it. Mobilization will begin this morning."

Karris opened her mouth, but had nothing to say.

"Now," the White said, turning to the Greyling brothers, "tell me what happened in the Prism's chambers last night."

Gill, the elder brother, cleared his throat and glanced at Karris.

"Don't spare her," the White ordered. "She might as well know the truth."

"Yes, High Lady. Um, Gavin and I were selected for guard duty last night. We've been short-staffed, and even though we're new, there were more experienced Blackguards down the hall guarding your room and down at the lifts, so it was allowed. The Prism arrived an hour before midnight. He greeted us and made some jokes with us—"

"Typical," Karris said under her breath. "Charm the new blood."

Gavin Greyling looked away. "I don't know about that. Anyway, he said something about...um, having been on a long trip with a woman he wanted and couldn't have." He licked his lips and studiously didn't look at Karris. "And he asked after his room slave. Gill and I talked about it this morning, and we couldn't remember exactly what he said."

"You interpreted that to mean what?" the White asked.

Gavin cleared his throat again and shifted from foot to foot. "That he, uh, wouldn't be averse to some, erm, companionship. So when the girl Ana showed up, we figured he'd sent for her. She certainly acted like he had. The Blackguards at the lift said they got a story from her that you'd sent for her, Mistress."

"So she lied. It's not the first time she's tried," the White said. "Go on."

"We let her in. We thought maybe it was a common—"

"Not interested in your thoughts on the point," the White said. "What happened?"

Gavin Greyling shifted again, glancing at Karris. "She hadn't been in there five minutes when Watch Captain White Oak came up. She said she had important business. We, uh, tried to dissuade her, but she seemed in a hurry, like she didn't want to be seen in the hall…"

"Tell the whole truth, you bastards," Karris said. Wooden, but even.

"She was wearing cosmetics, and perfume. Her hair was done, I don't know, all beautiful. Like a woman coming for an, an, what's the—" Gavin shot a look at his brother.

"Assignation," Gill said.

Gavin Greyling shifted from foot to foot.

"Back to when you let her in," the White said.

"When we opened the door, it was clear that the Prism had…uh, been woken enthusiastically by Ana. And that the watch captain was surprised by it. Watch Captain White Oak ran out, and the High Lux-lord Prism called after her. He seemed shocked. He ran after the watch captain and went down the lift to follow her before we could join him. We didn't know what to do, so we went back to our station, and he returned a few minutes later."

Orholam. Karris had a sick feeling in her stomach.

"He was absolutely furious with the girl, Ana. We, um, saw her when he went back in, and it was like she thought that they'd pick up where they left off. But he was having none of it. He shouted at her—"

"What did he say?" the White asked.

Gavin Greyling didn't look at Karris. "He said that Ana had cost him the woman he loved. That he'd thought she was Karris—er, the watch captain—and he wouldn't have touched Ana if he'd known who she was. That she disgusted him. The girl said some, uh, vile things about Watch Captain White Oak, and the Prism threw her out onto his balcony."

Oh, Orholam have mercy. Gavin had murdered that stupid girl because she'd insulted Karris? Karris felt like weeping, for Ana, for herself, for Gavin, for the whole stupid world and shipwrecked love.

"We saw…" Gavin swallowed and looked over at Gill, who nodded at him to go on.

"He was shouting and furious, and the girl was so frightened, she jumped off the balcony."

It sent a bolt through Karris. "She *jumped*?!" she asked.

"Yes, Watch Captain," the young man said. "He…he looked mortified immediately. I don't think I'll ever forget the look on his face. He said something like, 'Orholam have mercy, I've killed her.' And then he told us to go report it, and that he would be there when we got back. He looked so stunned that we believed him, Mistress. We didn't know what to do. One of us should have stayed with him. I'm sorry."

"Wait. He didn't kill her?" Karris asked.

"No, sir. She jumped," Gill said.

"And you are both completely certain of this?" the White asked.

"Yes, High Lady," they said at the same time.

"Certain enough to tell this tale to the Spectrum itself?"

Gavin paled, but Gill looked confused. If he was a liar, he was the better one. "Yes, Mistress. Why would we lie?"

The White said, "You would not be the first Blackguards to believe that their duty to protect the Prism extended beyond the duty to protect his life."

Gill blinked. "I understand, Mistress. But we barely know Lord Guile. We just started."

"And anyone who searches your belongings will not find any large gifts among them?"

His face hardened. "We're new to the job, Mistress, not to honor."

"Very well," the White said. "You're dismissed. Go get some sleep. You'll likely be wakened rudely for more questions from others, but you deserve what rest you can find."

She dismissed them and they left, grateful.

Karris turned to the White. "You seemed like you expected that."

"Of course I did. I already interviewed them earlier. I wanted to see if they'd changed their story. And...I wanted you to hear that the man you love was somewhat innocent of both crimes."

Karris blinked. The man I love? Both crimes? "What? What?!"

"He's rebuffed that girl at least twice before. And apparently he had good reason to believe you were coming to his bed last night, seeing as you did."

Karris squirmed, but had nothing to say.

"You know that Blackguards are forbidden to make love with their charges, don't you, Karris?"

"Yes, Mistress." She swallowed. She'd been stupider last night than she could believe. She was normally so rational!

"Have you spoken with Commander Ironfist about this matter?" the White asked. "Help me scoot down here, will you?"

Karris helped the White shift from sitting up in bed to lying down. "Um, no, Mistress. I—I'm afraid I acted impulsively last night, and before that I never thought it would be a, um, temptation." She had a sinking feeling in the pit of her stomach.

The White lay back. "Well, dear, if you had, Ironfist would have told you that he and I had a discussion about this very matter long ago. And then another much more recently."

"You did?" Karris asked.

"Don't interrupt, dear. We did. And we agreed that it's a good rule. Keeps lines clearer. Keeps waters from being muddied."

"Yes, Mistress," Karris said. She straightened her shoulders, took a breath. Her head was still a whirl, but this was the life she'd chosen. She was a Blackguard, through and through. It wasn't easy, but that was why she'd chosen it, because she'd known it was hard. Rules existed for a reason.

The White said, "And we also agreed that sometimes the exception proves the rule. And that you are that exception. If you wish to pursue a relationship with that impossible man, you may."

A sound that may have had some faint resemblance to a squeal jumped out of Karris's mouth. She froze, her lips pursed.

The White opened her eyes and grinned. "May Orholam have pity on us for whom we love, child. Now go find that incorrigible man, and keep him alive. I fear we're going to have great need of him in the coming days."

Karris hugged the old woman tight and ran from the room, pausing only to send the other Blackguards in.

Chapter 86

Gavin climbed out of the hell of his own making one foot at a time. The pulley and counterweights made it so he could go much faster, but the pulley made noise. From the depths, he couldn't know if the noise high above would make any difference, so he had to err on the side of caution.

Some time later, he got to the top. He climbed through the hole, reset the floor as quietly as possible, dissolved the yellow luxin board, and listened at the door. Nothing.

After listening for a full minute, he opened the door a crack. Then more.

There was no one in the room except Marissia, kneeling silently on the floor.

"Marissia," Gavin said, warmed by the sight of her. "I told you to go," he said gently.

She looked at him then, and he was surprised to see a wash of fresh tears run down her cheeks. "I knew you'd come back. Please, my lord, don't send me away. This is all I know. I—Please don't reject me."

Reject? "No, no, no," he told her. "I'm not sending you away. But...Marissia, I've given you your freedom. I would be a faithless man if I tried to take it back from you. It's a gift—"

"And I don't despise it, my lord. Not at all. I treasure it. But I can't accept it and still be your room slave. You would be lost without me, my lord." She ducked her head. "My apologies. That was very presumptuous."

"The truth often is. You're right. I need you. But you could become my secretary. Orholam knows, your duties have already included everything a secretary does."

"And more," she said quietly.

"Well, yes, of course. And the more has been accomplished with aplomb," he said, giving a little smirk. Then the smirk froze.

He'd just killed his brother, and the rest of life went on, not even pausing to notice.

"My lord..." she said, as if he was being dense.

"Yes?" he said.

"You love Lady White Oak."

"Yes, I do."

"It is one thing for a lady to tolerate the man she loves enjoying the companionship of his room slave. It is quite another for him to cheat on her with a free woman. Especially if you had made your favor obvious by freeing me."

Ah. It was so much easier to free a slave when you thought it wasn't going to cost you anything. Damn.

Good thing I don't have anything more pressing to deal with than my loins.

Gavin rubbed his jaw. Popped his neck right and left. "Marissia, I made you a promise, and I would be a small man to—"

"I have a solution, my lord!"

"A solution?"

"That doesn't dishonor the gift you've given me, but doesn't make me go."

Gavin cocked an eyebrow. "You want to stay? I mean, you *really* want to stay? Or are you just afraid of things being different? If you need more money..."

"My lord, I've already written up the contract. It's not manumission, but it's a promise that I can buy my manumission for one danar, whenever I want. That way, you've still given me the generous gift, and when I want, I can take it, without depriving you or making things difficult between you and Lady White Oak."

More difficult, anyway.

"I still don't...you're a room slave, Marissia. You don't even have rights to your own body. If you weren't a slave, you could be a satrapah, a merchant queen, whatever you wanted. Instead..."

"What could I do in this life that would have more meaning than serving you, my High Lord Prism?" she asked.

"How can you say that? You *know* me. You know what I am."

"Yes, my lord, I do. And I—" She closed her mouth, then said instead, "Please don't make me leave."

"I'm not going to make you leave," Gavin said. She was brilliant. An amazing woman. He walked over to his desk, signed the new contract, and brought it to her. She'd already torn up the old one.

Strangely, she was weeping. He handed her the new contract and she took it, still kneeling, and hugged his legs.

He'd slept maybe one hour last night. He'd had interrupted sex with a strange woman whom he'd then killed. He'd lost the love of his life.

He'd prepared himself to die. He'd realized everything he'd believed for the last twenty years at least had been a lie. He'd killed his own brother. He was fucking exhausted.

And yet, with this beautiful woman pressed against his groin, his body reacted. Sometimes he hated being a man.

After all the trouble you got me into last night, you're really going to do this to me?

Marissia noticed immediately, of course. But then, maybe she'd intended it. Usually she was reactive; there would be a question in her initial touches. Not now.

Gavin stepped back, and she stood smoothly in front of him, shrugging her wrap off her shoulders, leaving her sheathed in a pretty chemise. He said, "Maybe I should—"

She kissed his lips, pushed him backward, pulling his trousers down. She guided him to a chair and he sat abruptly as it hit his knees. And then she was on him, her eyes on his, holding him down, possessive. Her lovemaking was a whirlwind, hard and aggressive and fast and hot and sweaty and overwhelming. She rode him until he finished, light exploding in front of his eyes, but she didn't stop like she normally did. If anything, she bore down on him harder until he was worried the chair would break and spill them both on the floor. Her fingers were laced through his hair, holding his head in place, demanding he look into her eyes. Then those stunning green eyes flared and her hips bucked uncontrollably. Her fingers dug into his arm and twisted his hair painfully, and then she collapsed against him.

Gavin was left breathless and stunned. He stood and carried her to his bed. She burrowed into his arms, and gave him up only with a little mew of protest when he released her. He walked over to his own side of the bed and sat on the edge in the dim lamplight.

Though he'd reached his satisfaction, his body was still eager for more. Maybe it had just been too long on the trail with Karris. Maybe it had been Marissia's startling, utterly alluring intensity. He thought of taking her again and numbing his uneasiness. Tomorrow was going to be hell. He just wanted to sleep. For a few hours, he wanted to feel nothing.

Instead, he felt somehow like he'd done something wrong with Marissia. Try as he might, he couldn't think of what it was. Maybe he was just feeling guilty about Dazen.

He lay down, blinking at the ceiling, wondering how the hell he was going to dodge the many flaming arrows coming his way on the morrow. The Spectrum had either already met to discuss the murder or would do so the first thing tomorrow. There was nothing he could do about that now. And since the guards had already searched the room with their usual thoroughness, no one would think to look for him here.

Five minutes later—or at least it only felt like five minutes later—he woke. Marissia was gone. Working, no doubt. He lay in the quiet, idly picking up his problems, then setting them down with no particular urgency. He did some of his best work this way. He remembered that Demnos Jorvis didn't get along with his wife, Arys's sister Ela. He thought about the rate of growth of a bane. Balancing had been done manually before, drafters of one color being instructed to use more luxin for a year, drafters of the color out of control instructed to use less. The Chromeria had quite a reach. He thought of the High Luxiats, the men who determined doctrine that would be promulgated throughout the satrapies, who would no doubt be itching to meet with him after all the strange reports. They loved and feared him, but could he push through a change to the religion itself? He thought of Karris. He would win her back. It was possible now, he was sure of it.

And he thought of his dead brother. He sat up, and saw that Marissia had brought in the tray with the hard square loaves of special bread he'd dropped down the chute five thousand times. He didn't feel guilty. It was like looking into a mirror and realizing you're not a child anymore. But this day, Gavin could look at himself dispassionately. So this is who I am: Gavin Guile, fratricide. The man who'd had the will to kill his brother to save the Seven Satrapies. He was now the man everyone had thought he was for sixteen years.

Almost.

Marissia slipped in the door.

"My lord," she said. "Good, you're up. Your father wants to meet with you immediately. All Little Jasper is buzzing with news of the young lady's death. The Blackguard is being silent while they investigate—waiting for orders from the White, who's sleeping, after being up all night. The Spectrum had an emergency session last night and voted on the composition of the forces heading to Ru. They put your father in charge, but defeated his attempt to be named promachos. Grinwoody cornered me, my lord, and commanded me to get you. He refused to believe that I didn't know where you were."

There were tricks to ruling, tricks to winning and maintaining loyalty through even the fiercest fire. Gavin sometimes forgot that those were as effective on those who knew you well as on strangers. Karris was right: Gavin too often let those closest to him get the worst of him. So he drew a black line between himself and his worries and focused all his attention on the woman before him. "Marissia," he said. "That's no problem. You're marvelous. Superlative. If I make it through today without going to prison or the headsman, buy yourself something really, really nice."

She grinned. "As my lord commands."

Her joy lifted him. He was the Prism. He was Gavin Guile. What could he not accomplish in a year?

Chapter 87

"There are rumors you fought off an assassin last night," Andross Guile said.

"An assassin?" Gavin asked. He'd barely been able to get down here without being seen. He'd been tempted to use the shimmercloaks again, but he wasn't bringing those within a hundred paces of his father. Andross would know, somehow.

His father was sitting in the hellstone-dark room, but Gavin remained standing. He didn't want to be here any longer than necessary.

"There's another that you threw her off the balcony because she wouldn't indulge your curious perversions. Oh wait, I started that one." Andross Guile grinned mirthlessly.

"And who'd you spread that to? The mice? You're a shut-in."

"You think me toothless because I'm old?" Andross Guile asked.

That is generally when people lose their teeth. "I think you're opposing me for no good reason other than to show you can. And it infuriates me, as it would you, were you in my shoes."

"You are a stupid, stupid boy. How long have I been directing you? When have I done anything for no reason?"

Gavin was silent.

"You will marry, Gavin. Within the week. I've decided that—"

"Did you send that girl?"

"Pardon?"

"Did you send Ana Jorvis to my room last night?"

"That fool slattern was either trying to seduce you to salvage her family's chance at winning the marriage with you—which I'd already told them they'd lost—or..." Andross Guile shrugged. "Or she really was an assassin. I heard a rumor that the Order is recruiting young girls. Or perhaps she just thought you would finally succumb to her girlish lusts, which, as I heard it, you did, didn't you?"

"I thought..." No. Gavin wasn't going to talk to his father about whom he bedded, or wanted to.

"Ha! All cats are gray in the dark?" When Gavin didn't respond, the Red said, "Tisis Malargos, you'll marry her. One week. It's not ideal, but there's war coming, and everyone who matters is already here. It will save me a fortune, anyway. And we need allies badly. Why'd you have to throw that girl over the damned rail, anyway?"

"It was an accident," Gavin hissed.

The Red sat back in his chair, a look of triumph spreading over his face. "So you did throw her."

He said it like it was new information. Gavin cursed. Cursing was safe.

"How'd you get to the Blackguards? How'd you get them to lie for you? I tried to buy off those boys myself—did you already own them?" Andross Guile asked.

They'd lied for him. Gavin and Gill Greyling had lied for him.

"Pretty good lie, too: You, furious at being duped, shouting. She panics. She jumps. You blame yourself and flee. It doesn't defuse the enmity the Jorvises will feel, but it saves you from impeachment, and there were too many witnesses for you to have them swear she jumped off some lower balcony. Which brings us back to our need for allies."

The weight of grace was a punch to the face. Totally unexpected, totally undeserved. Ana had been a fool, but she didn't deserve death, and death was what Gavin had given her. Orholam have mercy.

Gavin took a deep breath. He took those feelings, boxed them up, and put them aside. I'll mourn you later, Ana, and make recompense to your family, you damned harlot. I'm sorry.

Today would be a test. If he could make it through five more minutes with his father, he might make it through today. If he could make it through today, he might live another month. If another month, a year was possible.

"No," Gavin said.

"And next time, for Orholam's sake, how about a little self-control?"

"Self-control is for those who can't control others," Gavin said. Then he realized who'd taught him that: this grimly smiling man. "The answer is no."

Andross Guile said, "You appear to be laboring under the mistaken assumption that I'm giving you a choice."

"No mistake: No." Gavin kept his voice level, civil, firm.

"If you choose not to obey me, you're choosing for me to disown you."

The threat literally took Gavin's breath away.

"You think I can't? You think because you're my only child that I won't? I'm not too old to have other children, you know. It was your mother who couldn't, after Sevastian. If you don't marry Tisis Malargos, I will. It's that simple. I don't know if she'd hate being married more to you or to me. Doesn't matter. She's a loyal girl. Loyal to her family. Practical. She'll do what she has to. An example you would do well to follow."

"So you don't need me?" Gavin said. "I'm the Prism. You think getting money is going to be hard for me? You think I'll lack for anything? You really want to start a fight with me?"

"Start it? If you hadn't been so busy fucking that little girl, I think you'd have noticed we've already started."

"What have you done?" Gavin asked.

"I made you, boy. In every way." Andross Guile sank back into the cushions of his chair. "You want to cross me? Look to what you love."

Chapter 88

"I heard that the wights are using hellhounds," Ferkudi said. "In Atash."

"And I heard the Eternal Flame in Aslal burned bright blue for two months straight!" Yugerten said. He was a gangly boy, and ranked low. No one paid much attention to him.

"Anyone can make a fire burn blue," Ferkudi said. "I'm talking hellhounds!"

The scrubs were walking together as a class to go do another real-world training. They didn't know any of the details yet, but after oversleeping, Kip had barely caught up with them before they got to the really bad neighborhoods.

"Burning dogs, made of luxin?" Teia asked dubiously.

Kip was trying to see who was watching them as they walked through increasingly narrow streets to Overhill.

"Hellhounds are a myth, Ferk," Tanner said.

"The man who told me wouldn't lie," Ferkudi said.

"Think, you moron, you're a drafter," Tanner said. "How would you even do such a thing? You could make a statue of a dog out of red luxin, but it wouldn't *do* anything, would it?"

"Well, I don't know. I guess not," Ferkudi said.

"They're not made of luxin," a voice interjected quietly. "But they are real."

It was Trainer Fisk.

The boys fell silent, looked at each other.

"The wights infuse red luxin into the coat and skin of a dog. They do it for practice, before they try it on themselves. It's a cruel, cruel thing, and worse is to set them on fire. But I've seen it happen. I saw Commander Ironfist put one down when we were cleaning up the wights from the False Prism's War."

Their respect for Commander Ironfist jumped up a few more rungs on the ladder to pure worship.

"But wouldn't a dog who'd been set on fire be just as likely to kill the men who sent it as that man's enemies?" Kip asked. "I'd think it would just go crazy."

Trainer Fisk spat. "Dammit, Breaker. It would be you, wouldn't it?"

"What?" Kip asked. He still wasn't used to being called Breaker.

But the trainer said nothing as they entered a small square and passed dirty merchants who stared at them with open hostility. This was a Tyrean neighborhood, but the people here didn't see a Tyrean when they looked at Kip, they saw only a Blackguard whelp.

When they'd passed out of the square and into the next street, Trainer Fisk said, "There's kinds of drafting we don't talk about much with younger drafters, because we lose enough of you as it is, and everyone thinks she's special and tries the things that we tell you not to try. But you all are going to be warriors, and maybe sooner than we'd like, so you deserve to know what's out there."

If he hadn't had everyone's attention before, he did now. The class bunched around him, hanging on every word.

"Breaker's right. You light a dog on fire, it'll go crazy. But drafting is about Will. You know that we use Will for everything we draft, that Will can cover over mistakes we make in matching wavelengths. Lots of theories as to how it really works, but basically, you can infuse your own Will in your work."

"Golems?" someone said.

Trainer Fisk grimaced. "Are almost impossible." He looked like he was sorry he'd started down this road. He looked at the girl who'd said it. "You're a blue monochrome, Tamerah. If you made a golem, it would just sit there in its harmonious blue-ness. A green golem would be totally uncontrollable, as has been demonstrated scores of times. They reject rules and control to the extent that they kill the foolish drafters who create them. So you have to be at least a bichrome to even attempt a golem, and they pretty much always go horribly wrong. Point is, for the question at hand, you can cast your will onto a living creature—in this case dogs. Usually those who've broken the halo—or plan to do so—will experiment on animals first to see how they might successfully change their own bodies. Hellhounds are one permutation of that."

"Permutation?" someone asked.

"Version!" Ferkudi said. "And shut up."

Trainer Fisk went on, reluctantly. "Infuse a dog with lots of red luxin, send enough Will into it to make it run at your enemies, and light it on fire. It's a sick and horrible way to die. They howl in pain and rage, impelled to attack even when they're so far consumed by the flames that you can't believe they're still moving. If you ever have to face one, take the legs off first, and then the head. That usually does it."

"Usually?" Ferkudi said, astounded.

"Enough of that," Trainer Fisk said. "Today, we're inviting trouble. As before, know that some of you may not come back from today's exercise. Of those who do, some of you may come back maimed. You may be knocked out of the Blackguard before you even get in, scrubs, and through no fault of your own."

It was like being dunked in cold water. The levity and wonder of the moment before was dashed.

"We can expect that the gangs have heard about the exercise the other week, and we can expect that they're looking forward to having another shot at you. Here's the setup: the top two teams will be teams of six. Five of you are Blackguards, one of you is a Color. The bottom team will be nine. As always, it is hard to stay on top. Those of you who are Blackguards are not allowed to draft. Your Color is allowed to draft but not allowed to fight. The Color will be carrying a purse with forty danars in it. Enough to attract some serious problems for you, but not enough to start a riot. We hope. The older classes and several full Blackguards will be along the route. If you need help, you call out for it, and they'll come. If you call for help, you fail and everyone in your team drops three places, but being a Blackguard means knowing when to beat a retreat. You start from here, the test is over when you cross the Lily's Stem. Got it?"

The scrubs nodded.

"First up, Teia and Kip, Cruxer and Lucia, Aram and Erato. Kip, you're the Color."

"Why does Kip get to be the Color?" Aram asked. Little bastard.

Trainer Fisk's jaw tightened for a fraction of a second, then he said, "Because Kip's slow. Our current Prism notwithstanding, usually the man or woman you guard is older, slower, and a worse fighter than you are. Part of what we do is deal with that, and protect them despite their weaknesses. That good enough, Aram, or do I need to explain myself to you further?"

Aram scowled, looking away.

It wasn't a bad team, Kip thought. Out of the twenty-one scrubs still left, Cruxer was first place, Teia was seventh place, Aram was eleventh but deserved to be in the top five, and Erato was ninth but deserved to be about fifteenth. Kip was fifteenth—and deserved to be about twenty-third—but that was neither here nor there. Cruxer's partner, Lucia, was ranked twenty-first. She was smart, pretty, and well liked, with short wiry hair and a heart-stopping smile, but not much of a fighter. No killer instinct. No matter how much extra training Cruxer did with her, she was probably going to fail out in the final test next week.

"Kip," Cruxer said. "You have any advice?"

Kip looked at Cruxer, shocked for a moment. Cruxer was a thousand times the man Kip was, and he was asking Kip for advice?

" 'Course he doesn't. Just cause he's Guile's get doesn't mean he's got half the brain his father does," Aram said.

"Head three blocks north and five blocks up, and go from there," Kip said quickly, flushing.

Cruxer said, "That's not exactly a straight route, Kip."

"Not straight? It's about as crooked as it could be," Erato threw in.

"I don't want to be in these slums any longer than I have to."

Trainer Fisk handed Kip the coin purse. "Go when you're ready," he said.

All of the approaches to this little wide spot between the houses and the wall were dark and narrow. There were men down every way, and no way to tell which curious eyes were hostile. Kip didn't see children, and there were few women. He guessed that meant the people here knew trouble was coming.

"Let's go," Aram said. "Straight south and we can cut to the main streets in just a few blocks. Come on!"

"It's not the distance that's the problem," Kip said.

"Kip, you gotta give me a better reason than that," Cruxer said. "We've gotta move. The longer we wait, the more time we're giving—"

"They're right, Kip," Teia said. "We only have to run a few blocks."

"I'm with Aram," Cruxer said. "Let's go! Wedge formation, don't let anyone within arm's length of Kip!"

They pulled Kip into a jog, and then suddenly he stopped.

"I'm the Color," he said.

"No shit," Aram said. "So stop making yourself an easy target!"

They all skidded to a halt, eyes skipping from the men in the alleys ahead of them and going to Kip, who was acting insane.

"You're protecting *me*," Kip said.

"We've established that. Two blocks, two!" Cruxer said.

"We could carry him," Lucia said.

"We'd give up two fighters to do that, at least."

Kip was the Color. They were his guards. They had to protect him. It was that simple. It wasn't a matter of who was the best, or smartest, or who had the highest rank, it was a matter of who was in control. And that was Kip. He was not only in control, he was right.

So he turned and ran the other direction.

More than one oath followed him—words hot enough to blister his ears—but he wasn't listening. In moments, they had surrounded him once more. They jogged past a puzzled-looking Trainer Fisk and the rest of the scrubs.

"It's the gangs," Kip said as they caught up with him. "We've got the Tyrean gangs to worry about first. We cut north three blocks, and we'll cross into Ilytian neighborhoods. Then we cut over into the markets, where the guards don't care where you're from, they don't want big armed gangs coming through regardless. We skip back and forth between gang territories, and they have to worry about each other instead of about us." He huffed. It was hard to talk while running. "Cruxer, give me your spectacles!"

The older boy handed him his blue spectacles. Kip held his own green spectacles up to his eyes first, and stared at the whitewashed buildings. Filling halfway up, he pressed that luxin into his right side, and drew in blue luxin and held it in his left arm.

He wasn't prepared for what it did to him. The calming, cool rationality of blue hit the wild restlessness of green like cavalry lines crashing together.

"Cruxer, you lead, you take it," Kip said. He was blinking rapidly, shaking his head. His temples were knotting up, an instant headache blossoming, radiating down his neck. With an effort of will, he tried to separate the luxins within him.

The alley ahead darkened as five men suddenly appeared, blocking it. They were armed with clubs and chains. The scrubs crowded ahead of Kip, blocking his firing lanes.

"Move or it's on your own heads!" Cruxer shouted. He didn't slow. The thugs blocking the alley didn't move.

"One and two!" Cruxer shouted, calling out his targets.

"Four!" Lucia said.

"Three!" Aram said.

"Five!" Teia said.

Which, of course, left Kip doing nothing.

One was the biggest, a fat, hairy brute who took up the center of the alley. He stood flat-footed, head-on, certain that these children would slow down. He must have weighed at least twice as much as Kip. He raised his club.

Cruxer sped up at the last second, turning to do a slippery side kick, left foot crossing behind his right, and then his right stabbing out with incredible force. It was a hard kick to do quickly when standing still, but its power was without equal. Kip had never seen anyone even try it when running.

But the kick was beautiful. It caught the fat man in the center of his chest and lifted his entire flabby mass off the ground, blasting him backward as if he'd been hit by a cannon blast of grapeshot. His descending club went spinning harmlessly away, and Cruxer was already uncoiling again. A spinning back kick, effortlessly high, his heel crashing across the neck of number two—who went down in a heap, smacking himself with his own chain.

Teia slowed down from her run before reaching her skinny opponent, but she acted almost as quickly, feigning a punch at the man's face, then kicking him in the groin. As he hunched over instinctively from the pain, his face met her rising knee with explosive results.

Lucia tried to engage her own target, but that man was more worried about Cruxer. Cruxer caught the man's descending club in an X block, brought his hands down to grab the man. But the thug snatched his hands back too quickly, barely holding on to the club.

It didn't matter. Cruxer connected one of his shin-strikes across the man's leg. The man went down, howling. Cruxer was on top of him in a moment, standing with one foot trapping the man's foot, and his other foot on the man's knee. He could cripple him in an instant just by shifting his weight.

Instead, Cruxer looked over to the rest of them. Kip hadn't even seen how Aram had dealt with his opponent, but the man was down. None of the others looked like they were going to put up any more fight.

Cruxer grinned, wild, elated, charming. It was the look of a boy who can't believe that all of his training actually works. That he is become what he has always hoped to be. It was, Kip knew, an innocent look. He felt a gulf open between him and the older boy. Cruxer was a warrior-in-training, but he wasn't a warrior yet. Cruxer would be an excellent warrior, but he was also a good man. He wouldn't lose his excellence, but he would lose this joy when he saw heads explode, when he watched friends try to hold in their life's blood as it pumped out of their guts, when he listened to his enemies whimpering and shivering as they died too slowly.

"Let's go!" Cruxer said. "Lucia, you guard the back next time."

"Give me shooting lanes next time," Kip said. "I've got luxin."

They ran on. Kip was getting tired, but he realized that just a few months ago he wouldn't even have been able to jog this far. Now he was keeping up with the others. He'd still be the first to tire, and the first to quit, but he wasn't quitting yet.

On the next block, they caught sight of a group of maybe a dozen men, trying to cut them off, and then stopping and cursing as the squad crossed into the Ilytian neighborhood.

Incredibly, they crossed through the Ilytian area with no trouble. Kip could only guess that the gangs here hadn't heard about them yet.

They didn't cross through the market, though. Kip hadn't realized how formidable his own group looked: the guards whom he'd thought would be unhappy to see an armed gang were definitely unhappy to see Kip and his friends. So Cruxer turned them south again.

"Men following," Lucia said. "Five or six of 'em. Seventy paces back."

Kip looked, and immediately felt dumb for doing it. Now they knew he knew. Stupid!

"Kip? You know this neighborhood?" Cruxer asked.

"Sorry."

"Anyone?" Cruxer asked. "If so, talk quick. I'm not feeling so great about this."

"I've been here," Aram said. "I think I can—Follow me."

He led them for several blessedly uneventful blocks, and Kip started to think they might make it back without any more fights.

Then they rounded a corner. What had looked like it would lead to an open, wide street was gated and chained. There was only the narrow street they'd entered from, and one alley out of the wide space between houses. In the alley, there had to be twenty men. Aram swore.

"Anyone feel like dropping three spots?" Kip asked.

No one answered. That was a no. Not this close to the final test. They'd take a beating if they had to, but none of them was going to just give up.

Kip stepped forward. He braced his feet.

"Semicircle," Cruxer said. "I got point. Kip, you stand on that rock, you should be able to keep drafting while we fight. The rest of us, don't let anyone into the middle of our semicircle."

They formed up as Kip gathered his will. The men in the alley were jogging forward now, constrained in the tight space. Kip didn't know what he was going to do until he was already drafting the big green ball into his fist. It was stupid. If he'd had the practicum, there would be a hundred different things he could do that would work better—but he hadn't. He knew how to do this. Fine. He was the ignorant boy from Tyrea who didn't know any better. He'd show them.

The ball swelled bigger than his head and Kip threw his hands forward with a yell.

The green luxin ball shot out at chest level at great speed. For once, Kip didn't fall on his butt from the recoil. In the confines of the alley, the men didn't have anywhere to dodge. The ball glanced off a man in the front row and then ricocheted back and forth. Five or ten went down as the rest surged into the open space.

Kip extended his other hand, gathering the blue into a spear point, ready to shoot it through the men.

You can't kill them! The blue rationality cut through the wildness, and Kip hesitated. He almost lost his concentration and the blue completely, but recovered. *Pop, pop, pop!* He shot little blue balls at the charging men, low, at their legs. One man tried to jump the projectile, got tripped in midair and landed on his face. Others took them in the knees, and the balls shattered, shooting glassine shrapnel through their clothing.

It was too much for simple street thugs. Even as they got into the range where Kip's drafting would be useless and their own numbers would give them the victory, the charge faltered. The thugs fled, not even pausing to help their injured.

Kip hurriedly put on his green spectacles—stupid! He'd forgotten to put them on before the fight!—and drew in more green. He drafted another green ball into his hands and just held it there, trying to look threatening.

The injured pulled themselves to their feet and followed after their comrades, but down the alley in the dark half-light between buildings, Kip saw one thin figure standing alone, lifting something, peering around the wounded men staggering through the alley.

"Kip," Lucia said, clapping him on the shoulder. She was grinning, impish, delighted. "You were amazing! That was the best—"

From the alley, the briefest flash, a puff of white smoke lit from behind as Lucia stepped into Kip's line of sight.

Something warm splashed over Kip's face, blotted out his vision.

He lost the green. Lucia fell into him heavily, but even as she hit him—in that fraction of a second—he knew something was terribly wrong.

They fell together. Kip caught her and she lay in his arms, half of her neck torn out by the musket ball, her body not yet aware death was a foregone conclusion, pumping blood, blood, blood.

They didn't move. Someone shrieked. For once, even Cruxer didn't know what to do. Desperately, he pulled Lucia out of Kip's arms and held her himself.

Within two minutes, the Blackguards arrived. Then it was orders, investigation, questions that Kip answered numbly. Blackguards armed with the thinnest description ran to see if they could apprehend the murderer. Kip stood, dazed. Someone had given him a towel and rubbed much of the blood off his face. He was still holding that bloody towel, limply, standing, not knowing what to do with himself.

He looked at Cruxer, still cradling Lucia's body, weeping, and he knew that the boy had been in love with her.

Orholam have mercy.

Kip couldn't stop thinking the stupidest thing: I didn't even hear the shot. I didn't even hear it.

Chapter 89

Karris thought she knew exactly where Gavin would be. If he wasn't in his room, that meant he'd drafted a bonnet and jumped off the Prism's Tower. He loved doing that. Show-off. And because no one had known he was fleeing, no one would have reported him leaving. They wouldn't have known it was important.

She checked the library first, though, just in case she was wrong. She walked past the practicum rooms, where she heard boys' voices, cursing as their drafting failed. She checked his personal training room below the tower. Then she headed up to the ground floor. She crossed the Lily's Stem, going against the flow of people who came in every morning with the dawn to work in the seven towers of the Chromeria, and cut down-island. She knew the other Blackguards had already fanned out across both islands, looking for him. With war declared, none of them were happy to have their Prism off by himself with no guards. The big idiot.

Still, Karris felt curiously alive. She felt as if, for the first time in years, she had a future. Life felt possible now. Promising.

She made her way toward the east bay. The fishing boats were already out, though it was barely light. Men and women were pressing seaweed flat to dry in the sun. The tide was just coming in, and she saw several drunken sailors staggering back toward their ships, doubtless overindulging to fortify themselves for the weeks or months of privation they'd face on the sea.

A gang of galley slaves, chained at their wrists to a long pole, were walking together toward the same ships. They looked gaunt and dirty, with long stringy muscles and no fat. One coughed a deep, unhealthy rattle as they passed.

A scent in the air arrested Karris, and she couldn't help but stop at a little storefront she hadn't been to in years. They kept slowly simmering pots of kopi, and at this time of morning it was fresh and beautiful. Especially when you'd been up most of the night.

"Ah, my favorite Blackguard!" Jalal said. He was a round little butterball of Parian. Karris thought he'd had more teeth the last time she'd been here. "Watch Captain..." He snapped his fingers.

"White Oak," she said, grinning.

"Ah, yes! But I find redemption here!" He grabbed a cheap clay cup and a fresh wedge of onion and ladled hot kopi into it. He poured out some of the steaming hot liquid into a clean saucer, swirled it, put it back into the cup, and repeated the saucering until the kopi was the perfect temperature. Then he fished out the onion wedge and spooned in half a spoonful of Ilytian sugar.

"Brilliant," Karris said. "You remembered."

"A kopi man never forgets." He tapped his forehead with his index finger thrice, thinking. "Ah, ah!" Then he produced the kind of small sweet roll that Karris liked. "Yes?"

She smiled. "You're a wonder." It was perfect. Exactly as she'd had years ago, and the kopi was wonderful.

She paid, feeling enlivened by the stimulant and the food, and headed toward Ebon's Hill. There was an estate there that had a

449

gorgeous view of the bay and the rising sun. Dazen had shown it to her when they were first courting.

He hadn't knocked on the door or anything so civil. Instead, he'd shown her how to climb up onto the fence, and from there onto the bulbous dome roof of a neighbor's house. It was quiet, peaceful, and for a young teenage girl, it had felt naughty.

They'd kissed there for the very first time, after holding hands all night, talking.

How was she going to broach the topic, though? "Gavin, you big idiot, I've known you're Dazen for months"? No. She'd merely sit down next to him, watch the sun rise, and then say, "I remember our first kiss here."

The thought of throwing Gavin so far off kilter was more than a little pleasing.

Truth was, they were going to have to do a lot of work. A lot of the lies he'd told her made sense to her now, but not all of them, and knowing why someone had lied to you was different than understanding it, different by far than forgiving it.

But still, she was eager to start living. Scary as it was. Besides, he'd said he loved her, hadn't he? It wasn't like she was going out on a limb.

She rounded the last corner and found herself on her ass, sitting on the ground. It took her a moment to realize she'd been hit in the face. And then a gang of men gathered around her, hitting, hitting, hitting.

She kicked, she swung, she screamed, but her training did little for her. There were a dozen men, all big, and they'd sealed off any form of escape. Her speed was no use to her on the ground. Her weapons expertise no good with her weapons torn away.

Her rage was undercut by humiliation, fear. She was a Blackguard. How could she let herself be taken off guard? How could she be so terrified? She tried to punch, tried to kick, but each of her limbs was trapped. She thrashed. A foot caught her in the kidney. Black stars exploded in white skies. She wasn't supposed to be afraid; men were supposed to fear her. A face leaned close, saying something, and she whipped her head forward, shattering his nose, making his blood explode all over her. She twisted an arm, shattered a man's elbow. Then her head rebounded off the paving stones from a blow she never even saw. And then all emotions faded as she lost her grip on consciousness—and still the beating continued, continued, continued.

Chapter 90

"Blackguards die. Death is our companion," Commander Ironfist said, addressing the scrubs in one of their little training buildings. "Yesterday, one of our own was killed. Lucia."

The remaining twenty scrubs had been given the night off after Lucia's death, but they had been told to be here in formation, first thing in the morning, or be kicked out. All had come.

"Lucia had little chance of making it into our company." The commander paused, letting that sink in. "That's right. In the harsh light of death, other people lie. Other people lie because they fear death, and fear that when they die, others will speak the truth about them. Our challenge is to live in such a way that the truth is no embarrassment. Lucia wasn't a great fighter, but she was brave and she was honorable and she didn't deserve to be murdered by some coward with a musket. We'll find him. We're out looking for him now. And when we find him, we'll kill him. In the meantime, we have work to do. We're the Blackguard. We always have work to do. Trainer?"

Trainer Fisk came before the class, but Kip looked over to Cruxer. The boy's face was like iron.

"War will be your teacher," Trainer Fisk said. "We're going to war. As some of you may know, the Spectrum has decided to send us to defend Ru. We've seen it coming. Now it's here. We'd planned to have two more weeks of training before we selected the trainees out of your class. Especially after Lucia was killed. But Blackguards don't stand still. Better we don't, anyway. The final round of testing is today. I know that some of you might be beat up from fighting yesterday. Sorry. Tough. Your class is down to twenty. Fourteen will become Blackguard trainees." He paused.

"Those of you who get cut, you can try again next season. And I hope you will. Despite that we're taking twice as many initiates as we usually do, this has been an unexpectedly fine class. Your odds to pass next time are very good. You'll be seeded at the top of that class, above the legacies." He scowled. "Now, all of you, to the grounds, double-time!"

When they arrived, jogging smartly in line, Kip saw that there were perhaps two thousand spectators ready to watch them. Of those, maybe only a third were full Blackguards or Blackguard trainees in the years ahead of Kip's class. Kip realized that he wasn't winded from the jog. He was a long way from the physical condition the best students were in, but he was getting stronger. Slowly.

He was also glad that Teia had told him today would probably be the final test. Kip had been able to hide the dagger in the Prism's training room, so he didn't have to wear it on his ankle. And no one could get in there.

As always, they took their places, and Trainer Fisk stood before them to give them the rules. "You pick your colors. No spectacles. No weapons. As before, you can challenge three places above you. You win their token, you can challenge again. Those at the bottom get to challenge first. Mercy or unconsciousness, as judged by me. We know you want to win, and that everything is riding on these fights for some of you, but anyone who maims an opponent during testing will be kicked out. Understood?"

"Yes, sir," the scrubs said in unison. There was a current in the air, like before a lightning storm. This test separated scrubs from Blackguards. Even if they washed out or got injured before final vows, if they made it through today, they would forever have that rare badge of honor: Blackguard. Those who were slaves who made it through today's test would have their contracts put in escrow by the Chromeria itself. Nothing would be allowed to interfere with their training until they washed out or stood to take their final vows and had their price paid by the Chromeria itself. The price they commanded would make their masters wealthy, but the sale itself wasn't voluntary. They would be instantly in a different class. They would, of course, still owe their obedience to the Blackguard, and would serve until retirement. But even a Blackguard slave was a Blackguard. Internally, there was no difference in duties or in privileges: a woman from a hundred generations of nobles like Karris White Oak served on exactly the same schedule as Pan Harl, whose ancestors had been slaves for eight of the last ten generations.

Today was everything.

As Kip and the others walked toward the ring they were each handed a token.

Trainer Fisk said, "If you make it into the Blackguard, you will keep the token you win this week. Whichever token you have at final vows, you will keep with you for life." Trainer Fisk pulled out a necklace he wore and showed them an old gold token with a four inscribed on it. "Those with the highest numbers will be your lieutenants, initially. Now get in line."

Kip got in line, an older trainee checking each name against the order list, and giving the top fourteen fighters gold tokens, those below that bronze. On the front of each coin was a number in Parian script with a verse of some ancient text Kip couldn't read. On the obverse was a fighter, each coin bearing a different etching. But Kip's coin was bronze, with an etching of a woman with a spinning staff on it and a Parian eighteen on the back.

Raising his voice, Kip said, "Sir, I'm fifteenth place, not eighteenth."

The entire circle got quiet. Not only the scrubs, but all the other Blackguards and Blackguard trainees. You didn't contradict a trainer. And indeed, Trainer Fisk's face darkened.

"You didn't check the list? Your cadre didn't finish yesterday. All of you are bumped down three spots."

"That's bullshit!" Kip said. He clapped a hand over his mouth. Blackguards guard their tongues.

"You just lost a color for that, son," Trainer Fisk said. "If you have anything else to say, you'll forfeit. You want to do that?"

Kip swallowed. Shook his head.

"You're counting our fight yesterday as a loss?" This time, the voice was Cruxer's. He came forward. "Did you see how Breaker fought? We made it through everything because of him. We *won*. There were only good neighborhoods left between where we were and where that bastard murdered Lucia. I'm sorry, sir, but Breaker's right. That is bullshit. You're making it nearly impossible—"

"Cruxer! You're still a scrub, and if you don't remember your place, so help me, I will bounce your ass out of here right this second," Trainer Fisk said. "The mission was to bring the money back to the Chromeria. You didn't do it. No excuses. You failed."

Kip had never seen Cruxer angry, much less furious, but the boy was now. For a second, Kip thought Cruxer was going to punch Trainer Fisk. A tremor flew through the crowd like a plucked chord on a psantria. Every Blackguard here had been trained to anticipate violence, and every one of them saw the same thing. But Kip stepped forward and put a hand on Cruxer's arm. "Orholam won't let injustice long stand, right?" Kip said.

Cruxer was religious. Kip thought using a luxiat's platitudes might redirect his classmate.

"A fact we all would do well to remember," Cruxer said. His tone was level, but his eyes didn't leave Trainer Fisk's. Then Cruxer turned.

"So, who's first?" Kip asked quickly. Oil on the waters, Kip, oil smoothing troubled waters.

Trainer Fisk glowered at him, then barked, "Winsen! You're up! Who do you challenge?"

Winsen was twentieth among the scrubs. Mountain Parian, but without their usual tall, thin build. He had a fair amount of baby fat and was one of the younger scrubs. He was an odd one—sometimes brilliant, sometimes terribly stupid. Teia thought that next year he'd be formidable. This year, though, his odds of making it were terrible. Not someone to be scared of. Kip scowled suddenly, realizing he was describing himself, too.

"Breaker," the boy said as they walked together toward the hellstone, "I'm going to stand still and try to draft. I'll fail. Just shoot me hard with one of those green balls of yours, would you? Knock the wind out of me. Get the submission."

"What?" Kip asked, incredulous.

"Try to make it look good, would you?"

Then Trainer Fisk was there. "Colors?" he asked.

"What?" Kip asked. He felt like he didn't understand anything.

Trainer Fisk said, "It's the final fight. Scrubs get access to all their colors; well, minus one for you. It's important that scrubs learn to deal with good luck and bad in the previous testings, but we want this to be a fair test of your real fighting skill. I know you drafted red that once, but you've never declared it."

"Oh, right!" Kip said. In his talks with Teia, they'd agreed that Kip should keep his polychromacy a secret as long as possible. Of course, if he kept it secret too long, he'd simply lose a fight that he could have won. Ante up and play. "Um, blue and green will be fine. So if I lose one...I'll keep green." It was possible that not everyone remembered him using red weeks ago in his fight with Ferkudi, or thought it a fluke, and if Kip kept fighting without other colors, he might confirm that speculation and give himself an edge later.

Winsen and Kip took their places in the dark. They pressed their fingers to the hellstone pillar to make sure they were drained of luxin, though Trainer Fisk didn't press their fingers down very hard. Then they stepped back, and a few moments later the shutters dropped from the colored crystals overhead and the circle was lit in blue and green spotlights.

Wondering if Winsen was setting him up somehow, Kip nonetheless drafted his trusty green bouncy ball of doom. He really needed to figure out more drafting techniques. He was supposed to be some kind of polychrome, and though the little bit he was doing with Teia and Ironfist had hardly taught him anything new, it *was* making him better at what he already knew, but he wasn't sure that would be enough. Strange how in becoming a drafter, it seemed like the last thing he had time to do was—

Across from him, Winsen had a blue staff forming in his hands. It was almost finished when he lost it. The luxin shimmered and broke apart, leaving Winsen stunned for one second.

The green ball was ready; Kip shot it straight into Winsen's gut.

The boy was struggling to draft again and Kip's ball blew through his hands, making him lose whatever he'd been drafting. He woofed and fell down, gasping, as if the wind had been knocked out of him.

Kip ran to the boy and put a foot on his neck. A whistle shrieked and a scattering of polite applause greeted Kip's victory.

Kip helped Winsen stand. The boy hung his head. "Thanks," he said, though, no sorrow in his tone.

"What the— What was that?" Kip asked.

"Don't say anything to the trainer," the boy said quickly. "I'm a slave, Breaker. My owner needs the money he'd get from me making it in. He needs it bad."

"And?" Kip said. So you throw the match?

"And fuck him."

The boy might not get another chance to get into the Blackguard.

"Do me a favor, would you?" Winsen said. "Get in. If I lost to a guy who eventually got in, it's not so bad."

"Do my best," Kip promised. "Hey, Winsen? How good are you?"

Winsen grinned. "On a good day? Top five. Light to you, Breaker."

They parted, Winsen heading toward an aghast, weeping noble. Kip would have felt sorry for the owner if he didn't know that for some reason Winsen hated the man enough to jeopardize his own future. And Winsen seemed like a good person.

It was a good reminder. Kip thought he was at the center of everything. Everything was about Kip—and there were tragedies and comedies passing right before his eyes that he didn't even see.

Nineteen was up next, and given that she was directly below Kip, he figured he'd get a rest. Nineteen was a girl named Tufayyur, and she was ranked appropriately, so far as Kip and Teia could guess. So she'd try for sixteen and then thirteen. Getting lucky twice was a lot more likely than getting lucky three or four times.

Kip took his place in the numbered line, starting to plot his own line of challenges. He wished that he had gotten to stand next to Teia, so he could talk it over with her. She understood this all better than he did. But then Tufayyur came to stand in front of him. "I challenge Kip," she said.

What? Kip looked at her in disbelief and she shrugged. He followed her eyes to who was above him—Barrel and Balder. A flash of understanding illuminated the outlines of something bigger going on, but Kip lost it.

He was the sensible challenge, he supposed. Again. He'd been planning on skipping Barrel and Balder himself. Neither of them should have been placed so low. He thought they should both be in the top fourteen.

But he had to go out to the middle of the ring again. If he lost once, he was out. Just like that.

The crowd didn't even fall silent for these early fights. Kip couldn't blame them, watching the worst fighters who won't even make it in isn't terribly interesting.

They went to the hellstone, and then took their place. The spotlights came on, blue and green, but Tufayyur wasn't interested in drafting. She charged. She aimed a kick at the side of Kip's head and he saw an opening to go for the knee of her other leg with a sharp low kick of his own—but that was a crippling blow. He hesitated. He absorbed her kick instead, his hesitation earning him ringing ears.

She used the opening to punch him in the face twice, light and fast, but enough to stun him.

Kip staggered backward. She hit him in the stomach, kicked for his groin—he barely deflected the latter with a knee but still took the shot in his thigh. She punched for his face again, but he ducked into the blow and her fist smashed against his forehead.

She yelped, but didn't stop. As he hunched, she threw flurries of blows at him. Then she snagged his arm and went for a submission hold.

Kip rushed into her and they both fell, as graceful as mating turtles.

Tufayyur went for a scissor submission with her legs, but her legs weren't long enough to get around Kip's girth and lock easily. Kip rolled on top of her, angling the whole of his body weight onto her torso. He grabbed one of her arms with both of his and then simply lay across her face.

The girl bucked, kicking her feet up to try to roll Kip off of her, but she wasn't strong enough. With her free hand, she went for Kip's nuts, but he pressed his hip down, and she wasn't strong enough to burrow underneath. She jerked, trying to get her hand away, failing.

Then she panicked, unable to breathe, flailing—and the whistle shrilled again.

There was a smattering of applause and laughter as Kip stood and offered her a hand, but she snarled at him and stormed away. "Way to go, fatty!" one of the older Blackguard trainees shouted.

Kip walked back to his spot, already tired, and was surprised to see Commander Ironfist himself waiting for him at the rail.

Oh, thank Orholam. Now that Gavin was back, the commander was going to march in and say, "Breaker is a special case. He's in, regardless," and Kip wouldn't have to go through the humiliation of getting his ass beat by fighters who weren't even going to be in the Blackguard.

As usual, the scrubs leaned in toward him, but the commander gave flat looks to a few and they all melted back. Kip came to stand before him. The commander's jaw was set and he looked so quietly intense that Kip swallowed.

"You think it's different because he's back?" the commander asked, clearly referring to Gavin, but not so much as gesturing toward the tower. Others would be watching. "It's not. You're still on your own," Ironfist said. Then he left.

Kip licked his lips. "Yes, sir."

And Kip was up next. He looked at the lineup. Some good luck, anyway, right? A tiny bit. He could skip over Barrel and Balder and take on Yugerten at fifteenth place. If anything, Yugerten should have been nineteenth or twentieth. Kip had a good chance, right? Sure.

Taking his challenge token, Kip brought it to Yugerten and set it on the rail in front of the boy, who didn't look surprised at all.

Kip took his time getting out to the circle, trying to catch his breath. He saw Teia scowling, thinking.

"We got a lot of fights today, Breaker. Get a move on," Trainer Fisk said.

Yugerten was tall but gangly and awkward, a monochrome blue. The boys took their spots, weighing each other. Then the lights went out—and back on, blue and green.

Kip drafted green as quickly as he could, and Yugerten seemed content to stand back and draft, too. But when Kip shot out a green ball, Yugerten dodged and straightened a moment later, having drafted a pair of t-batons. Kip had never fought with those weapons, but it was clear Yugerten had. With the handles in hand, he swung the batons in a quick circle and brought them to rest along his forearms.

Then the boy came at Kip fast, in order not to give him time to draft anything else.

Kip kicked at his leg, but Yugerten blocked, cracking a t-baton across Kip's shin, hobbling him. He stepped and punched for Kip's stomach. The other end of the baton extended beyond his fist, and it stabbed Kip's stomach hard.

Heaving forward, Kip deflected the follow-up punch and it only grazed his jaw rather than tearing his head off, and Yugerten lost one of the t-batons.

He let it go and punched Kip again. Kip tried to keep his balance and failed; he fell and Yugerten was on top of him in a moment, sitting on his chest, using his remaining baton to choke him.

Kip got one hand in front of his neck, but Yugerten was using both of his hands and all his weight to press down. Kip kept hoping the blue would shatter. Blue wasn't supposed to be good for this, but it didn't. He punched with his free hand, caught a shoulder. Punched, glanced off Yugerten's forehead. Punched, weaker.

The world was turning dark, stars blooming in Kip's vision. He couldn't breathe. He was staring into the spotlight—

He flooded blue luxin around the entirety of Yugerten's t-baton. He found the seals on the baton and opened them. The baton dissolved suddenly in a small cloud of chalk and resin.

Without the thing he'd been putting all of his weight on, Yugerten pitched forward, straight into Kip's forehead, and instantly went limp.

Kip rolled the boy off of him and stood.

When Yugerten was revived, there was applause. He'd just been knocked out, but he'd be fine. Kip walked over and grabbed the boy's challenge token. Still bronze, fifteenth place. This one depicted a man with crossed swords sheathed behind his back, unlimbering both.

Aram was at fourteenth, and was one of the best boys in the class. Tala, a yellow/green bichrome named after the hero of the False Prism's War, was at thirteen. She wasn't the greatest fighter, but she was an excellent drafter. Kip hoped she made it in.

That meant Kip had to go for number twelve, Erato, one of Aram's friends. Erato was actually the worst fighter out of Aram's friends, quick but unimaginative, so it was strange that she was the highest-ranked.

Kip paled, looked at the places again. If he and Teia had ranked everyone in the class correctly in their conversations, this was all wrong.

"You going to stand there all day, or are you going to challenge someone?" Aram asked. "Please pick me."

Fighting Aram was suicide, even if Kip did want to wipe that smirk off the boy's face. No. Kip wasn't seeing it. He needed a new perspective. The light in between the fights was full-spectrum—and so was Kip, right? He tightened his eyes and drafted superviolet. Superviolet was supposed to be alien, aloof, apart—and arrogant.

Oh shit. Kip forgot that the first time you draft a color, it exerts a lot more control over you. He walked up to Erato and slapped his challenge token down. "Trade you my bronze for your gold," he said.

Erato laughed at him.

"Colors?" Trainer Fisk asked.

"Green and yellow," Erato said.

"None," Kip said.

"What'd you say?" the trainer asked.

"I don't need any colors to throw out this trash."

"Ooh-hoo!" Erato said, her eyes gleaming.

"You get a bonus if you're the one who knocks me out?" Kip asked.

Her face went blank, stricken, for half a moment. Then she said, "What are you talking about?"

"Do you have any idea how much smarter I am than you?" Kip asked.

All emotions but hatred drained out of her face. "I'm going to enjoy this, Breaker."

They took their places in the middle of the large circle. It was twenty paces across. Stepping out for more than five seconds would result in disqualification. Neither of them had spectacles. They would get pure light from the great colored crystals above the huge underground chamber.

Trainer Fisk examined each of them in turn to make sure they hadn't already drafted, being more careful now that they were in the fights that mattered. "Eyes, palms." Satisfied, he stepped back and gestured that the crystals above be covered. He put their fingers on the hellstone, but didn't press hard enough—as he hadn't before.

Taking a deep breath, Kip rolled his shoulders, shook his head, loosening up. He took his spot across from her in the darkness.

"And...go!" Trainer Fisk shouted.

The shutters over the crystals dropped open.

Kip charged. He didn't try to draft the green or the yellow light streaming over him. Instead, he threw one hand forward and shot out the superviolet luxin he'd already drafted, poking Erato in both eyes.

She staggered backward, crying out, holding her eyes, plans blown.

Then Kip, sprinting, jumped straight at her, spearing her stomach with his head. She went down hard, air whooshing out of her lungs.

Landing on top of her, Kip scrambled to his feet and picked up the prostrate girl by the waist of her trousers and her collar, ran her to the edge of the circle, and heaved her out of it.

Kip heard gasps in the crowd, and a few claps. Trainer Fisk counted out the five as Erato struggled to get to her feet and failed, then called it. "Breaker wins! Take Erato to the infirmary. Breaker, you have one minute until your next fight." He came closer and lowered his voice. "So you can use superviolet now?"

"A little, sir."

"You know you're not supposed to pack luxin."

"Someone taught me to use every advantage and surprise I have." That someone, of course, was looking at him.

"You got it past me, but it won't happen again, Breaker. Smart not to declare your polychromacy, but you won't always get lucky and have opponents use your colors. Hope you've got other tricks."

"Always, sir," Kip said. Inside, he thought, Me, too. He shook out the last of the superviolet. The arrogance there hadn't cost him—but it should have. No colors? How stupid was he?

Trainer Fisk said, "Also, never do that spearing thing again. You'll break your damn neck."

"Yes, sir."

"Breaker, come here," Cruxer shouted. He stood at the edge of the circle.

Kip came over.

"You're not safe yet, you know that, right?"

"I know. I've got to win one more."

"You have a plan?" Cruxer asked.

"Might not be a good one," Kip said. "I..." He trailed off. He looked again at the placement. He was number twelve now. He had to finish the day at fourteen or better to stay in, but after he fought, everyone below him got to fight next. So if he won one more fight, he was safe, but if he lost this fight, the next fighter would be Balder. From his spot at eighteenth, he would challenge sixteenth, Yugerten, rather than take on his friend Aram at fifteenth. Yugerten had already failed out, so no problem there. Then Balder would take on Tala at fourteen. She was a great drafter, but she wasn't that fast, not yet. He'd take her out easily, clearing the path.

From there, he could either challenge Kip or skip right past him and challenge eleven.

Maybe he'd even climb higher, but that didn't matter. The only people who could climb after Balder went were the lower-ranked Aram and Barrel.

All of Barrel's fights could be against people who'd already lost. And he, too, could skip right past Kip.

Then Aram would go, again only having to fight people who'd already lost until he got past Kip.

If Erato hadn't bungled and lost to Kip, all four friends would still make it into the Blackguard training.

The more Kip looked at it, the more brilliant it seemed. Aram, Balder, and Barrel all belonged in the top ten. Even Erato was close. One or two of them might easily get unlucky and come to the final testing lower than they deserved, but *all* of them?

"Kip, you look like you just swallowed a lemon," Cruxer said.

And all of them, despite finishing low, were in places from which they could still make it into the Blackguard—and without ever being pitted against each other, or against Kip. If they'd made a pact to keep him out and had grouped themselves thirteenth, fourteenth, and fifteenth to make a ceiling beyond which he couldn't rise, the collusion would have been obvious. But this, this was subtle.

Hell, they'd guaranteed that twentieth and nineteenth places would both challenge Kip, so if he'd been a good boy and lost, they wouldn't even have had to fight him at all in order to knock him out of contention, and even if he won against nineteen and twenty, he'd be fatigued and easier to beat.

"It's a conspiracy," Kip said quietly. "And they don't even have to touch me."

"What?" Cruxer asked.

"Cruxer, can I win against nine, or eleven?" Teia was at ten; he wasn't going to take her on.

"Anything *can* happen."

"How about against Aram?" Kip asked.

"No."

"What happened to 'anything can happen'?"

"Not *anything*," Cruxer said.

"Kip, time's up," the trainer said. "Who are you challenging?"

For one mad moment, the green in Kip wanted him to challenge Aram—even though Aram was two spots below him.

That was stupidity. Kip could still be wrong. Or others might lose. It didn't have to be the way he'd foreseen.

"Kip, challenge me," Teia said, her tone flat.

He knew instantly what she meant. She'd let him win. He'd get in. It's who you know, not how good you are. Kip wanted to get in with his whole heart. They were going to bury him. But if he got in by cheating, it would taint everything he ever achieved. He would be no better than Aram and his friends.

And if Kip and Teia got caught cheating—which the trainers always looked for when partners sparred—both of them would get bounced. For him, it would be embarrassing. For Teia, it would be a total disaster.

Yet she'd offered. She was a friend. A real friend. Better than he deserved.

Kip stepped forward and challenged number eleven, Rig.

"Kip!" Teia said.

He ignored her, didn't look toward her at all even after he got into the ring. He asked for superviolet and blue for his colors. Rig had red and orange, but Kip knew he was finished. Red and orange weren't helpful in the kind of training fights the Blackguard did, because there was no safe way to light an opponent on fire. The training was naturally biased against Rig, which meant that he could only be ranked so highly because he was a great physical fighter.

It wasn't until Kip stepped into the ring that he realized an even worse blunder than picking Rig. He should have declared all colors. He had nothing to lose now. The whole point of not declaring the colors was so he could use them on his last fight, and in his rash idiocy and false heroism, he'd blown it. Teia had been trying to tell him—and he'd thought she was going to praise him for his nobility or something.

The whistle blew, and it went just as Kip expected. Rig would dart in and disrupt Kip every time Kip tried to draft, and soon he closed and they grappled. Rig slipped behind Kip, keeping his face down and batting aside every attack Kip tried with blue luxin until Kip was empty. Then Kip did the only thing he could think of: he filled Rig's mouth and nose with superviolet while imprisoning his hands.

But the boy didn't panic, didn't move: he snapped the superviolet with his tongue and teeth and choked Kip out.

And just like that, Kip's future was out of his own hands. He was twelfth out of fourteen. Rig helped him stand up. "Nice try there, Breaker. Best of luck making it in."

But Kip knew he'd already lost.

Chapter 91

~The Master~

Tap. Tap.

Hurtled into the pitch blackness of the chamber, Kip still somehow knew exactly where everything was.

I memorized the room. That was it.

Tap. Tap. Tap. And in. Boom.

Kip? Something about Kip? Why did that pass through my mind? I cock my head to the side. Odd. Doubtless, the whelp is asleep on the deck, recovering.

I take my gloves off and try to suppress the rage that floods me at the sight of my hands.

Damn them. Damn them all.

Thin threads of red luxin glimmer in the darkness, veins of fire through the dross of my skin. I push back my hood.

Where is the boy hiding it? I'd had his room searched, hired pickpockets to jostle his tubby body. Nothing.

Rage crests and I ball my fists, clamping my eyes shut. I can feel the room growing brighter, hotter. I'm going to make it to Sun Day. To hell with it.

I'm going to go now and find him. I'll beat the boy to death, injured as he is, if I have to. Maybe it is madness.

My hand is on the door before I remember my gloves and cloak. I pull on the gloves and snarl at the brief reflection of a man limned in red fire in the mirror. I pull the hood down and step into the hall.

"Captain!"

Chapter 92

Kip went to stand by Teia and Cruxer. At their prodding, he explained his conspiracy theory, and then, together, they watched it play out, exactly as he'd foreseen. Balder fought and beat Yugurten, then he fought and beat Tala, and for a moment Kip thought the boy would challenge him—and give him another chance—but instead, sneering, the boy challenged eleven and won.

That eleventh fight took a lot out of Balder, though, and he got smashed against nine. They reordered, and with Balder now at eleventh, Kip was moved down to thirteenth place.

Then Barrel was up. He fought as Kip had expected, too, skipping Aram and taking on fighters who were already out, and then skipping Kip, who spat at his feet. Barrel made it to twelfth, and lost to ninth.

Kip shuffled down to fourteenth. Aram challenged three up from himself, fifteenth, which was Erato. She was already out no matter what, so she conceded without fighting.

All Aram had to do was win one more fight, and if he did, Kip was out. He came up to the bar and looked over the prospects, standing almost directly in front of Kip.

"You *coward*," Kip said. "You're not smart enough to figure this out. Who did it? How much did they pay you to do this?"

A flash of fury came over Aram's face, quickly smoothed away.

"You *cheater*," Kip said. "What did you think, that you're some modern-day Ayrad? Ayrad didn't take money for what he did. He didn't use a team. You're *shit* compared to him. You're going to skip me. *Me*. The one you were hired to block. You think you're the best in the class, you think you're better than Cruxer, but you're afraid to take me on."

"I've got a lot of fights to win today, Kip. I don't need to tire myself on unnecessary—"

"So fighting me will tire you out? Thought you were amazing. Didn't Ayrad fight everyone in the class on his way up? And you won't even fight one fatty at fourteenth place. You're a legend all right, Aram. Aram the Unready, we'll call you. Aram the A-rammed." Kip had no idea what the latter meant, he just made it up. "Aram the—"

Aram slammed down his token in front of Kip. "I'm going to kill you," he said. He strode off into the middle of the circle.

Cruxer was at Kip's side an instant later. "Brilliant, now, Kip, after the back kick, Aram likes to throw a roundhouse punch, either stomach or face. He gets a lot of power into that thing, but if you can sidestep and come in, he'll be wide open."

"I've seen it," Kip said. "I'm just not fast enough to take advantage of it."

"Time!" Trainer Fisk announced. "Come forward."

"Anything else?" Kip asked Cruxer. "Please."

"He's a fast drafter, too," Cruxer said weakly. "Watch out for that... You're lucky, though, right, Breaker?"

"Very."

"Breaker, forward or out!" the trainer shouted.

"That's something then," Cruxer said.

"I didn't say it was good luck."

Kip turned to walk into the center of the circle. Then he saw the worst thing in the world. A ripple of recognition passed through the assembled Blackguards and trainees as someone came to the front rows to watch. Gavin. Gavin was here. Prism Gavin Guile himself had come to see his son test.

And Kip was about to fail.

Of course he'd come now. Of course he couldn't have come early enough to see Kip win the earlier fights. To see Kip do clever things. No, he came *now*, when Kip was out of ideas and out of luck. Just in time for Kip to shame him.

"Are you ill, Breaker?" Trainer Fisk asked.

Oh, and of course the Prism sat next to Commander Ironfist. Might as well let everyone down at once. Beautiful.

"I'm envisioning a great victory," Kip said.

"You arrogant little shit," Aram said, sneering.

"I didn't say it was mine," Kip said.

"Huh?"

"Not my... victory. Look, jokes don't work when you have to explain the— Forget it."

"Are you calling me stupid?" Aram asked.

Um, no, but shoe fits.

"I am going to punish you, *Kip*." Aram said it in such a way that he clearly intended using Kip's birth name to be offensive. Which it wasn't.

"I think we really don't understand each other at all," Kip said.

"Enough!" Trainer Fisk said. "Colors?"

"Green and yellow," Aram said.

"All colors," Kip said. No reason to hold back now.

"You're claiming to be a full-spectrum polychrome, Breaker?" Trainer Fisk asked.

There was a right answer here. "Um. Yes?" Kip asked.

"Bad time to announce that," Trainer Fisk said.

"What?" Kip asked. He'd thought it was the perfect time to announce it.

"Full-spectrum polychromes have such advantages over normal drafters that the Blackguards long ago established that to test their actual ability to be a Blackguard, they must be limited to share whatever colors their opponent chooses, plus one."

"What?" Kip said. "So by my saying I could draft more colors, you give me *less?*"

"Precisely."

"Well that's bull—" Kip stopped, barely.

Trainer Fisk arched an eyebrow.

Kip scowled. "That's very hard to take," he said. He cleared his throat. "And I don't think it's fair."

"I don't think it's fair, the Prism's bastard says. You little bitch," Aram said. "You shouldn't even be here."

"Aram, I don't know who bought you off, but I'm going to crush your face," Kip said. "You're going to beat me today. No doubt. But I'll be back."

"I'm going to hurt you, Kip. I'm going to make you blubber like the fat little piggy you are."

"Fuck you," Kip said.

"Breaker," Trainer Fisk said, "you are right on the line. Say one more word and you lose your extra color."

"Word," Kip said.

"Orholam damn you!" Trainer Fisk shouted. He grabbed Kip by his collar, and Kip heard the crowd gasp. "That's it! You lose your extra color. You know, boy, you have a choice: are you going to be Kip the Lip, the loser who always has the last word, or are you going to be

Breaker? I think you've made your choice for today. Maybe when you come back in six months you'll be grown up enough to choose differently." Trainer Fisk was seething. He turned to the crowd. Why was he so angry? Why was he so hostile suddenly?

Kip the Lip. He'd said Kip the Lip. Where—

Andross Guile. That would also explain why Trainer Fisk was so angry. He wasn't angry at Kip; he was angry about Kip. Andross Guile was forcing Trainer Fisk to make it as hard as possible for Kip to pass—forcing Trainer Fisk to betray his oaths. It didn't matter how. What mattered was that Kip was making what Andross Guile had asked Trainer Fisk to do all too easy. The trainer didn't even look at Kip now, as he announced, "Kip Guile has claimed to be a full-spectrum polychrome. There hasn't been one of those in the Blackguard for seventy years. There are rules. We've consulted them. Because of their innate advantages, full-spectrum polychromes get to choose only one color in addition to what their opponent chooses. For foul language, Breaker loses that choice. The colors for this bout will be green and yellow."

Ironfist's gaze was like a millstone. Kip looked away, and found his father's. Gavin Guile looked disappointed already.

Damn me. Damn me. Kip the Lip. I played right into his hands. Kip Almost.

That's who I am. Almost. I almost beat the Threshing, but I gave up. I was almost a hero, but I chose cowardice instead. I almost saved my village. I almost saved Isa. I almost saved Sanson. But I didn't even *almost* save my mother. Hell, *almost* is generous. I haven't almost avenged her. I swore I would. I took some little steps, telling myself I had to make it to the Blackguard to get access to the records in the library, but really, I've been happy to forget her. Some son. Some loyalty.

They might have conspired to keep me out of the top fourteen, but could I have really made it on my own? Probably not. Would I have made the top seven? Definitely not. The only good things in my life are the things that have been given to me. No wonder they hate me. I haven't earned anything.

"Why little Kip the Lip, are you crying?" Aram said.

"I'm going to kill you, you motherfucker," Kip said.

A backhand cracked across Kip's jaw, staggering him. Trainer Fisk said, "Kip, one more word, and I'll spare you the beating you're about to get and revoke your chance to try again in six months."

This time, Kip said nothing. He didn't even spit out the blood in his mouth, lest Trainer Fisk misinterpret it.

"Trainer," Aram said. "I'd like to withdraw one of my colors. I only need green."

The trainer nodded and gave the order. Then he said, "Hands."

Each boy in turn let his finger be pressed firmly on the hellstone and then took their places, illuminated only in white light.

Then the lights were shuttered.

"And..." Trainer Fisk said. Kip started running forward. He thought he had the timing just about perfect—"Go!"

Kip was already airborne as the lights came blazing on. Flying side kick. And miraculously, Aram was still standing right in line.

The boy's eyes went wide and Kip's foot slammed into his shoulder and chest. It launched Aram backward.

Kip fell, but popped back up to his feet in a moment. Aram had been shot all the way out of the circle. He rolled over, coughed, and for one moment Kip thought he'd knocked the wind out of his opponent. If Aram wasn't able to breathe for five seconds, Kip would win, just like that.

"One!" Trainer Fisk shouted, starting the count.

Aram jumped back to his feet and rushed back into the circle. Kip met him at the edge, determined to keep him out.

"Two!"

Back kick. It was fast. So fast Kip was lucky to jump backward out of its reach, which also meant he was safe from the follow-up punch, which also meant Aram got into the circle with no problem.

And there goes my chance.

Aram was still in pain, though, Kip could tell. Unless he was faking it to lure Kip into some kind of trap. On the other hand, why would he need to lure Kip into a trap? He had his color, speed, strength, and a lot more training.

As Kip moved in closer, Aram lashed out. A lightning-fast pop to Kip's nose. Too fast to stop. It wasn't hard, but it stunned Kip. Then Aram was on top of him. Kip didn't see the move that cut his feet out from under him, but he fell on his side, hard.

Kip had gotten halfway up when Aram hit him with a green luxin baton across the back.

"Come on, Breaker!" someone shouted.

Kip struggled up to his knees again. And grunted as another baton cracked across his back. But he didn't go down.

He saw the thought cross Aram's mind: he could crack that baton across Kip's head and put him out. But a shot to the head might leave Kip an idiot, and that would get Aram barred from the Blackguard forever.

For once, the rules were helping Kip.

Not knowing what else to do, Aram slammed the baton into Kip's back again. Harder.

Kip looked up at him and grinned. Don't you know what I am? I'm the fucking turtle-bear.

With a roar, Kip came to his feet as Aram was winding up for another swing. He caught Aram's hand in his own and pushed against him. Aram kneed Kip hard in the gut, but that only meant the older boy was off balance as Kip locked a foot behind his.

Kip landed on top of the boy, but lost him almost immediately. Aram slid around and got under one of Kip's arms and started battering his kidney with his fists. Kip tried to push off the ground, but somehow he couldn't get any leverage anywhere. Green luxin imprisoned his hands.

"I've got you, Kip. You feel that freedom?" Aram whispered harshly in his ear. "I'm giving you just enough so they don't call the fight. Just enough so I can punish you."

Pain stabbed through him, making it hard to think, impossible to plan. Aram let him slip a little out of the grip and then corralled him again, grinning fiercely.

Hands manacled behind his back as he rolled onto his side, Kip used the pain like hammer blows hardening his will. He stared up at the crystals above them, bathing them in green light—and fired tiny pebbles as hard as he could at them.

A fist crashed across his jaw and he rolled heavily onto his back. Then something cracked and the green crystal overhead shattered, plunging them into darkness and showering them with crystal rain. Kip had not only shattered the green filter, but also the mirror behind it that turned the light toward the practice field. Cries of alarm went up from the crowd.

Kip was ready for the darkness—and Aram wasn't. He lost his grip on the open green luxin he'd been using as Kip's manacles. The manacles broke open and Kip slipped out of Aram's grip and swung an elbow toward the boy's head that struck a glancing blow.

Then Kip was on his feet. He relaxed his eyes into sub-red, and he could see. Aram was on his feet, staring this way and that.

Kip slugged him in the stomach and stepped back quickly. Aram turned, recovered, grunting. Kip slid to the left and punched the boy's kidney.

Then, too soon, someone in the crowd cracked open a mag torch. No! Someone threw up a yellow flare. Kip tightened his eyes back to normal vision, and thought, Yellow, I can draft that if I'm—

But Aram's first thought was martial rather than magical. He hit Kip in the nuts and tripped him.

Kip's face bounced off the dirt, and then he was crushed by Aram's weight as the boy jumped on top of him.

Aram pummeled both of Kip's legs, hard punches right in the sweet spot in the middle of the thigh, rendering them useless.

Pain is nothing, pain is nothing, pain is nothing.

It didn't matter what Kip told himself. This wasn't pain; this was his body's simple refusal to obey orders.

Think, Kip, think! One shot can end a fight.

One lucky shot. Orholam, please! Give me one lucky shot!

He flopped over onto his stomach. Even with the few grappling classes Kip had attended, he knew it was a stupid move. Your hands and legs—your weapons—go forward, not backward. Not well, anyway. He presented one elbow as what he hoped was a tempting target, and then convulsed his whole body, jerking his head backward as hard as he could, hoping to smash Aram's face.

The back of his head glanced off the side of Aram's cheek. Not enough.

The circle lit up again with natural white light as other mirrors were shifted onto the field, and the yellow light was extinguished. Kip's one hope, dashed. He hadn't even had time to draft the yellow. Green filters flipped back on.

Then Kip's hands were trapped. Must have been trapped in luxin. A fist smashed his right ear. Another hit his left. Then his cheek. Then his mouth.

Right, left, right, left, right.

Kip was losing sense. But Aram had gone crazy. His leglock loosened as he concentrated solely on battering Kip to a pulp.

With a yell, Kip bucked and Aram lost his balance and fell forward. Kip wriggled to his knees, but Aram clamped down on him, smashing his fists harder and harder into Kip's face.

Crying, stupid with rage and pain, blood blinding him, Kip roared and stood—lifting the older boy into the air, half on Kip's back and half on his shoulders. He felt the boy stop punching him and his hands slip as he tried to collar Kip.

"You can do it, Breaker!" someone shouted.

The only thought in Kip's mind was to crush Aram like a bug. Screaming over the sounds of Trainer Fisk's incessant whistle, he lurched and threw himself toward the ground and—

Into a large red pillow. Inexorably, Kip's limbs were pulled away, and Aram's weight was borne away from him.

The clouds of dense red luxin faded, leaving Kip on the ground, still crying. Trainer Fisk examined him briskly to see how bad his injuries were, then stood.

"Aram wins. The top fourteen is decided. From here on up, we fight for placement. But Aram, you lost control. You damn near got yourself expelled. You're done for the day."

"No!" Kip shouted.

Trainer Fisk looked at him, then looked away, as if Kip was shaming himself.

Kip was weeping. Not from the pain, though everything was pain now. He'd been so close. He could have crushed Aram if they'd just let them finish the fight. He'd almost—

Almost. He was Kip Almost. Kip the Failure. Almost good enough. He was bleeding and weeping and snotting all over himself.

He looked up and expected to see Gavin leaving. Kip was an embarrassment. A weeping little girl where Gavin needed a son in his own image. Kip was nothing like his father. How could the acorn fall so far from the oak? Instead, Gavin held his gaze and beckoned Kip to come over.

Kip stood up and walked over toward the wooden bleachers where his father was sitting among all the trainees. He looked down, humiliated, humiliated by the tears dripping down his face, unable to stop, unable to hide.

Someone started clapping. Then others joined the one, and everyone was clapping. Kip looked to see if Aram was flexing or something. He wasn't. Everyone who was clapping was looking at him. Him?

Kip rubbed his forehead, trying to hold himself together. Him? For *him*?

Ah fuck. He started crying harder. He'd wanted to be one of the
Blackguards. They were the only people he respected. The only

people in the world he wanted to be like. And he'd failed them, but they gave him this.

He took a towel, ostensibly to wipe up his blood. He covered his head. Someone put an arm around him, and Kip saw his father.

"Father," Kip said. "I...if they hadn't blown the whistle...I almost..."

"The boy panicked, Kip. That grip he was going for is a neck-breaker. And I think he got it. If they hadn't blown the whistle, when you hit the ground, you'd have been dead."

Aram had gotten the grip. Kip had felt Aram's arms locking into place. If Aram had killed him, Aram would have been kicked out of the Blackguard. Not that it would have done Kip any good at that point.

"I failed," Kip said, not quite daring to look out from under the towel over his head.

"Yes," Gavin said. "He's better than you. It happens. Smart work with the crystal there. It almost worked. Now come on, let's go watch. It's good to learn from those who are better than you are. Looks like your nose is broken. Best to set it quick."

Kip touched his nose gingerly. Oh, that was *not* the right shape for a nose. "Is that the thing where it makes that sound and I scream?"

"Try not to," Gavin said. Heedless of Kip's sweaty hair, he reached behind Kip's head, holding him in place, and grabbed his nose, pulling on it.

Kip gasped, gasped, breathed. Orholam have mercy!

But he didn't scream.

Sure, *that's* the one thing I don't fail today.

He followed Gavin to the bleachers, but the only part of what his father had said that stuck with him was "almost" and "He's better than you."

A green drafter chirurgeon brought superviolet-infused bandages and tended to Kip's cuts as they watched the remaining fights. With tiny needles and thread of green luxin, the man stitched up Kip's right cheek and left eyebrow, then smeared stinging unguents on those and several other cuts.

Then he gave him what Kip thought was far too modest a dose of poppy tea. Kip was glad he was sitting, because he didn't think his legs were going to let him stand.

All in all, watching the fights was absolutely no good in teaching

473

Kip anything because he couldn't pay enough attention to learn. It was, however, a good distraction. Teia defeated a challenge, and then won two fights against boys who looked stunned at how fast she was. She ended up at seventh. Kip was proud of her. He could tell from her quiet grin that she was proud of herself, too.

They watched until the end. Watching Cruxer fight was art. He'd been bumped down to fourth by their "loss" in the real-world testing, too. He challenged third, second, and first—and won. Kip saw his father look over at Commander Ironfist, impressed. "He a legacy?" Gavin asked.

"Third generation. Inana's and Holdfast's son."

"Should have guessed. They still alive?"

"Inana is. She's been holding on. For this."

"He's amazing," Gavin said. "He might even be better than you were."

Ironfist raised an eyebrow.

Gavin grinned.

Ironfist grunted. It might have been assent. "If he lives long enough."

"I should go see Inana," Gavin said. "She was a gem."

The scrubs began lining up for the little ceremony that would see them become trainees. Kip's stomach turned. "Can we go now?" he asked.

Gavin said, "This is your friends' moment of triumph. Think about someone other than yourself. You turn your back on them now, and they'll remember it forever."

Kip blinked. Blinked. I'm a self-centered brat.

"Yes, sir," he said.

Commander Ironfist got up and went forward. All the scrubs were lined up according to their placement in the top fourteen. Except for Cruxer, who was down on both knees in the training circle, head bowed, one hand to his eyes and forehead in the sign of the three and the one, praying.

"Cruxer!" Trainer Fisk barked. He was standing in front of Aram at the bottom of the line, ready to pin the Blackguard pin to each scrub's lapel. "Time to pray later."

The scrubs were smirking, triumphant, accustomed to and amused by Cruxer's quirks. They all stood proudly, hands folded behind their backs, stances wide, chests out. All around the training ground, the older trainees and the full Blackguards were standing up, coming to attention themselves. Standing the same way.

"Yes, sir." Cruxer jumped to his feet and came toward the line. He was smiling, but Kip thought it was a tense smile.

As everyone was standing proud, Kip felt the gulf between him and them intensely. Outsider, loner, alien. They were all he would never be.

"Sir?" Cruxer asked, coming to stand in front of the trainer. He glanced coolly at Aram, who wouldn't meet his eyes.

"Yes, first?" Trainer Fisk said.

"A Blackguard's training is never done, but is the testing over for today?" Cruxer asked.

Trainer Fisk said, "Yes, of course, now get to your place—"

Cruxer said nothing, but he struck like a serpent, yelling his *kiyah* and giving his body the sharp countertwist that made his kicks so blindingly fast and powerful. Even Kip, who was looking straight at him, barely saw the strike. Cruxer's shin, gnarled and calcified by years of kicking against posts, crushed against Aram's knee. Crushed it backward.

The crunching squish of a joint being obliterated split the sudden silence.

Aram crumpled to the ground, gawping, gasping, eyes agape.

Cruxer dropped his hands instantly and stood in a narrow, non-threatening stance. Given that he was surrounded by hundreds of men and women attuned to violence and accustomed to stopping it by the most efficient means necessary, that was wise. "Training accident," Cruxer said loudly, coolly.

For a moment, even Trainer Fisk seemed as baffled as Kip. Finally he recovered. "What have you done?!" he shouted at Cruxer.

Cruxer's voice was cool, mechanical. "Permanent injuries inflicted during testing result in expulsion. Injuries during training do not."

"My knee! My *knee*!" Aram started blubbering. From the sound of his voice, he knew, like Kip knew, like everyone here knew—he would never fight again. He'd be lucky if he ever walked again. Knee injuries like that didn't heal. Aram was *crippled*.

Cruxer spoke loudly, clearly, and unapologetically. "I've wanted to be a Blackguard since I could walk. I value this brotherhood too highly to let in a man who destroys unity rather than builds it, a man who takes *money* to destroy one of his own. If the cost to remove him from the Blackguard is that I, too, am expelled, so be it." Emotion edged his voice for a moment, but he mastered it.

"What?!" Trainer Fisk demanded. "What are you talking about?"

"Aram's the second best fighter in our class," Cruxer said. "He took money to finish low. He took money to keep Breaker out."

"He's *Tyrean!*" Aram shouted. "He's a bastard! I would have done it for free! He's not one of us!"

"You would have done it for free? So you did do it for money," Trainer Fisk said, aggrieved, disbelieving. He shot a look over at Commander Ironfist. A straight admission of guilt. How stupid was Aram?

"He's not one of us!" Aram shouted.

"You mean, one of *you*," Commander Ironfist said, low and dangerous, stepping forward. "Because you'll never be one of *us*, Aram. Unlike Breaker."

The last word sent a shock through Kip.

"Breaker!" Trainer Fisk barked. "You heard the man. We got room for fourteen, and I only see thirteen up here. Get in line! Double time! Someone get this trash out of here."

"No! Noo!!" Aram shouted. But the chirurgeons were there instantly and they carried him away, blubbering.

Kip limped over to the line, not even close to double time, but he felt like he was floating all the way. How much poppy had that chirurgeon given him?

No, this wasn't the poppy.

Commander Ironfist stood in front of Kip. He took Kip's gold fight token and snapped it into a pendant. The front of the pendant was a black flame. "This is the Flame of Erebos. It symbolizes service and sacrifice. As a candle takes on flame and is consumed to give light and heat, so is a man who takes on duty. Day by day, we give our lives to serve Orholam and his Prism. Will you take this sacred duty, Kip Guile, Breaker?"

"I will." Kip felt little shivers.

"And will you forswear other loyalties, and have loyalty first to this body, to Orholam, and to his Prism?"

"I will."

"Then I declare you, Breaker, a trainee in the Blackguard."

"Break-er! Break-er!" the crowd chanted.

Ironfist let them go on for a few more seconds, then quieted them and worked his way down the line.

The rest of the ceremony passed like a dream. Each scrub was sworn in, and then the older trainees and the full Blackguards gathered around them to congratulate them.

They eventually decided to go to a tavern that the Blackguards preferred—all drinks on the new trainees, of course. Before he let himself be swept out into the evening, Kip looked for his father.

Gavin Guile was standing where Kip had left him, ignoring for the moment a messenger who'd come to him with something or other. He had eyes only for Kip. The Prism wore a bemused smirk, but maybe it was more than bemused. Maybe it was a little proud.

Chapter 93

Karris was dimly aware of the men leaving. She laid her face on the paving stones, praying they wouldn't come back, hoping for unconsciousness. It didn't come. She lifted her face and saw a pool of blood where her mouth had been. Her left eye was rapidly swelling shut, and the right doing the same, more slowly.

She felt sick from the blow to her head. There was a foul taste in her mouth along with the flat metal taste of blood. She realized they'd rolled her onto her side so she wouldn't drown on her own vomit.

Messily, she vomited again. She got it all over herself, but the spasms in her stomach kept her curled into a ball. She was heaving just to breathe, and heaving her guts up.

The spasms passed slowly, but her head still felt barely connected to her body, moving at its own pace, sloshing. She rolled onto her stomach again and somehow started crawling.

She could crawl. Good. Part of her noted that she hadn't broken either her arms or legs. Good, good. Her hands were slick with blood and worse, and the paving stones cut her knees. Her ribs ached every time she took a breath, but if any ribs were broken, they were merely cracked. She'd had broken ribs before, and that hurt worse than this.

Unless, of course, her body was masking the pain. Bodies did that. Damned things. Something caught in her throat and she spat up blood.

Still had her teeth, but she'd bit the hell out of her tongue. Something was burning around her neck. She was afraid to touch it, though. Couldn't, and still crawl.

She reached the intersection five or ten minutes, or a year, later.

What street was this? She'd just come down it, but she couldn't remember. Couldn't remember what part of town she was in. Not a busy street, though.

But she couldn't go any farther. Her right eye was completely shut now. She realized her butt hurt. They'd kicked the hell out of her butt. And her legs were starting to cramp up.

She retched again. Dry-heaved.

When she opened her one good eye, she saw someone walking toward her down the street.

The man turned aside and walked wide around her.

Others passed. Men, and women. A man with a cart. None stopped. Orholam, why didn't any of them stop?

Helpless. She might as well be naked out here. She couldn't do anything. At the mercy of anyone who passed. Anyone who wanted to take advantage.

She started crying, and hated herself for it. Everything just hurt so bad.

"Come now, sweetie," a man said over her. "Everything's going to be fine. Such a brave girl you are." Sounded Ilytian, by the accent. Karris hadn't had good luck with Ilytians. Didn't think much of them. "Dressed as a Blackguard, but white as a sail. You're Karris White Oak."

She couldn't answer. Stopping crying was all she could manage. Nodding her head was a victory.

"I'm going to pick you up. I want you to think about everywhere you hurt so we can tell the chirurgeons when we get to the Chromeria. Acceptable?"

"Y-yes." Something about him seemed familiar. But no, she was certain—

He picked her up, and she promptly passed out.

When she woke, she was in a bed. She could tell she'd been dosed with poppy, because she felt far too good. She heaved her head left, saw the world swim, and then heaved it right.

Gavin's room! Ha! She'd been here before. And oh-ho! There was the man himself, the Light of the Tower, the Star of Stars, the Moon's Right Hand. He was awfully handsome, standing there, that one wave of his hair falling in front of his eyes.

"Karris?" Gavin asked. He looked terribly concerned. "Can you hear me?"

"Mmm," she said. She smiled at him. She remembered seeing him without his shirt on at Seers Island. Mmm. "I want to see you naked," she said.

Oh dear! Had she really just said that? She laughed.

Gavin turned to a little man Karris hadn't noticed before. A chirurgeon in slave's robes. "I think we can ease up on the poppy," he said.

"Always trying to tell me..." Karris lost the thought. And consciousness.

Chapter 94

Tell her. You have to tell her.

Gavin rolled the little brown ball of opium between his finger and thumb. Karris was still asleep, and the people were scurrying every which way in the hall outside, preparing for war.

When the messenger had come to him at Kip's testing, Gavin had at first refused to understand the man's words, then nearly panicked. That Karris had been beaten had affected him far more than he would have expected.

"Look to what you love," his father had said.

They'd sail at high tide tomorrow. The mobilization was unbelievably fast because everyone had known that when the permission came, they would have to move fast. What was transpiring now was simply the last-minute orders. Still, there were a thousand decisions to be made. And though Gavin wasn't technically part of them, he still knew more than anyone here how to successfully put together an armada and an army.

But for now, he sat at Karris's bedside. When he'd first seen her, caked with blood, he'd thought she would be crippled by her injuries. Then, after the chirurgeons had tended to her and reported, he'd thought it was a miracle she wasn't hurt worse. Now he realized she'd been beaten expertly and exactly how much whoever did it had intended. She'd been meant to look awful—without incapacitating her permanently. It had been intended as a warning to Gavin, not a declaration of war.

His father had no idea.

He didn't have any proof it had been his father, of course. There were any number of possible suspects, but with this timing, this care, this precision? Gavin didn't need proof.

Seeing her on the bed, wrapped in bandages, unconscious, Gavin was made aware of how small she was. When she was awake, talking, her personality was so big you forgot. But here, she looked so vulnerable, a delicate flower, bruised.

"I'm going to rip their damn arms off. I swear it," Gavin said quietly.

"You talking to yourself, or am I that bad of a faker?" Karris asked, cracking one eye. The other opened a bare slit through the swollen blackness.

"You're back," Gavin said. His relief was like a crushing weight lifting.

"Did I...say something..." She trailed off.

"Something embarrassing while you were mudged on poppy? Like about seeing me naked? No."

She closed her eyes. "You're lucky it hurts to move, or I'd beat you bloody, Gavin Guile."

"Dazen," Gavin said quietly. That one word was the whole reason he'd come here. The whole reason he'd waited until Karris was lucid, but after all the buildup, he was still surprised to hear the word.

A bruised and swollen face and two black eyes and a split lip were not the easiest canvas on which to read emotions, and Gavin saw nothing. Karris's eyes were closed. Like she hadn't heard him. Maybe she hadn't. Maybe she'd passed out again.

A solitary tear leaked from the corner of one closed eye and tracked down her cheek.

The door's open. Nothing for it but to charge through now. Gavin said, "Corvan Danavis and I came up with the plan a month before the Battle of Sundered Rock. We'd made so many bargains with so many devils that even though I thought my original cause was just, I knew a victory would be disastrous for the Seven Satrapies. Corvan gave me a scar to match Gavin's, and a spy gave us the details of his battle dress." Gavin heaved a breath. "My mother knew it was me instantly, of course, but she didn't want to lose her last son so she coached me how to be Gavin. I thought if I could keep my disguise for even a few months that I would be able to stop most of the damage to the Seven Satrapies. I didn't realize how hard it would be with you. I didn't know how to even talk with you. I thought you loved Gavin. Marrying you—as him?—it was one betrayal too many, Karris. I couldn't. I just couldn't. But maybe what I did was worse."

The broken betrothal hadn't turned out so well. She'd disappeared, humiliated, financially ruined, and he'd thought he would never see her again. Part of him had been glad, the part that wanted to live. Surely Karris would be the one to see through his masquerade. The year she'd been gone had given him time to solidify his mask, to *become* Gavin Guile.

"Tell me," she said. She wouldn't look him in the eye, and she made no motion to clear away her tears. "Tell me everything."

Her tone gave him nothing. It was cold, flat, lifeless.

She already knew enough to get him killed, so he didn't know why it should be hard. In for a den, in for a danar, right? But the sick feeling in the pit of his stomach wasn't about life and death. Somehow, those were paltry things. This was about disgusting a woman who meant more to him than anything he'd ever known.

He drew a deep breath. Leaned back in his chair, leaned forward. Seven years, seven impossible goals. He'd failed at this goal every year for the past sixteen. If she killed him for this, at least he would have done something right.

So he talked. He told her about the fire at her family's house, how he'd found he could split light that night, and how he'd been wild with rage, thinking she'd betrayed him. He told of fleeing in shame. Of being pursued. Of having an army coalesce around him he wasn't even sure he wanted to have. And then of Gavin rebuffing his offers to surrender. He told her how he'd finally started fighting with his whole heart. Of putting Corvan Danavis in charge of his armies. Of fighting across the length of Atash, of promises from several Parian clans. Of how they'd needed those Parian reinforcements so badly they'd fled to meet them all the way into Tyrea—where they finally found out they'd been betrayed. The Parian clans weren't coming.

He said little about the final battle. He'd killed a lot of men that day, some of them brothers and sisters, sons and daughters of men and women he'd come to admire since.

Then he talked about the years since. How he'd faced the challenges of learning to be Gavin, and how he'd tried to right the wrongs that so few of the other members of the Spectrum cared to try to redress.

He spoke for more than an hour. And as he spoke, he could feel her softening, warming toward him, her expression opening. And finally, he'd reached the Battle of Garriston and its aftermath and how she'd slapped him and said she knew his secret, and how he was afraid she'd known the full truth. Quietly, he shared how he'd had to decide whether he should tell her the truth, or kill her.

Any warmth that had been gathering was dissipated like he'd thrown his windows open in winter. He saw the muscle in her jaw twitch. You were going to kill me, you asshole? it said.

"You wanted the truth," Gavin said. "Telling you means you could kill me."

"It makes sense, you bastard, just don't expect it to warm the cockles of my heart."

He had nothing to say. He realized he'd ground the little brown grain of opium to dust between his fingers.

"I am who I am, Karris," he said. Then he realized how ridiculous saying that was right now. "I mean, I am the Prism, so . . ."

"I know what you meant. So. Is that it?"

He hesitated. "No. That's not it, Karris. I killed Gavin last night."

"You mean metaphorically?" she asked.

So he told her. Then he backed up and told her about Ana, and he told her the truth.

"But the Blackguards . . . they said she jumped."

"They lied to save me, Karris. I didn't ask them to. I swear. Ana said some pretty foul things about you, and I knew I'd lost you forever. I threw her out onto my balcony—I, I don't think I was trying to murder her, but she hit the railing and tumbled right over. I went to the roof to try to balance. I can't anymore. So I went down to let Gavin out, to let him kill me." He couldn't look at her. Even with her battered face, he could read horror easily enough.

Finally, after telling her about Gavin, he said, "I didn't know what he did to you, back then. How he...humbled you. I should have figured it out, but I've been so worried about myself that I couldn't see even the most obvious things about those around me. I'm sorry, Karris, and I know I haven't acted like it, but I love you and I want to spend the rest of my life with you, if you can ever forgive me."

The silence was deep enough to drown in.

"Infuriating. Incorrigible. Inelegant. Inefficient. Incredible in both senses. But not, in the end, insincere, are you, Dazen Guile?"

"Huh?"

"Kiss me," Karris said.

"Pardon?"

"It wasn't a request."

He stood up from his chair and sat on the edge of her bed. She grunted with pain as his movement jostled her.

"Sorry," he mumbled. "Maybe—"

"Not a request."

"But your lips are cracked and—"

"Not a request."

"Ah."

He kissed her with the gentleness of a man kissing an invalid.

She pulled back, peering at him through swollenness-slitted eyes, disapproving. "That was horrible, Dazen Guile. That was *not* the kiss I've been waiting sixteen years for."

"Second chance?" he asked.

She looked unconvinced. "Hm. You don't deserve it."

"I don't," he said seriously.

"You don't," she said gravely, "but then, if you and I aren't about second chances, I don't know who is." She grinned a bit, though.

He kissed her again, tenderly, but drawing her in. But what began as a gift for her benefit, a smooth, strong seduction soon morphed. He folded her small form into his, wrapping protective arms around her. As they kissed, he could feel a tension loosening in him, a tension that had been knotted for so long he'd come to think of that pain as part of the pain of being alive.

She pulled back, and instantly back on guard, fearing rejection, Gavin pulled back, too.

But Karris murmured, "I'm afraid you've left me breathless, Lord Guile—"

"Well thank you." Relief beneath his grin.

"—because I can't breathe through my nose right now."

She laughed and he joined her ruefully. "You are so beautiful," he said. He felt as if his heart had swollen too large for his chest.

A dubious look. "I might be part blind right now, but *you* shouldn't be. I got beat up, what's your excuse?"

He chuckled. "I didn't mean particularly, precisely at this moment— You know what? I think my lips can make a more convincing case without words. Come back here."

They kissed, and kissed, and chuckled together about Karris needing to take little breaths and Gavin misreading her little moans of desire and her little moans of pain when he got too passionate. The world ceased. No worries, no cares. That knot Gavin hadn't known he carried eased and opened and disappeared, and he felt suddenly stronger than he had been in his entire life. Free. The power of the secret broken, chains shattered.

"Orholam have mercy, how I want to make love with you," she said.

"I can be persuaded," Gavin said quickly.

She made a little sound of frustration. "If only my body were so amenable."

"I could be...gentle," he offered, giving a roguish grin.

She pulled him close and whispered in his ear, "After sixteen years of missing you, Dazen Guile, the last thing I want from you is *gentle*."

He swallowed. Speechless. "Will you marry me, Karris White Oak?" Damn. He could have done better than that. Such questions should have some eloquence.

Then again with his history with Karris, perhaps a simple truth was better than an artful one.

"Karris, why are you crying?"

"Because it's past time for my pain medicine, you big idiot."

There was a knock on Gavin's door. "Oh, you have got to be joking," Gavin said, looking at the door like he could kill it with his eyes. He turned back to her. "Does that mean yes?"

"You've worn me down and taken advantage of my incapacitated state, so..."

"So that means yes?"

Another knock on the door.

"You stupid, stupid man, of course it does."

"I love you, Karris White Oak."

She smiled mischievously. "You ought to."

The door opened, and a Blackguard wheeled the White in. Gavin couldn't keep the huge grin off his face.

"Oh dear, have I interrupted something?" the White asked.

"No," Gavin said. At the same time Karris said, "Yes."

"I see."

"You were just the person I was hoping to see," Gavin said. "High Mistress White, would you be so good as to marry us?"

The White inclined her head, looking over the corrective spectacles she was wearing. "Well, Gavin Guile, it certainly took you long enough. And Karris White Oak! Slowest seduction in history! A woman with your charms." The White sniffed.

"Is that a yes?" Gavin asked.

"Of course it is," Karris answered for her. She was grinning from ear to ear.

"I imagine that Gavin's heading straight off to war, and that you'll want this done as soon as he gets back?" the White said.

"No," Gavin said. "Right now."

"Right now?" Karris said. "Don't you want to give this some thought? We have no idea what we're getting into."

"And when will we? Some things you can't know until you're in them. I'll be in it with you. That's more than enough for me." Gavin turned to the White. "Right now."

The White grumbled. "Figures." But she smiled. "Gavin, you're willing to have your father disown you over this?"

"I'm feeling invincible right now," Gavin said. "How'd you know about that, Orea?"

"Disowned?" Karris asked.

"I'll explain. Later," Gavin said.

"Me, too," the White said. "Karris, you know what this may mean for your tenure?"

"Yes," Karris said.

"Rules are made to bend for the right people," Gavin said.

"Promise me a big wedding when you get back," Karris said.

"Huge."

And so they were wed. The vows were simple. In the discharge of his normal duties as Prism, Gavin had prompted brides and grooms through the vows himself, but today *he* forgot them. And as soon as they were out of his mouth, they became a blur. He was barely aware even of the White, he had eyes only for Karris. He was filled with an inexplicable tenderness for this wild, frustrating, beautiful, stubborn, amazing woman.

He kissed Karris again, and she grimaced under her smile.

"Time for more medicine?" he asked.

She nodded, apologetic.

He found the tincture and poured her the dose. She accepted it gratefully and lay back on her pillows. "Come back to me, my lord. Come back soon, you hear me?"

"Yes, my lady," he said. He couldn't stop grinning.

She was asleep in less than a minute.

Finally, Gavin turned to the White. "Well done, Lord Prism," she said. "Perhaps I was right about you after all."

"I do my best."

"I hope your best is enough to save us."

And with the quiet moment, he remembered why he had worked so hard not to have quiet moments with the White. She would ask that they go to the roof and that he balance. She had all sorts of reasons. She would have heard all the stories that Marissia had told him. She would know what they meant.

"Do you know," she said, "I was on the roof the other day. And do you know what I saw? Cranes. Thousands of them, migrating. Have you ever seen them?"

"Not that I remember."

"They fly in Vs. Something about it makes it easier."

It was an odd thing to say. Like you'd explain to a child. Gavin had, of course, seen migrating birds before.

"This year, they weren't flying in a V. They were flying in a single line. Thousands of them. So odd. Cranes never fly over water for long when they migrate. I could see they were struggling. Without the efficiencies of their normal formation, birds were dropping out, falling, dying. They flew straight toward me. And then, suddenly, as they reached Little Jasper, that odd line broke apart. The cranes rested that day on the Jaspers, as they have not for many years. And when they left, they flew normally." She didn't really finish her story, she simply stopped talking. "Regardless, they were saved."

He'd broken the bane—and saved some cranes. Orholam's nipple.

"That's marvelous," Gavin said.

"Have you had a chance to go up to the roof yet?" she asked.

"Yes, yes I have." Face bland.

She studied him. Did she buy it? Surely, this was her telling him she knew. Unless—unless it was the ramblings of an old woman. Maybe senility came like this on a woman as bright as Orea. Maybe she had the pieces, and some part of her was desperately trying to put it all together by talking it out, out loud.

Or she was warning him, because of their friendship. Their friendship? Were they friends, after all? But she was utterly dedicated to the Chromeria, to her duties, to the Seven Satrapies. Her next words—he knew her next words were going to be: "Gavin, we need to talk about how to ease you into retirement."

"Gavin," she said, "the generals are in my room, planning the invasion. I think they could use your expertise."

Gavin took a deep breath. That meant his father would be there. Frying pan, fire. He stood, bent over to kiss Karris's forehead, and popped his neck right and left. "Very well, Orea, let's save the world."

Chapter 95

Gavin walked into Orea's room to find the generals and their aides gathered around a table on which a number of maps of different scales were laid out. "So you've got spies with the Color Prince's army," Gavin said.

"More than a dozen," a bearded, balding Parian general said. Caul Azmith was the Parian satrapah's younger brother. He was affable, polite, and not terribly bright.

"Projection or actual data?" Gavin asked. He wanted to know if he was staring at the positions the prince's army had been in eight or ten days ago, or if these were estimates of the current positions.

"Projection, on excellent data," the Blood Forest general said. He was also bald, though he was a young man, freckled and foolish. A political weasel who had no business leading a hunting expedition, much less an army.

"How old is this?" Gavin asked.

General Azmith said, "Ten days. Takes my handler two days to get to the smuggler who's carrying the letters. The smuggler had good wind. Earned himself a bonus for getting it here in seven days. It arrived last night."

"You using that smuggler for the return trip?"

General Azmith shook his head.

Which to Gavin meant that the smuggler had probably lied about how fast he'd made the trip in order to get his bonus. Most of the smugglers on the Atashian coast still used galleys so they couldn't become becalmed, with the low displacement that allowed the long wide ships to traverse bays that the pirate hunters couldn't. This time of year, the winds would rarely make it possible for a galley to come from Atash in seven days. Probably more like nine. Maybe ten.

If Gavin had been here, things could have been different. If Gavin were promachos, things still could be. But that was out of reach for now. His father had done that, and his father wasn't going to give it back for nothing. Gavin's own personal defiance, his own happiness in marrying Karris, was going to cost men their lives.

But that wasn't his fault. Gavin wasn't going to accept the blame for that. He would have, not so long ago. No, these generals had no business being generals, and they'd all been put into position by people who ought to have known better. There were plenty of veterans from the last war who could have been put in charge. Gavin had done the best he could by the people of Garriston. He couldn't make the right decisions for everyone else.

"How fast is your turnaround?" he asked.

The idiot Blood Forester spoke. "We're not actually going to start strategizing until your luxlord father arrives. He should be here any minute, Lord Prism."

"It doesn't matter," Gavin said.

"Lord Prism?"

"When you arrive in Ru, I think you'll find that the army is here." Gavin pointed to a little town called Voril, two days from Ru. "You'll find that the corregidor has maybe half the working guns he's told you, and less than half the powder, because he's always been more worried about his ego than about defense. So rather than look like a fool to you who are trying to save him, he'll act like one and lie to you, which you won't find out until it's too late. And I've marched through this country. If you're not being harassed and being made to pay for letting your wagons get spread out, this section is easy. I covered it in three weeks, but my brother had saboteurs and raiders who made us paranoid at every step. If they've been allowed to just march through here, they'll be on top of Ru before you know it.

"Your spies have been cataloguing the wrong things. What's important isn't the exact number of horsemen or who's a freed slave versus a volunteer. Those are good to know, but what you needed to know was how many anvils do they have, how many skilled black-smiths, how much scrap iron? Have veterans from the False Prism's War been put in positions of leadership, or have those slots gone to the Color Prince's favorites who don't know anything? How long are their supply lines, and how much food are they delivering every time? It's too late for a lot of those questions to be answered now. Too late for you to have raiders intercept the supply wagons, or to destroy the anvils or murder the blacksmiths and sabotage the wagons' wheels before they hit the Little Sisters' Pass. You could have bought yourself weeks, and only put a dozen men in danger to do it. The Color Prince hasn't led an army before either, and it's not your fault that none of you have—but it is your fault that you haven't asked the men who marched with me or my brother to advise you. You're going to ask those men to die, and not for good reason. The fact is, no matter what you do, you won't save Ru. It's already over. If you were wise, you'd send messages to tell them to evacuate the city and regroup at the neck of Ruic Head, and to take out of the city whatever supplies the Color Prince's army needs most. But you won't do that, because you're look-ing to win a battle instead of win a war. I've got my own fights, gentle-men. Fights that I can still win, and that will help you in ways you don't know. So good day, and I'll see you on the field."

Chapter 96

Gavin headed down to his own room. He spied his father coming up the lift just as he stepped into his room. Good thing the old bastard was blind. Grinwoody was with him, but the old slave had his back turned, helping the old man out of the lift.

Karris lay on his bed, asleep. In a chair beside the bed, Commander Ironfist sat. He rubbed his temples, and then his bald head as Gavin came in.

"Commander," Gavin said.

"Lord Prism." There was something oddly distant in the big man's voice.

"Is something the matter?" Gavin asked.

Ironfist looked at him levelly. "I almost lost one of my watch captains, one of my friends, in what appears to be a targeted attack. And someone murdered one of my students yesterday. A couple of the scrubs swear that the man was aiming at Kip and the girl stepped into the line of fire on accident. Do you have any comment, Lord Prism?"

"Can I trust you enough to bare my throat to you, Ironfist?"

Ironfist hesitated, as well he should.

"Well then," Gavin said.

Ironfist heaved a sigh and looked down at his hands. "We're doomed, aren't we?"

Gavin didn't follow. They were doomed because they didn't trust each other?

"The Chromeria is a lightning-struck tree. Still standing, but dead on the inside. That's why we're going to lose, I think," Ironfist said. "We have all the power in the world, but our faith is dead. If we don't believe in what we're doing for its own sake, we're just doing it to maintain power. And I think some of us are too good to continue throwing lives into the trough simply to feed the beast."

"Are we?" Gavin asked very quietly.

"When Ru falls, this will become a real war. And once it's a real war, and not simply an uprising of a few disgruntled madmen, then the questions begin. At some point, every one of us will have to ask if we're on the right side. If we've already decided our own side is wrong—that there's no Orholam, that the Chromeria is simply making the best of a bad situation—then where do men looking for certainty turn?"

"Maybe men shouldn't look for certainty," Gavin said.

"Should. Shouldn't. Doesn't matter. They do."

He was right. Of course he was.

Gavin quirked an eyebrow. "Why Ironfist, are you asking me to come back to religion?"

Ironfist met his levity with a flat stare. "My own faith is dead, Lord Prism. Not least because of you. I'd not ask you to embrace a lie, but I want my people to have a reason to die. I won't lie either. I can't tell them what we do matters. If that's beside the point, if you want us to die because it's our duty to die, I can accept that. That can be enough for me. That will be enough for the Blackguard. It won't be enough for everyone else."

"Does the Blackguard love me so much?" Gavin asked grimly.

Ironfist looked startled Gavin should ask. "We don't die for you. We die for each other, for our brothers and sisters. We die for the Blackguard." Then he grinned. "Looks the same from your side though, I suppose." Ironfist stood, looked at Karris, swallowed, then turned back to Gavin. "You should give her a ring, you know. Especially if you're going off to your death."

Of course. And he should make sure she was provided for, should he die. Damn.

Ironfist left, and Gavin followed him. Gavin got off at the level of his father's and mother's apartments, nodding amiably to the discipulae who passed him in the lift, on their way to do chores. He went into his mother's apartments.

He'd thought he'd accepted his mother's death, but going into her room and smelling the familiar, comforting smells of the place made him pause, barely inside the door. There was the wood polish, the waft of lavender, the stargazer lilies he'd always hated, a bit of orange, and spices he could never place. All that was missing was the smell of her perfume. A lump grew in his throat, threatening to choke him, making it hard to breathe.

"Oh, mother, I finally did it. I finally did the right thing with Karris. I wish you could see it."

"My lord?" a timorous voice intruded. "I'm so sorry, my lord. Should I withdraw?"

It was his mother's room slave. Gavin didn't even know the young girl's name. Different girl than last time. No wonder the room was immaculately clean, without even dust on the mantelpiece.

"*Caleen*," Gavin said. "You've done well. It's beautiful. It reminds me powerfully of her."

"I'm so sorry, my lord." She buried her face.

Gavin shook his head. The girl was young. His mother had always trained her help exquisitely, and had chosen only intelligent slaves, preferring that over physical beauty, unlike other leading families. But there are some situations you don't get around to training a fourteen-year-old girl for.

"Did my mother leave no instructions for you?" Gavin asked. Usually, like himself, his mother had kept at least half a dozen slaves in her household. She'd trimmed back in recent years, mostly manumitting those who'd provided long years of good service. Now Gavin knew why.

"She told me..." The girl blanched, then bulled forward. "She told me she was giving orders for my manumission to Grinwoody, seeing as how a slave can't deliver her own manumission to the records keepers. I hain't—your pardon, my lord—I *haven't* heard anything since then."

"You old bastard," Gavin whispered to himself. His father was still denying that his wife was dead, so he'd simply ignored the girl. The girl had been stuck here for four months, with nothing to do but dust the room and get fresh flowers and hope. "Did she leave you a letter?" Gavin asked.

"Yes, my lord," the girl said, her voice was barely a whisper, obviously picking up on Gavin's pique. "Believe Grinwoody put it in the lord's chamber."

"Of course he did." And they wouldn't appreciate Gavin breaking into his room.

But you know what? To the everlasting night with them. Gavin was more than half convinced that his father had orchestrated Karris's beating. The attempted murder of Kip seemed too heavy-handed, but at this point he wasn't going to excuse his father preemptively for anything.

Look to what you love indeed.

Gavin headed across the hall, drafted red luxin into the lock, jimmied it until he felt tumblers loosen, and then injected yellow luxin,

steeled his will, and twisted. The lock clicked open.

He might be half dead, but he wasn't neutered yet, thanks. He set a light to burning, casting a pale yellow glare through the Red's rooms. He went to the desk, rifled through the papers. Andross Guile was upstairs, and a council of war would surely take hours, even for a man as ignorant of war as his own father. Andross seemed to think that being brilliant meant being good at everything, and his generals would have to fill in the gaps in his knowledge carefully and slowly, lest they infuriate the old man. Considering how ignorant they themselves were, it ought to take a while.

It was almost comical how much excellent intelligence his father had left in the open. Gavin wished he'd come in merely to poke around. Andross was simply here so often that he clearly never thought about the danger of someone coming into his rooms while he was gone. He was never gone.

Gavin found the note about the slave girl quickly. His mother's handwriting was on the outside, a beautiful looping script that she hadn't lost even as age advanced on her.

We drafters are robbed of life before age can rob us of our faculties. Gavin didn't know if it was the greatest cruelty of all, or a small kindness. He glanced at the letter. It was as the girl had said, a simple, straightforward manumission, and a grant of four hundred danars. The girl would leave slavery with more in her hand than she would have earned at a servant's wages in two years. It was a fortune for a young girl. Enough for a dowry in those rural areas of the few satrapies where such things were still customary. The only unusual bit was the instruction that the girl be given an armed guard from the Cloven Shield mercenary company to take her home—Felia Guile had doubtless thought through the fact that sending a very young and attractive girl home with a fortune in hand would put her in grave peril. Of course, sending a guard from the Cloven Shield would cost more than two hundred danars, but they had a sterling reputation.

Like many socially conscious women, Felia Guile had always had deep reservations about slavery. Are we all not brothers and sisters under the light? she would ask. He could almost hear her voice as she talked through it: From Orholam's perch, what difference is a man's garment? And like so many others, she'd still had slaves. Impossible to think of a world without them. Men wouldn't volunteer for the galleys, or the silver mines, or the sewers, would they? And what does one do with the widows and orphans when a country is conquered?

Simply let them die at the first winter? Leave them as prey for slavers with less scruples than the civilized satrapies had?

Still, she'd say, it was dehumanizing. The beatings, the fathering of bastards, the jealousies and insecurities of the slaveholders themselves. Felia had never liked it. This manumission was generous, to say the least. But not uncommon to those owners who feared their dear slaves would be passed on to cruel mistresses or depraved masters, or to enemy families who might force them to reveal shameful secrets about their previous owners, or even to good families that might fall on hard times and have to rent their slaves out to work the mines or the brothels.

Gavin tucked away the letter. He looked around the room, wondering if there was anything else he should steal. Money? Gems? Should he try to read his father's correspondence? He opened the desk and found a box. He examined it briefly, then gave up trying to open that. Andross Guile lived and died by his correspondence. The box would yield to nothing less than a chisel and a smith's hammer. If that.

With a sigh, Gavin set it back into its place. It had felt heavy, too. In fact, some of the former contents of the box had been emptied out to make more room. Several jewels the size of songbird's eggs sat carelessly in the drawer among the feather pens and the cunning Ilytian ink-reservoir pen his father liked so much.

Gavin felt a perverse urge to steal something. He was going to get disowned anyway, so he probably ought to do something to earn it.

His eyes fell on the side table with its piles of Nine Kings cards. Apparently his father had been playing recently. It was one of the few things that gave the old man joy. Gavin had played him countless times in the past. The old man almost always won. He was a better player than Gavin, and he wasn't above cheating either, if he thought he could get away with it, though he'd been mortified the one time Gavin had caught him doing it, and had never cheated again so far as Gavin knew.

Instead of grabbing one of the decks on the table, though, Gavin headed for a cabinet. His father had once pulled an amazing deck out of the cabinet after Gavin had won three games in a row. There was a lock on the cabinet, but it was nothing serious. Gavin rummaged through old papers and his father's favorite books, and found an old jeweled deck box. He pulled it out, cracked it open. The cards were exquisite, but they didn't have the blind man's marks on them. Must have been his father's favorites from before he went into seclusion.

Gavin dropped the deck box into a pocket and headed back to his mother's room. The slave girl was standing there, wringing her hands. He handed her the letter and went to his mother's safe, a chunky Parian design that was hard to tell was arranged into numbers at all. He tried his own birth date. It didn't open.

Ah. He'd tried Gavin's birth date. Good: he was sinking back into the disguise.

Dazen's birth date worked. Thank you, mother. He grabbed some purses of gold, and her wedding ring, and some coin sticks. He gave the slave girl one of them, then a second. Her eyes went wide.

"Take this note to the west docks, the Bakers' Street, you know it? Blue dome building, houses the mercenary company the Cloven Shield. You ask to speak with One-Eye or Taya Vin. I'd advise One-Eye, he's kinder to young girls. You tell them Lady Felia Guile sent you. You can pay them up to three hundred danars to get you home, including all their expenses—any less that you can negotiate with them, you get to keep. Then book passage home—where are you from?"

"Wiwurgh, my lord."

"Paria? You don't look Parian."

"First generation, my lord. Parents fled the Blood War. It's not so bad. Lots of us in Wiwurgh."

"Very well. It's a long trip, you should pay forty danars for a stateroom. Cheaper to bunk below, but don't. Make your guard bunk with you. Man or woman doesn't matter, the Cloven Shield is safe. You can ask for a woman if you prefer, though. Also, take this note to a tailor. By nightfall tonight, you shouldn't be wearing a slave's garb. Understood?" Gavin scribbled a note. "You need to get on a ship tonight, though. This is my mother's wish, but my father isn't rational right now. You don't want to be around when he's angry, and I'm giving him good cause to be angry. He'll forget you within a week, but for now..."

He scribbled a second note and signed his own name on it. He dripped red luxin on it, pressed it with his will to make it stand in the shape of his seal, and then sealed it with luxin, barely even looking at it. "This tells anyone who might accost you that the Prism is going to check in on you, and if anything ill has happened to you, I will wreak vengeance on them. It may not be true. I don't know that I'll ever get to Wiwurgh, but if I live long enough, I'll try. You understand?"

The girl's wide eyes hadn't contracted in the least, but now she also looked on the verge of tears. "My lord... I don't know how to thank..." She swallowed.

"Go," he said. "It's very dangerous for you here." And me.

She left, and he followed. Then he went down the tower and hid his father's deck and Kip's deck in a spot he was certain his father would never check. He came back up to his own room.

Karris was asleep. Gavin slipped his mother's huge ruby ring on Karris's finger. She still didn't wake. Strangely, the ring fit perfectly. Gavin could have sworn his mother's fingers were wider than Karris's delicate digits. He looked at the ring.

His mother had resized it to Karris's ring size. Gavin smiled. Thank you, mother. He could just imagine her mischievous grin, knowing he would figure it out. He hadn't gotten all of his smarts from his father, she'd say. Still smiling as tears gathered in his eyes, he kissed Karris's forehead. He held his wife's hand and sat with her. His wife's hand. His wife.

After all they'd been through together. The fights with each other, against wights. The darkness and despair. He tucked a wisp of her hair behind her ear. Touched her face gently. Memorized her. He took a breath, and it was pure.

In a world where every danger was growing and his own strength was failing, Karris had his back. She'd always had his back. And somehow, dying though he was, power fractured, doom looming, he felt more whole than ever.

The yoke of responsibility lay hanging off the bedpost. Gavin kissed his sleeping wife's forehead, cracked his neck, rolled his shoulders, and picked the damn thing back up. Slipped it on. It felt good. It felt like it was made for him.

Marissia was waiting at the door. Her face was carefully composed, hands folded, ready to serve. Gavin handed her the note for the tower register to record his mother freeing her slave. Marissia took it silently, but there was a touch of hesitancy in her stance.

"Marissia," Gavin said quietly. "I... if you're gone when I get back, I understand, but you will always have a place here."

She bowed jerkily, and he could tell she was doing it to cover her sudden tears. She practically fled the room. Gavin rubbed the bridge of his nose and stepped into the hallway, doing his best not to look after her. Commander Ironfist was there, waiting silently.

"Commander," Gavin said. "How do you feel about doing a little skimming? Flirt-with-death dangerous."

Ironfist said nothing, but his mouth quirked up in a little grin.

Chapter 97

Though much is taken, much abides, Gevison had once said. Gavin hated poets. He and Ironfist had gathered food and weapons and taken a scull out into open waters.

"You going to suit up?" Gavin asked, pulling on armor.

"I've skimmed with you before," Ironfist said.

"And?"

"I prefer not to strap on weights when I may have to swim."

Ah yes, not everyone could swim in full armor. Benefit of being me.

"Rough weather today," Ironfist said.

That was all he said, but Gavin could tell he wasn't looking forward to going at extremely high speed over large waves. No wonder he didn't want his armor.

But in another minute, they were off across the waves. As before, Ironfist made an excellent partner on the skimmer, and their combined effort made them move quickly enough that Gavin was able to use the foils to lift the skimmer mostly free of the water. That was good, because the chop was rough today, up to two paces high. With the skimmer's foils just right, Gavin was able to keep the boat mostly level. If they'd been right on the surface, it would have been a horrendous trip, impossible, really.

After a few hours, though, they escaped the poor weather.

They found the Atashian coast, and Gavin skimmed west until he saw a bay that he recognized. Between the incredible speed at which they'd traveled and the impossibility of taking accurate navigational readings while in the middle of the chop, they'd ended up thirty leagues off course. That much error for a normal ship could mean an extra day at sea. Not for them.

They'd overshot the Color Prince's army, going too far south.

Ironfist drafted a binocle, and they saw several Ilytian ships. Traders, supplying the army. Civilians, but civilians possibly carrying guns and powder that would wreak havoc on the peaceful innocents of Ru.

Gavin looked at Ironfist. Ironfist shook his head.

He was right. Scout first. Fight later.

They skimmed through the emerald waters off Idoss, giving it a wide berth. People in towers with spyglasses with fine lenses would see them long before they could gather any intelligence. They passed more ships, almost all of them heading west, supplying the army, too, no doubt.

It wasn't good. A few Ilytian ships could simply be enterprising traders who knew they could make a quick profit. But seeing dozens of galleys from Idoss, coccas from Ruthgar (meaningless because many merchants owned those), and caravels from Garriston meant that whatever government the advancing army had left behind was actually doing its best to support the invasion. That meant reasonably good governance. As Gavin knew, the first sign of trouble is when those cities you've subdued stop sending you supplies. If Garriston had been turned into a city that could *export* goods in only a few months, that meant that the Color Prince was doing a better job governing it when he *wasn't* there than the rapacious Ruthgari governor had done when he *was* there. Not good news.

They spent the rest of the day scouting, not daring to head too near Ruic Head, where the fort would doubtless have good spotters, but taking note of exactly how many ships they passed, and the places where they might have missed ships. The biggest thing they learned simply from the positions of the ships was that Gavin had been right. The army was perhaps six days' march from Ru. That meant the ships coming to help from the Chromeria would arrive only a day before the Color Prince's army. If the weather cooperated.

Not enough time. It took men time to move barrels of powder into place in a city under siege. It took them time to figure where the best shooting angles were, and to train to remember the angles in the heat and panic of battle. It took time for men to establish infirmaries and barracks in the most logical places, and to determine which units would work with which, and for officers to figure out which of their ally's officers were morons. Coordination, logistics, backup plans, strongpoints, which places must be defended at all costs and which could be yielded and retaken at grievous cost to the enemy—all these took time. It wasn't enough to put a few thousand men in a city, and that was what Gavin was afraid his father was going to do.

Andross Guile, for all his intelligence, was a politician and a drafter, not a general. Gavin couldn't hate him for it. It was how he saw himself, too. Men like Corvan Danavis had different strengths, and Gavin had learned to trust him more than himself. At the Battle of Ivor's Ridge, he'd seen a platoon, cut down to half strength, isolated and hard pressed on his army's left flank. If they'd crumpled, the line would have shattered, and they'd been outnumbered at least three to one.

Dazen had called off the charge he'd been planning, in order to go reinforce them.

General Danavis had stopped him. "I know those men," he'd said. "They'll hold. Now go."

Dazen did, and had won the battle. Without his charge into the center, the center would have broken. He hadn't even seen it, hadn't known how bad the center was until he arrived there with two hundred horse and fifty mounted drafters. Corvan had, and he'd been right about the platoon on the flank, too. If Dazen had done what he thought instead, they'd have lost. He might have escaped after that battle, but his army would have been destroyed.

Andross Guile, on the other hand, would never trust anyone more than himself.

Gavin and Ironfist returned after sunset, sculling the last leagues to hide the skimmer. They didn't return to the Chromeria, though. Instead, they met the first ships of the invasion force.

Ironfist went off to check where his Blackguards were berthed, while Gavin went to find the generals. He briefed them on everything he'd found and ignored their questions about how he'd learned the exact locations of enemy ships, in real time, halfway across the sea.

Worse, he could tell that the fools didn't believe him.

Gavin made sure a secretary wrote it all down. "Just keep two sets of plans," Gavin said. "In one, do whatever you were already planning to do with what limited intelligence you have." Gavin meant it both ways, of course. "In the other, plan as if everything I say is true. Soon enough, you'll know which to use."

He left them then, and went to the cabin some noble had been evicted from as soon as the men on the ship saw Gavin arrive. Tomorrow, he would go back out and sink as many ships as possible. It was a damned thing, war. He didn't like killing merchants, and he liked killing the slaves forced to row their ships even less, but that which strengthens your enemy must be denied him.

Orholam, if you existed, if you walked the earth as a man, what would you do?

There was a knock at the door. Orholam was fast some days.

It was Kip. "Kip?" Gavin said, surprised.

"Yes, sir."

"I didn't mean I'd forgotten who you were," Gavin said.

"Yes, sir. I mean, no, sir. Of course not."

Gavin smiled, though he was exhausted, and beckoned the boy in.

"I'm sorry to disturb you, sir," Kip said. "The runts—I mean the Blackguard inductees—"

"I know what they call inductees, Kip," Gavin said. He smiled. It took a long time to gain respect among the Blackguard. Scrubs, runts, wobs, nunks—they had plenty of derogatory names that didn't stop until the last vows. Even then, the first year for a full Blackguard was usually hell.

"Yes, sir, of course." Kip blushed. "The commander said war's coming, and there's no way to prepare for war like being close enough to smell its breath, sir. We're to help move supplies and civilians. We'll be off the front lines, but not quite safe, he said."

He said it with such an adult tone and assurance that Gavin looked at his brother's bastard son with new eyes. Four months had changed the boy. He was still chunky—maybe always would be—but as only young men can do, he'd dropped at least a seven already. It was like watching a man emerge from himself. The fat that had rounded and softened his features was receding. The strong line of his jaw and brow was all Guile. He was broad-shouldered, and his arms, though still shapeless, were huge. His confidence was soaring today, of course, his having just gotten into the Blackguard. It would crumple again—a dozen times. Boys, especially athletes, can look like a man in a day—but it takes them longer to reconcile themselves to themselves. But this Kip, this was a glimpse of the Kip who could be.

And Gavin liked that Kip.

It takes some of us a great deal longer to reconcile ourselves to ourselves, does it?

Looking at his brother's son, Gavin was pierced with sorrow. He would never have his own son. Not even if he achieved his impossible goal, and that was looking less and less likely with every passing day.

Aware that he had paused too long, Gavin said, "It's a good plan. Tell the rest of the runts that we're going to lose this city, so they shouldn't get any heroic ideas in their heads. Heroism is a fine thing, but heroism wasted means you can't be there to help on the day you can make a difference."

"Yes, sir. Trainer Fisk has been saying the same thing to us. Except the part about losing." Kip frowned. "But thank you. For telling me the truth."

Thank you for telling me the truth. Now, if there wasn't some bitter irony in that statement, Gavin was a marsh mug.

"I want to go with you tomorrow," Kip said.

"And what makes you think I'm going anywhere tomorrow—other than the fact that all of us are already traveling, so you'll be going with me by default?"

"You're the promachos, sir. Whether they call you that or not. I want to fight with you."

So ready to fight. But was I any different? How many men did I kill before I really understood what it meant to kill? Gavin rubbed the bridge of his nose.

"I'm going to kill men tomorrow, Kip. Men who don't precisely deserve killing. It's one thing to kill a wight, or a murderer, or pirates, or a man invading your city or your home, ready to rape and murder and steal. It's another to kill a merchant whose goods will bring death, but who is himself simply trying to make a living. A man like that has children back home, a wife you're making a widow, and a destitute one at that."

"We all pick sides," Kip said.

"Simple as that?" Gavin asked.

Kip shifted from foot to foot, but nodded.

"We've heard from four different spies that Liv Danavis is with the Color Prince now. Part of his army. So tell me, Kip, if we see Liv Danavis on the deck of one of those ships, about to toss a grenado at us, you'll kill her? Without hesitation, before she can kill us?"

Kip swallowed. "Orholam's...beard, sir. I...I hope he would defend me from having to make such a choice."

"If Orholam defended us from such choices, we wouldn't be here, Kip."

"How could she go with them, sir? They're monsters. Literal, real, flesh and luxin monsters."

"Idealists mature badly. If they can't outgrow their idealism, they become hypocrites or blind. Liv has chosen blindness, fixating so much on the Chromeria's flaws that she believes those who oppose us must be paragons. That we're not perfect says nothing about our enemies, Kip. Nothing. As it turns out, they're mostly bad. Bad enough that their rule would be a cataclysm, but that doesn't mean they don't have some good points about us. It doesn't mean that every fool who works for them is evil. It simply means they have to be stopped. By killing them, if necessary. That's the life you're stepping into here, Kip. I leave tomorrow at dawn. I'll get permission from your commander for you to join me, but if you can't kill Liv if you need to, don't show up. I won't hold it against you as a man, but as a soldier, I won't want you covering my back either."

Kip didn't answer immediately, and Gavin respected him the more for it.

"Thank you, sir," Kip said eventually. "I don't like it, but I appreciate your honesty."

Honesty? When I tell the truth about this and lie about all else? Appreciate something else, boy. I'm a liar to the core.

Chapter 98

Dawn found Kip on the deck, waiting for his father. It was cold and the seas were choppy, but his Blackguard's runt clothes were warm enough. At least when combined with his fat. He pulled the gray cloak around himself, stamping his feet. He hadn't gotten much sleep. The idea of killing Liv—or of being killed by her—had kept him from that.

But Liv had made her choices. She'd believed the lies she wanted to believe. She'd gone over to the side of madmen. How could she be so stupid?

Maybe Kip hadn't known her at all.

The thought made him sick to his stomach. He thought of her smile. Her laugh when she'd made him think the walkway between the towers was snapping, the fine curves of her body as she'd walked in front of him.

The knot in his stomach eased when he saw his father come out of his room onto the deck, already speaking with Commander Ironfist.

The commander was in the lead, speaking over his shoulder. "Do you know what your wife will do to me if I let anything happen to you?" he asked.

"Wife?" Kip asked.

Commander Ironfist scowled quickly. "My apologies, my lord, I didn't—"

"It's not a secret, Commander," Gavin said smoothly. "I married Karris before we left, Kip."

"You wha—Oh, oh," Kip said. Clearly that relationship had been a little different than Kip had thought in the little slivers of it he'd seen. Which had included curses and slapping and jumping off a boat rather than be near Gavin. Kip closed his mouth, then realized not saying anything might look like he was passing judgment. He couldn't help but feel left out. That he hadn't deserved to hear about it right away, that his father was still holding out on him. "Uh, congratulations, sir?"

"Why thank you, Kip. And I'm very glad to see you this morning. I've asked you to fight not as a boy, but as a man, and you've responded. And I can tell you haven't slept, so you've responded appropriately. Well done, son."

Well done, son. The words were what Kip had ached to hear for his whole life, and doubly so since learning Gavin Guile was his father. But they were delivered perfunctorily, as if Gavin were checking items off a list, without emotion, without attention.

"Now, as we go this morning," Gavin said, "I want you to tell me about the assassination attempt."

Kip hadn't really thought of what happened in the alley that way, but Gavin said it so blithely that Kip knew he had to be right. Lucia had died because of Kip. Had stepped into the line of fire. It was, oddly, exactly what Blackguards were supposed to do, but she'd done it on accident. Kip wasn't sure if that made it better, or worse.

They walked to the stern and Kip saw that they weren't going alone. At the bottom of a pair of rope ladders, a dozen Blackguards stood on a skimmer the likes of which Kip had never seen. It was, of course, bigger so that it could hold seventeen of them, but it was also shaped differently, like a large flying wing, with eight scoops. Every Blackguard was armed with a bow and a large quiver and bandoliers of grenadoes. Some had spare spectacles. From there, each was armed according to his fancy and expertise. A couple had bucklers. One carried a notched sword-breaker. Most had a pistol. One had a *bich'hwa* like Karris often carried. And others had the forward-bent ataghans or the sweeping scimitars. The skimmer itself had grapnels and ropes aplenty.

Plus, every Blackguard was himself a considerable weapon.

Kip's awe and hesitancy must have shown on his face, because Gavin said, "Kip, you can't become who you need to be if I'm not willing to risk losing you. You still want to come?"

Cruxer was down there. Cruxer was coming! He saw Kip and lifted his chin in greeting. He looked pretty excited that he was being allowed to come.

It pained Kip to say it, but he said, "I don't bring much to the table, sir."

"Not yet. But you're about to learn from the best."

They climbed down the ladder and onto the huge skimmer. Gavin began giving the Blackguards instructions. "Biggest risk is you'll tear your arms off. You can't go from a standstill to full speed in a breath. If you have the skill, you can narrow the pipes at first. The luxin needn't be focused. This is one place you can be sloppy, whatever is the easiest band for you to draft will work." He continued, while Kip settled into his place.

They released the ropes holding the skimmer to the galleon and Gavin and Ironfist manned the pipes on the main platform, and soon Kip heard the familiar *whoop, whoop, whoop.* Soon, half of the other Blackguards joined in, while Gavin and Ironfist gave instructions, and thenceforth the men and women spoke back and forth to each other, giving tips and hints.

Gavin taught them how to do turns and showed how sharply they could do it. And Kip saw the same look of delight steal over the Black-guards' faces that had crept over his own the first time he'd experienced the wind and waves and the sheer, unbelievable speed.

Then, when things settled down, Kip told his father the whole story of the assassination attempt as they sped across the waves. This skimmer was modified to enclose the front, so the wind didn't obliterate their conversations.

"This...this is different than the skimmer before," Kip said. "Didn't you just make this up a little while ago?"

Gavin shrugged. "War always moves forward, and if you're not at the leading edge of what's possible, you might not live long enough to regret it."

They saw many ships, but didn't close with any of them until after noon. Gavin stopped, motioning to Ironfist to do the same, and peered at the horizon. He brought out a large glass binocle, which was odd. The last time he'd needed to see into the distance, he'd simply drafted disks of perfect blue luxin. Maybe the clarity of this glass was better.

"It's flying their flag," Gavin said. "Broken chains on a black background." He handed the binocle to Ironfist.

Ironfist was quiet. "That isn't just a big ship," he said.

"It's a great ship," Gavin said.

"I can't even count how many guns it has. They're not just on one deck," Commander Ironfist said.

Gavin said, "Forty-three heavy guns, one hundred and forty-one light guns, fifty-two paces long, holds up to seven hundred men."

"Are you joking?" Commander Ironfist asked. "You couldn't possibly have counted..."

"It's Pash Vecchio's flagship," Gavin said. "If he's brought his flagship here, he's thrown in with the Color Prince. He wouldn't have hired out that ship."

Kip understood that this was Not Good. "Pash Vecchio?" he asked.

"The pirate king," Commander Ironfist said.

"One of four," Gavin said. As if that made it less impressive.

"The most powerful of the four," Commander Ironfist said dryly.

"Could have sworn that ship was going down the last time," Gavin said.

"You've fought Pash Vecchio before?" Kip asked.

"No. I killed the previous owner of that ship and set it on fire. He   505 was a pirate king, too," Gavin said pointedly. "Good news: we won't be killing innocents."

"Great," Kip said, trying to muster some enthusiasm. "Did you say one hundred and eighty-four guns?"

"Relax, there's only eighteen on the stern," Gavin said.

Comforting.

"What do you think they're bringing?" Ironfist asked.

"Guns, or men, or just coming to blockade our ships from getting into Ruic Bay. Regardless, big obstacle. Needs removing."

"You always did love a simple impossible challenge, didn't you?" Ironfist said. He didn't sound like he thought he had a chance of dissuading Gavin.

Which, Kip knew, he didn't.

"Why do you think I let you bring so many Blackguards?" Gavin asked.

"Thought that was too easy," Ironfist grumbled.

Gavin turned to the Blackguards. "Ready to see what you can do?" he asked.

He got grins in return. The Blackguards were like children with a new toy.

"I should have given you more time to train with the . . . what are we calling them, Commander?" Gavin asked.

"Sea chariots."

Gavin nodded acquiescence. "Lots of guns, and let's guess that there'll be drafters on board, maybe numerous. Maybe wights. They'll have tricks you've never seen. Expect the guns to be loaded already, though we may get lucky with how fast we'll be on top of them. Staggered approach, try to cut their lines and set fire to the sails early. We circle sunwise so we don't have collisions. Sinking the great ship is the primary target. If any other ships join the fight, they're targets of opportunity, not worth dying for. Speed is your best defense, but expect to miss your first few shots. It's hard to adjust your aim to this much speed at first. You figure it out. If you slow too much, you've given away your advantage and you've become one drafter against a ship full of musketeers for all we know. There are blindages on every deck, so until those are set afire or removed, don't expect to toss grenadoes up top and have much effect. Four crow's nests big enough to hold multiple archers or drafters. Eight large guns pointed to stern, including two that can aim down far enough to hit close targets. Ten smaller gunport doors that won't open until they're ready to fire. Oh, and her name's the *Gargantua*. Questions?"

"Where and when do we regroup?" a skinny woman with hard eyes and dreadlocks asked.

"Roughly, here, in one hour. If more ships rush in, one league east of the eastmost ship. Ironfist and I have the binocle, we'll find you. If we go down, Watch Captain Blunt has another pair. If you're completely separated, work your way down the Atashian coast until you can find safe passage back to the Chromeria. Asif?"

A young man with a shaven head said, "Sir, I assume that every drafter we see is a target of opportunity as well? To keep knowledge of the sea chariots out of their hands?"

There was a pause, and Kip realized what the young man was asking. Did they specially set out to kill every drafter, because there was no way to take them prisoner—you couldn't disarm a drafter.

"Just seeing the chariots won't be enough for them to mimic them easily. Don't put yourselves at risk. Low priority, but yes. Each of you is more valuable to me alive than having fifty of them dead. Got it?"

They understood. They weren't primarily elite warriors, they were elite guards whose ranks had been decimated by the battle at Garriston. The Blackguard itself needed them alive.

"Then let's go sink some pirates."

The Blackguards gave a cheer, only Cruxer forgetting to join in, looking wide-eyed and tight-strung.

Gavin drew his priceless dagger-pistols and turned to Kip. "Would you hold these for me?"

Kip scowled, remembering how he'd nearly dropped them into the sea last time.

"Joking, Kip. Joking."

Kip grinned.

"This is for you." Gavin handed Kip a bundle.

Unwrapping it, Kip found it was a belt with a pouch meant to be worn across one hip, like a holster. In the pouch were seven spectacles, in spectral order, each in its own velvet-lined half-pocket. There were little runes in silver sticking out next to each pocket so that you could tell by feel which spectacles you were about to draw.

Kip looked up at his father, wide-eyed. The spectacles alone were worth a fortune, but this looked *old*.

"Do your best not to lose the sub-red and the superviolet. We don't know how to make spectacles like those anymore," Gavin said.

Drawing the sub-red and putting them on, Kip gasped as he saw what Gavin meant. Usually you had to relax your eyes and let them lose focus to see the heat of things. With these glasses, Kip could see in the sub-red spectrum and the visible spectrum at the same time.

"You'll still have to relax your eyes to *draft* sub-red, but it makes finding good sources much easier." Gavin buckled the belt onto Kip and showed him how he could draw a pair of spectacles quickly, flick his wrist to snap the earpieces open, and put them on. Then he flicked the spectacles to one side, which snapped one earpiece closed, and then hooked the other in, letting the pouch close the other and hold it firmly.

Gavin gave Kip the binocle and said, "You can draft when we get into the fight, but I want you to keep an eye out. It's easy to get tunnel vision. Even for me. I'm going to be steering and drafting and shouting orders and dodging fire and magic. You keep your head about you. If another ship is bringing its guns up to rake us with a broadside, I might not even see it. Head on a swivel, got it?"

"Yes, sir." Kip didn't know what else to say, how to thank his father for the spectacles, but Gavin didn't seem to require anything. He went to the pipes and motioned forward. With everyone on their own, the big skimmer picked up speed quickly.

In no time at all, they were hurtling across the waves at incredible speed, with the *Gargantua* getting bigger and bigger all the time.

Ahead of them, Kip saw the stern gunports yanked open, and big, big cannons pushed out the holes.

"On my signal," Gavin said. "Wait for it. Wait for it!"

Chapter 99

As usual, Liv woke next to Zymun. It was early, and the young man's breath was even, regular. He was a heavy sleeper. Their tent wasn't large, barely tall enough to stand in, and they slept on piles of furs and blankets on the ground. Liv rolled over, careful not to disturb

Zymun. He insisted she sleep naked, and sometimes he liked to start his day the way he liked to end it. It was flattering to be desired so much, but sometimes she thought she simply happened to be the most convenient way to sate his hungers.

She blinked, aware of some change in the atmosphere, a freer brush of the wind than a closed tent should allow.

The Color Prince stood outlined against the morning light in front of the open tent flap. He held up a finger so she didn't speak and wake Zymun. He motioned that she was to come with him.

A wave of shame went through her. She felt like a whore, caught by her father with a boy she didn't even love. The feelings crested, and she quickly drafted superviolet. It was like the first puff of ratweed in the morning, except the luxin made her think more clearly. The feelings were the vestiges of small-town religiosity. Besides, the Color Prince believed in freedom, free choices. She was young. She could do whatever she wanted. There was no need to feel shame here.

She stood, briefly forgetting in the superviolet rush that she was naked. Koios White Oak looked at her frankly, and she soaked up his regard as boldly as if it were light itself. She waited a long second until she saw the twinge of regret hit him, and moved as soon as she saw it, gathering up her shift and pulling on her dress so that he might think she hadn't seen it. There were other kinds of power than magic and the sword. But some power works best in silence.

In silence, she dressed in her most practical dress and held her long dark hair out of the way. The Color Prince buttoned the last buttons for her, then she followed him out into the camp.

As the Blood Robes had marched on, rolling over town after town, their ranks had swollen. Liv was never sure how many of those who joined them believed in their cause, or if they merely believed in victory and plunder. She wanted to despise those who joined out of convenience, but she was using superviolet too much to be more than coolly amused most of the time. Besides, men believe in power, and what is victory but the demonstration of power?

Parts of her still mourned it, but everywhere she looked, she saw that the Color Prince was right. Power. All human interactions came down to power.

The Color Prince gave sermons every day, and he had disciples now, both drafters and munds, who wrote down every word and did their best to make a coherent system of it all. He talked about Dazen 509 coming back and championing their cause. He talked about freedom. He talked about the tributes they all paid to the Chromeria. Though his words melded politics and religion and history and civics and science, Liv thought she discerned less of an incredibly nuanced system underneath his rhetoric, and more of a belief created simply by the strength of his believers' faith that it must be rational, or their great leader wouldn't profess it. She couldn't tell how much of it the Omnichrome believed, but she knew that if he was going to accomplish his great purposes, he needed loyal followers. And those followers needed something to believe in, to unify them.

He didn't preach to the mob about power, just as he didn't allow them to call him Koios. Familiarity and knowledge both were for the privileged. Sometimes Liv thought the Color Prince probably didn't give a damn what all the people believed, that he tapped the heresies he tapped because he figured he might as well exploit every resentment against the Chromeria.

"Have you figured out your great purpose yet, Aliviana?" the prince asked. He nodded to a group of green wights who barely stirred at his presence. Greens weren't much good at veneration either.

"Aside from bait for my father?"

"I told you from the beginning you were that, and no, I haven't given up all hope for Corvan. But a hostage needn't be given privileges or the freedom you have. Surely you've gone past that."

"I'm the best superviolet you've got. It has something to do with that," Liv said.

"A broad guess," the prince said. "But not long ago you would have said 'one of the best.'" He seemed amused.

"I've changed," she said. She was more confident now; she had cut away the Chromeria's false humility. "And I'm right."

"Mmm."

The Red Cliffs loomed above the whole camp. There were spidery trails everywhere up those cliffs, but the prince had opted to send almost everyone along the coastal road. Only his cavalry had traveled along the high road, foraging and ready to put down any armed resistance.

The army was big enough now that some days there were skirmishes that Liv didn't even find out about until after dark. The Atashian army had probed the Blood Robes for weakness, but with the number of drafters the prince had, they hadn't found much.

Zymun had speculated, though, that they were going to find out how much steel was in the Atashians' spines soon. The army was to reach the narrowest pass between sheer cliffs and the ocean tomorrow.

"Are they going to crush us at the Gates of Sand?" Liv asked.

"No," the prince said.

"Really? Zymun thought that was the best chance they had of stopping us before we get to the grasslands around Ru."

"It was. But you need naval support to hold the Gates, and our Ilytian allies crushed the Atashian navy five days ago."

Liv hadn't even heard a whisper of that. "Ilytian allies? But the Ilytians don't believe in anything."

"They believe in gold." The Color Prince gave a grim smile. Together, they climbed up an exposed rock promontory. The soldiers standing there snapped salutes. The prince reached the top and did something with his eyes. He expelled a disappointed breath. "Not yet. Maybe tomorrow."

"My lord?"

"Close your eyes, Liv. Can you feel it?"

She closed her eyes and tried to feel. She felt the coolness of the morning, smelled the latrines, the campfires, the cooking meat, her own body. She felt the hummingbird weight of light on her skin, light as a wind, passing in soft billows from the rising sun. She heard the sergeants calling out to training men, the clash of sticks on armor, the neighing of horses, the laugh of a woman, the tread of feet. She heard the faintly unnatural hiss of the Color Prince's breath.

Opening her eyes, she looked over to the man who was shaking the world to its foundations. Shook her head, disappointed in herself.

"Tomorrow. Tomorrow maybe you'll see it. Go now, and send up Dervani Malargos and Jerrosh Green."

They were the two best green drafters the Blood Robes had, the teachers for every green who hadn't yet broken the halo. Liv went down and called for them. They seemed to be waiting, and the two of them went up on the promontory.

Liv watched them as the prince spoke to them, wondering if they would see or feel what she had not, wondering if she was failing in some way.

"Good morning, beautiful. Always with the tests and mysteries, huh?" Zymun said, coming up beside her. He put a possessive arm around her. Sometimes that annoyed her, but she'd been worried

511

yesterday that Zymun was already losing interest in her, so she said nothing.

"I suppose," she said. "It's not capricious, though."

"You think," Zymun said. He was the only person Liv knew who dared to speak derisively of anything the Color Prince did. At first she'd wondered at that, but a little yellow and superviolet meditation had made it plain: Zymun was jealous. He felt threatened, less of a man around the most powerful man in all the world.

That was the mystery to her.

"So what was it today?" Zymun asked.

"Asked me if I saw something. I didn't."

"Looks like they didn't either," Zymun said, nodding toward Dervani and Jerrosh. "Those two hate each other, and both want to lead the greens. As if the greens can be led. Idiots and fools."

The men were bickering, faces turning red, furious. Liv could almost make out the words from here. But she watched the Color Prince instead. From the set of his overlarge shoulders, she could tell he was furious himself, though nothing else betrayed it. He raised one hand, as the people in the camp around seemed torn between watching and not being caught watching.

The two greens stopped abruptly. The Color Prince said something else, and they both dropped to their knees, apologizing. Odd to see a green on its knees.

Its. She'd thought *its* knees, not *his* knees. Wasn't that curious? Another remnant of my childish beliefs, that a person ceases to be a person when he breaks the halo. Our very language has been corrupted to make the murder of drafters palatable.

The Color Prince drew a pistol and shot Jerrosh Green between the eyes.

A spray of blood, atomized, drifted to the ground slower than the chunks of red-gray brain matter liberated from their bony home via lead. Jerrosh Green's body dropped backward and tumbled down the bare rock of the promontory. The camp was suddenly silent. Pistol still smoking, the prince bound a slender choker with a black jewel on it on Dervani's neck. He gestured for Dervani to stand.

The drafter stood and left without a word.

"Funny thing is," Zymun said, "I still can't tell which of those two is more brainless."

She looked at Zymun from deep within the grip of superviolet—she hadn't even noticed drafting it again, but now it was like a friend to her—and realized that the boy wasn't hard and callous. At least he wasn't only those. He was terrified. He was imagining his own brain painting the rocks.

He looked at her, and she saw in his eyes that he feared her, too. He was tiring of her, but not out of boredom or for her lack of enthusiasm under the blankets. He didn't want an equal; he wanted to be worshipped. Zymun was far more dangerous than she had realized. She would need to be rid of him, but carefully, cleverly, so he thought it was his own idea.

"I don't know how you do it," she said. She dropped the superviolet. He could sometimes tell by her voice when she was drafting it. "I don't know how you can see that and not be afraid." The shudder she let through wasn't wholly feigned. It also wasn't the shudder of desire she hoped he thought it was. She turned her eyes to his and moistened her lips and said softly, "Take me back to our tent. Right now."

Chapter 100

The big guns on the *Gargantua*'s top deck belched flame and smoke, the sight of hell's bounty outracing its sound. Two jets of water, fifty paces ahead of the skimmer, announced the miss an instant before the roar of the cannon revealed it had even been fired.

One of the guns on the second deck went off next, and Gavin shouted, "Now!"

Around the skimmer, Kip saw that the Blackguards were grouped into pairs, one at the reeds and one archer. Each team's archer had a rope in hand, and starting at the outside teams, they pulled.

Before Kip realized what was happening, the skimmer split, each team suddenly freed, one driver and one archer, the sea chariots breaking off from the skimmer smoothly and multiplying their force instantly. Two, four, six, and eight split off, leaving only Gavin and Ironfist and Kip on the now much smaller skimmer in the center.

The water behind them cratered and jetted as Kip heard the roar of the cannon again. Then it seemed the world turned to cannon fire. The *Gargantua* loomed larger and larger and the eight skimmers cut the waves with perfect grace, none so close to the others that a single cannon shell could hit two of them.

The seas were rough today, so Kip was glad that his father had made supports, both up behind his back so he wouldn't tumble off the stern and also handles so he could brace himself. Kip saw that the deck of the *Gargantua* was actually open, contrary to what Gavin had expected, but then, even in the few seconds that Kip was watching, the great wooden screens that were the blindages were brought down by scrambling sailors. Seen in sub-red through Kip's spectacles, the men glowed as if lit from within, still clearly visible despite the screen.

The skimmer cut hard to port and Kip barely caught himself. He didn't see any danger, but he decided that even as he was scanning the big ship and trying to keep an eye out for more distant dangers, he should copy his father's and Ironfist's stance. Each man had his legs set wide and knees bent, keeping his weight low.

The great rudder of the *Gargantua* turned hard, and the lumbering great ship, sails full, began to turn. Along the broadside, Kip could see gunports snapping open, on at least three different levels. Not all at once, but as each crew was ready.

There were a *lot* of guns.

From the nearest crow's nest, a ball of luxin the size of a cat arced out.

"Drafter! First crow's nest!" Kip called out.

The luxin ball split in midair and ignited. It landed on the water only a dozen feet from the starboard side in a curtain of flame—and floated, flames two feet high.

The first sea chariot cut hard to port, nearly plastering itself against the *Gargantua*'s hull. The next must not have seen the fire in the swelling of the waves, but those same swells saved it as the swells and the *Gargantua*'s wake made a ramp that flung the chariot into the air and neatly over the fire.

Gavin and Ironfist cut wide around the burning slick and then cut close to the ship.

"Musketeer! Third—fourth crow's nest!" Kip shouted. He couldn't even yell his warnings right.

There were half a dozen men along the high castle manning swivel guns. They had to aim between the bars of the blindage, but they didn't seem to be having much trouble. Kip threw sub-red at them, had no idea if he'd hit anything, and then hit the deck as one of the big cannons went off mere feet from his head as the skimmer pulled even to the ship. The world disappeared as cannons roared and great billowing clouds of black smoke and cordite gushed from their throats.

Seen through the sub-red lenses, the world was delineated into great flashes of exploding guns, the sharp tongues of spitting muskets, the muted bursts of the grenadoes, and the ghostly shadows of men.

Then they were out of the smoke. They immediately cut hard to port, passing in the very shadow of the beakhead. Gavin and Ironfist both hurled grenadoes into that deck overhead. Gavin's was wrapped in red luxin, and stuck; Ironfist's was spiked, and stuck. Twin explosions and showers of wood and flame announced their success. None of the cannons on the port side of the *Garguntua* had been fired, so Kip was able to see clearly once more.

Flames sprang up on the mainsail—and were immediately extinguished in sprays of orange luxin. A few of the lines had been successfully cut, but those that had been merely set aflame were also saved.

"Brace!" Gavin shouted.

The skimmer curved to starboard to get some separation, and just as they rose out of a trough, Gavin shot a huge ball of flaming red luxin at the first crow's nest. The drafter saw it coming and tried to blast it aside, but the ball merely shattered and drenched him and the crow's nest in flame.

But Kip barely saw that, because the concussion of Gavin throwing something so massive just as they went airborne threw the skimmer hard to the side, and had they not hit the crest of another wave, they probably would have capsized.

Instead, they simply slowed to a crawl as Ironfist and Gavin were thrown off the reeds for a moment, and the skimmer turned the wrong way, bobbing in the waves. Kip saw two men training swivel guns on them even as a man engulfed in flames pitched out of the crow's nest, tangling in the lines as he fell, shrieking.

Then the gunners disappeared in a wash of flame and exploding yellow light as four of the sea chariots closed around the Prism.

The port-side cannons began firing, and Kip saw one of the archers on the back of her chariot simply disappear. The blindage was afire, and Kip saw the sailors and soldiers above them struggling to throw it over the side. One of the Blackguards had painted a line of red luxin down the entire length of the *Gargantua*'s hull, and as the cannons roared, it lit.

Within seconds, Gavin and Ironfist had the skimmer back up to speed. Musket balls whistled past them, dimpling the water. Several of the archers were firing now at great speed. And Kip could tell that the soldiers were only beginning to make it to the deck.

"Birds!" Kip shouted as a flock of pigeons exploded from the deck of the *Gargantua*. Pigeons?

"Ironbeaks!" one of the Blackguard shouted.

Kip lost sight of the birds and the ship itself as the skimmer dodged in and out. In the sudden lurching, he thought he was going to be sick.

I'm going to be seasick? In the middle of a battle?

He looked to the horizon to try to steady his stomach. Two of the sea chariot drivers who'd both lost their archers had gone out the range of the guns and abandoned one chariot, pulling another cord that made the luxin fall apart at the seams. Gavin hadn't wanted the secret of how to make the chariots falling into enemy hands. But beyond them, Kip saw a galley coming, its triple oar decks moving the small ship quickly.

"Got a galley coming," Kip shouted. He pulled up the binocle and almost puked as the magnified vision seemed to magnify the swaying. "No flag."

Gavin shot a look up. "Probably pirates looking for an easy kill, not Vecchio's. Keep an eye on it."

Then they were back into the fight. They came out from under the stern galley onto the starboard side and saw an explosion blow one of the cannons on the lowest gun deck completely out the side into the water in a spray of wood and fire and smoke. One of the Blackguards— Kip though it was Cruxer—whooped.

An instant later, Kip saw one of the pigeons dive at Cruxer. It hit his chest, stuck.

Cruxer slapped the bird off his chest. It splashed into the water and less than a second later exploded.

Then Kip understood. Like the hellhounds Trainer Fisk had told them about, these birds were natural birds, but they'd been infused with a drafter's will to do one thing—attack the Blackguards. And in this case, they'd also been equipped with small grenadoes.

Which meant several dozen small flying bombs were circling the great ship—small, intelligent bombs.

As intelligent as pigeons, anyway.

And if that wasn't quite terrifying, seeing half a dozen of them hit a Blackguard team that had slowed to throw a grenado into a gunport was. A second later, both driver and archer were ripped apart by the explosions. The grenado the woman had thrown bounced harmlessly off the blindage—which hadn't been pulled off on this side of the ship—and exploded in the water, barely so much as scoring the wood of the hull.

The *Gargantua* was a floating castle. The fires weren't spreading. It was invincible.

"Reeds," Gavin said to Ironfist.

The big man seemed to know what he meant instantly, because he took Gavin's reed and began propelling the skimmer by himself.

"Kip, hold my feet down. All your weight."

Gavin was already weaving something between his hands. Kip practically dove onto his feet. Instant obedience. Then he followed Gavin's eyes.

The entire flock of the remaining ironbeaks was headed straight at them. With only Ironfist on the reeds, the birds were catching up.

Gavin didn't finish until the first bird was practically within arm's reach. Then he threw both hands out and a net of yellow luxin spun out from him. It engulfed all of the birds. Then Gavin yanked his arms down and was nearly pulled from Kip's grasp. But the pressure lasted only a second.

There was no such thing as action at a distance with luxin. To throw something, you had to throw it; to slap something down onto a deck, you had to yank it down. Gavin had made the luxin a lever, and he'd cast the entire net of the birds onto the deck of the *Gargantua*.

Where they exploded. Kip saw half a man and a helmet flying off the deck.

Not an empty helmet.

Gavin scrambled back into place, and Kip saw an orange drafter peek over the deck and spray luxin down on the burning hull, extinguishing the flames.

Ironfist saw him, too, and put a blue spike in his skull. The man tumbled into the sea.

"They're organizing into musket teams," Ironfist said. And the effect was almost immediate. The men on the decks must have started putting the best marksmen in front, while those farther back reloaded and gave them fresh muskets, because both the rate and the accuracy of fire increased.

A sea chariot driver just behind them crumpled, turning the pipes wildly to one side. Her chariot flipped, flinging her archer into the sea.

"Guard overboard!" Kip cried.

Ironfist's and Gavin's reaction was immediate. Catching a peak, they shot hard to starboard. The skimmer flipped completely backward before they hit the next wave.

All of them were nearly torn off the skimmer from the sudden change in direction, but neither Gavin nor Ironfist slowed. Kip thought he was going to tear the post behind him right off, but it held. Both men pulled grenadoes from their bandoliers and tossed them in high arcs. Then another.

"Sub-red on any muskets you see, Kip!" Gavin shouted.

They sped toward the swimming young man.

"I got the reeds," Gavin said. He took them both and headed straight for the Blackguard. Kip thought he was going too close, but as he popped over the last wave, Gavin turned slightly and they splashed barely a hand's breadth from the Blackguard. Ironfist reached down and between Ironfist's strength and the Blackguard's, the man popped out of the water in barely a second.

Kip hadn't seen what effect the grenadoes had on the deck, but the musket fire had slowed. Then he saw one of the swivel guns on a lower deck being turned toward them.

The other Blackguards on their sea chariots had rallied around them, and they were spraying red luxin everywhere, the yellows casting flashbombs to dazzle and distract, but the sheer number of them congregating in one sector was enough to encourage the cannoneers to turn the big guns.

The screams of the furious and the shouts of anger and the moans of the injured and the cries of urgent orders and the crackling of fireballs and the snapping of distant muskets and booms of cannons and the whistle of the big mortars and the snap of sails and the wash of the waves and hissing of the wind and the moans of the dying and the shrieks of the wights faded, grew distant, hushed. Kip could hear only the deep, slow whoosh of his own heartbeat, ludicrously slow, and around and beneath that a sighing, like the beach when the tide goes out. For a moment, he had a wild notion that he was hearing the sunlight hit the waves.

He saw one of the Blackguard archers drawing an arrow back. The string touched her lips and the arrow leapt out at the very moment a musket ball tore her jaw off.

Whoosh. The world looked beyond real. Kip realized he was seeing the whole spectrum at once. He could see dozens of guns. The skimmer was directly broadside to the *Gargantua.* And he could see the glow of men, the glow of matches and slow fuses. He could see the gleam of metal on the powder barrels through the open gunports, could see straight through the smoke.

He swept a hand out and fanned superviolet strands like spiderwebs out to every gun and barrel he could see. The superviolet was so fast and light, it hit its targets almost the instant he chose them. Then he swept his hand back, releasing little bursts of firecrystals so hot they burned his hand even as he shot them out at unbelievable speed.

Satisfaction swept through him even before the next big whoosh of his heartbeat rolled through his ears.

Struck by the firecrystals, every loaded musket and cannon on the starboard side of the *Gargantua* went off at once. Cannons that were in the middle of being loaded went off, muskets that men were standing over with ramrod in hand went off. Loaded muskets being handed up to marksmen went off. Some of the cannons hadn't been charged yet, and Kip felt vexed. Others, though, had been fully loaded but not yet pushed back into place, and they blew holes out of the sides of the gun decks.

The entire ship was rocked to the side from the simultaneous concussive force.

Not bad.

And then, on three different gun decks, powder barrels exploded. Flames and smoke and wood and cannons and men and parts of men blasted fresh holes in every deck.

The roar ripped over the Blackguards and Kip blinked. Time was back. He was back.

Men were screaming. Terrible, terrible screams. He could see men on fire, skin blackened and sloughing off, running to jump into the sea. Fires leapt out of all three gun decks.

The skimmer shuddered and Gavin and Ironfist threw their will into getting back up to speed.

"Four ships coming in, half a league," Kip said. He felt empty, stunned.

"Under the beakhead," Gavin said.

"Not so sure that's a good—" Ironfist said.

"Under the beak! The wights will be up on deck any second. We've got one chance at this!"

Ironfist acquiesced instantly and they sped in front of the ship, hardly any muskets barking now. They came under the front of the still-moving ship, and Ironfist took the reeds, maneuvering them so that the ship didn't plow right over them. The wooden beakhead loomed just above their heads, close enough that when the waves lifted them, it almost smashed Kip's head. Gavin wrapped one fist in fire and punched into the hull overhead.

When the wave receded, Gavin was yanked into the air, his fist still stuck into the wood. Kip lunged, but missed him.

"Leave him!" Ironfist shouted. "You see anyone, you light 'em up!"

Kip could see then that Gavin was drafting still, heedless of his body hanging by one arm.

I don't think I even could hold myself up by one arm.

Gavin was doing it and drafting—and drafting something horrendously complicated, if it was taking him this much time. Then he was done. When the skimmer rose on the next wave, Gavin touched down on the deck as gracefully as a dancer.

"Two minutes," he said. "We need to keep the drafters busy."

And so they circled again, Commander Ironfist giving hand signals to the three remaining sea chariots. They concentrated on hurling luxin and exhausted their grenadoes, some of them successfully tossing them into the huge holes Kip's explosions had created. Somewhere in the fighting, one of the teams had successfully cut all the rigging to the foremast, and another had set fire to the lateen sails, but the mainsail and mainmast were still whole.

The great ship seemed invincible.

Gavin swooped in and destroyed the capsized sea chariot, and then after perhaps thirty seconds they circled wider, out more than a hundred paces. With so many of the big guns silenced for the moment, it was close enough to still be a threat, but far enough away to be safer from all but the luckiest musket shot.

The Prism and one beefy female Blackguard were the only ones who had the strength and the endurance remaining to continue bombarding the *Gargantua* with magic. Everyone had gone through all their grenadoes. The archers had used up most of their arrows, and the four ships Kip had seen earlier—two small galleons and two caravels—were bearing down on them.

Gavin gave a quiet oath. "If it doesn't happen in the next—"

A deep whomping explosion drowned out his words. It seemed to shake the sea itself in its bed.

Kip shot a look at Gavin. His father looked oddly bereaved. "Their powder room was below the waterline. Makes it a lot harder for a stray shell to hit it, but...poor bastards."

When the smoke began to clear, Kip saw that both sides of the hull had been blown out right in the middle of the ship. With wood creaking and snapping, the mainmast plunged off to one side like a man jumping overboard, throwing men from both of its crow's nests and slashing through the weakened deck at the ship's waist.

Some few men were leaping from the decks, and fire was everywhere. Smaller explosions sounded like popping corn. Then the waist collapsed and the ship folded in on itself. The front half of the great ship went down almost instantly, far faster than Kip would have believed something made entirely of wood should sink. The stern rolled over on its side, open decks gaping like open wounds, swallowing the seas in great burbling gulps.

Deck by burning deck, the great ship plunged into the sea, hissing and spitting and vomiting up flotsam and broken men.

Before it even slipped under the waves, Ironfist asked, "Mop up the swimmers?"

Gavin looked toward the coming ships.

Mop up? Commander Ironfist meant, Should we kill the men who survived?

"You see any wights make it out?" Gavin asked.

"Didn't see any. Doesn't mean there weren't some," Ironfist said.

"I didn't see any either," the Blackguard they'd pulled out of the waves earlier said.

Kip watched the last of the *Gargantua* slip beneath the waves. There was a lot of junk afloat in the waves, but not many men. Gavin had said there were seven hundred men on board.

Orholam have mercy.

Because your Prism won't.

"No," Gavin said. "I'd rather be a mystery and a wild tale. We don't have it in us to sink four more. Let's go home."

They headed out two leagues to regroup, and the sea chariots came alongside and with difficulty in the heaving waves, they reformed the big skimmer. They'd lost seven Blackguards. Another had taken a ball in the elbow. She would be crippled. The rest had minor injuries: burns and little cuts and pulled muscles from maneuvering their chariots too sharply. One had a musket-ball burn in a streak along his neck that was going to leave a scar. He looked perversely pleased about it. A breath more to the left and it would have cut his carotid. Cruxer was wide-eyed, blinking a lot, but unhurt.

"Breaker," Cruxer said, "did you do what I think you did back there?" He looked at the Blackguards. "Am I the only one who saw him blow up half the ship?"

"I saw," one said. Others nodded, though not all of them.

"We saw," Ironfist said. "Well done, Breaker."

"Well done? It was fucking awesome!" Cruxer said.

The Blackguards laughed, and even Ironfist grinned and didn't reprove Cruxer for cursing.

"Did you blow up the whole ship, too?" Cruxer asked.

"No, that was him," Kip said. He'd been looking at his father already. Gavin was staring at him with a strange intensity that wasn't wholly approving. Kip thought he would be proud of him, but again, there it was, that sense that under everything, Gavin was holding out on Kip. Avoiding embracing him fully.

"How'd you do it?" a Blackguard asked Gavin. Kip thought his name was Norl.

Gavin looked displeased. For a moment, Kip thought he wasn't going to answer. But then Gavin's eyes passed over the rest of the Blackguards. They'd lost almost half their number today.

"I made a golem of a rat, and willed it to go to the powder keg to explode," Gavin said quietly. "It's the kind of thing a wight would think of, so there would have been one posted in the hall to stop any such thing. I figured the explosion gave me an opening. Figured right."

"But making golems is forbidden," Kip said. He knew it was stupid the second he said it. It had worked. It had probably saved their lives. It had definitely won the fight.

"I'll decide what's forbidden," Gavin said. But his voice wasn't strident; it was weary. "We'll eat here, dress the wounds we can, then head home."

They ate silently, everyone aware of the places that were empty. They'd won. They'd killed seven hundred men or more, at the cost of seven. By any measure, it wasn't only a victory, it was a great victory. And yet the Blackguards were silent, eating like automatons, not hungry but disciplined enough to know that their bodies needed the sustenance after a hard fight.

"You do this all the time," Ironfist said, "don't you?" They were sitting on the deck, munching hard biscuits and sausage.

"Sink ships?" Gavin asked. It sounded like he was making an effort to regain his levity. He was Prism; he needed to set an example. Ironfist refused to take the bait. "That ship could have sunk half our navy before we arrived in Atash, but we didn't even know it was here. The threat's gone, so to those idiot generals it will be like this never happened. We'll tell the story of what we did today, and some won't believe us. Most will believe we're exaggerating to make ourselves look good. But even those who do believe us won't know what we went through to do it. They won't understand what we faced here."

Gavin gave a little shrug.

"You do this all the time. You've been doing this since the war. You save people, without them even knowing. You've stopped wars, you've sunk pirates, you've put down wights, you've killed brigand companies single-handed. All without bragging or even asking for thanks. You are He Who Fights Before Us indeed," Ironfist said. "Promachos."

Gavin said nothing for a time. "Today we were *promachoi* together."

"The Spectrum granted you that title long ago, and then they took it away. They can take your title, my lord, but they can't take your name. We Blackguards know about secret names. We know about naming a thing what it is. You, Lord Prism, are Promachos."

"Promachos," the other Blackguards said quietly.

"Promachos," Ironfist said, sealing the name. "Thank you, Promachos. For all you've done that I don't know. For the prices you've paid that I can't understand. For doing what others couldn't, or wouldn't. Thank you. And know this, the Blackguard was created with twin purposes: to watch for and to watch the Prism. You've always distrusted us because of the latter, as well you should. But I tell you this day that the Blackguard will never turn against you so long as I draw breath. It is an honor to serve *you*, *Promachos*, and serve we shall, blood and bone."

"Blood and bone," said the Blackguards.

"Blood and bone," Ironfist said, sealing them to him.

Gavin couldn't meet their eyes. "I'm not the man you think I am," he said very quietly.

"Are you the man I've served these past ten years?" Ironfist asked.

"I am."

"Then perhaps, my lord, you're not the man *you* think you are."

Gavin flashed a grin and seemed abruptly himself once more. "You've got a stubborn streak a league wide, don't you?"

"And two leagues deep," Commander Ironfist said. "And don't you forget it." He stood up and turned to the Blackguards. "All right, you laggards, ready up! Let's go home. Tomorrow we do it again."

Chapter 101

"Your intelligence is abysmal," Gavin told the generals around the cabin. "Their plan—their first plan, at least—is simple. They stop our ships before we can get there. Without our troops and supplies, Ru will fall in days. You didn't come prepared for a sea battle. We've got a dozen warships; they have fifty."

"You've invented some new means of travel," Andross Guile said. He was the reason this room was bathed in blue light. "That's how you're scouting. Tell us about this."

Gavin ignored him and left to get some rest before the battle. He woke before dawn, and started laughing quietly. He dressed in the darkness and bound his hair back. A knock jostled the door in its loose hinges.

"Commander," Gavin said. They walked out onto the deck together where the Blackguards were checking their gear, some quietly joking, some doing the morning ka, whatever it took to soothe the pre-battle nerves. They'd taken down the biggest ship in the Color Prince's navy yesterday, but they were professionals; they knew they weren't invincible. A musket ball didn't care if it had been fired by a man on a great ship or an idiot in a dory. Anyone could die, anytime.

Kip was standing with them, looking like he was wound tight enough to thrum.

"I'm not going with you today," Gavin told Ironfist. He didn't bother lowering his voice. Let the Blackguards overhear. He was asking them to risk their lives. "I've other work to do that may give us some slim chance for victory. Probably not, but it's worth trying."

"Can I send anyone with you?" Ironfist asked.

"Not for this. I won't be in danger, though. Not physical danger anyway."

"Kip?" Ironfist asked.

Gavin turned and looked at the boy, who was eavesdropping and making a small attempt at pretending not to be. "Kip, you can't come with me. Not for this. You can make up your own mind about whether you want to go with the Blackguards to sink ships."

"I'll fight, sir."

Yes, you will.

"High Lord Prism?" a thick Blackguard asked. He was an orange/yellow bichrome named Little Piper. Gavin nodded for him to continue. "Will you look at a design we've put together?"

Gavin followed them over to a pile of munitions. Someone had designed great disks, bigger than a shield, with a grenado's trigger mechanism. Gavin didn't understand.

Little Piper pushed a tiny woman forward. "It's Nerra's design," Little Piper said.

She wasn't even one of the Blackguards who'd gone with them yesterday. She had to clear her throat twice before she was able to speak. "From hearing the stories, I figure the best advantage we have is that we can close quickly." She showed how the disk had teeth and red luxin on the bottom. "The driver brings the sea chariot right next to the ship, and the archer slaps this onto the hull."

Gavin took a breath. It was brilliant in its simplicity. But the design wasn't right. The disk could be hardened at the back so that most of the explosive force went into the hull. And there was no way you'd want such a short fuse on an explosive this powerful. And it needed shrapnel. And the red on the back side needed to be covered with a thin layer of yellow that could be stripped off just prior to placement so the red didn't lose its stickiness and so the disks could be stacked. Then the sea chariots would need to be— He was getting ahead of himself.

He started calling out for the items he needed, and the Blackguards delivered them promptly. Then Gavin made two different designs, one lighter and one heavier. He hefted both. The heavier one packed more explosive power, but power was no good if you couldn't get it where it was needed. He handed them around.

"The heavier," the Blackguards agreed.

Gavin gave them instructions then and they made a line, the Blackguards copying the backplate and filling the reservoir half full with nails and musket balls and forming the hooks. Gavin made the fuses and the yellow and red luxin mixture to fill the reservoir. A couple of reds applied the right amount of sticky red luxin to the backs, another drafter put a tiny layer of lubricative orange on top of that, and Gavin covered it with a thin plate of yellow.

"Hullwrecker," Gavin said, barely pausing as he checked that the fuses on every one were drafted correctly. Then he climbed down the rope ladder to the sea chariots and drafted a place for the hullwreckers to be stacked, and an extra support to keep whichever Blackguard placed the explosive from tumbling off the back of his own chariot. He'd replaced the sea chariots that had been destroyed yesterday, and even drafted extras. Today, fifty Blackguards would be able to head out at once.

"Well done, Nerra," Gavin said. She looked embarrassed. "You've saved a lot of lives today."

"But my lord, you made it a hundred times better."

"So I saved lives, too," Gavin said. "We're a team, right?" He smiled at her and she blushed.

Gavin moved to get onto his own sea chariot. It was slightly modified from the earlier versions. Another experiment. He was always experimenting. A young Blackguard was standing there to hold the boat steady when Gavin pulled it loose of the rest. It was Gavin Greyling.

It felt like a sledge hit the center of Gavin's chest. He met the eyes of the young man who'd lied to save his life. "I'll try to be worthy of it," Gavin said quietly.

The young Blackguard said nothing. His face showed nothing.

Gavin got on his sea chariot. He wanted to give more orders and advice to Commander Ironfist, but the man knew what he was doing. He would do the maximum damage with the minimum loss of life possible. He didn't need Gavin to tell him how to do that. So Gavin left.

He sped across the seas, which today were a great deal calmer than they had been yesterday. That fact alone would probably save more of the Blackguards than Nerra's and Gavin's invention.

For Gavin, it didn't mean much except that his trip was somewhat smoother and faster than it would have been.

The sun was past its zenith when Gavin turned the skimmer into the bay at Seers Island. He could see that his seawall was still in excellent order, and there were dozens of fishing dories out in the bay. People waved at him, greeting him like a returning hero. There was a town on the shore now, the jungle had been pushed back, and alongside temporary shacks, more permanent buildings were under construction. There were even farms.

The change was profound. Gavin wasn't sure why he was surprised, but he was. He hadn't even been gone very long, but he'd helped establish the fundamentals. They'd warehoused the tens of thousands of yellow bricks he'd made, and they'd obviously been putting them to good use. Fifty thousand people with purpose, good leadership, and all the tools they needed could do a lot of work in a short time. What didn't surprise him was that the Third Eye was waiting for him on the beach.

Being a Seer must be terribly handy.

Which was why he was here. He couldn't believe he hadn't thought of it sooner. He was going into battle and he'd spent—perhaps wasted was more accurate—several days scouting out their positions. While he knew a Seer. A True Seer who didn't couch what she saw in mystical jargon and vague pronouncements.

Gavin beached the skimmer and jumped lightly onto the sand. The Third Eye was dressed in a simple white dress, belted with a golden sash. She'd once said that she was usually modest. It was, he'd come to see, actually true. She held a hand out, and Gavin kissed it. She smiled, delighted, and Gavin thought there was something softer about her this time.

"My apologies about last time," she said.

"My lady?"

"If I spoiled your marriage for you, the last time you washed up on my beach. I try to not ruin futures for people, but I was under some stress. I make mistakes."

Gavin looked at her radiant face and was glad she had reminded him he was a married man. He was terribly in love with Karris, but this woman tugged at him on several layers beneath the rational. "Me, too," he said. He knuckled his forehead. "Just exactly how much do you..."

"Hold on, Corvan is right down on the pier. I think he's been so busy he may not have seen you come in."

She offered her arm and he took it, escorting her through the crowds. The people noticed, and they stared, and many of them bobbed their heads to both of them, but Gavin knew this kind of deference. It was the kind of respect men on campaign give to their general. The protocol peeled back to its bare, necessary layers. These people were hard at work, and they had worked alongside the Third Eye for months. They adored and respected her, maybe loved her, but they had work to do.

And she had no bodyguards now. That spoke either to an unprecedented level of peace here or perhaps to her prescience. Hard to kill a Seer, one would guess.

They walked together out to the pier, where Corvan Danavis was speaking to three men who were gesturing to what appeared to be plans for a shipyard.

He turned and looked shocked. He ran—literally ran—over to Gavin and embraced him. Gavin loved him for that. He embraced his one true friend hard, and then released him. "Corvan, you old dog, you look well."

Corvan was growing out his mustache again, though it wasn't yet long enough to dangle beads in. He looked ten years younger. "Do you know how hard it is to negotiate with people who can see the future, Lord Prism? I can't believe you did this to me. But yes, I suppose that working twenty hours a day agrees with me. Or perhaps it's the company I get to keep during the other four." He grinned.

Gavin had no idea what he was talking about. Then he saw the ring on Corvan's finger a moment before the man stepped over to the Third Eye and kissed her, picked her up, and spun her in a quick circle.

Gavin laughed. "No disaster?" he asked the Third Eye.

She smiled mischievously. "It was...a political necessity," she said with mock gravity, teasing Corvan.

"A duty. A burden," Corvan said gravely.

Gavin couldn't believe he hadn't seen it. Of course it probably *had* been a political necessity. Corvan the leader of the invaders; the Third Eye not quite the leader but the most respected among the island's inhabitants. Both single, both desperately needing to bind their people together. It *had* been a duty. But sometimes fate is kind, and that which is your duty is also exactly what you were made for.

It also would have made things incredibly awkward if Gavin had bedded the woman his best friend ended up marrying. A disaster.

"Are you going to tell him?" the Third Eye asked.

"Tell him?"

"Men!" she said. "You went to the Spectrum and..."

"You know?" Gavin asked. "Oh, of course. Orholam, that's unnerving. You haven't told him?"

"I hate spoiling the future. Besides, you're the one who paid the price for it. It's only right you should get to tell him."

"Tell me what?" Corvan asked.

"You're a full satrap, High Lord Danavis," Gavin said.

"I'm a— What? What?" Corvan said.

"Full satrap, full responsibilities, full privileges. You get to name your own Color. A small flotilla of ships carrying supplies and diplomats is already on its way here."

"Three weeks out," the Third Eye said, "and bringing along more than a few problems, along with their lifesaving goods and medicines."

"You knew about this?" Corvan asked.

"You didn't think I'd marry some mere washed-up general, do you?" the Third Eye asked.

Gavin could tell it was an inside joke. Corvan smiled fondly and shook his head. "A satrap? You said it would be honorary at best. That getting votes would be the work of future generations."

"Meh." Gavin shrugged. "They stabbed me in the back. I replied in kind. By the way, you voted for war."

"Did I have good reason?"

"Mmm."

"Color Prince?"

"None other."

"You left me here, you know. Abandoned me. Do you know how hard it is to be married to a woman who knows everything?"

"Almost as hard as it is to be married to a man who exaggerates," the Third Eye said.

They were deeply in love. Smitten. At their age. Sad.

"I hear you finally came to your senses," Corvan said to Gavin.

"She told you about Karris?" Gavin asked.

"Orholam is kind," Corvan said.

Orholam? I thought you barely believed in him. "Corvan, I'd love to spend the next six months here, but I need to speak with your wife. The war's moving on, and I need to leave within two hours to make it back before I run out of light."

They went to a tavern nearby and sat outside—"Absolute necessity for civilization," Corvan had said when Gavin commented sardonically—and took seats in the back. Gavin filled them in on everything that had happened. Everything, from destroying the blue island to throwing that girl off the balcony. He was glad to see that the Third Eye hadn't known all of it.

Then he asked her, "Can we save Ru?"

"The real question is if we can save the Seven Satrapies."

"Can we save Ru?" he insisted.

"One time in a thousand," she said. "Your father would have to think that he was the brilliant mind coming up with half a dozen strategies that you simply aren't in a good place to feed to him." She touched Gavin's hand, and the yellow luxin eye tattooed into her forehead glowed. She took a deep breath, continued to hold his hand, and the glow brightened, brightened until it was blinding.

She threw Gavin's hand away from her like it was a serpent. She stood abruptly and went out. Gavin stood, bewildered, but Corvan was faster. "Stay," he said. "I'll take care of this."

He was gone for five minutes. Gavin tried some of the ale that a very nervous woman handed him. It was surprisingly good. If he hadn't known that the Third Eye was the real thing, he would have been suspicious. The skeptic in him was stirring even now. This seemed perfectly orchestrated to paralyze or terrorize him.

The Third Eye came back in unsteadily. She avoided looking Gavin in the eye as she sat across from him.

"You want to know the disposition of forces at Ru. I can tell you that."

"Are you trying to scare the hell out of me?" Gavin asked.

"Gavin, listen to your mother."

"Now that, *that* is the kind of thing I expect from a charlatan," Gavin said. "I thought you weren't big on parlor tricks."

"You remember Koios White Oak?"

"I remember seeing a wall fall on him sixteen years ago."

"He's the Color Prince."

"I saw a *wall* fall on him. A burning wall."

"He's the Color Prince."

"I saw a wall—"

"I'm not the moron in this conversation, Guile. Please don't speak to me as if I am. How many times have you escaped certain death? You think your enemies might never have the same good fortune?"

Gavin's mouth went suddenly dry. "What—but I—does Karris know this?" Koios. That night when Karris had wept about her dead brothers, she'd said his name. She'd been trying to work up the nerve to tell him. But even telling him would have felt like betraying her brother.

"Have you told Karris all your secrets?"

Fair question. He'd told her most of them, but no, not all.

"You're wasting time," the Third Eye said. She was suddenly hard and cold, like it was all she could do to get herself through this. "You need to go back to the Chromeria and get Karris."

"She's injured."

"Stop interrupting. She'll be well enough to fight. The men your father sent to beat her were very careful, very professional. They were told to inflict pain, not injury."

"It *was* my father? That piece of—"

"That part isn't important right now. If you don't get her... just get her."

"Tell me," Gavin demanded.

"Telling you *changes* things," she said tensely. Her golden eye was glowing.

"Tell me!"

"If you don't get her, you'll die. A musket ball tomorrow or a green wight the next day. If you do . . . the old gods waken, Gavin."

"The old gods waken?! That's all you tell me?"

"You've lost green. You know what happens. This battle to save Ru, it's noble, but it's the wrong battle. You already know that."

"There's a green bane, like the blue?"

"You can't stop them all, Gavin. It's impossible."

"Where is it?" he insisted.

"If I tell you, you'll be in the wrong place."

"Tell me."

"If I tell you, you'll die, you damned fool," she said, temper flaring. "Ask the right questions!"

"Am I going to—" He balled his fists. "What do I need to do?"

"Mercy isn't weakness, and love carries a heavy price."

"I think I'm more the kind of a man who—"

"If you don't figure out exactly what kind of man you are, there's no hope for you at all."

"If you were going for ominous, that was pretty good."

"I do omens for a living. You want better? Then go now and bed your wife. Bruised and broken as you are, it may be your last chance."

"Now that, *that* was ominous." Gavin stood with a bravado he didn't feel. He'd learned things, but not the way he'd wanted to.

"Gavin," the Third Eye said, "you came to ask where their forces are. They've taken the fort on Ruic Head, though they haven't put up their own flag. They hope to sink your fleet at the neck. And Ru has several hundred traitors already in the city, including the mercenaries the Atashians hired to protect them. The prince's men have been hard at work."

Gavin hesitated. "How long until I lose the rest of my colors?"

"That depends on what kind of man you are."

"What would you guess?" Gavin asked, irritated.

"If you're as good of a man as I think you are, you don't have as much time left as you think you do." Her eyes were full of compassion—except for that pitiless third eye, which saw only truth.

Gavin walked out the door, and saw Corvan. The man had been weeping, but had dried his eyes and was trying to pretend he hadn't been.

Orholam's great hairies, it couldn't be that bad, could it?

The men embraced. Said nothing. Walked together down to the beach. The Third Eye followed them. People had gathered, realizing who Gavin was. They watched from a distance. They knelt. It was like they didn't know how to tell Gavin what he meant to them. It was just as well, because he didn't know how to take it. He waved to them, nodded.

"You said before that you were sometimes wrong, right?" he asked Corvan's beautiful wife.

"Sometimes," she said sadly.

One in a thousand. He'd faced worse.

"Dazen," Corvan said quietly. He swallowed, looking out to sea, looking at nothing. "My lord, she tells me if I go with you, I can only make it worse. Otherwise, I'd...My lord, it's been an honor."

And then, as Gavin got onto the skimmer and Corvan pushed the boat out into the gentle surf, The Third Eye said, "Orholam guide you back, Lord Prism."

He was sure that she didn't mean back to the island.

Chapter 102

"I'm going to kill him, someday. But he's good at what he does. I'll give him that," Zymun said, rising from their bed in the predawn darkness. Liv was already up and dressed, almost finished fighting her hair into some order. "I'll let him do the work of uniting the satrapies, and then take it from him. Unless he threatens to botch it, of course."

"What are you going to do? Once you become king, I mean." She slid the hairpins in place, adjusted the bit that was falling in front.

"Emperor," Zymun said, correcting her. "And whatever do you mean? What will I do? You're not very smart, are you?"

Not smart enough to avoid you in the first place, clearly. She froze. His charm had been slipping more and more frequently. He was a lizard beneath it. There was something wrong with him. Something thin, an essential *shallowness*. How had she not noticed before? When he touched her now, her flesh grew cold. Her body had known. She'd told herself that she was extricating herself carefully, but she wasn't: she was afraid. Afraid to be a woman alone in an armed camp. Such fear didn't befit a drafter. Such fear didn't befit a woman. He wanted to treat her like she was nothing? Hatred coiled in her breast.

It took all of her self-control, but she turned and looked at him with a mask of cool condescension. "Zymun, Zymun, Zymun. Emperor? Please. There is no trace of greatness in you."

She slipped out of the tent deftly. She was shaking. What about your big plan to make him tire of you? To escape his clutches and make him think it was his idea?

All in pieces now. *Shit.*

Knowing the smart thing to do and having the makeup to do it were two different things. To hell with him.

Liv went directly to the Color Prince's tent. He was gone. She found him instead on the outskirts of the camp, greeting new drafters who'd abandoned Ru or other Atashian towns. At least half of them were on their last year or two of life. Cowards, Liv thought.

But armies are composed of those who join for bad reasons as well as good, and the prince despised no one who helped him. Liv approached him, bowed deeply, and said, "Magnificence, may I have a private word with you?"

The prince measured her, then excused himself.

"Zymun is planning to betray you," she said without preamble.

"Thank you. Will you teach this class of recruits for me?"

"What?" she asked. " 'Thank you?' That's all?"

He looked at her sharply.

"My apologies, my prince. I didn't mean to raise my voice."

He favored her with an indulgent smile. "When did you find this out?"

"I'd suspected he had an...overlarge opinion of himself, but he didn't say anything treasonous until this morning."

"And you came straight to me."

"Yes, my lord."

A retainer emerged from the ranks and started coming toward the prince. He lifted a hand, telling the man to wait.

534 "You knew," Liv said.

"I knew."

"So . . . Did you send me to spy on him?"

"You tell me," he said. Another servant looked ready to come forward, and again he motioned to the woman not to interrupt. Running an army meant making decisions from dawn until dusk and beyond.

"You weren't testing him. You were testing me," Liv said.

"Oh?"

"You knew he'd betray you; you didn't know if I would. So I passed. Was Zymun in on this?" If he had been, that would mean that he was still favored by the Color Prince, and the way Liv had left him wasn't simply over her loyalty to the prince. She might have just made a powerful enemy, without at the same time making a more powerful friend.

"Do you know what happens to an egg, when you keep it warm?" the prince asked.

"It hatches?" Liv said.

"And when you make it hot?"

"I'm not sure I—"

"It cooks." He smiled, indulgent, magnanimous. "Everything has a proper time and season. Some things rushed are spoiled. This is why so many of the Chromeria's wights go mad and become dangerous, not because wights are innately so, but because their drafters get to the end of their human span and then panic. Panicked people do shoddy work. If instead they worked deliberately, over a course of years, to prepare themselves for the transition, their odds of success increase dramatically. If they had people to teach them what to do, just imagine what we might accomplish."

"That's—that's . . . wise. And that's what you're doing with Zymun?"

"Zymun is incredibly gifted, and very, very dangerous. There is no human warmth in him. Only a fool would trust a man like that, but by using him? I've found that I can trust you. Now, did he know you were coming here?"

"I'm—I'm afraid he might. I've made a terrible enemy of him, my lord."

"Forgive me for this, but raise your voice now and swear that Zymun's a traitor, that you wouldn't lie to me, and so forth." The prince's face twisted. "Do it. Now."

"My lord! I swear it to you! Zymun is a traitor—I would never lie to you! You have to believe me!" Liv threw herself at the Color Prince's knees.

He backhanded her across the cheek hard enough it rattled her teeth, and she fell to the ground, weeping.

Two guards lifted Liv and pulled her away, just around a tent, out of sight, but still close enough that she could hear a little of what was said. She heard Zymun speaking, his voice oily slick as usual, totally unafraid. His back must have been toward her, because she couldn't make out his voice.

"Zymun," the Color Prince said, "I'm giving you a small force, drafters and soldiers, whatever composition you want, but only twenty men, and make sure you bring along gunners in that number. I want you to cross the neck at midnight, climb the cliffs, and take Ruic Head. There may or may not be ropes waiting for you. We have spies, but they're criminals and prone to hysteria. Not trustworthy. Regardless, take Ruic Head and keep flying the Atashian flag. The Chromeria's fleet is two days out. Let the scout ships through unaccosted, only open up when the main fleet first starts through the neck. I expect you to sink at least a dozen ships. At least. Oh, and take no greens with you. Take blues. The bane will be disorienting until Atirat is come."

Zymun said something.

"No. Absolutely not. I have need of her."

Something else. Liv cursed to herself for not being able to hear, but she couldn't without exposing herself.

"Zymun," the Color Prince said, raising his voice as if the young man was farther away. "I trusted you with a vital mission once and you failed. You lost a magic worth more than ten of you. It was my mistake to trust you with that, so I didn't punish you for it. I had hoped to abort this war before it began. I thought it worth the risk. You're one of the very best I have, Zymun. You know that I've been lenient with you and why. For a privileged few, I tolerate one failure. *One*. Understood?"

Chapter 103

Commander Ironfist had Kip and Cruxer join him on the central skimmer. Instead of heading directly for Ruic Bay as Gavin had, Commander Ironfist had them work their way up the Blood Forest coast.

Though they had only been skimming for two hours, Kip was feeling antsy. He didn't like being trapped on a boat. He tried to enjoy the salt spray and the speed and the small towns they passed. The sea today was much calmer, and the sky was blindingly blue. The sea itself changed color with every bay and shallow.

They came upon the scout ship so fast they barely had time to split the sea chariots off. They rounded a point, and there it was, approaching the point from the opposite side, flying its broken-chain flag. Commander Ironfist was shouting orders and two of the sea chariots darted off in front of the rest of them.

The cocca was a small ship. Twenty-five paces long, with a crew of perhaps twenty and lateen sails, and six medium guns per side, balanced on the gunwales the old way instead of outfitted with gunports. It didn't get a single shot off. A single sailor was manning the swivel gun on the front, trying to load it, when the two sea chariots passed on either side. One set its hullwrecker near the prow, the other on the opposite side near the stern. Then they broke away.

Kip could hear men shouting, and for what seemed forever, he thought that the explosives had failed.

Then they went off at the same moment. Muffled thumps blew all the way through the cocca's hull and out the opposite side as well. There was fire, but it was quenched quickly as the ship went down.

With four wide holes in the hull, it didn't take long. At Commander Ironfist's piercing whistle, the sea chariots regrouped and sealed their individual boats back into place. By the time they were finished, the cocca was underwater. A dozen men and women were paddling in the water or clinging to debris.

"Commander, should we take captives for interrogation?" Watch Captain Beryl asked.

Ironfist looked at the people in the water and judged how far they were from shore. It wasn't far. Leaving them wouldn't be a death sentence, but Kip knew that they didn't have the space to take captives and still continue to sink ships. "Our mission's elsewhere," the commander said. "By the time they could bring word back to their generals, our battles will be finished, I think."

They left and hadn't gone half an hour farther up the coast before a putrid smell rolled over the skimmer. It was death.

"There's a village a league or two from here," one of the Blackguards said. "Weedling, it's called. I grew up just a few bays down."

The skimmer cruised slowly into Weedling Bay and Kip was relieved to see that the village wasn't burned to the ground. But there were hundreds of gray shapes crowded onto the beach so thickly that there was hardly any sand visible. Perhaps a dozen locals were walking across the backs of the shapes, carrying machetes and buckets.

"Are those beached whales?" Cruxer asked.

"Orholam have mercy," someone said.

The wind brought a blast of putrefying flesh and blood to the skimmer and Kip almost gagged. He felt funny. Not just sick or disgusted, but trapped. He wanted to jump into the waves and swim. He wasn't even sure where. It was a crazed, caged animal feeling.

"Commander," one of the Blackguards said, "I don't feel so good."

"It's just dead fish," Ironfist said. "Kalif and Presser, draft us some oars."

They drafted oars and oar locks and the Blackguards rowed the ship in. When they got within forty paces, the villagers finally noticed them. Some fled outright, while the others merely watched them with hooded eyes.

A tall older man with some kind of long-bladed spear that he had been using to cut into the thick whaleskin stood on a half-butchered whale with one hand on his hip. "Well, the sea she brings us all sorts of insanity, don't she?" he said.

"Are you the conn here?" Commander Ironfist asked.

"Such as we have," the man said.

"I'm Commander Ironfist of the Chromeria Blackguard."

"Ironfist? Aye, we've heard that name here. Curious boat you have. I'm Conn Mossbeard."

He didn't, so far as Kip could tell, actually have moss in his beard, but it was dyed a pale lichen green.

"What happened here?" Ironfist asked.

"Something's been building for a couple weeks, though it's not near so strong today," the conn said. "Livestock acting like there were coyotes in the yard, but none were, you know what I mean? Plowhorses and oxen shying from their harnesses. Horses spooked. Pigs attacking like all the sudden they thought they were javelinas. We had people injured by the score, by beasts they'd known their whole lives. We're farmers and fishermen here, we knew something wasn't right. Still don't know what, though. They say great powers clash, small folk suffer, I don't know." He spat.

Ironfist didn't interrupt, gestured for the restive Blackguards not to speak either. If the stench of the decaying whales hadn't been so overpowering, Kip would have jumped off the boat.

What's gotten into me?

"Whales beached yesterday. Heard of it before. Never seen it, and never heard of so many doing it at once. Handy placement if they're going to do it, I thought at first. We could get enough meat and oil to last us years, but..." He pulled his tunic up and Kip saw that he had a bandage around his side. It was bloody. "I started giving orders, like I done a thousand times. People here know you got to work together for big jobs like this. But they attacked me instead. Men and women I've known my whole life. Attacked me and run off. The animals are gone, too. It's like a madness came. 'Cept it didn't hit us all. The steadiest men and women, we're all still here. Coro over there, he used to be an idiot, had fits when he didn't get exactly one biscuit at dawn, exactly two pieces of bacon at lunch. Now he's as right as you or me. But them's were normal, most of them are long gone. Don't know where. Don't know what to do but butcher what we can and hope this all blows over like a squall."

"Did any of the people act...um, oddly before they went?" a Blackguard named Pots asked. He turned to Commander Ironfist. "Your pardon, Commander."

"We're good people here," the conn said. "Decent. Devout."

"People do strange things when they're not in their right mind. Things that aren't truly their fault," Pots said.

The conn grimaced. Spat again. "Seemed like folk lost all sense of dec...of decoration, if you take my meaning. I saw...I saw." He spat again. Avoided eye contact. "Folks were rutting like animals. Folks walking about nekked. Folks grunting and howling and barking.

Barking. You heard people called barking mad? I thought it was jus' something people say. I saw men I've known forty years barking at each other. Scared me half to death. Like they was made animals in all but body."

"Whatever it is, it's driving the animals mad, too," Commander Ironfist said.

"You feel it?" Pots asked.

Most of the Blackguards mumbled agreement.

"I think we better leave," Commander Ironfist said.

"Kip, you feel it?" Pots asked.

"Absolutely," Kip said.

"Nerra, you?" Pots asked.

"No."

"Commander?" Pots asked.

"Maybe a little."

"Wil, you?" Pots asked.

Wil swallowed. "I feel half mad, to tell you the truth."

"It's the greens," Pots said to Commander Ironfist. "It's something wrong in green. Lust, loss of self-control, rebellion against authority. The Color Prince has poisoned green."

"Atirat," someone mumbled ominously.

"Whatever it is, it's not only affecting drafters; it's hitting munds and even animals," Pots said.

"Mossbeard!" Commander Ironfist called out. "We're doing what we can to stop it. Your folk may come back yet. All may be restored to you yet."

Conn Mossbeard looked at them with steel eyes. "Restored? I caught my wife with another man, and when she saw me, she just laughed and kept on. I looked into her eyes and couldn't tell if it was madness plain and simple or if the madness was letting her do what she'd always wanted."

Ironfist said nothing.

"Go play at your wars. Go visit your plagues on someone else. It's always the little man as pays the piper. I killed my wife, sir, the woman who stayed with me through drought and blight and fire and the death of four daughters for twenty-four years. There's no restoration here."

They rowed away and Mossbeard went right back to slaughtering the whale he stood on without giving them another look.

"Greens," Commander Ironfist said without looking at any of them, "you tell me if it gets too bad. If you feel like you're going to turn on us, tell us. I'm not going to lose anyone today, through madness or death. Understood?"

"Yes, sir," Kip said with the rest of them.

They went all the way up the Atashian coast that day, almost as far as Ruic Head, and they sank half a dozen ships. On many of them, the sailors were in disarray, unwilling or unable to follow orders and act as coherent units. It made them easy targets, and they sank them without any trouble.

It was, frankly, frightening how easy it was. With the combination of their speed and the explosive power of the hullwreckers and the fact that the ships they were preying on were distracted and had never seen anything like the sea chariots—much less prepared for them— they sank ship after ship. But their feeling of invincibility was broken when Pots took a ball in the shoulder. They bound him up, and made it all the way to Ruic Head, where a fort towered on top of the red cliffs there, bristling with artillery that could reach far out into the narrow neck of the Ruic Bay. They approached only close enough to look at the fort's flags—it was still flying the Atashian colors.

Commander Ironfist turned them back toward the fleet, and they made it back an hour before dusk, which was a good thing, because it took them another hour of consulting the sextant and compass and skimming and guessing and consulting the sextant and compass again to find the fleet, which was making good progress toward Ruic Head. Three days out now. Kip and the other greens were relieved to get away from the Atashian coast, though, and he could feel the madness receding as they got farther away.

They talked, and they couldn't be certain, because measuring feelings of growing dread wasn't exactly as simple as sliding beads, but they thought that whatever was causing the madness had to be coming from the Color Prince's camp itself. Or from one of his ships nearby. No one seemed to want to talk about the prospect of fighting a battle when men were as likely to jump off their ships as they were to obey an order. It seemed an invitation to chaos and slaughter.

Gavin didn't come back that night. Kip wondered if he'd died somewhere, far away and alone.

The next morning, Commander Ironfist headed out again, but this time he wouldn't let anyone who could draft green come with him.

Kip was left alone. He waved to Cruxer and grimaced at his own ill fortune. When he turned to go inside, he found himself staring at Grinwoody.

"Young master," the slave said. "Luxlord Guile finds himself with a spare hour. He wishes to play Nine Kings with you. Attend me, please."

It wasn't, of course, a request.

"And if I won't come?" Kip asked.

Grinwoody smiled his unpleasant smile. "Long swim home."

Chapter 104

Gavin barely made it to the Chromeria before nightfall, the skimmer going slower and slower as his eyes strained for light. At least the waters were still enough that he was able to land directly on the back side of Little Jasper, where there was a tiny dock, rather than having to draft an entire dory by starlight and row in to Big Jasper and walk.

Stepping onto the creaking wood, he disintegrated the yellow skimmer. He rubbed his arms and shoulders, hoping they didn't cramp. The muscles were trembling and weak from his journey even though the last two hours had been slow going. He was starting to feel a sick foreboding that yellow was getting harder to draft. He hoped it was simply the gathering night, and not that he would wake tomorrow unable to draft yellow at all. If so, he was going to have a hard time getting back to the fleet before the battle was over.

He tried to smile over the rising terror. At least he was going to spend tonight in Karris's arms. To the evernight with everything else. What had the Third Eye said? "Bruised and broken as you are, it might be your only chance"? Gavin was sore and fatigued, but he was neither bruised nor broken, so either she had meant the "you" to mean Karris or she was simply wrong. Regardless, he wasn't going to solve the mysteries of prophecy and he didn't care to. He just wanted to see his wife. His *wife*. How odd that phrase seemed. And yet how he'd missed her. He felt it keenly now, now that she was so close and his mind wasn't crowded with fighting, plotting, doing, doing, doing.

Some part of him thought that she was going to be snatched away if he didn't hurry. He opened the lock on the stout oak door. The hinges were rusty. Pulling the door open made him aware again of how tired his arms were. He tried to lift a hand over his head and couldn't.

The door opened to a long, claustrophobia-inducing tunnel, barely wide enough for one man to pass with his shoulders turned. Gavin touched his hand to one of the ingenious sub-red switches, and from the heat of his hand, it triggered a reaction that opened panels of yellow down the length of the tunnel. Sometimes it was the simple, elegant things that could be done with magic that impressed him far more than his own brute-force behemoths.

Five minutes down the tunnel deposited him at an iron gate with a different lock. He opened that and took a narrow staircase up into the front yard of the Chromeria. By the time he reached the lifts, two Blackguards had fallen in step beside him. He grinned at them. "Gentlemen."

"Lord Prism," they said.

He took the lift up, and then the second lift to his own floor, walked past the Blackguards, who didn't look surprised in the least to see him—how did they do that, anyway? He walked to his own door, then, thinking he heard something, he looked down the hall. The White's door was closing, very slowly.

She must be asleep. Her guards are being careful not to wake her.

But still Gavin hesitated. You should go check that out. For a second he was aware of himself, poised between going in to a beautiful woman and going to an old crone. What kind of an idiot even thinks that's a choice?

Cursing himself for a fool, he left his door and strode quickly down the hall. It was rude to enter anyone's room filled with luxin; it was treated like coming in with a pistol leveled at your host's head, and if Gavin could get away with many things, that wasn't one of them. Not with the White. So he drew in superviolet. What they couldn't see couldn't be rude, could it?

He opened her door as stealthily as it had just been shut. A crack, and then more. Bodies wearing Blackguard garb lay on the floor and a figure was treading slowly toward the White's bed, clad all in black.

The light streaming in from the well-lit hallway betrayed Gavin. The figure spun, drawing a pistol from his belt in a smooth, fast motion. 543

Gavin blasted the door open with his shoulder and dove into the White's room, shouting, "Assassin!"

The pistol roared. Its ball shattered wood and whined, ricocheting off the stone behind it.

A gray ball nearly two feet across shot out of the man's hands, catching Gavin's first Blackguard as he was jumping into the room and drawing his pistol. It knocked him horizontal and back into the other Blackguard.

The assassin had dropped his first pistol and drew another, turning to kill the White, who was awake and scrambling to get off her bed.

From the floor, Gavin shot the tiniest spotlight beam of superviolet out, and as the assassin turned, Gavin's superviolet played over the man's hand. Then Gavin shot the rest of his superviolet.

Superviolet is delicate. All the superviolet Gavin held probably weighed only as much as a hairpin, and it wasn't strong, but even a hairpin flung at great speed can have some effect. The superviolet burned the air and slammed into the back of the assassin's hand, cracking bones and flinging the pistol out of the man's grip.

Gray-white light flooded the chamber from a dozen sources. Gavin popped up off the floor, instinctively drawing in light to hurl blue spears at the assassin.

He was all the way up and throwing his body forward to ready itself for the massive recoil of the magic he was about to throw when he realized he hadn't drafted anything.

The assassin's counter of another ball of gray light caught Gavin full in the chest. It launched him backward and he slammed into a wall, the impact driving his breath from him.

Green, his brain told him helpfully. He's not drafting gray, that's *green*. I just can't see it anymore.

The assassin pulled out another pistol and leveled it at Gavin. From this range, with Gavin still trying to suck in his first breath, the man couldn't miss.

A sunburst of white-gray light lit the man, and Gavin saw the White standing in her bedrobe, a cloud of tiny glowing particles floating in front of her, like motes of dust. Her hands snapped forward, and so did the entire cloud. The sound of the tiny flechettes hitting the assassin was like the sound of Blackguards at archery practice, when an entire volley studded the targets.

The assassin froze, and a moment later, tiny droplets of blood formed on his skin, everywhere. His back had been turned to the White, and the tiny glassine flechettes had gone all the way through him. The assassin blinked bloody eyes, confused, knowing only that something was terribly wrong, and then he collapsed on the floor and began convulsing.

The world didn't stop. Even as the man was falling, Blackguards were bursting into the room, whistles were shrilling. A sword descended on the assassin's convulsing wrist, separating his still-loaded gun and gun hand from his body.

The sudden press of bodies was almost a relief. The Blackguards had their priorities. Subdue the threat, secure the area, check the health of the guarded, check the health of the downed guards, notify the chain of command, and so forth. Gavin let it roll over him. He'd taken a good shot, and he'd be lucky if it turned out he hadn't cracked a rib, but he was alive, and so was the White.

Oddly enough, it seemed that both of the Blackguards who'd been guarding Orea Pullawr were alive, too. One was still unconscious, and the other could only remember being grabbed from behind and having a foul-smelling rag pressed over his face. Apparently whoever had sent the assassin was trying to make some point about the vulnerability of the entire Chromeria by making the assassination as clean as possible. The guns and magic had only come out when the assassination was threatened with failure.

They found the White's balcony door cracked open, and climbing ropes hanging past it. The ropes were hanging from the roof. The assassin must have tied the rope above and, finding the White's balcony deadbolted, decided to go to the roof and enter through the door. It was a bold plan that would allow the assassin to escape after the murder by opening the balcony door from the inside and sliding down the rope without alerting anyone. It would have given the assassin valuable minutes to escape alive. This had been no suicide mission. The Blackguard immediately began going down the tower to check every room that had a window or balcony on the north side, looking for accomplices.

Gavin was shaken. A few months ago, he would have killed that assassin by himself. This time, his color-blindness had almost gotten both him and the White killed. He looked at the gray lights burning everywhere in the room. They weren't gray; they were blue and green. The White had been a blue/green bichrome, so she'd obviously put in colored lux torches so that if something like this happened, she could immediately have light available to draft in a heartbeat. With a lesser assassin, the sudden flood of light itself might have bought her a few seconds. Not this one. But regardless, between Gavin and the Blackguards interrupting, it had worked.

He wondered if the White was well. She hadn't drafted in years, and she wasn't in particularly good health to begin with.

Gavin stood with the Blackguards' help just in time for Karris to come in the door and crash into him. She grabbed him so fiercely, it almost knocked him off his feet. Then he recovered his senses and hugged her back.

"I heard there was an assassination attempt and you were involved and—and you scared me half to death, Gavin Guile!"

"You changed your hair," he said stupidly. She'd bleached to blonde from its previous dark Tyrean hue. He liked it blonde.

"You like it blonde," she said.

"He saved my life," the White said. She walked over. Walked, instead of being wheeled over. Gavin couldn't see the halo in her gray eyes, but he could see that her eyes were no longer washed out, desaturated. Now they looked like a drafter's eyes again. And there was fine red color in her cheeks. She looked stronger, younger, and yet her halos were still intact. Mercifully. "They say he spoke before he died. He said, 'Light cannot be chained.' Do you know what that means, Gavin?"

"It means we have a problem," Gavin said quietly.

"It means the Order of the Broken Eye exists and is choosing to reveal itself. And *that* means we have a problem. The Order has risen. They mean war. Now go, I know you've other things in mind for tonight, and I'll be up until all hours telling my story and giving orders and taking questions. I'll handle all this. You..." She waved him toward Karris. "You handle all that." And then she winked.

"Thank you," Gavin said. He might have blushed a little.

"No, Gavin, thank you," the White said. "Thank you."

Of course, it wasn't as easy as simply going back to his room. The room had to be searched—and Gavin held his breath when they searched the closet—and then guards had to be posted. Marissia sat on her little slave's stool by the door, looking like she was trying to be invisible to Karris, but didn't want to leave without being dismissed in case Gavin needed anything. Gavin absolutely refused to have a Blackguard in the room with him. "Karris is here. She's a Blackguard." While he argued, he gave Marissia a glance and a tiny wave. She looked grateful, and slipped out the door silently.

"Mmm, we're assuming she might be...preoccupied, Lord Prism," Watch Captain Blademan said dryly. What, did Ironfist offer a class in that attitude? "Someone attacked the White by climbing up to her balcony; we're not leaving you in danger."

In the end, they posted two Blackguards out on the balcony and pulled a curtain. The men were both given heavy wool cloaks and hats and told not to come inside until Gavin rapped on the glass—*if* he rapped on the glass. Other guards were posted outside the definitely-not-soundproof doors.

Being worth killing was a real pain in the ass.

"How are you?" Karris asked as she closed the door.

He barely heard her. He was taking the chance to look at her, really look at her for the first time. It seemed he'd been gone forever. He hadn't noticed earlier, but she still moved gingerly. The blackness and swelling had faded, though not completely. Karris healed fast. "Your eyes are healing well, how's the rest of you?" he asked.

"My eyes? I look like a raccoon!" She scrunched her face up like a rodent and made little chirping sounds that Gavin supposed were supposed to be a raccoon.

"Do that again," he said.

She laughed, embarrassed, and he laughed with her.

"You're the prettiest damn raccoon I ever saw."

"Oh, Gavin Goldentongue," she teased. "With that kind of eloquence, you're going to charm my— Oh, look at that." By some feminine magic, without apparently using her hands, her undergarments slid down her legs. She kicked them aside with a *hmm*, and grinned a self-satisfied grin at him. She looked positively devilish.

Gavin's mouth went dry. She opened her robe and let it slide down her shoulders and then pool on the floor and she walked toward him. Her chemise was a silk confection, clinging to her lean curves, barely coming down to her hips.

"Are you well enough for me to have my way with you, my lord?" she asked.

"A bit bruised and broken," he said. He suddenly smiled. Damn

Seers. "And a lot pungent. I've crossed the seas entire today. And I see that—" No, no don't mention Marissia. "I see that there's a bath drawn. I could—"

"You come back and find me half-naked and you want to take a bath?" she asked. But she was teasing.

Instead of matching wit for wit, Gavin looked straight into her eyes and said, "I want this to be perfect for you."

"I don't want perfection. I want you, Dazen Guile."

There was a right answer to that. Gavin cupped her cheek with a hand and pulled her lips to his. She was all that was warm and soft and safe in all the world. He pulled her into his arms and she pulled into him, glorying in the muscles of his shoulders and arms, his sheer size in comparison to hers. He obliged her by enfolding her completely in his arms. Then she squeaked.

"Ow, ribs, ribs," she said, breaking their kiss. Bruises. Right.

She used the interruption to grab his shirt and pull it over his head. He gasped. "Shoulder, shoulder," he grunted. She freed the shirt more gently, and they grinned at each other.

"Whew," she said. "You are stinky."

"Hey, I—"

"Teasing!" she said.

"Oh shut up and get back here," he said.

She grabbed his belt, tugging it loose, but he grabbed her and kissed her again. He slid his hands over the silk, gently, back to waist to hips to ass, and then up to cup her ass beneath the nightgown. He made a sound low in his throat and suddenly picked her up and carried her to their bed.

Karris held him as they made love. Held him with her lean muscular legs, pulling him into her, into her. Held him with her sex, writhing against him. Held him with her arms, glorying in his muscles and in him, digging her fingers into his back and subtly guiding him to what pleased her most. And she held him with her eyes, the intensity of her hunger startling him, the intensity of her desire for him inflaming him, and the intensity of the connection almost too much for him to bear. But when he looked away, she grabbed his chin, pulled him back, kissed him, and then nipped his lip in punishment. She held him, and held him tight as he climaxed, and held him in place afterward, running her fingers through his hair, playing with his ear.

548   He'd never felt so known and accepted in all his life.

When the capacity for reason came back to him, he propped himself up on an elbow and caressed her body. Her skin was aglow in the golden lamplight and she made no effort to cover herself, instead enjoying his gaze. There were a million ways he wanted to praise her beauty, but none of his words seemed adequate to the task. How could words tell her how she fascinated him, inflamed him, awed him? He remembered an old Blood Forest wedding vow. "With my body, I thee worship," he said. He leaned over and kissed her neck, her breasts, her lips.

They made love again wordlessly, and he gave his all to please her, interpreting every sigh and stretch and curled toe to guide him. And he took his reward. Repeatedly. She only shook her head and laughed when she saw his familiar pleased-with-himself grin. They lost themselves in each other for hours, talking, holding each other, crying, talking, making love again, finally bathing together when they were sure they could make love no more, and then just holding each other, skin to skin, her back to his stomach, watching as the dawn light rose.

"I love you so much I hate you, Dazen Guile," she said.

"I love you, too, Karris Guile."

She sighed, pensive. "Can we run away?" she asked.

"Where do you want to go?" he asked.

She harrumphed. "You stupid man, you broke the first rule of running away, and we haven't even gotten dressed yet."

"We have to get dressed? Then forget it," Gavin said.

Her elbow into his ribs would have been a gentle nudge if he hadn't been flung into a wall last night.

"Ouch!" he said.

"Serves you right," she said.

"So what's the first rule of running away?" Gavin asked. The dawn was red, magnificent, and he had a beautiful woman in his arms. This seemed to be the best place in the whole world.

"You can't bring logic or practicality into running away. Everyone knows that."

"Ah. So we *can* go naked?"

"You're impossible."

"True, but on the other hand, you can't say you didn't know what you were getting yourself into."

"No. That's true." She said nothing for a while, and Gavin thought she might have drifted off to sleep. What was the saying about a red sky in the morning? Something about storms coming? Thanks, Nature, I appreciate some omens with breakfast.

"I..." She sounded tentative. "I know that you've been trying, with Kip I mean. I heard you went to his testing."

"While I should have been with you. Protecting you."

"Protecting me? Don't make me hurt you." She rolled over, braced her head on an elbow. "You were exactly where you should have been."

He said nothing.

"So... how's it going?" she asked.

"He's a good boy. Smart. My plan is working perfectly, so far. He has no idea how talented he is. I put him with the best young fighters in the world, and he's hanging in there. By his fingernails, but hanging in."

"He's not that good of a fighter, is he?" Karris asked. "Without previous training?"

"No, he's not. But he's made the right friends, and he's got the respect of the right people. They've made it possible for him to stay in—which is as much a success in my eyes as if he'd been the best fighter there. The point of him being in the Blackguard wasn't to teach him to fight; it was misdirection; it was so he would measure himself against the best people rather than against the best whisperers and the best drafters."

"You're brilliant, and your plans always work, my lord husband, but that wasn't what I was asking about and you know it. Misdirection indeed."

He was glad she could catch him, glad to be known that much by this amazing woman—but not glad to be caught. His face fell. How's it going? "He's a good boy..."

She waited for the but. He could tell she knew it was coming.

"But he's not my son." It was a failure to speak it. "He grins this quirky grin and I see his father."

"All of you Guile men have that grin. Even your father used to charm—"

"I killed Kip's father, Karris. The boy is so desperate not to be an orphan he's latched on to me. So desperate to please he'll do anything I ask. What will he do if he ever finds out the truth? If he came after me, tried to kill me, who could call *him* the betrayer? I'm raising him and making him formidable, and the more he loves me, the more he'll hate me when he finds out I've deceived him from the beginning.

Through no fault of his own, he's a viper, Karris. And the tighter I hold him to me, the more likely he is to bite me."

Karris studied him quietly. "All true. All beside the point. You kept a secret for sixteen years from *me*. Keeping it from a boy who hasn't known you and will never know your brother? Child's play. What's really going on?"

"Look, this soul-searching is deeply meaningful and everything, but what I did before, I'd do again. Karris, if you were falling off a cliff, and I could save only you or me, I'd save you. No question. Because even though I know that I can do things for the world that you can't, I don't care. I knew I should kill you, that you were the person most likely to destroy me. I knew that this...this was incredibly unlikely. But I love you, so I didn't care. When I look at Kip? I'd make the rational choice. And I feel bad about that, but I feel bad when I send soldiers into war. I like Kip; I wouldn't want to lose him. I want to get to know him more. But I don't love Kip, and there's nothing I can do about that."

Someone pounded on the door. "Lord Prism."

"One minute!" Gavin called.

Karris had an odd intensity in her eyes. "My lord, I was never helplessly in love with you—well, maybe when we were children I was. But in the years since, my feelings for you have come and gone. But my admiration for the man I saw you to be never changed. You twisted me in knots because the good man I felt you were—my Dazen—and the man I thought I *knew* you to be—Gavin—were so different. But I saw that you were the kind of man who was worthy of my love. I knew the man I would marry would be good and strong and gentle and honorable and smart and stubborn enough to handle me and...Hold on, I know there must be *some* other virtue," she teased.

"Charming? Never forget charming."

"Sometimes I could do with less of that," she said. She got serious. "I chose you."

"Ah, you couldn't resist me."

"Yes, yes I could," she said flatly. "I *chose* you."

"How startlingly...unromantic," he said. He was reminded of her affinity for the blue virtues, despite being a red and a green, for thinking things through, for making the columns add up.

"I love you body, soul, and breath. Is that unromantic? Love is not   551 a whim. Love is not a flower that fades with a few fleeting years. Love is a choice wedded to action, my husband, and I chose you, and I will choose you every day for the rest of my life."

There was another knock on the door. "Lord Prism! The Spectrum is meeting right now, and they wish to speak with you. Lord Prism?"

"Dazen," Karris said suddenly, "no matter what happens, I love you." Something about her voice was raw, as if she were right on the edge.

Gavin had a sudden intuition. "Karris, what are you talking about? What's going on?"

"I just—"

"What did the Third Eye tell you?"

Silence. He'd hit it; he could tell.

Karris moved to get up, but Gavin grabbed her hand. "Karris, please..."

She looked back at him, then looked away. "I'll tell you, but I'm not telling you anything else no matter what you say, understood?"

"Understood," Gavin said. He grimaced, but he knew Karris when she got stubborn.

"She hedged, of course, said she doesn't see everything perfectly..."

"The Third Eye, with less than helpful help? Yes, I'm familiar with—"

"She told me when you're going to die," Karris said in a rush. Then she stood and threw a robe around her shoulders. "Now get up, lazybones, we've got a long day ahead of us." She smiled, but it didn't touch her eyes.

Chapter 105

"I lured you here under false pretenses," Andross Guile said as Kip came into his dark cabin. The Red had of course taken the captain's cabin, and though he'd put curtains on the windows, it wasn't nearly as pitch dark as his own apartments back at the Chromeria. Kip had forgotten to soak up superviolet light before coming in, so he was at the mercy of the dim light and his ears. But Luxlord Guile seemed to be in unusually good spirits, and that put Kip on his guard. "I don't want to play a game with you. I want to apologize," Andross said.

Kip remembered the glasses he carried, and put the sub-red on. It didn't help that much. "For what?" he asked. He could think of a dozen things for which the old monster should apologize, but he couldn't imagine the man apologizing for any of them.

"For trying to have you killed."

"I'm sorry, what?" Kip asked.

"Believe me, I thought you *did* owe me an apology for refusing to die. But this is me apologizing to you."

"You're going to have to do better than that," Kip said.

Outlined against the thin light coming beneath one curtain and glowing in sub-red, Kip saw Andross Guile tense, his fists ball. "Remember what you are, boy!" He relaxed with an effort. "You'd just come to the Chromeria and my son barely knew you. If you'd cracked under the pressure and jumped to your death, it would have been a very brief scandal, brought up idly, revived some six months later when I had new evidence 'found' that the woman who'd claimed to be your mother confessed to lying, having taken money from a rival family to smear Gavin. Then it would have been forgotten. You would have just been another attack on a family that has endured a thousand, an anecdote of an attempted smear on a great house."

"Mistress Helel? You sent that fat woman who tried to throw me out of the tower?" Kip asked. Andross kept talking, but Kip was still struggling to come to grips with what he'd said first.

"Was that her name? Oh, and while I'm clearing the air...I paid those idiots in your Blackguard training class to block you. No harm done, right? Regardless, I'm sorry."

"You're *sorry*?" Kip asked, incredulous. Like that was enough?

Kip saw an eyebrow rise above one of the big lenses, as if the man was wondering how stupid this fat boy was. Andross Guile raised his index finger. "I want you to know, Kip, I haven't apologized to *anyone* in twenty years."

"I'm honored," Kip said.

The old man chose to ignore the sarcasm. "Well, if that's behind us, perhaps you would like to play some Nine Kings?"

"What? What? No! You tried to kill me! You can't—you can't just try to kill people because they're inconvenient."

Andross Guile's head tilted like a dog's, trying to understand this odd, odd boy. "Reality begs to differ."

But Kip felt the world going gray. "This is all a screen. A distraction. You killed Lucia," he said. Kip saw her again, stepping into the line of fire. He saw her face bloody, neck torn open by a musket ball, pumping blood, blood, blood. Kip shivered.

"Who?" Andross asked.

"The girl in my Blackguard class who took the bullet you meant for me!"

"What are you talking about?" Andross asked.

Kip's rising rage wavered. "Someone tried to shoot me, during training. They killed her instead."

The old man shook his head, like Kip was a moron. "Why would I go to the trouble and expense to block you from the Blackguard if I intended to kill you before you could get in? I meant you to be a failure, not a corpse."

"Maybe you were making doubly sure you stopped me."

"It's nice that you have such a high opinion of yourself, but use that puny brain of yours. All these accusations. Again! If *you* were killed, there'd be an investigation. The boys who agreed to block you from the Blackguard would come forward. After all, it's one thing to make someone fail and have to try again next season, but something else altogether to kill them. You start killing people, and consciences get pricked. You think I'd leave my seal where it could be seen like that? You think I would fail twice the same way? No, boy, believe me, if I wanted you dead, you would be."

As insulting as it was, Kip thought it was probably true. In fact, he thought it was more likely true because Andross Guile had been insulting him when he said it. "So why'd you try to block me from the Blackguard?"

"To foil my son. He has plans for you, and he was defying me. He needed to be punished, and reminded of certain...verities."

"So why tell me now? What do you want?" Kip had no doubt that the loathsome old man did have a plan. He wanted something from Kip. "I could go tell..."

"Tell whom? Please." Andross Guile waved it away, and Kip realized that the man could confess with impunity. He was right. No one was going to take Kip's word, especially not with an utter lack of evidence. "Kip, I have to tell you something, and I don't expect you'll believe me, but maybe you will someday. I owe you my life, boy. Oh, not in any melodramatic sense, of course. My wife—your grandmother—left me and committed suicide. Albeit the suicide of the Freeing. I loved her. I lived for her. And she rejected me, preferring to die rather than spend another day in my company. Have you ever faced a rejection so profound?"

Kip thought of his mother, choosing to blast her brain on haze or any other intoxicant she could get until she was able to forget him, committing a slower, less noble suicide day by day. But Andross Guile wasn't looking for commiseration.

"I wanted to die. I considered following her and laying open my veins in the bath. And do you know what saved me?"

"Me?" Kip asked dubiously.

"Ha! Don't flatter yourself. Nine Kings. Distractions saved me. Even this old heart takes time to muddle through grief, but those distractions kept me alive long enough to do it. My petty tortures of you kept my mind occupied, gave me something to look forward to. Would Kip fail here? What could I come up with to take away from him when he lost our game tomorrow? How else could I test the boy, in ways that strained you but gave you some chance for victory?"

"You did not let me win. Don't even pretend you—"

"Bah! You think your wits are a match for mine? Well, I'll let you wonder. Now shut your mouth, I'm trying to thank you."

Kip fell into sullen silence, feeling abruptly like a child again. Robbed of his rage, he felt powerless in Andross's august presence.

Andross sighed. "Well, there. Thank you. That is all."

"That's it?" Kip asked.

The man sank down lower in his chair. Grimaced. "You've earned my respect, Kip. You've overcome adversity that would have crushed lesser men. You've surprised me. Not once, but several times. When I think of you, I'm disgusted and disappointed that my son could make...this. And yet, despite this blubber and this loud mouth and this utter lack of self-control, these Tyrean manners and..." He waved a hand, as if there was much more objectionable about Kip but that it was a tangent. "Despite it all, Kip, you consistently *win*." His voice grew scratchy. "I have lost my wife and all my boys now, one way or another. Perhaps I am to blame for some shred of that. But

you, Kip, you have proved you are a Guile. I will hinder you no more."
He turned away and gestured Kip to go.

Kip walked to the door slowly, bewildered.

"Perhaps," the lonely old man said in the darkness, not turning,
"perhaps someday we could play that last game you owe me."

Kip left the cabin and closed the door under Grinwoody's disapproving eyes.

Chapter 106

Gavin knocked on the door out to the balcony and let two very cold
Blackguards back in. They didn't make eye contact, but they did grin
at the floor. "Well done, sir," one said beneath his breath. "Woman's
got some lungs," the other said to the first, clearly intending to be
overheard.

The first winked, not at all stealthily, at Karris, who covered her
face and laughed ruefully. They were like her brothers. Gavin wasn't
going to get in the middle of that. That relationship would change
now that she was his wife. But Gavin didn't want to kill her joy. Let
things change in their proper season. He rang the slaves' bell.

Marissia and another slave, a skinny old woman with Ruthgari
skin tanned so leathery she looked Atashian came in and began laying
out their clothing at Karris's direction.

"I didn't even realize you'd moved all your things in," Gavin said.

"I wanted to wait for you; it seemed presumptuous to invade without being asked, but my kin in the Blackguard kicked me out."

Gavin laughed. He noticed as Marissia dressed him that Karris was
watching him closely, watching how he looked at Marissia. Hiding it
well, but jealous. For her part, Marissia was a cipher. Professional,
calm, more rumpled this morning than usual, but that was because
she'd probably slept in the hallway, rather than in her closet-sized
room off Gavin's quarters, where she slept when she didn't share
Gavin's bed.

In his years as Prism, Gavin had grown used to having very little privacy, at least not from the Blackguard or from Marissia, but what had seemed amusing when the Blackguards had teased him about overhearing him and Karris making love all night, sometimes loudly, seemed less humorous when he saw Marissia's carefully blank face and deeply shadowed eyes.

There are nations at stake, and I'm thinking about a slave's feelings. Gavin cursed inwardly.

After getting dressed—Karris picked out his clothes, something that Marissia had done for ages—Gavin went downstairs. He stopped only to say, "Twenty minutes, meet me at the back door, packed and ready for war."

Karris nodded grimly. It was almost daylight, and they couldn't afford to burn too much of that.

Facing the Spectrum was almost a relief. Gavin thought it was definitely better than being stuck between two jealous women who both had good cause to be angry at him. It was a fight that Marissia couldn't have, of course, because it was a fight she would lose spectacularly, but that didn't mean she couldn't feel, or that she was wrong to. Orholam have mercy. Four Blackguards accompanied him. It was understandable, given the assassination attempt last night, but it still made Gavin feel like a prisoner.

"You have me for ten minutes," Gavin said.

"Pardon?" Delara Orange asked.

"There's going to be a battle for Ru in two days, and I need to be there."

"And how are you going to do that? We thought you were with the fleet," the Blue said.

So Gavin explained, concisely. He could travel across the sea in a day. There was already a map on the table with the disposition of forces that they had guessed. Gavin moved and added and subtracted forces until it was accurate.

"How do you know all this?" Delara asked.

"I'm the Prism," Gavin said. "Five minutes."

"You can't treat us like this. We aren't slaves to take your orders. What will you do if we don't let you go?" Klytos Blue asked.

Turning cold eyes on the little man, Gavin said, "I'll kill you and piss on your corpse." He meant it.

Klytos Blue's mouth dropped open. His wasn't the only one.

"I came here as a courtesy," Gavin said. "But thousands of people are going to die if I don't leave, so tell me, is there anything wrong—anything at all—in valuing thousands of warriors over one spineless worm?"

Klytos spluttered, "Are you...are you calling me a worm?"

"That's the kindest thing I have to call you right now."

Klytos opened his mouth, and Gavin pointed a hand at him and shrouded it in flame. "Try me," he said. "'Cause I really need to piss."

The White intervened. "Gavin, Lord Prism, what do you intend to do?"

So he told them. Delara Orange looked distraught that he was already considering Ru lost, but he told her if things went well, they might be able to save the city after all. He didn't believe it, but it placated her. And then he left.

No one tried to stop him.

Karris was at the back dock. Together, with four more Blackguards, they crossed the seas. The ships of the fleet had anchored less than five leagues from Ruic Bay.

The battle would begin tomorrow.

Chapter 107

It was still night when Kip was summoned to the deck. He dressed quickly, pulling on his trainee's garb. He strapped the dagger sheath to his calf, and checked that the slit he'd cut in his trouser leg allowed him to grab it. It was more obvious than he would have liked, but people probably wouldn't be looking at his leg today. He put the lenses pouch on his right hip. He ran a hand through his unruly hair and stumbled up to the deck.

The *Wanderer* was under way, though only the foresails and mizzen were raised. The sailors worked silently, apparently aiming to get the ship into a different position before dawn. The Blackguards were gathered on deck around Commander Ironfist.

"How well did you study those black cards, Kip?" Commander Ironfist asked.

"Sir?" Commander Ironfist had seen the new cards, but how did he know about the black cards?

"Not many secrets on Little Jasper, Kip."

"Uh, pretty well, sir."

"You see any of the apotheosis cards?"

"I have no idea what that means, sir."

"Maybe they're just a rumor, then. Never seen any of them myself."

The commander moved to address everyone, but Kip interjected, "Sir? Um, I know that after we were inducted, there wasn't really time to file papers and everything. I wanted to—I'm technically, or was technically, I guess? Teia's owner, anyway."

"Are you worried about your payout? Now?"

"No, sir! I mean, if I die, sir, I want Teia to get it all. I didn't even really realize until we were fighting the *Gargantua* that if I died she wouldn't get anything. She needs it more than the Guiles do, sir." Kip was suddenly embarrassed, and he wasn't completely sure why.

The commander looked at Kip for a long moment, then nodded. It would be taken care of. He turned to the Blackguards. "All right, form up." He barely raised his voice, but everyone moved smoothly into rows. They put the trainees like Kip up front. Commander Ironfist picked up a bowl where a fistful of shiny black berries had been crushed. "Trainees," he said. "I expect some of you have full pupil control, but if you don't, dab a finger in this and touch the corner of each eye. One dab will serve for both eyes. It's belladonna. It'll dilate your pupils for you. It should wear off by full sunrise, but you'll be extremely sensitive to light until then. More isn't better. This stuff'll make you go blind." He handed the bowl around, and almost everyone but Kip dabbed a finger in. Kip drew out his sub-red spectacles instead.

Cruxer goggled at him. "You have Night Eyes?" he asked. "Can I see them?"

Kip handed over his sub-red spectacles. Night Eyes? Cruxer put them on. He cursed aloud. It was only the second time Kip had ever heard the boy swear. "What?" Kip said.

"Orholam's beard, Kip, there's only like ten pairs of these in the world. Some people say Lucidonius himself made every pair. This is amazing. I can see everything!"

The rest of the trainees drifted out of the lines and even quite a few full Blackguards were craning their necks. Commander Ironfist snapped his fingers and glowered at Kip, and Cruxer, who very quickly took them off and handed them back to Kip, resuming his at-attention posture. "Sorry, Commander," he said quietly.

Kip put his glasses on.

"I'm afraid that's not the only wonder we're going to see today," Commander Ironfist said. "I can't leave any of you greens behind, but I'd like to. Truth is, you might be more of a danger to your fellows back here."

He let that sink in, and Kip didn't like it. Nor did any of the other greens he could see. For that matter, the Blackguards who weren't greens didn't seem particularly enamored of the thought either.

"You've all felt it. Even I can feel it now, and I'm no green. Our scouting tells us that there's a bane somewhere, probably in the crook of the coast. Those of you who haven't heard of that may have heard it called a lightbane. It's a temple to the false gods, *loci damnata*, in this case Atirat. A bane corrupts light itself, and drafters more strongly than most. The good news is that if the power is wild like this, it means there's no false god in place yet. Questions? I know you've got 'em, so make it quick."

One of the full Blackguards, a broad-shouldered, lean warrior with wild hair, coal skin, and intense blue eyes named Tempus said, "The luxiats says Lucidonius made it so there wouldn't be bane anymore. It shouldn't be possible."

Ironfist nodded to him. "We have no idea what the heretics have done to make it possible. Today we may find out, Orholam help us."

"Effects on drafting?" an Ilytian who barely came up to Kip's shoulder asked.

"Green should be much easier to draft large amounts of, but may be much harder to control. It may be different closer in. In addition, none of us have dealt with color wights on the scale we will today. There are stories about the bane perfecting wights. Don't know if it's true, but if I've heard it, so will have a lot of green wights. You're going to see things you've never seen, things that you think are impossible. These wights have had time to work together, to learn from each other. No wights have done that for hundreds of years. Remember, whatever shape they're trying to take, they're still men underneath, and you're doing them a favor by putting them down. Orholam have mercy on them, because we can't. Greens, if you find yourselves losing control or believing that you don't need to obey my orders, I won't hold it against you. Of your own volition and in your own minds, decide right now that you want to put an end to this menace. If you come up with your own way to fight this, you're welcome to it. Sink their ships, kill their wights, save our men. The Blackguard has made every one of you elite warriors, so fight as you know best. Follow my orders as long as you can bear it. I don't question your loyalty, but I know I can't trust you to obey orders. I'm putting you all in second squad under Watch Captain Tempus. First squad, take the center. Second squad, you're with them. Third squad, the Prism says that the fort on Ruic Head is held by the rebels. The generals don't believe him. The fort's guns can reach halfway across the neck. If it is held by rebels, we need to silence those guns before they can wipe out our fleet. If he's wrong, we make sure that the rebels *don't* take it, and then come out and assist. If the bane is in range of the big guns, we'll do our best to kill it, sink it, whatever. Everyone got it? Go."

The third squad with Teia and Commander Ironfist headed out. Kip nodded to her as she went, wondering if he'd see either of them again. As they did, the Prism came skimming in on one of the sea chariots with Karris. They saluted the departing squad. The Prism's face looked haggard, and there were dark circles under his eyes. He brought his chariot into place with the skimmer and handed it off to a Blackguard to seal it to the greater ship.

Gavin started immediately: "Squad one, squad two, our mission is to destroy the bane. We do that, sanity returns. Destroying the bane will weaken our greens, but it will weaken their wights much more. Its loss will incapacitate any green wight for a few minutes at least. We can expect the temple to be swarming with greens. In the center, there will likely be twelve greens standing inside luxin pillars. If we can get past them without waking them, that would be best. Unlikely, though. And though we can't see it from here, there may be a central spire. We climb the spire, we kill Atirat's avatar—hopefully before he or she wakes—and it all disappears. So if you can't swim, find something that floats quick."

The Blackguards were looking at him oddly.

"What?" Gavin asked.

"Lord Prism, how do you know this?" Tempus asked.

"Because I killed the blue bane by myself a couple months ago."

Tempus rubbed his temples. Other Blackguards shuffled their feet. Kip heard a few mutter "Promachos" as if it were a quiet curse. At first Kip thought it was because they didn't believe Gavin, then he realized it was because they did.

My father's a giant, a god among men.

"Promachos," Tempus asked. He hesitated. "If we're too late, and the avatar wakes..."

Gavin pursed his lips. "Whoever it is, they won't know much more about it than we do. It will certainly be a drafter of incredible power, seemingly able to draft infinite amounts from the smallest amount of light. It may be able to control the green drafters in its vicinity. Your bodies, at least. It can control the green luxin that's become part of your body over your years of drafting. Maybe your minds, eventually. But if we get to it today, it shouldn't have time to learn the full extent of its power. Best if we kill it before it wakes and keep this all theoretical, eh?" Gavin quirked a smile. "Light's rising," he said. "Let's take it to them. We cut through the lines first and find the temple. Greens won't be at strength until full light."

They took to three skimmers. Gavin took the center of one with Karris and Kip with him, Watch Captain Tempus took the center of a skimmer dominated by green drafters, and Watch Captain Blademan took the last. Ironfist hadn't let any of the greens be drivers, even in Tempus's group. They'd be archers on each of the sea chariots when they split.

With the light barely gray in the east, the skimmers set out in a wide formation. The light was so weak that not all of the drafters could help propel the skimmer, even with their eyes dilated, so their progress wasn't as fast as usual. Gavin's skimmer, even with fifteen people on it, was easily the fastest, and he didn't wait for the others.

They cut across the sedate waves, barely making any noise. Up ahead, Kip saw their ships looming larger. It wasn't yet dawn, but to Kip the disposition of the ships seemed odd. They knew that the Color Prince's army had seized the battery across from Ruic Head, of course. Between those cannons and the cannons in the fort on Ruic Head, the Atashians' field of fire covered almost the entire entrance to Ruic Bay. Of course, the Color Prince held the fort on Ruic Head now—and he didn't know that Gavin knew that. But if he had seized the fort, it would seem better strategy to beef up the middle of the neck here, to force the Chromeria's ships to head along either coast, where it would be easier to shoot them.

They hadn't done that. Instead, the center of the prince's line was weak. There were a number of ships, but they were caravels and coccas and naos, small vessels. Quicker, more agile, sure, but not with many guns. Was the prince simply trying to bait the trap and not reveal that he did hold the fort on the north side?

That had to be it. Once they saw the Chromeria's forces commit to going along the northern shore, the prince's line would be reinforced and crush them against the fort's guns.

Whatever corrupting power the green had, it didn't seem to be exerting it yet. Kip supposed it must have something to do with there being no ambient light. After dawn, it would surely become more and more intense.

They passed the first ships and heard alarum bells ringing only after they passed. A luxin flare shot out over the sea, illuminating them. There was a rattle of muskets and a couple swivel guns, but at the speed they were traveling, none came close. Kip saw one of the superviolets on the skimmer tracking the flare. It took her several seconds with the bouncing of the skimmer over the waves, but finally the beam of superviolet she was shooting out caught the flare and encapsulated it, extinguished it, plunging them back into darkness. The other two skimmers came through in darkness, unseen.

As the light rose in the east, they traveled faster, and they passed more ships, too quickly for them to get off credible shots. As the sun peered over the horizon, Kip caught his first glimpse of Ru's Great Pyramid, rising red and green in the morning.

But there was no sign of any rising green spire. The skimmers spread out as they went deep into the bay. The distant sounds of the battle starting rolled over the leagues behind them. And still no temple, no spire, and Kip was only beginning to feel the restless energies of green pulling at him.

They came fully in sight of the city. Kip could see the towns outside the walls still smoking, having been burned down the day before. The base of the great stepped pyramid was only blocks from the waterfront. Though constructed of the local reddish stone, the pyramid was whitewashed aside from the great red stripes painted in zigzags up each of its four sides, and covered with greenery. At the top rested a giant curved mirror. Clearly, the makers of the Chromeria's Thousand Stars had stolen the idea from the Great Pyramid. Behind the city, the Red Cliffs loomed a thousand feet over the city. Smoke rose from whatever towns had once rested up there, and Kip saw a single trebuchet bombarding the city from on high.

It must have been difficult to get the catapults up to the top of the cliffs, or to find materials to build them up there, but there was no way to stop them once they made it there. And if the Blood Robes brought one up, surely they would now bring more. There was no defense against that.

The trebuchet loosed another shot. It looked to Kip like it was nearly random. It was such a long distance that it might take them days to breach the walls—but days of raining death into a city were days of terror for those inside.

The walls of the city still looked whole, though the entire waterfront was burning, and hulks of burned-out ships rested in the shallows everywhere. Apparently the Color Prince's rented pirates had done good work.

But Gavin obviously didn't care about the city right now. They pulled in a broad arc, seeing that the army had entirely encircled the city and seized all the towns around it.

"Greens, anyone got a feel yet?" Gavin asked. The sun had fully cleared the horizon now. Musket shots were crackling from the shore, aiming at them, but they were three hundred paces out.

"If anything, it feels weaker here than out—" one of the men started.

"Shit!" Gavin said before he could even finish. "Of course! 'Most of the times,' she tells me! Most of the times." He turned the skimmer sharply back out to sea. Karris made hand signals to the other skimmer.

"What is it? What is it?" Kip asked, and he could tell he was speaking for some of the others, too.

"The bane's huge. If it's nearby, but it isn't here, where is it?" Karris said.

Kip still didn't understand. Up ahead, he saw the guns of the fort on Ruic Head open up, pillars of black smoke blowing out with every shot. It had to be home to the biggest guns Kip had ever seen. Below, the Chromeria's fleet had taken a tentative course. They weren't hug-

564

ging the north coast closest to the fort, but neither had they gone straight for the middle.

Now, as the guns opened up, cratering the waters around their fleet, the Chromeria's ships were reacting quickly, tacking to the middle. But instead of the Color Prince shoring up the middle to keep the Chromeria's ships in range of his guns, they were melting away instead. One Chromeria ship was afire and had lost its mainmast, but the rest were fleeing.

Sure of salvation, the Chromeria's ships were heading straight for the gap, amazed at their own escape.

The fort's big guns set half a dozen of the smaller ships aflame, though. Men were screaming, and Kip saw shapes moving through the water faster than they should have been able to, jumping out and hurling luxin. Birds—ironbeaks, no doubt—crowded the air.

But when Kip took his eyes away from the individual stories unfolding before his eyes—the men dying, the fires started, the amazing shots hit, the luxin bent into shapes he'd never seen—he saw that the Color Prince wasn't even trying to hold the center. No ships were rushing to shore up the defenses there.

And Kip was feeling wild. What the hell?

It was getting harder to think strategically. Kip wanted to kill, he wanted to run, he wanted to move—and though he was flying at greater speeds than most men know in their whole lives, it wasn't enough. He wanted to move like this as his own master, under only his own control.

What had Karris said? "If it isn't here"?

It is here.

"The bane float," Gavin said. "Most of the times!"

As soon as Kip realized was that meant, he saw that everyone else had already figured it out. Gavin had turned the skimmer toward the middle of the strait. There, lost among the fires coming from each shore, were a dozen rowboats—boats filled with the Color Prince's drafters and wights.

"Split!" Gavin said. "Kill them before they can finish!"

Finish what?

The skimmer split into its component parts—six sea chariots and the central skimmer, leaving Kip with Gavin and Karris, who were each manning one of the reeds. Kip took off his sub-red spectacles with one hand and tucked them into their case, but the skipping of the skimmer was so jarring that instead of drawing another pair to ready himself for the fight, he had to use both hands to grip the railing.

The snap of muskets firing sounded in Kip's ears and a torrent of every color of luxin flew between the sea chariots and rowboats. Half the drafters in the boats seemed to be there solely to defend the others, and Kip saw massive shields of green luxin springing up around every one of them, far more powerful than the drafters should have been able to make. Fire and luxin and even musket balls were absorbed easily. The other men on the boats were heaving at great green chains that disappeared into the depths below them, and even as Kip watched, something seemed to give. First one crewman fell down and the tight chains suddenly went slack, and then another and another.

The sea chariots and the skimmer closed on all of them.

Something enormous moved beneath the waves and Kip saw a tangled, coiled mass rising toward the surface with terrible speed.

And then the entire sea exploded into the sky.

Chapter 108

Teia's skimmer hissed across the water in the darkness. Her right hand was clamped to the railing in a death grip as the boat skipped from wave to wave at great speed. She felt blind for several minutes, too tense to relax her eyes into sub-red and paryl. Terror was sufficient to dilate the pupils, but apparently mere crippling anxiety did not suffice. She looked around and saw that not a few of the others also had white-knuckled grips on the rail, but among the more dour expressions, not a few of the Blackguards were grinning eagerly, some at the amazing speed and the wind whipping their ears, others no doubt at the prospect of putting their training to the test. Most of the Blackguard runts had been kept back, just as Trainer Fisk had promised, but at the last moment, Commander Ironfist had decided that Teia's gifts might serve a purpose.

Now she had to prove herself, and she wasn't ready. She knew she wasn't ready.

Gradually, she relaxed marginally. She realized her other hand was clenched on the front of her own tunic and on the vial she wore beneath it. She hadn't gotten rid of it yet. Wouldn't until the papers were signed and filed and the money sticks were in her hands. Somehow, it felt like it could still be snatched away from her. She'd do something today to disgrace herself, and the Blackguard would change its mind and reject her. She unclenched her fist and let the vial go.

There wasn't much to see except misty waves and the rock looming ever higher in front of them. People were going to die here today, and Teia couldn't help but have the premonition that she was going to be one of them.

They were approaching Ruic Head directly. The Head was five hundred feet tall, with only narrow goat tracks up the bare face of the cliffs on this side. They would be guarded, and a single alarm would be enough to doom the entire attack.

But Commander Ironfist seemed to know exactly what he was doing. He turned them north and approached the coast, then came back south, mere feet from the rocks. Then he brought them up against a rock. He squatted and the others came close. "There's a dock two hundred paces from here around the corner. It'll be guarded. I'm going to bring us to a spot forty paces from it. Tlatig, Tugertent, Buskin, you're the best archers. String your bows." The two Archers and the man did so immediately as the commander continued, "You'll get up on the rock and take your shot from there. Teia, can you spot if the guards are wearing mail beneath their cloaks from forty paces?"

She nodded. "I could, but I don't have enough paryl right now to..."

"Over there." He pointed.

He continued giving orders to the others while a Blackguard showed Teia a tiny white mag torch. The woman beckoned Teia to sit cross-legged on the deck of the rocking skimmer. She draped several cloaks over her head.

"It'll burn for ten seconds. If you need a second torch to fill up, let me know," the woman said.

It felt odd to put on dark spectacles and then use a mag torch, but

Teia knew even from her brief time with Magister Martaens that she couldn't look directly at a mag torch without risking blindness, so she huddled down and snapped the tiny torch. It burned brilliantly, white-hot. She filled herself with paryl easily in a few seconds and had to wait while the tiny torch burned itself out. She knew such a thing must have cost a small fortune, and it seemed a waste. If she relaxed, even at night she could fill herself with paryl within a few minutes. Then she realized that fifteen lives depended on that little torch, and that time was of the essence. Maybe not a waste after all.

When the tiny torch sputtered out, Teia came out. Having stared into the white-hot magnesium flame even indirectly, she was, she realized, completely night-blind now. She thought of forcing her eyes to relax, but maybe overcoming her body's defenses wasn't always best. The Blackguards had pulled out oars wrapped in wool and were paddling the skimmer slowly forward. They reached a rocky point that must have been what provided the protection from the sea for the dock beyond it. The waves, even on this calm morning, were such that the Blackguards had trouble keeping the boat in place. With the waves and the height of the good grips, Teia had to be helped up onto the top of the rock. The three archers were taller, even Buskin, who'd gained his nickname for wearing heeled shoes to compensate for his diminutive stature. They all came up nimbly.

Teia crawled forward to the top of the rock—and with the barest tread of leather to warn her, found herself staring at a boot less than a hand's breadth away as a man stepped out from behind the rock outcropping. He saw her.

He was so surprised to find a little girl that he didn't even raise his voice. He said, "Hey, there, what are—"

His head shot backward as an arrow punched through his eye and popped his helmet off.

Tlatig dove under the man even as he fell, and caught his helmet before it could clang on the rocks. The dying man fell across her outstretched body, cushioning and muffling his fall.

Rolling the man off of Tlatig carefully, Buskin turned the spasmodically twitching man facedown. He drew a knife and drove it into the guard's neck at the base of the skull. The twitching stopped immediately. Buskin turned expressionless eyes on Teia and motioned for her to get to work. Still shocked, she returned to the spot and peered south. There were three soldiers standing on the dock, chatting with each other and enjoying the rising dawn. All three had bows, but all were unstrung, as if they expected to have warning.

They're dead and they don't even know it yet.

The dock was barely fifteen paces long, and had two small rowboats tied to it, bobbing in the waves and creaking as they rubbed and bumped against the wood of the dock.

Shooting out a beam of paryl light, Teia could see that all three men were wearing full mail and helmets. She wasn't going to be much help. "All of them have full—"

A bowstring thrummed above her. She rolled over and saw Tlatig drawing another arrow smoothly from her quiver. She'd been looking farther to the right. Teia had been so focused on the dock, she hadn't even noticed that there was a little shack for the guards. And two men there were down—in full sight of the men on the docks.

Tlatig was already turning toward the docks.

"Three," Tugertent said. It wasn't a count of the guards; it was a countdown, and moments later, three arrows jumped into the air as Teia watched.

The guard farthest left took an arrow through the side of his neck. It must have cloven his spine, because he fell instantly, limply, straight into the water. A second guard grabbed the side of his neck, which was spurting blood like a fountain. A dim whine sounded as the third man turned, his helmet deflecting the arrow intended for his neck. It spun his helmet in front of his eyes and he slapped at it, already moving. The archers all loosed another volley. Teia couldn't see if they'd hit the man or not, but when he dove into the water, his dive looked purposeful.

"Go!" Buskin hissed. The three archers ran down the trail, arrows fitted to their bows.

Teia drew her knife and followed them, not knowing what else to do. She turned the beam of paryl onto the little hut. The paryl light cut through the leather flaps over the windows. She saw a man in mail moving toward the door.

"Hut!" she whispered. "Front door!"

Tlatig was already headed toward the hut, and as the front door opened, Teia saw her loose an arrow from five paces into the darkness beyond. In the paryl light—the leather window flap dimming her vision only as much as silken gauze would—she saw him fall to the floor.

Buskin and Tugertent were out on the dock, searching the water. It was still dark enough that the sun didn't help them at all. Teia ran out to join them. The archers were moving up and down the length of the dock, peering into the depths as well as they could.

Teia's paryl beam cut through the water, scattering, but much better than visible-spectrum light.

"There!" She pointed. "Swimming!" The man was swimming—underwater—twenty paces distant. Heading for the shore to the north.

"Balls," Tugertent said. "Swimming in full mail. Didn't think you could even do that." She drew an arrow. "I got this one." From where she was, standing right next to Tugertent, Teia thought she saw a tiny shimmer around the fletching of her arrow.

The swimming soldier reached the shore seventy paces distant or more and surfaced slowly, silently. Tugertent's arrow met his bare head, and he slumped back into the water. Teia swore that the arrow had curved slightly in the air. What the hell?

"Brave," Tugertent said. "And crazy strong." She cursed in appreciation.

"Double-check he's dead," Commander Ironfist said.

Tugertent saw Teia looking at her, the question obvious in her eyes. She put a finger to her lips. Quiet. Teia let it go. There were more important things.

Tlatig gave a signal from the cabin that Teia thought was the all-clear, and Buskin motioned something back to her. Buskin trotted back down the line.

"You can see through walls and water?" he asked. He was old for a Blackguard, one of the ebon-skinned, blue-eyed Parians who usually only came from noble families, but he was almost painfully thin where Commander Ironfist was thick. His halos were red, and streaked out in lines through his irises.

"Only if they're close enough, and thin enough," Teia said. "I saw through the leather at the windows."

Commander Ironfist said, "Teia, you go first up the trail, start now. Look for men and traps. Tugertent will be with you in thirty seconds. Their relief might be coming down at any time. I want to be up before they start coming down."

The Blackguards were already carrying the bodies toward the dock to throw in the water.

Teia stopped them, found the smallest man, and stripped off his sword belt, floppy hat, and jacket. She pulled the jacket on over her own clothes, strapped on the sword, and pulled the hat over her hair. There was blood on the jacket. She put it out of her mind.

The Blackguards looked at her oddly, but she ignored them. She refilled her hand with imbalanced paryl to make a torch. Her mouth was dry and it was hard to swallow, but all she had to do was jog and look. She could do that. She moved to the head of the trail, and when Tugertent joined her, she felt overwhelmingly grateful.

"Let me go around corners first," she said.

The rest of the Blackguards gathered behind them. She took the lead and the three archers followed thirty paces behind her. The rest were ten paces behind them. The path itself soon changed from a goat track winding around trees and bushes to one cut into the rock of the head itself. It was barely three feet wide, and Teia saw that some of the men behind her had to turn their shoulders sideways to slide along the wall. The wall itself was worn smooth from decades or centuries of other soldiers doing the same. They ascended sharply in long switchbacks, back and forth across the face of bare rock wall.

Teia kept her paryl beam cutting left and right, expanding her pupils to see, searching for booby traps or alarm wires, then tightening them back to the visible spectrum. Magister Martaens had said that her mistress's master had navigated completely by paryl light? There was so much noise in that spectrum, Teia could barely believe it. But she found no traps.

She stayed half a switchback ahead of the Blackguards, and when they were all about halfway up the cliffs, Teia heard voices above them.

"—says, 'She would of if I were rocking her boat!' "

At least four men laughed, including the speaker.

Teia glanced back. In contrast to her own panic, the Blackguards behind her looked calm. But the soldiers were behind and above them, and coming down, as if racing them for the corner of the switchback. The archers didn't have any angle to shoot them, and if they waited until the soldiers rounded the corner, the soldiers would certainly have time to sound an alarm.

Retreating back around the corner, out of sight, Teia looked back for orders.

"Get a count," Buskin mouthed to her.

Both parties were walking toward the same switchback corner, a hundred paces away, and the two trails got closer and closer as they neared each other. In another forty paces, if the descending soldiers looked down, they'd be able to see the ascending Blackguards.

Teia held up four fingers, five fingers, shrugged. Commander Ironfist was already coming forward, his tall, muscular body somehow weaving around the other Blackguards on the trail as if certain death wasn't beckoning at the slightest wrong step. He came to the center of the line. In his hand, he held a long green luxin rope. Behind him, struggling more to make it around the Blackguards because she was shorter, came the smallest of their number, a woman named Fell.

Ominous name right now, Teia thought. Ironfist helped Fell wrap the rope tightly around her waist, then threw the ends of the rope down the rest of the line. Everyone grabbed the rope except for the two Blackguards immediately beside Ironfist, who grabbed on to his belt. It was as if they were able to communicate volumes without speaking a word.

Commander Ironfist looked at Teia. "Exact count. Signal when they're directly above us."

Teia squared her shoulders, pulled the hat down in front of her eyes, and tried to remember the dead soldier's gait. She rounded the corner, walking quickly, but making sure her feet were wider apart than usual to minimize the motion of her hips. She kept her head down, held her shoulders tight, as if they were bigger and more muscular than her own, and kept glancing out to sea to make it believable that she didn't see the soldiers coming toward her.

"Arvad!" one of the men called out. "What are you doing coming up early?"

Teia bobbed her head up toward them. Trick with faking a man's voice was not to try to become a bass—go for an easy tenor, and keep it short. "Rogue wave! Was knocked off the dock! He's hurt!" She pointed a hand down toward the dock, standing close enough to the edge that the Blackguards could see her hand. With her fingers and thumb outstretched: five. Then she brought the other fingers in to point with her index finger alone. Plus one. Six.

She gestured for the soldiers to follow her before they could ask more, and turned her back. She got to the corner and pointed again to the dock, her arm outstretched. Then as the soldiers came directly above the Blackguards, Teia dropped her arm.

The descending soldiers weren't fifteen feet away from the Black-guards. Ironfist turned his back to the wall, his feet pointing out, and Fell stood in front of him, in almost a hug, facing his big chest. His big hands wrapped around her hips.

After a quick count, Ironfist flung Fell up into the air and she landed with her feet in his hands at shoulder level, then he pressed straight above his head. Blue luxin blazed out from her hands, blast-ing her back against the green rope out over the abyss, but still she shot out more. The stretchiness of the green rope allowed her to push back and back, and Ironfist leaned out and out to be able to continue holding her feet, his body going diagonal to the trail, held only by the tension of the green rope and the two men holding on to his belt.

Fell didn't try to blast each of the men with luxin spears or missiles. Instead, she shot a blue frame against the wall behind them, and merely made it so thick that there was no space to stand on the trail. It nudged them off. With nothing to hold on to, it didn't take much.

As one, six men tumbled off the trail above the Blackguards. Only one gave so much as a squawk of surprise as he plunged to his death. But that nearest man hit the green luxin rope as he fell. The man flipped and continued his fall, but Fell was yanked hard to the side. At the same time, she stopped shooting out blue luxin, so she rebounded toward the wall. Ironfist leaned crazily over to one side, but couldn't run to the right because the Blackguards were crowded thick on the ledge. Instead, he pivoted, put both of her feet in one hand, and extended that hand along the side of the ledge as both of the Black-guards on either side of him had to let go of his belt lest it throw both them and him off the ledge.

Ironfist set Fell down gently, the motion costing him his own balance—and fell off the ledge.

His big fingers slapped on the lip, slipped, and then held. The Black-guards pulled Fell in among them, and before Teia could blink, numerous luxin ropes were already around the commander. With their help, he levered himself up and stood. He didn't seem fazed in the slightest. "They're all dead," he said. "But we need to hurry."

He'd been calmly inspecting their work while he was dangling off the ledge? Bloody flux!

The sun rose to full light as they jogged up the path. When they neared the top of the path, Teia scouted ahead and saw that around the last bend, there was a stout wooden gate, ten feet tall, with sharpened spikes at the top. In the paryl light, through small gaps, she could see that it was reinforced with iron, and there were four men behind it. The drop-off beside the gate wasn't sheer like the rest of the cliff they'd just traversed, but it was too steep to climb while armed men were above you. She thought she could make out the shapes of spears and muskets among the men stationed there, too.

She had barely reported back when the cannons above began firing out on the water. During the whole climb, Teia had been so focused on merely staying on the path and watching for booby traps or pitfalls or approaching soldiers that she'd barely looked out to sea. Their view was astounding. Gorgeous: the sun barely up, the bay blue and deeper blue-green, the sails of the ships unfurled, and now thick clouds of smoke rolling out from the broadsides as the Chromerian fleet tried to enter the bay. There were only a few small ships holding the center of the Color Prince's lines. They fired back a volley.

"Lem," Commander Ironfist said. "Up front."

A small, twitchy man came forward. "Hello," he said to Teia. He glanced at her nonexistent chest, up to her eyes, away. "Name's Lem. True name Will. You know, Will to Willum, to Lum to Lem."

"Sure," Teia said. I guess.

"Thing that's special about Lem isn't that he's crazy," Lem said. "We're all all sorts of crazy. But Lem is crazy in one particularly valuable way."

"And you're going to tell me what it is," Teia said as he glanced at her chest again. She couldn't tell if he was being creepy or if he just never looked at people's eyes.

"Lem here believes he can do anything in the service of the Blackguard. Lem here believes rock is like butter, in front of him. He's a bit slow, which is good, because otherwise he'd probably be dangerous as all hell. That's what the trainers said. See, Lem can punch grips in the rock for us, no problem. Got a will that'd make Andross Guile weep like a little boy. True name *Will*, you see."

"Right," Teia said.

Lem filled himself with blue luxin, then leaned over conspiratorially to Teia. "There's something in the water," he said.

How did this freak get into the Blackguard?

He's a valuable freak. Like me.

Lem extended a hand and waited. He was chanting numbers under his breath. "Forty-one, fifty-three, forty-seven, fifty-nine, no, fifty-three, fifty-nine, sixty-one, seventy-one, no..."

A hammer of blue luxin shot from his hand and pierced the stone. It stuck, a horizontal bar connected to a spike sunk deep into the stone. The bar would make a good hand- or foothold. He checked it, pulling on it to make sure there was no play, then took a deep breath. He swept a hand down and eight more of the spikes leapt from his hands in order. It would make an admirable ladder.

Blue luxin—shot into *rock*. Holy hells. Just when Teia thought she couldn't get any more impressed with the Blackguards.

Lem smiled at Teia; then, as if noticing he was making eye contact, he looked away. "True name Will, you see."

Teia saw.

At Commander Ironfist's gesture, Teia climbed the makeshift ladder. She was almost to the top when she heard the scrape of iron over rock and someone inside barking orders. The window was an open slot above her head. Then she saw a cannon poke out of the window. She clamped her hands over her ears an instant before the cannon fired.

The pressure wave nearly blew her off the makeshift ladder. And that shot was followed by half a dozen others, all around the semicircle of the fort. The cannons all rolled back out of sight from the kick of the shots, but when Teia raised her head to see if she could get a count of the men loading the cannons through the thick smoke— paryl cutting through it easily—she saw that the windows were barred. There was enough space for the cannons to be rolled forward and poke through the bars but not enough for the Blackguards to climb in. Maybe, maybe after a shot, a person could crawl through the wide area in the bars that the cannon occupied when it was forward.

So, crawl in front of a cannon and hope there was enough space, and attack armed men who would all be looking your way.

Teia felt rather than heard another set of handholds shiver into the rock next to her, going around the great windows up to the top of the fort. Looking down, she waved to Commander Ironfist that they wouldn't be able to get in through the windows. Lem was already firing out another ladder to bracket the other side of the windows.

Above the rock, the fort continued in several floors of wooden towers. Teia was glad she wasn't afraid of heights, because it was getting dizzying. There was a flat spot wide enough for three people to stand where rock and wood met. The heavy timbers of the fort's wooden walls were sunk in deep holes drilled directly into the red rock. Teia used her paryl to look through the walls. She couldn't see through the wood itself, but in the spaces where bark pressed against bark, she could catch glimpses. Even then it was cloudy—but she couldn't see anyone on the other side.

A Blackguard joined her, and she saw that others were clambering up the ladder on the other side. Teia looked down and saw the soldiers still standing by the little gate below them, looking out at the sea. If those men turned around to watch their guns fire—and it was quite a sight, so it was entirely possible—they would see the Blackguards in full view. But for a moment as the fort's guns pounded, Teia looked at what the soldiers were watching unfold on the waves. Ships were afire—mostly the Chromeria's ships that had sailed too close to the fort.

The rest of the fleet was heading for a gap at the middle of the neck. The Color Prince's small ships—Teia didn't know enough about ships to identify them—were fleeing from that area. But most of the Chromerian fleet wasn't going to make it. Teia had seen how far the fort's guns reached, and with some of the fleet only turning now, they'd be in range of the guns for ten or fifteen more minutes. The fort would manage hundreds of shots in that time. Orholam have mercy. Teia turned away and, far to the west, thought she could see the whisper of two skimmers crossing the waves, coming back to join the battle. Had they not found the green bane?

"How many soldiers?" the Blackguard asked Teia. He meant inside. She shook herself. She could do nothing about the crises and stupidity out there except help stop the guns up here.

"I don't see *any*," she whispered.

"Maybe we have a chance then." The man gestured over to the other team, and Teia saw that there were eight people lined up on that ladder, and six more below her. The Blackguard—Teia didn't know his name—was drafting a charge against the wooden wall, placed off to the side as far as he dared.

The other team was drafting another ladder, this one merely propped against the wood like a traditional ladder. They climbed it rapidly and Commander Ironfist gave the go-ahead.

Pushing Teia to the side, the Blackguard ignited the charge. It blew, and for a moment, Teia was surprised that no one cried out in alarm from within the fort.

Of course. They're firing cannons of every size. An explosion wouldn't alarm them.

With prybars of luxin, the Blackguards quickly tore out the remaining wood and poured into the fort. There were dead bodies everywhere. Atashians, mainly, but also scruffy men with no uniforms at all, and drafters, even a few color wights. There'd been a battle here yesterday.

The fort was huge, covering Ruic Head in a spiky wooden crown and sunk deep into the rock. But there was hardly anyone in sight. There were two men standing watch at the gate, looking out the opposite side of the fort. Blackguard archers killed them, arrows punching through their mailed backs. The Blackguards who'd climbed the other side found a cannon crew on top of the fence and killed them in seconds.

Teia ran with them, going down a staircase into the fort proper, down a wide hallway to a wooden doorway. It was dark and smoky, but Teia had no trouble seeing in sub-red.

"Four on the left, five on the right. Looks like a wight giving orders in the middle," she whispered. Then she ran down the hallway on tiptoe even as the cannons roared to where another team stood outside the door to another battery. "Three right, six left."

Ironfist gestured that she should stay where she was. He quietly drew a long, gorgeous scimitar that she'd never seen before. The grip was inlaid with turquoise and abalone, and there was something that looked like burned wood inset along the spine of the blade. Ironfist didn't look at the blade, as if he couldn't stand the sight of it, but he presented it to Buskin, who reached a hand out from his spot in the stack and touched the wood on both sides of the scimitar.

As the atasifusta wood burst into flame, both teams burst into action. The Blackguards stormed the rooms simultaneously, Ironfist visible through the thick gunsmoke as a giant wielding a bar of flame. Teia heard shouts, anger, terror—and pistol fire. Her own pistol was drawn in her sweaty hand, cocked and ready.

A door opened on the opposite side of the hall, and a drafter poked his head out into the hallway, looking confused. He saw Teia.

The pistol rose of its own volition, the flint snapping down, sparks flaring, the shockingly hard kick and the hot smoke. Teia blinked and saw the drafter on the ground at her feet, his left eye and a quarter of his skull blown off.

He wasn't dead.

"Reload," Commander Ironfist said in her ear. Somehow back already. She flinched and found her hands doing what she'd been told: swabbing, popping her powder horn open, tamping the wadding. The commander peeked into the room from which the drafter had come, then, finding no one, jabbed his flaming scimitar down into the man's back, into his heart, pulled it out, and jogged down the hall.

She ran after him, barely having charged her musket, but suddenly not wanting to be left behind. They stumbled straight into ten enemy drafters. Teia lurched to a stop, but Commander Ironfist was already flowing through the steps that looked like the *yeshan* ka, scimitar in one hand, luxin in the other, killing men left and right. The other Blackguards joined him a moment later, blasts of light painting the walls.

Teia waded in at the same time as the Blackguard who'd blown open the fence for them. Zero. His name was Zero, she remembered now. They faced two drafters who were already gathering light. "You take the green, I got the red!" Zero shouted. He moved before Teia could say anything.

Teia attacked the drafter on her side—the same man Zero attacked. The drafter on the other side shot a blade of luxin into Zero's torso. He stumbled and fell and looked at Teia as if he couldn't believe she'd been so stupid.

I'm color-blind, damn it!

Zero fell, but then both enemy drafters were down, killed by the other Blackguards.

A snarling red wight lit himself on fire, and Commander Ironfist roared, shouting for Teia to go after—*someone*—she couldn't understand the words over the shouting and the fires.

Then she saw a young man running away, and she went after him. He was dressed in a white shirt and cloak, both with thick bands of many colors on it: one of the Color Prince's polychromes. He ran down the halls and disappeared. Teia followed as fast as she could.

Rounding a corner, she ran right across his extended foot and into his shoulder and went flying. Ambushed! She slid across the smooth stone floor and saw that he had her pistol in his hand. She thought he'd broken her finger from tearing it out of the trigger guard. The boy was perhaps seventeen years old, his face bloody where his spectacles had been shattered, the glass cutting his cheeks and his hawkish nose. He pointed the pistol at her, and she froze.

On her knees, she watched as a dozen soldiers armed with muskets ran up to join the young man. They must have been on some other gun emplacement or in the barracks. He tucked her pistol away. He grinned at her and said, "Kill her, then go reinforce the men inside."

Teia didn't want to die. But there was nothing she could do. Orholam, there was nothing she could do. Then, even as three of the soldiers raised their muskets, she felt something vast beyond comprehension passing by her, over her, through her like a rushing wind. It whispered: *Like this.*

She could suddenly hear Magister Martaens saying, "You'll burn to death." But Teia felt serene. No fear. Her hands came up, fingers spread. Rapid pulses of open color streamed out of her—something beyond paryl, or paryl in a way she'd never considered trying to draft it.

It felt like she'd dipped her hands in fire. The soldiers screamed, ducked, dropped their weapons. Two fled. Several fell and curled into balls.

Teia heard the steps of running men coming up behind her and she snapped a hand out toward them, ready to kill.

They were Blackguards. She stopped, her eyes instantly tightening back to the visible spectrum. She looked at her hands. They were untouched, unburned but still tingling. She turned back to the soldiers she'd incapacitated, expecting them to be charred husks. They were unharmed, dazed, then scrambling for their weapons as the Blackguards fell on them.

Teia jumped to her feet. The boy in charge was one of the ones who'd fled, shielded from her blast by the bodies of the men in front of him. She ran after him.

She got to the yard in time to see him slipping out of a gap in the gate.

Damn. She wasn't going to go after him.

And just like that the fight seemed to be over. Teia went down to the battery, rubbing her tingling palms. The Blackguards weren't taking any time to celebrate their victory, they were already loading the cannons under the watchful eye of one of the men who'd worked with big guns before.

Teia said, "Commander, is Zero going to—"

"Dead," Commander Ironfist said. He'd extinguished his sword, but there was smoke and soot and blood and bloody hair on the blade. "The boy? The polychrome?"

"I didn't— He was able to get—"

Commander Ironfist held up a finger and walked toward the window. "Am I seeing things?" he asked.

A line of Blackguards joined him. Vanzer, a green, said, "Oh no. I can feel it."

The battle on the sea was still going strong. The Chromeria's fleet didn't seem to have even noticed that the fire from the fort had ceased. Every ship was still under way, heading for the center. And the Color Prince's fleet had yielded the center completely.

But the Blackguards were looking at the sea itself. It was a different color in a vast circle, at least a league across, directly under the center.

"They've lured us right to the middle of the neck," Ironfist said. Right into the center of that great dark circle.

A spire as wide across as a tower shot up out of the water, causing huge waves that battered the ships around it. Then smaller towers shot up hundreds of paces away, in a circle. One of them pierced right through the hull of a galleon and lifted it entirely out of the water until its hull split and rained men and matériel into the sea.

Then it seemed the sea itself jumped in a disk an entire league across and the bane surfaced. The waters jumped, and then crashed down, swamping entire ships, crushing others—and then the waters went racing off the sides of the newly surfaced island in vast torrents in every direction.

It looked like some of the ships fortunate enough to be turned in the right direction would race right off the island, but vines as thick as tree trunks lashed out as the island surfaced. A forest of vines, living, grabbing like the tentacles of a kraken, whipped out—not in one single place, but in hundreds. The bane was a living, writhing carpet.

Though Teia's eyes couldn't tell her, she had no doubt what color this was. The wildness of green, undampened by the seas, now hit the drafters like a slap in the face.

The ships that weren't crushed were beached on the green island, leaning over crazily, immobilized.

In one minute, the Chromeria's fleet was simply gone. The defense of Ru aborted. Thousands killed. The battle lost.

From the island itself, Teia saw hundreds of men—small as burrowing insects from up here—emerge. They pointed their hands at the sky, and light shot up from hundreds of green color wights. A tiny group in the center of that burgeoning army was fighting them, hurling every other color around them.

"Those are Blackguards," someone said. "The Prism's down there. Fighting. Against all that."

Orholam have mercy. They didn't stand a chance.

Chapter 109

"Five minutes until sunrise," the orange drafter announced. He was nervously, noisily sucking his spit back and forth across the khat he had tucked under his lip.

A dozen orange and yellow drafters were gathered at the base of Ru's southern wall, waiting for dawn, nervously commanding Liv and her team to be quiet. Liv's team was made of four drafters and four soldiers. With her, they made the holy number of nine. Liv would have preferred to make the holy number of ninety-nine. She would have preferred to have fighters who could draft and drafters who could fight, but the Blood Robes were years away from having anything remotely as good as the Blackguard.

The Blood Robes' army was awake and armed, but the closest of them were four and five hundred paces back from the wall. The Atashians surely had guns that could reach that far, but they'd decided to conserve their powder. Liv could only guess that their situation was nearly as dire as the Blood Robes'. The Color Prince's battery on the south side of the neck had only enough powder for one shot from each gun. His hope was that the Chromeria's fleet would avoid that shore altogether and instead hug the opposite coast, which they believed their Atashian allies still held.

Liv wouldn't know how that turned out until it was all over, if ever. Her own mission was the next thing to a suicide mission. Her soldiers were dressed in scored and scarred leather armor and faded blue cloaks of the Blue Bastards, a mercenary company that had been hired by Ru. Mercenary companies rarely took bids volunteering to endure sieges, so Ru must have paid them a fortune.

And as might be expected of men whose primary loyalty was to their purse, they'd been willing to come to an understanding with the Color Prince. They had refused to fight for him, fearing that a reputation as turncloaks would interfere with future contracts. But they did agree to grease the skids for Liv's team in return for leniency when the Blood Robes took the city.

Like every leader, the Color Prince hated mercenaries and still had to use them. He was convinced that the pirate lord Pash Vecchio had betrayed him. The weedy pirate had sworn that his great ship would hold the south shore, herding the Chromeria's fleet straight into their trap. They'd had word that his ship had been seen, so maybe he'd show up at the last moment. More likely, he was waiting at the outskirts like some of the other pirates, hoping to swoop in on the wounded ships after the battle and take slaves and plunder.

The sound of distant guns, rumbling over the sea, came before dawn did. Liv wondered if people she knew were dying out there. She turned back to look at the wall, watching the sunlight creep down its face.

"I thought this was impossible," she said to the orange-eyed khat chewer.

"Chromeria trained, aren't ya? Chromeria lies, princess."

Of all the colors, only the Color Prince's orange drafters were better than the Chromeria's. Their illusions crafted into the depths of other luxins were as good as Chromeria students', but they also did something that Liv had heard rumors about, but that the Chromeria denied was possible: they cast feelings. You had to see the object on which they'd cast the hex, and you had to be susceptible to such things—the more emotional you were, the more powerfully you would experience the hex. But this wall was their masterpiece in two parts. First, the Color Prince's men inside the city had cast hexes on every building and street and on the wall itself for several blocks around here. The hexes could be cast thin enough that the eye wouldn't even pick them out, especially against backgrounds with lots of colors or patterns. But the effect remained—going right past the mind, straight to the guts, blanching the liver, putting water in the stomach. In one small neighborhood on the opposite side of this wall, everyone felt dread.

It wasn't an alien feeling for someone to experience in a city under siege, and it accomplished what it had been intended to—people avoided this area. That meant they studied the wall less closely than they would, which meant the illusion held.

Liv asked how they did it. They said they cast their will into the creation, the same way golems were made. It made the magic alive in some sense. Forbidden by the Chromeria, of course. The luxiats thought that tearing part of your will off to make magic tore part of your soul off, and that such lost parts of your soul were never regained.

The Blood Robes knew better. So they said.

The trebuchet on the Red Cliffs above threw its great stones on every quarter hour, and it threw stones close to this neighborhood. The oranges had reached the wall, and when they set their charges, they timed them to go off when the trebuchet's stones rocked the earth.

One Atashian captain had been assassinated, and another bought off, guaranteed safety for himself and his family when the city fell. They'd burrowed a hole in the wall, then covered it with an illusion. Blue luxin, overlaid with red and yellow and orange, twisted into illusions that looked nearly the same as the wall itself. It would fool a quick glimpse from twenty or thirty paces, but not a close inspection.

The drafters and sappers had worked through every night, with thick wool blankets draped over them to hide the light of the mag torches, emerging exhausted and coated in sweat every morning. But in mere days they'd made an unseen gate, with supports drafted to hold up the wall above them, wide enough for five men to pass abreast.

It wouldn't be wide enough to let in the entire army, and it was too short for horses to pass, but that wasn't the strategy. An hour after Liv's team entered the city, the Color Prince would send five hundred of his best drafters and warriors through this tunnel, with instructions to open the city's south gate and let his armies in.

Ultimately, Liv didn't see how it could fail. The Color Prince hadn't been so sure. He'd wanted to deal with the Chromeria's fleets on one day and Ru the next in case the fleet landed ashore and attacked him from the rear instead of trying to bring supplies directly in to Ru. But he'd made his gamble: to spring his trap, he needed to do both things today.

If things didn't work out, Liv was going to find herself very, very alone in a hostile city.

"Time!" the orange barked. As the sun drenched them, he and a blue and a yellow all touched the wall in slightly different places, reaching the control nodes that they'd left on the surface. They pulled back the illusion like a curtain.

"Remember what our prince has said," Liv said. "What we do today, we do for mercy. The price of freedom is always paid in blood. And if the price must be paid, better that it be paid by few. Let us be swift and implacable."

It wasn't much of a speech, but Liv had never done this before. Her men nodded, then they went into the wall first. She was second to last. If she died, their entire mission would fail, so they would protect her above all. The price and privilege of being a superviolet.

She ducked in behind them. The wall was eighteen paces thick at its base. Immense. This was the reason they hadn't bombarded the wall straight on with the trebuchets—it would have taken them months to break through. Cannons could have done it, but they didn't have the amount of powder necessary, nor easy access to saltpeter mines to make more. But whoever had told the Color Prince that five men could pass abreast had been lying. The space was so short that Liv had to stoop deeply to get through, and five men abreast? She could reach each wall with her outstretched fingers. It was enough for their purposes, and Liv was momentarily glad that she was going into the city first, rather than in the middle of five hundred men straining to get through this tiny hole while under fire and magic.

Grateful to be going alone into an enemy city. I'm mad.

And then they were out. Some of the men were dusty. One, a seven-footer named Phyros, was dabbing his head, which was bleeding freely from smacking it on the roof of the tunnel. They slapped off the dust from their faded blue shirts—the closest thing to a uniform the

Blue Bastards had—and bound a bandage quickly around Phyros's head.

"Follow me," Phips Navid said. He was a cousin of Payam Navid, the gorgeous magister Liv and every other girl at the Chromeria had half loved. Phips had grown up in Ru, though his father and older brothers and uncles had all been hanged after the Prisms' War. He'd been twelve years old, and narrowly avoided the noose himself.

They jogged through the streets. Near the wall, because of the dread hex, there was no one at all out. But soon they jogged past some soldiers, who merely nodded at them. They swung one block wide to avoid a troop of the Blue Bastards—only the top few commanders of the mercenaries knew their plan. Any underlings who saw them would ask what they were doing.

Most of the city was untouched as yet by the war. The Color Prince wanted a new power base for his war, not another drain on his resources, so he'd had the trebuchets on the Red Cliffs concentrate their stones on a few neighborhoods, and the artillery batteries. There were whole markets and palaces that remained untouched. The buildings were whitewashed adobe with flat roofs that served as extra rooms, especially on hot nights, just as they did in Tyrea. But here there were far more palaces built around central courtyard gardens. Whatever damage had been inflicted on Ru during the Prisms' War had long ago been scrubbed away by their wealth.

But the people on the streets didn't look like they felt fortunate. They looked like dread hexes had been painted on every wall. As she passed beneath three- and four-story-tall palaces, Liv spied men with long lenses on not a few of those palaces, peering out toward the sea. The sound of cannons was barely audible down in the maze of streets, though.

They passed unmolested all the way to the temple district. The Great Pyramid of Ru suddenly towered above them. Liv instantly saw both its kinship and its rivalry with the ziggurats of Idoss. The Idossians had gone for height, and their great ziggurat was taller and steeper than the Great Pyramid, but for sheer mass and grandeur, it couldn't compare to this: whitewashed limestone laid out precisely on the cardinal points of a compass, with great brass braziers burning day and night up each corner, the great steps up the east face sheathed in burnished copper, shining like red gold in the sun, the pinnacle itself sheathed in electrum, the great mirror like a star held high. Every season, the facings of all four sides were changed—though this year, with the army approaching, they hadn't gone to the expense to change to the autumn trappings. Every summer, the pyramid was made a garden, a veritable mountain of flowers, the design given over to a new director every year, with a noble family underwriting the costs.

This late in the year, the flowers should have been withered and dying, the full splendor long passed. Instead, every plant was still in bloom, an effect of the green bane, the Color Prince had said. This year, the gardens had been designed to evoke a sun resting on the pinnacle of the Great Pyramid, in the jagged, runic old Atashian art style. Lilies and gardenias and white irises and white hydrangeas yielded to daisies and buttercups and marigolds. In zigzag steps, orange roses and lilies and tulips represented the rays of the sun, stabbing through a sky of hyacinth and bluebells. A forest of vibrant greens took up the middle, and the base was a maze of rhododendrons, camellias, and roses of every color. Streams came down every side, even passing over the great steps in whimsical aqueducts. Fountains spat water from heights to land in pools a dozen paces below. And all of this was temporary, to be switched out next season for something equally lavish. The noble families did this to compete with each other.

The sheer scale of the wealth necessary for such a display simultaneously enthralled and sickened Liv. This city was wealthy, but they'd passed their share of beggars and slatterns and cripples and orphans, even in half an hour.

"Staring," Phips Navid said gently.

Liv pulled her eyes away. No one seemed to have seen her gawking. Idiot. Gawking was a sure way to break their disguise.

But everyone else seemed busy, concerned with their own business and keeping their heads down. In another two minutes, Liv and her men were at the base of the great steps. One of the commanders of the Blue Bastards was there, a bent-nosed blue-eyed old goat with no front teeth named Paz Cavair, talking with one of the city captains who was guarding the base of the pyramid with six men.

"Liv!" Paz shouted. "Was hoping I might see you. Come here."

Liv scowled and jogged over with her men. "Sir," she said, "I was headed over to check how much powder—"

"Never mind that. I got a message I want you to take up to Lord Aravind up top."

Grimacing, playing dumb, Liv said, "Can I send one of my men?"

"No, it's important. Him only. Besides, how are you going to keep that little ass of yours so tight if you don't sweat a bit?"

The captain laughed with Paz, and Liv's men snickered quietly, as if trying to suppress it.

Liv looked at her men. "I don't know what you boys are laughing about. If I gotta go up, you're coming, too."

That shut them up.

The captain laughed, but then looked uncomfortable. "I'm afraid I can only let two of you up there. We could take the message for you if you want, but I can't let armed parties up the Great Pyramid."

"We're in the middle of a war. You're joking, right?" Paz Cavair said.

"I hate to be a stickler, but orders and all," the captain said. He was a young man. Dark-haired, beautiful blue eyes, beaded beard. "You know how it is."

"I do," Paz Cavair said. "Jump."

"Huh?" the captain asked.

It was the code. Paz Cavair's one guard and all of Liv's attacked the Atashian soldiers, drawing knives and stabbing them through mail, breaking necks and savagely hacking into the flesh of the captain and all his men. It was over so fast, and the bodies carried away so swiftly, that there was no immediate outcry.

The murder done, Paz Cavair flipped his cloak around. He had the eagle sigil of Ru stitched on the other side and he took up position as if he was a soldier himself. Liv and all her men flipped their cloaks around as well. Paz Cavair's bodyguards stripped the cloaks off the other guards, and they piled several others on top of each other and hid them as well as they could. "Five minutes to reach the top if you run. You need to get there before the guard's changed."

"This was supposed to be the new guards," Liv said.

"Their relief is late. Nothing we can do about it now. Go!"

So they ran, straight up the steps. It would only be a matter of time before Lord Aravind's men saw them. If they were lucky, their cloaks would buy them peace until they reached the top—most of the city's soldiers had little official insignia, but only elite soldiers were supposed to approach Lord Aravind en masse. But it was war, and the old way of doing things always breaks down in war.

Liv ran.

Cannons went off to the south, and she could see part of the Color Prince's army massing, charging toward the gates. It was mostly a distraction—for her.

"Liv," the Color Prince had said last night. "I've been testing you. To see if I can trust you with something."

"I know. I'd say, of course you can trust me, but I suppose I would say that regardless."

He smirked. It was a little gruesome with his burn scars, but she barely even saw those anymore. "Not testing your loyalty, not now." The sun was setting early, lighting up the Red Cliffs, making the shadows of the trebuchets stretch out forever. "Your competence. It's a test that I'm forced to give you because I have so few superviolet drafters, and I need a good one for this. The best one. I'd like to keep you safe, but instead, I need to risk you so that we might be victorious. If you succeed, I will reward you more highly than you can imagine."

"What do I need to do?" Liv asked.

And here she was, sweating, heaving, feeling like she was going to throw up. She stopped for a moment and looked out to sea, feeling something, thinking she'd heard something.

A vast green island had risen from the depths of the sea and now floated in the middle of the neck. Ships, small specks, were crashing and capsizing. Huge waves were rolling out from it. An enormous spire rose out of the center of the island. Her heart soared and she swore she felt suddenly wild and strong. The green bane.

To the south, she could hear the sounds of battle. Cannons and muskets were being fired from the wall, shaking the city. The soldiers at the top of the pyramid hadn't seen the bane or Liv's team yet, their vision narrowed to the battle playing out in front of the walls.

But despite feeling wild and strong, sprinting up the steps was exhausting. Liv slowed and the men on either side of her each grabbed one of her arms and helped her up the rest of the way. They didn't harass her for it. They were fighters and their bodies were trained for this. She wasn't. It made her feel weak and helpless—and some small part of her felt trapped and wanted to wrench free. But she suppressed the urge.

They slowed as they came close to the top of the pyramid. Almost invisible from below, there was a square patio at the pyramid's penultimate level, where lords could gather and religious rituals be carried out. It was from here that the men and women of Ru's royal family had been slaughtered and thrown down the steps. Fuschias hung from baskets and pools of water and fountains kept the nobles cool, slaves brought fruit and wine from within the pyramid itself.

The drafters in Liv's team had all pulled on their spectacles, and she did the same. She drafted a shell of superviolet and filled it with liquid yellow, as Gavin Guile himself had shown her. It felt like so long ago now.

"Who are you?" a voice asked from above. A soldier, challenging them.

A spear of blue shot through the man's nose and into his face, and blood exploded from his eyes. Liv's team charged.

There were more people on the top of the pyramid than Liv had guessed, but no drafters. She shot her flashbomb into the middle of the crowd and it burst, blinding the half of the men who were looking their way. Liv's men were ferocious—easily some of the best drafters and fighters she'd ever seen. Phyros spun two axes that looked like halberds with their hafts shortened, and everywhere he went, men died, slaves died, women died. The blue drafters shot spikes through faces and necks, left and right. Phips Navid charged Lord Aravind, shouting vengeance, and was cut down by the noble's bodyguards.

Liv stood back and shot flashbombs, feeling vaguely cowardly, but knowing that she was irreplaceable, and her flashbombs did their work. She only had to draw her pistol once, when a crazed slave had rushed her with a flowerpot. The woman had dropped at Liv's feet, powder burns around the bloody hole in the center of her chest.

Then, abruptly, it was done. Men and women were moaning, but there was no fight. Liv's team was down to five, somehow, and each of them was checking bodies, dispatching wounded enemies who were scrambling to hide or to find weapons.

"Got ten soldiers coming up the outer steps," Phyros said. "I'll hold the inside steps."

Phips Navid was whimpering over by the throne. Liv walked over to him. His left eye was crushed, and there was a spear all the way through his stomach and coming out his back, and his knee was bent the wrong way.

"We get him?" Phips asked. "That swine Aravind? We get him?"

"Yes," Liv said. "Looks like he took a spike in the groin. Phyros just opened his throat."

<hr/>

Phips barked a laugh, but it ended in a whimper. "Good, good. Fourteen years I been hunting that bastard. Wish I could have done it myself. Wish...wish I hadn't needed to. You believe in heaven?"

"I believe in hell," Liv said.

He looked like he tried to laugh, but his face twisted in pain. "Do me the favor, will you? I'll go find out for both of us." He grinned again fiercely and held that grin stubbornly against his pain and fear. She told herself it was mercy, but she couldn't move until she drafted superviolet once more. It had to be done.

She did it, blade slicing neatly through carotid and jugular. She stepped back on shaky legs. Turned away before she could watch what she'd done.

"Ladder's back here," Phyros called.

Liv hurried back to him and climbed up the ladder. There was a small ledge beneath the great polished mirror. But as soon as Liv approached it, she knew it was no ordinary mirror. Not only was this mirror massive—fifteen paces across at least—it was spotlessly clean. There was no dust, no scratches on its face. There were old, old runes carved into the iron frame, black with age.

From the top of the pyramid, Liv could see the battle unfolding at the walls. The Prince's five hundred, decimated, had made it through the bloody smoky hell of that tunnel, and were pushing against soldiers in every street in that neighborhood. The black smoke of muskets rattling and the sound of men screaming rose even to here. But the Blood Robes were pushing in, gaining ground. In another half a block, they would push into a market, giving their superior skills a wider battle front. After that, Liv couldn't imagine it would be long before they would reach the gate. But the fight wasn't over yet, and it seemed that the Atashians on the top of the wall had a limitless supply of loaded muskets, pulling them out, shooting, being handed new ones, shooting, shooting, raining ceaseless death on the attackers.

Liv tore her eyes away. Her fight was here. She tightened her eyes to slits. The mirror seemed to hum in her vision. Strange. She looked down at the base and saw a black panel. She probed it with fingers of superviolet and felt the mirror shudder. It felt like there were little invisible levers inside it.

What am I doing? She looked at the soldiers coming up the pyramid. This was her last test. This was what she was made for. If she did this, the Color Prince would give her more than she'd ever dreamed. She'd never again be inconsequential. She could never again be ignored, despised, powerless.

They were going to win the battle for the city, but out there, somehow, the battle for the sea would turn on what she did here. This was her chance to pay back the Chromeria for every sneer, for using her against her father, for making her break her oaths, for defiling everything.

The tendrils of her superviolet luxin sank into the black box, found levers within, pulled—and the mirror swung, almost taking her head off. She let go of the luxin, and the mirror stopped abruptly. She drafted again and pulled another and the mirror tilted. She pulled another, and the mirror shimmered and turned blue.

"Quickly, my lady, they're almost upon us!" one of the men cried.

"Working!" she shouted.

With the superviolet controls, Liv pulled another lever, and a green filter bubbled to the mirror's surface. From there, it was a simple matter of pushing and pulling the first two levers. She caught the sun's rising light in the huge mirror and shot it out over the bay. She turned it left and right and up and down, wondering if she would have any idea when she finally got it right, or if she was *already* getting it right. She felt something when the beam was aimed far out to sea, over Ruic Head, but that must have been her trying too hard. That wasn't even remotely the right direction. She turned it over the bay, up and down, searching.

Then something vibrated—she lost it. She reached again and turned the beam back, the tiniest bit. It caught, and hummed. In a moment, the mirror went from a mirror to something else entirely.

The mirror collected all the sun and was sending a vibrant emerald beam out to the bane. It was visible in the very air, burning bright green. That wasn't right; it wasn't even possible. Mirrors never shone so bright that you could see the beam during the day. Maybe in fog, or smoke, or at night, the light might be visible, but not an hour after dawn.

And yet it was.

But as it vibrated on that perfect frequency, humming like music, Liv's perception was pulled through the great lens itself—and suddenly, she could see the tower shivering up out of the sea, growing, right in front of her, as if it were only a hundred paces away, not thousands.

As she saw, she knew that Koios White Oak had been wrong. She'd passed the test of competency easily. This *was* a test of loyalty. For she saw Kip, and Karris, and Gavin Guile himself on the bane, and she knew that if she obeyed the Color Prince, she would doom them all.

If she was to have the power to change the world, if she was to save ten thousand naïve young women in the future from the sharks and sea demons, she must let her friends die. She had begged the Color Prince to save Kip and Karris before—had traded Blood Robes' lives for theirs in Garriston. Not half a year ago, her friends had been worth her oath and the lives of a few strangers. Was saving them *now* worth the dream of a new, changed, pure world?

"Do you know what Atirat needs, Aliviana?" the Color Prince had asked her last night.

"Sacrifices?" she hazarded.

"Light. Every god is birthed in light."

And, weeping, light she brought.

Chapter 110

The first great wave came from behind the skimmer.

Gavin shouted something, but it was lost in the roar of water falling and crushing and sweeping over the back of the skimmer. His body language was unmistakable, though. He threw himself at the reeds and threw luxin down them as hard as he could. The Blackguards followed his example, and the skimmer jumped forward.

But they weren't as fast as the great swell that swept Kip off his feet. He grabbed on to the rail with both hands, and as it flipped him around, he saw the spire rising out of the sea behind them. Already, it was hundreds of feet high. It was the origin of the great wave and the pounding water falling from the sky both.

Then Kip was crushed down against the deck. He heard the sound of luxin snapping and ripping loose and he saw Gavin flying off the front of the skimmer. He'd shot luxin so hard, he'd torn the reeds off. They were all suddenly airborne. Kip lost the railing—or maybe it disintegrated. He could see nothing except water. Whatever had hurled the sea upward had stopped, and now the seas dropped again with all the chaos of a waterfall. Kip fell and fell and fought for one deep breath. When he landed in the water, it was into a current that blasted him sideways. He hit something, scraped something else. It was no use trying to fight, he was being tumbled head over heels. He had no idea which way was up.

Feeling something beneath him, he grabbed it, missed, slipped. The current was forming swift rivers, and he knew that he needed to avoid the deeper current. He grabbed again, catching what felt like a tree branch, and walked himself hand over hand toward the weaker current. His lungs were burning, and the water was so fouled that he couldn't see anything but green. He fought down his panic, fought down the wildness. Hand over hand, Kip. He grabbed root after root and kept going, going.

Moments later, he felt the temperature change on his back. Air. Wedging his feet in among the roots, he lifted his head and breathed.

The current almost pulled him into the depths and he staggered, but caught himself. He was standing on a new island, and everywhere, water was sluicing off in great rivers back into the sea. The land, if land it was, wasn't uniform. In some places the water had no way to seek lower ground, and it stood in ponds and lakes.

Green. Every possible shade from the slate green of lichen to the red-tinged green of a ruby leaf. Radiant emerald greens that glowed from within and the dull, earthen greens of roots; spruce and sage and seaweed and olive and sea foam and mint green. The entire island was an amalgam of living vegetation and green luxin. Kip was standing on roots pulsing with life. He saw an entire galleon, mysteriously unbroken, wedged between the branches of what looked like a fallen tree, fifty feet in the air. But even as Kip stared in wonder, he saw branches climbing up the galleon's hull like an ivy shoot. They wrapped over the galleon's waist, thickened, and crushed the decks, spilling sailors everywhere.

The entire island was living vegetation, and it was waking.

Searching for the Blackguards, Kip saw the black-garbed figures rising, spread over five hundred paces. He only saw eight of them, but there were more in the water, swimming, fighting. Gavin stood a hundred paces away, waving, and pointing toward the spire. He looked urgent.

Kip ran toward him.

Coming to a channel of swiftly flowing water that was too wide to jump across, Kip threw green luxin down at his feet, making a plank to run on like he'd seen Commander Ironfist do before. It was easier than any drafting he'd ever done. The green light seemed to press itself physically into his eyes; he barely had to open the tap, and it flowed out just as easily. He felt the wild joy and freedom of green, a joy without terror, a joy without anchor—

Kip didn't think it was his own joy he was feeling.

Gavin wasn't waiting for Kip; he was sprinting for the spire. That he didn't wait first hurt Kip's feelings, then terrified him. Gavin would wait, if he could. If there wasn't some absolutely desperate need, if seconds weren't absolutely crucial, he would gather up his forces. Not only Kip, but everyone. Gavin would want to have his whole team together for both humane and tactical reasons. That he thought there was no time for either—

A sound like a thousand sighs swept across the bane—air being released, the hollow echo of bubbles opening. Kip ran straight over a rising cocoon yawning open, its membrane tearing as a jade green hand clawed the air. Commander Ironfist had been right. Green wights had flocked here by the hundreds or thousands to be perfected by the bane itself. And now they were rising. Kip hurdled over the color wight rising from its gooey cocoon and ran faster than he'd run in his entire life.

"Load the cannons," Commander Ironfist said. He was looking out over the bay at the new island through the mounted long lens that the battery's gunners had used to sight targets. His face was as hard as Teia had ever seen. "Hezik! You have some experience?"

A Blackguard with shoulders like a buffalo stepped forward. He had only one ear, a thick scar down the left half of his face testimony to a sword stroke. "Yessir, mother commanded a pirate hunter in the Narrows."

"Recommendations. Time's short."

"Don't load all the guns. Only these two can hit that damn thing at all, and only this one with any sort of accuracy." He gestured to the big bronze culverin. "Six thousand paces, but from this height, and with this powder, nice big grains rather than fine, wrap the first shot in sacking to help me get the range..."

"Your command, Hezik. Take out the big tower."

Hezik was silent for a second, thinking, then he began pointing to men. "Inventory. I want to know how much of this grain of powder we have, and what shot. Do we have any shells? You, weigh that ball on the scales over there, then measure out four-fifths of that weight. You, there should be some gunners' notes somewhere. Find 'em!"

Gavin had set fire to the huge yellow sword he'd drafted and was throwing flames with his left hand and slashing green wights with his right, still running toward the spire. Karris was hard on his heels, her ataghan cutting necks and stomachs as wights' eyes were drawn by Gavin's figure in front of her. As always, Kip brought up the rear, short of breath, but able to do anything with green empowering him.

Before they could reach the spire, dozens of wights rose up. They'd been kneeling, worshipping before the spire, but seeing these interlopers, they ran to intercept them. The spire was still growing, twisting higher toward the heavens. The wights themselves were growing, too. The green bane was making all of them stronger. Every one of them used the power differently. Some went green golem, wrapping themselves in green armor that made them three times as wide. Others looked like saplings, stripped of bark, a thin green skin replacing their own skin, green over red, skeletal and all the more alien for being so close to human. Others made themselves hugely tall. Others drafted huge claws or great, springy frogs' legs. Others, less imaginative, drafted thick shields and cudgels and helms.

Kip felt a thump reverberate dimly through the ground at his feet and a second later heard the sound of a cannon. A dim trail of smoke from a crater more than a hundred paces away pointed back toward the battery up on Ruic Head, where a much larger plume of black smoke was blowing away.

"To me, to me!" Gavin shouted.

After a moment of resistance at being ordered to do something, the green in him rebelling, Kip realized it was what he wanted to do anyway. In seconds, he and five Blackguards joined Gavin.

"They're making a god. We kill it," Gavin said. He drafted another yellow sword, handed it to a Blackguard who had lost her weapons. "No matter what. No matter how. Got it?" He made another yellow sword, and another, tossed one to a Blackguard and one to Kip. Then he started running toward the wights. His hands were surrounded with glowing knots of yellows and reds.

As the first green spear came shooting toward Gavin, he dropped under it and rolled on the ground, came up to his knees and threw his hands forward. A fan of yellow missiles blasted out from him, each trailing chains of flame. The missiles stabbed dozens of the wights and the chains whipped around them, wrapping some in flame and scoring the wights behind.

But Gavin barely slowed. He popped back up to his feet and kept running.

A frog wight Kip hadn't even seen descended, huge claws raking downward. Karris dodged to the side and swept her ataghan under its armpit.

Then, still fifty paces from the base of the spire, they ran into a veritable wall of green wights. Gavin crashed through a few, killing, spinning, killing—and almost got separated from the Blackguards. A Blackguard named Milk had his entire arm and shoulder ripped off by a big claw. A woman named Tisa was knocked aside as she drafted a stream of fire and accidentally shot a gush of pyrejelly down her own stomach and leg. It flamed and she screamed.

But she didn't forget herself. As a green golem eight feet tall settled between Gavin and the rest of them to cut him off, Tisa hurled herself onto the golem's back, taking both of them down in a sudden intense wash of fire.

Kip slashed back and forth, trying to keep up with the others. Something twisted his yellow luxin sword and he lost it.

The three remaining Blackguards reunited with Gavin, who fought with the flaming sword in one hand and luxin of alternating colors in the other. They were stuck, surrounded by dozens of wights, stopped.

A shell rocked the ground, exploding with a deafening roar. Kip felt the pressure wave and almost fell. A smoking hole cratered the green island, thirty paces away. The wights around it had been vaporized, those farther out torn to pieces.

The Blackguards and Gavin recovered first. The crater and the hole in the wights' lines wasn't directly between the Blackguards and the tower, but it offered movement. Freedom.

Even then, they never would have made if it the greens could tolerate order—if they'd organized their defenses. But with the help of the chaos, Gavin and his people cut through the staggered creatures and ran into the gap created by the shell, stepping on bodies and slipping on released green luxin that was evaporating as the once-men holding it died. Kip almost tripped over a woman's bare torso—nothing else of her remained. Red and green ran in rivers next to each other, filling the crater with blood soup.

Crashing into the still-recovering lines on the opposite side of the crater with Karris, Gavin, and the remaining three Blackguards, Kip remembered his knife, still strapped to his calf, and pulled it out, stumbling. He lashed out at a big wight who was holding his bleeding eyes, weeping. Kip's knife cut through the wight's shell and kidneys with ease.

He felt instantly, stupidly guilty. The man hadn't been able to defend himself, and Kip had cut him like a—

"Incoming!" Gavin shouted. He knocked Kip down.

They heard the thump and the explosion, but it was a good seventy paces away this time—no good to them, but no danger either.

By the time they stood, a man with a green bull's head on his shoulders was charging them. Gavin leapt aside and cut the man's back as he passed. The wight went down, but his horn caught Karris, who hadn't jumped far enough. It spun her hard and slammed her into the ground.

Kip jumped on the bull and stabbed in through the top of its head, twisting his dagger in its brain and ripping it out. He grabbed Karris and pulled her to her feet. There was blood on her arm and chest, but instead of skewering her, the horn had passed under her armpit. She was winded, gasping for air, but not wounded. Lucky.

Gavin threw his sword into the chest of a woman who had the form of a harpy and spun, pulling his dagger-pistols from his belt. The guns spun in his hands as he pointed at Kip. Both pistols cracked and Kip ran on, certain that two wights behind him and Karris were dead.

A Blackguard was hamstringing two giants at the base of the stairs when one caught him with a war hammer in the shoulder. He staggered sideways, trying to catch himself, and met the other's battle axe. It cut all the way through his chest.

Gavin shot yellow spears into their brains, one-two-three, in rapid succession, but it was too late for the Blackguard.

"Up," Gavin shouted, "up!"

They ran up the stairs as if hell was on their heels. Kip was at the back. The tower was growing even as they mounted the stairs, twisting higher like a growing tree.

"What was that?" Gavin asked.

What? Kip hadn't seen anything. He was exhausted, and they were only halfway up the tower. He looked down and saw that the wights had decided to follow them. He didn't slow.

A clash of arms up ahead told Kip that they had encountered defense. It was all that allowed him to catch up. But Gavin had barely slowed. Kip heard screams descending, and when he passed the same spot of the winding stair, he saw wights far below, their bodies broken.

A great beam of green light hit the top of the tower, and the whole thing bucked and shivered. It nearly hurled them off the stairs.

"What the hell is that?" Commander Ironfist asked.

No one answered. No one knew. The green itself felt different suddenly, not affecting all of them so much as being gathered elsewhere. Teia was holding a pair of binocles. Through them, she could see more than most. "It's coming from the Great Pyramid," she said. "Or going to it, I can't tell."

"Is it a weapon?"

"I don't know!"

Men were scrambling around the room, the gunners swabbing out the smoking hot bronze barrel, cooling it and making sure no bits of burning powder remained in the breech that would ignite the charge. Others were weighing the powder for the next shot. The Blackguards who were tasked with muscling the great thing back into place were taking a well-deserved rest. Though the carriage was wheeled, the culverin was still massive. Hezik was staring alternately at a list of numbers he'd scribbled on a piece of parchment someone had passed him and down at the green island, lips moving silently, doing mental sums.

Everything was chaos, happening all at once.

"There's a green man on top of the tower," the spotter on the long lens called out.

Whatever was happening between the Great Pyramid and the bane was definitely helping the invaders. The tower was getting more massive by the second. "Why would the Atashians be helping the bane?" Teia asked.

"Sir," the spotter said, "if I didn't know better— Sir, that thing is Atirat."

"Because the city has fallen," Commander Ironfist said grimly. He walked over to the spotter, who moved aside for him.

"What?!" Hezik shouted to a Blackguard reporting to him. Not asking about the city.

"We didn't see it before. It was at the bottom of the pile." The Blackguard turned one of the shells over. The side was stove in, spilling all its powder out, and making it as effective in flight as a one-winged bird.

"Commander," Hezik said. "We've only got two shots left. One shell, and one ball. Which do you want us to load?"

They'd been shooting the shells, and Hezik had honed his accuracy through practice. He was now hitting within forty paces of where he aimed, and he had done much better than that twice. But Gavin and the others were almost to the top of the tower. An exploding shell, that close? It would kill all of them.

On the other hand, the balls weighed more and flew differently. They'd shot a few of those earlier to get range before they started shooting the shells into the wights, but they hadn't had as much practice.

Commander Ironfist said, "Use the ball."

Hezik hesitated. "Sir, I'm only accurate within maybe twenty paces with the ball. It's not a matter of skill at this distance, sir. We'd have to get very lucky."

Teia had seen him shoot. He was being wildly optimistic.

Commander Ironfist's face didn't shift. "I trust you. Use the ball. Kill that god."

By the time Kip reached the top of the tower, wheezing and so exhausted he thought he was going to vomit, the others were already fighting. The top of the green spire was something between a tower and a tree. Twelve smaller towers ringed it, like merlons on a crenellated wall. From each of those merlons, a giant was emerging. Four of them were already out, fighting Gavin, Karris, and the last Blackguard, Baya Niel.

The others were waking. Kip felt a shiver in the merlon next to him. The giants within the merlons were still men, but men who'd descended so deep into green that they'd rebuilt themselves, and the blasting green light from Ru seemed to be helping. Even as Kip looked, he saw green skin covered with tiny scales shimmer over the giant's naked muscle on his arms. His chest was thickening, legs elongating.

In a paroxysm of revulsion, Kip stabbed his dagger into the creature. The dagger punched through the cocoon like it was wet paper. The giant's green, green eyes shot open, its mouth opened on the other side of the glass, and then it slumped and its eyes dimmed.

Six of the giants were now out, fighting Gavin and Karris. One died as Kip watched, its head wrapped in flames by Gavin and then taken off by Baya Niel. But the others were still emerging. It seemed that those who were full in the green light from Ru had already awakened, but those who were shaded from it by their merlons were slower.

For one second, Kip considered joining the fight in the middle. Gavin and Karris were doing their best to get to the middle of the tower, where the green light was focused and reflecting so brightly it hurt Kip's eyes. The other giants were blocking Gavin and Karris from getting there. Gavin and Karris had their hands full. Kip would barely be a help to them—but he could keep them from facing even worse odds.

So he ran around the edge of the tower instead, circling to the great cocoons. He rammed his dagger into another giant's chest. As before, its eyes opened, bulged, dimmed. Kip ran on. He stabbed a third. This one punched its fist through the cocoon and groped for

Kip, but Kip pulled the dagger out and ducked. The giant crumpled, tearing through the cocoon and falling on the ground in a splash of goo.

The next three cocoons were already empty, and as Kip ran toward the next, his eyes lifted to the fort on Ruic Head, where he saw a flash of light and a gout of smoke. One thousand one. One thousand two...

Kip didn't have time to worry about it. As he ran toward one of the awakening giants, another came from the side to intercept him. More than eight feet tall, this one had drafted a sword for his right arm. Green luxin shouldn't hold an edge, but either different rules applied to the giants or it wouldn't matter because getting hit with all the force in the giant's massive arm would tear Kip to pieces regardless, edge or no edge.

Fumbling with his lenses at his hip, Kip put the red spectacles on his face, intending to wreathe the big bastard in flames—but he'd put the wrong glasses on his face. Orange splattered harmlessly across the giant's chest and it drew back its huge sword arm and roared, charging at full speed.

Kip threw orange at the ground and leapt hard to the side. He felt something whistle past his ear. The giant stomped right next to him, his foot splattering in the slick orange luxin as he tried to change direction. His nonsword arm wheeled crazily and, slipping, he shot right off the edge of the tower.

Kip watched him spin into space with grim satisfaction. Fat kids know how hard it is to stop once you get up to a sprint.

The nearest merlon was empty.

Without warning, the empty merlon exploded in scraps and shrapnel of green luxin that hit the side of Kip's face and his left arm like a swarm of hornets as the cannonball struck it.

One thousand six, I guess.

Still standing, stunned, bewildered, and bleeding, Kip heard the delayed, distant roar of the cannon. Those bastards up there really were trying to kill them. If he had been two steps closer, he'd be dead.

But there was no time. Gavin was bleeding from a slash down his chest, and Karris was literally smoking as if she'd recently been on fire. Baya Niel's nose was streaming blood. Several giants were dead on the ground behind them, and the light at the center of the tower was dimming, revealing a figure. That should be a good thing. Kip didn't think it was. He ran to the next merlon, stabbed the fully formed giant there, and ran on to the last one.

This giant was awake, pulling herself out of the merlon, getting her bearings.

Kip leapt at her, slashing.

The giantess brought up her forearm and blocked the slash, her arm catching Kip's forearm. Kip's momentum carried him forward into his own hands, his doubled fists smacking into his face.

He dropped at her feet, stunned, blood pouring into his eyes. He saw death in the giantess's twisted visage.

"A miss!" the spotter cried. "Fifteen paces long, twenty paces left. Tore off a tower on the southeast. Nearly killed Breaker."

Curses went up, but there were no recriminations. Everyone knew that merely hitting the top of the tower from five thousand paces was an incredible feat. There was skill, and there was art, and there was simple luck. They were operating at the uttermost of the first two. The last couldn't be counted on.

But the crews didn't slow. Men were already swabbing out the culverin. The powder was already measured.

"We're certain that there's no more shot?" Commander Ironfist asked.

"Triple-checked, sir," Hezik said. "Just the one explosive shell. If by some miracle I hit the tower, it'll kill all our people, too."

Commander Ironfist's face was grim. A second passed. Everyone looked at him.

"Load it."

A cannonball right about now would be nice, Kip thought, looking up at Death.

But there was no shot. No rescue. Even if they fired a ball right now, it would be six seconds before it saved Kip—and in six seconds, he'd be dead.

He flailed, slashed. His dagger punched into the giantess's calf muscle.

He thought it was over then. He'd hurt her, but not badly, and now she would kill him. But the giantess didn't do anything. She stood as if locked in ice. Through the blood in one eye, Kip blinked up at her. She was blanching—literally desaturating from the head down as if he'd poked a straw into her and was sucking out all the color. The green luxin that covered her features was unraveling. Her green hair fell off, the green mask of perfection over her face drooped, sloughing off, dissipated in a smoke redolent of fresh cedar. Her jade eyes sank, her body shrank, deflating. In moments, a woman with the rags of a dress torn by her recent huge size and now draped over emaciated limbs stood over Kip. The broken green spars of her halos shimmered in the whites of her eyes and disappeared. The green in her irises shimmered and disappeared. Her skin was bleached to its natural Ruthgari-pale hue.

Limp, she fell across Kip, her motion tearing the dagger out of her bleeding calf.

He pushed himself up to his knees. She raised her hand as if to draft.

Kip slashed her throat, and she sighed. Her eyes rolled back in her head and she relaxed into death.

She'd raised her hand to draft, to kill Kip. He'd had to do it. Or had she raised her hand in supplication?

The green light from Ru went out.

"Enough," a voice said. It wasn't loud, but it seemed to cut through everything. It shook Kip to his bones.

The dead woman forgotten, Kip looked to the center of the tower, where a new god stood.

Atirat, the queen of lasciviousness, the green goddess, the consort of heaven, the lady of moonlight, was supposed to be many things, some of them contradictory. But whatever else this goddess was, it wasn't a she. Unlike his twelve giants, he was no taller than Gavin. Apparently he thought real power didn't need to be vulgarly demonstrated in superior size. Though avoiding vulgarity didn't seem to particularly concern Atirat otherwise.

He had no human flesh left. Everywhere, luxin knit so thin it could be silken cloth formed his skin. Long, intertwined figures were incised atop the vast hempen ropes of his muscles, seeming to copulate with every motion of his arms or legs. His hair, worn long, was a tapestry of vines and serpents. A gold choker around his throat held a single black jewel. As he moved, his muscles split and slid past each other, revealing seams of scarlet that might have been the bark of the red birch, or simply veins unprotected by his luxin skin. He was bare-chested, living vines forming a kilt. Moss curled on his chest as hair, and leaves and grass bloomed and withered spontaneously on every surface.

It was so good, even Gavin couldn't tell if it was real or illusion.

The god's eyes were chips of flint, and he seemed lit from within, with power, with light, with magic, with life. Gavin supposed it all would have been far more impressive if he could see green. But something about the way he moved was familiar. Oh, Orholam have mercy. The spies had been right.

"Dervani Malargos," Gavin said. "Never thought I'd see you wearing a dress. I'd ask what you've been up to since the war, but I suppose I can probably hazard a guess." A cockroach emerged from the god's armpit and disappeared into his arm. "Nice beetle. Be careful of termites."

Inside, Gavin's heart was lead. He'd fought beside Dervani Malargos. He, Dazen, not he Gavin. His mother had confessed to sending an assassin after the man. Apparently the assassin had lied about his success. Dervani was Tisis's father. Either way, Dervani had no reason to love Gavin—nor, truth be told, Dazen.

Dervani had been worth killing because he had known Dazen. He'd been there, right at the end at Sundered Rock. He might have seen everything. If Felia Guile had been right, he might unmask—

But then perhaps I should be more worried about him killing me now than ruining my life in some hypothetical future.

Atirat raised his hands and Gavin felt the giants behind him lifted and pushed backward.

"Gavin," Karris said. "Gavin!" She was reloading her pistol, already fitting the lead ball in wadding and ramming it home. Though he couldn't see green, Gavin could see the darker thread of luxin from her eyes down to her hands. "Gavin," she said, "I'm not doing this. Run!"

"You won't shoot me," Gavin said.

"Damn you! It's not me!"

"You'll stay," Atirat said in a voice like stones rolling together.

Atirat pointed a finger at Gavin and a spidery thread of luxin crawled up from the very ground at his feet. Gavin batted it away. "What's this?" Atirat laughed. "So that's how we've succeeded. You've lost green. You are a broken Prism, and yet you've held your office. I suppose I should thank you for your stubborn pride, Guile. Thank you, and goodbye."

Karris raised her pistol like a marionette and fired at Gavin's head.

He slapped her hand aside at the last moment. The bullet burned a crease along his neck. Vines shot up his legs and he slashed at them with his sword, freeing himself. A cudgel the size of a tree limb blasted him off his feet. Gavin rolled, stood, and found himself right at the edge of the tower. He whirled his arms in circles.

The tower grew saplings with spear points at the edge. They stabbed at Gavin. He dodged one, took another into the meat of his shoulder, and grabbed another. When it pulled back, it pulled Gavin back, too.

He rolled on the ground, slashed the spears off near the ground, and ran.

Karris was still rooted in her spot, reloading her pistol. The last Blackguard, Baya Niel, was similarly rooted to his spot—he, too, was green, and thereby susceptible to Atirat's control, though mercifully he'd lost his pistols. The tower was trying to grab Gavin, even anticipating where he was going to run and sprouting thorns. The remaining three giants were all standing sentinel, content to watch until ordered otherwise. Across the tower, Kip was staring wide-eyed by a dead woman. Gavin could only pray that the boy had the sense to play dead. Kip could draft green, too.

Another tree trunk swept toward Gavin's feet and he leapt over it. He threw streams of fire toward Atirat, but couldn't see whether they'd had any effect. He landed, jumped as two more thorn-spears tried to impale him. He tried to remember anything useful about Dervani Malargos.

There was no hint that Gavin's fire had done anything. A throne was rising behind Dervani, and his hands were raised. Gavin slashed at the thorn spears, burned the vines that tried to entangle him. Rolled, dove, staggered left and stutter-stepped right, throwing missiles and fire and blasts of pure heat, trying ever to work his way toward the god.

Then the god cheated. The floor disappeared. The green luxin holding Gavin up simply disappeared at his next step, and then reformed on every side of him. It pulled him back to the surface, locking every limb in an iron embrace.

But Gavin wasn't helpless. Most drafters grew accustomed to drafting from their hands, the outlets forming at their wrists or fingertips. But you didn't have to do things the way drafters usually did.

Gavin split the skin all along his shoulders and arms and threw reds and sub-reds into the luxin holding him captive. It hissed and smoked and burned and for one second he pulled free, and then the green reformed. Gavin threw everything into it, screaming and splitting skin along his arms, down the sides of his chest, down his legs, and poured fire into his bonds.

He staggered free and raised his hands toward the god to draft a yellow spike through Atirat's brain. He threw all the vast power of his will—into nothing.

He stared down at his hands. No luxin. What the hell?

No yellow.

The green shot up his legs and imprisoned him in a moment. Only then did Gavin see his mistake. Atirat had drafted a bubble all the way around the top of the tower. A thin, green, translucent bubble. A lens that blocked out every color Gavin could use.

But no lens was perfect, and Gavin wasn't about to give up and die. He drew in sub-red, but that only made the green around his hands smoke, and the luxin grew back as fast as he could burn it. Drafting through that lens was like breathing through a reed that was too long, too thin.

Gavin was too weak.

"How does it feel, Gavin Guile? To be mortal, I mean. Surrounded by light, and yet helpless?"

Gavin Guile. Not that it mattered now, but Dervani didn't recognize him. Felia Guile had tried to murder a man who actually wasn't a threat—and because she had failed, he now actually was a threat.

Gavin's wry smirk seemed to irritate the new god. "I thought you died," Gavin said. He'd seen Kip back there. Maybe the boy could make something happen if Gavin kept Atirat's attention.

"I very nearly did. There was a small conclave of us. Drafters who survived the war but were so damaged that you would force us to suicide. You'd taken enough from us. We weren't willing to die on your command. So some of us learned to remake ourselves with light. The burned, the scarred, the amputees. We became new. Because light cannot be chained, Gavin Guile."

"How did you—" Gavin started to ask. Kip was creeping on his hands and knees directly behind the throne that had blossomed for Atirat.

"There is only one question, Gavin Guile," Atirat said. "Do you want to be killed by the woman, or the boy?"

Kip froze. "Father," he said. "I can't move."

"Gavin," Karris said. Her teeth were gritted and there were tears in her eyes as she fought the green luxin that suffused her body. "I can't—I can't…"

"I can make the shot," Hezik said, tense, eager.

"Making the shot means killing them all, you idiot!" Buskin shouted.

Hezik said, "We can't save them! This is our only chance. It's a *god*!"

Commander Ironfist ignored both; words he thought he'd forgotten came unbidden to his lips: "Mighty Orholam, giver of light, see me now, hear my cry. In the hour of my darkness, I approach your throne." The commander watched himself say the words as if he were a bystander. He'd not prayed the prayer of supplication since he was thirteen years old. His chest felt hollow. He could see his mother bleeding out her life in front of him as the words spilled forth. "Lord of Light, see—" A sudden thought interrupted his prayer.

"One slot up, two slots right," he told Hezik.

"Sir, I've got it right—"

"Now!" he shouted.

Three clicks, instantly, as Hezik moved the cannon to the slots commanded. Ironfist took the smoking linstock and lit the fuse himself.

The roar filled the battery, and Ironfist swore every man counted the seconds.

"I wish you could know what it's like, Gavin," the god said. "I can feel every living, growing thing in the world. And my senses are only expanding, second by second."

Atirat sounded drunk, but regardless, Kip couldn't move. His muscles flexed and tightened at his command, but his bones themselves were locked in place. He'd almost made it. He'd almost saved them all. Kip Almost.

Gavin said something, but Kip couldn't hear it. He saw Atirat tense, warned by some sixth sense. He turned, and Kip saw the blast of smoke from the cannon from the fort on Ruic Head.

One thousand one.

Atirat rolled his shoulders. Laughed. "Friends of yours?" he asked. "Don't they know cannonballs are more likely to kill you than me? I should almost let it land, just to see." He raised his hands, aiming, as if he could track a ball through the air itself.

One thousand five.

"Almost," he said. Something shot out of Atirat's hands and intercepted the ball in midair, not twenty paces above them.

He hadn't expected a shell.

The shell exploded with a thunderous roar and concussion that shook the tower. The green bubble covering the tower shattered. The giants were thrown off their feet. Kip was bowled over.

Kip scrambled as he landed on his face, reaching for the dagger. Everyone else reacted instantly. Kip heard the snap of Karris's pistol going off, saw Gavin throw yellow spikes into each of the giants and straight at Atirat. Flames billowed off Gavin's hands—

—and were quenched.

Even as his giants died, Atirat batted aside the attacks directed at him as if they were smoke. Hands left, right. Gavin was locked down, the bubble reformed, snapping in place. Gavin overwhelmed, buried in green sludge, Karris falling, Baya Niel fallen.

Kip could feel the steel in his joints re-forming. He leapt toward Atirat's back, extending the dagger, and felt his bones lock in place in midair.

Fat kids know all about momentum.

Kip's dagger punched straight into the back of Atirat's head.

The luxin freezing Kip's bones blew apart like mist. He tackled Atirat, landed on top of him. He twisted the dagger in the god's head, hearing bones crunch and squish.

Still on his knees, Kip looked at the dagger in his hand. The green and blue jewels on the blade were glowing hot, bright for one instant. Kip heard bodies falling: the giants, robbed of form and life.

Karris laughed and Kip realized how suddenly quiet it had grown up here. He tucked the dagger away, stood.

"Orholam's beard, Kip," Gavin said. "Well done." At their feet lay a man—or some hideous thing that had been a man. Without the green luxin that he had woven into every part of his body, Dervani Malargos was a skinless, hairless tangle of meat, brains, and blood oozing out of his destroyed skull.

The tower shook and sank five paces suddenly, almost throwing them all into the sea.

"Does that mean that the entire island is about to collapse?" Karris asked.

"Afraid so," Gavin said.

"I would think that's really great," Karris said. "If I weren't about to fall to my death."

Gavin laughed. "I can help with that. Get over here."

And the lovely, lovely sound of Gavin drafting filled Kip's ears.

"We did it!" Hizek shouted. "We saved them! I told you I could make that shot!"

The Blackguards were cheering, watching the great tower slump into the sea with no fear. Gavin Guile had stopped a god; they had no doubt he would be able to escape a mere collapsing tower.

But Teia couldn't take her eyes off Commander Ironfist, who stood stock still. And then he dropped to his knees like a ton of bricks.

Teia had never seen a man quite as big and frightening as Commander Ironfist. She'd certainly never seen a man his size weep.

"*Elrahee, elishama, eliada, eliphalet*," he said, over and over, clearly some Parian prayer. He fell on his knees and, seeing Teia's bewildered look, said, "He sees me. He hears. He hears even me."

Then, heedless of what his people would think, the huge Parian lay prostrate, weeping, weeping.

Chapter 111

Andross Guile's flagship had survived the naval battle. Of course, he hadn't brought it in close enough to risk losing it. His ship did assist in the rescue efforts after the green island broke apart and sank into the sea. It had been another ship that had first come across the Prism, Karris, Kip, and Baya Niel, but they'd been transferred over after the remnants of the fleet had picked up whatever survivors they could find.

It had been a race between the Chromeria's ships and the circling pirates, who were searching the wreckage for loot, or picking up men to press-gang or sell as slaves.

Now, after dark, Gavin and Kip sat on the forecastle of the big ship, huddled around a brazier. Kip's clothes still weren't dried out. He knew how to dry them with sub-red now, but after how much he'd drafted today, he didn't even want to see luxin, much less draft it. He was going to be lightsick tomorrow, he had no doubt. Gavin had been given new clothes and bandages for all his cuts immediately, of course. But then, that's what being the Prism gets you.

They sat on the deck for a long time in companionable silence. Gavin dismissed his exhausted Blackguards. The men who were guarding him now had helped take the fort on Ruic Head and after fighting for hours had then assisted the rescue efforts all day; they deserved the rest. From time to time, men would come up to the Prism and congratulate him. Some even congratulated Kip. Kip Godslayer, one called him. Kip didn't appreciate it. He was Godslayer only in the most technical sense. He'd delivered the final blow only because he'd been the least threat, only because he'd been beneath notice.

Gavin simply said, "You do what you have to do, Kip. Let people call you what they will. You can't change it. People want heroes, and if every once in a while that title sticks to you, just make sure you don't believe in it too much yourself." He shook his head, as if the words weren't coming out right. "You were brave today, Kip. You lived up to the highest ideals of the Blackguard, and I'm proud of you." He handed Kip the mulled wine.

Kip grimaced, taking it. It hadn't been him. It had been the knife.

He still hadn't told his father about the knife. He needed to. He'd been trying to work up to it all afternoon.

Karris came up to their brazier. She sat beside Gavin and put her hand on his thigh. She smiled over at Kip. "Hey there, Godslayer," she said. She was teasing, but she meant it in a good way. Somehow, when she said it, it seemed nice. Kip mumbled evasions below his breath.

"I really need to teach you to knife fight, though," she said. "Sloppy technique, sloppy." Again, kidding. But Kip grinned. It was the kind of ribbing that told him she wanted to spend more time with him in the future. It was about the nicest thing he could ask for.

"I'm exhausted," she said to Gavin. "I'm going to go below. You going to be an hour or so?"

"Andross asked to speak with me, and the generals always have business. We have to see if we can keep these bane from recurring," Gavin said glumly. "At least an hour."

"I'm proud of you," she said. "For this."

Gavin seemed to know what she was talking about, but Kip didn't. For sitting at a brazier with Kip?

"Someone told me something about love once," Gavin said. "Still sounds silly to me, but I'm giving it a shot." He was teasing.

Karris's smile lit the deck. "I love you," she said, her voice warmer and softer than Kip had ever heard it. She had it bad.

"Is there an action wedded to that choice?" Gavin asked.

"I'm going to go below and sleep for a while," she said. "But, uh, wake me." She didn't try very hard to hide her wink, and Kip blushed.

"Mmm," Gavin said appreciatively as she got up and left. He watched her go. "Kip," he said. "If you ever find a woman like that... don't be an idiot like your father."

"Yes, sir." Kip grinned. "So... what happens now?"

"You mean with the satrapies?"

Kip nodded.

"We've lost two satrapies. Tyrea didn't matter to the other satrapies, but Atash?" He shook his head. "I'm afraid we were so eager to avoid war, we've made it all but certain."

He said "we." Even though Kip knew his father had fought for all he was worth to get the Chromeria to move before it was too late, he still shared responsibility for the failure. His father, he decided again, was a great man.

Kip hadn't had much time to think today, but he'd had enough. The dagger was important, as in Important. It had sucked the luxin right out of that giant. Kip should have told his father about the knife immediately. But volunteering to have his father mad at him seemed impossible.

Every time, just when things are going well, you open your big mouth, Kip.

But at least usually it was an accident. This time he had to do it on purpose.

He was within a breath—or maybe a minute or two—of speaking when a greasy voice said, "Sirs?" Grinwoody. "Luxlord Guile awaits your pleasure. He heard you were topside and climbed up, with considerable effort to his person."

"Then where is he?" Kip asked. Oops. Kip the Lip. Maybe it was all this Kip the Godslayer talk. Or maybe it was the mulled wine warming him.

"On the stern castle, sirs. He only demanded the Lord Prism's presence, however."

"You can come if you want to, Kip. But it won't be pleasant," Gavin said. "Father and I have some hard words to exchange."

Grinwoody's mouth thinned to a tight line, but he said nothing.

"I'd rather stay with you, sir," Kip said.

Gavin and Kip climbed down, Kip having to take extra care on the steps. Apparently he'd had more wine than he'd thought. They crossed the ship's waist and climbed up the steps to the stern castle.

Something about the scene tickled Kip's memory. Andross Guile was turned away from them. There were only dim slivers of light from the moon, penetrating the scattered clouds. Andross was wearing a cowl and dark-lensed spectacles. It hit Kip like a millstone. He'd seen something like this in the Nine Kings card Janus Borig had given him. The figure who'd been writing had been wearing that cowl.

"I see you managed to botch our entire operation and get our fleet wiped out," Andross Guile said. "But I am so happy you've come back safe. With your bastard no less. And I hear we've a wedding to celebrate. To a woman I forbade you to marry."

It's treason, but only if I'm caught, he'd thought, his mind a whirl of passions. The "-os" he'd been writing to could only be Koios White

Oak, the Color Prince, addressed by his first name. As one would address a friend. Conspiring about Dagnu. The Red, conspiring about being made the red god. Andross Guile had made common cause with their enemy. And there was more.

"You're a red wight," Kip said quietly, almost to himself.

"Gavin," Andross said, either not noticing or not caring to notice what Kip had said. "You've disobeyed me for the last time. I've started the process to strip you of your office. You should know I have the votes. You've bullied the Spectrum for the last time."

"You're a red wight," Kip said again.

"Kip," Gavin said. "I think you've had too much wine. Why don't you—"

"You traitor!" Kip shouted at Andross. "You monster!"

"Grinwoody, get the young drunkard out of here," Andross said. "Now!"

He *was* a red wight. How couldn't everyone see it? So maybe reds usually went insane in more conspicuous ways, but how could it have gotten past them? Did they just not dare to ask? Were they all too afraid, hoping someone else would take the risk first? Surely there should be ways to deal with old drafters who hid themselves away.

But the rules didn't apply to Andross Guile. The rules never had. He was the man whose mansion that he never even visited was taller than mansions were allowed to be. He was the man who'd raised two sons who had become Prisms, who'd held on to a seat on the Spectrum without even bothering to go to the meetings. But he was no man; he was a monster.

Grinwoody seized Kip by the front of his tunic and hauled him away. Kip didn't know what came over him. He broke Grinwoody's hold, just as he'd learned in his training, and stabbed his fingers for the man's eyes. Grinwoody brought his hands up, palms forward. Kip snagged two of the man's fingers with each hand and yanked down in a fingerlock.

The wiry old man dropped to his knees, surprised, and Kip kicked him in the chest, sending him flying, tumbling down the steep stairs to the ship's waist.

Kip charged Andross Guile to tear off his hood and spectacles, to show Gavin what Kip was certain of. He was almost on top of the old man when he saw the knife Andross drew.

It was too late to stop. The old man jabbed the small blade straight at Kip's stomach. Kip swept it aside and crunched into the old man and into Gavin, who'd stepped in to intervene.

Kip tore the old man's hood back and felt the knife cut along his ribs. Andross Guile was spitting fury, deep in the grip of red, attacking as fast as he could, determined to kill. He grabbed Kip's tunic with one hand.

It was a tangle of limbs. Gavin was trying to knock Andross Guile's attacks aside so he didn't skewer Kip. Kip landed a punch on Andross's face, then couldn't reach him as Gavin wedged his shoulder in front of Kip's right arm. Another stab got through, piercing Kip's left arm.

Andross Guile's spectacles, knocked askew by Kip's punch, now fell off as the fury raged through him. He attacked like a madman. Gavin drove him back until all three hit the railing.

A whistle was screeching, sailors were screaming, the muffled percussion of Blackguards' boots coming up steps from the cabins belowdecks. They'd never make it in time. Kip only saw Andross Guile's eyes—the halos broken, red throughout. A red wight.

Kip didn't even remember drawing his own knife. Didn't know how it had gotten into his hand. Letting Gavin get between himself and Andross Guile, he swung his right hand out behind and around his father and stabbed the old bastard. He caught him in the meat of the shoulder.

The old man's eyes lit up. He screamed.

Something cracked across the back of Kip's head and the weight of another body joining the fray crushed them all against the railing. When Kip turned, he saw it was Grinwoody. Grinwoody, old but Blackguard trained. Two bare knives were in the middle of the circle between eight grasping hands. The tangle of limbs became a momentary deadlock.

Kip's knife was the longer by far, and while he was trying to keep Andross from stabbing him with the smaller knife, both Grinwoody and Gavin looked to the longer blade at the same time. It was in a bad position. Kip was straining it toward Andross, but if someone pushed it up and twisted instead—Kip had no leverage to stop from impaling himself.

In a split second, Gavin's eyes flicked up to Kip's. Kip saw that his father had the same thought—but then the desperation in Gavin's eyes was replaced by an odd calm. A decision reached. A choice made. Peace.

A flurry of motion as both Grinwoody and Gavin released their holds at the same time. Grinwoody's hands got there first, and Kip's knife shot up, straight at his chest—only to be diverted at the last second by Gavin's pull. Pulling the knife into his own chest.

Everyone stopped fighting, but not all simultaneously. Kip staggered backward, horrified. His release of the dagger meant Andross Guile's force was unopposed. The dagger slammed all the way to the hilt in his son's chest.

Gavin's mouth opened in a silent scream and even Andross drew back, aghast. Gavin sagged against the railing. Then his eyes widened, and widened again, as if something new was hurting him. And so it was. The dagger was *growing*.

Andross Guile didn't see it. He was pulling his cowl back over his face and picking up his spectacles. When he turned and saw a full-length sword through his son, he merely said, "The Blinder's Knife. Excellent. Grinwoody, retrieve it." Whatever momentary humanity had afflicted him, it was gone now.

Gavin's face was a study of pain and betrayal. He was dying, and his own father was only worried about a knife.

Kip was rooted in place. His father had saved him, had sacrificed himself—for Kip. It was so fast, he didn't know whether to attack Andross again or go to his father. It wouldn't make any difference now, anyway.

Gavin pushed himself up on the railing that had been supporting him, tried to speak, but couldn't. He glanced at Kip as if in apology, in farewell, then pushed himself over the edge.

He splashed into the water in the darkness and was lost. The ship was still under sail, a firm breeze helping them speed along steadily. The first young Blackguards reached the stern castle, spread out, bewildered, the sailors shouting, Grinwoody shouting and pointing in the wrong direction, distracting, causing chaos, the whistle from the crow's nest still shrilling.

Kip didn't think, didn't hesitate. He dove into the water.

Chapter 112

The water was cool and the light of the moon and stars did nothing to penetrate its depths. Under the surface, Kip could see nothing. He relaxed his eyes and looked for heat.

There!

Kip swam. He wasn't an accomplished swimmer, but though his target was facedown and unmoving, Gavin wasn't sinking yet.

That changed before Kip reached his father's body. Gavin slipped beneath the waves and Kip took one deep breath and managed to snag his tunic before he got too deep. Kip pulled him to the surface, nearly skewering himself on the sword still protruding from his father's back. He flailed in the water, but the truth was, he was barely a good enough swimmer to float by himself, even with all his blubber. Swimming for two was damn near impossible.

He wasn't even able to cry out for help. The flagship gave no immediate signs of turning either. Kip was a good hundred and fifty paces away before the bell started ringing.

Andross Guile didn't want to find him. He'd delayed the Blackguards as long as he could. The bastard.

Kip finally found a position floating on his back where his buoyancy and one flailing arm mostly kept him afloat and able to breathe. Almost every swell would crest over his head, but if he breathed at the right time, he wouldn't inhale water.

He shouted, "Help! Man overboard!" But he had no hope that the flagship was going to hear him. It was only now lighting up and beginning to turn. A ship of that size wasn't going to get back to Kip for ten or fifteen minutes, if it ever found him at all. If any Blackguards had jumped into the water after him, Kip couldn't see them. More to the point, they wouldn't be able to see *him* unless he was lucky enough to get a sub-red.

Kip tried to fight the panic clamping down on his chest. It made it hard to breathe. He took a wave at the wrong time and hacked and coughed to clear his lung, almost losing his father's body. Dear Orholam. Dear Orholam, no.

Gavin Guile was dead. Dead. Dear Orholam, no. Father, why? Why'd you do it?

When he regained some calm, he realized he'd soaked up some light during the fight. He hadn't even been aware of it. He supposed that like his testing, the fear and anger had dilated his eyes. He'd soaked up luxin without even being conscious of it.

He had a little red and a little yellow. There were other ships out here, he knew it. He just had to let them know he was here. Someone would save him.

After taking a deep breath, he shot sparkling yellow out of his finger. Even that small action pushed him under the waves and left him gasping.

He wondered if there were sharks. He wondered if sharks could smell luxin. He knew they could smell blood, and his father's blood would be drawing them.

He didn't panic, though. He didn't have anything left in him to panic with. After a minute, he held up his hand and drafted red luxin around his finger. With a few tries, he was able to light it with the yellow.

But he couldn't hold it up and hold his father and swim. He tried to light it again after bobbing in the waves a bit, but too much had washed away.

He heard the ship before he saw it. It came up behind him and blocked out the light behind. A net was thrown over him, and within a minute, he and his father were pulled up, rolled onto the deck.

"What have we? What have we?" A man started cackling. "Ceres!" he shouted. "Ceres, you fickle wench! You beautiful bitch, Gunner loves you! Thank you! Apology accepted! Boys, gather 'round. See what Captain Gunner's luck has brought us."

Kip was lying on his back, exhausted. All he had strength to do was breathe.

Gunner? Kip's thoughts were slow. Gunner was the man on the pirate ship Gavin and Kip and Liv and Ironfist had sunk outside of Garriston, wasn't he? Gavin had said he hadn't killed the man because he was an artist. Was this the same man?

Captain Gunner, a night-black Ilytian bare-chested under a waistcoat—a different waistcoat than last time—rolled Gavin over as far as the protruding blade allowed. It *was* the same Gunner. Oh hell. "Bugger me," Gunner said, looking at the blade. He tore it out of Gavin's body and held it aloft.

Kip's blade was not what it had been. His knife was now a longsword. 617

No, more. The wide blade was three and a half feet long, and whiter than ivory, single-edged with twin black whorls crisscrossing up the blade. Bracketed by those black, twisting, living whorls, every one of those seven jewels now burned with inner light, each one its own color from sub-red to superviolet. The spine of the blade was a thin musket, except for the last hand's breadth, which was pure blade.

Gunner swung the blade back and forth. "Light," he said. "Lighter than should be possible." But when he saw the musket, how the single cutout in the blade was positioned to give space for fingers to steady the barrel, he positively chortled.

The sound of vomiting made Kip and Gunner both turn from their inspection of the blade. Murmurs shot through the crew as Gavin puked water onto the deck.

He rolled over, gasping and coughing.

"Alive? Take him below," Gunner ordered. "Feed him, tend to his wounds, and bind him. Don't let him escape. He's a fighter." The men lifted Gavin and carried him belowdecks. Captain Gunner shouted again, "Ceres! Ceres! I'm no miser! You share with me, I share with you. I could use this man." He was talking about Kip, Kip realized. "He's a drafter. You saw! You know how bad I been wanting a drafter! Good drafter's hard to find on the sea, Ceres. But you done me right."

Oh shit.

"I do this, we call it straight between us? Fair? You gave me two. I'll give you one back!" Gunner said. "Boys?"

Hands descended. Kip tried to fight, but he only got a bloody nose for his trouble. He was so weak there was no resisting. With a heave, the men tossed him back into the sea.

He surfaced in the darkness, hearing only the sweep of oars and the distant sound of Gunner giving orders and laughing.

Kip swam, barely having the energy to keep floating on his back, out of light, unable to draft, certain that someone would come.

No one did.

Chapter 113

Koios White Oak the Color Prince came the next morning to the palace in which he'd installed Liv. He seemed jubilant as he beckoned her to join him on the roof.

Together, they looked out over the city. There were some fires in a few neighborhoods. Fighting still continued in pockets. It would be weeks, probably, until the city was pacified. The Color Prince was offering clemency to those rebels who laid down their arms in the next two days. Those who continued fighting would be subject to retributive rapes, the killing of family members, and all the horrors his men could dream up. He didn't invent war, he said, and he would do anything to end it quickly. Sharp, quick brutality was better, he said, than tolerating protracted lawlessness.

"Did it work?" Liv asked.

"Birthing Atirat?" the prince asked. "Oh yes. You succeeded marvelously. The failure was Atirat's own—and Zymun's. We'll retake the fort on Ruic Head tomorrow and perhaps we'll learn what happened. It seems he did capture it, but he must have botched something, because they knew he had it. And then he lost it. If he lives, I don't expect he'll come back to camp. You're free of him."

That was a relief, though Liv felt weak for feeling it. She'd turned the tide of a battle, and she was afraid of a sniveling teenaged boy?

"There's more good news," the prince said. "Aside from your tremendous success and us taking the city. Your father wasn't fighting for them."

"I know," Liv said.

"Has he been in communication with you?"

"No."

"Then how do you know?" Koios White Oak asked.

"Because we won."

The prince laughed, but Liv could tell her answer peeved him. "Let us hope we never have to test your confidence in his abilities, then. But there's more. Can you feel it?"

He meant magically. "No. I don't have your senses," Liv said.

"The Prism is dead. The colors are free."

"I don't understand," Liv said. She felt sick. Her senses had been shut off as soon as Atirat had taken shape. She'd missed the climax of the battle, and she'd hoped that somehow she'd been wrong, that Kip and Karris and Gavin had lived.

"This . . ." Koios swept a hand toward the bay. "This was a setback. The bane rise spontaneously, Aliviana. All we need to do is wait, and there will be another. Another blue, another green, another one of *every* color, now."

She looked over at him sharply. No wonder he wasn't very upset.

"It will take time, but they can't stop us now, Liv. The only trick for us is to make sure that as each bane rises, a drafter we trust is at the center of it."

"A drafter we trust? You mean that any drafter can . . ." She'd seen Atirat atop the bane, of course, but—Dervani Malargos?

"Any sufficiently talented drafter, yes. In centuries past, it led to bloodbaths, as every green would tear every other apart, each in their quest to become a god. And then the gods would war with each other. But that time is past." He smiled magnanimously. He opened a hand, and there was a choker in it with an odd, throbbing black jewel at the center. "I told you that I had a purpose in mind for you, Aliviana, a great purpose befitting the greatest of my superviolets. So tell me, can you now guess what it is?"

Chapter 114

Andross Guile stood in his cabin, examining himself. He stood, shirtless, with no hood, no cowl, no dark spectacles, the curtains open. He looked at his hands, his arms, and then, last, he looked at his eyes. The broken red halo he'd been hiding for months was gone. He still had all his colors—sub-red, red, orange, and yellow—entwined halfway through the irises of his shocking blue eyes, but they were in balance now.

He'd seen the Blinder's Knife work before—and it didn't work like this. That knife killed. But when he looked at his shoulder, it was flawless, not even the skin broken. He looked at his eyes again, certain it was some trick. But there the halo was, stable. And he felt hale. He felt better than he'd felt in fifteen years, twenty. He'd had to sink into his own discipline in order to keep the red from driving him mad— and at the end there, he wasn't sure he was winning.

Now he was simply a drafter again. A polychrome with a good ten years left in his eyes.

This, this changed *everything*.

Sometime not long before dawn, Kip washed ashore. He couldn't take credit for swimming in. He'd barely had the strength to float and breathe for the last few hours. He crawled far enough up the sand not to get pulled out to sea and collapsed like a beached whale.

He woke to someone picking at his pockets, around noon. He floundered, slapping their hands away, afraid he was under attack. He sat up, and saw that there were at least a dozen bodies washed up on the beach around him.

The looter started laughing. Kip blinked up at him, but the young man had the blinding noonday sun burning over his shoulder. He was dressed in a dirty white tunic and cloak adorned with many bands of color. He also had a pistol dangling from his hand.

"Oho, I stopped at the right beach, didn't I?" the young man said. "Lucky, aren't I?"

Kip looked down the beach and saw the young man's dinghy on the beach. He must have seen all the dead from the water and decided to loot what he could. Kip was thirsty. "You have any water?" he croaked.

"In the boat. Food, too."

Kip stood with difficulty. The young man didn't help him up. Then it hit him. He knew that voice. He squinted against the brightness. "Oh no," he said.

"Bit slow, aren't ya?" Zymun said. He stepped forward and punched Kip in the face.

Kip fell and sat heavily in the sand. He checked his nose, eyes streaming. On the bright side, it wasn't broken. He stood slowly, walked over to the dinghy. He halfway emptied the skin. He had a headache that he thought was a hangover. He hadn't had one of those before. Plus he was lightsick. Every part of his body hurt. He had a gash along his ribs and his left arm was throbbing from being stabbed.

Kip considered attacking Zymun, who was rubbing his hand: punching Kip had hurt his fist. But Zymun had a *gun*. He would see if Kip tried to draft—which right now sounded as appetizing as gargling sewage—and Kip was feeling about as agile as a hundred-and-twelve-year-old man. Kip had seen the boy draft, long ago. He had no doubt that Zymun had the will to use that pistol. He got in the boat.

"Take off that belt and give it to me. Then tear off a strip of your shirt and tie it around your eyes," Zymun said. "Slowly."

Kip did both. He felt Zymun push the dinghy into the water. Kip lunged forward, tearing off his blindfold.

Zymun was clinging to the prow with one hand, bobbing in the water, halfway to climbing into the boat, and he had the pistol leveled at Kip's face. "Back. Back!" he said. "I can't hold on here for long, so if you're not seated and blindfolded in five seconds, I'm going to put a bullet in your face."

Settling back onto his bench, Kip pulled the blindfold back up, defeated. He'd *almost* done it. Almost. The cloak of failure draped easily around his slumped shoulders. Kip Almost. Again.

No. That wasn't true. He wasn't that Kip anymore. He wasn't stupid. He wasn't weak. He wasn't a coward. He wasn't rejected.

He had gotten into the Blackguard. He had been accepted by the best drafters and fighters in the world. He had been accepted by his father. He had fought a king and wights and a god. He'd made huge mistakes: he'd been stupid and weak and cowardly and rejected. Without him, his father wouldn't have been stabbed. But he also had pulled his father from the waves, had saved his life when no one else could. Kip had donned Almost as his spectacles. There was a middle path, a golden mean between the whore's son and the Prism's. He wasn't really Kip Godslayer, but he also wasn't the boy who'd knuckled under to Ramir. Not anymore. I am what I do, and I am Breaker.

He who looks through only one lens lives in darkness. He who has

ears, let him hear.

It's time for me to break that old lens.

"Take the oars," Zymun said. As Kip reached blindly for them, he heard Zymun slip into the boat. Then he felt luxin encase his hands, locking them around the oars. "You row for an hour, and then I'll give you food and more water. Go on! We got a long way to go, brother."

Kip started rowing. His left arm did not appreciate it. "Brother?" he asked. His voice came out calm, unafraid, unashamed.

"My grandfather Andross Guile's summoned me to the Chromeria. He said the rest of his family hadn't turned out. Said he's considering adopting me. Said he has big plans." He paused. "What, didn't you know? I'm Karris and Gavin's son. I'm Zymun White Oak."

Kip's heart dropped out of his chest, punched a hole in the deck, and killed a dozen fish on its way to the sea floor.

He heard a metallic scrape of the pistol being examined, and he thought that maybe Zymun had decided to kill him after all. Then Zymun barked a laugh. "Holy fuck am I lucky," he said to himself. "Would you look at that? This gun wasn't even loaded."

Chapter 115

Gavin woke to someone slapping his face. He felt awful. The cabin was dark and stank of men who hadn't washed in ages and bilgewater and seaweed and fish and human waste. There were manacles on his wrists, and he was naked except for a breechclout.

Another slap cracked across his cheek, hard enough to put the taste of blood in his mouth. He opened his eyes. He looked at the man in front of him. His lungs and throat felt raw from the seawater he'd tried to breathe.

"Gunner, you son of a bitch," Gavin said. His voice was raw, too. Last night was a dim memory. "What are you doing?"

"Can't draft, can ya?"

Gavin held up his hands, empty, helpless. It was so dim in the cabin it would take him a couple of minutes to draft enough to be a threat to anyone. And summoning the will would be a problem, too, with how terrible he felt.

"Give me a couple minutes," he said. His left eye was swollen. There was—Oh, Orholam! Gavin checked his chest. It was uninjured. What the hell kind of nightmares had he been having? Thinking he'd been stabbed? Had he been drugged and smuggled off the flagship?

"Your eyes are as blue as Ceres's, Lord Guile. Not a touch of halo in 'em. Always hated luxlords putting on airs. Ordering people around. Not willing to pull their own weight." He laughed low, as if he'd said something clever. "But I gots my own solution to the little injustices life brings under my purview. It ain't quite the ship of state, but she is a stately ship, is she no?"

"This your boat?" Gavin asked, still disoriented. He was seated on a bench next to a skinny man with white hair and beard, big eyes, half clothed. All of the men down here were skinny and half clothed, all drinking water or tearing into hardtack. All wearing chains. All watching him.

"Yes, my *boat*. The *Bitter Cob*, I call her, for how she'll leave your nethers raw. She belongs to me, and now you belongs to her. Serve well, Guile. For if this old girl goes down, you go down with her."

The other end of his manacles snapped shut around the oar.

"Gunner..." Gavin said, warning.

"*Captain* Gunner, Number Six. Or you get a whipping."

"Orholam damn you, don't you know who I am?!" It had been almost two decades since Gunner had worked for Gavin. Maybe time had changed him too much for the man to recognize him without his rich clothes.

Gunner grinned. "He who asks, 'Don't you know who I am?' is the one who doesn't know the answer. But here's the thing, Gavin Guile. I'm going to give you the opportunity to find out."

"Not Gavin," Gavin said defiantly. "Dazen. My name is Dazen Guile."

Gunner threw open the door and daylight poured in. "Whatever guile you use makes no matter to me. You're Galley Slave Six. Third row, middle seat. But don't worry, you row strongly and obey alacritously, and you'll get a head seat in six months. Good to have goals, ain't it?" He grinned toothily. "Boys?"

Gavin said nothing. He didn't resist, for in the open door he'd seen something worse than bondage. In the dim near-night of the reeking cabin, he hadn't noticed: colors were always muted by darkness. But with the opening of that door, with the sky and the birds and sails, and the pure puissant light that Gavin had been waiting to soak up to use to break these chains and escape, he saw something worse. He couldn't split the colors from that pure white light. He couldn't split the colors because he couldn't draft the colors. He couldn't draft the colors because he couldn't *see* the colors. The ignorant speak of subchromacy as color-blindness, when it really is only color confusion.

But Gavin *was* color-blind. All the world was gray. It was as Gunner had tried to tell him. In one instant, everything that was special about Gavin Guile had been stripped away. He not only wasn't the Prism anymore, he wasn't even a drafter. The door to the deck slapped closed, and chains rattled through the handles, trapping Gavin in a blacker darkness than any he had ever known.

Acknowledgments

From millimeter waves to martial artists to *Magic: The Gathering*, I needed a lot of help with this one. In addition to those I've thanked in previous books (whom I still owe), a few people deserve repeated or new thanks. Thank you first to my wife, Kristi, without whom I'd be working some job I hated. Thanks for tolerating the six-day workweeks for the last couple years, honey. I'll try to be more sane... eventually. Thank you to Elisa, for taking on so many of the business duties so that I can write more. Thank you to Don Maass, Cameron McClure, and the rest of DMLA for finding the right people for us to work with, for guidance, for expert explanations, and for excellent story advice and encouragement. The writer's life is too often solitary, and you've been sanity and wisdom.

Thank you to Orbit Books (Devi, Anne, Alex, Tim, Susan, Ellen, and Lauren P. especially), who all continue to amaze me with the hard work they do, their innovation, and their responsiveness. I hear horror stories from writers who landed elsewhere, and I'm glad to call Orbit home. Thank you to all those behind the scenes who make the whole machine run so smoothly.

Thank you to Mary Robinette Kowal (*Shades of Milk and Honey*) for being my first ever beta reader. Excellent feedback, and great catches. You made the book better. Plus, that one thing, that place in book 3 where things look really bad, and you suggested something to make it utterly horrible? Yeah, I'm totally stealing that.

Thank you to mathematics professor Dr. N. Willis, who read *The Black Prism* and immediately asked me if I'd played *Magic: The Gathering*. (His sneaky way of seeing if I would play with *him*, without admitting his geekery straight out.) I had never played *MtG*, but soon saw the mathematical beauty of the game. The seed for the in-world game Nine Kings was planted there (though the mechanics and play are different). To forestall some emails I know I'll get about this: Yes...but it'll be years. Thanks also for helping me structure the Blackguard trial, which somehow got incredibly complicated. Go figure.

Thank you to a certain special forces friend of mine, E.H., who got me the (declassified, totally legal!) brief on millimeter wave technology. Who says fantasy can't use cutting-edge science?

A big thanks to Sergeant Rory Miller, whose books on violence should become necessary texts for those who wish to depict violence convincingly in their fictional worlds, and for those who wish to avoid it in the real one! (Start with *Meditations on Violence*.) For one thing only I don't forgive him: talking about rates of adrenaline release in a world and time period that doesn't yet have the word "adrenaline" was hell. (Thanks to Peter H. at Powell's for hand-selling that book to me—and hand-selling mine to others!)

Thank you to Alfred, Lord Tennyson, whose "Ulysses" I quoted briefly in both *The Black Prism* and *The Blinding Knife* as being written by Gevison. Immortal lines, sir. Meant to acknowledge you in the last book and overlooked it. My apologies.

Last, thank you to my readers. I love what I do, and I get to keep doing it because of you. That's a huge privilege and an honor, and I feel a debt of gratitude to you. I can't promise you much except that I'll work my hardest to tell you the best stories I can. How about I do that, and you keep forcing my books on your friends. Deal?

—*Brent Weeks*

Character List

Adrasteia (Teia): A student at the Chromeria. She is slave to Lady Lucretia Verangheti of the Smussato Veranghetis; a Blackguard candidate and a drafter of paryl.

Aheyyad: Orange drafter, grandson of Tala. A defender of Garriston, the designer of Garriston's Brightwater Wall; dubbed Aheyyad Brightwater by Prism Gavin Guile.

Ahhanen: A Blackguard.

Aklos: A slave of Lady Aglaia Crassos.

Amestan: A Blackguard at the Battle of Garriston.

Aram: A Blackguard scrub. His parents were Blackguards, and he has been training in martial arts since he could walk.

Arana: A drafting student, a merchant's daughter.

Aras: A student at the Chromeria, a Blackguard scrub.

Arash, Javid: One of the drafters who defended Garriston.

Aravind, Lord: Satrap of Atash. Father of Kata Ham-haldita, corregidor of Idoss.

Arias, Lord: One of the Color Prince's advisers. He is an Atashian in charge of spreading news about the Color Prince.

Arien: A magister at the Chromeria. She drafts orange and tests Kip on Luxlord Black's orders.

Ariss the Navigator: A legendary explorer, discoverer.

Asif: A young Blackguard.

Asmun: A Blackguard scrub.

Atagamo: A magister who teaches the properties of luxin at the Chromeria. He is Ilytian.

Atiriel, Karris: A desert princess. She became Karris Shadowblinder before she married Lucidonius.

Ayrad: A yellow drafter. He was a Blackguard scrub years before Kip entered the class. He started at the bottom of his class (forty-ninth) and worked his way up to the top, fighting everyone. It turned out he'd taken a vow. Became commander of the Blackguard and saved four different Prisms at least once before someone poisoned him.

Azmith, Caul: A Parian general, the Parian satrapah's younger brother.

Balder: A Blackguard scrub who has it in for Kip.

Bas the Simple: A Tyrean polychrome (blue/green/superviolet), handsome but a simpleton, sworn to kill the killer of the White Oak family.

Ben-hadad: A Ruthgari student at the Chromeria. He has been accepted into the Blackguards in an earlier class. A blue/yellow bichrome who has created his own mechanical spectacles that allow blue or yellow lenses to be used, he's highly intelligent.

Big Ros: A slave of Aglaia.

Blademan: A Blackguard watch captain. He leads one of the skimmers in the battle at Ruic Head, along with Gavin and Watch Captain Tempus.

Blue-Eyed Demons, the: Mercenaries who fought for Dazen's army.

Borig, Janus: An old woman. She is bald, smokes a long pipe, and is apparently a Mirror.

Bursar: The Omnichrome's most important adviser. She is constantly doing figures with her small abacus and is in charge of one-third of the chits for the soldiers to use for prostitutes.

Burshward, Captain: An Angari captain (from beyond the Everdark Gates).

Burshward, Gillan: Captain Burshward's brother.

Buskin: Along with Tugertent and Tlatig, the best archer Commander Ironfist has on the approach to Ruic Head.

Caelia: A dwarf servant of the Third Eye.

Carver Black: A non-drafter, as is traditional for the Black. He is the chief administrator of the Seven Satrapies. Though he has a voice on the Spectrum, he has no vote.

Carvingen, Odess: A drafter and defender of Garriston.

Cavair, Paz: Commander of the Blue Bastards at the Great Pyramid of Ru.

630   *Cezilia:* A servant/bodyguard to the Third Eye.

Clara: A servant/bodyguard to the Third Eye.

Companions' Mother: Head of the Omnichrome's army's prostitute guild.

Coran, Adraea: Blessed. Said "war is a horror."

Cordelia: A willowy female Blackguard.

Corfu, Ramia: A powerful young blue drafter. He is one of the Color Prince's favorites.

Corzin, Eleph: An Abornean blue drafter, a defender of Garriston.

Counselor, the: A legendary figure. Author of *The Counselor to Kings*, which advised such cruel methods of government that not even he followed them when he ruled.

Crassos, Aglaia: A young noblewoman and drafter at the Chromeria. She is the youngest daughter of an important Ruthgari family, a sadist who enjoys the pain she inflicts on her slaves.

Crassos, Governor: Elder brother of Aglaia Crassos; the last governor of Garriston.

Cruxer: A Blackguard scrub. He's the third generation to enter the ranks; his parents are Inana and Holdfast.

Daelos: A Blackguard scrub.

Dagnar Zelan: One of the original Blackguards. He served Lucidonius after converting to his cause.

Danavis, Aliviana (Liv): Daughter of Corvan Danavis. She is a yellow and superviolet bichrome drafter from Tyrea. Her contract is owned by the Ruthgari, and she is supervised by Aglaia Crassos.

Danavis, Corvan: A red drafter. A scion of one of the great Ruthgari families, he was also the most brilliant general of the age and the primary reason for Dazen's success in battle.

Danavis, Ell: The second wife of Corvan Danavis. She was murdered by an assassin three years after their marriage.

Danavis, Erethanna: A green drafter serving Count Nassos in western Ruthgar; Liv Danavis's cousin.

Danavis, Qora: A Tyrean noblewoman; first wife of Corvan Danavis, mother of Aliviana Danavis.

Delara, Naftalie: A woman Andross was going to "let" Gavin marry.

Delara Orange: The Atashian member of the Spectrum. She represents Orange and is a forty-year-old orange/red bichrome nearing the end of her life. Her predecessor in the seat was her mother, who devised the rotating scheme for Garriston.

Delarias: A family in Rekton.

Delauria, Katalina: Kip's mother. She is of Parian or Ilytian extraction and is a haze addict.

Delclara, Micael: A quarryman and a Rekton villager.

Delclara, Miss: The matriarch of the Delclara family in Rekton. She had six sons who are quarrymen.

Delclara, Zalo: A quarryman, one of the Delclara sons.

Delelo, Galan: A master sergeant in the Omnichrome's army. He escorts Liv to the gates of Garriston.

Delmarta, Gad: A young general of Dazen's army who took the city of Ru and publicly massacred the royal family and their retainers.

Delucia, Neta: A member of the ruling council of Idoss (i.e., a city mother).

Djur: Along with Ahhanen, he is on duty as a Blackguard when Karris and Gavin leave the refugee ship.

Droose: One of Gunner's shipmates.

Elessia: A Blackguard.

Elio: A bully in Kip's barracks. Kip breaks his arm.

Elos, Gaspar: A green color wight.

Erato: A Blackguard scrub who has it in for Kip.

Essel: A Blackguard woman who broke the fingers of an Atashian nobleman when he began to take liberties.

Euterpe: A friend of Teia's who was a slave. Her owners lost everything in a drought and rented her to the Laurion silver mine brothels for five months. She never recovered.

Falling Leaf, Deedee: A green drafter. Her failing health inspired a number of veteran drafters to take the Freeing at Garriston.

Farjad, Farid: A nobleman and ally of Dazen's once Dazen promised him the Atashian throne during the False Prism's War.

Farseer, Horas: Another ally of Dazen's, the bandit king of the Blue-Eyed Demons. Gavin Guile killed him after the False Prism's War.

Fell: A female Blackguard, the smallest in the force, she excels at acrobatic moves.

Ferkudi: A Blackguard scrub, a blue/green bichrome who excels at grappling.

Finer: A Blackguard seen in one of the cards.

Fisk, Trainer: He trains the scrubs with drills and conditioning. He just barely beat Karris during their own test to enter the Blackguards.

632 *Flamehands:* An Ilytian drafter and defender of Garriston.

Gaeros: One of Lady Aglaia's slaves.

Galaea: Karris White Oak's maid, and betrayer.

Galden, Jens: A magister at the Chromeria, a red drafter.

Galib: A polychrome at the Chromeria.

Gallos: A stableman at Garriston.

Garadul, Perses: Appointed satrap of Tyrea after Ruy Gonzalo was defeated by the Prism's forces in the False Prism's War. Perses was the father of Rask Garadul. He worked to eradicate the bandits plaguing Tyrea after the war.

Garadul, Rask: A satrap who declared himself king of Tyrea; his father was Perses Garadul.

Gazzin, Griv: A green drafter who fought with Zee Oakenshield.

Gerain: An old man in Garriston who exhorted people to join King Garadul.

Gerrad: A student at the Chromeria.

Gevison: A poet (long deceased).

Golden Briar, Eva: A woman Andross was going to let Gavin choose to marry.

Goldeneyes, Tawenza: A yellow drafter. She teaches only the three most talented yellows each year at the Chromeria.

Goldthorn: A magister at the Chromeria. Barely three years older than her disciples, she teaches the superviolet class.

Gonzalo, Ruy: A Tyrean satrap who sided with Dazen during the False Prism's War.

Goss: A Parian Blackguard scrub, one of the best fighters.

Gracia: A mountain Parian scrub. She's taller than most of the boys.

Grass, Evi: A drafter and defender of Garriston. She is a green/yellow bichrome from Blood Forest, and is a superchromat.

Grazner: A Blackguard scrub. Kip breaks his will in a bout.

Green, Jerrosh: Along with Dervani Malargos, he is one of the best green drafters in the Omnichrome's army, and a Blood Robe.

Greenveil, Arys: The Sub-red on the Spectrum. A Blood Forester, she is a cousin of Jia Tolver, and her sister is Ana Jorvis's mother, Ela. Her parents were killed in the war by Lunna Green's brothers. She has twelve children by twelve different men.

Greyling, Gavin: A new Blackguard. He is brother to Gill Greyling, named after Gavin Guile. He is the handsomer of the two brothers.

Greyling, Gill: A new Blackguard. He is elder brother to Gavin Greyling, and he is the more intelligent of the two.

Grinwoody: Andross Guile's chief slave and right hand. He is barely a drafter, but Andross pulled strings to get him into training for the Blackguard, where he made friends and learned secrets. He made it all the way through Blackguard training, and on oath day decided to sign with Lord Guile instead, a betrayal the Blackguards remember.

Guile, Andross: Father of Gavin, Dazen, and Sevastian Guile. He drafts yellow through sub-red, although he is primarily known for drafting red, as that is his position on the Spectrum. He took a place on the Spectrum despite being from Blood Forest, which already had a representative, by claiming that his few lands in Ruthgar qualified him for the seat.

Guile, Darien: Andross Guile's great-grandfather. He was married to Zee Oakenshield's daughter as a resolution to their war.

Guile, Dazen: Younger brother of Gavin. He fell in love with Karris White Oak and triggered the False Prism's War when "he" burned down her family compound, killing everyone within.

Guile, Draccos: Andross Guile's father.

Guile, Felia: Married to Andross Guile. The mother of Gavin and Dazen, a cousin of the Atashian royal family, she is an orange drafter. Her mother was courted by Ulbear Rathcore before he met Orea Pullawr.

Guile, Gavin: The Prism. Two years older than Dazen, he was appointed at age thirteen.

Guile, Kip: The illegitimate Tyrean son of Gavin Guile and Katalina Delauria. He is a superchromat and a full-spectrum polychrome.

Guile, Sevastian: The youngest Guile brother. He was murdered by a blue wight when Gavin was thirteen and Dazen was eleven.

Gunner: An Ilytian pirate. His first underdeck command was as cannoneer on the *Aved Barayah*. He later became a captain.

Ham-haldita, Kata: Corregidor of Idoss, the Atashian satrap's son.

Harl, Pan: A Blackguard scrub. His ancestors were slaves for the last eight of ten generations.

Helel, Mistress: She masqueraded as a teacher in the Chromeria and tried to murder Kip.

Hena: A magister at the Chromeria who teaches a class on luxin construction.

Hezik: A Blackguard whose mother commanded a pirate hunter in the Narrows. He can shoot cannons fairly accurately.

Holdfast: A deceased Blackguard. His son is Cruxer and his widow is Inana, another Blackguard.

Holvar, Jin: A woman who entered the Blackguard the same year as Karris, though she is a few years younger.

Idus: A Blackguard scrub.

Inana: Cruxer's mother, and a Blackguard. Widow of Holdfast, a Blackguard.

Incaros: One of Lady Aglaia Crassos's room slaves.

Ironfist, Harrdun: Commander of the Blackguard, thirty-eight years old, a blue drafter.

Isabel (Isa): A pretty young girl in Rekton.

Izem Blue: A legendary drafter and a defender of Garriston under Gavin Guile.

Izem Red: A defender of Garriston under Gavin Guile. He fought for Gavin during the False Prism's War. A Parian drafter of red with incredible speed, he wears his ghotra in the shape of a cobra's hood.

Jalal: A Parian storekeeper who sells kopi.

Jevaros, Lord: A young idiot who could become the next Blackguard commander and Andross Guile's tool.

Jorvis, Ana: A superviolet/blue bichrome, student at the Chromeria, one of the women Andross Guile would allow Gavin to marry.

Jorvis, Demnos: Ana Jorvis's father, and Arys Greenveil's brother-in-law, married to Ela Jorvis.

Jorvis, Ela: Sister of Arys Greenveil, wife of Demnos Jorvis, Blood Forester, mother to Ana Jorvis.

Jumber, Norl: A Blackguard.

Jun: A Blackguard scrub. Partners with Ular during a scrubs test to get across town with money.

Kadah: A magister at the Chromeria; a green drafter who teaches drafting basics.

Kalif: A Blackguard.

Kallikrates: Teia's father. He ran the silk route as a trader before losing everything due to his wife's lavish lifestyle.

Keftar, Graystone: A green drafter and Blackguard scrub. He's an athletic, dark-skinned son of a rich family that paid for him to be trained before he came to the Chromeria.

Klytos Blue: The Blue on the Spectrum. He represents Ilyta, though he is a Ruthgari through and through. A coward and Andross's tool.

Laya: A Blackguard who drafts red, present at the Battle of Garriston.

Lem (Will): A Blackguard, either simple or crazy, a blue drafter with incredible will.

Leo: A Blackguard scrub, hugely muscular.

Lightbringer, the: A controversial figure in prophecy and mythology. Attributes that most agree on are that he is male, will slay or has slain gods and kings, is of mysterious birth, is a genius of magic, a warrior who will sweep, or has swept, all before him, a champion of the poor and downtrodden, great from his youth, He Who Shatters. That most of the prophecies were in Old Parian and the meanings have changed in ways that are difficult to trace hasn't helped. There are three basic camps: that the Lightbringer has yet to come; that the Lightbringer has already come and was Lucidonius (a view the Chromeria now holds, though it didn't always); and, among some academics, that the Lightbringer is a metaphor for what is best in all of us.

Little Piper: An orange/yellow bichrome Blackguard.

Lucia: A Blackguard scrub. She is the prettiest girl in the class and is Cruxer's partner. They have a close friendship.

Lucidonius: The legendary founder of the Seven Satrapies and the Chromeria, the first Prism. He was married to Karris Shadowblinder and founded the Blackguards.

Lunna Green: The Green on the Spectrum. She is Ruthgari, a cousin of Jia Tolver. Her brothers killed Arys Greenveil's parents during the war.

Lytos: A Blackguard, a lanky Ilytian eunuch.

Malargos, Aristocles: Uncle of Eirene and Tisis Malargos; didn't come back from the wars.

Malargos, Dervani: A Ruthgari nobleman, Tisis Malargos's father, a friend and supporter of Dazen during the False Prism's War. He is a green drafter who was lost in the wilds of Tyrea for years. When he tried to return home, Felia Guile hired pirates to kill him so that he wouldn't reveal Gavin's secrets.

Malargos, Eirene (Prism): A matriarch, the Prism before Alexander Spreading Oak (who preceded Gavin Guile). She lasted fourteen years, though Gavin has only the barest memory of her from Sun Day rituals in his youth.

Malargos, Eirene (the Younger): The older sister of Tisis Malargos. She took over the family's financial affairs when her father and uncle didn't come back from the war.

Malargos, Tisis: A stunningly beautiful Ruthgari green drafter. Her father and uncle fought for Dazen. Her older sister is Eirene Malargos, from whom she will likely inherit the wealth of a great trading empire.

Marissia: Gavin's room slave. A red-haired Blood Forester who was captured by the Ruthgari during Dazen's war, she has been with Gavin for ten years, since she was eighteen.

Marta, Adan: An inhabitant of Rekton.

Martaens, Marta: A magister at the Chromeria. She is one of only a handful of living paryl drafters, and she instructs Teia.

Mori: A soldier in the Omnichrome's army.

Mossbeard: The conn of a village on the Blood Forest coast near Ruic Bay.

Naheed: Satrapah of Atash. She was murdered by General Gad Delmarta during the False Prism's War.

Nassos: A Ruthgari count in western Ruthgar. Liv Danavis's cousin serves him.

Navid, Payam: A good-looking magister at the Chromeria; Phips Navid is his cousin.

Navid, Phips: Cousin to Payam Navid. He grew up in Ru, and later joined the Omnichrome's army. His father and older brothers were all hanged after the False Prism's War when he was just twelve years old. He wants vengeance on Lord Aravind.

Nerra: A Blackguard who designs great explosive disks for sinking ships.

Niel, Baya: A green drafter and Blackguard.

Nuqaba, the: Keeper of the oral histories of Parians, a figure of tremendous power. She resides in Azûlay.

Oakenshield, Zee: Andross Guile's great-great-grandmother, a green drafter. She was the founder of Guile house, despite the name coming from another side of the family.

Omnichrome, Lord (the Color Prince): The leader of a rebellion against the rule of the Chromeria. His true identity is known by few, as he has re-formed almost his entire body with luxin. A full-spectrum polychrome, he posits a faith in freedom and power, rather than in Lucidonius and Orholam. Also known as the Color Prince, the Crystal Prophet, the Polychrome Master, the Eldritch Enlightened, and the Lord Rainbow. He was formerly Koios White Oak, one of Karris White Oak's brothers. He was horribly burned in the fire that triggered the False Prism's War.

One-Eye: A mercenary with the Cloven Shield company.

Onesto, Prestor: An Ilytian banker at Varig and Green.

Orholam: The deity of the monotheistic Seven Satrapies, also known as the Father of All and the Lord of Light. His worship was spread throughout the Seven Satrapies by Lucidonius, four hundred years before the reign of Prism Gavin Guile.

Orlos, Maros: A very religious Ruthgari drafter. He fought in both the False Prism's War and as a defender of Garriston.

Or-mar-zel-atir: One of the original Blackguards who served Lucidonius.

Oros brothers, the: Two Blackguard scrubs.

Payam, Parshan: A young drafter at the Chromeria who attempts to seduce Liv Danavis as part of a bet. He fails in spectacular fashion.

Pevarc: He proved the world was round two hundred years before Gavin Guile, and he was later lynched for positing that light was the absence of darkness.

Philosopher, the: A foundational figure in both moral and natural philosophy.

Phyros: A member of the Omnichrome's army. He is seven feet tall and fights with two axes.

Pip: A Blackguard scrub.

Pots: A Blackguard.

Presser: A Blackguard.

Ptolos: Satrapah of Ruthgar.

Pullawr, Orea: See White, the.

Rados, Blessed Satrap: A Ruthgari satrap who fought the Blood Foresters although he was outnumbered two to one. He was famous for burning the Rozanos Bridge behind his army to keep it from retreating.

Ramir (Ram): A Rekton villager.

Rassad, Master Shayam: Completely blind in the visible spectrum, he allegedly could navigate with sub-red and paryl; taught Marta Martaens's teacher in paryl.

Rathcore, Ulbear: The late husband of the White, he has been dead for twenty years. An adroit player of Nine Kings.

Rig: A Blackguard legacy. He is a red/orange bichrome.

Rud: A Blackguard scrub. He is a squat coastal Parian who wears the ghotra.

Running Wolf: A general for Gavin during the False Prism's war. He was thrice bested by smaller forces commanded by Corvan Danavis.

Sadah Superviolet: The Parian representative, a superviolet drafter, often the swing vote on the Spectrum.

Samite: One of Karris's best friends. She is a Blackguard and a bodyguard for Kip, and one of the strongest female Blackguards.

Sanson: A village boy from Rekton.

Satrap of Atash: See Aravind, Lord.

Sayeh, Meena: Cousin to Samila Sayeh. She was just seven years old when she was killed in Gad Delmarta's purge of the royal family at Ru.

Sayeh, Samila: A blue drafter for Gavin's army. She fought in the defense of Garriston under Gavin Guile.

Selene, Lady: A Tyrean blue/green bichrome. She is in charge of the greens in Garriston so that they can dredge the key irrigation canals.

Sendinas, the: A Rekton family.

Shadowblinder, Karris: Lucidonius's wife and later widow. She was the second Prism. See also Atiriel, Karris.

Sharp, Master: One of Andross Guile's agents. He wears a necklace of human teeth.

Shayam, Lord: One of the lords of the air, set to oversee redistribution of the city of Garriston by the Color Prince.

Shimmercloak, Gebalyn: Vox Shimmercloak's former partner. She seems to have died in a fire while on an assignment.

Shimmercloak, Niah: An assassin. She is the partner of Vox and a lightsplitter.

Shimmercloak, Vox: A green drafter and assassin. He was kicked out of the Chromeria at thirteen; he worships Atirat.

Shining Spear: Originally called El-Anat. Once he converted to the Light, he became Forushalzmarish, then Shining Spear so the locals could pronounce it.

Siluz, Rea: Fourth undersecretary of the Chromeria library and a weak yellow drafter. She knows Janus Borig and directs Kip to meet her.

Small Bear: A huge archer with just one eye. He served Zee Oakenshield.

Spear: A commander of the Blackguards when Gavin first became Prism.

Spreading Oak, Alexander: The Prism before Gavin. Likely a poppy addict, he spent most of his time hiding in his apartments.

Stump: A Parian Blackguard.

Sworrins, the: A Rekton family.

Tala: A drafter and warrior in the False Prism's War. She was also a defender of Garriston. Her grandson is Aheyyad Brightwater, and her sister is Tayri.

Tala (the Younger): A yellow/green bichrome. Named after the hero of the False Prism's War, she is an excellent drafter, though not yet an excellent fighter.

Talim, Sayid: A former Prism. He nearly got himself named promachos to face the nonexistent armada he claimed waited beyond the gates, forty-seven years ago.

Tamerah: A Blackguard scrub, a blue monochrome.

Tana: A Blackguard legacy, a scrub.

Tanner: A Blackguard scrub.

Tarkian: A polychrome drafter.

Tayri: A Parian drafter and defender of Garriston. Her sister is Tala.

Tazerwalt: A princess of the Tlaglanu tribe of Paria. She married Hanishu, the dey of Aghbalu.

Temnos, Dalos the Younger: A drafter who fought in both the False Prism's War and the defense of Garriston under Gavin Guile.

Tempus: A Blackguard put in charge of greens during the battle at Ruic Head.

Tep, Usef: A drafter who fought in the False Prism's War. He is also known as the Purple Bear, because he is a discontiguous bichrome in red and blue. After the war, he and Samila Sayeh became lovers, despite having fought on opposite sides.

Third Eye, the: A Seer, the leader of Seers Island.

Tiziri: A student at the Chromeria. She has a birthmark over the left half of her face.

Tizrik: The son of the dey of Aghbalu. He fails the Blackguard testing, though not before Kip breaks his nose for being a bully.

Tlatig: One of the Blackguard's most skilled archers.

Tolver, Jia: The Yellow on the Spectrum. An Abornean drafter, she is a cousin of Arys Greenveil (the Sub-red).

Tremblefist: A Blackguard. He is Ironfist's younger brother, and was once the dey of Aghbalu.

Tristaem: The author of *On the Fundaments of Reason.*

Tufayyur: A Blackguard scrub.

Tugertent: One of the Blackguard's most skilled archers.

Ular: A Blackguard scrub, Jun's partner.

Usem the Wild: A drafter and defender of Garriston.

Valor: A Blackguard scrub. He partners with Pip during a Blackguard test. They fail when thugs stop them.

Vanzer: A Blackguard and green drafter.

Varidos, Kerawon: A superchromat, magister and head tester of the Chromeria. He drafts orange and red.

Varigari, Lord: A gambler from the Varigari family, originally fishermen before they were raised in the Blood Wars. He lost the family fortune and lands to his habit.

Vecchio, Pash: The most powerful of the pirate kings. His flagship is the *Gargantua.*

Vena: Liv's friend and fellow student at the Chromeria; a superviolet.

Verangheti, Lucretia: Adrasteia's sponsor at the Chromeria. She is from the Ilytian Smussato Veranghetis.

Vin, Taya: A mercenary with the Cloven Shield company.

Wanderer, the: A legendary figure, the subject of Gevison's poem *The Wanderer's Last Journey.*

White Oak, Karris: A Blackguard; a red/green bichrome; the original cause of the False Prism's War.

White Oak, Koios: One of the seven White Oak brothers, brother to Karris White Oak.

White Oak, Kolos: One of the seven White Oak brothers, brother to Karris White Oak.

White Oak, Rissum: A luxlord, the father of Karris and her seven brothers; reputed to be hot-tempered, but a coward.

White Oak, Rodin: One of the seven White Oak brothers, brother to Karris White Oak.

White Oak, Tavos: One of the seven White Oak brothers, brother to Karris White Oak.

White, the: The head of the Spectrum. She is a blue/green bichrome, but currently abstains from any drafting in order to prolong her life. Her name is Orea Pullawr, though it is rarely used. She was married to Ulbear Rathcore before his death.

Wil: A green drafter, and a Blackguard.

Winsen: A mountain Parian, and a Blackguard scrub.

Wit, Rondar: A blue drafter who becomes a color wight.

Young Bull: A blue drafter who fought with Zee Oakenshield.

Yugerten: A gangly Blackguard scrub, blue drafter.

Zid: Quartermaster of the Omnichrome's army.

Ziri: A Blackguard scrub.

Zymun: A young drafter and member of the Omnichrome's army.

Glossary

Aghbalu: A Parian city.

alcaldesa: A Tyrean term, akin to village mayor or chief.

Am, Children of: Archaic term for the people of the Seven Satrapies.

Anat: God of wrath, associated with sub-red. See Appendix, "On the Old Gods."

Angar: A country beyond the Seven Satrapies and the Everdark Gates. Its skilled sailors occasionally shoot the Everdark Gates to enter the Cerulean Sea.

aristeia: A concept encompassing genius, purpose, and excellence.

Aslal: The capital city of Paria.

ataghan: A narrow, slightly forward-curving sword with a single edge for most of its length.

Atan's Teeth: Mountains to the east of Tyrea.

atasifusta: The widest tree in the world, believed extinct after the False Prism's War. Its sap has properties like concentrated red luxin, which, when allowed to drain slowly, can keep a flame lit for hundreds of years if the tree is large enough. The wood itself is ivory white, and when the trees are immature, a small amount can keep a home warm for months.

Atirat: God of lust, associated with green. See Appendix, "On the Old Gods."

Aved Barayah: A legendary ship. Its name means *The Fire Breather.*

aventail: Usually made of chain mail, it is attached to the helmet and drapes over the neck, shoulders, and upper chest.

Azûlay: A coastal city in Paria; the Nuqaba lives there.

balance: The primary work of the Prism. When the Prism drafts at the top of the Chromeria, he alone can sense all the world's imbalances in magic and can draft enough of its opposite (i.e., balancing) color to stop the imbalance from getting any worse and leading to catastrophe. Frequent imbalances occurred throughout the world's history before Lucidonius came, and the resulting disasters of fire, famine, and sword killed thousands if not millions. Superviolet balances sub-red, blue balances red, and green balances orange. Yellow seems to exist in balance naturally.

bane: An old Ptarsu term, could be either singular or plural. It may have meant a temple or holy place, though Lucidonius's Parians believed they were abominations. The Parians acquired the word from the Ptarsu.

beakhead: The protruding part of the foremost section of the ship.

beams: See Chromeria trained.

Belphegor: God of sloth, associated with yellow. See Appendix, "On the Old Gods."

belt-flange: A flattened hook attached to a pistol so it can be tucked securely into a belt.

belt knife: A blade small enough to be tucked in a man's belt, commonly used for eating, rarely for defense.

bich'hwa: A "scorpion," a dagger with a loop hilt and a narrow, undulating recurved blade. Sometimes made with a claw.

bichrome: A drafter who can draft two different colors.

Big Jasper (Island): The island on which the city of Big Jasper rests just opposite the Chromeria, and where the embassies of all the satrapies reside.

binocle: A double-barreled spyglass that allows the use of both eyes for viewing objects at a distance.

Blackguard, the: The White's bodyguard. The Blackguard was also instituted by Lucidonius both to prevent the Prism's overreaching power and to guard the Prism from external threats.

blindage: A screen for the open deck of a ship during battle.

Blood Plains, the: An older collective term for Ruthgar and Blood Forest, so called since Vician's Sin caused the Blood War between them.

Blood War, the: A series of battles that began after Vician's Sin tore apart the formerly close allies of Blood Forest and Ruthgar. The war was seemingly interminable, often starting and stopping, until Gavin Guile put an end to it following the False Prism's War. It seems there will be no further hostilities. Also known as the Blood

Wars among some scholars who differentiate between the various campaigns.

Blue-Eyed Demons, the: A famed company of bandits whose king Gavin Guile killed after the False Prism's War.

blunderbuss: A short musket with a bell-shaped muzzle that can be loaded with shrapnel. Useful at short distances only, such as against mobs.

brightwater: Liquid yellow luxin.

Brightwater Wall: Its building was an epic feat. This wall was designed by Aheyyad Brightwater and built by Prism Guile at Garriston in just days before and while the Omnichrome's army attacked.

Broken Man, the: A statue in a Tyrean orange grove. A Ptaru relic?

caleen: A diminutive term of address for a girl or female slave, like "girl" but used regardless of the slave's age.

Cannon Island: A small island with a minimal garrison between Big Jasper and Little Jasper.

cavendish: Tobacco-like fruit leather.

Cerulean Sea, the: The sea at the center of the Seven Satrapies.

cherry glims: Slang for red-drafting second-year students.

chirurgeon: One who stitches up the wounded and studies anatomy.

Chosen, Orholam's: Another term for the Prism.

Chromeria, the: The ruling body of the Seven Satrapies; also a term for the school where drafters are trained.

  Chromeria trained: Those who have or are training at the Chromeria school for drafting on Little Jasper Island in the Cerulean Sea. The Chromeria's training system does not limit students based on age, but rather progresses them through each degree of training based on their ability and knowledge. So a thirteen-year-old who is extremely proficient in drafting might well be a gleam, or third-year student, while an eighteen-year-old who is just beginning work on her drafting could be a dim.

  - *darks:* Technically known as "the supplicants," these are would-be drafters who have yet to be tested for their abilities at the Chromeria or allowed admission to the school.
  - *dims:* The first-year (and therefore lowest) rank of the Chromeria's students.
  - *glims:* Second-year students.
  - *gleams:* Third-year students who are fairly advanced.
  - *beams:* Fourth-year students.

cocca: A type of merchant ship, usually small.

Colors, the: The seven members of the Spectrum. Each originally represented a single color of the seven sacred colors, and could draft that color, and each satrapy had one representative on the Spectrum. Since the founding of the Spectrum, that practice has deteriorated as satrapies have maneuvered for power. Thus a satrapy's representative, though usually appointed to a color corresponding to his abilities, could be appointed as Luxlord Green, but not actually draft green himself. Likewise, some of the satrapies might lose their representative, and others could have two or even three representatives on the Spectrum at a time, depending on the politics of the day. The term is for life.

color matchers: A term for full-spectrum superchromats. Sometimes employed as satraps' gardeners.

color-sensitive: See superchromat.

color wight: A drafter who has broken the halo. They frequently remake their bodies with pure luxin, rejecting the Pact between drafter and society.

conn: A title for a mayor or leader of a village in far northern Atash; more common in Blood Forest.

Corbine Street: A street in Big Jasper that leads up to the Great Fountain of Karris Shadowblinder.

corregidor: A Tyrean term for a chief magistrate; from when Tyrea encompassed eastern Atash.

Counselor to Kings, The: A manuscript, noted for its advocating ruthless treatment of opponents.

Cracked Lands, the: A region of broken land in the extreme west of Atash. Its treacherous terrain is only crossed by the most hardy and experienced traders.

Crater Lake: A large lake in southern Tyrea where the former capital of Tyrea, Kelfing, sits. The area is famous for its forests and the production of yew longbows.

Crossroads, the: A kopi house, restaurant, tavern, the highest-priced inn on the Jaspers, and downstairs, allegedly, a similarly priced brothel. Located near the Lily's Stem, the Crossroads is housed in the former Tyrean embassy building, centrally located in the Embassies District for all the ambassadors, spies, and merchants trying to deal with various governments.

cubit: A unit of volume. One cubit is one foot high, one foot wide, and one foot deep.

culverin: A type of cannon, useful for firing long distances because of its heavily weighted cannonballs and long-bore tube.

dagger-pistols: Flintlock pistols with a blade attached, allowing the user to fire at distance and then use the blade at close range or if the weapon misfires.

Dagnu: God of gluttony, associated with red. See Appendix, "On the Old Gods."

danar: The currency of the Seven Satrapies. One danar at an expensive inn on Jasper Island buys a cup of kopi. The average worker makes about a danar a day, while an unskilled laborer can expect to earn a half danar a day. The coins have a square hole cut in the middle, and are often carried on square-cut sticks. They can be cut in half and still hold their value.

    tin danar: Worth eight regular danar coins. A stick of tin danars usually carries twenty-five coins, that is, two hundred danars.

    silver quintar: Worth twenty danars, slightly wider than the tin danar, but only half as thick. A stick of silver quintars usually carries fifty coins, that is, one thousand danars.

    den: One-tenth of a danar.

darks: See Chromeria trained.

Dark Forest: A region within Blood Forest where pygmies reside. Decimated by the diseases brought by invaders, their numbers have never recovered, and they remain insular and often hostile.

darklight: Another term for paryl.

dawat: A Parian martial art.

Dazen's War: An alternate name of the False Prism's War, used by the victors.

Deimachia, the: The War of/on the Gods. A theological term for Lucidonius's battle for supremacy against the pagan gods of the old world.

Demiurgos: Another term for a Mirror; a half-creator.

dey/deya: A Parian title, male and female respectively. A near-absolute ruler over a city and its surrounding territory.

dims: See Chromeria trained.

discipulae: The feminine plural term (also applying to groups of mixed gender) for those who study both religious and magical arts.

drafter: One who can shape or harness light into physical form (luxin).

drafter-tailor: A profession that disappeared overnight during the Guile brothers' childhood. These tailors could, with enough will, craft luxin flexible enough to be fashioned as clothing and seal it.

Elrahee, elishama, eliada, eliphalet: A Parian prayer.

Embassies District: The Big Jasper neighborhood that is closest to the Lily's Stem, and thus is closest to the Chromeria itself. It also houses markets and kopi houses, taverns, and brothels.

epha: A unit of measurement for grain, approximately thirty-three liters.

Ergion: An Atashian walled city a day's travel from Idoss.

Everdark Gates, the: The strait connecting the Cerulean Sea to the oceans beyond. It was supposedly closed by Lucidonius, but Angari ships have been known to make it through from time to time.

evernight: Often a curse word, it refers to death and hell. A metaphysical or teleological reality, rather than a physical one, it represents that which will forever embrace and be embraced by void, full darkness, night in its purest, most evil form.

eye caps: A specialized kind of spectacles. These colored lenses fit directly over the eye sockets, glued to the skin. Like other spectacles, they enable a drafter to see through their preferred color, allowing them to draft more easily.

False Prism, the: Another term for Dazen Guile, who claimed to be a Prism even after his older brother Gavin had already been rightly chosen by Orholam and installed as Prism.

False Prism's War, the: A common term for the war between Gavin and Dazen Guile.

Fealty to One: The Danavis motto.

Ferrilux: God of pride, associated with superviolet. See Appendix, "On the Old Gods."

firecrystal: A term for sustainable sub-red, though a firecrystal doesn't last long when exposed to air.

firefriend: A term sub-red drafters use for each other.

Flame of Erebos, the: The pin all Blackguards receive, it symbolizes sacrifice and service.

flashbomb: A weapon crafted by yellow drafters. It doesn't harm so much as dazzle and distract its victims by the blinding light of evaporating yellow luxin.

flechette: A tiny projectile (sometimes made of luxin), with a pointed end and a vaned tail to achieve stable flight.

foot: Once a varying measure based on the current Prism's foot length. Later standarized to twelve thumbs (the length of Prism Sayid Talim's foot).

Free, the: Those drafters who reject the Pact of the Chromeria to join the Omnichrome's army, choosing to eventually break the halo and become wights. Also called the Unchained.

Freed, the: Those drafters who accept the Pact of the Chromeria and choose to be ritually killed before they break the halo and go mad. (The closeness of this term with "the Free" is part of the linguistic war between the pagans and the Chromeria, with the pagans trying to seize terms that had long had other, perverted, they thought, meanings.)

Freeing: The ritual release of those about to break the halo from incipient madness; performed by the Prism every year on Sun Day.

frizzen: On flintlocks, the L-shaped piece of metal against which the flint scrapes. The metal is on a hinge that opens upon firing to allow the sparks to reach the black powder.

gada: A ball game that involves kicking and passing a ball of wrapped leather.

galleass: A large merchant ship powered by both oar and sail. The term later referred to ships modified for military purposes, which included adding castles at bow and stern and cannons that fire in all directions.

gaoler: One in charge of a prison or dungeon.

Gargantua, the: Pirate king Pash Vecchio's flagship.

Garriston: The former commercial capital of Tyrea at the mouth of the Umber River on the Cerulean Sea. Prism Gavin Guile built Brightwater Wall to defend the city, but his defense failed, and the city was claimed by Lord Omnichrome, Koios White Oak.

Gatu, the: A Parian tribe, despised by other Parians for how they integrate their old religious customs into the worship of Orholam. Technically, their beliefs are heresy, but the Chromeria has never moved to put the heresy down with anything more than harsh words.

gemshorn: A musical instrument made from the tusk of a javelina, with finger-holes drilled into it to allow different notes to be produced.

ghotra: A Parian headscarf, used by many Parian men to demonstrate their reverence for Orholam. Most wear it while the sun is up, but some wear it even at nighttime.

giist: A colloquial name for a blue wight.

gladius: A short double-edged sword, useful for cutting or stabbing at close range.

Glass Lily, the: Another term for Little Jasper, or for the whole of the Chromeria as a collection of buildings.

gleams: See Chromeria trained.

glims: See Chromeria trained.

gold standard: The literal standard weights and measures, made of gold, against which all measures are judged. The originals are kept at the Chromeria, and certified copies are kept in every capital and major city for the adjudication of disputes. Merchants found using short measures and inaccurate weights are punished severely.

Great Chain (of being), the: A theological term for the order of creation. The first link is Orholam himself, and all the other links (creation) derive from him.

Great Desert, the: Another term for the Badlands of Tyrea.

great hall of the Chromeria, the: Located under the Prism's Tower, it is converted once a week into a place of worship, at which time mirrors from the other towers are turned to shine light in. It includes pillars of white marble and the largest display of stained glass in the world. Most of the time it is filled with clerks, ambassadors, and those who have business with the Chromeria.

great hall of the Travertine Palace, the: The wonder of the great hall is its eight great pillars set in a star shape around the hall, all made of extinct atasifusta wood. Said to be the gift of an Atashian king, these trees were the widest in the world, and their sap allows fires to burn continually, even five hundred years after they were cut.

Great River, the: The river between Ruthgar and Blood Forest, the scene of many pitched battles between the two countries.

great yard, the: The yard at the base of the towers of the Chromeria.

Green Bridge: Less than a league upstream from Rekton, drafted by Gavin Guile in seconds while on his way to battle his brother at Sundered Rock.

green flash: A rare flash seen at the setting of the sun; its meaning is debated. Some believe it has theological significance. The White calls it Orholam's wink.

Green Forest: A collective term for Blood Forest and Ruthgar during the hundred years of peace between the two countries, before Vician's Sin ended it.

Green Haven: The capital of Blood Forest.

grenado: A flagon full of black powder with a piece of wood shoved into the top, with a rag and bit of black powder as a fuse.

grenado, luxin: An explosive made of luxin that can be hurled at the enemy along an arc of luxin or in a cannon. Often filled with shot/shrapnel, depending on the type of grenado used. Smaller grenadoes are sometimes carried in bandoliers.

Guardian, the: A colossus that stands astride the entrance to Garriston's bay. She holds a spear in one hand and a torch in the other. A yellow drafter keeps the torch lit with yellow luxin, allowing it to dissolve slowly back into light, acting as a kind of lighthouse. See also Ladies, the.

Guile palace: The Guile family palace on Big Jasper. Andross Guile rarely visits his home in the time Gavin is Prism, preferring to reside at the Chromeria. The Guile palace was one of the few buildings allowed to be constructed without regard to the working of the Thousand Stars.

habia: A long man's garment.

Hag, the: An enormous statue that comprises Garriston's west gate. She is crowned and leans heavily on a staff; the crown and staff are also towers from which archers can shoot at invaders. See also Ladies, the.

Hag's Crown, the: A tower over the west gate into Garriston.

Hag's Staff, the: A tower over the west gate into Garriston.

Harbinger: Corvan Danavis's sword, inherited when his elder brothers died.

Hass Valley: Where the Ur trapped Lucidonius.

haze: A mind-altering drug. Often smoked with a pipe, it produces a sickly sweet odor.

Hellfang: A mysterious blade, also known as Marrow Sucker and the Blinder's Knife. It is white veined with black and bears seven colorless gems in its blade.

hellhounds: Dogs infused with red luxin and enough will to make them run at enemies, and then lit on fire.

hellstone: A superstitious term for obsidian, which is rarer than diamonds or rubies as few know where the extant obsidian in the world is created or mined. Obsidian is the only stone that can draw luxin directly out of a drafter if it touches her blood directly.

hullwrecker: A luxin disk filled with shrapnel. It has a fuse and a sticky side so that it will adhere to a ship's hull and explode once the soldiers have gotten away from the ship.

hurricano: A waterspout.

Idoss: An Atashian city, ruled by a council of city mothers and a corregidor.

incarnitive: A term for incorporating luxin directly into one's body.

Inura, Mount: A mountain on Seers Island, at the base of which the Third Eye resides.

ironbeaks: A term for luxin- and will-infused birds, used to attack opponents at distance and then explode.

Ivor's Ridge, Battle of: A battle during the False Prism's War, which Dazen won primarily because of Corvan Danavis's brilliance.

jambu: A tree that produces pink fruit. Found on Seers Island.

Jasper Islands/the Jaspers: Islands in the Cerulean Sea that hold the Chromeria.

Jasperites: Residents of Big Jasper.

javelinas: Animals, good for hunting. Giant javelinas are rare. Both species have tusks and hooves and are nocturnal.

ka: A sequence of fighting moves to train balance and flexibility and control. Frequently uses combinations of movements that might be used together in combat. A form of focusing exercise or meditation.

Karsos Mountains, the: Tyrean mountains that line the Cerulean Sea.

katar: A blade that instead of a hilt uses a cross-grip while the hilt extends up on either side of the hand and forearm. With its reinforced tip and allowance for the fist shape of the hand, it is extremely useful for punching through armor.

Kazakdoon: A legendary city/land in the distant east, beyond the Everdark Gates.

Kelfing: The former capital of Tyrea, on the shores of Crater Lake.

khat: An addictive stimulant, a leaf that stains the teeth after chewing, used especially in Paria.

kiyah: A yell used while fighting to expel the breath and empower the body's movement.

kopi: An addictive stimulant, a popular beverage. Bitter, dark-colored, and served hot.

kris: A wavy Parian blade.

Ladies, the: Four statues that comprise the gates into the city of Garriston. They are built into the wall, made of rare Parian marble and sealed in nearly invisible yellow luxin. They are thought to depict aspects of the goddess Anat and were spared by Lucidonius, who believed them to depict something true. They are the Hag, the Lover, the Mother, and the Guardian.

Laurion: A region in eastern Atash known for its silver ore and massive slave mines. Life expectancy for the enslaved miners is short, and the threat of being sent to the mines is used to keep slaves in line.

league: A unit of measurement, six thousand and seventy-six paces.

lightbane: See bane.

lightsickness: The aftereffects of too much drafting. Only the Prism never gets lightsick.

lightwells: Holes in the Chromeria's towers that are positioned to allow light, with the use of mirrors, to reach into the interior of the towers late in the day or on the dark side of the towers.

Lily's Stem, the: The luxin bridge between Big and Little Jasper. It is composed of blue and yellow luxin so that it appears green. Set below the high-water mark, it is remarkable for its endurance against the waves and storms that wash over it.

linstock: A staff for holding a slow match at one end. Used in lighting cannons, allowing the cannoneer to stand out of the range of the cannon's recoil.

Little Jasper: The island on which the Chromeria resides.

Little Jasper Bay: A bay off Little Jasper Island. It is protected by a seawall that keeps its waters calm.

loci damnata: A temple to the false gods. The bane. Believed to have magical powers, especially over drafters.

longbow: A weapon that allows for the efficient (in speed, distance, and force) firing of arrows. Its construction and its user must both be extremely strong. The yew forests of Crater Lake provide the best wood available for longbows.

Lord Prism: A term of address for the Prism.

lords of the air: A term used by the Omnichrome for his most trusted blue-drafting officers.

Lover, the: A statue that comprises the eastern river gate at Garriston. She is depicted in her thirties, lying on her back arched over the river with her feet planted, her knees forming a tower on one bank, hands entwined in her hair, elbows rising to form a tower on the other bank. She is clad only in veils. Before the Prisms' War, a portcullis could be lowered from her arched body into the river, its iron and steel hammered into shape so that it looked like a continuation of her veils. She glows like bronze when the sun sets, and the entrance to the city comes through another gate in her hair.

luxiat: A priest of Orholam. A luxiat wears black as an acknowledgment that he needs Orholam's light most of all; thus he is commonly called a blackrobe.

luxin: A material created by drafting from light. See Appendix.

luxlord: A term for a member of the ruling Spectrum.

Luxlords' Ball, the: An annual event on the open roof of the Prism's Tower.

luxors: Officials empowered by the Chromeria to bring the light of Orholam by almost any means necessary. They have at various times pursued paryl drafters and lightsplitter heretics, among others. Their theological rigidity and their prerogative to kill and torture have been hotly debated by followers of Orholam and dissidents alike.

magister: The term for a teacher of drafting and religion at the Chromeria.

mag torch: Often used by drafters to allow them access to light at night, it burns with a full spectrum of colors. Colored mag torches are also made at great expense, and when made correctly give a drafter her exact spectrum of light, allowing her to eschew spectacles and draft instantly.

match-holder: The piece on a matchlock musket to which a slow match is affixed.

matchlock musket: A firearm that works by snapping a lit slow match into the flash pan, which ignites the gunpowder in the breech of the firearm, whose explosion propels a rock or lead ball out of the barrel at high speed. Matchlocks are accurate to fifty or a hundred paces, depending greatly on the smith who made them and the ammunition used.

matériel: A military term for equipment or supplies.

merlon: The upraised portion of a parapet or battlement that protects soldiers from fire.

Midsummer: Another term for Sun Day, the longest day of the year.

Midsummer's Dance: A rural version of the Sun Day celebration.

Mirrormen: Soldiers in King Garadul's army who wear mirrored armor to protect themselves against luxin. The mirrors cause luxin to disintegrate when it comes in contact with it.

Molokh: God of greed, associated with orange. See Appendix, "On the Old Gods."

monochromes: Drafters who can only draft one color.

Mot: God of envy, associated with blue. See Appendix, "On the Old Gods."

Mother, the: A statue that guards the south gate into Garriston. She is depicted as a teenager, heavily pregnant, with a dagger bared in one hand and a spear in the other.

mund: A person who cannot draft. Insulting.

murder hole: A hole in the ceiling of a passageway that allows soldiers to fire, drop, or throw weapons, projectiles, luxin, or fuel. Common in castles and city walls.

nao: A small vessel with a three-masted rig.

Narrows, the: A strait of the Cerulean Sea between Abornea and the Ruthgari mainland. Aborneans strangle trade between the Narrows by charging high toll fees to merchants attempting to sail the silk route, or simply between Paria and Ruthgar.

near-polychrome: One who can draft three colors, but can't stabilize the third color sufficiently to be a true polychrome.

non-drafter: One who cannot draft.

norm: Another term for a non-drafter. Insulting.

nunk: A half-derogatory term for a Blackguard inductee.

Odess: A city in Abornea that sits at the head of the Narrows.

old world: The world before Lucidonius united the Seven Satrapies and abolished worship of the pagan gods.

oralam: Another term for paryl, meaning hidden light.

Order of the Broken Eye, the: A reputed guild of assassins. They specialize in killing drafters and have been rooted out and destroyed at least three times. They are thought to have re-formed each time with no connection to the previous incarnation of the Order. Some say paryl drafters worked with the Order hundreds of years earlier. Shimmercloaks were the pride of the Order, always working in pairs.

Overhill: A neighborhood in Big Jasper.

Pact, the: Since Lucidonius, the Pact has governed the Seven Satrapies. Its essence is that drafters agree to serve their community and receive all the benefits of status and sometimes wealth in exchange for their service and eventual choice to die just before or after breaking the halo.

parry-stick: A primarily defensive weapon that blocks bladed attacks. It sometimes includes a punching dagger at the center of the stick to follow up on a deflected blow.

petasos: A broad-brimmed Ruthgari hat, usually made of straw, meant to keep the sun off the face.

pilum: A weighted throwing spear whose shank bends after it pierces a shield, preventing the opponent from reusing the weapon against the user and encumbering the shield greatly. They are becoming more rare and ceremonial.

polychrome: A drafter who can draft more than two colors.

portmaster: A city official in charge of collecting tariffs and the organized exit and entrance of ships into his harbor.

Prism: There is only one Prism a generation. She senses the balance of the world's magic, can balance the magic, and can split light within herself. Her role is largely ceremonial and religious, not political, except for her balancing the world's magic so that wights and catastrophes don't result.

Prism's Tower, the: The central tower in the Chromeria. It houses the Prism, the White, and superviolets (as they are not numerous enough to require their own tower). The great hall lies below the tower, and the top holds a great crystal for the Prism's use while he balances the colors of the world. The annual Luxlords' Ball is held there.

promachia: The institution of a person named to the office of promachos. It gives great, nearly absolute powers during wartime.

promachos: A title given the Prism during war. It allows for his absolute rule and can only be instituted by order of the entire Spectrum. Among other powers, the promachos has the right to command armies, seize property, and elevate commoners to the nobility. It is an ancient term meaning He Who Fights Before Us.

Providence: A belief in the care of Orholam over the Seven Satrapies and its people.

psantria: A stringed musical instrument.

pyrejelly: Red luxin that, once set alight, will engulf whatever object it adheres to.

raka: A heavy insult, with the implication of both moral and intellectual idiocy.

Raptors of Kazakdoon, the: Flying reptiles from Angari myth.

Rath: The capital of Ruthgar, set on the confluence of the Great River and its delta into the Cerulean Sea.

Rathcaeson: A mythical city, on the drawings of which Gavin Guile based his Brightwater Wall design.

ratweed: A toxic plant whose leaves are often smoked for their strong stimulant properties. Addictive.

Red Cliff Uprising, the: A rebellion in Atash after the end of the False Prism's War. Without the support of the royal family (who had been purged), it was short-lived.

Rekton: A small Tyrean town on the Umber River, near the site of the Battle of Sundered Rock. An important trading post before the False Prism's War.

Rozanos Bridge, the: A bridge on the Great River between Ruthgar and the Blood Forest that Blessed Satrap Rados burned.

Ru: The capital of Atash, once famous for its castle, still famous for its Great Pyramid.

Ru, Castle of: Once the pride of Ru, it was destroyed by fire during General Gad Delmarta's purge of the royal family in the Prisms' War.

Ruic Head: A peninsula dominated by towering cliffs that overlooks the Atashian city of Ru and its bay. A fort atop the peninsula's cliffs guards against invading armies.

runt: An affably derogatory term for a new Blackguard inductee.

Salve: A common greeting, originally meaning "Be of good health!"

Sapphire Bay: A bay off Little Jasper.

satrap/satrapah: The title of a ruler of one of the seven satrapies.

sev: A unit of measurement for weight, equal to one-seventh of a seven.

seven: A unit of measurement for weight, equal to a cubit of water's weight.

Sharazan Mountains, the: Impassable mountains south of Tyrea.

shimmercloak: A cloak that makes the wearer mostly invisible, except in sub-red and superviolet.

Skill, Will, Source, and Still/Movement: The four essential elements for drafting.

Skill: The most underrated of all the elements of drafting, acquired through practice. Includes knowing the properties and strengths of the luxin being drafted, being able to see and match precise wavelengths, etc.

Will: By imposing will, a drafter can draft and even cover flawed drafting if her will is powerful enough.

Source: Depending on what colors a drafter can use, she needs either that color of light or items that reflect that color of light in order to draft. Only a Prism can simply split white light within herself to draft any color.

Still: An ironic usage. Drafting requires movement, though more skilled drafters can use less.

slow fuse: A length of cord, often soaked in saltpeter, that can be lit to ignite the gunpowder of a weapon in the firing mechanism.

slow match: Another term for a slow fuse.

spectrum: A term for a range of light (for more information on the luxin spectrum, see the Appendix); or (capitalized) the council of the Chromeria that is one branch of the government of the Chromeria (see Colors, the).

spidersilk: Another term for paryl.

spyglass: A small telescope using curved, clear lenses to aid in sighting distant objects.

star-keepers: Also known as tower monkeys, these are petite slaves (usually children) who work the ropes that control the mirrors of Big Jasper to reflect the light throughout the city for drafters' use. Though well treated for slaves, they spend their days working in two-man teams from dawn till after dusk, frequently without reprieve except for switching with their partner.

subchromats: Drafters who are color-blind, usually men. A subchromat can function without loss of ability—if his handicap is not in the colors he can draft. A red-green color-blind subchromat could be an excellent blue or yellow drafter. See Appendix.

Sun Day: A holy day to followers of Orholam and pagans alike, the longest day of the year. For the Seven Satrapies, Sun Day is the day when the Prism Frees those drafters who are about to break the halo. The ceremonies usually take place on the Jaspers, when all of the Thousand Stars are trained onto the Prism, who can absorb and split the light, whereas other men burn or burst from drafting so much power.

Sun Day's Eve: An evening of festivities before the longest day of the year and the Freeing the next day.

Sundered Rock: Twin mountains in Tyrea, opposite each other and so alike that they look as if they were once one huge rock cut down the middle.

Sundered Rock, Battle of: The final battle between Gavin and Dazen near a small Tyrean town on the Umber River.

superchromats: Extremely color-sensitive people. Luxin they seal will rarely fail. Far more common among female drafters.

tainted: One who has broken the halo, also called a wight.

thobe: An ankle-length garment, usually with long sleeves.

Thorikos: A town below the Laurion mines on the river to Idoss. Serves as the center for arriving and departing slaves, the bureaucracy necessary for thirty thousand slaves, and the center for the trade goods and supplies necessary, as well as the shipping of the silver ore down the river.

Thorn Conspiracies, the: A series of intrigues that occurred after the False Prism's War.

Thousand Stars, the: The mirrors on Big Jasper Island that enable the light to reach into almost any part of the city for as long as possible during the day.

Threshing, the: The initiation test for candidates to the Chromeria.

Threshing Chamber, the: The room where candidates for the Chromeria are summoned to test for their abilities to draft.

Tiru, the: A Parian tribe.

Tlaglanu, the: A Parian tribe, hated by other Parians, from whom Hanishu, the dey of Aghbalu, chose his bride, Tazerwalt.

torch: A red wight.

translucification, forced: See willjacking.

Travertine Palace, the: One of the wonders of the old world. Both a palace and a fortress, it is built of carved travertine (a mellow green stone) and white marble. Notable for its bulbous horseshoe arches, geometric wall patterns, Parian runes, and chessboard patterns on the floors. Its walls are incised with a crosshatched pattern to make the stone look woven rather than carved. The palace is a remnant of the days when half of Tyrea was a Parian province.

Tree People, the: Tribesmen who live (lived?) deep in the forests of the Blood Forest satrapy. They use zoomorphic designs, and can apparently shape living wood. Possibly related to the pygmies.

Umber River, the: The lifeblood of Tyrea. Its water allows the growth of every kind of plant in the hot climate; its locks fed trade throughout the country before the False Prism's War. Often besieged by bandits.

Unchained, the: A term for the followers of the Omnichrome, those drafters who choose to break the Pact and continue living even after breaking the halo.

Unification, the: A term for Lucidonius's and Karris Shadowblinder's establishment of the Seven Satrapies four hundred years prior to Gavin Guile's rule as Prism.

Ur, the: A tribe that trapped Lucidonius in Hass Valley. He triumphed against great odds, primarily because of the heroics of El-Anat (who thereby became Forushalzmarish or Shining Spear) and Karris Atiriel.

urum: A three-tined dining implement.

vambrace: Plate armor to protect the forearm. Ceremonial versions made of cloth also exist.

Varig and Green: A bank with a branch on Big Jasper.

vechevoral: A sickle-shaped sword with a long handle like an ax and a crescent-moon-shaped blade at the end, with the inward bowl-shaped side being the cutting edge.

Verdant Plains, the: The dominant geographical feature of Ruthgar. The Verdant Plains are favored by green drafters.

Vician's Sin: The event that marked the end of the close alliance between Ruthgar and Blood Forest.

Voril: A small town two days from Ru.

warrior-drafters: Drafters whose primary work is fighting for various satrapies or the Chromeria.

water markets: Circular lakes connected to the Umber River at the center of the villages and cities of Tyrea, common throughout Tyrean towns. A water market is dredged routinely to maintain an even depth, allowing ships easy access to the interior of the city with their wares. The largest water market is in Garriston.

Weasel Rock: A neighborhood in Big Jasper dominated by narrow alleys.

Weedling: A small coastal village in Ru close to Ruic Head.

wheellock pistol: A pistol that uses a rotating wheel mechanism to cause the spark that ignites the firearm; the first mechanical attempt to ignite gunpowder. Some few smiths' versions are more reliable than a flintlock and allow repeated attempts to fire. Most, however, are far less reliable than the already unreliable flintlocks.

Whiteguard, the: The original term for the Omnichrome's personal bodyguard.

widdershins: A direction; counter-sunwise.

willjacking/will-breaking: Once a drafter has contact with unsealed luxin that she is able to draft, she can use her will to break another drafter's control over the luxin and take it for herself.

Wiwurgh: A Parian town that hosts many Blood Forest refugees from the Blood War.

wob: A term for a Blackguard inductee.

zigarro: Rolled tobacco, a form useful for smoking. Ratweed is sometimes used as a wrapping to hold the loose tobacco.

Appendix

On Monochromes, Bichromes, and Polychromes

Most drafters are monochromes: they are able to draft only one color. Drafters who can draft two colors well enough to create stable luxin in both colors are called bichromes. Anyone who can draft solid luxin in three or more colors is called a polychrome. The more colors a polychrome can draft, the more powerful she is and the more sought after are her services. A full-spectrum polychrome is a polychrome who can draft every color in the spectrum. A Prism is always a full-spectrum polychrome.

Merely being able to draft a color, though, isn't the sole determining criterion in how valuable or skilled a drafter is. Some drafters are faster at drafting, some are more efficient, some have more will than others, some are better at crafting luxin that will be durable, some are smarter or more creative at how and when to apply luxin.

On Disjunctive Bichromes/Polychromes

On the light continuum, sub-red borders red, red borders orange, orange borders yellow, yellow borders green, green borders blue, blue borders superviolet. Most bichromes and polychromes simply draft a larger spectrum on the continuum than monochromes. That is, a bichrome is most likely to draft two colors that are adjacent to each other (blue and superviolet, red and sub-red, yellow and green, etc.). However, some few drafters are disjunctive bichromes. As could be surmised from the name, these are drafters whose colors do not border each other. Usef Tep was a famous example: he drafted red and blue. Karris White Oak is another, drafting green and red. It is unknown how or why disjunctive bichromes come to exist. It is only known that they are rare.

On Outer-Spectrum Colors

There is a small and controversial movement claiming that there are more than seven colors. Indeed, because colors exist on a continuum, one could argue that the number of colors is infinite. However, the argument that there are more than seven draftable colors is more theologically problematic for some. It is commonly accepted that there are other resonance points beyond the seven currently accepted ones, but those points are weaker and much more rarely drafted than the core seven. Among the contenders is one color far below the sub-red, called paryl. Another equally far above superviolet is called only *chi*.

But if colors are to be so broadly defined as to include colors only one drafter in a million can draft, then shouldn't yellow be split into liquid yellow and solid yellow? Where do the (mythical) black and white luxins fit? How could such (non)colors even fit on the spectrum?

The arguments, though bitter, are academic.

On Subchromacy and Superchromacy

A subchromat is one who has trouble differentiating between at least two colors, colloquially referred to as being color-blind. Subchromacy need not doom a drafter. For instance, a blue drafter who cannot distinguish between red and green will not be significantly handicapped in his work.

Superchromacy is having greater than usual ability to distinguish between fine variations of color. Superchromacy in any color will result in more stable drafting, but is most helpful in drafting yellow. Only superchromat yellow drafters can hope to draft solid yellow luxin.

On Luxin (with sections on physics, metaphysics, effects on personality, legendary colors, and colloquial terms)

The basis of magic is light. Those who use magic are called drafters. A drafter is able to transform a color of light into a physical substance. Each color has its own properties, but the uses of those building blocks are as boundless as a drafter's imagination and skill.

The magic in the Seven Satrapies functions roughly the opposite of a candle burning. When a candle burns, a physical substance (wax) is transformed into light. With chromaturgy, light is transformed into a physical substance, luxin. Each color of luxin has its own properties. If drafted correctly (within a tight allowance), the resulting luxin will be stable, lasting for days or even years, depending on its color.

Most drafters (magic-users) can only use one color. A drafter must be exposed to the light of her color to be able to draft it (that is, a green drafter can look at grass and be able to draft, but if she's in a white-walled room, she can't). Each drafter usually carries spectacles so that if her color isn't available, she can still use magic.

PHYSICS

Luxin has weight. If a drafter drafts a luxin haycart over her head, the first thing it will do is crush her. From heaviest to lightest are: red, orange, yellow, green, blue, sub-red,* superviolet, sub-red.* For reference, liquid yellow luxin is only slightly lighter than the same volume of water.

(*Sub-red is difficult to weigh accurately because it rapidly degenerates to fire when exposed to air. The ordering above was achieved by putting sub-red luxin in an airtight container and then weighing the result, minus the weight of the container. In real-world uses, sub-red crystals are often seen floating upward in the air before igniting.)

Luxin has tactility.
   Sub-red: Again the hardest to describe due to its flammability, but often described as feeling like a hot wind.
   Red: Gooey, sticky, clingy, depending on drafting; can be tarry and thick or more gel-like.
   Orange: Lubricative, slippery, soapy, oily.
   Yellow: In its liquid, more common state, like bubbly, effervescent water, cool to the touch, possibly a little thicker than seawater. In its solid state, it is perfectly slick, unyielding, smooth, and incredibly hard.
   Green: Rough: depending on the skill and purposes of the drafter, ranges from merely having a grain like leather to feeling like tree bark. It is flexible, springy, often drawing comparisons to the green limbs of living trees.

Blue: Smooth, though poorly drafted blue will have a texture or can shed fragments easily, like chalk, but in crystals.

Superviolet: Like spidersilk, thin and light to the point of imperceptibility.

Luxin has scent. The base scent of luxin is resinous. The smells below are approximate, because each color of luxin smells like itself. Imagine trying to describe the smell of an orange. You'd say citrus and sharp, but that isn't it *exactly.* An orange smells like an orange. However, the below approximations are close.

Sub-red: Charcoal, smoke, burned.

Red: Tea leaves, tobacco, dry.

Orange: Almond.

Yellow: Eucalyptus and mint.

Green: Fresh cedar, resin.

Blue: Mineral, chalk, almost none.

Superviolet: Faintly like cloves.

***Black:** No smell/or smell of decaying flesh.*

***White:** Honey, lilac.*

(*Mythical; these are the smells as reported in stories.)

METAPHYSICS

Any drafting feels good to the drafter. Sensations of euphoria and invincibility are particularly strong among young drafters and those drafting for the first time. Generally, these pass with time, though drafters abstaining from magic for a time will often feel them again. For most drafters, the effect is similar to drinking a cup of kopi. Some drafters, strangely enough, seem to have allergic reactions to drafting. There are vigorous ongoing debates about whether the effects on personality should be described as metaphysical or physical.

Regardless of their correct categorization and whether they are the proper realm of study for the magister or the luxiat, the effects themselves are unquestioned.

LUXIN'S EFFECTS ON PERSONALITY

The benighted before Lucidonius believed that passionate men became reds, or that calculating women became yellows or blues. In truth, the causation flows the other way.

Every drafter, like every woman, has her own innate personality.

The color she drafts then influences her *toward* the behaviors below. A person who is impulsive who drafts red for years is going to be more likely to be pushed farther into "red" characteristics than a naturally cold and orderly person who drafts red for the same length of time.

The color a drafter uses will affect her personality over time. This, however, doesn't make her a prisoner of her color, or irresponsible for her actions under the influence of it. A green who continually cheats on his wife is still a lothario. A sub-red who murders an enemy in a fit of rage is still a murderer. Of course, a naturally angry woman who is also a red drafter will be even more susceptible to that color's effects, but there are many tales of calculating reds and fiery, intemperate blues.

A color isn't a substitute for a woman. Be careful in your application of generalities. That said, generalities can be useful: a group of green drafters is more likely to be wild and rowdy than a group of blues.

Given these generalities, there is also a virtue and a vice commonly associated with each color. (Virtue being understood by the early lux-iats not as being free of temptation to do evil in a particular way, but as conquering one's own predilection toward that kind of evil. Thus, gluttony is paired with temperance, greed with charity, etc.)

Sub-red drafters: Sub-reds are passionate in all ways, the most purely emotional of all drafters, the quickest to rage or to cry. Sub-reds love music, are often impulsive, fear the dark less than any other color, and are often insomniacs. Emotional, distractable, unpredictable, inconsistent, loving, bighearted. Sub-red men are often sterile.

Associated vice: Wrath

Associated virtue: Patience

Red drafters: Reds are quick-tempered, lusty, and love destruction. They are also warm, inspiring, brash, larger than life, expansive, jovial, and powerful.

Associated vice: Gluttony

Associated virtue: Temperance

Orange drafters: Oranges are often artists, brilliant in understanding other people's emotions and motivations. Some use this to defy or exceed expectations. Sensitive, manipulative, idiosyncratic, slippery, charismatic, empathetic.

Associated vice: Greed

Associated virtue: Charity

Yellow drafters: Yellows tend to be clear thinkers, with intellect and emotion in perfect balance. Cheerful, wise, bright, balanced, watchful, impassive, observant, brutally honest at times, excellent liars. Thinkers, not doers.

Associated vice: Sloth

Associated virtue: Diligence

Green drafters: Greens are wild, free, flexible, adaptable, nurturing, friendly. They don't so much disrespect authority as not even recognize it.

Associated vice: Lust

Associated virtue: Self-control

Blue drafters: Blues are orderly, inquisitive, rational, calm, cold, impartial, intelligent, musical. Structure, rules, and hierarchy are important to them. Blues are often mathematicians and composers. Ideas and ideology and correctness often matter more than people to blues.

Associated vice: Envy

Associated virtue: Kindness

Superviolet drafters: Superviolets tend to have a removed outlook; dispassionate, they appreciate irony and sarcasm and word games and are often cold, viewing people as puzzles to be solved or ciphers to be cracked. Irrationality outrages superviolets.

Associated vice: Pride

Associated virtue: Humility

LEGENDARY COLORS

Chi (pronounced KEY*):* The postulated upper-spectrum counterpart to paryl. (Often referred to in tales as "far above superviolet as paryl is below sub-red.") Also called the revealer. Its main claimed use is nearly identical to paryl—seeing through things, though those who believe in chi say its powers far surpass paryl's in this regard, cutting through flesh and bone and even metal. The only thing the tales seem to agree on is that chi drafters have the shortest life expectancy of any drafters: five to fifteen years, almost without exception. If chi indeed exists, it would mostly be evidence that Orholam created light for the universe or for his own purposes, and not solely for the use of man, and would move theologians from their current anthropocentrism.

Black: Destruction, void, emptiness, that which is not and cannot be filled. Obsidian is said to be the bones of black luxin after it dies.

Paryl: Also called spidersilk, it is invisible to all but paryl drafters. It resides as far down the spectrum from sub-red as most sub-red does from the visible spectrum. Believed mythical because the lens of the human eye cannot contort to a shape that would allow seeing such a color. The alleged color of dark drafters and night weavers and assassins because this spectrum is (again, allegedly) available even at night. Uses unknown, but linked to murders. Poisonous?

White: The raw word of Orholam. The stuff of creation, from which all luxin and all life was formed. Descriptions of an earthly form of the stuff (as diminished from the original as obsidian supposedly is from black luxin) describe it as radiant ivory, or pure white opal, emitting light on the whole spectrum.

COLLOQUIAL TERMS

Students at the Chromeria are encouraged to use the proper names for each color, but the impetus to name seems unstoppable. In some cases, the names are used technically: pyrejelly is a thicker, longer-burning draft of red that will burn long enough to reduce a body to ash. In other cases, the reference becomes precisely the opposite of the technical definition: brightwater was first a name for liquid yellow luxin, but Brightwater Wall is solid yellow luxin.

A few of the more common colloquialisms:

Sub-red: Firecrystal
Red: Pyrejelly, burnglue
Orange: Noranjell
Yellow: Brightwater
Green: Godswood
Blue: Frostglass, glass
Superviolet: Skystring, soulstring, spidersilk
Black: Hellstone, nullstone, nightfiber, cinderstone, hadon
White: Truebright, starsblood, anachrome, luciton

On the Old Gods

Sub-red: Anat, goddess of wrath. Those who worshipped her are said to have had rituals that involved infant sacrifice. Also

known as the Lady of the Desert, the Fiery Mistress. Her centers of worship were Tyrea, southernmost Paria, and southern Ilyta.
Red: Dagnu, god of gluttony. He was worshipped in eastern Atash.
Orange: Molokh, god of greed. Once worshipped in western Atash.
Yellow: Belphegor, god of sloth. Primarily worshipped in northern Atash and southern Blood Forest before Lucidonius's coming.
Green: Atirat, goddess of lust. Her center of worship was primarily in western Ruthgar and most of Blood Forest.
Blue: Mot, god of envy. His center of worship was in eastern Ruthgar, northeastern Paria, and Abornea.
Superviolet: Ferrilux, god of pride. His center of worship was in southern Paria and northern Ilyta.

On Technology and Weapons

The Seven Satrapies are in a time of great leaps in understanding. The peace since the Prisms' War and the following suppression of piracy has allowed the flow of goods and ideas freely through the satrapies. Cheap, high-quality iron and steel are available in every satrapy, leading to high-quality weapons, durable wagon wheels, and everything in between. Though traditional forms of weapons like Atashian bich'hwa or Parian parry-sticks continue, now they are rarely made of horn or hardened wood. Luxin is often used for improvised weapons, but most luxins' tendency to break down after long exposure to light, and the scarcity of yellow drafters who can make solid yellows (which don't break down in light), means that metal weapons predominate among mundane armies.

The greatest leaps are occurring in the improvement of firearms. In most cases, each musket is the product of a different smith. This means each man must be able to fix his own firearm, and that pieces must be crafted individually. A faulty hammer or flashpan can't be swapped out for a new one, but must be detached and reworked into appropriate shape. Some large-scale productions with hundreds of apprentice smiths have tried to tackle this problem in Rath by making parts as nearly identical as possible, but the resulting matchlocks tend to be low quality, trading accuracy and durability for consistency and simple repair. Elsewhere, the smiths of Ilyta have gone the other direction, making the highest-quality custom muskets in the world. Recently, they've pioneered a form they call the flintlock. Instead of affixing a burning slow match to ignite powder in the flashpan and thence into the breech of the rifle, they've affixed a flint that scrapes a frizzen to throw sparks directly into the breech. This approach means a musket or pistol is always ready to fire, without a soldier having to first light a slow match. Keeping it from widespread adoption is the high rate of misfires—if the flint doesn't scrape the frizzen correctly or throw sparks perfectly, the firearm doesn't fire.

Thus far, the combination of luxin with firearms has been largely unsuccessful. The casting of perfectly round yellow luxin musket balls was possible, but the small number of yellow drafters able to make solid yellow creates a bottleneck in production. Blue luxin musket balls often shatter from the force of the black powder explosion. An exploding shell made by filling a yellow luxin ball with red luxin (which would ignite explosively from the shattering yellow when the ball hit a target) was demonstrated to the Nuqaba, but the exact balance of making the yellow thick enough to not explode inside the musket, but thin enough to shatter when it hit its target, is so difficult that several smiths have died trying to replicate it, probably barring this technique from wide adoption.

Other experiments are doubtless being carried out all over the Seven Satrapies, and once high-quality, consistent, and somewhat accurate firearms are introduced, the ways of war will change forever. As it stands, a trained archer can shoot farther, far more quickly, and more accurately.

extras

orbit

meet the author

BRENT WEEKS was born and raised in Montana. After getting his paper keys from Hillsdale College, Brent started writing on bar napkins, then on lesson plans, then full time. Eventually, someone paid him for it. Brent lives in Oregon with his wife, Kristi. He doesn't own cats or wear a ponytail. Find out more about the author at www.brentweeks.com.

introducing

**If you enjoyed
THE BLINDING KNIFE,
look out for**

THE BROKEN EYE
Lightbringer: Book 3

by Brent Weeks

Chapter 1

The two Blackguards approached the White's door, the younger rhythmically cracking the knuckles of his right fist like he did when he was nervous. The Greyling brothers stopped in front of the door, hesitated. Pop, pop, pop. Pop, pop, pop.

The elder brother Gill looked at his little brother, clearly trying to emulate Commander Ironfist's sledge-gaze. Gavin hated it when Gill did that, but he quit popping his knuckles nonetheless.

"We gain nothing by waiting," Gill said. "Put that fist to use."

It was early morning. The White usually didn't emerge from her chambers for at least another two hours. With her declining health, the Blackguard were doing all they could to make her last months easy.

"How come it's always me who—" Gavin asked. At nineteen, Gill was two years older, but they were the same rank.

"We have no idea how long this will last. If you make her miss it because you're arguing with me…" Gill let the threat hang. "Fist," he said. It was an order.

Scowling, Gavin Greyling knocked on the door. After waiting the traditional five seconds, he opened the door. The brothers walked inside.

The White wasn't in her bed. She and her room slave were praying, prostrate on the floor despite their age, facing the rising sun through the open eastern doors to the balcony. Cold wind blew in around the two old women on their knees.

"High Mistress," Gill said. "Your pardon. There's something you must see."

She looked at them, recognizing them immediately. Some of the nobles and luxlords didn't treat the youngest of the full Blackguards seriously. It was a judgment that cut because it was partly deserve. Gavin knew he wouldn't have been promoted to full Blackguard at seventeen even a year ago. But the White never treated him like he was less than anyone. He would gladly die for her, even if someone told him that she'd die the next day of old age.

She broke off her prayers, and they helped her into her wheeled chair, but when the old room slave waddled over to close the balcony doors on bad hips, Gill stopped her.

"She needs to look from the balcony, *caleen*," Gavin said.

Gavin wrapped the White in her blankets gently but efficiently. They'd learned exactly how much delicacy her pride would stand, and how much pain her body could. He pushed her out onto the balcony. She didn't complain that she could do it herself, another sign that the end was coming.

"In the bay," Gill said.

Sapphire Bay was resplendent below them. Today was the Feast of Light and Dark, the equinox, and it was turning into one of those autumn days one hopes for: the air chilly, but the sky blindingly blue, the waters calm instead of their normal chop. The bay itself was conspicuously underpopulated. The fleet was still gone to fight the Color Prince at Ru and stop his advance. Surely by now, the battle had taken place, and all that remained was to wait to hear whether they should rejoice in their victory or brace for a war that would tear the Seven Satrapies apart. Thus the White's prayers, Gavin supposed. Can you pray about the outcome of an event after the fact? Do they do anything then?

Do they do anything in the first place?

The White waited silently, staring at the bay. Staring at nothing, Gavin was afraid. Had they interrupted her too late? But the White trusted them; she asked nothing, simply waited as the minutes stretched out.

And then, finally, a shape coming around the bend of Big Jasper. At first, it was hard to get a sense of the size of thing. It surfaced a hundred paces from the high walls of Big Jasper, which were lined with people jostling each other to see. The sea demon was visible at first only by the wake it left, plowing waters to the left and the right.

As the sea demon came closer, it sped up. Its cruciform mouth, half open, swallowing the seas with its ring-shaped maw and jetting them out through its gills along the whole of its body, now opened full. With each big gulping pulse, its mouth opening wide now, water splashed out to the sides and back in great fans every fifty or so paces, then went still as the massive muscles contracted, the water behind it hissing with churned air and water.

The sea demon was approaching the sea wall that protected

Sapphire Bay. One galley was making a run for the gap in the sea wall, trying to get out. With how fast the sea demon moved, the captain couldn't have known it was precisely the wrong direction to go.

"The damn fool," Gill muttered.

"Depends on if you see this as a coincidence or an attack," the White said, eerily calm. "If the sea demon gets inside the sea wall, every last boat inside will be smashed. Orholam forfend."

The galley slaves lifted their oars as one, trying to make as little disturbance on the seas as possible. Sea demons were territorial, but not predators.

The sea demon passed the galley and kept going. Gavin Greyling expelled a relieved breath and heard the others do the same. But then the sea demon disappeared in a sudden cloud of mist.

When it reappeared, it was red hot. The waters were boiling around it. It veered out to sea.

There was nothing they could do. The sea demon went out to sea, then it doubled back, accelerating. It aimed directly at the prow of the galley, as if it wanted the head-to-head collision with this challenger.

Someone swore under their breath.

The sea demon rammed the galley with tremendous speed. Several sailors flew off the deck: one into the sea, the other flying until he crunched against the sea demon's knobby, spiky head.

For one instant it looked like the ship would somehow hold together, and then the prow crumpled. Wood exploded in shards to every side. The masts snapped.

The entire galley—the half of it that was left—was pushed backward, ten paces, twenty, thirty, jetting huge fans of spray into the air. The sea demon's forward progress was only briefly slowed. Then the galley was pushed down into the waves as that great hammerhead rose even higher out of the water and kept pushing. Abruptly, the fire-hardened wood hull smashed like a clay pot thrown against a wall.

The sea demon dove, and attached to that great spiky head by a hundred lines, the wreckage was dragged down with it.

A hundred paces away, a huge bubble of air surfaced as the last of the decks gave way underwater. But the ship never rose. Flotsam was all that remained, and not nearly as much of that as one would expect. The ship was simply gone. Perhaps half a dozen men out of a crew of hundreds were flailing in the waves. Most of them couldn't swim. Sailors, and they can't swim. Gavin Greyling had learned to swim as part of his Blackguard training, and that most sailors couldn't had always struck him as insanity.

"There it is," Gill said, pointing. "You can see the trail of bubbles."

It hadn't gotten trapped inside the sea wall, thank Orholam. But what it seemed to be heading for was worse.

"High Mistress," a voice broke in behind them. It was Lux-lord Carver Black, the man responsible for all the mundane details of running the Chromeria that didn't fall under the White's purview. He was tall man with in Ilytian hose and dou-blet, with olive skin and long dark hair streaked liberally with white. "Your pardon, I knocked but got no response. The beast has been circling the Jaspers, five times now. I've given orders for the guns on Cannon Island not to fire unless it attacked. They want to know if they should consider this an attack." The defense of Little Jasper was technically in his portfolio, but Luxlord Black was a cautious man, and he liked to avoid blame wherever possible.

What could a cannonball do against such a beast?

"Tell them to wait," she said.

"You heard her!" the Black bellowed, cupping a many-jeweled hand to his mouth. There was a secretary on the roof, one floor above the White's balcony, holding a polished mirror a pace wide, leaning out over the edge to listen.

"Yes, my lord!" the man hurried to flash the signal, and a younger woman replaced him at the edge, trying to listen without appearing to be listening to the wrong things.

Girl has a future as a courtier.

The sea demon was now hugging the coast, swimming through waters so shallow its back was visible. It rammed through the port master's dock without even appearing to notice it. Then it reached the far southern tip of Big Jasper.

"Oh shit." The thought was everyone's, but the voice was the White's. The White? Cursing? Gavin Greyling didn't think she even knew curses.

The people on the Lily's Stem had lost sight of the beast as it had come in to shore, and the sea demon was bearing down on the bridge before any of them could react.

The Lily's Stem floated at exactly the height of the waves. Without supports, the yellow and blue luxin formed a lattice that looked green. It had withstood battering seas for hundreds of years, the chromaturgy required to make such a thing now beyond perhaps even Gavin Guile himself. More than once it had served as a wavebreak for ships trapped outside the sea walls and had saved hundreds of lives. But the sea demon's first, incidental contact with the bridge rocked the entire structure. It threw hundreds of people off their feet.

The vast shape slid along the smooth luxin for ten, twenty paces, then stopped, seeming confused by contact. Confusion lasted only an instant though, as fresh billows of steam rose around it. The sea demon's head plunged into the waves and it sped out to sea, its vast tail slapping the water beside the Lily's Stem and sending geysers over almost the whole length.

Then, out to sea, it turned again.

"Tell Cannon Island to fire!" the White shouted.

Cannon Island sat in the bay on the opposite side of the Lily's Stem. The likelihood of the gunners there making the shot was remote.

But a slim chance at distraction was better than nothing.

The first culverin fired immediately; the men must have been waiting for the order. The shot was at least a thousand paces, though. They missed by at least a hundred. The island's other five guns facing this way each spoke in turn, the sound of their fire reaching the tower at about the same time they saw the splash. Each missed. The closest was more than fifty paces off target. None deterred the sea demon.

The crews began reloading with all the speed and efficiency that could be imparted with relentless training. But they wouldn't get off another volley in time. The sea demon was simply too fast.

The Lily's Stem had become chaos. Not only people had been thrown off their feet—a team of horses had fallen, panicked, and turned sideways with their cart within the confines of the bridge itself, blocking all but a trickle of men and women from getting out onto Big Jasper. Some were climbing over and under the flailing, biting horses.

A stampede flowed out of the other side of the bridge, people falling, being trampled. Some few would make it in time.

"Carver," the White said, her voice clipped. "Go now and see to the dead and wounded. You're faster than I, and I need to see how this ends."

Luxlord Black was out the door before she was done speaking.

Four hundred paces out. Three hundred.

The White reached a hand out, as if she could ward off the sea demon by will alone. She was whispering prayers urgently under her breath.

Two hundred paces. One hundred.

A dark shaped streaked under the bridge from the opposite side, and a colossal collision with the sea demon set jets of water a hundred feet into the air. The sea demon was launched into the air, bent sideways. It wasn't alone. A black shape, massive itself but dwarfed by the sea demon, had hit it from below. Both crashed back into the water, not twenty paces from the Lily's Stem.

The sea demon's momentum carried its turned body all the way into the bridge itself, shooting a tidal wave of water over the top of tube and rocking the whole edifice—but not shattering it.

A fan-shaped spray of water and expelled breath, flukes and a black tail surfaced. The tail smashed down on the sea demon's body, and then the whale darted away into Sapphire Bay. Out, away.

"A whale," the White breathed. "Was that…"

"A sperm whale, High Mistress," Gill said. He'd loved stories of the sea's pugilists. "A black giant. At least thirty paces long, head like a battering ram. I've never heard of one that big."

"There haven't been sperm whales in the Cerulean Sea for—"

"Two hundred years," Gill said. "Your pardon," he added.

She didn't notice. They were all too engrossed. The sea demon was obviously stunned. Its red-hot body had turned blue and sank beneath the waves, but even as the sea calmed from the aftershocks of the collision, they could see the red glow begin again. The waters hissed.

A swell of that big body underneath the waves, and it turned and began to move—chasing after the whale.

The White said, "That kind of whale is supposed to be quite aggress—"

Four hundred paces out from shore, another eruption of water as the two leviathans collided again.

Sperm whales had been the only natural enemies of sea demons in the Cerulean Sea. But the sea demons had killed them all, long ago. Supposedly.

They watched, and again the giants collided, this time farther out, farther south. They watched, in silence, while the rescue operations below worked to clear the Lily's Stem.

"I thought those whales were usually...blue?" the White asked Gill, not turning from the sea.

"Dark blue or gray. There are mentions of white ones, possibly mythical."

"This one looked black, did it not? Or is that my failing eyes?"

The brothers looked at each other.

"Black," Gill said.

"Definitely black," Gavin said.

"Bilhah," the White said, addressing her room slave by name for the first time that Gavin remembered. "What day is today?"

"Today is the beginning of autumn, mistress. 'Tis the Feast of Light and Darkness, when day and night war over who will own the sky."

The White still didn't turn. Contemplative, she said, "And on a day when the light must die, when there is no victory possible, we're saved—not by a white whale, but by a black one."

Gavin felt like a significant moment was passing him by, as the others nodded sagely. He looked from one to another. "Well?" he asked. "What does it mean?"

Gill slapped the back of his head. "Well, that's the fuckin' question, ain't it?"

Chapter 2

Gavin Guile's palms bled warm, thick gray water. He'd thought he had respectable calluses for a man who worked mainly with words, but nothing prepared you for ten hours a day on an oar.

"Strap!" Number Eight said, raising his voice for the foreman. "More bandages for *His Holiness*."

That elicited a few pale grins, but the galley slaves didn't slow. The big calfskin drums were thumping out a cetaceous pulse. It was a pace the experienced men could maintain all day, though with difficulty. Each bench held three men, and two could keep the pace for long enough to allow their seatmate to drink or eat or use the bucket.

Strap came over with a roll of cloth. She motioned for Gavin to present his hands. Strap had only half a tongue. She didn't speak often, and when she did, you wished she hadn't. Gavin pulled his bloody claws off the oars. He couldn't open or close his fingers, and it wasn't even noon yet. They would row until dark; five more hours, this time of year. She unrolled the cloth. It seemed crusty.

Gavin supposed there were worse things to worry about than infection. But as she wrapped his hands with efficient motions, albeit without gentleness, he smelled something vibrant, resin overlaid with something like cloves, and heard the tiny shivering splintering of breaking superviolet luxin.

For a moment, the old Gavin was back, his mind reaching for how he could take advantage of their foolishness. It was difficult to draft directly from luxin breaking down, but difficult was nothing for Gavin Guile. He was the Prism; there was nothing he couldn't—

No, there was nothing he *could* do. Not now. Now, he was

blind to colors. He couldn't draft anything. In the threadbare light of the slowly swinging lanterns, the world swam in shades of gray.

Strap finished tying the knots at the back of his hands and growled. Gavin took that as his sign and lifted weary arms back to the oar.

"F-f-fights infection," one of his oarmates. He was Number Eight, but some of the men called Fukkelot. Gavin had no idea why. There was a loose community here with their own slang and inside jokes, and he wasn't part of it. But it was perhaps the first time Gavin had heard the man put two words together without one of them being a curse. "Down here in the belly, infection'll kill you quick as a kick."

Superviolet luxin fighting infection? The Chromeria didn't teach that, but that didn't make it wrong. There was plenty they didn't know. But he thought instead about his brother, Dazen, who had slashed his own chest open. How had Dazen not succumbed to infection down in the hell Gavin had made him?

Not that it mattered now. He saw again blood and brains blowing out of Dazen's skull, painting the wall of his cell after Gavin had shot him.

Gavin put his bandaged hands back on the well-worn oar, the grip lacquered with sweat and blood and the oil of many hands.

"Back straight, Six," Number Eight said. "The lumbago'll kill ya if you do it all with your back." Now that many words with no cursing was just a miracle.

Eight had somehow adopted Gavin. Gavin knew it wasn't pure charity that led the wiry Angari to help him. Gavin was the third man on their oar. The less work Gavin did, the more Seven and Eight would have to do to keep time, and Captain Gunner wasn't taking it easy on the speed. He wasn't keen on

extras

staying close to the site of The Fall of Ru. In another week, the Chromeria would have pirate hunters out: privateers given writs to hunt the slave takers who'd swept in upon the wrecks of the invasion fleet, saving men in order to pressgang them. They'd look to ransom those who claimed relatives with means, but many would doubtless head straight back to the great slave yards of Ilyta, where they could offload their human cargo with impunity. Others would seek out nearer slave markets, where the unscrupulous would forge the documents saying these slaves were taken legally in far distant ports. Many a slave would lose his tongue so he couldn't tell the tale.

This is what I led my people to. Gavin had killed a god, and still lost the battle. When the bane had risen from the depths, it had smashed the Chromeria's fleet, their hopes thrown overboard like so much jetsam.

If I had been declared promachos, it wouldn't have happened.

The truth was, Gavin hadn't been too hard; he'd been too soft. He shouldn't have only killed his brother, he should have killed his father, too. Even up to the end, if he'd helped Kip stab Andross Guile instead of trying to separate them, Andross would be dead, and Gavin would be secure and in his wife's arms right now.

"You ever think that you weren't hard enough?" Gavin asked Seven.

The man rowed three big sweeps before he finally answered. "You know what they call me?"

"Guess I heard someone call you Orholam. Because you're seat number seven?"

"That ain't why."

Friendly sort. "Why then?"

"You don't get answers to your questions because you don't wait for 'em," Orholam said.

"I've done my share of waiting, old man," Gavin said.

Two more long sweeps, and Orholam said, "No. To all three. That's three times no. Some men pay attention when things come in threes."

Not me. Go to hell, Orholam. And the one you're named after, too.

Gavin grimaced against the familiar agony of rowing and settled back into the tempo, walking through the two and a half paces that the sweeps covered at his end of the oar. *The Bitter Cob* had a hundred and fifty rowers, eighty men in this deck and seventy above. The oars interlaced at the big outrigger that minimized the fouling, and openings between decks allowed the sound of drums and shouted orders to pass between the upper and lower galley decks.

But not only sound passed between the upper and lower decks. Gavin had thought his sense of smell was deadened after a few days, but there always seemed some new scent to assail his nostrils. The Angari fancied themselves a clean people, and maybe they were—Gavin hadn't seen any signs of dysentery or sweating sickness among the galley slaves, and each night, two buckets made the rounds of the slaves, the first full of soapy water for them to slop on themselves and the second full of clean sea water to rinse themselves. Whatever slopped free, of course, dribbled down on the slaves in the lower hold and, dirtied further, into the bilge. The decks were always slippery, the hold hot and damp, the sweat constant, the portholes providing inadequate ventilation unless the wind was high, the dribbles of liquid from the deck above that dripped onto Gavin's head and back suspiciously malodorous.

Footsteps pattered down the stairs, the light step of a veteran sailor. Fingers snapped near Gavin, but he didn't even look over. He was a slave now; he needed to act the part or be beaten for his insolence. But he didn't need to cower. On the other hand, he *did* need to row, and that took all his strength.

Strap took Gavin's hands off the oar, unlocked the manacles, whistled to Number Two. Numbers One and Two were at the top of the fluid slave hierarchy, allowed to sit up front and rest, running errands without chains on and only required to row if another slave got sick or fainted from exhaustion.

After Strap manacled his hands behind his back, Gavin looked at Captain Gunner, standing at the top of the stairs out of the hold. Gunner was Ilytian, with midnight black skin, a wild curly beard, a fine brocaded doublet worn open over his naked torso, loose sailor's pants. He was handsome in a batshit-crazy sort of way. He talked to himself. He talked to the sea. He admitted no equal on heaven or earth—and in the firing of guns of any size, he was justified in that. The last Gavin had seen of him, he'd been jumping off a ship Gavin had just lit on fire and poked full of holes. Gavin had spared Gunner's life on a whim.

The good you do is what kills you.

"Come on up, little Guile," Captain Gunner said. "I'm running out of reasons to keep you alive."